The Magazine of Philip José Farmer

The Magazine of Philip José Farmer

Edited by Michael Croteau

THE BEST OF FARMERPHILE
The Magazine of Philip José Farmer
Edited by Michael Croteau

Meteor House

ISBN 978-1-945427-07-7

First Trade Paperback Edition

To the Wizard of Peoria, Philip José Farmer, the kindest,
most generous hero a fan could wish for.

TABLE OF CONTENTS

Nonfiction by Philip José Farmer

Nonfiction by Guest Contributors

Fiction by Philip José Farmer

INTRODUCTION
MICHAEL CROTEAU

FarmerCon II was held in Peoria, Illinois, in August 2007. At our dinner banquet we were giving out our first annual "Farmerphile" awards and I introduced George H. Scheetz as the winner of the "Retroactive Farmerphile" award. Describing George, I mentioned he was the publisher of the first fanzine devoted to Philip José Farmer, *Farmerage*, and he also published *Riverworld War: The Suppressed Fiction of Philip José Farmer*. A fledgling publisher myself, I joked that while everyone else in the room wanted to be Philip José Farmer, I wanted to be George Scheetz!

You should have seen the look on his face.

But it was true. While most of the people there dreamed of being a professional writer—several already were, and some others have become so since—I knew I never would. The closest I would come to creating a book, was to publish it. I had already published five issues of *Farmerphile*, but at that time I had no idea I'd go on to be one of the founders of Meteor House and publish over twenty books—most of them having to do with Philip José Farmer in one way or another.

And about that word, "publisher." It turns out what I really wanted was to be an editor, but I didn't know what the word meant at the time. My understanding of what an editor did was closer to a copyeditor's job.

That is just the tip of the iceberg of what I learned publishing fifteen issues of *Farmerphile*. Luckily I had a lot of help, and from

13

people who knew the difference between a publisher, editor, and copyeditor. Paul Spiteri, Christopher Paul Carey, and Win Scott Eckert all took turns as coeditor. Keith Howell designed the cover layout of the first issue and he and Charles Berlin contributed illustrations for nearly every issue. Together I believe we made *Farmerphile* something Philip José Farmer could be proud of.

Farmerphile had three goals. The first was to publish never-before-seen material by Farmer himself. That we did in spades: over a dozen short stories, plus articles, letters, speeches, excerpts, and even a serialized novel (not included in this collection).

The second was to preserve as much history about Phil's life and career as we could. That was accomplished by printing his letters and speeches, and by printing essays about him by his friends and fans, many of them fellow science fiction authors. One of the most popular regular features was Bette Farmer's peek behind the curtain in her column, "The Roller Coaster Ride with Phil Farmer." All of her columns are included in the first section of this book.

The third goal was to examine his body of work. From deep dives into the Wold Newton Universe in the "Creative Mythography" columns; to "Bibliophile" examinations of individual books; to essays dissecting his short stories; to finding hidden links between seemingly unrelated works; to articles so knowledgeable they can only be compared to Phil writing about Tarzan.

Some notes on the format of this book: Many of the pieces have an introduction giving some background or context. We have mostly left the introductions intact so you get the feel of the fanzine as it was. Also, several articles in this book were later expanded and used elsewhere—as bonus material in Titan Books reprint series for example. In those cases we have used the latter versions of the articles to give you the most up to date content.

Many of the pieces in *Farmerphile* had illustrations. Regrettably we were not able to reproduce them in this collection for a number of reasons. This really is a shame as the artwork was certainly a big part of *Farmerphile*'s appeal and success. I wish I could have shared all the interior illustrations and cover art drawn by Keith Howell, Charles Berlin, Jason Robert Bell, Chuck Loridans, Karl Kaufman, Shannon Robicheaux, Joey Van Massenhoven, Henry Covert, John Streleckis, and Vladimir Verano. As it is, the only remnant of all this wonderful artwork we have in this collection is the frontispiece, an illustration by Charles Berlin for the story, "The Face that Launched a Thousand Eggs." And of course the collage of covers used for the trade paperback edition, and Keith Howell's cover from *Farmerphile No. 12* we used for the hard-cover limited edition.

Going through all this material to write this introduction brings back a flood of memories and reminds me just how remarkable *Farmerphile* was; how proud we were of each issue and what we were able to share with the world. It also reminds me how much I miss Phil and Bette, and how lucky I was to get to know them, spend time with them, and, I hope, do something special for them.

The Roller Coaster Ride with Phil Farmer
Bette Farmer

Farmerphile No. 1

As I stood at my locker in the basement of Bradley Hall, there was suddenly a loud crashing behind me. I turned and saw that a man had fallen down the stairs. I turned to help him and saw that he was grinning from ear to ear, and that it was a guy I had wanted to meet. Embarrassed, I turned back to my locker, knowing he was all right. There was another crash, and there he was again. I turned around and said, "You're going to kill yourself." He jumped up and started a long diatribe about how he had looked at me from afar for so long and it was like viewing a beautiful sunset or some such thing. He has started many stories through the years with just such an opening BANG!

I went to Bradley on two scholarships, one in music and one in science. They said that didn't happen very often. I was soloist in choir, and prepared for lab tech training, too.[1] I met Phil in my first semester as a Freshman at Bradley University. It was about Nov. of '40. He told me he was going to give me his fraternity pin the next night. I waited several nights and finally asked him just when he planned to do that. It was in the middle of a basketball game and he just reached in his pocket as if he'd been waiting for me to ask, pulled out the pin and put it on me. The next semester he told me he was transferring to the University of Missouri. I was heartbroken, but he said he could get much better Journalism courses there, so I said no more. After he got down there I started getting these beautiful letters. (No, Mike, you can't print those!) Many of them spoke of "when we get married." I hadn't heard anything about that. He came home almost every Friday night. He would skip his last English class on Friday and hitch-hike home. He said he just got too lonesome for me. Then we would have to figure out some way to get him back. Someone in the family would always come through.

I got a letter in April inviting me to a fraternity dance. I was very excited, and my mother and I spent a lot of time planning what I would wear. I was invited to stay at the Pi Phi house which

Fall 1941, Stamford Texas shortly after Phil joined the Army Air Force

was across the street from Phil's Lambda Chi house. It was a very exciting trip. The first night I arrived was the dance. About 11:30 that night someone tapped Phil on the shoulder and said it was time to go.

I asked, "Go where?"

He said, "To get married!"

I said, "Married?"

His friend said, "You don't think I'd come all the way from Kansas City for anything else, did you?"

With that, we all piled into cars and drove to Boonville, Missouri and by the time we arrived it was almost midnight. We had to get our license before midnight, so we could get married the next day. We woke a Justice of the Peace and, after giving us our license, he asked if we'd like to be married by a minister. I said we would, so he sent us across the street, where he woke another couple, a minister and his wife. After getting married we drove back to Columbia, Mo. and I went to the sorority house and Phil to the frat house for the night! The reason for this was that we didn't want anyone at home to find out. The next day I told the girl I was staying with that I felt it was too much of an inconvenience for me to stay there (of course she didn't believe me) and Phil and I drove back to a hotel in Boonville and that's where we spent our honeymoon.

Farmerphile No. 2

We first became aware of the yearly Science Fiction Conventions in '52, and went to Chicago to attend the Worldcon being held there. Phil had just had "The Lovers" published and, of course, we were very excited since we had never met any of the people in Science Fiction.

We met a lot of writers at the convention. One strange man and woman followed us around, smiling, for the whole evening, but never spoke. Later, when we went to our room, we found a note under our door. It was from Forry Ackerman, offering his services as an agent, but Phil already had one. Later, when we lived in Los Angeles, we became good friends of Forry and Wendy and enjoyed their company.

One young man, wearing a beanie cap with a propeller on top, came up to Phil and said he'd read the "The Lovers" and didn't think it was so great. This young man became an excellent writer, who gets very angry with me when I mention the above and denies it vehemently. But then Harlan Ellison is vehement about many things, but we both love him dearly and consider him a good friend.

I started to sit on a chair at a lecture, and jumped up immediately. Someone's thumb was on my chair. I turned around to look and *it belonged to Isaac Asimov.* Since then I don't think I ever sit down without looking behind me to be sure my chair is empty.

We met many wonderful people at the Con in '52. It always seemed better than the later Cons because they got so large while this one was around three hundred people. We didn't know anyone when we arrived, but by the time we left we had made many friends, among whom were: Doc Smith, Fred Pohl, Tony Boucher, Fritz Leiber, Bob Bloch, Bob Tucker, Lester del Rey, George O. Smith, Ted Sturgeon, Randall Garrett, Harry Harrison, and I believe, Arthur Clarke was there, too.

Achievement Awards Winners: Ed Emshwiller, John W. Campbell, Willie Ley, Evelyn Gold, Phil Farmer, Forrest J. Ackerman and Hannes Bok.

Phil met Sam Mines, editor of *Startling Stories*, Jerry Bixby, assistant editor, Ted Dikty, and Mel Korshak to talk about doing a hard cover of "The Lovers." They told him about the Shasta Prize Novel Contest, and he came home and wrote *River Of Eternity* in less than 30 days. He would write a page, hand it to me and I would type out the final copy. He just made it. That is a long story that most of you know, so I won't go into that.

In December, Randy Garrett phoned and asked if he could come for Xmas. He stayed several years. Finally Phil told him he would have to go and gave him the money to go to New York where I later heard that he was living with Bob and Barb Silverberg. Randy was a very talented man, but when it came to writing, I either had to tie him to a chair to get him to sit at the typewriter, or he was out to the nearest bar within the hour.

The following year we attended the Worldcon held in Philadelphia. This was the first year they gave out awards and Phil was nominated for the "New Discovery" that year along with Bob Sheckley.

When we got there, we were introduced to Horace Gold's wife, Evelyn. Horace seldom left his home in those days, so he sent her to represent *Galaxy,* one of the magazines that had turned down "The Lovers." She was very friendly to me and by the next day was asking me if Phil was going to win. I honestly told her I didn't know. But Phil did. He had been told that afternoon, but was afraid I would tell someone, so *I didn't know.* I was glad, because I was impressed by Mrs. Gold's friendliness and might have told her. So, that night at the banquet, when the awards were to be given out, Mrs. Gold sat at Bob Sheckley's table, and when Phil's name was called as the winner she had a very surprised look on her face. When they announced Phil's name, he turned to me and said he'd known all afternoon. Phil can really keep a secret, but I felt this was going too far. Needless to say, we were very happy.

Phil won the award mostly because of "The Lovers" and it had been a hard story to get published because it was so different. Of course, John Campbell turned it down for *Astounding*. John really didn't publish much about people or biology, just straight science for the most part. I remember that some of the "Purists" in SF were very unhappy to have Women in their universe. It was amusing. But the good reception of "The Lovers" was amazing. Sam Mines published letters in *Startling Stories* about it for over a year, and almost all praised the story.

Farmerphile No. 3

In October, 1952, we received a phone call from Pekin, Illinois from Vernell Coriell. He had just read "The Lovers" and wanted very much to come up and meet Phil and bring a friend, Jack Cordes.

Vern was a devoted Tarzan fan and at that time was editor of The Burroughs Bibliophiles. We kept up that friendship for many years, and after Vern passed away, Jack continued to come to our house. So we've kept that friendship alive for over fifty years. Jack now presides over our weekly movie club. Vern was a member of the famous Coriell family acrobatic team for many years. After he retired from that, he did lectures and demonstrations of acrobatic prowess for high schools. One day he came to our house with a unicycle, which he was learning to ride so he could take it with him on his tours of the high schools. At the same time, another friend of ours, Burke Martin, stopped by. He had taken a job with the Post Office for the Xmas holidays, so he came in with his mail bag to have a cup of coffee and rest and visit with us. Time flew by and suddenly Burke remembered his mail route. Vern said he had to go too, so we all went out on the porch and Vern did a double flip down the six steps from the porch, jumped on his unicycle, and rode down the street and back. Suddenly we noticed that many neighbors up and down the street were out looking for their mail. They saw all the "goings on" at the Farmer household, as Vern went by on his cycle. Their mouths dropped open . . . those "kooky" Farmers were at it again.

In 1962 we were living in Scottsdale, Arizona. Phil was working as a tech writer for Motorola. During his vacation we drove back to the Midwest to attend the convention in Chicago again. One night there was a rumor going around that Hugh Hefner was going to invite some of the authors, etc. to the Playboy mansion for a party later that night. During the evening, one by one this author and that editor etc. would be invited. Finally we got our invitation and I was so excited. We were invited for a late evening, early morning breakfast, served by a number of University of Chicago students. The apartment was fascinating, especially the indoor swimming pool. You could watch people dive on the main floor and then walk downstairs and watch them swimming in the pool. I was impressed. During the evening I asked Mr. Hefner to point out the ladies room. He said I would never find it, and walked me down the paneled hall, stopped, pressed one of the panels and there was a beautiful bathroom!

I consider myself to be one of the few people I know who has been ushered to the bathroom by Hugh Hefner.

We moved to L.A. around 1965, from Phoenix, Arizona, where we had lived for almost seven years. We didn't know many people when we arrived so Bob Bloch introduced us into the Pinckard Salon, a group of about thirty people who met once a month to hear a fantastic lecturer. We made many close friends who came to our house frequently. Among them were: A.E. van Vogt and wife, Mayne, Wendy and Forry Ackerman, Bebe and Lou Behren, who introduced electronic music to the industry, Bob and Ellie Bloch and our old friends Lil and Arnold Schindler and Lil Nevil. When we'd meet for birthdays, Harlan Ellison would often be there.

While we were living there, Phil received an invitation to the Rio Film Festival.[2] Harlan called Phil and asked if he could get him an invitation. Phil called and suggested they might want a very prominent writer and suggested Harlan and so Harlan was invited. The committee told Phil that the SF group of writers was the nicest group they had ever dealt with. Everyone helping everyone else out to get there. Harlan did many things for Phil and other writers during the time we lived there and still is. He really is not all bluster.

Farmerphile No. 4

Gary and Dede Wolfe used to come to Peoria on a weekend now and then and we would play pool and just have a wonderful time. There was one particularly funny event that happened while they were here. Phil and Gary had been invited to speak at Bradley University, and the man who had asked them phoned beforehand that he would like to take them to dinner. Since we assumed he wanted to talk about the speech, Dede and I weren't invited. Well, we thought that was pretty bad manners, but we would show them. So we called for reservations at the same restaurant. We didn't tell Gary and Phil. This restaurant is huge, with many little corners and two floors and a balcony, and it never occurred to us that we'd see each other. The waiter led us to our table in a very winding way, upstairs, around corners here and there and finally to our table. We sat down, looked at the table across from us and burst out laughing. He had seated us right across from Phil and Gary's party. The man who was taking them looked very embarrassed, while we explained that we didn't know they were there! Dede and I laughed all through the meal.

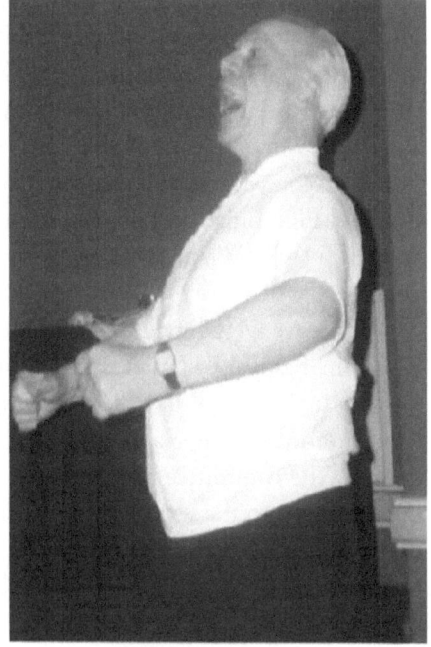

Later Gary was able to talk Phil into going to Florida to the conference. Gary has written about that in his article [page 269], but I will just say that we were both very glad we had gone. We hired a boat to take us to a restaurant, The 17th Street Fisheries, where we had great food and fun. I asked the pilot of the boat who owned all the beautiful mansions along the way, and he said, "It's drug money." Suddenly the beauty went out of the houses for me. I'm sure he was exaggerating somewhat, but I couldn't forget his words.

One thing Gary didn't mention was that before Phil gave his Tarzan yell, he put both hands on the edge of the stage and swung himself up to the platform. He was seventy-five at the time.

Farmerphile No. 5

For three weeks of my life, I enjoyed listening to laughter coming from Phil's office as he wrote *Venus On The Half-Shell*. He was so thrilled when Mr. Vonnegut gave him permission to write it, with the promise that he would not tell anyone that he was the author.

We arranged with a friend to come over with a wig she had, which we used for the beard, and she took pictures of Phil in our basement. In my favorite, he was sitting in front of a poster of the Marx Brothers. The publisher objected to that one because another company was bringing out a book about them and they felt that would constitute advertising for a competitor, so we used another picture.

The book sold very well, and the argument started as to whether Mr. V. had written it, or another author. Many were suggested, but not Phil for a long time. In the meantime Mr. V. was getting angry. I never was sure why. Some people said it was the worst thing he had written and some said the best. I'm not certain which idea angered him the most. However, he notified Phil that he had to tell the public that it was his book. We were on our way to Los Angeles where Phil was to speak at Harlan Ellison's program, "Ten Tuesdays Down A Rabbit Hole." The day Phil spoke The UCLA newspaper came out with absolute proof that Vonnegut had written the book. When Phil got up to speak, he announced that at Mr. Vonnegut's request he was announcing that he had written it. It was too bad. Everyone had had so much fun trying to figure it out. To this day we still run across people who think Vonnegut wrote Venus. It started out as a wonderful, joyous thing, because Phil admired Mr. V. so very much. It ended with lies and insults and hurts. A movie company wanted to make it, but Mr. V. said "No." He said Phil had enough money! Since when has an SF writer been really wealthy?

I have read that 225,000 copies were sold the first month. Naturally, we were very excited and waited for the first royalty check. When it was very low, we phoned the editor who had told us how well it was doing. He had been fired, and we were told it hadn't sold well. We know that wasn't true.

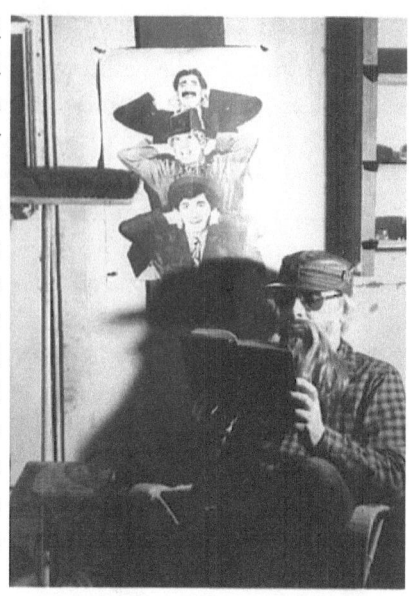

In spite of all the grief attached to that book, we are both still happy that *Venus* was written and published, and is still out there to be enjoyed. All writers have problems at one time or another, and that was one of ours.

Farmerphile No. 6

Phil had finished *Tarzan Alive* and he decided he wanted to write about Doc Savage. He needed to refresh his memory about "Doc," so he approached his friend, Jack Cordes. Jack had a complete collection of Doc Savage Magazines, and they were priceless. Jack was generous, and a good friend, so he allowed Phil to borrow all of them while he wrote the Doc Savage book. Phil read all one hundred and eighty-one of the magazines once, and went on to read some of them two or three times so that he would have a better idea of what Lester Dent, the author, was trying to say. Both the Tarzan book and Doc Savage required a lot of work, but he enjoyed writing them.

While writing it, Jack and Phil and I drove to La Plata, Missouri, the home of Lester Dent. Lester had been gone a few years, but we went to visit his wife. She was a lovely person and showed us all over the house, including his writing area. She was pleased that Phil was writing about Lester's hero, Doc Savage. Jack found that she didn't have some of Lester's stories, so as soon as we came home he sent her a couple of duplicates he had. Then he contacted someone at *Astounding* and told them of her problem. They contacted dealers who had the magazines, and it wasn't long before Mrs. Dent had a complete set. She was very pleased.

One time when we were in Dallas at a convention, Phil decided he would go shopping with me. Now that in itself should have alerted me, but I was so pleased that we went. Then I found this beautiful, very expensive dress that I looked just great in, but it cost too much. Phil insisted that I buy it and I insisted it was too expensive. At that point an old lady (about my present age) came over and whispered in my ear that I shouldn't be a fool . . . buy the dress! So I did. When we returned to the hotel, Phil asked me to write a check for a very large amount for him, as he had bought two paintings (the Shadow and Doc Savage paintings below). And then it hit me why he wanted me to get the dress! In order for him not to feel guilty, I had to too! Well it worked out well. We both were happy with our purchases, and enjoyed them for many years.

Photo courtesy of Patti Perret, *The Faces of Science Fiction*, Blue Jay Books, 1984.

Farmerphile No. 7

Walt Liebscher was a good friend of ours for many years. While we were still living in Los Angeles, Walt was horrified that our granddaughter, Kim, had never been to Disneyland, and said he and Phil would take her there. Somewhere I have many pictures of Phil and Walt and Kim and Minnie Mouse. At one time Walt was writing an article about strange names . . . funny ones . . . and we would spend many hours laughing at Walt's new names. Someone must know if he ever had that published. I'd love to see it.

Even after we came back to Peoria from L. A. he came to visit us as long as he could. He said he moved out of the Midwest because of his fear of tornados. Well, that got to be a joke because shortly after we left Los Angeles they had a major earthquake. Walt's bedroom was in the basement, and he was sleeping when it happened. When the shaking started, he tried to get upstairs to the main level, but he had bookcases lining the walls of the stairwell, and all the books were falling down into his pathway. He did finally make it up to the street, got in his car and drove to our friends' house, Lil and Arnold Schindler. The five of us were very close and spent a lot of time together.

One day Walt went to see his doctor and told him he had had strange dizzy spells, etc. and the doctor made him an appointment with a neurologist for the following Monday. As Walt was going out the office door, he had a major stroke. He didn't walk or talk much for a long time. Lil helped him a lot. We'd go to the Schindler's for dinner, and Lil would ask Walt a question. You could not understand his answer, and Lil would say, "Come on, you can speak plainer than that!" At first I thought it was being too hard on him, but she really got him to talking. He was very brave after the stroke, and soon learned to drive the car and talk to people.

Walt often wrote for Ed Connor's fanzine *Moebius Trip*. Ed became a member of our Sherlock Holmes group and we saw him every month at the meetings. He had a habit of always calling Phil to tell him about insulting reviews he had read. Finally, if I answered the phone and it was Ed, I would remark that he must have seen a bad review about Phil, and he would very casually say, "Yes," and be delighted to tell Phil about it. He never called with the good reviews. He was an odd man. He started collecting stray cats after his mother died, and later, when he was killed in an accident, his family found forty-five stray cats in his house. I don't really know of anyone who got very close to Ed, so it would be difficult for me to write a lot more. He really enjoyed Sherlock Holmes, as we all did, and we often picked him up and took him to meetings. But he never talked about himself, so it was hard to get to know him.

Farmerphile No. 8

"*There are no time machines. Like it or not, Miniver Cheevy, you have to live in this, your time.*" A quote from "Riders Of The Purple Wage," which reminds me that no matter how much we wish something could occur again, it can't. It can't? Well, it is going to do just that, and if you will bear with me, I'll tell you how we can go back to the night "Riders" opened in Chicago.

Phil had been contacted by director Arnold April, who wanted to make a play out of the book. We talked about it and I told Phil I could not imagine how they could make a play out of that story unless they had an actor on stage telling the audience what was going on. They were very clever. They put a window to the right of the stage, covered with a Venetian blind. When the actor was speaking to the audience, he would open the blinds. When he was done talking, he would close them. It was very clever.

Eric Barnes wrote the words and the music. I was told that he did it in one week, and if so, he is a genius, because he wrote some hilarious dialogue and Arnold did some great directing.

We went to Chicago for the opening. Gary Wolfe and his wife, Dede, went with us. I will never forget how excited I was, as we drove to the theater that opening night. Imagine my surprise when we drove up to this tiny building across from a cemetery and they told me that was the theater. Then someone said, "Bette, Hair started out in a place like this." Then I felt better. It was a dinner theatre and as we sat down to eat I saw a friendly face from Peoria. It was Jerry Klein and his wife. Jerry was doing a review and we hadn't known he was coming. Then I got nervous, because Peoria is a conservative town and "Riders" is not a conservative play. I needn't have worried as Jerry laughed all the way through and wrote a glowing review for the paper the following week. I had great hopes that it would "take off" and become a big success. But it snowed and snowed and snowed, and we had no advertising, and by the time people became aware of it, the theater had already been rented for the next month. So it just had a one month run. I will always believe that it could have been another "Hair" because it was so much better. Of course, I'm not prejudiced.

Now I will tell you how we are going to get in that time machine and go back. Our great grandson, Zachary Gittrich, came to me one day and asked where all the info about the play was. I said I had no idea. I couldn't tell him who wrote or directed it, or where the tape was or anything. He loves theater and wanted to put it on. Rather, he thought maybe he could sell the Lab theatre with the idea with only one stipulation. He got to play the lead. He worked very hard. He made long distance calls until he found out all he needed to know. Then he got permission from the directors in Chicago. He made copies of the tapes for the Board of Directors, and he waited. They turned him down because they said they had no place to put it this year. That's what they said. I think it was just a bit much for Peoria, but Zach says I'm wrong. Well, Zach is a wonderful great-grandson and an admirer of his great-grandfather's work, and he was on a mission. He called Mike Croteau to ask if he had any information about the "Riders" play or knew where to find any. Mike said he recalled seeing a copy of the script in a certain box in our basement. I didn't think we had received a copy of the script, but sure enough, Zach found it. This is just one more good thing that came from Mike searching our basement files gathering material for *Farmerphile*. I called Gary Wolfe and got the name of the play-write, and Zach called him. He got permissions from everyone, and nothing was going to stop him. Have I mentioned that Zach was seventeen at the time? Well, now he is eighteen. He finally called Bill Knight and Bill led him to the people who would give him permission to rent the Apollo Theater.

So the first two weekends in June we will all get in our time machines and go back and watch the play again. Mike is the guy to contact if you want to come to this year's Farmercon and attend the play. I think we can "fill the house" and all have a great time.[3]

Farmerphile No. 10

It is so quiet here since everyone left that I am thinking of having a monthly Farmercon. It was the best meeting we've ever had. I guess practice makes perfect, after all. What a wonderful time we all had.

The party started here on Friday afternoon with the arrival of Gary K. Wolfe from Chicago. Shortly after that, in came the Spiteris; Paul, Claire, Gina and Maddie. We already had some local guests, Julie and Lynn Carl and Julie's mom, so the party had a good start.

Saturday morning my oldest friend in Peoria came by to meet everyone. Jeanne Schroeder was the first person who knew Phil and I had eloped at the University of Missouri. That was sixty-six years ago, so you might say our friendship has lasted. She brought a plate full of delicious homemade chocolate brownies which everyone enjoyed.

Saturday morning everyone got busy to get everything ready for our Sunday party. Paul and Claire went to the store to pick up the food I'd ordered plus extras. John, our caregiver, did a great job getting the lower level ready by setting up the tables so they would be ready for the food. In the meantime, my helper Vui and I got a picnic lunch together and when the Spiteris returned we took off for Grand View Drive, which Teddy Roosevelt called "The most beautiful drive in the world." We found picnic tables overlooking the river so we could enjoy the view. It was great picnic weather. After we ate, we drove over to the park playground so the girls could play a while. They enjoyed that, as did a few of the adults!

We returned home, sat on the back porch and drank iced tea and lemonade and just talked. It was one of the nicest parts of the whole weekend. John served those who wanted it, some Lithuanian beer. He and several others enjoyed that.

About 6 P.M. we all left for Jonah's restaurant on the river in East Peoria. We had our own private room, bar and bartender, and a lovely view of Peoria from the other side of the river. We also had a very good meal. After dinner we had a number of speakers. Paul Spiteri introduced the speakers and did a wonderful job of that.

Some people who could not make it wrote letters of regret, which Win Eckert read aloud to the group. Among them were Phileas Fogg, Tim Howller, Greatheart Silver, and Kilgore Trout. We were so sorry they couldn't make it. Maybe next year. Thank you, Win, for reading those to us.

Thirty years ago, Phil was guest of honor at a con at the University of Copenhagen, and there we met Hans and Hanne Kiesow. Imagine our surprise when they came to our party this year. That was a very special part of the con to us, what a nice surprise.

Thank you to Chris Carey, who announced that thanks to Bob Barrett we will have an 11th issue of *Farmerphile*. And thanks to Mike looking through our file cabinets, we have had the first ten issues. But the real thanks go to Phil, who wrote them all in the first place. I'm so glad that Phil and Bob were friends, so we could get hold of those stories. My favorite is the one Chris read aloud at the banquet, "The First Robot." I had read this one just a few days before and actually cried. I wonder how many of us women in the group . . . especially writers' wives . . . feel like the first robot?

Phil and I were both presented with lovely framed awards. I was a bit embarrassed because so many of you have done much more than I have for this publication, and I want you to know that I have gone through life with Phil getting the awards, and it has made me very happy. One time as Phil had been autographing for several hours at a convention, a young man came up to where I stood and said, "Mrs. Farmer, he also serves who stands and waits." I assured him I had always known that, but as a matter of fact, one time Phil autographed for seven hours in a book store in England. As people would get their books autographed, they would come up to the front where I sat on a high stool, and talk with me. You can't imagine what interesting conversations I had with readers, and not about books! One young man who was a student at Cambridge invited me up to visit. Another man struck up a conversation on the British museum. It's amazing how interesting it can be to "Stand and wait!" I do like people and enjoy talking to them.

Joe Lansdale presented Phil with a "Maker of Universes" award. He also reminded us of the first time we all had met at a con, and told how much Phil's words helped him.

On Sunday everyone came to our house. All the food was put out on the lower level, which goes to a patio. We had chairs out there and inside and on the porch upstairs. People would take turns coming up to visit with Phil and he thoroughly enjoyed the whole day. Everyone ate and drank, and during that, we all started signing each other's programs. That did get to be funny, because eventually I looked down as I signed one, and saw my name at the top and in the middle of the page. I realized I was signing my own program for the second time! But it was like a shark feeding frenzy. We were all eager to get our programs signed, no matter what.

When it was over I said we couldn't wait a whole year for another FarmerCon and Mike suggested doing one after the Windy City Pulp and Paper Con in April. How I would love to get up to that. It really isn't impossible, so I'll keep it in mind.

People wonder why we settled back in Peoria. Our friends in L.A. gave us a lavish party when we left there. The hit of the party was a huge cake with "Why Peoria ???!!!" written across the top. Well, we had several reasons, one of them being that my family was here and we could live much cheaper, and Phil wanted to try to just write. That was scary. I recall one time when a check was long overdue and I complained about it. Judy Benjamin, an editor at Del Rey, wrote me and said I should stop complaining or the company I was talking about might stop publishing SF. I wrote back and told her that I had a bill from Sears in front of me, and I was going to write them and tell them that if they didn't stop billing me, I wouldn't buy anymore from them. Her husband, Lester, who was a writer first, told her I was right and we should be paid. No more from Judy. Yes, we did get our check.

But we had a stronger reason for choosing Peoria. We had lived in New York, Scottsdale, Ann Arbor, and Los Angeles, but the most fun we ever had was right here in good old Peoria. Right after WW2 many veterans and their wives came back here to go to college at Bradley, where Phil and I went. They all lived in Quonset huts on the campus and they were very small. But we had a house, so every weekend on Friday night the party would begin. It would end Monday morning. I never knew who I would find on my way to work, but I would just put a toe in their ribs and say, "Go to class," and they would get up and leave. But this group was very special. They were all intelligent people with a great sense of humor. My daughter used to say that she had difficulty finding a husband because there was no one out there both intelligent and crazy. For example, one New Year's Eve we were partying when a couple of my more dignified friends walked in. Phil and his friend, Bob, decided to play a trick. Bob came up the basement stairs shuffling and babbling and bent over like the Hunchback of Notre Dame. Phil introduced him as his retarded brother whom he allowed to live in our basement. At that point, Bob went over to the one lady and started patting her and babbling. She turned and left right away. When she had gone, those crazy guys rolled on the floor with laughter. And that is the crazy Peoria we knew. Those friends are all gone, but the Farmers go on.

Back around 1965 the *Saturday Evening Post* did a series of articles about towns that had "cleaned themselves up." Peoria was chosen one month as a city that had cleaned up its gambling and prostitution. Well, we had a good friend at the library who was a notorious gambler, and I worked for the VD clinic as a lab technician. We got a good laugh out of the publicity because our friend still gambled around the corner from the library, and I still checked out all the prostitutes for VD every week. The police would stop the girls from working, arrest them and collect fines. A week later they let them go back to work. The city did quite well that year, I'm sure. I always knew when they had gone back to work because I had to pick Phil up late at night from his job, and the red lights would be shining brightly again.

Farmerphile No. 11

When we moved from Los Angeles to Peoria we made it a habit to go back there every winter. We always stayed with Lil and Arnold Schindler for about three weeks. Phil's birthday party was always put on by Ellie (wife of Bob) Bloch. She would put on this wonderful dinner and a beautiful cake, and invite various people. Sometimes just Farmers and Schindlers, but if Florence Russell was in town from England, she would be there, too. I recall once when Forry Ackerman was there, and Lil Neville (wife of Kris) was always invited. For those of you who are too young to remember Kris, he was the author of a famous short story, "Bettyann."

Bob Bloch and I celebrated the same birthday, April 5th, so Ellie would get a small cake for Bob and me, because we wouldn't be there in April. They were wonderful people and we miss them a lot. Lil Neville and I speak now and then on the phone and can't believe we are all that's left of our group.

In the spring or summer, Lil and Arnold would come and visit us for three weeks. We took a lot of trips together. I recall one year when they came and it was raining over the whole United States except Virginia. So Lil and I went to the travel bureau and asked what they had in Virginia and they suggested Williamsburg, so Lil and I bought plane tickets, and went home and told Phil and Arnold we all were leaving the next day for Virginia. We had a great time.

When Phil's 80th birthday came along, I decided to have a big bash of a birthday party for him. I hired a guy in an ape suit to come to the door about half way through the party. When he knocked at the door, I said, "Phil, there's someone at the door, would you get it?" He opened the door and this huge ape put out his hand and said, "Mr. Farmer, Happy Birthday from Tarzan."

You have never seen an expression like the one on Phil's face! He was really dumbfounded. And then he started to laugh. Nobody else at the party knew this was going to happen either, so there were a lot of amazed looks. Gradually everyone realized what was going on and then even the "Gorilla" started having a good time, but for a while there were about forty-five amazed people. I was pleased that it worked out so well.

As a matter of fact, our lives are full of great times and a lot of it is connected to the SF world, naturally. We had the usual, and some unusual, problems of every couple, but our lives were so full of interesting happenings that I must say it has been a great sixty-six years we have spent together. All the great trips, the Guest of Honor trips particularly, have been wonderful. So here's to the next ninety years, Phil.

Farmerphile No. 12

As many of Phil's fans will know, we lived in California in the late 1960s before returning to Peoria. Before we left L.A. Phil had been laid off with about 30,000 other people who wrote theory and operation manuals for the moon landing, because the men had landed on the moon. I didn't know it but the company had found Phil another very good job and we could have stayed, but Phil wanted to write and said he wanted to move to Peoria because it would be cheaper to live here. So I flew ahead to Peoria, found the cheapest little house in a nice area, flew back, packed up 20,000 books and we moved back to Peoria. We had been gone from Peoria for about fifteen years. We lived in Syracuse, NY, then moved to Scottsdale, Arizona. During the seven years we were there, Phil was transferred to Ann Arbor, Mich., where we lived about four months before that contract was canceled and we moved back to Scottsdale.

We stayed there until about 1965 when we moved to Los Angeles. Needless to say, I got very used to moving. I really liked it. I get bored after about seven years, so it's time to move. I'm afraid I don't have the energy I used to have so I'll probably stay where I am now. Anyway, the last day Phil worked, he was given several severance checks, which he put in his top dresser drawer. That night I remarked to Phil that I had just heard the gates across our driveway clang. He got up and went out and looked all round three sides. The 4th side was the driveway next door, and our bedroom windows were on that side. They were casement windows and opened to the floor. I had opened them to let air in and as I walked in to close them I noticed muddy footprints on the carpet. I backed out of the room, went into the kitchen and called Phil. He grabbed a knife and went in to check on the children. I called the police. When they came they asked me to check my purse and I brightly told them I was sure they hadn't taken anything out of it, because as I walked out of the bedroom, I had noticed my purse on the chair and had gone back and put it on the floor behind a chest. Well, they insisted and when I lifted my purse, I knew. It was so light. I quickly went to the dresser to see if Phil's checks were there and they were. So I was glad my purse had been there. There was far less in that. The man was caught. If I had walked in on him I would have fainted. He was a very scary looking guy who had escaped from prison. If you have ever had an experience like this you'll know the fear you feel for a long time. This happened to us right after the Manson murders. All of L.A. was on edge until they were found.

After we had been in Peoria for several years Phil decided to start a local scion society of Baker Street Irregulars, The Hansoms of John Clayton. Being a female Sherlockian is quite different from being a male. Mainly, we did the cooking so everyone could eat after taking their exam, and oh you needed a meal after those exams. You cannot imagine some of those questions.

Like, where did Sherlock sit when smoking his pipe? Or how many steps did Sherlock take walking from his carriage to the house? And of course, many more detailed questions concerning the particular story we had read for that evening. I decided, the time our quiz was on the novel *The Sign of Four*, that I had to see if I could win. It was like studying for an exam in college in one of my science classes. But I won. After that I never tried to win, just to enjoy the story. It was more fun. You really needed a good memory.

So, we would take our test, find out who the winner was and then have our refreshments while discussing the story from that evening. We always had a lot of fun, and I'm glad they established the group. It was a good group and an interesting one, rather like SF groups.

Phil, Bob Burr, George Sheetz and I got together one evening in Peoria and started it off. Most of the female members did "kitchen duty" at each meeting. Why were men running the show? I could just see them in an apron, and who knows what sort of food we would have ended up with! So we were the "Mrs. Hudsons" of the group.

There were a lot of "different" and interesting people in the group. I had gone to college with one particular woman. She had taken the picture for the Kilgore Trout book, and when it came out she wasn't given credit. Phil contacted New York and reminded them to put her name in the book. When it came out, she was shocked at having her name in a Science Fiction book. She was a strange lady. For instance, one time she had the meeting at her house and when it came time for food, nothing happened. When we were done discussing the story, we waited for the smell of coffee and noises of food being prepared. And we waited, and we waited. Finally someone leaned over and whispered in my ear, "Would you like to go over to the restaurant and get cup of coffee?" I agreed, and we got up to leave. She liked to play tricks on friends so I guess this was it for us. She was very amused as we left. I turned to her and asked if she would like to go with us for coffee. She smiled her enigmatic smile and turned us down. I always hoped she got pleasure from that, but I couldn't see how. We went to the restaurant, had a bite and talked about the story. I was always sorry she didn't join us. We had fun.

[1] There is an old saying in SF, that all you needed to be a writer was a tweed coat, a pipe and a wife who worked. I worked as head of hematology for several years before we left Peoria and then on for twenty more in various cities, last working in Beverly Hills for three internists.

[2] Phil wrote a travelogue about this trip which appeared in the fanzine *Luna #6* (1969) and was reprinted in *Pearls from Peoria* (2006).

[3] Despite all of Zach's hard work, "Riders of the Purple Wage" never played in Peoria.

CREATIVE MYTHOGRAPHY
THE FARMERIAN HOLMES
WIN SCOTT ECKERT

"These are much deeper waters than I had thought."
—Sherlock Holmes
"The Adventure of the Reigate Squire"

D edicated followers of this column know that Philip José
Farmer's Wold Newton Family originated in 1795 with a
radioactive meteor and generations of cross-breeding, resulting
in an extended tree of crime-fighting adventurers, detectives,
explorers, and arch-criminals. Casual followers of the mythos,
however, may not be aware of the significant role the Canon of
Sir Arthur Conan Doyle's Sherlock Holmes tales plays in the
Wold Newton backstory outlined in Phil's *Tarzan Alive* and *Doc
Savage: His Apocalyptic Life*.

Of course, Phil patterned his first biography, *Tarzan Alive*, on
William S. Baring-Gould's *Sherlock Holmes of Baker Street*. Phil also
adopted Baring-Gould's theory that detective Nero Wolfe was
Sherlock Holmes' son (*Sherlock Holmes of Baker Street* and *Nero
Wolfe of West 35th Street*). In addition, Phil expanded the Holmes
family tree by placing Sherlock Holmes as a descendant of Dr. Siger
Holmes, who was present at the Wold Newton meteor strike, and
postulating that Sir Denis Nayland Smith (the protagonist of Sax
Rohmer's Fu Manchu books) was Sherlock Holmes' nephew.

The Sherlockian connections, however, are woven into the history of the Wold Newton Universe with a degree of complexity which transcends fictional genealogy. Phil's initial tour-de-force Wold Newton essay, "A Case of a Case of Identity Recased, or, The Grey Eyes Have It" (Addendum 2, *Tarzan Alive*), is based on Professor H. W. Starr's foray into Holmes-Tarzan scholarship, "A Case of Identity, or, The Adventure of the Seven Claytons" (*The Baker Street Journal*, New Series X, i, January 1960; reprinted in Addendum 1, *Tarzan Alive*). Starr sets the stage by suggesting that the hansom cab driver John Clayton from the Holmes novel *The Hound of the Baskervilles*, must be a member of a lineage in which all first sons are named John Clayton, and in fact the cab driver is the fifth Duke of Greyminster. Starr explains that Greyminster is the real name of the family called "Greystoke" in the Tarzan stories by Edgar Rice Burroughs; the family is also called "Holdernesse" in the Holmes tale "The Adventure of the Priory School."

Tarzan's father, of course, was named John Clayton, as was Tarzan himself. While it might initially seem ridiculous that a member of the nobility would choose to spend seven years as a London cabby, Starr makes a convincing case for John Clayton as enlightened radical, abandoning his wealth and title in a gesture of support for the underprivileged. Starr also proposes the Clayton genealogy, but as Phil makes some alterations in his follow-up, we'll focus on Phil's version.

Phil bolsters Starr's contention that the fifth duke was the cab-driver by conflating the duke with Sydney Trefusis, the protagonist of George Bernard Shaw's *An Unsocial Socialist*. He then explains that the fifth duke was the father of John Clayton, who was married to Alice Rutherford. These were Tarzan's parents, who were lost at sea and presumed dead in 1888, as told in Burroughs' *Tarzan of the Apes*. Shortly thereafter, in 1889, the fifth duke was murdered and the title passed to his brother, the sixth duke.

In May 1901, the sixth duke's son, Arthur, Lord Saltire, was kidnapped and Sherlock Holmes was called in to solve the case. Dr. Watson and his editor Doyle memorialized the incident as

"The Adventure of the Priory School," calling the sixth duke the "Duke of Holdernesse." The sixth duke's illegitimate son, James Wilder, was involved in the crime and immediately left England. Phil tells us that Arthur was later known as "William Clayton," the seventh Duke of Greystoke and a cousin to Tarzan (John Clayton), as seen in *Tarzan of the Apes* and *The Return of Tarzan* (which collectively cover events occurring 1909-1910). In *Tarzan Alive*, Phil explains that his real name was William Cecil Arthur Clayton.

When William Clayton was killed at the conclusion of *The Return of Tarzan*, the title passed to Tarzan, the grandson of the fifth duke. Tarzan became the eighth Duke of Greystoke.

Phil also edited one of Watson's Sherlock Holmes manuscripts, publishing it as a novel under the title *The Adventure of the Peerless Peer*. The novel resolves a lingering question raised by Phil's researches in *Tarzan Alive*: how did Tarzan respond to the publicity surrounding the discovery that he, an English peer, had been raised by apes? The answer, as Holmes deduces in 1916, is that Tarzan avoided the issue. In order to save himself unwanted attention, he passed himself off as the late seventh duke, William Clayton, whom he resembled greatly. Thus, although Tarzan was legitimately the eighth duke, he was known to the world as the seventh duke, William Clayton.

Holmes garners a hefty fee from Tarzan in exchange for his and Watson's silence on this matter.

In *Doc Savage: His Apocalyptic Life*, Phil explains that three years after the Priory School case, in 1904, the sixth duke hired Holmes to check up on his wayward son, James Wilder. Phil gives us Wilder's real name, James Clarke Wildman, and we learn that Wildman is the father of pulp hero "Doc Savage" (James Clarke Wildman, Jr.). And the sixth duke's estranged wife, named as "Edith Appledore" in "Priory School?" According to Phil, her real name was Edith Jansenius and she was the woman Holmes and Watson secretly observed eliminating the "worst man in London" in Watson and Doyle's "The Adventure of Charles Augustus Milverton."

Phil's reprinting of excerpts from Burke's *Peerage* (Addendum 3, *Tarzan Alive*) lists Edith as deceased, June 1907. However, a partial manuscript and outline entitled *The Evil in Pemberley House*, recently unearthed from a filing cabinet in the basement of Phil's house in Peoria, demonstrates that Edith, the dowager Duchess of Greystoke, was alive as late as Spring 1973, age 103. In the manuscript, the dowager duchess encounters Patricia Wildman, the granddaughter of her late husband's illegitimate son, James Wildman. Sparks ensue. In "Further Sketches from the Ruins of My Mind!" by Robert R. Barrett (*Farmerphile No. 11*, January), my fellow Creative Mythographer states that Doc Wildman (or Doc Savage, if you prefer) shared his life with his cousin, Pat Savage, rather than marrying a former con-woman as stated in *Pemberley House*. Mr. Barrett speculates that Phil created the *Pemberley House* manuscript as a fictional element designed to protect Pat Savage, concluding that, "We will probably never know!"

With respect to my fellow *Farmerphile* contributor, I believe that we probably will know. It's clear that Phil discovered the information in *Pemberley House* while interviewing Patricia Wildman during preparation of the book *Doc Savage: His Apocalyptic Life*. While Phil is a trickster and has been known to plant small misdirecting bits of information (such as the June 1907 death of Edith Jansenius), I doubt he would devote the time and effort to writing several false chapters and a fake outline, and then effectively bury them in his basement for thirty-plus years, with a goal of creating disinformation to protect Pat Savage. When and if the *Pemberley House* manuscript is completely reconstructed, readers will see that the document is consistent with the overarching Wold Newton mythos and Sherlockian backstory, and will be able to make their own determination.

It should also be noted that in *Pemberley House*, Patricia Wildman encounters Sherlock Holmes and Dr. Fu Manchu on the train from London to the village of Lambton in Derbyshire. Recalling that *Pemberley House* takes place in early 1973, it's obvious the Royal Jelly life-extension elixir which Baring-Gould posited that Holmes developed was quite effective. Of course Fu Manchu also had his own immortality brew, called the Elixir of Life.

The Other Log of Phileas Fogg is another prominent entry by Phil which relies and builds upon the Holmesian Canon. In fact, the primary villain is none other than the man who would go on to become Holmes' arch-nemesis, Professor James Moriarty. The premise (lifted from Professor H. W. Starr) that Professor Moriarty was also the man called "Captain Nemo" in Jules Verne's *20,000 Leagues under the Sea* is certainly controversial, as is the dismissal of Verne's sequel, *The Mysterious Island*, as completely fictional. Even if one disagrees with that premise, however, the novel can still be interpreted as a Moriarty adventure, with references not only to the villainous Professor, but also his brother, Colonel Moriarty (also named James) from Watson and Doyle's "The Final Problem."

As long as we're discussing Professor Moriarty, it's worth noting here the daughter that Phil created, Urania Moriarty, to help fill a genealogical slot. In *Doc Savage: His Apocalyptic Life*, Phil speculated that Urania was married to John Clay from Watson and Doyle's "The Adventure of the Red-Headed League." Phil informs us that Clay was the son of the Countess Cagliostro and Sir William Clayton. Sir William Clayton was the uncle of John Clayton, the fifth duke and erstwhile cabby from *Hound* (more on the prolific Sir William later). John Clay was the same person as Colonel Clay, the master of disguise in Grant Allan's *An African Millionaire*. According to Phil, John Clay and Urania Moriarty were the parents of Dr. Caber, Joseph Jorkens' nemesis in stories by Lord Dunsany, and Carl Peterson, Bulldog Drummond's arch-enemy from the novels by H. C. "Sapper" McNeile.

Phil also edited another manuscript of a Holmes adventure, but one not originally set down by Watson. Rather, this tale was recorded by master cracksman A. J. Raffles' amanuensis, Harry "Bunny" Manders. The case is "The Problem of the Sore Bridge—Among Others" and it provides the solution to the disappearance of "Mr. James Phillimore, who, stepping back into his own house to get his umbrella, was never more seen in this world." Phillimore's vanishing act is mentioned in Watson and Doyle's "The Problem of Thor Bridge." Both *Peerless Peer* and "Sore Bridge" were recently reprinted in the collection *Venus on the Half-Shell and Others* (Subterranean Press, 2008).

Phil also began to edit another Holmes manuscript, but sadly never completed the process. Typed and handwritten notes (again from the treasure chest that is the filing cabinet in the basement) indicate that the untold tale "Sherlock Holmes in Mecca," taking place during the period of Holmes' global travels from May 1891–April 1894 known as "the Great Hiatus," was a whopper, with Holmes teaming with Ludovick "Sandy" Gustavus Arbuthnot's uncle on an Arabian mission assigned by Sherlock's older brother, Mycroft Holmes. Sandy Arbuthnot is from the Richard Hannay series of novels by John Buchan. The "Mecca" case may have involved the Islamic holy relic, the Black Stone. In typically humorous fashion, Phil's notes contain some possible alternate titles: "The Adventure of the Meccan Mechanic"; "The Adventure of the Mute Meccan"; "The Adventure of the Huge Haji"; "The Adventure of the Copped Kaaba"; and "The Adventure of the Half-Arsed Hafiz" are but a few examples. Perhaps some day an intrepid Farmerian Sherlockian will piece this case together.

Mixed in with Phil's notes for "Mecca" is a final page which reads: "SH & JW investigate the Loch Ness Monster." Intriguing, although this would not have been related to the "Mecca" case, since during the time of the Great Hiatus, Dr. John Watson thought Holmes was dead. An elderly Holmes and Watson also make a small cameo appearance in *Doc Savage and the Cult of the Blue God* (originally titled *Doc Savage: Archenemy of Evil*), the screen treatment Phil wrote in the 1970s for the second, and unfilmed, Doc Savage motion picture.

One of Phil's more outré Sherlockian outings is the short story "A Scarletin Study." Here, he edits Jonathan Swift Somers III's manuscript of the first case of the genius talking canine detective Ralph von Wau Wau. Wheels within wheels, Somers is also an editor, the case actually being written in first person by Dr. Weisstein. The beginning of the tale parallels in humorous and exacting detail Watson and Doyle's first Holmes novel, *A Study in*

Scarlet, with Ralph standing in for Holmes and Weisstein filling the Watson role. The Ralph von Wau Wau stories take place in the Wold Newton Universe, as Phil incorporated the canine genius in *Doc Savage: His Apocalyptic Life*. Both *Cult of the Blue God* and "A Scarletin Study" were most recently published in the collection *Pearls from Peoria* (Subterranean Press, 2006).

Although Phil devoted several volumes of writing to his heroes Tarzan and Doc Savage, his lifelong fascination with Sherlock Holmes obviously runs through many of his works. It's a fascination he's passed on to many post-Farmerian Wold Newton writers as well.

In my own "Who's Going to Take Over the World When I'm Gone?" (*Myths for the Modern Age: Philip José Farmer's Wold Newton Universe*, MonkeyBrain Books, 2005), I devote a whole section to the lineage of "The Malevolent Moriartys." Dennis E. Power reconciled two different version of Phil's Sherlock Holmes crossover novel (the Holmes-Tarzan *Peerless Peer* and the Holmes-Mowgli *The Adventure of the Three Madmen*) in his essay "Jungle Brothers, or, Secrets of the Jungle Lords" (*Myths*). Rick Lai added characters from the works of John Buchan and Robert Louis Stevenson to the Moriarty family in "The Secret History of Captain Nemo" (*Myths*). Brad Mengel's "Watching the Detectives, or, The Sherlock Holmes Family Tree" (*Myths*) goes a few steps further, creating a whole tree for the Holmes family, using Phil's work as the jumping-off point.

Speaking of *Myths for the Modern Age*, and returning to Phil's own investigations into the Sherlockian Canon, another brief but effective bit of research is his "The Two Lord Ruftons" (originally published in the *Baker Street Journal*, December 1971; reprinted in *Myths*). In this essay, Phil discusses the Lord Rufton who is the father of the title character in Watson and Doyle's "The Disappearance of Lady Frances Carfax," and the Lord Rufton in Doyle's Brigadier Gerard story "How He Triumphed in England." Phil concludes that the Lord Rufton in the Gerard tale is the grandfather of Lady Frances Carfax. The Wold Newtonian connections should be noted. In *Doc Savage: His Apocalyptic Life*, Phil placed Brigadier Gerard as a distant (and non-Wold Newton irradiated) ancestor of James Bond. The Carfaxes also appear in the reproduction of the Greystoke lineage from Burke's *Peerage* (Addendum 3, *Tarzan Alive*):

> He [Sir William Clayton] m. 4th 1832 Lorina, dau. of Lord Dacre by Jane Carfax, dau. of Lord Rufton, and by her had issue,
>
> 1. Phileas, b. 1832, and
> 2. Roxana, b. 1833.
>
> His wife divorced William in 1835 and m. Sir Heraclitus Fogg [Bt.], an eccentric inventor and owner of a vast estate, Fogg Shaw, in Derbyshire. Sir Heraclitus adopted his two stepchildren, William not objecting.

Additionally, in Phil's novel *Traitor to the Living*, Professor Gordon Carfax (who is the same person formerly known as private detective "Herald Childe" in Phil's *Image of the Beast* and *Blown*) has an uncle named Rufton Carfax. Rufton Carfax is likely descended from Lord Rufton from "Lady Frances Carfax."

I would be remiss indeed if I didn't mention Phil's short essay "What Happened to Black Michael?" (Addendum 4, *Tarzan Alive*; based on an original idea by Dale L. Walker; developed by John Harwood; additional notes by Farmer). In this piece, Phil reconciles the sailor Black Michael from Burroughs' *Tarzan of the Apes* with a ship's captain, Black Peter Carey, from Watson and Doyle's "The Adventure of Black Peter," providing yet another connection between the Canon and the Tarzanic Epic. Phil also informs us that Peter Michael Carey was responsible for the murder of the fifth Duke of Greystoke.

Phil concludes with the following paragraph:

> Be it also noted that Holmes, strong as he was, could not drive a harpoon all the way through the body of a pig. He concluded that the man who pinned Carey to

the wall with a harpoon was very strong and probably a professional harpooner. Cairns [a character in "Black Peter"] was such, but he would have had to use both hands to do it. Tarzan, of course, could have performed the feat with one hand and without drawing on all his strength.

"The Adventure of Black Peter," in which Holmes investigates Black Peter's murder, takes place in July 1895. Tarzan was born in November 1888. On the one hand, Phil's final remark is meant to reinforce our image and understanding of Tarzan's enormous strength. On the other hand, it seems odd for him to mention that Tarzan "could have performed the feat" when Tarzan was less than eight years old and living undiscovered in the African jungle, being raised by apes. My fellow Creative Mythographer, Christopher Paul Carey, has remarked on this curiosity to me and is currently probing his family records for further information on his infamous relative. A mystery remains, one worthy of Holmes himself.

Deep waters, indeed.

CREATIVE MYTHOGRAPHY
EXCESSIVELY DIVERTED,
OR, COMING TO PEMBERLEY HOUSE
WIN SCOTT ECKERT

On July 4, 2005, I met Philip José Farmer for the first time. That, in and of itself, would have been—and was—sufficient to render me mute and senseless. Contrary to the popular cliché, one should always try to meet one's hero; the experience just might turn out to be better than one could ever have hoped.

Something else happened that day, though. In addition to the invitation from Mike Croteau, webmaster of *The Official Philip José Farmer Home Page*, to come to the mountain, I was invited into the deep caverns below the mountain containing many hidden treasures: The Basement. Little did I know at the time, but in The Basement, just behind the library in the den, which was decked out with many awards and original cover art for various Phil Farmer books, was located what is now affectionately—and reverentially—called The Magic Filing Cabinet. Mike and I spent several engrossing hours poring over files, clippings, and memorabilia, in an effort to locate more previously unpublished material for *Farmerphile: The Magazine of Philip José Farmer*.

And boy, did we find some unpublished material.

Fans of Farmer's work with Tarzan, Doc Savage, and the Wold Newton Family know that Farmer gave us several tantalizing hints of Lord Greystoke's fate after Edgar Rice Burroughs ceased chronicling his exploits. Greystoke visited Opar one last time and dismantled it (*Tarzan Alive: A Definitive Biography of Lord Greystoke*); he granted an interview with Farmer just prior to faking his death and assuming a new identity ("An Exclusive Interview with Lord Greystoke"); he traveled back in time (*Time's Last Gift*) and lived forward 14,000 years, even making brief appearances in prehistoric Africa (*Hadon of Ancient Opar, Flight to Opar*, and *The Song of Kwasin*).

However, until July 4, 2005, we didn't know that Farmer also had information on the post-pulp career of Doctor James Clarke "Doc" Wildman, Jr. In fact, the source of Farmer's information for the partial manuscript and outline of *The Evil in Pemberley House* was Patricia Wildman herself; she also supplied Farmer with some of the information he needed to complete the biography of her father entitled *Doc Savage: His Apocalyptic Life*.

It is worth noting, however, that sources other than Farmer have also purported to reveal information on the post-canonical careers of Greystoke and Doc. Some of these also provide information about other children and even grandchildren of the two super-men. If they did have other descendants, then why was Patricia Wildman identified as the sole heir to Pemberley House?

Greystoke and his descendants are fairly easy to explain. Most of them participated in the Jungle Lord's overall plan to fake their deaths, or at least disappear, and assume new identities. They all had access to the wealth the ape-man had discovered in an African hidden city, and they all had partaken of the life-extension elixir he had discovered. None had any need or desire for the wealth of the Greystoke estate, and the peerage title was mostly a burden rather than an honor, especially for those who were effectively immortal.

Greystoke and Jane had three biological children, Charlotte Clayton, b. 1911 (mentioned in Burroughs' non-series book *The Man-Eater*); John Paul "Jack" Clayton, b. 1912 (*Tarzan Alive: A Definitive Biography of Lord Greystoke*); and Penelope Alice Clayton, b. 1919[1] (see Chuck Loridans' "The Daughters of Greystoke," *Myths for the Modern Age: Philip José Farmer's Wold Newton Universe*,

Win Scott Eckert, ed., MonkeyBrain Books, 2005). The first two faked their deaths at different times and eventually reunited with their parents and family, along with Jack's son John Clayton (b. 1943) and his own family. Penelope had long since changed her name when she moved to America in the mid-1930s, but she too, along with her husband, Mr. Smith, eventually disappeared from public view and reunited with the larger Greystoke clan.

There were also two adopted sons. One's story was actually told in Burroughs' *The Son of Tarzan* (for the full story of the biological son Jack Clayton vs. the adopted son John Drummond-Clayton, see Farmer's "The Great Korak-Time Discrepancy" in *Myths*). John Drummond-Clayton (b. 1898) would not have been entitled to the Greystoke title. In any event, he and his descendants—with one exception to be noted below—joined the Greystoke clan in faking their deaths and disappearing in, or before, 1972.[2]

The other adopted son's tale was recounted by J. T. Edson in a series of four novels beginning with *Bunduki* (and a couple of short stories that take place very shortly before the first novel). In *Bunduki*, which can be dated to 1972,[3] James Allenvale "Bunduki" Gunn (b. 1949), a second adopted son of Lord Greystoke, is mysteriously transported to the planet Zillikian, a "counter-Earth." Also transported is Bunduki's cousin, Dawn Drummond-Clayton (b. 1950), the granddaughter of John Drummond-Clayton, who was the *first* adopted son of Lord Greystoke. The inexplicable disappearances of Bunduki and Dawn removed them from consideration for inheriting Pemberley; neither would have been eligible to inherit the titles.

Interestingly, *Bunduki* reveals that the rest of the Greystoke clan is living in Pellucidar, the inner world described in Edgar Rice Burroughs' series starting with *At the Earth's Core*. When the Greystokes faked their deaths, they must have traveled to Pellucidar to cover their tracks.[4] The savage inner world would have suited Lord Greystoke perfectly, but for reasons yet untold, by the late 1980s he and Jane had returned to the surface world, using new identities.

The jungle lord also had two other children, although he

didn't know it.[5] Chuck Loridans uncovered the story behind one child, conceived with a priestess named La when Greystoke was suffering from amnesia. The child, born in 1938, eventually became known as "Modesty Blaise," although she never knew who her parents were ("The Daughters of Greystoke," *Myths*).

The other child was Jean Raoul de Coude; he was conceived with Countess Olga de Coude during the events of Burroughs' *The Return of Tarzan*, before Greystoke reunited with Jane, and was born in 1910. By 1988, Greystoke had long since faked his death and taken a new identity, but de Coude managed to get to him nonetheless, tormenting the Jungle Lord before finally being killed (*Tarzan the Warrior*, Malibu Comics, 1992). Perhaps if de Coude had known that Pemberley House was up for grabs in 1973, he would have made a claim for it, but it would have been rejected due to his illegitimacy.

Moving on to Doc Wildman, the Man of Bronze, it will be most instructive to begin with a set of documents pertaining to him; specifically, an essay, a transcript, and some reproduced newspaper clippings, all of which appeared in *Farmerphile No. 6* (October 2006) in a piece I titled "Doc Wildman: Out of Time." Much of the documentation refers to Doc under a name he was known to use on occasion, particularly when operating in Europe, "Doctor Francis Ardan."[6]

The information provided in "Doc Wildman: Out of Time" reconciles the other children and grandchildren of Doc Wildman with the existence of Patricia Wildman by explaining that Doc went back in time several decades and then lived parallel to himself in a second time-track; it doesn't explain why the other descendants were not identified as his heirs in *The Evil in Pemberley House*.

Doctor Justine Ducharme (b. 1928) was never publicly revealed as Doc's daughter. Both Doc and Justine's mother felt, despite Doctor Natas' discovery of the familial relationship as described in the tale "The Vanishing Devil,"[7] that it was nevertheless best to maintain as much secrecy as possible in order to protect Justine against further threats aimed at getting to Doc.

Doc's son in time-track #1, Clark III, was portrayed as being killed in 1966 in the mini-series "The Heritage of Doc Savage" (*Doc Savage*, volume 1, issues 1–4, DC Comics, 1987; collected as *Doc Savage: The Silver Pyramid*, DC Comics, 2010). Brad Mengel's essay "The Incredible Adventures of Clark Savage III"[8] proposes that Clark III faked his death and became a vigilante under the alias Richard Joseph Camellion. Either way, Clark III was not available as an heir.

Clark III left behind a son who was born in 1967, Clark IV, nicknamed "Chip." After the tragic events surrounding Clark III's apparent death, Doc's remaining aides felt it wisest to quit New York and raise the child in secrecy at one of Doc's arctic fortresses. The world never knew of Clark IV's existence until long, long after the 1973 events of *Pemberley House*.

If one believes my outlandish theory that Doc's archenemy, "Jean Lumière du Soleil," was also his son,[9] then he would be a potential heir, but for the fact that he died in 1937 in the pulp novel *The Devil Genghis* (or, if one prefers, a year later in the Doc Savage pastiche miniseries *The Monarch of Armageddon*, Millennium Comics, 1991). In Doc's time-track #1, Lumière du Soleil was briefly resurrected in 1989 in the DC Comics story "Sunlight Rising" (*Doc Savage*, volume 2, issues 11–14, DC Comics, 1989), but that cannot have had any impact on Patricia's inheritance in 1973.[10]

It's worth mentioning that Doc had other grandchildren, although he didn't know it. In 1949, the nefarious Doctor Natas briefly kidnapped Doc's daughter Justine Ducharme and extracted samples of her DNA. A few years later he succeeded in cloning Justine, and then one of his henchmen, Pao Tcheou, impregnated the clone as a test. A successful pregnancy ensued, and the daughter, Ducharme, became Natas' concubine in the 1970s.

Natas then impregnated the clone; Natas' son, Shang Chi, was born in 1951; his adventures in the 1970s and '80s were documented in the pages of the Marvel Comics series *The Hands of Shang Chi: Master of Kung Fu*.

Even if Shang Chi had known he was Doc's biological grandson, he wouldn't have been interested in the Pemberley estate.

Finally, it should be noted that Doc's cousin (called "Pat Savage" in the pulp novels and later known under the name Patricia Hazzard after her marriage to Captain Rex Hazzard, as seen in Lin Carter's Prince Zarkon novel *The Earth-Shaker*) and her granddaughter Pamela Hazzard (from the DC Comics series) have no claim to Pemberley; they are descended from the brother of the woman who had an affair with the sixth Duke of Greystoke, which resulted in the illegitimate birth of "James Wilder," aka James Clarke Wildman, Sr.

Eliminating non-canonical descendants from consideration might seem like an over-the-top exercise, but it is part and parcel of The Game. It's literary archaeology—or rather the Wold Newtonian brand of it, Creative Mythography.

As always, the blame and the credit for my obsessions in this area rest with Phil Farmer.

Documenting the historical events in *Pemberley House* required much research and a bit well-educated speculation to ensure that I correctly documented the proper passage of the Pemberley Curse from generation to generation. Juggling the various descents of the Curse, the Greystoke title, and the Pemberley estate, and ensuring that all the players were accounted for in all three regards, led to headaches on more than one occasion.

A reconciliation of the family tree as laid out in the manuscript and Farmer's notes with the established Wold Newton Family tree was also necessary. There were slight differences, indicative that Phil may have made his initial notes before his research on the genealogy of the Greystoke lineage was solidified in *Tarzan Alive*. Of course, Phil's sometimes contradictory notes are easily explained when one remembers that he conducted his own research before meeting Lord Greystoke and Patricia Wildman, and Phil confirmed that my various researches and reconciliations were, to the best of his recollection, accurate.

One example of a contradiction is that when Farmer wrote the initial short synopsis of *Pemberley House*, he thought the Claytons and the Darcys were of the same lineage. His deeper research into the dukes of Greystoke in *Tarzan Alive* showed this not to be the case; although a female Darcy married the fifth Duke of Greystoke, this marriage did not cause the Pemberley estate to transfer to the Greystoke/Clayton line. Phil discovered that Sir Gawain Darcy sold the estate to a member of the Clayton family.

Despite the fact that Pemberley House and the associated estate came into the Claytons' hands through purchase from a Darcy, rather than inheritance, Patricia Wildman is still a lineal descendant of the Darcys. As Farmer outlined in *Tarzan Alive*, Ursula d'Arcy was married to Ralph Arthur Caldwell-Grebson in about 1667. They are ancestors of both the Greystokes and the Darcys.

There were a few other minor reconciliations, such as changing the date of death of Patricia's grandfather from 1932 to 1931 in order to be consistent with Farmer's "Doc Savage Chronology" which he put together for the 1973 publication of *Doc Savage: His Apocalyptic Life*. A reference to the sixth Duke of Lambton was changed to the sixth Duke of Greystoke, and William Cecil Darcy was changed to William Cecil Clayton; these were relics of Farmer's original theory that the Darcys and the Greystokes were one and the same. Beyond these slight changes, the corpus of his research for *Pemberley House* hangs together and synchs up with *Tarzan Alive* amazingly well.

Or perhaps not so amazing. We are talking about Philip José Farmer, after all.

---

[1] Although only male heirs can inherit the peerage, female children could inherit the Pemberley estate, and so all descendants, male and female, are included here.

[2] Wold Newton scholar Dennis E. Power disagrees with me to a certain extent, maintaining that the immortality elixir eventually ran out and that John Drummond-Clayton died at an old age. See "The Royal Jelly Problem: An Exploration of the Causes and Prevalence of Immortality in the Wold Newton Universe" at Power's *The Wold Newton Universe: A Secret History* website, www.pjfarmer.com/secret/Immortal/royal-jelly.htm.

[3] In "Ouroboros, Part II" (*Farmerphile No. 5*, Christopher Paul Carey and Paul Spiteri, eds., July 2006), I dated *Bunduki* as occurring in 1974; subsequent research has revised the date, placing it and the following three novels in the series in early 1972.

[4] Farmer dismissed Burroughs' crossover novel *Tarzan at the Earth's Core* as complete fiction due to the physical improbability of the inner Earth described in the Pellucidar series. Perhaps Pellucidar was not exactly as described in Burroughs' books, with an eternal sun hanging in the center of a hollow globe, but rather was a series of interconnected underground caverns teeming with primitive and prehistoric life. Those whose credulity is strained in this regard are free to reject Edson's assertion that the Greystokes moved to the inner world after faking their deaths in 1972.

[5] Dennis E. Power maintains there is a third child: Diana, Princess of the Amazons, conceived while Lord Greystoke/John Gribardsun was posing as the historical Hercules, after he traveled back in time in Farmer's *Time's Last Gift*. See "Marvelous, Fantastic Tales of the Wold Newton Universe: Wonder Woman" on Power's website, www.pjfarmer.com/secret/marvelous/wonderwoman.htm. Gribardsun fathered countless children while living from 12,000 BCE to the present (see also "Sahhindar through the Centuries" by Eckert and Power in *Farmerphile No. 13*, Paul Spiteri and Win Scott Eckert, eds., July 2008; revised as "Gribardsun through the Ages: A Chronology of Events Pertinent to *Time's Last Gift*" in the Titan Books edition of *Time's Last Gift*, 2012 [page 79]); since estate laws undoubtedly do not account for potential heirs conceived while time-traveling, we can safely ignore Diana and the rest, at least in terms of their right to inherit property or titles.

[6] See *Doc Ardan: City of Gold and Lepers* by Guy d'Armen, adapted and retold in English by Jean-Marc and Randy Lofficier, Black Coat Press, 2004. The novel, in which Ardan battles the nefarious Doctor Natas, can be interpreted as an early adventure of the Man of Bronze versus Doctor Fu Manchu.

[7] A short story by Win Scott Eckert in *Tales of the Shadowmen, Vol. 1: The Modern Babylon*, Jean-Marc and Randy Lofficier, eds., Black Coat Press, (2005).

[8] Available at *An Expansion of Philip José Farmer's Wold Newton Universe* website, Win Scott Eckert, ed., www.pjfarmer.com/woldnewton/Pulp2.htm.

[9] Briefly, the theory goes that in April 1919, nine months after Doc's escape from the prison camp Loki (see Farmer's Doc Savage novel, *Escape from Loki*), a child is born to Lili Bugov, the Countess Idivzhopu. The child is raised as the son of Baron Karl von Hessel (Doc's grandfather, aka Wolf Larsen, who will go by the moniker Baron Karl by the time of the Doc Savage novel *Fortress of Solitude*). However, given young Clark Savage's intimate encounter with the Countess Idivzhopu in July 1918, there can be little doubt as to the true parentage of this child, who will grow up to menace the world, not to mention his own hated father, as "John Sunlight."

My colleague Christopher Paul Carey, in his article "The Green Eyes Have

It—Or Are They Blue? or Another Case of Identity Recased" (*Myths*), gathers and documents an incredible amount of evidence about the Countess, von Hessel, and Doc's archenemy "John Sunlight." Carey concludes that John Sunlight is either Lili Bugov posing as a man, or that she underwent a sex-change operation to become Sunlight. Carey evocatively points out both Bugov's and Sunlight's unusually long fingers. Keeping in mind all the physical similarities between Bugov and Sunlight that Carey documents, as well as the behavioral differences, I am led to a different conclusion. I believe Sunlight is Lili Bugov's son.

However, if Sunlight were born in April of 1919, he would be only eighteen years old in August of 1937 (*Fortress of Solitude*). This could pose a problem, in terms of his believability as a villain. On the other hand, Baron von Hessel/Baron Karl has been mentoring him in the ways of evil for those eighteen years. And Doc made a believable hero at age sixteen, just as many other Wold Newton Family members started their careers early in life. It is stated in *Fortress of Solitude* that, "He was not a young man . . ." but I believe this to be blatant misdirection on writer Lester Dent's part, in order to help Doc conceal the terrible secret of Sunlight's parentage. In short, Sunlight's age is not an insurmountable issue. (It is interesting to note that, based on textual evidence in *Fortress of Solitude*, Sunlight escaped from the Siberian gulag at approximately age sixteen or seventeen—the same age at which his father escaped from a similar inescapable prison camp.)

Further, I do not believe that Farmer would have noted the sexual encounter between Clark and Lili without reason. Sunlight, like Doc, emits a strange sound in times of excitement or stress, although Sunlight's takes the form of a low, evil growl, rather than Doc's cool, exotic trilling. Sunlight's inhuman strength, derived from unspecified sources, and his incredible stamina and will power, a result of his magnificent brain, are extensively described in *Fortress of Solitude*. The derivation of Sunlight's formidable intelligence is easily understood once it is revealed that he is possibly of the Moriarty lineage (per another theory promulgated by Dennis E. Power, which holds that Wolf Larsen was a son of Professor Moriarty; this theory was adopted in my "Who's Going to Take Over the World When I'm Gone? (A Look at the Genealogies of Wold Newton Family Super-Villains and Their Nemeses)" in *Myths*, but was contradicted in my tale "The Wild Huntsman" in *The Worlds of Philip José Farmer 3: Portraits of a Trickster*, Michael Croteau, ed., Meteor House, 2012; *Tales of the Wold Newton Universe*, Eckert and Carey, eds., Titan Books, 2013; nonetheless, if "The Wild Huntsman" is correct, then Sunlight's lineage via his grandfather Wolf Larsen is still extraordinary), as well as of the Wildman and the Clayton lines. In my estimation, the physical similarities between Countess Idivzhopu and Sunlight, coupled with Sunlight's Wildman-like strength, vocal habits, and brain power, undoubtedly point to a familial relationship, one made possible by Doc's indiscretion with the Countess.

In any event, whether one agrees with my theory, Chris Carey's, or neither, it has no bearing on Sunlight's ability, or rather lack thereof, to inherit Pemberley House.

[10] In the years since this essay was written, there have been two additional Doc Savage comic series. DC Comics incorporated Doc into their 2010 *First Wave* series; the stories took place in an alternate DC universe where Doc interacted with The Bat-Man, The Spirit, and other characters. Next, Doc tales were published by Dynamite Comics. This series, like the 1980s DC stories, brought Doc forward to the modern day, but in a completely different continuity from the 1980s DC version. Reconciling these alternate continuities with the Wold Newtonian history of Doc Wildman and Pat Wildman would not be instructive and is beyond the scope of this article.

Creative Mythography
Only a Coincidence:
Phileas Fogg, Philip José Farmer,
and the Wold Newton Family
Win Scott Eckert

Phileas Fogg lives!

And so do Sherlock Holmes, and the jungle lord, and Doc Savage, and the insidious Doctor Fu Manchu.

In 1844, Fogg participated in an Eridanean blood-sharing ceremony, which granted him a lifespan of one-thousand years.

Philip José Farmer points out that there is no record of Sherlock Holmes' death.[1] One of Holmes' biographers, William S. Baring-Gould, revealed that the Great Detective developed a Royal Jelly bee pollen elixir which extended his life[2]; he probably perfected the Royal Jelly treatment in 1921.

The jungle lord is immortal. As shown in one of the canonical stories recounting his adventures: he was given an immortality elixir by an African witch doctor in 1912. Later on, in 1933, the jungle lord, his wife, and a few others gained access to Kavuru pills which halted the aging process. The jungle lord shared these with his cousin, Doc Savage, "the Man of Bronze," who analyzed and synthesized the pills, resulting in an unlimited supply to be shared with both their families and their closest associates.[3]

Doctor Fu Manchu independently developed his Elixir of Life in 1929.[4]

In addition to the common thread of immortality, or at least very long life, there is another tie which binds together these amazing men: they are all members of the extensive Wold Newton Family.

The Wold Newton Family takes its name from the cosmic event that spawned it. On December 13, 1795, at 3:00 P.M., a meteorite came plunging to the earth, landing near the English village of Wold Newton. The impact site became part of the local folklore in the countryside of the Yorkshire Wolds in the East Riding of Yorkshire. Pieces of the Wold Cottage meteorite[5] are held in the Natural History Museum in London, and in 1799, Edward Topham built a brick monument to commemorate the event:

Here
On this Spot, Decr 13th, 1795
fell from the Atmosphere
AN EXTRAORDINARY STONE
In Breadth 28 inches
In Length 30 inches
and
Whose Weight was 56 Pounds
THIS COLUMN
In Memory of it
was erected by
EDWARD TOPHAM
1799

History also records that several people observed the object in the sky. "Topham's shepherd was within 150 yards of the impact and a farmhand named John Shipley was so near that he was forcibly struck by mud and earth as the falling meteorite burrowed into the ground."[6] A contemporaneous account observes that:

In the afternoon of the 13th of December, 1795, near the Wold Cottage, noises were heard in the air, by various persons, like the report of a pistol; or of guns at a distance at sea; though there was neither any thunder or lightning at the time:—two distinct concussions of the earth were said to be perceived:—and an hissing noise, was also affirmed to be heard by other persons, as of something passing through the air;—and a labouring man plainly saw (as we are told) that something was so passing; and beheld a stone, as it seemed, at last, (about ten yards, or thirty feet, distant from the ground) descending, and striking into the ground, which flew up all about him: and in falling, sparks of fire, seemed to fly from it.

Afterwards he went to the place, in company with others; who had witnessed part of the phænomena, and dug the stone up from the place, where it was buried about twenty-one inches deep.

It smelt, (as it is said,) very strongly of sulphur, when it was dug up: and was even warm, and smoked:—it was found to be thirty inches in length, and twenty-eight and a half inches in breadth. And it weighed fifty-six pounds.

(Remarks Concerning Stones Said To Have Fallen from the Clouds, Both in These Days, and in Antient Times by Edward King, ESQ. F.R.S. and F.A.S, 1796.)

What many historians fail to adequately record is the presence of eighteen other persons in the immediate vicinity at the time of the Wold Newton meteor strike. We know about these eighteen people through the extraordinary and singular work of one historian. This historian, in fact, has engaged in a rather in-depth treatment of the subject in two scholarly biographical tomes. However, despite the fact that this historian's biographies are often appropriately shelved in the Biography section of libraries, his revelations are generally regarded as fictional.

The historian to whom I refer, of course, is Philip José Farmer, and the biographies of which I speak are *Tarzan Alive: A Definitive Biography of Lord Greystoke* (1972) and *Doc Savage: His Apocalyptic Life* (1973). In the course of his researches into the life of Lord Greystoke, Farmer extensively traced the jungle lord's ancestry, and came to discover the ape-man was closely related to several other august historical personages. The nexus of this relationship was the Wold Cottage meteor strike in 1795.

As Farmer uncovered, seven couples and their coachmen "were riding in two coaches past Wold Newton, Yorkshire . . . A meteorite struck only twenty yards from the two coaches . . . The bright light and heat and thunderous roar of the meteorite blinded and terrorized the passengers, coachmen, and horses . . . They never guessed, being ignorant of ionization, that the fallen star had affected them and their unborn." (*Tarzan Alive*, Addendum 2, pp. 247-248.)

The eighteen present were:[7]

Coach Passengers (14)

JOHN CLAYTON, 3rd Duke of Greystoke, and his wife, ALICIA RUTHERFORD—*ancestors of the jungle lord*

SIR PERCY BLAKENEY, and his (second) wife, ALICE CLARKE RAFFLES—*Blakeney is from Baroness Emmuska Orczy's* The Scarlet Pimpernel *and sequels*

FITZWILLIAM DARCY, and his wife, ELIZABETH BENNET—*from Jane Austen's* Pride and Prejudice

GEORGE EDWARD RUTHERFORD (the 11th Baron Tennington), and his wife, ELIZABETH CAVENDISH—*ancestors of Professor George Edward Challenger, from* The Lost World *by Edward Malone, edited for publication by Sir Arthur Conan Doyle*

HONORÉ DELAGARDIE, and his wife, PHILIPPA DRUMMOND—*ancestors of Hugh "Bulldog" Drummond from H.C. "Sapper" McNeile's (and later Gerard Fairlie's) novels*

DR. SIGER HOLMES, and his wife, VIOLET CLARKE—*ancestors of Sherlock Holmes, from the stories and novels by John H. Watson, M.D., edited for publication by Sir Arthur Conan Doyle*

SIR HUGH DRUMMOND and his wife, LADY GEORGIA DEWHURST—*ancestors of Hugh "Bulldog" Drummond from H.C. "Sapper" McNeile's (and later Gerard Fairlie's) novels*

Coachmen (4)

LOUIS LUPIN—*ancestor of Arsène Lupin, from novels and stories by Maurice Leblanc*

ALBERT LECOQ—*ancestor of Monsieur Lecoq, from the novels by Émile Gaboriau*

ALBERT BLAKE—*ancestor of Sexton Blake, from the stories by Harry Blythe and countless others*

1 UNNAMED by Farmer

The meteor's ionized radiation caused a genetic mutation in those present, endowing many of their descendants with extremely high intelligence and strength. As Farmer stated, the meteor strike was "the single cause of this nova of genetic splendor, this outburst of great detectives, scientists, and explorers of exotic worlds, this last efflorescence of true heroes in an otherwise degenerate age."[8] (*Tarzan Alive*, Addendum 2, pp. 230–231.)

In addition to the jungle lord and the Man of Bronze, Farmer concluded that influential people whose lives were chronicled in popular literature were part of the Wold Newton Family, including Solomon Kane (a pre-meteor strike ancestor); Captain Blood (a premeteor strike ancestor); The Scarlet Pimpernel (present at meteor strike); Fitzwilliam Darcy and his wife, Elizabeth Bennet (present at meteor strike); Sherlock Holmes and his nemesis Professor Moriarty (aka Captain Nemo); Phileas Fogg; Monsieur Lecoq; The Time Traveler; Allan Quatermain; A.J. Raffles; Professor Challenger; Arsène Lupin; Bulldog Drummond and his archenemy, Carl Peterson; the evil Fu Manchu and his adversary, Sir Denis Nayland Smith; Sir Richard Hannay; G-8; Lord

Peter Wimsey; The Shadow; Sam Spade; Doc Savage's friend and associate Monk Mayfair, his cousin Pat Savage, and his daughter Patricia Wildman; The Spider; Nero Wolfe; Mr. Moto; The Avenger; Philip Marlowe; James Bond; Lew Archer; Travis McGee; and many more.

Farmer's researches, uncovering the cosmic explanation for the almost superhuman nature and abilities of these amazing men and women, heroes and villains, are meticulous, well-sourced, and representative of all his historical endeavors. He not only studied the jungle lord's life, but he actually met and interviewed the ape-man himself,[9] after spending uncounted hours poring over Burke's *Peerage* to uncover his real name, titles, arms, and forebears. He applied a similar depth of focus when researching the life of Doc Savage, discovering Doc's real name, ancestors, and current relatives, as well as the family arms.

After writing the two biographies, Farmer continued to chronicle previously unrevealed exploits of Wold Newton Family members in novels and short stories; often these tales have been mistaken for fiction, but they are entirely consistent with the information he had already uncovered, and many are similarly sourced from newly discovered, and unpublished, manuscripts and diaries.[10]

Among the first of these was *The Adventure of the Peerless Peer*, edited by Farmer in 1974 from Dr. John H. Watson's unpublished manuscript, and reissued by Titan Books in 2011. Another, *The Other Log of Phileas Fogg* was first published in 1973, and derived from Phileas Fogg's secret notes.

Further books in Farmer's Wold Newton series include *Time's Last Gift* (1972; revised 1977) and *Hadon of Ancient Opar* (1974).[11] *Hadon of Ancient Opar* kicks off the Khokarsa trilogy, which is rounded out by *Flight to Opar* (1976) and *The Song of Kwasin* (2012), the latter coauthored with Christopher Paul Carey.

Ironcastle (1976) is Farmer's translation and retelling of J. H. Rosny Aîné's *L'Étonnant Voyage de Hareton Ironcastle* (1922), which has several prominent Wold Newton references. Farmer's

The Lavalite World (1977), the fifth entry in the World of Tiers series,[12] solidly connects to the Wold Newton series. This is not an accident; more on this in a moment.

Farmer also wrote several Wold Newton short stories and pieces in the 1970s: "Skinburn," "The Problem of the Sore Bridge—Among Others," "The Freshman," "After King Kong Fell," "A Scarletin Study," "The Doge Whose Barque Was Worse Than His Bight," "The Obscure Life and Hard Times of Kilgore Trout," "Extracts from the Memoirs of 'Lord Greystoke,'" and others more peripherally connected to the series.

He also continued to write short biographical pieces, including "A Reply to 'The Red Herring,'" "The Two Lord Ruftons," "The Great Korak-Time Discrepancy," "The Lord Mountford Mystery," "From ERB to Ygg," "A Language for Opar," and "Jonathan Swift Somers III, Cosmic Traveller in a Wheelchair: A Short Biography by Philip José Farmer (Honorary Chief Kennel Keeper)."[13]

Farmer returned to the Wold Newton series in a big way in the 1990s, starting the decade with the authorized novel *Escape from Loki: Doc Savage's First Adventure* (1991), and rounding it out with the authorized *The Dark Heart of Time: A Tarzan Novel* (1999). 2009 saw the publication of the Wold Newton series novel *The Evil in Pemberley House*, coauthored with Win Scott Eckert. Farmer passed away on February 25, 2009, after the completion of *The Evil in Pemberley House* but before publication. The following year Wold Newton short fiction was authorized by Farmer's estate, and new stories based on his research appeared.[14]

Returning to *The Other Log of Phileas Fogg*, it's worth noting that not only is Fogg a Wold Newton Family member, but so too is his primary adversary, Nemo (aka Professor James Moriarty). In fact, they are half-brothers. The dalliance that led to Moriarty's birth also caused Phileas' mother, Lorina Dacre, to divorce his biological father, Sir William Clayton. Lorina Dacre was the daughter of Lord Dacre and Jane Carfax, who in turn was the daughter of Lord Rufton.

Nemo also has several Capellean assistants: Colonel James

Moriarty (the very tall dark man with a heavy stoop); Colonel Sebastian Moran; a man named Vandeleur; and a henchman who is "the dissolute wenching young baronet, Sir Hector Osbaldistone."

Colonel Moriarty is the Professor's elder brother. That two brothers Moriarty share the first name James is an oddity found in Dr. Watson's accounts of Sherlock Holmes. In "The Final Problem" Watson refers to Colonel James Moriarty, and in "The Adventure of the Empty House," Holmes mentions Professor James Moriarty.

Colonel Moran was Professor Moriarty's lieutenant and appeared in Watson and Doyle's "The Empty House." Vandeleur appeared in Robert Louis Stevenson's short story "The Rajah's Diamond," which was published in the collection *New Arabian Nights*. Sir Hector Osbaldistone is a descendant of Sir Francis Osbaldistone, who was seen in Sir Walter Scott's *Rob Roy*.

Fogg's secret log also indicates that before joining Fogg, his valet Passepartout was a valet for Lord Windermere. Oscar Wilde wrote a biographical play about Lord Windermere's wife: *Lady Windermere's Fan: A Play About a Good Woman*. The log also refers to Lady Jane Brandon of Brandon Beeches. Brandon Beeches also appeared in George Bernard Shaw's *An Unsocial Socialist*.[15]

Finally, Fogg's notebooks discuss the Rajah Dakkar of Bundelcund, a renegade Capellean who is killed. This cannot be the Prince Dakkar of Jules Verne's *The Mysterious Island*, which H.W. Starr dismisses as wholly fictional in his essay "A Submersible Subterfuge, or, Proof Impositive."[16] However, if there is a kernel of truth in *The Mysterious Island* (or more than a kernel), then maybe Rajah Dakkar is the Prince's father.

Perhaps the greatest mystery to be found in *The Other Log of Phileas Fogg* is not resolved by Fogg's secret diaries, but rather is contained in Farmer's cryptic concluding comment: "That Phileas Fogg's initials and your editor's are the same is, I assure you, only a coincidence."

What precisely is Farmer hinting at here? That *he is* Phileas Fogg?

Perhaps, but there are many established facts about Farmer which probably preclude this delightful notion.

But might Farmer be implying something else, something related to the Wold Newton Family? What follows does not purport to be the final answer to the puzzle of Farmer's enigmatic remarks, but is one potential resolution.

There are many science fiction writers in the Wold Newton Family, some accomplished, successful, and well-known like Farmer; others, not so much. Among these are Leo Queequeg Tincrowdor, Kilgore Trout, and Jonathan Swift Somers III, all three of whom are on a branch of the Family descended from the Shawnessys. Of course, there are numerous other writers in the Family, but many of these are adventurers who have recorded their own deeds and published them with the assistance of other editors and writers. Philip Marlowe and Travis McGee come to mind. Tincrowdor, Trout, and Somers, on the other hand, are of the breed who made writing their primary career, rather than a happy side-effect of lives of daring and bold exploits.

Tincrowdor was born in New Goshen, Indiana, when his parents were on the way to a Terre Haute hospital, in 1918.[17] He attended the University of Shomi.

Somers was from Petersburg, Illinois; he was born on January 6, 1910. He shares a birthday with Sherlock Holmes.

Trout was born in 1907 and spent much time in the city of Ilium, a code name for Troy, New York.

Farmer was friendly with all three men, writing of Tincrowdor's experiences in *Stations of the Nightmare* (1982), and penning brief biographical sketches of Somers and Trout.

In any event, there doesn't seem to be a place for Farmer in the Shawnessy line. Doubtless Farmer attended various Family reunions and gatherings, although perhaps Trout didn't make as many of the reunions as Midwesterners Tincrowdor, Somers, and Farmer.

However, there are others to whom Farmer is more closely related. While he shares with Tincrowdor, Somers, and Trout the experience of being a working writer, he has had some parallel experiences with Tim Howller, Tom Wode Bellman, and Paul Janus Finnegan.

Peoria native Tim Howller was also born in 1918. He appeared in Farmer's short stories "After King Kong Fell" and "The Face that Launched a Thousand Eggs." Like Tincrowdor, he attended the University of Shomi ("Shomi" = Missouri) and he experienced similar college hazing incidents to Farmer, who attended the University of Missouri. It appears as though Tim Howller was an autobiographical version of Farmer himself.

Tom Wode Bellman's roots are in Busiris, Illinois. Bellman, also a science fiction writer, appeared in Farmer's short story "The Light-Hog Incident." Busiris is a code-name Farmer used for Peoria.

As for Paul Janus Finnegan, also born in Terre Haute in 1918, let's back up a few steps.

The image to the right is cropped from Farmer's "The Fabulous Family Tree of Doc Savage (An Extension of the Wold Newton Family Chart of *Tarzan Alive*)" in *Doc Savage: His Apocalyptic Life*. The branch in question is one of many begat by the prolific Sir William Clayton (1799-1902). Sir William's father, John William Clayton, the third Duke of Greystoke (1750-1801) was one of those irradiated when the Wold Newton meteor struck.

According to both *Doc Savage: His Apocalyptic Life* and *The Other Log of Phileas Fogg*, Phileas Fogg (b. 1832) was the biological son of Sir William Clayton. Phileas had a sister, Roxana (b. 1833). These birth dates are clearly documented in *Tarzan Alive*. In 1835, when Phileas and Roxana were very young, their mother, Lorina Dacre, divorced Sir William and married Sir Heraclitus Fogg, who adopted both of the children.

In both *Tarzan Alive* and *Doc Savage: His Apocalyptic Life*, Farmer states that the daughter of Phileas Fogg and Aouda Jejeebhoy, Suzanne Fogg, married French Foreign Legion Captain Armand Jacot. Suzanne and Armand's daughter, Jeanne Jacot (aka "Meriem"), married John Drummond Clayton, the adopted son of the jungle lord.

At the conclusion to *The Other Log of Phileas Fogg*, Farmer writes that, "Fogg retired to Fogg Shaw in rural Derbyshire, where he tinkered around in his laboratory and raised a number of *children*, all as handsome as he or as beautiful as their mother" (emphasis added).

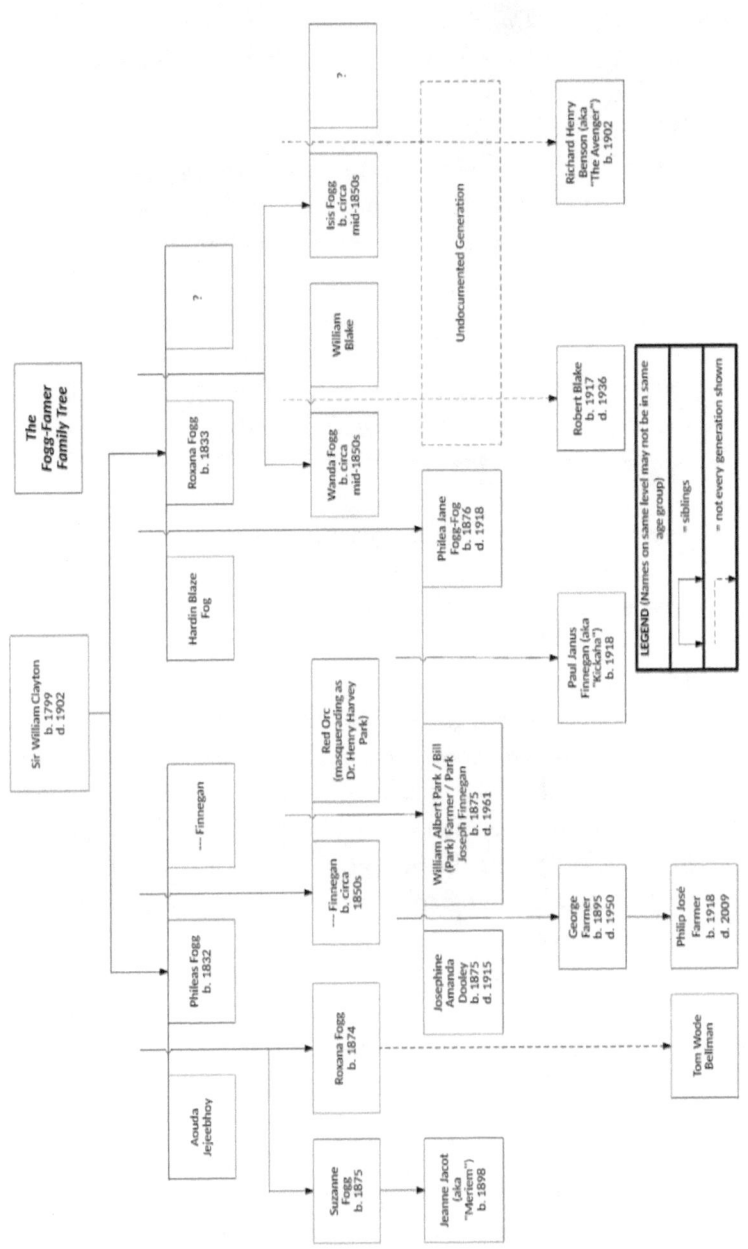

The Fogg-Farmer Family Tree

Sir William Clayton
b. 1799
d. 1902

Phileas Fogg
b. 1832

Hardin Blaze
Fog

Roxana Fogg
b. 1833

?

?

Isis Fogg
b. circa
mid-1850s

William
Blake

Wanda Fogg
b. circa
mid-1850s

Undocumented Generation

Richard Henry
Benson (aka
"The Avenger")
b. 1902

Robert Blake
b. 1917
d. 1936

Phileas Jane
Fogg-Fogg
b. 1876
d. 1918

Paul Janus
Finnegan (aka
"Kickaha")
b. 1918

Aouda
Jejeebhoy

Roxana Fogg
b. 1874

— Finnegan

— Finnegan
b. circa
1850s

Red Orc
(masquerading as
Dr. Henry Harvey
Park)

William Albert Park / Bill
(Park) Farmer / Park
Joseph Finnegan
b. 1875
d. 1961

Josephine
Amanda
Doodey
b. 1875
d. 1915

George
Farmer
b. 1895
d. 1950

Philip José
Farmer
b. 1918
d. 2009

Tom Wode
Beltman

Suzanne
Fogg
b. 1875

Jeanne Jacot
(aka
"Merriem")
b. 1898

LEGEND (Names on same level may not be in same
age group)

= siblings

= not every generation shown

Suzanne Fogg, at least, is mentioned in the text of both *Tarzan Alive* and *Doc Savage*, but neither she, nor the other Fogg children, are reflected on any of the family tree graphics included in those biographies.

Why?

It should also be mentioned that in *Tarzan Alive*, Farmer refers to Suzanne, Phileas, and Aouda as "late," as in deceased. Yet he concludes *The Other Log of Phileas Fogg* with this:

> *Whatever happened to the distorters, the important thing is that Fogg and Aouda and Passepartout and Fix lived happily for many years. They may still be living for all anybody knows [due to the alien life-extension process which conferred one-thousand-year lifespans].*
>
> *Fogg may even have thought that, after a hundred years, the public could be informed of the true story.*
>
> *That Phileas Fogg's initials and your editor's are the same is, I assure you, only a coincidence.*

If Farmer is not implying that he is Fogg, then is he insinuating that he's related to Fogg? The illustrations of Fogg in the Tor Books edition of *The Other Log of Phileas Fogg* (1982) show a character that looks exactly like Farmer. In fact, when Christopher Paul Carey had Farmer sign this edition for him a few years ago, he asked, "Could you please sign your picture?" and Farmer promptly placed his autograph directly under the picture of Fogg on the frontispiece.

Fogg is also very closely related to Kickaha (Paul Janus Finnegan) from Farmer's World of Tiers series. Kickaha also shares Farmer's initials, and is also from Terre Haute, Indiana, where Farmer was himself born on January 26, 1918. Kickaha's parents were Philea Jane Fogg-Fog (a daughter of Roxana Fogg and Hardin Blaze Fog), and Park Joseph Finnegan. Park Finnegan deserted Philea Jane upon learning she was pregnant, and she died shortly after Paul's birth, after which Paul was adopted and raised by Ralph Finnegan, a cousin of Park Finnegan.

Perhaps Farmer is connected both to the Wold Newton Family and the family of Lords from the World of Tiers series. Based on the descriptions in the books, Paul Janus Finnegan (Kickaha) is the spitting image of Farmer, and Finnegan also greatly resembles the Lords called Urthona and Red Orc. In fact, Red Orc strongly implies that Kickaha is half-Lord, and that Kickaha may be his own offspring. Wold Newton scholar Dennis E. Power has speculated that Red Orc was Park Finnegan.[18] However, a Wold Newton researcher very close to Power, Coyle T. Ravin, theorized that Park Finnegan was Red Orc's son, and thus Kickaha is his grandson.[19]

If so, this doesn't negate Kickaha's membership in the Wold Newton Family, which he derives from his mother, a Fogg. As Power noted, Kickaha's mysterious acrobatic knife-throwing uncle was likely Jean Passepartout.

Interestingly, there are incidents in the history of Farmer's family which parallel those in Kickaha's.

Farmer's great-grandfather was Dr. Henry Harvey Park, who was married to Dr. Lida Park. Henry's son, William Albert Park, was either abandoned in 1877 at age two by both of his parents and turned over to a distant relative, George Farmer, or was turned over to George Farmer by Henry Park's wife, Dr. Lida Park, upon Henry's death in 1883. Lida Park took off for Texas with two older daughters and became the world's first female osteopath.[20]

The record is unclear regarding whether or not Lida Park was William Albert Park's mother. But if William was Henry Park's son by a prior relationship, that may explain her willingness to leave him behind.

William Albert Park, Farmer's grandfather, later called Bill (Park) Farmer, deserted his wife Josephine Amanda Dooley and their children in 1912. In 1915, Josephine died in an accident eerily similar to that in which Philea Jane Fogg-Fog perished. George Farmer, Farmer's father, never forgave his own father.

Parallel historical events don't dictate a genealogical relationship, but there are indications that Paul Janus Finnegan and Philip José

Farmer could easily be cousins. Kickaha is described as six feet, one inch tall and weighing 190 pounds, muscular, and broad-shouldered; his face is strong and craggy with a long upper lip. His voice is a rich baritone. Without a doubt, this could be a description of Farmer. (It would be interesting if they had met in 1946 while Kickaha was going to college on the G.I. Bill. Perhaps they did, and that's how Farmer later came to write of Kickaha's adventures.)

Did William Albert Park, later known as Bill Farmer, even later go by the name Park Joseph Finnegan? Both William Park/Bill Farmer and Park Finnegan had a marry-them, love-them, and leave-them-with-children *modus operandi*.

Let's return to the Foggs for a moment. Farmer tells us that Philea Jane was the youngest of the three daughters of Roxana Fogg. Philea Jane was born when her mother was forty-three. In the World of Tiers novel *The Lavalite World*, Farmer tells us that Philea Jane was born in 1880. If so, then her forty-three year-old mother Roxana would have been born in 1837. However, *Tarzan Alive* indicates Roxana was born in 1833, a year after her brother Phileas. If so, then Philea Jane must have been born in 1876. Philea Jane would have just about been of childbearing age, at forty-two years old, when her son Paul Janus "Kickaha" Finnegan was born in 1918.

As we will see, the discrepancy in Philea Jane's birth year is not the first fact regarding the Foggs that Farmer casts in a shroud of—dare I say it?—fog.

Furthering the confusion, as Dennis E. Power and others have noted, Farmer provided two conflicting lineages for Paul Janus Finnegan. First, Paul Janus Finnegan was the great-nephew of Phileas Fogg by his descent through Phileas' sister Roxana (*Doc Savage: His Apocalyptic Life*). Second, Paul Janus Finnegan was the great-grandson of Phileas Fogg through Phileas' daughter Roxana (*The Lavalite World*). Much later, Farmer told Christopher Paul Carey that the lineage in *Doc Savage* was the correct version. Nonetheless, we do have a clue that Phileas Fogg had a daughter Roxana, named after his sister.

Philea Jane's two older half-sisters, Wanda and Isis,[21] were born sometime between 1854 and 1871—probably much closer to 1854, since Roxana married her first husband in 1853, when she was 20, and he died in 1871. Yet Farmer tells that Wanda's son Robert Blake was born in 1917. Even applying the most generous interpretation to the numbers, and supposing that Wanda was born in 1871, she'd be forty-six at the time of Robert's birth, which is highly unlikely. And given that a mid-1850s birthdate is much more probable for Wanda, she cannot be Robert Blake's mother. The same argument might apply to Isis Fogg's son, Richard Henry Benson (aka The Avenger), who was born in 1902. If Isis was born in the 1860s, then Richard Benson could be her son. However, if Isis was born any earlier, then it's unlikely that she's Benson's mother.

The evidence is overwhelming that Farmer omitted a generation between Wanda Fogg and Robert Blake, and possibly omitted a generation between Isis Fogg and Richard Benson.

In *Doc Savage*, Farmer also lists Wanda and Isis with their mother's surname rather than their father's, and does not provide their father's name, thus presenting yet another mystery to be solved at a later date. (He did the same with Wanda and Isis' younger half-sister, Philea Jane, only later revealing, in the novel *The Lavalite World*, the details about her father.)

At this point, Farmer's obfuscations regarding the Foggs appear purposeful. He was too detailed and meticulous in his research for it to be otherwise.

Again, why?

Because Farmer himself is a Fogg.

If Park Joseph Finnegan was a half-human, half-Lord, the son of the Lord called Red Orc, then who was his human mother? A Fogg, a child of Phileas, although the chronology prevents Aouda Jejeebhoy from being the mother of this child. Phileas must have had a daughter, probably sometime in the 1850s. Dennis E. Power suggests that Phileas Fogg met her mother in Ireland while creating the identity of the Irish born sailor Patrick M'Guire, an identity he would use again years later as part of the *Nautilus* crew.

Miss Finnegan, the mother of Phileas' daughter, then traveled to America and lived with other Finnegan relatives (see the prior reference to Ralph Finnegan).

Phileas Fogg's daughter would also have been quite young when she was seduced by the Lord, Red Orc, who was using the identity "Dr. Henry Harvey Park," resulting in the birth of Park Finnegan/William Albert Park/Bill Farmer in 1875. Through some as-yet undiscovered machinations, Red Orc saw to it that the child ended up in the care of the real Henry Park.

If Philip José Farmer is the great-great-grandson of Phileas Fogg, it's obvious why he chose not to disclose this when revealing the genealogy of the Wold Newton Family; he certainly would not want Red Orc to know he knew of their relationship. And although the Eridanean-Capellean conflict ostensibly ended in 1872, he wouldn't want any potential Capellean agents to know he was aware he was descended from a key Eridanean agent.

As for Farmer's shared and parallel experiences with his fellow Family members, I refer you to the blurb Tim Howller—or rather Farmer himself?—provided for an advertisement for the Farmer collection *Venus on the Half-Shell and Others*: "Finally confirmation of my long-debunked many-souls theory of quantum mechanics . . ."

In fact, Christopher Paul Carey has speculated that Farmer and Kickaha are soul-twins: "Perhaps they are twins, the same soul living out two different lives on two different worlds. This is also a theme in the World of Tiers books, with the two Earths, both experiments of Red Orc to see how they would diverge. Perhaps Red Orc was experimenting by leaving one twin (Farmer) on our Earth, and creating the circumstances whereby the other twin (Kickaha) traveled through the gate into the World of Tiers."

If this is the case, then Red Orc was probably behind the freakishly similar "accidental" deaths of Josephine Dooley and Philea Jane Fogg-Fog, as part of a dark design to create similar backgrounds for his soul-twins.

Since Philip José Farmer is a Wold Newton Family member via his descent from Phileas Fogg (and Fogg's father, Sir William

Clayton), it's worth noting that his other children and grand-children, are also Family members. Farmer's time-traveling daughter, Josie Bauer, from Spider Robinson's Callahan's series, may not have been his biological daughter.[22]

Farmer's membership in the Family explains a lot. When Farmer interviewed the jungle lord, the latter claimed not to know about the Wold Newton Family. Is that likely? The jungle lord was intelligent and educated. He was a member of the British peerage. Surely he knew of the events in his family's past and about the Wold Newton meteor. So why did he grant only Farmer an interview?

Of course Farmer had done amazing research to track down the ape-man, and that was to be rewarded.

But the other reason the jungle lord granted the interview was because Farmer was part of the Family.

[1] Foreword to Farmer's *The Further Adventures of Sherlock Holmes: The Peerless Peer*, Titan Books, 2011.

[2] *Sherlock Holmes of Baker Street*, Bramhall House, 1962.

[3] This is recounted in Philip José Farmer's *Tarzan Alive: A Definitive Biography of Lord Greystoke*, Doubleday & Co., 1972; University of Nebraska Press Bison Books, 2006.

[4] *The Mask of Fu Manchu* by Shan Greville, edited for publication by Sax Rohmer (1930); part of Titan Books' Fu Manchu series.

[5] The meteorite is named after the Wold Cottage, the house owned by Edward Topham, who was a poet, playwright, landowner, and local magistrate. Apparently Magistrate Topham was instrumental in the Wold Cottage meteorite's role in promoting worldwide acceptance of the fact that some stones are not of this Earth. The Wold Cottage is still privately owned, and is currently the site of an excellent bed and breakfast; nearby is the Wold Top Brewery, where one can procure the local brew, Falling Stone Bitter.

[6] See the *Wold Cottage* website, fernlea.tripod.com/woldcottage.html.

[7] It has since been revealed, by researchers inspired by Farmer's original discoveries, that there may have been several more persons present that fateful day, not named by Farmer. I restrict myself herein to Farmer's original findings.

[8] Of course, not all the Wold Newton Family members were heroes. Some turned the genetic advantages with which they had been blessed toward decidedly nefarious pursuits.

[9] On September 1, 1970, Philip José Farmer conducted "An Exclusive Interview with Lord Greystoke." (Originally published as "Tarzan Lives" in *Esquire*, April 1972; reprinted in Farmer's *Tarzan Alive: A Definitive Biography of Lord Greystoke*, University of Nebraska Press Bison Books, 2006.) The interview ostensibly took place in Libreville, Gabon, West Africa, but Farmer later revealed that the interview actually occurred in Chicago. ("I Still Live!" in *Farmerphile: The Magazine of Philip José Farmer No. 3*, January 2006; reprinted in the Farmer collection *Up From the Bottomless Pit and Other Stories*, Subterranean Press, 2007.)

[10] Farmer's prior publication of *A Feast Unknown* (1969), *Lord of the Trees* (1970), and *The Mad Goblin* (1970) (all part of Titan Books' series of Farmer reissues) may have also added to the impression among some readers that the Wold Newton biographies, novels, and stories are works of fiction. These novels are also sourced, from the memoirs of Lord Grandrith, and cover the exploits of Grandrith and Doc Caliban. Grandrith is also a jungle lord, while Caliban is also a Man of Bronze. However, unlike Greystoke and Savage, who are cousins, Grandrith and Caliban are half-brothers. They share a common history which is not based on the Wold Newton meteor strike. Among Farmer's followers there are several explanations for the discrepancies: (1) The novels are highly fictionalized adventures of the real Greystoke and Savage, and Farmer published the books before uncovering and revealing the true backgrounds of these men in *Tarzan Alive* and *Doc Savage: His Apocalyptic Life*; (2) Grandrith and Caliban's escapades occurred much as Farmer documented them, based on Grandrith's memoirs; the two heroes coexist alongside their more famous analogues in the Wold Newton Universe; or (3) Lord Grandrith and Doc Caliban exist in a universe which is parallel, but very similar, to the Wold Newton Universe. Perhaps this alternate universe shares a common past with the Wold Newton Universe, but diverged from it at some point in prehistory. The latter alternative begs the question how Farmer came into possession of Grandrith's memoirs, but solving such a mystery is not insurmountable.

[11] Both volumes are part of Titan Books' reissues of the Wold Newton series. Christopher Paul Carey discusses Farmer's research and sources for *Time's Last Gift* and the Khokarsa trilogy in an afterword to *Time's Last Gift*, Titan Books, 2012.

[12] *The Maker of Universes* (1965), *The Gates of Creation* (1966), *A Private Cosmos* (1968), *Behind the Walls of Terra* (1970), *The Lavalite World* (1977), *Red Orc's Rage* (1991), and *More Than Fire* (1993).

[13] These have been collected in *Myths for the Modern Age: Philip José Farmer's Wold Newton Universe*, Win Scott Eckert, ed., MonkeyBrain Books, 2005.

[14] "A Kick in the Side" by Christopher Paul Carey and "Is He in Hell?" by Win Scott Eckert, *The Worlds of Philip José Farmer 1: Protean Dimensions*, Michael Croteau, ed., Meteor House, 2010; "Kwasin and the Bear God" by Philip José Farmer and Christopher Paul Carey, *The Worlds of Philip José Farmer 2: Of Dust and Soul*, Michael Croteau, ed., Meteor House, 2011.

[15] Lady Jane Brandon, the widow of Sir Charles Brandon, became Sir William Clayton's twelfth wife after his eleventh wife perished in 1874. Sir William, a Wold Newton Family member, was the biological father of Phileas Fogg.

[16] There is a split among post-Farmer Wold Newton researchers regarding the veracity of *The Mysterious Island*, and the validity of many points made in Starr's essay. A few even go so far as to challenge the authenticity of Fogg's notebooks, casting them as an elaborate forgery; others take a more moderate view, and have proposed lines of research which reconcile aspects of *The Mysterious Island* with *The Other Log of Phileas Fogg*.

[17] Interestingly, Farmer was born in Terre Haute in 1918. At age five, the Farmer family moved to Peoria, Illinois, and Farmer spent much of his life there.

[18] "The Conundrums of Kickaha." *Farmerphile: The Magazine of Philip José Farmer No. 7*, Christopher Paul Carey and Paul Spiteri, eds., January 2007.

[19] "The Stars Are but Reflections." *The Wold Newton Universe: A Secret History.* Dennis E. Power, ed. (pjfarmer.com/secret/contributors/no-stars.htm).

[20] Philip José Farmer. "Maps and Spasms." *Fantastic Lives.* Martin H. Greenberg, ed., 1981. *Pearls from Peoria.* Paul Spiteri, ed., Subterranean Press, 2006.

[21] Furthering the confusion, *The Lavalite World* indicates that one of Philea Jane's two older half-siblings was a brother, but since the actual names Wanda and Isis are supplied in *Doc Savage*, we'll assume that Philea Jane's two older half-siblings were sisters. The reference to a brother is a tantalizing hint worth further investigation.

[22] Josie Bauer is seen in Spider Robinson's *Time Travelers Strictly Cash* and others. Paul Spiteri has speculated that the Eridanean-Capellean conflict continued into the twentieth century, and that the Eridaneans recruited Farmer for some missions involving time travel for ten-year periods. Due to the resemblance

between Farmer and Phileas Fogg, the Eridaneans once asked Farmer to pose as Fogg. (See "The Time Distorter" by Paul Spiteri, *Farmerphile: The Magazine of Philip José Farmer No. 15*, Paul Spiteri and Win Scott Eckert, eds., January 2009, and "Le Maréchal" by Paul Spiteri, *The Worlds of Philip José Farmer 1: Protean Dimensions*, Michael Croteau, ed., Meteor House, 2010.) Dennis E. Power's research indicates that Josie Bauer was an adopted daughter of Philip José and Bette Farmer, and the biological granddaughter of the time-traveling Doctor Omega. (See Power's "Bronze Lady Down" in *Doctor Omega and the Shadowmen*, Black Coat Press, 2011.) She must have been adopted during one of Farmer's ten-year sojourns back in time, one in which Farmer's wife Bette accompanied him. When Phil and Bette Farmer had to return to their present time, Josie was probably then cared for by, and later inducted into, the Time Police.

Gribardsun through the Ages:
A Chronology of Major Events Pertinent to Time's Last Gift
With selected entries from Philip José Farmer's Tarzan Alive and other sources
Win Scott Eckert and Dennis E. Power

In Philip José Farmer's novel *Time's Last Gift* (TLG), John Gribardsun travels back in time with an expedition from the year 2070 to 12,000 BCE. 2,000 years after Gribardsun's prehistoric arrival, circa 10,000 BCE, a Gray-Eyed Archer God called Sahhindar, god of plants, of bronze, and of time, makes several fleeting appearances in the civilization of Khokarsa, as described in Farmer's *Hadon of Ancient Opar* and *Flight to Opar*, as well as the concluding book of the trilogy, *The Song of Kwasin* by Farmer and Christopher Paul Carey.

We know from a multitude of clues in *Time's Last Gift* that Gribardsun is a well-known jungle lord, and from the Khokarsa books that he is Sahhindar. In fact, Sahhindar is the Khokarsan pronunciation of "Zantar," which, as Farmer pointed out in *Tarzan Alive*, is actually how the jungle lord spoke his name.

With that in mind, what follows is a timeline of this extraordinary man, excluding the detailed chronology of the ape-man's life from 1888 to 1946 that Farmer provided in the biography *Tarzan Alive* (TA). Relevant information from *Tarzan Alive*, *Time's Last Gift*, and other sources is included, as well as a few speculative additions by post-Farmerian scholars.

December 13, 1795
Wold Newton meteor strike: Seven couples and their coachmen "were riding in two coaches past Wold Newton, Yorkshire . . . A meteorite struck only twenty yards from the two coaches . . . The bright light and heat and thunderous roar of the meteorite blinded and terrorized the passengers, coachmen, and horses . . . They never guessed, being ignorant of ionization, that the fallen star had affected them and their unborn." *Tarzan Alive*, Addendum 2, pp. 247–248. The meteor strike was "the single cause of this nova of genetic splendor, this outburst of great detectives, scientists, and explorers of exotic worlds, this last efflorescence of true heroes in an otherwise degenerate age." Id., pp. 230–231.

The jungle lord is a descendant of John Clayton, third Duke of Greystoke, and his wife, Alicia Rutherford, who are both present at the meteor strike. (TA)

May 11 or 23, 1888
John Clayton II (son of the fifth Duke of Greystoke) and his wife Alice sail from Dover for Freetown. (TA)

June 1888
The Claytons sail on the *Fuwalda* for an Oil Rivers port. (TA)

Late June 1888
The Claytons are stranded in the jungle of French Equatorial Africa (Gabon) by mutineers. (TA)

November 22, 1888
John Clayton III (the future eighth duke of Greystoke) is born. He becomes the jungle lord and is a member of the Wold Newton Family. (TA)

1888–1946
Events of the jungle lord's life as documented by Philip José Farmer in *Tarzan Alive*.

February–June 1916

The jungle lord's adventures with Sherlock Holmes in the land of Zu-Vendis, as told in *The Peerless Peer* by John H. Watson, M.D., edited by Philip José Farmer (Titan Books, 2011). Watson marries Nylepthah, the granddaughter of both Sir Henry Curtis and Captain John Good. Wold Newton researcher Rick Lai has noted that according to Watson's manuscript, "Watson married the granddaughter of both Sir Henry Curtis and Captain John Good in 1916. The Zu-Vendis brides of those two Englishmen could only have given birth to children no earlier than 1887. This means that the parents of Watson's wife had a child when they were both about fifteen years old, and Watson may have married a fourteen-year old girl. Maybe the Zu-Vendis language was misunderstood by the jungle lord and Holmes, and Watson's wife was only the daughter of Curtis or Good." Curtis is a more likely candidate since Haggard never mentioned Captain Good marrying.

September 1, 1970

Philip José Farmer conducts his groundbreaking "An Exclusive Interview with Lord Greystoke." (Originally published as "Tarzan Lives" in *Esquire*, April 1972; reprinted in Farmer's *Tarzan Alive: A Definitive Biography of Lord Greystoke*, University of Nebraska Press Bison Books, 2006.) The interview ostensibly takes place in Libreville, Gabon, West Africa, but Farmer later revealed that the interview actually occurred in Chicago. ("I Still Live!" in *Farmerphile: The Magazine of Philip José Farmer No. 3*, January 2006; reprinted in *Up From the Bottomless Pit and Other Stories*, Subterranean Press, 2007.) Farmer learns some key information for his in-progress biography, as well as information that will eventually form the basis of *The Dark Heart of Time: A Tarzan Novel*.

1972

The jungle lord, his wife Jane, and various family members fake their deaths and take new identities. They continue to have some adventures, at least through the 1990s, as documented in various comic strip and comic book pastiches.

2008

Jane is killed and immediately put into a cryogenic chamber for potential revivification. The jungle lord is gravely injured in the same accident, but recovers. (TLG)

2070–12,000 BCE

The jungle lord, now calling himself John Gribardsun, is part of the expedition of the time vessel *H. G. Wells I* which travels back in time from 2070 to 12,000 BCE. Among his fellow scientists on the expedition is Rachel Silverstein. They arrive at the Vezeres River Valley, France. Through Gribardsun's efforts he brings together two divergent Neolithic tribes whose combined language becomes the basis for the Khokarsan language and also the roots of the Indo-European language group. (TLG)

Note that in this novel Farmer used 1872 as the jungle lord's/ Gribardsun's birthdate. This was before he definitively settled on an 1888 date in conjunction with his theory about the jungle lord's adopted son [see his "The Great Korak-Time Discrepancy," *Myths for the Modern Age: Philip José Farmer's Wold Newton Universe*, MonkeyBrain Books, 2005], and reflects the debate among Burroughs fans about whether 1872 or 1888 is the correct date. When reading *Time's Last Gift*, the reader should substitute 1888 anytime 1872 is mentioned.)

c. 12,000 BCE

Gribardsun appears among the proto-Khokarsans, known as the Khoklem, as they are spreading out on the north shore of the Kemu, Africa's northern landlocked sea. The locals call him Sahhindar and venerate him as the Gray-Eyed Archer God. During a number of visits over a period of fifty years, he teaches the Khoklem how to domesticate plants, how to mine copper and tin to make bronze, and how to make bricks and mortar, among other wondrous innovations. This propels the Khoklem almost instantly from the Old Stone Age to the Bronze Age, thus launching the Khokarsan civilization, which Gribardsun regards as his own private project. (See *Hadon of Ancient Opar*, *Flight to Opar*, and *The Song of Kwasin*.)

c. 10,000 BCE

As the Ice Age wanes in Europe, the dwarf Pag (rendered "Paga" in the Khokarsan tongue) crafts the Ax of Victory from meteoritic iron for the hero Wi. Wi leaves his tribe and heads south with his love Laleela ("Lalila" in Khokarsan); the faithful Pag accompanies them. (See *Allan and the Ice-Gods* by H. Rider Haggard).

c. 10,011 BCE

Gribardsun reappears in Khokarsa as Sahhindar. The events of *Hadon of Ancient Opar* begin. Hadon is a warrior of the ancient city Opar, the ruins of which will be/were discovered in Africa by the jungle lord in 1909. Paga and Lalila arrive in the Wild Lands on the outskirts of the empire of Khokarsa and come under Sahhindar's protection. After parting with Sahhindar, Paga gives the Ax of Victory to Kwasin. (See *Hadon of Ancient Opar*, *Flight to Opar*, and *The Song of Kwasin* for the adventures of Hadon and his giant cousin Kwasin, both of whom are descendants of Gribardsun.)

c. 8000 BCE

Gribardsun is present, in disguise, when a second expedition on the *H. G. Wells I* arrives in 8,000 BCE. (TLG)

c. 5,000 BCE

Gribardsun is the historical Hercules. (TLG) This is the most likely date for the Age of Heroes in Greek mythology.

c. 3100 BCE

Gribardsun takes a photograph of the first Pharaoh, who was Menes or Narmer. (TLG)

c. 3,500 BCE

Gribardsun is there when the third *H. G. Wells I* expedition arrives in the Mesopotamian valley in 3,500 BCE. He assumes the name Terah and marries Rachel Silverstein, a crew member on the third expedition. They are the parents of the biblical Abraham. So in a sense Gribardsun is the father of Judaism, Islam, and Christianity. (TLG)

c. 2600 BCE

Although it is not mentioned in his memoirs, could Gribardsun have been Gilgamesh, the Sumerian epic hero and king who sought immortality, or Enkidu, the wild man whom Gilgamesh befriended? Perhaps Gilgamesh and Enkidu were one person, dual aspects of Gribardsun rendered as separate entities for mythological purposes.

c. 1440 BCE

Gribardsun takes a photograph of the historical Moses. The Exodus is dated differently by various scholars. The date most widely held by those who think it was a true event is 1446–40 BCE. It is not known if Gribardsun took a photograph when Moses was in Egypt or not. (TLG)

c. 1334 BCE–1135 BCE

Somewhere in this time period the historical Trojan War occurs. Gribardsun takes a photo of Odysseus and also the city of Troy. He was also a merchant-ship captain supplying the Achaean army during the Trojan War. (TLG)

c. 1200 BCE–600 CE

Gribardsun is given the name Quetzalcoatl by the Aztecs. (TLG) These dates reflect the earliest period of the Aztec civilization.

c. 753 BCE

Gribardsun takes a photo of the actual founders of Rome. According to Gribardsun, Romulus and Remus did not exist, which is unfortunate since it would have been interesting for these feral men to have met. (TLG)

c. 630–562 BCE

This is the date of the reign of Nebuchadnezzar the Great, famed for the great civilization of Babylon and for his conquest of Jerusalem and Judah. Gribardsun's memoirs relate that Nebuchadnezzar was one of the people Gribardsun photographed. (TLG)

c. 221 BCE–?

Gribardsun takes a photo of several of the Early Chinese Emperors. (TLG) This date is the one attributed to the start of the first emperor's reign. How long Gribardsun stayed in China is unknown, although to have taken the photographs of several emperors he would have been in China for decades or else left and returned periodically.

c. 100 BCE–44 BCE

Gribardsun takes a photograph of Julius Caesar. (TLG) However, Caesar was fairly long-lived and well-traveled. We do not know at what point in Caesar's life Gribardsun took the photograph or in what location. Caesar traveled to Rome, Greece, Gaul, Britain, and Egypt. If Gribardsun took the photograph during Caesar's invasions of Britain, in 55 or 54 BCE, it is interesting to note that he may have encountered Phra the Phoenician, who, it has been speculated, was later known as Captain Carter of Virginia. ("John Carter: Torn from Phoenician Dreams [An Examination Into the Theories that John Carter was Phra the Phoenician and Norman of Torn]" by Dennis E. Power and Dr. Peter M. Coogan, *Myths for the Modern Age: Philip José Farmer's Wold Newton Universe*, MonkeyBrain Books, 2005.)

88 BCE

The probable birth of Phra the Phoenician at Tyre. In *Edgar Rice Burroughs: Master of Adventure*, Richard Lupoff noted the similarities between the openings of *Phra the Phoenician* by Edwin Arnold and *A Princess of Mars* by Edgar Rice Burroughs. Both are about immortals who have only a hazy recollection of their origins, both citing they have always seemed to be about thirty years of age. Lupoff, possibly in jest, suggested that Phra the Phoenician was

Captain Carter of Virginia. In his short essay entitled "John Carter is Phra the Phoenician," www.pjfarmer.com/woldnewton/Articles5.htm#PHRA, Peter Coogan built on Lupoff's suggestion, and pointed out physical similarities between Phra and Carter. Both Phra and Carter had black hair and tawny skin and both were immortal. We do not know the color of Phra's eyes, but Carter's were gray. If Phra was indeed the earliest identity of Carter, and we take in all the factors of his physical attributes and his inexplicable immortality, then it is not too much of a leap to suggest a close familial tie between Phra and Gribardsun, if not father and son then perhaps grandfather and grandson.

c. 7 BCE–36 CE
Gribardsun takes photos of Jesus. (TLG) This is the widest range of dates attributed to the life of Jesus of Nazareth. When Gribardsun took the photographs of Jesus is unknown.

c. 300–800 CE
According to Gribardsun, he was the first person to set foot on Tahiti, beating the Polynesians by a week. (TLG) The exact date the Polynesians arrived in Tahiti is unknown. This five hundred year spread is the current theorized arrival date.

c. 400–600
These are the dates attributed to the reign of King Arthur. According to historical speculation, there may have been several men who were the inspiration for the Arthurian legends. Therefore, there may have been a few men whose exploits have come down in history as those of King Arthur and the members of his court. Jeffrey Diehl speculates that Gribardsun made an appearance in Britain during the Arthurian age as Myrddin the Wild. ("The Connecting Factor," users.frii.com/asacat/dr.htm) If Gribardsun was active in England during the Arthurian epoch, he may have encountered, perhaps for the second time, his fellow immortal, Phra the Phoenician, who has been speculated to be one of the men to whom some of the Arthurian legends are attributed.

449–585

Gribardsun takes a photo of the historical Beowulf. (TLG) These dates reflect the internal dates in the poem *Beowulf.*

742–January 28, 814

Gribardsun photographs Charlemagne. (TLG) These dates reflect Charlemagne's reign. Although Gribardsun states that he stayed out of conflict, one has to wonder, given his proximity to Charlemagne, if perhaps he was not one of Charlemagne's twelve peers, perhaps even the superlative warrior and knight Roland.

982

Gribardsun beats Eric the Red to America by six months and waits behind a bush for him to arrive, taking a photo of him as he lands. (TLG)

1138–1193

Gribardsun photographs Saladin, the great diplomat and leader of the Muslims during the age of the Crusades. (TLG) These dates reflect Saladin's lifetime. Exactly when Gribardsun took the photograph is unknown; however, if the speculation in the next entry has any validity, Gribardsun probably did not accompany Richard the Lionheart on the Crusades.

1190–1215

According to Art Bollmann ("Two Streams in a Wood Converging," www.pjfarmer.com/secret/contributors/tz-jc.htm), Gribardsun was Little John of the Robin Hood tales. Most versions of these take place during the reigns of King Richard and King John. According to some speculation, Robin Hood was also one of the identities of Gribardsun's fellow immortal, Phra the Phoenician. ("The Lives and Times of John Carter of Mars" by Dennis E. Power and Peter Coogan, www.pjfarmer.com/secret/Immortal/phra2.htm) Jeffrey Diehl's "The Connecting Factor" speculates that Gribardsun acted as Herne the Hunter in Anglo-Saxon England during the Crusades.

1207–1213

Gribardsun is Sir William Marshal, 1st Earl of Pembroke; during these years, he resides in the Province of Leinster, Ireland, and builds Carlow Castle. (See the short story "No Ghosts Need Apply" by Win Scott Eckert in *The Phantom Chronicles 2*, Moonstone Books, 2010, and the short story "Le Marechal" by Paul Spiteri in *The Worlds of Philip José Farmer 1*, Meteor House, 2010)

1266

Gribardsun takes photos of Kublai Khan and Marco Polo. (TLG) This is the date when Polo was at Kublai Khan's court. It is not known if Gribardsun accompanied Polo on his voyages or if he happened to be in China during one of his periodic visits.

1564–1616

Gribardsun photographs William Shakespeare. (TLG) These are the dates of Shakespeare lifetime. It is not known at what point in this time period Gribardsun took the photographs.

1592

Sir John Gribardsun kills the sorcerer Baron de Musard. (*The Evil in Pemberley House* by Philip José Farmer and Win Scott Eckert, Subterranean Press, 2009.)

December 13, 1795

Wold Newton meteor strike: Seven couples and their coachmen "were riding in two coaches past Wold Newton, Yorkshire . . . A meteorite struck only twenty yards from the two coaches . . . The bright light and heat and thunderous roar of the meteorite blinded and terrorized the passengers, coachmen, and horses . . . They never guessed, being ignorant of ionization, that the fallen star had affected them and their unborn." *Tarzan Alive*, Addendum 2, pp. 247–248. The meteor strike was "the single cause of this nova of genetic splendor, this outburst of great detectives, scientists, and explorers of exotic worlds, this last efflorescence of true heroes in an otherwise degenerate age." Id., pp. 230–231.

It is probable that Gribardsun comes to witness this event, which imbued his ancestors, and passed on to him, the qualities of supermen. He may even have been an invitee at the Conclave called by Sir Percy Blakeney, and held in Wold Newton, in December 1795. (See the short story "Is He in Hell?" by Win Scott Eckert, *The Worlds of Philip José Farmer 1: Protean Dimensions*, Meteor House, 2010.)

1798
Gribardsun, as Sir John Gribson, attends the funeral of Lady Marguerite Blakeney. (See the short story "Marguerite's Tears" by Win Scott Eckert, *Tales of the Shadowmen 8: Agents Provocateurs*, Black Coat Press, 2011.)

November 1872
Gribardsun is on the *Mary Celeste*. (TLG) Thus, he is on the periphery of the events described in Philip José Farmer's *The Other Log of Phileas Fogg* (Titan Books, 2012).

1873
Allan Quatermain discovers the lost city of Kôr, founded by Kohr, the son of Hadon of Opar sometime after the great catastrophe that destroyed the Khokarsan civilization. While there, Quatermain runs across a giant named Rezu (compare this name to that of the Khokarsan sungod "Resu"), who, strangely, bears a striking resemblance to Kwasin, once owned the Ax of Victory, and believes he is the sungod. The great Zulu warrior Umslopogaas, son of Chaka Zulu, brings the ax once again to Kôr, many millennia after Hadon's son Kohr first carried it there when he founded the city. (See *She and Allan* by H. Rider Haggard.) The story of how Umslopogaas inherited the ax, which he calls Inkosikaas, is told in the novel *Nada the Lily* by H. Rider Haggard.

1883
Allan Quatermain and Lady Luna Ragnall take the *taduki* herb and get a glimpse into the lives of Lalila, Paga, and the hero Wi circa 10,000 BCE. (See *Allan and the Ice-Gods* by H. Rider Haggard.)

c. 1883–1885

Ludwig Horace Holly and Leo Vincey visit the lost city of Kôr. (See *She: A History of Adventure* by Ludwig Horace Holly, edited for publication by H. Rider Haggard.) Holly is a member of the Wold Newton Family. (TA)

1886

Allan Quatermain, Sir Henry Curtis, and Captain John Good discover the lost land of Zu-Vendis, which was founded by immigrants from the Khokarsan city of Wentisuh after the great catastrophe that destroyed the Khokarsan civilization. Umslopogaas shatters the Ax of Victory upon the sacred altar stone in Zu-Vendis. (See H. Rider Haggard's *Allan Quatermain*). Also in this year, the medium Bayrolles communes with the spirit of Hoseib Alar Robardin, who imparts to him details of "the ancient and famous city of Carcosa"; the name of this city is a transposition and corruption of "Khokarsa," the capital of the mighty Khokarsan Empire. (See "An Inhabitant of Carcosa" by Ambrose Bierce.)

1888–2070

In this time period, there are two jungle lords living at the same time. Gribardsun's memoirs state that he took great pains to avoid his younger counterpart. While we don't know exactly what Gribardsun was doing year-by-year during this time, there are a few possibilities . . .

1895

Sherlock Holmes, a Wold Newton Family member, investigates the murder of Black Peter Carey ("The Adventure of Black Peter" by Doyle and Watson), a former seaman killed by a harpoon that nailed him to the wall. In the short essay "What Happened to Black Michael?" (*Tarzan Alive*, Addendum 4; based on an original idea by Dale L. Walker; developed by John Harwood; additional notes by Farmer), a convincing argument is made that Black Peter Carey was the same person as the Black Michael who seemed to have befriended the jungle lord's parents in Burroughs'

Tarzan of the Apes. In *Tarzan Alive*, Farmer speculates that Black Michael wanted to save the Greystokes' lives and maroon them so he could sell their location for a ransom. Black Michael attempted to extort money from the fifth duke of Greystoke, but he ended up killing him instead. When the sixth duke refused to pay the ransom, Black Michael refused to divulge the location of the Ape Man's parents and so they died in the jungle. According to Holmes' investigation, a man named Cairns whom Carey had blackmailed was the guilty party in the harpoon murder of Carey. In *Tarzan Alive*, however, Farmer makes an interesting comment that, "Tarzan, of course, could have performed the feat with one hand and without drawing on all his strength." This appears to be idle speculation, but is it really? Wold Newton researcher Christopher Paul Carey suggests otherwise. In 1895, the jungle lord was only seven years old and of course could not have known that Black Michael had killed his grandfather and marooned his parents. However, Gribardsun would have known.

January 1899
At Carlow Castle in Ireland, Colonel Sebastian Moran is attacked by the "ghost" of Sir William Marshal—possibly Gribardsun exacting revenge on Moran for the latter's involvement in a blackmail scheme involving Gribardsun's shipwrecked parents. (See the short story "No Ghosts Need Apply" by Win Scott Eckert in *The Phantom Chronicles 2*, Moonstone Books, 2010.)

November 1929
Hareton Ironcastle discovers an ancient ax called the Reaver of Worlds that was made from a shattered half of the Ax of Victory. (See the short story "Iron and Bronze" by Christopher Paul Carey and Win Scott Eckert, *Tales of the Shadowmen 5: The Vampires of Paris*, Black Coat Press, 2009.)

1973
Philip José Farmer edits another version of the jungle lord's memoirs. These are published as "Extracts from the Memoirs of 'Lord Greystoke.'"

September 1990

Gribardsun and another time traveler calling him- or herself by several names ("J. Bauer," "the Farmer's daughter," and "Doctor Omega") snatch Doctor James Clarke Wildman (the real name of "Doc Savage") from September 1990 and convince Wildman to go back in time to 1950 in order to preserve the timeline. Bauer, speaking to Gribardsun, chastises him about "that time in Khokarsa," implying that Gribardsun has either previously time-traveled with Bauer, or that Bauer visited Khokarsa when Gribardsun was there as Sahhindar. (See "Doc Wildman: Out of Time" by Win Scott Eckert, *Farmerphile: The Magazine of Philip José Farmer No. 6*, October 2006.) Note that the 1990 date applies to Wildman's personal timeline; it is not clear when on Gribardsun's personal timeline this event occurs.

"J. Bauer" is Josie Bauer, the time-traveling daughter of Philip José Farmer, as seen in Spider Robinson's *Time Travelers Strictly Cash*. Doctor Omega is a time traveler from the novel *Doctor Omega* by Arnould Galopin, adapted and retold by Jean-Marc and Randy Lofficier, Black Coat Press, 2003.

1990–2070

Although in *Time's Last Gift* Gribardsun specifically states that he did all he could to prevent a time loop from occurring and tried to prevent the creation of the *H. G. Wells I*, he was probably being misleading. He undoubtedly knew that not only did his own personal history depend on him traveling back in time, but that the history of the world did as well. In this period he is in the shadows helping to finance and influence the creation of time-traveling technology. In fact, he likely contacts his younger self, because Gribardsun knew exactly when he was supposed to go to which historical places, in order to get the best photos and ensure he filled his position in history. According to a theory propounded by Andrew J. Brook, Gribardsun is given an itinerary by his future self during the period they are concurrently alive in the 20th and 21st centuries. Recalling that Gribardsun's memoirs state that he went out of his way to avoid his other self, perhaps he leaves his other self messages with instructions without actually meeting face to face.

Post-2070

There are two editions of *Time's Last Gift*, one published in 1972 and a revised version published in 1977. The revision is mostly an epilogue which tells what happened to Gribardsun after 2070. Gribardsun should have only known of events up to 2070 when he traveled into the past and this is reflected in the original edition of *Time's Last Gift*. Yet what was the origin of information added to the second edition? Perhaps, as a time traveler, Gribardsun became associated with the Time Police; the information in the 1977 edition (and all subsequent editions) of *Time's Last Gift* reflects information Gribardsun could have gleaned from this association.

2073

World Central University scientists release a rejuvenation process allowing almost everyone to regain and maintain their youth. Although *Time's Last Gift* does not specify the origin of this breakthrough in technology, we can speculate at least two sources which, combined, create the rejuvenation process. In *The Other Log of Phileas Fogg*, the Capelleans, the Eridaneans, and their terrestrial adoptees have thousand-year life spans due a life extension treatment. This is one source. As for the other, Gribardsun lived 14,000 years without aging, as noted in the canonical books about the jungle lord, and by Gribardsun himself: "As you know now, I was fortunate enough to be given an elixir by a witch doctor who was the last man of his tribe. He belonged to a family the original head of which, some generations before, had discovered how to make the elixir, a vile-tasting devil's brew, from certain African herbs, blood, and several other constituents I will not even hint at. He had a high regard for me because I saved his life and also because he thought I was some sort of a demigod. He knew of my rather peculiar upbringing."

Gribardsun's body therefore must be capable of great regeneration. The rejuvenation technique is probably a combination of both of these sources and its creation was no doubt aided by Gribardsun for one specific purpose, as seen in the next entry.

2108
Jane is revived and her mangled body is rebuilt. (TLG) Although not specifically stated in *Time's Last Gift*, the ability to regenerate Jane's mangled body probably was a modification of the afore-mentioned rejuvenation process.

2140
Gribardsun—now known as "Commander Rhys"—and his wife Jane depart for Capella, in a cryogenic sleeper ship. (TLG) Perhaps they eventually encounter some of the Capellean "Old Ones," from *The Other Log of Phileas Fogg*.

The 22nd Century and Beyond
Gribardsun still lives . . .

WHEN DAY BREAKS THE STONE GOD AWAITS
DENNIS E. POWER

Philip José Farmer's *The Stone God Awakens* is the story of Ulysses Singing Bear, a physicist who was accidentally "stoned." Singing Bear worked on Project Niobe, the goal of which was to create a matter-freezer, a device that could cease the motion of the atoms and subatomic particles in an object. The frozen matter would become like an indestructible stone that nothing could destroy.

To Singing Bear it seemed as though he were sitting in his laboratory one instant and the next he was plunged into the middle of a war; a war between sentient, anthropoid raccoons and Siamese cats. He quickly discovered that he had been turned to stone and had been in such a state for twenty million years. Singing Bear eventually learned that he was in fact the last human being alive on Earth.

Farmer would later utilize the concept of "stoning technology" in the short story "The Sliced-Crosswise Only-on-Tuesday World" and his Dayworld series, which consists of the novels *Dayworld*, *Dayworld Rebel* and *Dayworld Breakup*. Stoning technology was the crucial technology of this series. It was a boon for the ever increasingly overpopulated world of the future. Stoning not only allowed for the creation of low cost indestructible materials for permanent housing, it could forever preserve food, which meant abundant food supplies could be kept indefinitely for times of need. To further help the world's strained resources stoning technology reduced the human population in a humane and safe manner. First it allowed people to leave the Earth. Stoning technology was invaluable for low cost and low risk space travel; passengers never needed food or oxygen. Before take off they were stoned and after arrival they were destoned. And if some rare calamity occurred and the ship was destroyed the passengers' indestructible molecularly frozen bodies would be unharmed and would float in space until relocated. Stoning technology's major benefit, however, was that it transformed society and reduced the world population by a seventh.

A citizen of the Dayworld spent one day a week as a living breathing human being; the other six days he or she existed as a stone statue. Each day one seventh of the world was destoned to live out a normal day while the majority of the population remained stoned. The stoner culture greatly reduced the "demand for food, amount of pollution, and living space required."

One has to wonder—at least I always have—were the worlds of Ulysses Singing Bear and the Dayworld series the same? One strong argument against this notion is that Ulysses Singing Bear was not destoned until struck by lightning twenty million years after he had been stoned. However, in the course of his travels Ulysses Singing Bear came across the ruins of a museum where he had once been prominently displayed before being stolen by the Seal People. In the Dayworld series it is not uncommon for famous people to retire due to ill health or age by being stoned. They would then be displayed like the statues that they had become.

I suggest that Ulysses Singing Bear had this prominent place in the museum because he was the father of stoning technology. However, the process for destoning was not invented until several years after Singing Bear's accident. The reason why he was never destoned may have been that the stoning process that he developed was incompatible with the process that could stone and destone objects and living beings at will. His process, however, was the breakthrough that demonstrated that stoning could be accomplished. The incompatibility of the technologies was the reason why he had never been destoned. Or at least this may have been the official reason that the world government propounded. When the stoner technology was perfected the world was undergoing an overpopulation crisis and a serious shortage in natural resources; the government may have felt that destoning Singing Bear at a time when people were being stoned to save natural resources would have been unfair. He also would have been a man out of his time and element so they may have felt he better served as a petrified icon of this world saving technology.

During the course of the Dayworld series, protagonist Jefferson Caird discovers that by 3414 the human population has dwindled and that most natural resources have been replenished so stoner technology is no longer necessary. The world government was aware of these facts but continued its policies in order to maintain control of the world society. Caird and others brought about the end of the Dayworld society and by the conclusion of *Dayworld Breakup,* stoning was fast becoming a thing of the past.

In the years after *Dayworld Breakup* the stoner technology may have become lost over the ages. In the ruined museum that had once contained his petrified form, Ulysses Singing Bear saw a holographic display that depicted that mankind had overpopulated the world and depleted the Earth's natural resources, yet stoning technology was not depicted in the holographic images. There was also a short depiction of the scientists who attempted to de-petrify Ulysses Singing Bear. Either the stoner technology had been lost or, as previously speculated, he was not able to be destoned with the Dayworld's destoning technology because his particular molecular freeze was incompatible with that technology.

After being destoned some twenty million years in the future Ulysses Singing Bear became a major figure in a battle for control of the Earth, a war of animal versus vegetable. Before becoming extinct the human race had forcibly evolved various animal species into sentient anthropoids. They had also created living computers that could store the vast history and knowledge of the human race. These living computers were giant trees, Sequoias with cellulose circuitry. As plants often do, one of these trees grew larger and absorbed some of the other trees of knowledge and gained sentience. Growing ever larger and absorbing all of the other trees of knowledge, it finally straddled the world like the mythical Yggdrasil. When Ulysses Singing Bear appeared on the scene The Tree immediately perceived him as a threat. The sentient tree viewed its mission to keep the various sentient species in a state of barbarism so that they would never achieve a degree of civilization that could threaten the planet. The Tree wiped out any civilization it deemed a threat by sending vast armies of sentients loyal to the God-Tree to make war on the threatening civilization.

The theme of The Tree replacing humanity as the dominant species on Earth in *The Stone God Awakens* thematically ties Ulysses Singing Bear to another of Farmer's works, which may provide clues to not only how Ulysses Singing Bear came to be petrified but also what happened after the *Dayworld Breakup* and how the trees were first created.

Farmer, ever being the trickster, often buries his important clues inside jokes. In the novel *Dayworld Rebel*, there is a small passage in which Jefferson Caird and his other fellow "rebels" watch a film called "The Martian Rebellion," which tells the story of a rebellion on Mars, which forty years previously had been defeated through the efforts of three bumbling and accident prone men named Moses, Curleigh and Lawrence. These three men were staunch supporters of the government, therefore staunch advocates for the stoner culture.

In Farmer's polytropical paramyth entitled "Only Who Can Make a Tree?," there are three scientists Dr. Mough, Dr. Kerls and Dr. Lorenzo who attempt through a series of bizarre experiments to end the perils of pollution and overpopulation. In the end they accidentally release a virus that turns every human being, excluding one, into a tree.

Of course most people reading the books will get Farmer's joke that these three men in both cases were written to be allusions to The Three Stooges. Yet perhaps there is more than meets the eye.

Although it is undated, "Only Who Can Make A Tree?" seems to be set around when it was written in the late 1960s, while the

Dayworld series is set in 3414. Even if these characters were not merely allusions to the Three Stooges how could these three men have possibly lived that long? The Dayworld series provides us a couple of methods. Stoning greatly expands the chronological life span since one Dayworld year is equivalent to seven calendar years; therefore an average lifespan of sixty-five years would encompass 455 calendar years. Another method is that one of Caird's ancestors created a life extension process that retarded aging and added centuries to the life span. This life extension treatment was available only to a relatively few chosen people who made up the extended family of Dr. Immerman, the scientist who discovered the treatment.

If these scientists were Immers the stoner technology could easily have extended their lives from the twentieth to the 35th century. If these men were scientists in the late 20th century dedicated to finding a means of reducing pollution and overpopulation as depicted in "Only Who Can Make a Tree?," and if their bumbling, accident prone natures had a basis in reality then, it is possible Farmer was hinting that they were responsible not only for the existence of the Dayworld but also for the shape of the world in the aftermath of the *Dayworld Breakup*.

Neither Farmer nor Ulysses Singing Bear details specifics about the laboratory accident that petrified Singing Bear, other than to say it seemed due to a power surge of some sort. However, Singing Bear was not the only person in the room: "Suddenly, the needle of the big power meter had swung around to the red. The operators had cried out, and one had jumped up," yet Singing Bear was the only one petrified. It is not too difficult to imagine that these three men could have joined Project Niobe, seeing it as a means to achieving their goals of reducing pollution and overpopulation. Well intentioned, they may have tampered with the equipment, seeking to accelerate the program but only succeeded in stoning Singing Bear. Yet out of this accident the stoner technology was born, although it took years to fully develop.

These three intrepid scientists may have been part of the team that made de-petrifaction possible, although it may have been through another fortuitous accident. They may have created the process without fully understanding the science behind it. Because of their pioneer efforts in creating stoner technology they may have been among the first recipients of Immerman's age slowing process.

Like most of the Immers they eventually had to adopt new identities and so moved to Mars. Although their participation in the revolution was probably as Farmer described it, the anecdote about them in *Dayworld Rebel* seems to serve three functions. Jefferson Caird shows his companions the film as a clue about his future plans. The anecdote about the trio called Moses, Curleigh and Lawrence may have been metaphoric. They sought to prevent the revolution and so maintain the status quo of the civilization that they had created. Yet they were too public at least for the Immers and so were later arrested on charges of data bank embezzlement and sent to rehabilitation, meaning that they were stoned and stored away.

Criminals were probably the last of the people to be de-petrified and the technology was discarded as a tool of oppression. By the time the three had been de-petrified they could see that mankind was once again on a track to deplete natural resources and overcrowd the planet. They set to work to ensure that mankind would live with Nature by creating organically derived technology, such as the organic engines used by the Neshgai, in *The Stone God Awakens*, and the computer trees.

Their botanical work in the 1960s and in the post-Dayworld era may also not have been entirely their own. These three "scientists" may have learned of a pair of special trees that once grew in Africa. In Philip José Farmer's Tarzan novel, *The Dark Heart of Time*, Tarzan encounters a gigantic tree, alien in nature. This tree was a communications device and a sort of computer/archive attended by a priestess who was still young but over a hundred years in age. She had become the caretaker of The Tree when its original caretakers had returned to the stars. The Tree seemed to have a symbiotic relationship with its surrounding area, causing biological and environmental changes. In one drastic case it seems to have altered a terrestrial frog into something akin to The Tree's original world. Tarzan's companion Rahb, a bear-man, may have also have been from one of the resulting humanoid species created through The Tree's hybridization process, as were the Kwagana (The Stunted Men) and the Goura-Zannkas (The Men of the Stars) encountered by the Ironcastle expedition.

Such fusions between animal and plant were also referenced in Farmer's translation of J. H. Rosny Aîné's *Ironcastle*. Hareton Ironcastle speculated that the section of Africa called Gondoroko had once been struck by a meteorite or asteroid brimming with life. In most cases when alien life forms are introduced into a new area, the alien life form either is quickly wiped out or thrives, the latter instance causing severe damage to the ecosystem. Such cases include the introduction of rabbits and European mice to Australia as well as the threats posed currently by the introduction of zebra mussels and snakehead trout to the rivers and lakes of the United States. However, in the case of Gondoroko, the alien species that were introduced were very adaptable and crossbred with native terrestrial plants and animals, creating new and unique hybrids comprised of both animal and plant species. Yet this growing area of hybridization also posed a threat to terrestrial life as native species became wiped out through hybridization.

At the end of *Ironcastle*, the explorers found a large crystal ship buried deep in the African soil that they speculated was the source in this area of hybridization between mineral, animal and vegetable. However, what Ironcastle thought was the origination of the hybridization may have been just a branch root of another larger tree. The Crystal Tree in *The Dark Heart of Time* may have been the source of this bizarre hybridization. Consider for a moment that they might have been in a real sense the seeds for an invasion. As The Tree grew it generated an area of hybridization through its roots and stems. The branching plants arising in this area were hybrids of mineral, animal and vegetable designed to protect and feed The Tree. By the time they reached maturity the trees would have a large fertile area filled with hybrids, which would provide fertile ground and protection for the Crystal Tree.

Upon reaching full maturity The Tree would send out a signal and more seeds would follow the signal to earth. The new seeds would flourish and the areas of hybridization would then spread rapidly, overwhelming the native plants and overriding the terrestrial biology.

This was avoided when Tarzan inadvertently destroyed the Crystal Tree in 1918. Without the source roots the area of hybridization stopped expanding and by 1920, when the main events of *Ironcastle* took place, this area was already dying out. By destroying The Tree, Tarzan had literally saved the world.

In the years to follow, Dr. Mough and his two companions learned of The Tree and located one of the branch roots, possibly the same one mentioned in *Ironcastle*. In the post-Dayworld era, using sophisticated plant cloning techniques they were able to create viable hybrids between oaks and the alien Crystal Tree. In their hubris they may have believed that they could control the hybrids but, as with many mad scientists, their creations took on a life of their own.

Underneath the joke, "Only Who Can Make a Tree?" can be seen as a cautionary tale, a tale of warning that these three men were eventually responsible for creating the sentient trees that ultimately replaced humanity as the dominant species on Earth in *The Stone God Awakens*.

(Special thanks to *Farmerphile* editor Christopher Paul Carey: our discussions about *The Dark Heart of Time* and *Ironcastle* allowed me to see even further connections.)

Philip José Farmer and
The Case of the Two Jungle Lords
Dennis E. Power

In 1976 I was browsing through a local bookstore and saw a paperback cover that rooted me to my spot. The cover had a beautifully painted picture of Sherlock Holmes and Dr. Watson and Tarzan. The book was titled *The Adventure of the Peerless Peer* and had been written by Philip José Farmer. I knew then without even reading the cover blurb that this was going to be a great read about Tarzan meeting Sherlock Holmes. I was not disappointed and even more thrilled when it had cameos by G-8 and The Shadow. *The Peerless Peer* remained one of my favorite Farmer books.

I found the hidden pun in the book's title very amusing. The obvious interpretation of the title of *The Adventure of the Peerless Peer* is that it refers to Tarzan, who is Lord Greystoke. This makes him a Peer of the Realm. Obviously Tarzan is unique and has no equal, hence is Peerless. Thus we have the Peerless Peer. Another interpretation, at least one that occurred to me, had to do with the villain of the piece, Von Bork. British scientists had developed a bacteria that could eat sauerkraut, but the fiend Von Bork had stolen the formula for the bacteria and destroyed the sample, greatly extending the war. All through the adventure, Holmes could never discover where Von Bork had hidden the formula. It turned out that Von Bork had a glass eye and had inscribed the formula on its surface. The glass eye is the second Peerless Peer, the eye that cannot see. Oddly enough most of the people I have talked to about the book did not get the pun, so perhaps I just have an overactive imagination.

A few years later I read a collection of Philip José Farmer's short stories called *The Grand Adventure* which had in it a story titled "The Adventure of the Three Madmen." In his foreword to the tale Farmer recounts how the Burroughs estate withdrew their permission to use the character of Tarzan. Farmer had rewritten *The Adventure of the Peerless Peer* and substituted Mowgli of Rudyard Kipling's *The Jungle Book*. While I was disappointed that Tarzan had no longer met Sherlock Holmes, I thought that Farmer had done a very nice job in fitting Mowgli into the existing tale.

Years later when I was rereading *The Grand Adventure*, one passage from Farmer's introduction to "The Shadow of Space" struck me. He said "I have this strange thing about my stories. I believe that they did happen or will happen. I'd be tampering with reality if I altered a story to any significant extent once it's been printed." My immediate thought was that well, then both *The Adventure of the Peerless Peer* and "The Adventure of the Three Madmen" must be true. Yet how could they be? My first thought that was that *Peerless Peer* and "Three Madmen" might be a Rashômon type situation, with two divergent accounts of the same story deriving from the differing perspectives of the story-tellers. However, I immediately realized that this could not be the case, since John H. Watson supposedly wrote both accounts. Was one then a true account and the other just a red herring?

I went to the source and read both *The Adventure of the Peer-less Peer* and "The Adventure of the Three Madmen" back to back. After a few readings, I began to see some very telling textual clues. Not all of the differences in the text could be accounted for by Farmer rewriting the novel to plug in Mowgli.

I realized after comparing the two texts that they fit together, perhaps not as seamlessly as a deck of shuffled cards but more like a jigsaw puzzle. With a gamester like Philip José Farmer the analogy of the jigsaw was very apt. He provided clues that both *The Adventure of the Peerless Peer* and "The Adventure of the Three Madmen" took place concurrently; Sherlock Holmes met Tarzan and he also met Mowgli!

There were two key passages that led me to this perhaps controversial conclusion. In both *Peerless Peer* and "Three Madmen" natives who resembled Persians capture Holmes and Watson and take them to their village. A day later, two Germans are shoved into the hut with them. They tell identical stories in both versions. They had heard a strange cry and hurried to see what the cause of it was. There were five dead men lying in a clearing. Six men were running in one direction away from the clearing and four others were running in another direction. Three of the dead men had arrows in them, two had their necks broken. Our clue to consider here is the presence of the arrows.

Mowgli was not depicted as having a bow and arrow previous to this incident although the German offered the suggestion that he had taken the bow from one of the natives. Another German mentioned Mowgli was seen standing over a dead body with a bloody knife in his hand, a bow was not mentioned. While it may be that Mowgli had acquired proficiency with the bow and arrow after his career was chronicled in *The Jungle Books*, in *The Jungle Books* themselves he used his teeth, nails and knife. As he apparently did in this case as regards to the broken necks and bloody knife. If Mowgli had not shot the arrows, where had they originated?

Another clue was found where the text differed between the versions. In *Peerless Peer*, Tarzan told Holmes and Watson how he went to check out a rumor that a white woman, an Englishwoman, had been captured by a tribe of blacks. He states he fought his way to her, killing a dozen men, and fought his way out carrying her with him, killing a dozen more men. When Tarzan had removed the gag he had put on her so she would stop screaming, she had told him that she was perfectly happy living with the Sultan and could he please return her, immediately.

Mowgli did not rescue a woman in "Three Madmen," but

rather wished to get away from one. This is Liza Borden, Mowgli's co-star in the film epic *Mowgli's Revenge*. She was a loud-mouthed, spoiled woman who claimed that Mowgli had ravished her, over and over again. Watson was immediately suspicious of her story since she used dialogue from her films. Mowgli claimed that it was she who had chased him, not the other way around. Liza Borden departed from the action of the novel shortly after she was introduced, having gone off to relieve herself and then disappearing. We are told that she eventually made her way back to England but not how she got there or what happened to her in the interim.

When I realized that Liza Borden was probably the woman whom Tarzan went to rescue, the jigsaw pieces fit together nicely. Once I had the pieces in place I reconstructed the story of how Sherlock Holmes had interacted with both Tarzan and Mowgli. This reconstruction was the basis for my article "Jungle Brothers" In *Myths for the Modern Age: Philip José Farmer's Wold Newton Universe* (MonkeyBrain Books, 2005).

Interestingly enough, Holmes considered both Tarzan and Mowgli to be impostors. In both *Peerless Peer* and "Three Madmen," Sherlock Holmes made some rather accurate deductions about the Jungle Lords' claim to their peerage. Tarzan of course was the Duke of Greystoke and Mowgli was the heir of Sir Jametsee JeJeebhoy, the Parsee Baronet of Bombay. Aouda JeJeebhoy, of Jules Verne's *Around the World in 80 Days,* was also supposed to be a relative of Sir Jametsee. In both cases Holmes was hired by the supposed impostor to investigate this possibility. Given a large retainer and told not to begin the investigation until instructed to do so. In essence Holmes was bribed to keep his thoughts to himself.

While examining *Peerless Peer* and "Three Madmen" to see if it was possible that both could be true, I started to look at "The Adventure of the Three Madmen" on a different level. Farmer's choice of Mowgli as the replacement Jungle Lord struck me as bit odd. Now mind you I understand that Mowgli was Tarzan's precursor as the feral child, so it seems a natural replacement. Yet since Mowgli was a native of India he was as out of place in Africa as Holmes and Watson. It might have seemed more natural for Farmer to have rewritten the story more completely and place it in WWI India, possibly replacing Zu Vendis with the lost city of the Nine, from Talbot Mundy's *Jimgrim* series. However, if Farmer was set on retaining the African locale, due to Zu Vendis, a more seamless choice for the jungle lord character would have been someone like Ka-Zar or Ki-Gor. The last one would have been very appropriate since the Ki-Gor stories were written by John Peter Drummond, and according to Farmer Tarzan's son Korak was actually John Drummond, the brother of Hugh Drummond. Yet for some reason, Farmer chose Mowgli to replace Tarzan, rather than another feral man raised in Africa.

Tarzan Alive is fiction that purports to be true, or perhaps it is truth disguised as fiction. Had Farmer taken advantage of Burroughs Inc.'s refusal to let him reuse the character of Tarzan to shed some light on a hidden truth found between both versions of his Sherlock Holmes in Africa tale? Had Holmes' investigations into both Lord Greystoke's and Mowgli's backgrounds revealed a truth that even Farmer could only hint at? Wondering what this might be I reread the Mowgli stories in *The Jungle Book* and then carefully once more read through *Tarzan Alive*. I found an odd similarity. Mowgli's parents had been killed by a lame tiger. He had then wandered into the woods to be raised by wolves. John Clayton, Tarzan's father, had served in India and during the course of it he had been attacked and mauled by a tiger. The tiger had been run off by a shot from Colonel Moran. (Although Moran was later revealed to be a Capellean agent, the tiger attack does, on the surface at least, seem to have been legitimate.)

Was this lame tiger that killed Mowgli's parents the same one shot by Colonel Moran? In *The Jungle Books* Shere Khan is obsessed with killing Mowgli because he had escaped him. Yet it might have been more than that, possibly Shere Khan blamed Mowgli for his lameness. Was it possible that Shere Khan had killed only one of Mowgli's parents, his mother, while his father escaped with some injuries? Did Sherlock Holmes' investigation uncover a connection between Mowgli and John Clayton that for some reason was never disclosed?

Although Kipling's dates for Mowgli did not exactly jibe with John Clayton's service in India, the connection seemed too fitting not to be true. Like Tarzan, Mowgli may have been large for his age and seemed a few years older than he actually was when Kipling first heard of him. A slight bit of evidence for Mowgli to have been a bit younger than Kipling had stated could be in how he was depicted in "Three Madmen." By Kipling's dates he would have been forty or more and without the benefit of an immortality serum. By my reckoning he would have been just over thirty. I can tell you from personal experience, there is a world of difference between thirty and forty.

If my deductions about Mowgli were correct, then when Farmer rewrote *The Adventure of the Peerless Peer*, making Mowgli the replacement for Tarzan does not seem that odd at all. If you would like to see if you have arrived at the same conclusion that I did, please check out my article in *Myths for the Modern Age*.

Bibliophile—a discussion on
The Other Log of Phileas Fogg
Paul Spiteri

"Gentlemen, here I am"

For over two hundred years two extraterrestrial races, known as the Eridaneans and the Capelleans, have been fighting a secret battle on, and for, Earth. Both races promise utopia for the people of Earth once their enemy is defeated. It is the Capelleans who first landed a scout ship on Earth, closely followed by the Eridaneans. In the ensuing battle their spaceships are destroyed and the extra-terrestrial visitors are stranded. With no hope of escape the two separate parties go underground and undergo surgical modification in order to blend in with their new surroundings.

Over the years, as the underground war wages, all the females of both species are targeted and killed. With no way to keep their bloodlines pure the aliens interbreed and adopt so as to keep their respective races alive.

Jules Verne, chronicler of the famous journey described in *Around The World in Eighty Days,* probably knew nothing of the power struggle, the fight for mankind, that existed behind the seemingly harmless, though fantastic, exploit undertaken by our Victorian hero.

The covert war is in full force at the time Verne wrote of the Englishman's epic journey. And while so many readers devoured with joy the regular instalments describing in real time this journey as described by Verne, none but a very select few could have known about the secret mission that sparked, and coincided with, the dash across the globe. For Phileas Fogg, seemingly eccentric Englishman, with looks Verne describes as "like a bearded Byron," is in fact an Eridanean agent embarking on a mission which may result in the end of the war with the Capelleans. Readers of Verne's chronicles know that Fogg is a fastidious man; proof of that comes early when Fogg dismisses his manservant for bringing his shaving water that is 2 degrees colder than he has stipulated. Rather than a costly mistake by the manservant, this is actually a coded message which allows Fogg to bring in Jean Passepartout; another Eridanean agent and one most suited for what is to come. Not that Fogg is yet aware of his mission; for that he visits his habitual daytime refuge, the Reform Club.

Here, via coded messages delivered during a game of cards, Fogg receives instruction and engineers the wager that starts in train two adventures; the one told so expertly by Verne and the parallel one that was only revealed a hundred and one years later, in 1973, on the publication of Phil's exposé. Fogg is to circumnavigate the globe in 80 days, a feat that has only recently become feasible due to the completion of a cross Indian railway. The wager is for twenty thousand pounds, equivalent to some five million dollars today.

That this story behind the story should ever come to light is due to two spectacularly important finds. First, in 1947, Fogg's own secret diary is found hidden in his house in Savile Row. Unfortunately the book was unreadable and it was initially assumed it was written in code, although analysis eventually proved it was an unknown language. Even with that revelation the book was still beyond the grasp of scholars. It was only after the second find, a series of notebooks written by Sir Heraclitus Fogg (a true blood Eridanean and adoptive father of Phileas), that the diary of Phileas Fogg was translated. These notebooks had translatory notes (possibly this was a primer for the passing on of the Eridanean language to adoptees) which allowed Sir Beowulf William Clayton, 4th Baronet, to translate a good chunk of the diary.

Phil learned of the translation during his researches (for *Tarzan Alive*) into the life of General Sir William Clayton, Phileas Fogg's biological father. This allowed Phil to reconstruct the amazing story behind *The Other Log of Phileas Fogg*.

Although ideologically separated (though this, as becomes apparent, is obviously a fine line) the two races do share a technological ability superior to that prevalent on nineteenth century earth. One of their most important tools is known as a disruptor, a device that allows the immediate transportation of people and goods between two of them. Passepartout has one disruptor and part of their mission is to retrieve others or, at least, destroy them so as to keep them from the enemy.

As is the norm with Phil Farmer you read more about the privations and sacrifices endured by the heroes that others tend to gloss over. Farmer's heroes are heroes for sure but they also have human failings that we can all relate to—it is recognising them as men but glimpsing what they *can* achieve that makes them a Farmer hero—truly the greatest type of hero.

Whereas knowledge of the original adventure does give a framework for Phil's additional information, that is by no means required. Phil skilfully gives the unfamiliar reader an overview of the famous story and expands on the adventure where the "true" story is not narrated by Verne. Phil shows how these side adventures fit neatly into the better known version of the journey. Phil is a wonderful storyteller but his skill here is in his role as narrator of the fantastic story behind the wondrous venture we all know so well. The way Phil blends together the two adventures, giving us an insight into the true nature of this journey, an adventure story layered on an adventure story, really ups the intrigue, and the enjoyment. Part of the added joy of this book is noting how seamlessly Phil blends the two stories, illustrating with apparent ease how the two stories sit alongside each other in the same timeline.

Three major adventures are described that are Eridanean/ Capellean in nature which Verne knew nothing about (or possibly failed to report if he did know about them). The first occurs toward the start of the journey while Fogg and Passepartout are in India. Riding a war elephant through the jungle our intrepid duo leave their party and sneak off in the night (yes, on an elephant!) so that they can use the distorter to transport themselves into the palace of the Rajah of Bundelcund. The Rajah, a Capellean agent, has gone rogue and has acquired a distorter for himself. Fogg and Passepartout wish to recover it and using their own distorter they transport themselves into the palace. Here they find themselves in a situation only Phil could describe adequately! A most bizarre battle ensues during which the Rajah is killed and Fogg makes a startling discovery. One of the Capellean leaders is in the palace, himself after the distorter. This man is none other than another Verne protagonist: Captain Nemo! Nemo is not the disillusioned, embittered and idealistic Indian Prince we are led to suppose he is from reading *Twenty Thousand Leagues under the Sea* and *The Mysterious Island*. Rather he is a ruthless pirate and power hungry Capellean who is sworn to kill all Eridaneans. Up until this point Fogg had assumed the captain to be dead, having served with him (in disguise) on the *Nautilus* and being instrumental in the destruction of the ship.

As Farmer scholars will know, Phil contends (in *Tarzan Alive*) that Nemo, the name meaning "no-one," is none other than the arch-enemy of Sherlock Holmes, James Moriarty! This second nefarious "career" for the Capellean is first evidenced in 1891, some twenty years after the events described here, and is chronicled in the Sherlock Holmes story "The Final Problem" (published 1893).

The battle is successful for Fogg for although they are not able to acquire the Rajah's distorter they do succeed in destroying it and escaping with their lives. They return to their camp with their travelling companions none the wiser of this nocturnal adventure.

Readers of *Around the World in Eighty Days* will know how subsequently Fogg and Passepartout encountered the Rajah's funeral procession and rescued his widowed wife from being sacrificed on the funeral pyre. Though we know that Fogg fell in love with the beautiful Aouda, what isn't known is that she was an Eridanean agent, sent to spy on the Rajah. It was Aouda who had supplied the Eridanean command with information on the Rajah's palace and in so doing aided Fogg and Passepartout to successfully complete their mission.

From India the racing journeymen (with Aouda in tow) travel to Japan and catch a boat to take them to San Francisco. It is whilst on this voyage that the group embark on their second great adventure. They transport themselves onto the *Mary Celeste*, thus explaining the reasons behind the enigma of the brigantine. Any reference to the *Marie Céleste* is erroneous and owes more to Conan Doyle's fictional story, "J. Habakuk Jephson's Statement." Doyle's story drew very heavily on the original incident, but included a considerable amount of fiction.

Tables are turned and counter-turned as Fogg and Passepartout battle with Nemo on the infamous ship (including a vivid description of a cat-and-mouse chase). Their mission accomplished and another enemy distorter disposed of, Fogg and Passepartout return to their ship.

Landing in San Francisco the journey continues across the American continent as described by Verne. Here are many adventures too, including a duel aboard a moving train as well as an attack by the Sioux! As always on this journey the Capelleans are trailing Fogg, intent on capturing or disposing of him.

Running behind schedule the party arrives in New York too late to catch the ship that will get them to England in time to win the bet. Desperate, Fogg hires a steamer to cross the Atlantic. Pushing the engines too hard the ship uses up all its fuel and the deck is torn up to feed the fires.

Further problems delay the Fogg party at Liverpool, meaning they miss their train to London. This is rectified when Fogg commissions a private service to get him to London. A curiosity in Verne's book is that when Fogg arrives in London all the clocks of London strike at ten minutes to nine; the answer is within the pages of this book.

In Verne's original it is at this point that Fogg arrives in London minutes late to claim his prize. He returns dejected to his home in Savile Row and it is only the next day that he realises that having crossed the International Date Line he has a day in hand and so races to the Reform Club and thus wins his prize. The truth is that Fogg knew he had an extra day and this is where the third major adventure occurs. Arriving at Savile Row he is trapped in his home by Nemo and his men; Fogg, Passepartout and Aouda manage to fight their way out (Aouda being injured in the fray) and get to the Reform Club in time. The bet is won and Phileas utters the immortal line used in this article as a subtitle.

Verne hinted at Fogg's immortality; Farmer confirms it as a benefit of being an Eridanean agent. Fogg may still be with us and clues certainly point to the fact that he was around in 1973, the centenary of his adventure, for at the end of the book Phil makes a point of saying that it is just coincidence that his initials are the same as Phileas Fogg's. Can we really be so sure? After all, the drawings of Fogg bear a striking resemblance to the author himself. It is also worth noting that the back cover blurb on *Father to the Stars* (1983) is attributed to Phileas Fogg though anyone reading these words will recognise the distinctive style.

A quick Google search will throw up many expansions to Phil's story. Notably, Farmer scholar Dennis Power has written an essay expanding on the hidden history of the Capellean and Eridanean's sojourn on earth: "Aliens Among us! Capelleans and Eridaneans" (www.pjfarmer.com/secret/aliens/capellean-Eridanan-revised.htm) and an ingenious piece of writing it is.

Bibliophile—a discussion on
Jesus on Mars
Paul Spiteri

"Christopher Columbus, you should be here"

P hil says that dreams inspire about one in thirty of his stories. He also tells us (in the Author's Preface to *Riverworld War*) that he had a dream featuring a bookshelf in a vast library. The shelf was packed with leather bound hardback books but Phil could only make out one title: *Jesus on Mars*. As Phil was looking at the book a huge hand reached up and took the volume.

Just that enigmatic title was the inspiration for probably the oddest titled novel in the Farmer canon. Darrell Schweitzer called it "one of the silliest-sounding titles of all time" but nonetheless it is "a superior idea" that "certainly keeps you reading." (Again, words from Darrell.)

The book was sold to Pinnacle but George Scithers, editor of *Isaac Asimov's Science Fiction Magazine*, was sent a copy and liked it. Rather than serialise the novel, George decided to print an abridged one-shot version. Due to a lack of communication the novel ended up hitting print before the short story was due. This scuppered the magazine deal and Phil was left with the abridged script and associated artwork.

At this point George Scheetz (famed as the editor of the short-lived but excellent *Farmerage*) stepped in and suggested the abridged story, plus artwork, should be published as a collector's item. (This became *Riverworld War*, and included some excised chapters from *The Magic Labyrinth*.)

Jesus on Mars tells the story of Earth's first manned mission to the Red planet. Sparked by an automated rover's discovery of a buried metallic structure, four Marsnauts are despatched. The *Barsoom* is captained by Richard Orme, a black Canadian Baptist, the other members of his crew being a Jew, a Moslem and an atheist. All the religious bases covered!

No sooner have the Marsnauts discovered that the artifact is in fact a buried spaceship than they are captured by what turns out to be the inhabitants of Mars. But even greater surprises are in store, for these are not beings indigenous to Mars but rather the descendents of humans, and an extraterrestrial race known as the Krsh, who crash landed on Mars some two thousand years ago.

The Krsh are an ancient race, technologically much further advanced than Earthlings, who, over two millennia ago, started to explore the galaxy. They encountered a couple of planets with life before Earth but it is in our solar system that they start to take an interest in events. The Krsh are ethically advanced too (it's always pleasing to note that Phil's technologically advanced aliens are normally also ethically advanced) and only reveal themselves to people they have rescued from mortal danger. During this process they pick up a group of early Christians, including the replacement apostle, Matthias. These humans agree to accompany the Krsh back to their home planet but before the journey can be started the Krsh ship is attacked. The assailants are from one of the planets previously visited by the Krsh and have followed the explorers to our solar system. An epic battle ensues. The Krsh are able to defeat the attackers but in the process are marooned on Mars.

Using the technology on hand the Krsh and humans build an underground sanctuary. This sanctuary expands to forty caverns and a population of over a million by the time Orme and his crew enter the picture.

But finding an interbred, homogenous human race under the surface of Mars is not the last surprise for the Earthmen and woman. As well as Matthias and his disciples, the spirit of Jesus was picked up from Earth and is now in residence on Mars. All the inhabitants of Mars, including the Krsh, are Jewish (whether by birth or conversion) and for the most part would be considered orthodox. However, they do recognise Jesus as the adopted son of God and revere and worship him as the true Messiah.

For the most part Jesus "lives" in the energy source that provides light to the main cavern (sunlight during the day, moonlight by night) and descends to spend time with his followers—and his wife!—at regular intervals.

Jesus is cagey about his origin and drops hints to Orme that he may be an energy being who hitched along with the Krsh when they visited his planet. How else explain that this "being" likes to reside in nuclear reactors! Is this any easier or harder to believe than he is the true Messiah?

The presence of Jesus had a profound effect on the Krsh; rather than "convert" the humans to an atheistic, scientific based philosophy they are converted to Judaism. It's as if the overriding evidence before their eyes is too much to counter. And the same effect is evident on at least two of the crew from Earth. However, Madeleine Danton, the professed atheist, steadfastly refuses to believe that her conscious decision to deny the existence of God, and his son, is now proven to be wrong. We can only imagine the turmoil she is going through. Both Avram Bronski and Nadir Shirazi, the Jew and the Moslem, respectively, accept what they see and convert to the Martian version of Christianity (or is it Judaism?).

From a narrative viewpoint we are more closely involved, and witness to, Orme's turmoil. Brought up in a strictly religious household he has tended to drift away from his beliefs in adulthood. Now he is faced with empirical proof of the existence of Jesus and the message he brings. Or is he? As he struggles with his conscience he believes he may have been visited by the "true" Jesus in a dream. Or is this just his mind playing tricks on him? In the end he has to face his demons and decide how he must be true to himself.

Although the Krsh have adopted the religion of their fellow castaways they have not forsaken their science. The inhabitants of Mars enjoy longevity, memory improving drugs and superior health care. Mars is as close to Utopia as we can imagine. There appears to be no downside—or none that we are made aware of. Maybe that's just Phil's point; heaven on earth would be perfect!

However, not all are content on Mars and as with every culture there are those who dissent. Such rebellion is small scale, is known about, and tolerated, by the leaders of the colony. In much the same way that the youths in the Farmer story "The Blasphemers" are allowed some latitude, the same is true on Mars. At one point in the book Orme is taken to an illegal drinking party, away from the main civilization hub, and is pleasantly surprised to see normal, adolescent behavior among the group.

The visit by the Earth party has been anticipated for a long time and with the help of Orme and his crew the Martians plan a return to Earth. Jesus wants to spread his message back on the world where he has so many followers. But he will not go empty handed. He has gifts; food generating machines to put an end to world hunger, the promise of immortality and the prospect of one day raising the dead (these latter two themes being close to Phil's literary heart). But he also has might. He is able to disable all of Earth's atomic weapons.

We are left to wonder how Earth will change. After all, the melding of a small group, isolated on another planet with spiritual and scientific leadership is a far cry from attempting to mold a planet of several billion. Is Earth welcoming Christ, the anti-Christ or an alien life form beyond our comprehension? No matter where your religious affiliations lie, Phil has given all of us something to ponder. As Arthur C. Clarke has said, "Any sufficiently advanced technology is indistinguishable from magic." Are the miracles that Jesus shows us in this story "magic" or advanced technology?

In the closing scene of the book Orme faces his own doubts and endures the ultimate test of his faith. As surprising and shocking as the ending is, it gives us a deeper insight into this Jesus and leaves us to consider whether the vehicle really matters if the message is the right one.

Once, while discussing this book with Tracy Knight, he showed me his own copy which Phil had inscribed. He'd humorously written "To Tracy Knight from Philip José Farmer—author also of Joseph Smith on Mercury and Buddha on Venus." These titles may not have been in Phil's dream and we can only regret that a series of books describing religious figures appearing throughout our solar system was never actually realized. Based on what we do have, it would have made enlightening as well as entertaining reading.

As an aside, the Pinnacle version of *Jesus on Mars* contains a bonus. The last four pages contain an essay by Harlan Ellison® on Doctor Who. Being a Brit I grew up with the Doctor and still can vividly recall Saturday evenings of science fiction televisual joy. The Doctor may have been from the planet Gallifrey but in many aspects he was quintessentially English. Eccentric, lacking in clothes sense and slightly menacing, Doctor Who was the one show you had to see to have any sort of street cred come playground discussions on a Monday morning. The show was cancelled sixteen years ago but recently made a comeback starring Christopher Eccleston (David Tennant in Season 2) as the eponymous Doctor. If you haven't already, do try and catch it; you won't be disappointed.

Bibliophile—a discussion on Lord Tyger

Paul Spiteri

"Things went their own way"—Boygur

In Ras Tyger, Phil gives us one of his more three-dimensional characters. A character that features in a story ranking amongst the finest he has written. Ras, whose name means "Lord" in Amharic, is a melting pot of emotion, of ability, of thought. He is a poet, an artisan, a wooer of women and at the same time he is a hunter, a killer and a man driven by the lust of an innocent. He experiences fear and loss but has bravery to more than compensate. He is skillful but prone to flamboyancy, practical but apt to show off. Fundamentally he is a man, albeit a superman. Ras is one who excels in his world as he would in any environment. But is it the jungle environment, his upbringing, that has made this superman or is it the superman that can thrive in the jungle environment?

Phil successfully evokes the sounds, smells and sights of the jungle valley. This valley is a pocket universe and Phil has populated it as such. (Anyone questioning the fauna here should wait for the book's conclusion when certain idiosyncrasies are explained.) Ras is the hero and he must assume ultimate responsibility for his acts of free will without any certain knowledge of what is right or wrong, good or bad. We are given an insight into Ras' thoughts in a similar way we get to know the inner thoughts of Ramstan in *The Unreasoning Mask*.

Living a seemingly idyllic life in the African jungle, Ras has loving foster parents and spends his youth exploring his domain and either taunting (the men) or bedding (the female) members of a nearby native village. His view of the world, his world, has been molded by his foster parents and by Igziyabher—the unseen being he knows as God. Limits are put on where he can travel, boundaries that Ras knows he will one day break through. He is fortunate in that his God—Igziyabher—lives atop a tower built straight up out of a nearby lake. Igziyabher keeps an eye on Ras and feeds instructions to him via his foster parents, but, however hard he tries, Ras never manages to discern how these divine instructions are given. Igziyabher periodically sends out his angels, who fly in big black birds, to swoop over the valley and keep an additional eye on Ras.

Ras' orderly life is shattered when a scientific group comes into the valley. They are shot down but there is one survivor, Eeva, a Finnish anthropologist. Initially it is Eeva who helps Ras as he recovers from a fearsome battle that sees the local tribe decimated. It is Eeva who first gives Ras an insight into the world beyond his own. Although a smart and capable woman, Eeva grows to rely on Ras, he is the master in this world. Ras in turn grows fond of the woman and cannot understand it when she will not sleep with him. In the end Ras has to force the issue. (Making erotically inventive use of a crocodile's heart—a crocodile he has just killed with only his knife. One overtly masculine act to another.)

Although Igziyabher does everything to protect and nurture Ras, he has no such feelings for others in the valley. Trying to get away from the black bird, Eeva is chased into the jungle and may have been consumed by a napalm bomb. Ras' foster parents' home is ransacked and both are presumed dead.

Reunited with Eeva, who suffered bad burns from the napalm attack, but managed to survive, he sets off to challenge his God.

The journey Ras and Eeva make includes passing through a

fearsome swamp, being imprisoned by a lost civilisation, escaping in dramatic fashion and travelling down a dangerous river to an encounter with Igziyabher. This encounter is not face-to-face but rather via a closed circuit link they find on an island's sacred hut. Igziyabher has been using this structure, coupled with psychedelic drugs, to influence the course of events in the valley and surrounding areas for many years. The tribes' holy men visit the hut and whilst under the influence of the drug undergo suggestive influence. Ras himself is almost induced to murder Eeva after inadvertently taking the drug but manages to escape before the full force of the suggestion can take effect.

Nearing the structure Ras knows as the home of God, the tower, he is ecstatic to come across Yusufu, his supposedly dead foster father. Yusufu is a captive of a party of men, but with Ras' help escapes and is deliriously happy at being reunited with his son. Together the three journey to the tower situated in the middle of the lake. Ras has tried before to climb the virtually sheer wall of the tower but this time his drive is the strongest it has ever been and he manages to make it to the top. There he finds Igziyabher. Igziyabher turns out to be Boygur, an insane multi-millionaire who believes he is creating a real life Tarzan.

Dennis E. Power has postulated that Boygur is a mortal son of XauXaz, one of the Nine (see www.pjfarmer.com/secret/tarzan/cloamby.htm) and it is XauXaz who has provided financial and political backing to his son's monstrous experiments. It is further suggested that the family that Boygur uses as his nursery is in fact descended from XauXaz (and so would have had some of the same genetic stock as Lord Grandrith!).

In an interview with Paul Walker for the September '74 issue of *Luna Monthly*, Phil acknowledges that Boygur is a caricature of himself as the mad scientist who tries to raise his own Tarzan and continually has to compromise with reality. Phil also reveals that the inspiration for the name Boygur comes from "Peer Gynt." The Bøyg is a mysterious voice in the darkness that tells Peer what to do.

Ras extracts all the answers he needs from Boygur. How he

and his two brothers before him were kidnapped from the same family, driving both his genetic parents to an early death in the process. How the two "experiments" before him resulted in failure and how Boygur hired dwarfs to pretend to be apes and had Ras raised by them. Boygur is shocked and appalled when the jungle superman he has raised is far from innocent. Boygur sadly notes that "things went their own way."

Hearing enough, Ras passes judgment and sentence on Boygur for the pain he has inflicted, directly or indirectly, on Ras and the people he has loved. By the closing chapters Ras is leaving the valley he has known all his life and his future is reminiscent of Heinlein's Michael from *Stranger in a Strange Land* (incidentally, a book dedicated to Phil). An innocent when it comes to western civilisation but possessing the self-knowledge, the confidence, the inherent ability to get what he wants wherever he wants it. Any thoughts that Ras will suffer in our modern world evaporate; Ras may not know what to expect from media moguls and the L.A. scene but he is looking forward to it, to the new challenge. Ras Tyger is ready for the West but is the West ready for Ras Tyger?

At the end of the book our relationship with Ras is complete; we may only be along for the ride, an observer much like Doktor Krempe in the early pages of "Evil, Be My Good," but we feel a kinship with the young man. What would such a superman have become if he had been born in a "civilised" society? An explorer, a soldier, an Olympian? Or a criminal, a murderer, an outcast? True, his genetic background is good and noble so one would assume a worthy life, but Ras is obviously a unique individual by any standard.

This book is dedicated to ERB and it really is a tribute to him despite what some may see as parody. Lord Tyger is an homage to Phil's favourite hero and demonstrates the fundamental impossibility of that character as conceived by ERB. Phil's genius is in devising a way in which a feral man could truly come to exist. In the real world, one of unpredictability, Boygur's experiment was always doomed to fail. But what a failure!

Through the Seventh Gate:
Pursuing Farmer's Sources in Savageology
Christopher Paul Carey

Everyone knows that long ago, on a fateful day in 1970 in a Chicago motel room, Philip José Farmer met Tarzan of the Apes. Farmer's interview of Lord Greystoke is a matter of public record. But did Farmer, the Grandmaster of Science Fiction, ever meet Doc Savage, the Bronze Hero of Technopolis and Exotica?

Never does Farmer mention this in either of his biographies, *Doc Savage: His Apocalyptic Life* (Doubleday, 1973) or *Tarzan Alive* (Doubleday, 1972; rpt. Bison Books, 2006), or in any of his many books, short stories, articles, or interviews from his half-a-century-spanning career. Farmer *does* reveal he learned and deduced some of the Savage family history during his genealogical researches into Lord Greystoke's lineage, connecting James Wilder from Sir Arthur Conan Doyle's "Adventure of the Priory School" with Lester Dent's Clark Savage, Sr. (or as Farmer names him, James Clarke Wildman). And yet how to account for the abundance of "new" information presented above and beyond the Doyle connection in Farmer's Doc Savage works—information not revealed to Dent or any of the other "Kenneth Robesons" in the biographical supersagas of the Man of Bronze? To believe that Farmer made it all up is, of course, absurd.

Yes, we could suppose it is possible that Farmer received the exclusive information he presents in *Doc Savage: His Apocalyptic*

Life, *Escape from Loki* (Bantam Books, 1991), and *Tarzan Alive* from a meeting with Clark Savage, Jr., himself, or perhaps one of Doc's aides or even his knockout cousin, Pat. But Farmer does not tell us this, and unless he is endeavoring to protect the identity of the still living Doc and/or his aides (which remains a possibility), he received his information from another source.

First let us look at the "new" or "exclusive" information Farmer presents regarding Doc Savage, and from there attempt to elucidate his source or sources. In *Tarzan Alive*, Farmer reveals that Lord Greystoke sent a number of Kavuru elixir pills to his cousin for analysis. Savage then synthesized the formula, and that is why Doc and his aides have not aged since 1933. We may guess this story came to Farmer via "Lord Greystoke." But when? The information about the Kavuru pills and Doc's involvement with them does not appear in Farmer's interview with Greystoke on September 1, 1970. In that interview, Farmer was allowed to look at photostats from the diary of Greystoke's father, but was told that he must not take the photostats with him. Presumably those were the only documents Farmer observed during the interview, so when did our intrepid biographer learn about Doc's synthesis of the Kavuru pills? What other contact did Farmer have with Lord Greystoke?

Presumably a fair amount. For example, in Chapter Four of *Tarzan Alive*, Farmer has intimate knowledge of the report, archived in the British files, that details Lieutenant Paul d'Arnot's first encounter with Tarzan in West Africa. From this we see that Farmer's sources are extensive, and since no other known Tarzanic scholar has been able to locate the British files on Tarzan, the conclusion is that Farmer got the files directly from Lord Greystoke himself. There are numerous other instances of exclusive data re Lord Greystoke in *Tarzan Alive* that indicate Farmer must have had much more extensive contact with the Ape-man, at least in terms of an exchange of documents, correspondence or phone conversations, than just his 1970 interview, but to list these would go beyond the scope of this article. We do know for certain that after the 1970 interview Greystoke agreed to mail "portions of his memoirs" to Farmer (see *Mother Was a Lovely Beast*, Chilton, 1974), one extract of which has been reprinted in the new Bison Books edition of *Tarzan Alive*.

The point remains that some of Farmer's sources on Doc Savage came directly via Lord Greystoke. But may we assume that all of it did? I do not believe so.

In *Tarzan Alive*, we next learn from Farmer that Doc's mother was Arronaxe Larsen, and that "[t]here is little doubt that Arronaxe's father was Wolf Larsen" from Jack London's *The Sea Wolf*. This information seems to have come from Farmer's research into the Wold Newton family utilizing Burke's *Peerage*, as well as the comparative study of eye-color in literary characters. However, certain evidence supports the conclusion that those sources may have been only Farmer's cover, or, at most, merely his secondary sources.

Farmer himself, I believe, alludes to his main source for his exclusive information on the life Clark Savage, Jr., in *Doc Savage: His Apocalyptic Life*. In fact, he states the source outright, though he does not claim to have had access to it. Lester Dent, Doc's first biographer, was also privy to this source, though if he had full access to it, he did not divulge much of its contents in the Doc supersagas.

Farmer's source for most of his exclusive information on Doc Savage is, I believe, the same top secret intelligence files that Dent references in the Doc Savage supersaga, *The Golden Man* (Street & Smith, April 1941). In this story, a mysterious "golden man" appears from the sea who can predict future events and knows many things from the past that he cannot possibly know, including Doc's origins. The golden man says that he knows Doc was "born on the tiny schooner *Orion* in the shallow cove at the north end of Andros Island." Doc is shocked, as he is the only living person who should know this information about his past. The golden man also knows that Baron Orrest Karl Lestzky is dying in Vienna that night. Lestzky is the only other person alive at the time who really understands the intricacies of Doc's brain operating technique to cure criminals. At the end of the adventure, Doc discovers the golden man is really Paul Hest, an intelligence agent of an unnamed country (presumably Germany) who had temporarily suffered from amnesia.

How may we surmise that Farmer himself has seen this intelligence file on Doc? Because of a name Hest cites from the files: *Baron* Orrest *Karl* Lestzky (italics mine). As I have illustrated elsewhere (see my "The Green Eyes Have It—Or Are They Blue?" in *Myths for the Modern Age: Philip José Farmer's Wold Newton Universe*, MonkeyBrain Books, 2005), the character Baron Colonel von Hessel from Farmer's Doc Savage novel *Escape from Loki* is an analogue for the character Baron Karl, the so-called Playboy Prince from the original Doc Savage supersaga *Fortress of Solitude* (Street & Smith, October 1938).[1] Baron von Hessel, like Baron Orrest Karl Lestzky, is a surgeon with exceptional skills who knows Doc. The two barons are, I propose, one man. Hest calls Lestzky Doc's "friend," but surely this is a facetious remark. They are more like nemeses. Doc certainly would have been keeping tabs on Lestzky, the man who, as Baron Karl, worked in such close quarters with Doc's other grand nemesis, John Sunlight. This is why Doc is moved by news of Lestzky's death—not because they are friends, but because Doc has been following the baron's career very closely since he first matched wits with him in Camp Loki in 1918. Those still in doubt need only reference *Escape from Loki* to see that von Hessel was privy to secret intelligence files on Doc and his family. "'Our Intelligence has a dossier on you and Doctor Clark Savage, Senior,'" von Hessel states. "'Quite a lengthy one.'" Again, Doc is astounded.[2]

Now we begin to understand how extensive the German intelligence files truly were, and because Farmer cites the files in both *Escape from Loki* and *Doc Savage: His Apocalyptic Life*, it becomes clear that this is where he garnered his exclusive information on Doc. It is no wonder Farmer chose to write about Doc's adventure in Germany during the Great War: the Germans' files on Doc would have certainly concentrated on those years.

However it was that Farmer managed to get extensive access to the dossier, there can be little doubt this is where he corroborated the research he had sussed out of Burke's *Peerage* on the Savage/ Wildman genealogy. There, in the top secret German files, he learned that Hubert Robertson and Ned Land were aboard the *Orion* when it sank less than a year after Doc's birth. He confirmed that Doc's mother's name was Arronaxe, and that her father was the blue-green eyed master of the *Sea Wolf*. And in those files, he read about the slippery Baron von Hessel, a man of many names, who would one day again duel with Doc. Further, perhaps something in the files led Farmer to another source, one which told him the story of the adventurous daughter of James Clarke Wildman, Jr., as recently uncovered in the unfinished tale, *The Evil in Pemberley House*.[3]

How I would love to have a look at those files—what more might we learn about the history of the Man of Bronze! But something tells me, Farmer had a good reason for disguising their contents as fiction. Some things are better left to the imagination.

[1] The two supersagas featuring Doc's nemesis John Sunlight, *The Fortress of Solitude* and *The Devil Genghis*, have been released in a convenient double-novel edition (Nostalgia Ventures, 2006).

[2] Rick Lai, in his excellent work *The Bronze Age: An Alternative Doc Savage Chronology* (Fading Shadows, 1992; reprinted and expanded as *The Complete Chronology of Bronze*, ACES, 1999), points out the intelligence dossier mentioned in *Escape from Loki* must be the same as that referred to in *The Golden Man*; I am sure other dedicated Doc Savage readers caught the reference as well.

[3] Completed by Win Scott Eckert and published in 2009 by Subterranean Press.

THE ARCHAEOLOGY OF KHOKARSA
SOURCES IN FARMER'S ANCIENT
OPARIAN MOTHERLAND
CHRISTOPHER PAUL CAREY

"'Good stranger,' I continued, 'I am ill and lost.
Direct me, I beseech you, to Carcosa.'"—Bierce

When Philip José Farmer's *Hadon of Ancient Opar* and *Flight to Opar* hit the bookshelves in the mid-1970s, faithful initiates of the Burroughsian tradition no doubt winked at one another conspiratorially when they brought the books home and read of Hadon navigating the tunnels under Opar, climbing a narrow flight of spiral steps, and emerging on the top of an enormous boulder. They knew that this was the same path Tarzan of the Apes had trodden in *The Return of Tarzan* (1913), and that the apeman would one day stand upon that same giant boulder (although by Tarzan's day the rock had weathered into a kopje). Similarly, readers of H. Rider Haggard no doubt smiled at the names Lalila, Paga, and Wi (characters drawn from Haggard's 1927 novel *Allan and the Ice-Gods*), and how they must have chuckled when, on multiple occasions, Farmer uses the adjective "haggard" to describe beauteous though fatigued Lalila! In crafting his ancient Khokarsa—the prehistoric empire that spawned Tarzan's Opar—Farmer drew on many more sources than just these examples. The present article seeks to examine such less well-known sources or those hitherto unknown altogether.

In terms of developing theme in his series about life and death in ancient Africa, one of Farmer's strongest influences was Jessie L. Weston's classic examination of Arthurian legend, *From Ritual to Romance* (1920). A precursor to the work of Joseph Campbell, Weston's book takes a cross-cultural approach to determine a myth's essential meaning, and in one chapter the author discusses a particular theme common to both the tales of King Arthur and ancient Indian *Rig-Veda* hymns. Weston calls this theme "The Freeing of the Waters," in which the fate of the land is tied to the actions of the people who inhabit it, and above all, the deeds of its hero. "Tradition relates," writes Weston, "that the seven great rivers of India had been imprisoned by the evil giant, Vrita, or Ahi, whom Indra slew, thereby releasing the streams from their captivity." Anyone who has seen the movie *Indiana Jones and the Temple of Doom* will immediately recognize this theme, whereby the hero completes his mission and miraculously drought and famine are replaced by blessed rain and an abundance of crops.

Those who have read *The Return of Tarzan* may recall La's recounting of Opar's history to the apeman, in which she states that more than ten thousand years ago a "great calamity" occurred to her city's distant motherland. This is the impending sense of doom which hovers constantly over Farmer's Khokarsan civilization. At any moment the reader expects La's great calamity to rattle apart the island of Khokarsa, and indeed many tremors and convulsions of the earth do occur throughout the series. Each quake is seen as "Kho's wrath" upon the inhabitants of Khokarsa, who have sought to place the impudent sungod Resu above the righteous mother goddess. Similarly, when the pile city of Reba burns to its embers in *Flight to Opar*, it is the wickedness of the people who are to blame. Just as in Weston's thesis, the fate of the lands is determined by the actions of its inhabitants. Farmer goes further to amplify this theme by having his characters possess accurate and repeated premonitions of doom, which occur in visions, dreams, or feelings of general foreboding.

Since Farmer's series ended prematurely, the reader ultimately never gets to witness the great calamity and how the hero's actions might have influenced or diffused the impending disaster. However, because it is known that the city of Opar survives in the time of Tarzan, the reader does have an understanding that Hadon, in some sense, must have succeeded in his task. His people have endured the cataclysmic eruptions that sank the motherland, although in due course the Oparians must have faced great hardships. Eventually, the survivors will be forced to intermingle with the native paranthropoids, and the high priestess of Opar will forsake Kho and become Resu's high vicar. Still, the reader knows that Hadon's bloodline survives over ten thousand years into the future through Tarzan's La, a prediction made by the oracle at Kloepeth in *Flight to Opar*. Following Weston's theme, this was due to the successful completion of Hadon's task in bringing his daughter to be born in Opar.

"The Freeing of the Waters" theme is also inversely illustrated in Plato's story of Atlantis, and one can only imagine that Farmer had this in mind as he wrote *Hadon* and *Flight*. In the *Critias*, Plato writes of the once righteous and semidivine inhabitants of Atlantis:

> So long as these principles and their divine nature remained unimpaired the prosperity which we have ascribed to them continued to grow. But when the divine element in them became weakened by frequent admixture with mortal stock, and their human traits became predominant, they ceased to be able to carry their prosperity with moderation. (*Timaeus and Critias*, trans. Desmond Lee, Penguin, 1981)

Though Burroughs does not state that Opar is a lost colony of Atlantis in *The Return of Tarzan*, he does make the claim in *Tarzan and the Golden Lion* (1923). However, ERB scholars such as John Harwood and Frank Brueckel, with whom Farmer consulted during the creation of his Khokarsa, argue that Burroughs' "Atlantis" was not located on the Atlantic Ocean but rather on a great inland sea that existed in Africa circa ten thousand years ago (*Heritage of the*

Flaming God, eds. Alan Hanson and Michael Winger, Waziri Publications, 1999). Farmer also covers this ground in his *Tarzan Alive: The Definitive Biography of Lord Greystoke* (1972), though by the time he wrote his Ancient Opar series he had pushed the date back to twelve thousand years ago. It seems likely that Farmer's decision to emphasize Weston's thesis was at least partially an attempt to explain Burroughs' conflation of the legendary Atlantis with Opar's ancient motherland. Interestingly, Pierre Benoit, a French author following the Burroughs and Haggard traditions, also placed Atlantis in inland Africa in his 1919 novel *L'Atlantide*.

Just as Plato relates in the *Critias* that the Atlanteans were once gods who had lost their divinity and fallen victim to their more mortal vices, so Farmer portrays his Khokarsans. Hadon's giant cousin Kwasin is said to be "like a hero of old," emphasizing that the glory days of the Khokarsans have long since passed and the empire has begun to weaken; and though Kwasin bears some of the attributes of a god, his character, like many in the land, is deeply flawed by greed, lust, and overbearing ego. The fate of Kwasin, who is last seen swinging his mighty ax in a battle with Minruth's soldiers, is never learned, but unless he manages to miraculously redeem himself his destiny will doubtless follow that of Plato's Atlanteans and be very bleak indeed.

Early in his plans for his series, Farmer decided he would have two heroes appearing alternately throughout the books: Hadon of Opar and his cousin Kwasin of Dythbeth. Now that it has come to light that Farmer based his main theme on Weston's thesis in *From Ritual to Romance*, this makes perfect sense. Hadon, succeeding in his quests by his exhibitions of honesty, loyalty, and integrity, would succeed in "freeing the waters." By his valiant actions of heroism, he would save his home queendom of Opar from utter destruction in La's great calamity. Conversely, Kwasin, by his very vanity, rage, and undisciplined nature, might have unwittingly contributed to the total catastrophe that was surely to have befallen Khokarsa at the series' conclusion. After all, he is a native of the island of Khokarsa.

When conceiving the series, Farmer originally intended that Hadon would "slay the dragon" that stalked the jungles along Ancient Opar's southern inland sea. Again, this was to echo Weston's "Freeing of the Waters" theme, although this time very literally as Hadon freed the Kemuopar of a terrorizing monster based on the ancient Babylonian creature known as the *sirrush*. Farmer had been inspired by a chapter he had read in Willy Ley's book *Exotic Zoology* (Viking Press, 1959). Ley claimed that the dragon-like beast depicted on the Gate of Ishtar at Babylon was based on a living animal, reported to have been seen in modern times in central Africa. The idea of the *sirrush* also appears in the deuterocanonical Biblical parable *Bel and the Dragon*, in which the Babylonians are seen to worship one of the beasts as their deity before Daniel decrees it a false god and poisons it. Not the first modern author to entertain writing a story based on the *sirrush* legend, Farmer was preceded by L. Sprague de Camp's *The Dragon of the Ishtar Gate* (Lancer, 1968). The *sirrush* in that story is also said to exist in Africa (and one may only conjecture that de Camp had also read Willy Ley's book), although the creature in the end turns out to be a hoax. Farmer's story of the *sirrush* would certainly have featured a living creature and much heroic adventure, but for whatever reason he abandoned the storyline, though not the idea. The *sirrush* still appears, albeit offstage, in the form of the diorite and basalt statues of the *r"ok'og'a* that Hadon encounters as he arrives at the city of Khokarsa in *Hadon of Ancient Opar*.

If Farmer had proceeded as originally planned, Hadon's quest to slay the dragon would have echoed very closely the quest of Jason and his Argonauts to retrieve the Golden Fleece. In that myth, Jason sets out to retrieve the Fleece, which is guarded by a dragon, so that he may be placed on the throne of Iolcus in Thessaly. Similarly it may be imagined that Hadon, in this early conception of the story, would have been sent out by Minruth to slay the dragon that hunted along the shores of the great inland seas. While this plot point never occurs in Farmer's published book, the idea of a quest that would put Hadon on the throne of Khokarsa survives in the form of his mission to retrieve Lalila,

Abeth, and Pag from the Wild Lands, and in its way that plot point remains a tribute to the ancient Greek myth of Jason and the Argonauts.

Throughout the two Ancient Opar novels, allusions to the myths of various cultures abound. For instance, the frequent plagues which sweep across the empire are inspired by the Ten Plagues of Egypt as described in the book of *Exodus*. Much of Farmer's Khokarsan religion comes directly from Robert Graves' *The White Goddess* (1948), which proposed a common origin for the majority of European goddess figures as well as their ousting by the worshipers of a monotheistic god. And Farmer's descriptions of the oracle of Kho come straight out of Euripides' *Ion* and other ancient accounts of the Greek Oracle of Delphi, in which an old hag sits within a temple upon a three-legged stool, breathes in intoxicating gas that rises from a crack in the floor, and utters vague prophecies that will shake the foundations of the empire.

Many of the characters in the novels also stem from ancient, and sometimes modern, myth. Kwasin, while originally to be called Khonan by Farmer as a play on Robert E. Howard's barbarian hero Conan, was in the end based on the enormously strong Greek hero Heracles (or the Roman Hercules) and the Sumerian hero Gilgamesh. Further, Kwasin's (and Hadon's) travels through the Wild Lands echo the wanderings of Greek Odysseus, and the name of the series' antihero is derived from Kwasind, Hiawatha's Indian strongman friend from Longfellow's *The Song of Hiawatha* (1855). In his "The Purple Distance" (*Pearls from Peoria*, Subterranean Press, 2006), Farmer cites many similarities between the characters Hiawatha and Tarzan of the Apes, so it is not surprising the author decided a character based on Kwasind would feel at home in a series sparked by a lost city discovered by the Lord of the Jungle.

By using Haggard's Laleela (Lalila) as a character, Farmer may have meant to draw reference to the Akkadian mother goddess A-a (which perhaps Farmer took as a derivation of "Lalila," i.e., "Lalila" → "a-a"), whose name meant "night," hence alluding to the meaning of Lalila's own name, "moon of change." This also may have been Farmer's subtle cue that Lalila was a predecessor to

Haggard's Ayesha, as another spelling of A-a is Aya (i.e. Aya →
Ayesha). It should be noted that A-a was the consort of the Akkadian sungod Shamash, thus reinforcing Farmer's own Khokarsan
dichotomy of Kho and Resu.

As alluded to at the start of this article, Lalila and Paga feature
prominently in Haggard's *Allan and the Ice-Gods*, which serves as a
sort of prequel to *Hadon of Ancient Opar*. While much attention has
been given to the Burroughs connections in Farmer's Ancient Opar
novels, the available literature on the books' Haggardian elements
is scattered and sparse. This is unfortunate, as one of the important
subplots of the book and more than one significant theme stem
directly from Haggard. The important subplot is the Ax of Victory,
which Paga crafted from meteoritic iron for the hero Wi in *Allan
and the Ice-Gods*.[1] Haggard went to great lengths to recount the
history of the ax in his novels, from its creation by Pag in *Ice-Gods*,
to its inheritance by the great Zulu warrior Umslopogaas when he
became leader of the "People of the Ax" in *Nada the Lily* (1892), to
the fateful role of the ax during the battle against the giant Rezu in
She and Allan (1921), and finally ending with the ax's destruction
by Umslopogaas in the climactic scene of the classic adventure *Allan
Quatermain* (1887). Farmer had once planned to write as many as
twelve books in the Ancient Opar series, including the story of how
Hadon's son Kohr eventually acquired the ax and brought it with
him when he founded the city of Kôr, which appears as a lost city
in Haggard's novels (see David Pringle's interview with Farmer in
Vector #81, June 1977). By bringing the ax within his own series,
Farmer managed to fill in the missing story of the legendary
weapon; but more than that, its inclusion may have brought new
retrospective meaning to Haggard's work.

In his article "Astar of Opar: The Secret Origin of Sumuru" (*The
Wold Newton Universe* website, www.pjfarmer.com/woldnewton/
Astar.pdf), pulp expert and creative mythographer Rick Lai points
out that the giant Rezu from *She and Allan* bears a striking
resemblance to Farmer's character Kwasin. Even more curious is
the fact that Rezu's Achilles' heel is Umslopogaas' Ax of Victory
and that Rezu seems to be a near-immortal. The present article

does not seek to employ the methods of creative mythography, but any reader of Farmer who has read *She and Allan* is left wondering if perhaps Kwasin somehow survived the great calamity of Khokarsa and partook of a longevity treatment similar to that of Tarzan or Ayesha.[2] Or Rezu may be a descendant of Kwasin, perchance through one of the many children he spawned while roaming the Wild Lands. In any case, if it is Kwasin himself, by the time of *She and Allan* he has for some unknown reason turned against his upbringing and forsaken the mother goddess in favor of the sungod.

Of course, the name Rezu itself appears in Farmer's Khokarsa as "Resu" the sungod. This provides an interesting insight into the author's "reverse engineering" world building. By tying in Haggard's ancient cultures with his own, Farmer ingeniously creates a faux history that justifies Burroughs' lost race cultures (and also "explains" some cultural survivals in real life cultures, such as sun worship in ancient Egypt). Just as Brueckel and Harwood proposed that the lost cities discovered by Tarzan were the remnants of a single motherland culture (Central African Atlantis, i.e., Farmer's Khokarsa), Farmer goes further to illustrate that Haggard's lost cities are also post-deluge remnants of that same ancient motherland. What is ingenious here is that Farmer picked up on a little observed thread flowing through both Burroughs' and Haggard's lost races: the similarity of their matriarchal-based religious structures. Here we see Farmer not just writing simple pastiche but rather innovating within tradition on a quite sophisticated level. The matriarchal element repeats itself frequently in Haggard's fiction, from the tales of Ayesha, to the Zu-Vendis of *Allan Quatermain*, and on to *The Ivory Child* (1916), in which the "Oracle of the Child" (the "Child" being a sacred idol in the story) is always a woman with a half-moon birthmark—thus correlating with Farmer's Khokarsan oracles, who are always female and have religious ties to the moon. In this latter novel, the religious matriarchy is balanced against a male ruling class headed by a king who is addressed as Simba, meaning "lion." (Interestingly, Farmer originally planned to use a word meaning "great lion" to represent the King of Khokarsa, though he later dropped this idea.) Perceiving the strange mix of matriarchy and patriarchy throughout the lost races of Burroughs and Haggard, Farmer decided to incorporate Haggard's work into his own and in this way caught the spark of a grand tradition.

Because Haggard explained the correlation between some of his lost cities and ancient Egypt, Farmer's merging of Haggard's lost races into his own served to flesh out the entire historical landscape of fictional Africa in a way that was anthropologically and almost uncannily sound. In Farmer's creative fusion of Burroughs, Haggard, Brueckel, and Harwood, the destruction of Khokarsa in the great calamity gave birth to numerous lost cities across the African continent in which the struggle between the mother goddess and the sungod existed in a diverse spectrum. In some of the cities, either the priests or the priestesses continued to rule. In others, like Tarzan's Opar, a compromise had been reached in which the priestesses presided over religious functions while worshiping the sungod. In yet other lost cities, like Ayesha's Kôr, the battle between the priests and the priestesses still raged twelve thousand years after the fall of Khokarsa.

If one were to superimpose the "Map of Ancient Africa" from *Hadon of Ancient Opar* overtop the map of post-great calamity migrations devised by Brueckel and Harwood for their essay "Heritage of the Flaming God," a tiny glimmer of the depth and scope of Farmer's collaborative world building emerges. One sees that the survivors from Wentisuh migrated to the southeast and founded the city of the Kavuru (doubtless also related to Farmer's Kawuru) from Burroughs' *Tarzan's Quest* (1936), and to the south to found Xuja from *Tarzan the Untamed* (1920). The survivors of Siwudawa migrated to the southeast and founded Cathne and Athne from *Tarzan and the City of Gold* (1933), while the former inhabitants of Miklemres migrated to the southwest and those of Bawaku migrated to the southeast and founded Tuen-Baka from *Tarzan and the Forbidden City* (1938). Without reference to Brueckel and Harwood, Farmer located Haggard's Kôr in the back regions of Portuguese South East Africa based on descriptions of Allan Quatermain's journey in *She and Allan*.

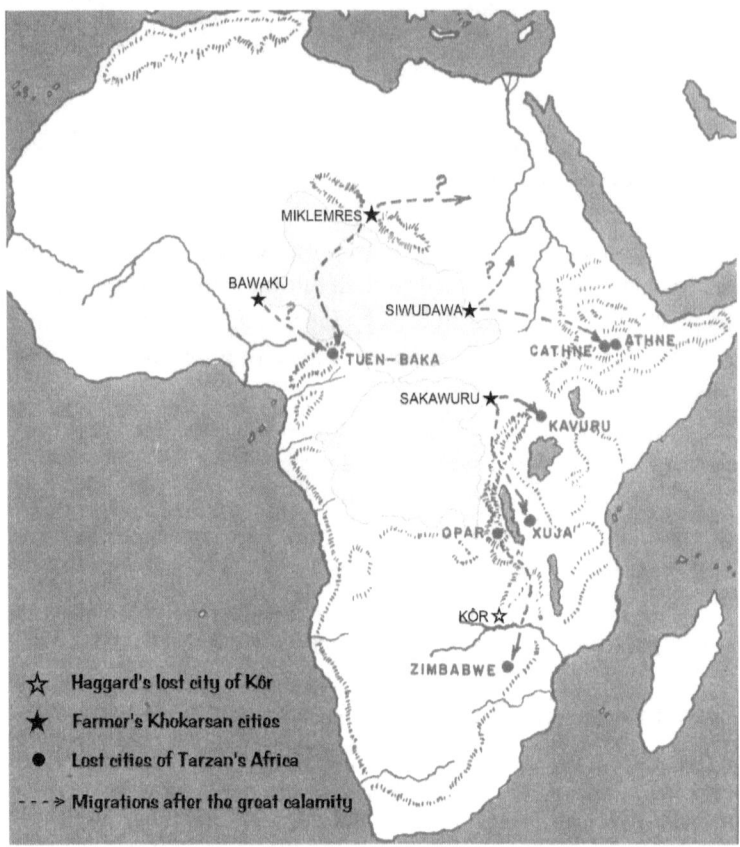

☆   Haggard's lost city of Kôr

★   Farmer's Khokarsan cities

●   Lost cities of Tarzan's Africa

- - -➤ Migrations after the great calamity

But the lost cities of Burroughs and Haggard were not Farmer's only inspirations for his ancient African civilization. The name Khokarsa itself derives from Ambrose Bierce's classic tale of mysticism and horror, "An Inhabitant of Carcosa" (1886). In Bierce's story, a medium channels a spirit that drifts back in time to a forlorn age and witnesses the ruins of dead civilization. That civilization, in Farmer's view, is ancient Khokarsa, the ancient motherland of Tarzan's Opar. The passage of time, or perhaps a faulty transmission by the medium, has undoubtedly inverted the syllables of "Car-co-sa" into Farmer's "Kho-kar-sa"; and the monoliths erected to the dead heroes of the Great Games in *Hadon of Ancient Opar* may indeed be meant to be Bierce's "number of weather-worn stones" that were "broken, covered with moss and half sunken into the earth" and were "obviously the headstones of graves."

In conclusion, a survey of the sources drawn upon in the creation of the Ancient Opar novels indicates that Farmer was working within a tradition that stemmed from both classical antiquity and modern literature. The degree to which he fused the two, in conjunction with a deep understanding of history and anthropology, signifies a major achievement in literary world building that places Farmer as a legitimate heir to the lost race tradition of Burroughs and Haggard.

[1] While spelled "axe" by Haggard, this article will follow Farmer's usage: "ax."

[2] As concerns Rezu, such a treatment is mentioned in *She and Allan*, although it seems to have occurred much later than 12,000 years ago.

THE MAGIC FILING CABINET
AND THE MISSING PAGE
CHRISTOPHER PAUL CAREY

Sometimes the Great Whangdoodle appears just when you need Him. What follows is the story of how two Farmerian mysteries came to be solved.

I was in Peoria, Illinois, for Farmercon II, happy to be back among the living after having undergone surgery earlier in the year, and overjoyed to be in the presence of my favorite living writer. In fact, I was near ecstatic because I was editing a new collection, *Venus on the Half-Shell and Others*, by The Wonderful Wizard of Peoria himself. The book's contents had already been selected, the text of Philip José Farmer's scintillating fictional-author stories had all been scanned and converted to electronic format, I had read and re-read the stories, and now I was preparing to write the introduction and story headers.

I already had some idea of what I was going to write, *Venus* and the fictional-author stories being some of my favorites among Phil's work, but I figured I might pick the brain of the Grand Master and his lovely wife Bette while I was visiting for the convention. Most of all I wanted to tie up the loose ends of the two mysteries alluded to above.

The first mystery is broader than the second, and its answer is, I believe, of great interest to science fiction history. It concerns a long-running hoax perpetrated by Phil that you can read about in much more detail in the introduction to the new collection (no, that's not a mystery; I did manage to complete the introduction). Suffice it to say that word of mouth, and a couple of brief mentions in printed but unsourced articles, had it that Phil was going to edit an anthology of fictional-author stories by other writers. But was this just hearsay? Or had perhaps someone mistaken something said by Phil when he had spoken elsewhere about publishing his own fictional-author stories? And even if it were true, who were the authors Phil was considering to solicit for the anthology? Philip K. Dick was an author who came up in one of the unsourced articles, but was this true? And who else would have been included, and did Phil actually contact any of them? No one seemed to know.

There stood the first mystery.

The second mystery had to do with "The Impotency of Bad Karma," a story selected for the lettered edition of the book, one which even many hardcore Farmer fans have had a hard time tracking down. In fact, despite having scoured eBay for many a year, I had only ever seen a photocopy of its original publication in the extremely limited-run preview issue of *Popular Culture*, which Mike Croteau had obtained from the defunct magazine's publisher, Brad Lang. Problem was, the photocopies Mike had obtained ended with the words, "They did send his blood pressure up, though in a healthy manner." Anyone who has read the more readily available rewritten story "The Last Rise of Nick Adams" will know this is not where that version of the story ends, and that in fact these words end just before the story's climax (pun very certainly intended). Was this a printing error in *Popular Culture* or was there a missing page? I shot off emails to the top Farmerian experts, but even über-Farmer-collector Rick Beaulieu, and the kind and knowledgeable webmaster of the exhaustive *Philip José Farmer International Bibliography*, Zacharias Nuninga, hadn't a clue. In fact—and this says something about the tight-knit though global community of Farmer collectors—these two gentleman had the very same photocopied version as Mike and I. To further the mystery, Mr. Lang had told Mike, upon graciously sending him the photocopies several years prior, that the story had definitely ended with that line. Further, it could not have been a typographical error, or Phil would have certainly let Mr. Lang, who had copyedited the story himself, know about it.

But how could the story end there, with . . . well . . . literally no climax?

And there, mystery number two.

Farmercon, it would seem, is the perfect place to tackle the nebulous questions of metafiction. In truth, at the first Farmercon I was able to meet and converse with the very real Eric Clifton from Phil's *The Lavalite World* and *More Than Fire*, as well as Hans Kordtz from *Escape from Loki*. I kid you not. So I fully believed I might have a good chance of solving both mysteries while I was in Peoria in August 2007. With such a gathering of Farmerphiles (the fans, I mean, not magazines) I held high hopes that someone among them would have some answers for me. This did not turn out to be the case. And yet, before I even had the chance to sit down with Phil and Bette on the day following the convention, Mike Croteau called me aside and showed me what he had found in The Magic Filing Cabinet.

Let me back up. For those who don't know, The Magic Filing Cabinet is The Wizard of Peoria's secret weapon, kept in a well-hidden subterranean chamber and sealed tight from unwanted intruders by magical enchantment. Inside The Cabinet, the intrepid Farmerian explorer will find a treasure trove of mojo-laden folders bearing age-yellowed parchments upon which are written the secrets of the pluriverse. From it comes much of the wealth that is published in *Farmerphile*, as well as rare gems in the form of partial manuscripts and outlines like *The City Beyond Play*.

And so on that summer day, Mike (who possesses a Secret Key bequeathed him by The Wizard) opened The Magic Filing Cabinet and showed me a folder that bore the mind-blowing title "FICTIONAL-AUTHOR PERMISSIONS." After getting permission from The Wizard to look through the folder myself, it was indeed as if my mind had exploded in a supernova of splendor. In the folder were all the answers to the first mystery, and much more.

The Great Whangdoodle had cawed, and the illuminations thus revealed may now be read in the introduction to *Venus on the Half-Shell and Others*. I'll give you a hint so you don't want to banish me to some hellfire pocket universe of Red Orc's devising: In addition to all the answers poised above about Phil's proposed fictional-author anthology, the introduction also includes a list and description of several hitherto unknown fictional-author stories Phil either had begun writing and never finished, or ones he planned to write but never did. And in case you're still considering that not-so-nice pocket universe for me, here's a bonus tidbit that didn't make the cut for the intro: Did you know Phil once planned to write a biography of Oz, and that he received permission from L. Frank Baum's estate to do so? You do now.

As to the mystery of the missing page, Phil took a look at the photocopies I brought of the story and told me that to his knowledge there was indeed an absent portion of text. That mystery was not solved in Peoria, but rather about a week or so later when I finally managed to track down Brad Lang, the editor of *Popular Culture*. I presented the conundrum to him again and lo and behold the missing page magically appeared: it had been in that issue of *Popular Culture* all along, but before now, for some unfathomable reason, it had previously eluded Brad! Seems there was still a bit of magic floating about that must have stuck to my clothes and luggage from when I had visited Peoria. Or was that a distant cawing I heard?

Oh, by the way, there is a third mystery: that of how the very real Tom Wode Bellman, who appears in fictionalized form in Phil's "The Light-Hog Incident," came to write the foreword to *Venus on the Half-Shell and Others*. But that, I am afraid, is a story I will have to leave to Mr. Bellman.

A Box Within a Box:
Philip José Farmer as Maxwell Grant as . . .
Danny Adams

The year is 1932; the world is choking under the depths of the Great Depression, and everywhere it seems as if savage shadows are closing in on the light of civilization. The suffering millions are begging for a hero. A hero like . . . Kenneth Robeson?

Well, not quite. Perhaps Maxwell Grant . . . or rather, that is to say, Philip José Farmer. And it's not quite 1932, and the story in question was not actually written in 1935 as it claims, but 1977—an era some may consider a dark time in our history for other reasons, perhaps, but notable in annals of science and pulp fiction. For after publishing several "fictional author" stories, Phil Farmer became a pulp double agent, writing as a fictional author who was himself a fictional author who was writing about another fictional author . . .

Maybe I should explain.

The story in question is the first of "The Grant-Robeson Papers," titled "The Savage Shadow," originally published in *Weird Heroes*, Volume 8 (edited by Byron Preiss, Jove/HBJ) and now finally reprinted in *Pearls from Peoria*. On a cold and cloudy day in December 1932, Kenneth Robeson is a struggling pulp writer who needs to pitch a smashing idea to the legendary publishers Street & Smith so they'll give him an advance so that he won't be kicked out of his apartment in three days. He's gone to the observation platform of the Empire State Building hoping the view of New York City will inspire him. There he sees an attractive young blonde trying to calm down her elderly and increasingly hysterical father—then some thugs, followed by medical personnel bearing straitjackets, bearing down on the couple. Robeson leaps to the couple's defense and winds up being struck on the head from behind for his troubles.

He wakes up to the blonde and a policeman staring down at him, and a desire to find out what is going on—not just because the blonde is a knockout, but also hoping her story might give him an idea he can pitch to Street & Smith.

What's going on is that her father, Professor Winston Burke, was a moralistic and brilliant scientist who believed he had invented an elixir—or perhaps *vaccine* would be more appropriate—to cure hostility. But when the good professor tried it on himself he went mad and started believing he was being followed by an evil shadow. Eventually he was turned over to the care of one Doctor Von Adlerdreck of the Restful Meadows sanitarium. But his daughter, Patricia, suspected something very sinister was happening at Restful Meadows.

Like any good pulp story, Robeson agrees to help the damsel in distress. Likewise, sinister things really *are* going on. And in the best pulp tradition, Robeson will eventually meet face to face with the gun-wielding thugs, German spies, more gangsters, humorous sidekicks who always come through in a pinch, and of course, car chases and shoot-outs.

Except . . .

. . . Kenneth Robeson is best known as the author of the *Doc Savage* and *Avenger* series.

. . . and Maxwell Grant, the purported author of "The Savage Shadow," is the author of the *Shadow* tales.

. . . and there's one further twist: both men were themselves fictional authors, pseudonyms for various authors Street & Smith hired to write those series. (Perhaps as a heads up to this, Farmer never actually gives us a description of what Robeson looks like in "The Savage Shadow.")

Fortunately, Phil Farmer wrote a fictional introduction to this cleverly convoluted story as well. In 1935, he tells us, four years after the appearance of the first Shadow novel, one Mr. D*** convinced Grant and Robeson to each write a story with the other as the protagonists (and offering a lot of money to sweeten the offer). Supposedly sixteen stories were written for this wealthy eccentric, which were then locked away in a Manhattan safe until 1977, when Phil Farmer, as "editor," brought them to light.

So let's recap. In "The Savage Shadow," Phil Farmer is writing as Maxwell Grant, who is purportedly writing a story about Kenneth Robeson, though the latter two men never existed either except as bylines on covers and shadows, er, "house names" in the offices of Street & Smith.

Got it? Good, because unsurprisingly, this being a Farmer story, there's more. This is a Farmerian "box within a box" story, as Christopher Paul Carey puts it, "mixing fiction and reality in a really weird blur."

Every element within it relates to something else in the original Doc Savage or Avenger tales or both. Every new twist becomes a morsel for Robeson's imagination that he will eventually incorporate into some of the most famous pulp series of the 20th century. Doc Fauve (Fauve meaning "wild beast" in French, as the story points out) is transformed into Doc Savage, Fauve's yellow eyes becoming Savage's "magnetic whirlpools of molten gold." The lovely Patricia (Trish) Burke and one of the aforementioned sidekicks, ex-stripper Patricia Coningway is crafted into Robeson's template for Doc Savage's cousin Pat Savage; and Il Vendicativo, Ricardo Bensoni, reincarnates into Richard Benson, the Avenger. Each of Robeson's sidekicks in his adventure has the best of him or herself brought out to the light, promoted to the greatest person they could possibly be—from a sergeant to a colonel, pharmacist to one of the world's greatest chemical engineers, and so on—and is made a hero to beat back the darkness of the Great Depression. To offer a little extra hope from an unlikely venue. Robeson's characters reached the pinnacles of achievements in their fields—just as Phil Farmer's pulp characters did too, whether writing as Farmer or as Maxwell Grant.

For that matter, Farmer doesn't even let us off the hook in

his introduction. As Win Eckert wrote, "J***** D*** is Jimmie Dale, a character from Frank L. Packard's *The Adventures of Jimmie Dale* and other novels. Jimmie Dale's alias was The Gray Seal. L***** C******* is Lamont Cranston. In the pulp novel continuity, the wealthy millionaire Cranston is not really The Shadow. The Shadow merely uses Cranston's identity because it is convenient for him. The real Cranston is usually off traveling overseas or something, although [he] does appear from time to time in the pulp novels. The Shadow's real identity is Kent Allard, as revealed in [the 1937] *The Shadow Unmasks*."

Even the last quote in the "backwards logic puzzle of a story," as Christopher Paul Carey put it, is hardly there by accident (as no piece of a Farmer story is accidental, but one bit of a puzzle that fills in three dimensions rather than just a flat picture). Doc Fauve drinks from his mug and slightly paraphrases Act Four of Shakespeare's *The Tempest*: "They're such stuff as dreams are made on." *The Tempest*, of course, gave us the character of Caliban, and "The Savage Shadow" was published a few years after Farmer's Doc Caliban stories . . .

. . . Another article, maybe. For now, the quote sends Robeson off onto a literary adventure; climaxes a shadowy (and tempestuous) niche of the world he had never known before but can now draw on to make his heroes flesh and blood; and spins off from those shadows Maxwell Grant's most famous hero.

The Shadow, of course, could see what evil lurked in the hearts of men. An evil we all may possess, in this case revealed and thrust in our faces, impossible to ignore, by Professor Burke's concoction. Our own personal invisible savage shadow whispering evils we would like to think we're incapable of, the harshest way to keep ourselves within a moral center. And on another level, a meeting—if only as shadows—between two great pulp heroes as only Phil Farmer could imagine it.

With many thanks to Win Eckert and Chris Carey for their contributions to this article.

Remembering the Eyre Incident
Three Decades Later
Danny Adams

Busiris, Illinois: an ordinary-looking city of one-hundred and fifty thousand people, built atop three bluffs stretching six miles along the beautiful and historic Illinois River, named for a city in ancient Egypt that was a cult center of the god Osiris—the Egyptian god of life, death, and fertility, who is best remembered as being chopped up and resurrected. Busiris is often confused for its twin, Peoria; not hard to reason why, as scientists have repeatedly demonstrated through alternate dimension theories that in various realities the two often occupy the same physical space.

But three decades ago, specifically in 1972, this sleepy Midwestern city was home to a bizarre and powerful man—if you could call him a man—named Paul Eyre, who healed thousands of people just by looking at them . . . and killed those who would do violence against him, often without even being consciously aware that he was exercising this power. Some believed him a Messiah, some an Anti-Christ, and many more were convinced that he wasn't even from Earth at all.

The brief but indelible chronicle of Eyre's extra-human existence in Busiris was most notably recounted by Peoria science fiction writer Philip José Farmer, with the unwitting and perhaps posthumous help of Busiris SF author Leo Queequeg Tincrowdor, in four novellas: "The Two-Edged Gift," which appeared in

Continuum I, edited by Roger Elwood (1974); "The Startouched," *Continuum II*, ed. Elwood (1975); "The Evolution of Paul Eyre," *Continuum III*, ed. Elwood, and "Passing On," *Continuum IV*, ed. Elwood (1975). These were published as an all-inclusive 1982 collection from Tor Books titled *Stations of the Nightmare*. (As many Busiris residents know, however, Tincrowdor and his wife Morna had long since disappeared themselves by then, and so did not get to enjoy the fruits of their collaboration with Farmer.)

By all accounts from Eyre's surviving neighbors—not many, as Eyre lived across from a nursing home and next door to a large veterinary office—his life was entirely ordinary until his unprecedented transformation. In his mid-fifties with two grown children, he did engineering work for Trackless and was a decade away from retirement. He enjoyed hunting, fishing, reading newspapers and sports magazines—nothing remotely hinting at the unearthly events of later. So how did it happen?

Early theories connected Eyre to an unusual and little-known part of England called Wold Newton. A meteor struck there in the late 18th century and some believe that its ionized radiation endowed those nearby with superhuman abilities which they then passed down to their descendants. While there have been alleged connections with Wold Newton and Busiris in the past, however, Leo Tincrowdor's sketchy and often confusing final notes suggested a more localized phenomenon.

According to Tincrowdor, Eyre was hunting in the woods near the city alongside his dog Riley when he discovered a saucer-like object and, thinking it was a bird, fired on it. An investigation soon proved that it was no bird, or even anything remotely resembling a terrestrial animal, but rather a saucer which infected Eyre with microscopic pathogens that acted as seeds. Or sperm, perhaps, as only one out of the millions survived and that one subsequently gave birth to Eyre's remarkable life-and-death abilities.

The healing and death-dealing weren't Eyre's only abilities, however. According to Tincrowdor, the reason Eyre never allowed anyone to see him at night was due to the fact that he could also metamorph—that is, to shape shift—into a saucer creature himself, one capable of crossing through the Earth's atmosphere and outer space with equal facility. Tincrowdor insisted that Eyre had visited the moon and several planets during these night time excursions. These journeys lasted only very briefly, however; according to Tincrowdor, Eyre was insistent on finding a mate of his own "kind," or at least half of his own kind—the half that was the saucer creature.

Despite the fact that thousands of people witnessed Eyre's apparent miracles and claimed healing from them, however, some of Tincrowdor's notes strain belief. He claims, for instance, that the microbes in Eyre's body—including the one that survived—were shaped like rounded gold bricks, and that Eyre had visions of a gleaming green city beyond a field of red flowers. If that sounds familiar, it should—a yellow brick road and a field of poppies leading to the Emerald City of Oz. And the symbolism continues: the creature that Eyre believed was the saucer's mother (and thus his mother, after a fashion) was a leotaur, half human and half lion, the second most famous dual-combination creature in terrestrial mythology (beaten out in sheer recognition only by the centaur).

What became of Paul Eyre has grown to become one of the greatest mysteries of modern times; a Google search on his name will bring back nearly two million web pages. Naturally, Tincrowdor offered an answer, which doubled as the explanation for the existence of his notes found shortly after his disappearance: he said that guilt drove him to record Eyre's fate because that fate was one crafted by Tincrowdor himself. According to the scrawled pages, Eyre's killing power was nullified by taking saucer form, and the military tricked him, by using a fake report of a flying saucer crashing in Los Alamos, New Mexico, into believing that a potential mate had found the Earth. Instead, a nuclear warhead awaited Eyre and, according to the Busiris science fiction writer, Eyre could not soar away quickly enough to escape being lethally irradiated.

The military, of course, denies this. Eyre's family—his wife Mavice (now a resident of the nursing home across the street from the house she shared with her husband) and children Roger and

Glenda—have consistently refused to speak of their father over the years, citing an oath of secrecy to the federal government and the military. Nor can Tincrowdor come forward to affirm or recant his strange explanation. Eyre's disappearance washed out the subsequent smaller mystery of both Tincrowdor and his wife Morna going missing days later. To this day many people suspect foul play; Tincrowdor reportedly was heavily involved in the Eyre Incident, and conspiracy theories abound that the writer was "silenced" permanently. Yet others claim that moments after Tincrowdor was seen for the last time, taking a drink of Kentucky Bourbon with his wife at Von Richtofen's on Sheridan Avenue, two more saucers hovered over Busiris for a few all-too-brief seconds before launching into a cloudless, star-filled sky.

This is a fate Tincrowdor himself may have appreciated.

Whatever the true story behind Eyre's brilliant moment in the world's eye, Busiris flows along as it always has—maybe with still-untold stories lurking beneath the surface, or others yet to be that will prove amazing enough to make even the Eyre Incident fade from its residents' memories.

(Note: *Stations of the Nightmare* only covers the events leading up to the death of Eyre and Tincrowdor's discovery of the Eyre's saucer body. The rest is the speculation of this author and witness reports as published in the Busiris *Ledger-Sun*.)

Star Trek's Loss is Your Gain
From Screen Treatment to Short Story
Danny Adams

While it may be hard to imagine now—particularly after so many science fiction authors have repeatedly expressed their disdain for it over the years—*Star Trek* was seen by many in the SF community as a golden gift (and opportunity) when it debuted in 1966.

The reason is simple: at that point, feature length films (as we would now call them) had been around for a half-century, and television had been widespread for over a decade, and yet almost no one in the visual media took science fiction seriously. Especially TV, where even the unexpected success of *The Twilight Zone* found few in the industry who were interested in repeating it. In fact, many TV execs dug for reasons why an SF show wouldn't work even after Serling's best-known masterpiece did: "*The Twilight Zone* was an anthology show, and nobody wants those anymore," they would say. And those who were willing wanted action shows that were short on brains—the kinds of shows most SF authors and readers couldn't stand.

Star Trek, then, was the first SF TV show—and close to the first SF in any visual media—that relied just as heavily on brains as it did brawn. It was the first time an SF series with recurring characters and no-twist endings was taken seriously on TV. So in the beginning it was met with cheers and optimism by many writers—including Philip José Farmer.

The problems came shortly afterwards, of course. After Phil decided that he despised the constraints television would clamp on his prose, his treatments became "The Shadow of Space," which has obvious *Trek* parallels, and "Sketches Among the Ruins of My Mind," one of the most dizzying stories he ever wrote.

"Space" possesses elements where you can trace a straight *Trek* line from Point A to Point B: the strong starship captain—one having woman troubles, no less. Engineer Scotty becomes Engineer MacCool; Navigator Sulu becomes Navigator Wang. The physicist chief Van Voorden is logical, not exactly Vulcan but possessing shades of a certain Federation first officer. The starship is preparing to embark on a history-making ground-breaking experiment, as the *Enterprise* did several times in the original series.

But this being a Farmer story, legends and myths creep in—fittingly, since these explorers are on an epic voyage which could someday become legend. The captain doesn't have a short punch of a name like Kirk, but rather the Scandanavian "Grettir"—as in Grettir the Strong, an Icelandic folk hero who had his own saga written about him. The original Grettir was a courageous rebel, much like Kirk. The Icelander finds himself outlawed, yet his muscle and wits allow him to survive the proscribed twenty years. Likewise the starship's name, *Sleipnir*, comes from the greatest of all horses, Odin's eight-legged steed, who carried Odin not only over terrestrial realms (including the sea and the air), but also on round trips to the land of the dead. If you want to match a powerful ship with an equally powerful captain, Grettir and *Sleipnir* would be the perfect combination.

Ironically (though no Farmer fan should be surprised by this show of prescience), by the late 1980s *Star Trek: The Next Generation* might have been a better fit for the story. Captain Jean-Luc Picard is better known for solving problems with his mind (though he's been known to use muscle when the situation called for it); many of *TNG's* storylines were far more surreal—or at least less concrete—than the original series; and most of the special effects by this point were done on computer, so punching through universes and a galaxy being destroyed by slamming into someone's forehead wouldn't have been out of the reach of the electronic artists. (Though, admittedly, several more Trek series later, the idea of a starship going into a gigantic woman's mouth—or other body part—might still be hard for some viewers to swallow—no pun intended.)

"Sketches Among the Ruins of My Mind," on the other hand, is most decidedly *not* a story one can easily pin to *Star Trek*—in fact, the difference is so great we may never have known the connection save for getting Phil Farmer's word on it. He related that the original tale involved Captain Kirk finding an idol on a distant planet . . . but in refashioning the story from treatment to story, the distant planet becomes Earth and the distant future becomes not-far-from-now. The idol transforms into a giant black Ball orbiting the Earth; the starship captain is now an ordinary domestic man-turned-chronicler named Mark Franham with a wife and two kids. Instead of a Captain's Log, Franham is obliged to make tape recordings every day due to the fact that the Ball wipes everyone's memories for three days out of every four.

Franham, in fact, is James T. Kirk's opposite in some ways: settled instead of exploring, hoping for the best instead of taking direct action. One can hardly blame Franham, though—the Ball is sending everybody's memory backwards even while they're still aging forward, forcing them to live a bipolar existence of objective and subjective time. Even the redoubtable Captain Kirk himself would find himself back to his pre-Academy days, back to child-hood, as Franham does; the fact that Franham not only survives but escapes madness once human beings' memories are no longer being skewered shows a strength and will no less solid than any starship commander's.

Then with "The Rebels Unthawed" you have the third . . . but wait. Didn't Phil only submit two screen treatments for *Star Trek*? That's the way the story goes, yet while we don't know when "Rebels" was written, it looks remarkably like *Trek*—including a starship captain who is a champion fencer (more prescience—fencing was one of Jean-Luc Picard's favorite activities) and an alien First Officer. This time the crew rescues a dozen men and women from Earth who were lifted away by extraterrestrials during America's Civil War. The two officers, Rawson and Kegan, are from opposing sides, yet call a truce in order to secure control both Americus, the new world that Captain Kinnison takes them to, and with the love—or at least the body—of the ship's chief doctor's assistant, Paula Eden.

What "Rebels" gives us is one of science fiction's early "alternate histories" regarding what might happen if two Earth cultures, vastly separated by time and attitudes, met. Like Kirk, Kinnison is a strong leader who isn't afraid to use force if necessary but prefers diplomacy, and he manages to win over many of the temporal castaways . . . except Rawson and Kagan, who consider him enough of a threat to unite against him and the enlightened future he represents. But the story is still more Farmer than Roddenberry—and again, complete with mythical elements. The ship's name, *Enkidu*, for instance, harkens to the friend and traveling companion of the ancient Sumerian king Gilgamesh.

Unfortunately "Rebels" was made into neither a TV episode or a short story—a loss for *Trek* and Farmer fans alike . . . until now, that is!

I STILL LIVE!
75TH ANNIVERSARY DINNER KEYNOTE ADDRESS
PHILIP JOSÉ FARMER

On October 21, 1989, Phil was a member of a hearty group of Edgar Rice Burroughs enthusiasts to travel to Chicago, Illinois, to commemorate the 75th anniversary of the first hardcover publication of *Tarzan of the Apes*. The event was hosted by a group known as the "Normal Beans" of Chicago ("Normal Bean" being ERB's tongue-in-cheek pseudonym when he wrote his first novel, *A Princess of Mars*, misprinted by his editor as "Norman Bean") and a dinner was held, appropriately enough, at The Adventurers' Club. Chicago was chosen as the setting of the gathering for a number of reasons. Not only was it ERB's birthplace, but it was also where he penned *Tarzan of the Apes*, as well as the city where the book was published by A.C. McClurg & Co. in 1914. But there was one more reason the location was so very appropriate: as Phil would reveal here for the first time, Chicago was also the place where Phil had interviewed Lord Greystoke in the flesh. What follows is Phil's keynote address, with the notes from his original manuscript included.

L adies and gentleman (if you'll pardon me this now old-fashioned form of address), Mr. Tom Willshire, who's the organizer of this festive occasion, Normal Beans and all gathered here who don't fit into the three categories above:

Greetings from Lord Greystoke, aka John Clayton, Tarzan, Lord of the Jungle, the River Devil, The Apeman, Munango-Keewati, John Caldwell, and a dozen other more-or-less fitting titles!

This salutation does not come directly from Tarzan. I am assuming that, if he knew of this gathering, he would transmit greetings through me. However, since I last talked to him, I have not heard from him. That was in 1970, when I briefly interviewed him. Our meeting did not take place in Libreville, Gabon, West Africa as I described in an article for Esquire magazine and in my biography, *Tarzan Alive*. Because of security reasons, Lord Greystoke asked me to say that the meeting was in Libreville. But he told me that, after a few years, I could reveal that the meeting actually occurred in a motel room in Chicago. I don't know why security demanded that the truth be held back for a while. I didn't ask His Lordship, and I'm sure he wouldn't have given me any specifics if I had asked. It may have been more for my safety than his that he made this request. Probably, he was involved in some British government work, undercover, of course, or perhaps some personal enemies were after him.

Some day, we may find out just why this deception was necessary.

In any event, it was in Chicago, not far from here, that I talked to Tarzan. It was appropriate that this city be the place where I met him. His chief biographer, Edgar Rice Burroughs, was born in Chicago on Sept. 1, 1875.

Thus, it's fitting that we celebrate here the Diamond Jubilee of the printing of ERB's first hardcover book, the 101st birthday of Tarzan, born Nov. 22, 1888, and 114th birthday of Edgar Rice Burroughs. We're a little premature in gathering here for Tarzan's birthday and little late for Burroughs'. But nothing is perfect except in our imaginations.

However, we're not far off the mark in celebrating on this date the first appearance in print of *Tarzan of the Apes*. This was in the October issue of *All-Story Magazine*, 1912. And, remember, it was in Chicago that Burroughs first heard of Tarzan from the unnamed man who told Burroughs about The Apeman, the last incarnation of the heroes of ancient mythology.

As a side note, I did ask Lord Greystoke about his wife, Jane Porter. He replied briefly that she was still living and in good health. I assume that she, too, still looks young and is the gorgeous blonde undiminished by age, whom he married. Height, five feet seven inches; bust, 38; waist, 19; hips 36. What used to be called an hour-glass figure. And she's still the same courageous, tough and strong-minded lady.

I wish I could reveal just how I discovered who the "real" Tarzan was. I had plans for describing this complicated procedure—which used mainly *Burke's Peerage*—in the revised edition of *Tarzan Alive* (not my title). The book is out of print just now, but I have hopes that, in a few years, it'll appear in a corrected and up-to-date edition. I would prefer that it also give Lord Greystoke's real identity. But, until I get his final permission, I can't do that. I mentioned a minute ago that Tarzan was the last incarnation of the heroes of ancient mythology. I'll get to an elucidation of this statement in a moment. First, however, allow me a digression that is really not a digression. I have here some pages of a report from a professional astrologer, Susan Gillis, on the horoscope of a certain individual. This was done after the biography, *Tarzan Alive*, was published. Just for kicks, I had a friend who believes in astrology—I don't—act as middleman in the preparation of this horoscope. The astrologer was given the birth date and birthplace of an unnamed person. Using this data, she came up with the pages I have here, some of which I'll read to you.

Not until after the horoscope had been prepared was she told the name of the individual. While I'm reading this, keep in mind Tarzan's, Lord Greystoke's, characteristics as revealed in Burroughs' semi-biographical, more than somewhat fictionalized chronicles of the Apeman's life.

Interpretation of Horoscope

Personality

The Native [*est. but he's an African native*] is a powerful individual who demands independence and freedom. He resents authority. There is a great persistence and determination. He finishes what he sets out to do. When he makes a promise he feels obligated to carry it through and will do so. [*right*] However, the Native tends to shun responsibility; [*prefers jungle life*] therefore he avoids committing himself. In other words he knows that he will feel an obligation to carry through any promise that he makes, and so prefers to avoid making a promise. [*right*] His feelings are likewise with other responsibilities. He has great self-control. He truly knows himself and can determine his own fate. He is a humanitarian [*not in large sense, just towards those he knows*] but at the same time demands his own privacy. The native feels a need to get away from people to think things out and contemplate. [*Jungle Tales—ponders on Nature of Creation & the Creator, searching for identity as a human & formulation of his own philosophy*] What one sees of the Native's surface personality is not what is within. The Native outwardly presents a light and bolder type of personality. His true inner personality is extremely deep and intense. His mind works in a deep and intense fashion as well. The native enjoys intense research, delving, and learning. [*teaching himself to read when he didn't know English*] When he finds something that interests him, the Native will carry through to a successful conclusion. He has this tremendous self-control. He does not like to show his emotions outwardly, so people are not aware of the intensity of the emotions with the Native. However, the Native does get involved with the emotions and problems of friends. The Native will never lay his own emotions out on the table, or his own problems, for friends. The Native is intelligent, curious and skeptical to a healthy degree. [*right, Jungle Tales of Tarzan*] there can be disappointments in friends, though, due to misplaced trust. The Native is analytical and critical. Deep within there is a basic lack of emotional security and self-confidence. [*wrong*] He is an extremely physical person. He loves the outdoors, sports and animals. He has extreme physical coordination and dexterity. He has tremendous energy, and a love for travel. There is writing ability, as he communicates better through the written word than he does through the spoken word. [*silent—again learned to read—taught himself*]

Love Life

The Native is more physical than the emotional in his sex life and love life. This is due to his physical and emotional makeup, as previously mentioned. He is not quick to settle down and marry, but when the Native does marry, it is for good. There is no divorce

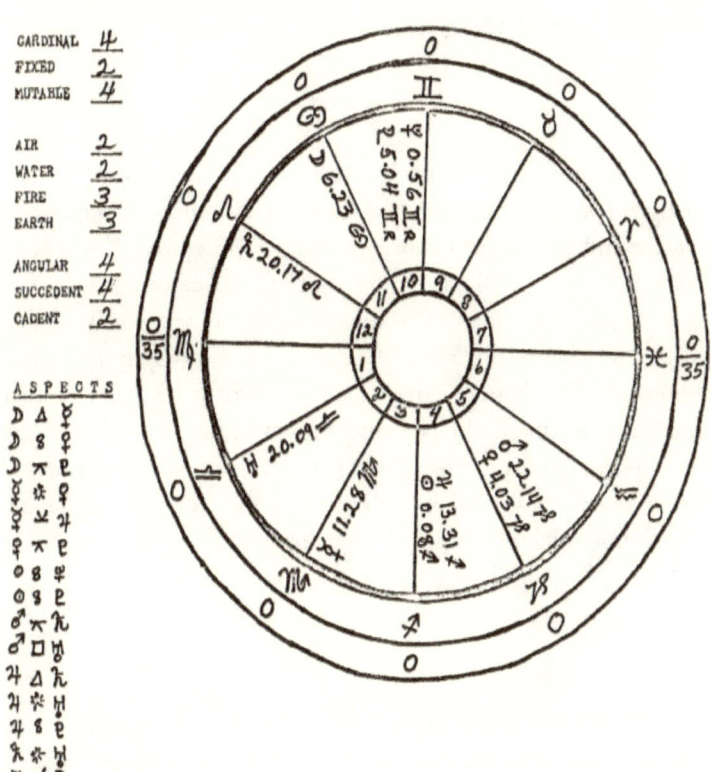

163

shown in the chart. There is a broken marriage engagement shown in the chart of the Native however. [*not quite true—unless we talk of La of Opar, Nemone, the Countess de Coude or Teeka*]

Home

The Native does not know his father due to the death of the father or a separation from the father when the Native was very young. There is a stepfather in the Native's chart. There are problems relating to the Native's parents. No specific problem is indicated in the Native's chart, but general difficulties are indicated. These difficulties could include an early separation from the natural parents, and/or the Native's resentment towards the stepfather. [*Tublat—Dum-Dum, Tarzan 13 years old. Tublat goes mad, corners Kala, Tarzan kills him with his real father's knife. In a sense recreated the original oedipal situation*]

Career

Upheavals in the Native's career are indicated. [*plenty of those, one great danger after another*] Conflict is indicated between the Native and his employers or superiors. [*Tublat and Kerchak*] The Native attracts public attention through his career. [*ERB's books and movies*] His financial status is never on an even keel. [*loses money in investments more than once, back to Opar to refill his exchequer*] The Native can go back and forth between financial stability and financial chaos many times in his career. The Native has a potential for acting, [*posing as aged, his various pseudonyms and identities assumed*] as well as an ability for writing. There is career potential for the Native's great physical coordination and dexterity. [*not an Olympic contender—too much publicity*]

Health

The Native is extremely health conscious. He strives to keep himself physically fit. He would be aware of a proper diet and would use health foods. The Native knows that good nutrition keeps him healthy. [*A Feast Unknown*] Any health problems would most likely be in the Native's legs; particularly the thigh and knee regions. [*? mostly his head, concussions*]

As you can see the astrologer came close to the mark on most counts.

While writing *Tarzan Alive*, I did my own research in astrology. I'm a mere tyro in it, but there were enough reference books available for me to figure out the horoscope. And, amazingly or not, the astrology did work out. Tarzan, a Sagittarius, but born on the cusp between Sagittarius and Scorpio, also has many of the characteristics of the Scorpio. The persona of Tarzan, as described by Burroughs, and the natal chart as worked out by the astrologer, agreed in most respects.

Once, I got a letter from a reader of *Tarzan Alive*. He had the brass to accuse me of having worked out Tarzan's birth date from the characteristics and life of Tarzan. That is, I did it backwards in order to find the most suitable birth date and, hence, the astrological data. I was hurt and somewhat indignant for a while at this accusation. But I've cooled off since then. After all, a healthy skepticism is to be admired, and both Tarzan and myself are skeptics. But I assure you that the birth date came first. I got it from Lord Greystoke himself. Of course, he could have been misleading me, but I see no reason why he should have.

We return to the statement that Tarzan is the last incarnation of the heroes of ancient mythology. Mythology, as those familiar with the works of Joseph Campbell and Carl Gustav Jung know, derives ultimately from the archetypes in the mass unconscious mind of human beings. Not just in the minds of Westerners but in the minds of all races, tribes, and nationalities.

There's not enough time here to develop this theme, but those who have read my *Tarzan Alive* have been given enough to highlight this theme. Allow me, however, to read a paragraph relevant to this premise, one which I pursue in a number of sections in the book. Page 93:

Tarzan was indeed magnificent. He looked like the hero of classical myth, and, like them, he had been hidden in a far-off corner. He had been biding his time until he had fully developed his powers. Then he would come out to astonish the great world and perform feats of wonder and be the savior of peoples. He was like Hercules, Samson, Theseus, Achilles, Hiawatha, Gilgamesh, Finn McCool and the young Arthur. Burroughs may or may not have been consciously aware of the similarity of young Tarzan to the heroes of old. But there is no doubt that in his unconscious, where artistry is born, where archetypes live, he was aware. He was reporting on the last of the heroes, the final great son of Mother Nature, her gift to the twentieth century, and her reminder that the demigods were not yet all dead.

One of the appeals of the Tarzan books is to our unconscious, where dwell the gods, and goddesses, the spirits, the succubi and incubi, the djinns, the monsters of Chaos, the wizards and witches, the wise old man, the Great Mother, the great enchantresses and seductresses (ERB's *La of Opar* and HRH's *She-Who-Must-Be-Obeyed* to name only two), Old Man Death Himself, and the saviors and heroes of old.

This is not the only appeal. A strong fascination is the image in the reader's mind of living like Tarzan in the jungle, free of inhibitions, constraints, obligations and responsibilities of civilized life, freedom from traffic, traffic lights, traffic jams, paying taxes, paying off the mortgage, hospital and doctor bills, free of doing what your neighbors and the government, which also lies to you, requires you to do. Freedom! Being your own ruler, living in a state of blissful anarchy.

This freedom is doubtless an illusion, but it glows brightly in the imagination and makes us envy Tarzan.

There are also the adventures Tarzan experiences. We live in them vicariously, and we have fun, without the danger. Let's not forget fun.

However, the evoking of archetypal images while reading Tarzan is a very strong one. I gave some space to that in the biography. But a professor of Classics at the University of Iowa, Doctor Erling B. Holtsmark, devotes much more space to this theme—and others—in his *Tarzan and Tradition: Classical Myth in Popular Literature*, Greenwood Press, CT, first published in 1981. It may still be available from Greenwood Press. I strongly recommend this study, which not only stresses the classical and preliterate myths evident in Tarzan's life but also makes a keen literary analysis of Burrough's writings.

Holtsmark claims—and cites evidence—that Burroughs is much more than the inspired hack writer so many critics and academics think he is.

Allow me to quote briefly from the description in the front inner flap of the dust jacket.

"Holtsmark finds Burroughs' own extensive classical education evident in the Tarzan books. The first six books that is. Burroughs' language and narrative style reflect the central premises of ancient Greek and Latin literary technique. His thematic concerns also parallel those of the classical authors. Tarzan himself is a surprisingly complex literary persona whose clear roots in the mythical heroes of antiquity, notably Odysseus, are combined with features borrowed from American Indian traditions . . . Holtsmark also explores the erotic and Darwinian elements in Burroughs' thematic structure."

Holtsmark has an extensive bibliography. He seems to have covered all items re Burroughs and Tarzan that he could find. Strangely enough, there is no mention of my book, *Tarzan Alive*, which preceded his by nine years. I don't know how he missed it. But our conclusions re the thematic elements in the Tarzan books and the development of Tarzan's character—he does change in his attitudes and behavior during the course of the early books and in the final chronological volume—Holtsmark and I find the same elements, come to the same conclusions.

However, Holtsmark's study also stresses the literary elements and analyses them almost to the molecular level. Again, I highly recommend this book. Not just to readers of the jungle saga but to academics who make comments about Burroughs and Tarzan which display their own ignorance despite their claim to be scholars.

Now, in the same vein, I'll read a copy of a letter of mine which appeared in the editorial column of the *Philadelphia Inquirer*, April 29, 1972. The *Philadelphia Inquirer* is not connected to the *National Inquirer*.

Book character distorted

Tarzan Still Lives—and is no bigot

To the Editor:

I read Art Peters' column of April 14 concerning my book "Tarzan Alive" and Peters' stand against comic books. If Mr. Peters had read my book, he'd know that there is almost no connection between Tarzan of Burroughs (the book Tarzan) and the movie, TV, and comic book images of Tarzan.

If Mr. Peters had read my book, he'd know that Tarzan is not racially prejudiced. How could he be? Prejudice is judging before you know the facts. Society establishes an emotional bias towards certain subjects in the infant. The adult continues to reinforce his early-life conditioning with rationalizations that have no basis in reality.

Tarzan never saw a human being until he was an adult. And, as Burroughs makes clear in the twenty-four books about him, Tarzan could care less about skin color. Black or white, man or beast, it was the individual that counted.

If Mr. Peters had read my book, he'd know that Tarzan had a Jewish grandmother. This won't set well with the many anti-Semites among whites and blacks. But Tarzan also had black forebears. And he was descended from Mohammed, who, you may remember, was an Arab.

Contrary to what Mr. Peters says, Tarzan did mature. (The book Tarzan of course; I'm not speaking of the movie or comic book person.) In the beginning, he's a simple ape-man, sometimes cruel, prone to solve problems with violence. But he is highly intelligent, and though he makes mistakes, he learns.

He not only matures; he evolves. He learns the rules of civilization, though he doesn't always obey them nor does he ever groove on civilization.

In the final book of his adventures, it is he who restrains an American soldier from slaughtering surrounded Japanese troops. It is he who says that hate never does any good. It is he who has learned to laugh at many things, including himself.

He is still, in one sense, the Noble Savage, but he is also an ideal civilized man, that is, he is a true gentleman. Of course, he'll still eat worms if he gets a chance, but that's because he has no prejudice against eating them.

American readers are too likely to confuse the present white-black situation here with the relations between Tarzan and blacks in Africa. There is no correlation.

Just as there is no correlation between my book and Mr. Peters' comments on it.

Philip José Farmer
Peoria, Ill.

So, there, you asshole! I thought as I finished that letter.

I have a few tag ends re *Tarzan Alive* that you might find amusing.

One, when *Tarzan Alive* came out, a Boston TV station called the publisher to get my address. The station wanted to invite me to Boston for an interview about Tarzan and, mainly, about his being a real, that is, nonfictional character. The dolts at the publicity department of the publisher told the caller that the book was a hoax! This really pissed me off. The least the publicity people could have done was phone me and ask if Lord Greystoke really did live. That incident, by the way, was one more in the long list of things I had against this particular publisher.

Two, several years ago, I got a call from a would-be Olympic athlete who wanted Tarzan's address. The athlete desired training tips from Tarzan, whom he figured, rightly, was the world's greatest athlete. And all without steroids, too.

I had to tell this athlete that I did not have Tarzan's forwarding address. I still don't.

I also received a number of letters, one from as far away as Australia, inquiring about getting in touch with Tarzan.

Once, at a convention, an attendee asked me if I really believed that Tarzan did exist. I replied, "You believe in God, don't you?" I let him figure out the ambiguities in that statement.

But I say to you, in one sense or another, TARZAN STILL LIVES!

Hayy ibn Yaqzan[1] by Abu ibn Tufayl
An Arabic Mowgli
A paper presented at the 1990 Conference for the Fantastic in the Arts
Philip José Farmer

Phil is an expert on the subject of humans raised by animals. Not only has he written a Tarzan novel authorized by the Burroughs estate and a novella featuring Kipling's Mowgli (not to mention the Lord Grandrith adventures and numerous other pastiches of the Lord of the Jungle), he has also edited an entire book on the subject under the weighty title *Mother Was a Lovely Beast: A Feral Man Anthology, Fiction and Fact About Humans Raised by Animals* (Chilton, 1974). Thus it will not be surprising to learn that when Phil was invited to the International Conference on the Fantastic in Arts, he chose to address this familiar theme. The reader will quickly see that this speech, while it makes frequent comparisons to Burroughs' Tarzan and Kipling's Mowgli, is about quite a different kind of feral man.

Phil's readers may perk up at his mention of the name Rabi'a in the speech. Rabi'a also appears as Alfred Jarry's spiritual teacher in "Coda," the third and final installment in what might be called the Doctor Faustroll/Alfred Jarry cycle (see *Tales of Riverworld*, Warner Books, 1992, and *Quest to Riverworld*, Warner Books, 1993). Sufism is another theme to which Phil has oft returned, notably in the mind-blowing SF adventure *The Unreasoning Mask* (Putnam, 1981) and with the character Nur ed-Din el-Musafir in the Riverworld series.

The paper that follows, first printed in the *Journal of the Fantastic in the Arts, Volume 3, No. 3*, 1994, was given in Ft. Lauderdale, Florida, in March 1990. Phil began his presentation, appropriately enough, by beating his chest and unleashing the victory cry of a bull-ape.

The myths, legends and folktales about human infants reared by animals probably originated not long after *homo sapiens* developed language. There is no way to determine that this assumption is valid, but it seems likely. If we believe the psychologists and the anthropologists, we believe that humankind circa 40,000 or so years ago was "closer to nature." The Old Stone Age people, we are told, did not draw a sharp physical and spiritual line between human beings and animals. Ancient literature abounds with such tales, and the oral myths and legends of pre-literate groups indicate that feral-person stories began in the "dawn" of humankind. By no means the earliest is the Roman legend of the raising of abandoned babies, Romulus and Remus, by a she-wolf and a woodpecker. This is familiar to every Western schoolchild or, at least, used to be.

Thus, the fascination of such tales of abandoned or lost children who are adopted and raised by beasts or birds is deep. So deep that it must be part of the mass unconscious mind postulated by Carl Jung and others. This fascination has led to many fictional works about such children. The most popular tales of these and the most enduring have been written by Rudyard Kipling and Edgar Rice Burroughs. Kipling's Mowgli character, raised by Asiatic Indian wolves and other animals, first appeared in *The Jungle Book* in 1894. Burroughs' character, Tarzan, raised by African great apes, initially stepped onto the stage in the October, 1912 issue of *The All-Story Magazine*. The expanded and revised book version, *Tarzan of the Apes*, was published in 1914.

The Mowgli book is ninety-six years old; the Tarzan seventy-eight. Whatever their rank in world literature or the estimation of the academic critics, they have flourished long enough to be counted as a permanent part of world literature. They still live.

The oldest feral-human story not of mythic or legendary origin but a fictional product seems to be "Salaman and Absal."[2] This oldest known fictional version was written by the great Persian philosopher and physician, Abu ibn Sina, who lived A.D. 980–1037. He is better known in the West under his Latinized name, Avicenna. The feral man in his story was raised by a female deer.

Abu ibn Tufayl, the author of *Hayy Ibn Yaqzan*, plucked the basic story idea from Avicenna and also used the names of Absal and Salaman in his work. But ibn Tufayl completely restructured the situations in his predecessor's work and added many of his own. Tafuyl's intent was to restate Avicenna's philosophy in the light and thought of another Muslim theologian and mystic, the Persian, al-Ghazali, A.D. 1058-1111. It was al-Ghazali's great work, "The Revival of the Religious Sciences," that made Sufism acceptable, more or less, to orthodox Islam.

Abu ibn Tufayl was born circa A.D. 1110 in a little town fifty miles northeast of Granada in Muslim Spain. He was a notable Sufi, a great physician, and a master of state for the ruler of Granada, Abu Yaqub Yusuf, and for several succeeding governors of the Almohad dynasty. Ibn Tufayl also encouraged Averroes in his philosophical studies and his immense project of integrating Islamic theology and philosophy with the thought of Aristotle and Plato.

Ibn Tufayl was a Sufi. Though it may be safely assumed that the readers of this publication are well aware of the Sufi discipline and its aims, it will not hurt to remind some readers of some its aspects. For instance, though Sufism is usually identified with Islamism, it is supposed to have existed before the birth of Mohammed, who lived circa A.D. 570-632.[3] It is mystical in intent and philosophy and chiefly strives to attain "oneness" with God, though this oneness is not a pantheistic identification with the Creator or "becoming" God. Though the discipline requires the novitiate to be guided by the Master in the early and middle phases, the Sufis admit that there are also natural-born Sufis. These, however, are very few.

The Sufis from the beginning were regarded suspiciously by the fundamentalist Muslims. The Sufis' view is that many parts of the Koran are to be interpreted as symbols or metaphors and are not to be taken literally. Also, the Sufis admitted women to their ranks, and the orthodox Muslims were scandalized by Sufi meetings in which men and women freely mingled. One of the great female Sufis was Rabi'a who lived A.D. 717-81, an ex-slave who became an Islamic saint.[4] Nor is Sufism confined to Mohammedans. A Sufi may be a Christian or Jew, or indeed, anyone who believes in a single God.

Ibn Tufayl wrote *Hayy Ibn Yaqzan* as a Sufi didactic story. The hero's name is a touchstone of this intent. "Hayy" is, in Arabic, "life," "ibn" means "son of," and "Yaqzan" means "awareness" or "wholly awake." Thus, Life, son of Awareness, is the protagonist, as contrasted with Mowgli, meaning "Frog," a name given him by his lupine fosterparents, and with Tarzan, meaning "White Skin," given him by the great apes who reared him.

Ibn Tufayl writes that Hayy may be the child of a sister of a king of an island off the coast of India. Despite her brother's insistence that she not marry until after he had, she secretly wed a kinsman. The princess bore a child, and then, fearful that she and her baby would be killed for defying her brother, put the infant in a tightly sealed ark and cast it onto the sea. The ark drifted to another island, inhabited only by animals and birds. After the baby managed to get out of the box, he was nursed by a doe who had lost her own fawn. This casting away in an ark reminds one of Moses and other mythical and legendary heroes. The adoption by the animal is similar to Tarzan's. At the age of one, his parents dead, he was given suck by Kala, the great ape who had just lost her own child. Mowgli was just barely able to walk when a tiger made his parents flee for their lives, leaving the infant behind. He was saved from the tiger by a male wolf and his mate, who was nursing her cubs and allowed Mowgli to share the milk with them.

However, ibn Tufayl allows the reader to choose between two stories of Hayy's appearance on the island. The alternative which ibn Tufayl seems to prefer is that the island was unique in that human newborn infants could be produced from the soil by spontaneous generation. Like the Gernsbackian science-fiction writer, he goes to great length in describing how this could be possible. In any event, this is possibly the first fictional work in which the protagonist could have been born from Mother Earth herself. It is also, as far as I know, the last.

Hayy, Mowgli, and Tarzan, respectively the children of a royal Indian Muslim couple, a low-caste Indian Hindu couple, and the scion of British nobility, were alike in that all had a high intelligence, adaptability, and curiosity. Hayy, unlike Mowgli and Tarzan, had no contact with language-users until he was an adult. He had no mentor except himself whereas Mowgli had the wolves, Baloo the brown bear, Bagheera the black panther, and Kaa the python; Tarzan had his great-ape fostermother and her tribe. Mowgli's lupine fosterparents and Tarzan's anthropoid fostermother loved and cared for their human adoptees. In a more limited way, Hayy's corvine fostermother cared for him in a gentle and instructive, though mute, fashion. Hayy could not have survived without her, but most of what he learned he taught himself.

Mowgli and Tarzan, though they, too, had to teach themselves much of what they learned, did get the benefit in their childhood of jungle lore and the social forms and mores of lupine and anthropoid society. Also, their societies were language-users, albeit in a rather restricted way.

Note that, contrary to the claims of some Arabic scholars, ibn Tufayl's work is not a Robinson Crusoe story. Hayy Ibn Yaqzan, and also Tarzan and Mowgli, are cast into a totally feral society before they are able to talk. They have no contact with other human beings until they are adults. Robinson Crusoe, on the other hand, is not isolated upon an island until he is fully grown. He has been formed by human society, and his thoughts and actions are the products of human education and cultural conditioning. Though he has to work out many problems and be ingenious in solving them, he has the knowledge and ability to use tools. He has been given these, and, though the environment is different from that in which he was raised, he adapts his knowledge to his new environment. Hayy, Tarzan, and Mowgli have to learn how to make and use tools by themselves. Their feral companions are unable to help them in these undertakings.

All three feral men do eventually wear garments to hide the genitals. But each one does this for different reasons. Tarzan eventually took to wearing a loincloth because he observed that the local blacks were, like himself, human. Humans were superior to beasts, though he later changed his mind about that, and they wore genital-concealing garments. Therefore, he would emulate "men." Mowgli wore no genital-concealing garment until he was forced to do so when he first encountered humans en masse in the village of his biological father. Having to wear clothes annoyed him very much. Hayy had no more sense of shame than Tarzan or Mowgli, but he was disturbed and unhappy about his nakedness. This came about from his observing that the animals' sex organs were much better concealed than his. Thus, he desired to wear a garment about his waist because he wanted to emulate the creatures around him.

Mowgli seems to have had little curiosity about the nature of gods or God. The Law of the Jungle, learned from the wolf pack, was deity enough for him. But both Hayy and Tarzan were eager to know what God was all about, eager, in fact, to meet Him face to face, as it were. Hayy came to the concept of a Creator through both inductive and conductive logic. Tarzan got his idea that there might be a Creator from the books in his dead parents' cabin.[5] He had, however, a very hazy idea of God's attributes. And he also thought that God must be a person of some sort. His quest led him to conclude that the Creator was a rather impersonal Being or force responsible for all the beauty and goodness in the world. God had originated such feelings as self-sacrifice, compassion, and the ability to see goodness and practice it.

However, Tarzan could not figure out why God had made that terribly dangerous and utterly repulsive creature, Histah the snake. After that, there is no record of Tarzan being interested in First Causes or a Supreme Being. It should be noted that the Ape-Man's loathing of snakes does not originate from a genetic tendency. His great ape tribe and his experiences with the deadly limbless creature taught him that. Mowgli, on the other hand, though he detests poisonous cobras for excellent reasons, is a friend of the python and especially his mentor, Kaa.

Hayy ibn Yaqzan, unlike Tarzan, untiringly pursues a quest for the Creator, the One, the Truth, the Ineffable, the Way. He was born Sufi, and his solitary life exemplifies the processes and various stages by which Sufis, born or instructed, spiritually evolve.

When Hayy is no longer a child, he works via his intelligence through the Wooden Age and then Stone Age, making artifacts suitable for each period. Some of these are tools to dissect animals while he is searching for their animating principles, their souls. Eventually, when he is thirty-five years old, after much experimentation, research, and philosophizing, he concludes that God is a Being Whose perfection is infinite, Who is beyond perfection, goodness, and beauty, though He includes these in the Divine Persona.

He also concludes that, to be fully aware of this Being, to know him in a mystical sense, is to know "joy without lapse, unending bliss, infinite rapture and delight." Hayy's intellectual and spiritual odyssey ends in the rapture of "being one" with the Necessarily Existent, the Truth, the One.

Ontogeny recapitulates phylogeny. Hayy is, in ibn Tufayl's work, the living embodiment of this maxim. But he has progressed beyond the physical and mental evolution of the species to a spiritual being. From feral man, one like the beasts, and thence to *homo sapiens*, he has gone on to union with God. He has become the Ultimate Human Being though he is, in a sense, now more than human. But this superior-to-man state does not mean that he is now God. He is exalted only because he rides on the waves of emanations from God. He has seen the One, the Ineffable, yet he has not become the One. No human being may do that, though some are deceived into thinking that they are.

[1] Translated from the 12th-century Arabic by Lenn Evan Goodman, *Classical Arabic Literature* (Vol. 1), Twayne, 1972. This paper was first delivered at the International Conference on the Fantastic in the Arts, Ft. Lauderdale, Florida, 1990.

[2] See Goodman's Introduction to *Hayy Ibn Yaqzan*; see also Richard Lupoff's *Edgar Rice Burroughs: Master of Adventure*, Ace, 1965 *re* Professor Altrocchi's unpublished manuscripts on feral-human stories.

[3] *The Sufis*, Indries Shah, Doubleday, 1971.

[4] See Margaret Smith, *Rabi'a The Mystic*, reprinted, Philio Press, Amsterdam, 1974.

[5] See "The God of Tarzan," *Jungle Tales of Tarzan*, 1919.

Works Cited

Burroughs, Edgar Rice. "The God of Tarzan." *Jungle Tales of Tarzan*. Chicago: McClurg, 1919
____. *Tarzan of the Apes*. Chicago: McClurg, 1914
Kipling, Rudyard. *The Jungle Book*, 1894
Lupoff, Richard. *Edgar Rice Burroughs: Master of Adventure*. NY: Ace, 1965.
Shah, Indries. *The Sufis*. NY: Doubleday, 1971.
Siba, Abu ibn. "Salaman and Absal."
Smith, Margaret. *Rabi'a the Mystic*. rpt., Amsterdam: Philo Press, 1974.
Tufayl, Abu ibn. Hayy ibn Yaqzan. Lenn Evan Goodman, trans., *Classical Arabic Literature*, Vol. 1, NY: Twayne, 1972.

Why Do I Write?
Writer Guest of Honor Speech
1992 Conference for the Fantastic in the Arts
Philip José Farmer

Two years after presenting his paper on Hayy ibn Yaqzan, "the Arabic Mowgli," Phil was asked back to the International Conference on the Fantastic in Arts, this time as Guest of Honor. The topic of Phil's second presentation before the conference was not to be feral humans, though from what you will read, it is clear Phil considers a writer's imagination to be more than just a little wild.

Jim Seels, author of "Collecting Philip José Farmer," *Firsts*, October 1991, was kind enough to provide *Farmerphile* with a copy of this speech to be printed here for the first time.

M embers of the International Association for the Fantastic in Arts and honored guests, I'm pleased to be here as your professional-writer guest of honor. Like all of you, I love the "capital W" Word and make my living from words. Which is not to say that the members are wordy—though I suppose a few are. A few hundred.

The title of this speech is "Why Do I Write?" That derives from the title of the text of an entire publication issued in May of 1985. The title was "Why Do You Write?" Or, in the language in which it was published, "Pourquoi Écrivez-Vous?"

This was in a French super-size magazine with the overtitle of *Liberation*, edited by Daniel Rondeau and Jean-Francois Fogel.

As far as I know, it was a single-shot publication. Subtitled: *Des Grandes Signatures Venues de Monde Entier.* That is, great signatures from all over the world. Subsubtitled: *400 Écrivains Repondent.* That is, 400 authors respond.

Historically, the first time the question, Why Do You Write? was proposed by a French publication was in 1919. The replies from a hundred authors were printed in three issues of the revue *Littérature* starting in November 1919. That is, when I was a year and eleven months old. The authors who were asked the question, Why Do You Write?, were all French except for the Italian poet, Giuseppe Ungaretti, and the Norwegian novelist, dramatist, poet, and winner of the Nobel Prize, Knut Hamsun.

In 1984, sixty-five years after the first inquiries, a French magazine, *Liberation*, sent the same question to authors. But, this time, it went to over four hundred authors all over the world. Those who replied included a Samoan, two Zimbabweans, a Trinidadian, Palestinians, Israelis, and a Sudanese. Not included were authors from Greenland, Patagonia, Albania, and Lower Slobbovia.

Most of these I had never heard of before—or since. So much for my ignorance.

The Etats-Unis or U.S.A. section included such mainstream names as Mailer, Irving, Coover, Malamud, Barth, Carver, Highsmith, Oates, and Lurie. Five writers whom people think are science-fiction/fantasy writers were included. These were Asimov, Bradbury, Wm. Burroughs, Farmer, and Vonnegut. Burroughs and Vonnegut would object to being thus labelled. In fact, I object, but a lot of good it does me.

The shortest reply in the publication was from Charles Bukowski. He said, "If I knew why I write, I would surely no longer be able to write." Bravo for him!

To tell the truth, I didn't know why I wrote and I suspected that none of the four hundred authors knew. But I was willing to try to figure out the why by writing an essay. So I did.

Under my name on page fifty-two was an editorial comment. "One of the fathers of science-fiction."

This is not true. I'm one of the children. I didn't originate any school of s-f unless, as my critics claim, it was the school of bad taste. Perhaps the editor meant that I'd fathered the school of erotic extrapolation in s-f.

The second editorial comment is "Born in 1918." This is true, if I am to believe my parents.

The third editorial comment is "A work to make libraries collapse." The verb is "plier," which means to fold or to bend or to yield. I translate it as "collapse." What the editor means here is that I've written a hell of a lot of books.

Follows the text. This was written in English by me and translated by the editors into French. Unfortunately, I lost the original and could not, after so many years, reconstruct it in English. So, I had to translate the French back into English. Let's see how I've done though you must keep in mind that my original somewhat colloquial English has been slightly Frenchified, and, thus, spavined. I just couldn't help it. I've also shortened the text and I will add comments now and then.

The text begins: In the night of a wet space (my mother's womb) a spermatozoon was racing along with millions of others of his kind. During this microcosmic marathon, all except one died. And the victor ceased to exist when it fused with the egg, both forming one: the other.

The spermatozoon landed upon the ovum as if it were an astronaut and the ovum was a distant planet. That day, Flash Gordon not only dropped in onto the unknown planet, the ovum, he fused with it.

From this fusion was created an Other (in the existential sense) named Philip José Farmer. Nine months later, this entity began his exploration of another unknown planet: the Earth. His story after crash-landing on Earth was a science-fictional one, in fact, every baby's story is science-fictional. And the newcomer fell into the hands of strangers who spoke an incomprehensible language and certainly did not think as he did.

His history is of a savage battle to survive on this planet while trying to become a complete human being, that which the Chinese call a "round man."

Aside: In one sense, I have certainly become a round man. I should weight 180 pounds. I do weigh 225.

But the entity which crash-landed, more or less human, a semi-robot, was doomed to labor all his life to become not-quite-human-enough. The realization of this would come at the end of his odyssey on this planet. Many have tried to become human. Few have succeeded, if, in fact, anybody has done so. And for all, apparently, the end is death.

Why then keep on trying to live? Perhaps because it's necessary to live a certain amount of time to develop one's self as fully as possible, to strive to become a round man, that is, a truly compassionate and empathetic person. And is death another forced landing, a crash-landing which also results in a fusion where we become an Other? Or where we combine with Some Thing to become Something Other? And if our free will doesn't overcome our semi-robot deterministic physical and mental mechanisms so that we can at least get close to being a real human being, a round man, will that prevent us from becoming an afterlife Other? Providing there is an afterlife, of course.

Human infants are semi-robots who possess, however, a limited though vigorous free will. Some of them become adults who use free will as much as possible. But the majority use their free will only once in their lives, that is, at the moment they unconsciously decide they won't ever use their free will.

I consider myself a born writer whose genetic drive to write was influenced by the environment. Since the age or eight or nine I've known that my main goal in life, aside from surviving, was to write fiction. This heritage influenced by the unique environment directed this semi robot toward the goal of being a writer and particularly toward the new genre of literature born of the industrial electronic era. That is, the genre of science-fiction. In the same way that the egg absorbed the spermatozoon, I absorbed the *Bible*, the *Iliad*, the *Odyssey*, Swift, Twain, fairy tales, the legends and myths of the ancient Mediterraneans, of the Medieval Norsemen, and of the native Americans. I absorbed also the boys' literature of the 1920's and 1930's. Also, the *Thousand and One Nights*, L.

Frank Baum, Edgar Rice Burroughs, A. Conan Doyle, Robert Louis Stevenson, and some of Dickens' works. All these I read while in grade school.

In high school and college I absorbed too many classic, popular, and (so-called) subliterature works to list here. I thank God or Chance (one or the other) that my parents did not restrict my reading to the classics or works approved by the school authorities. A writer (or scholar) cannot truly know the literature of his nation unless he knows the popular literature also.

The books cited above (and many more) influenced me to a lesser or greater degree. And so did the silent films of my child-hood and the talkies of my youth. Among a dozen or so films I saw while in grade school or before school, the most formative were the *Black Pirate*, the *Thief of Baghdad, Robin Hood, The Lost World* (which was based on Doyle's novel), and a week-end serial, *The Green Archer*. These made as much impression on me as any book I was to read. After all, I saw most of them more than once before I could really read. This influence of the movies demonstrates the power of environmental forces on genetic destiny. If I had existed in a time before movies existed, I would have been a somewhat different writer.

Also, whoever dealt me my genetic cards gave me a touch of earthiness, a dab of vulgarity. This streak of vulgarity, of earthiness, plus a horror of and yet fascination for the irrational behavior of Homo sapiens, led me to be particularly fond of the tales of the native American, who we called American Indian when I was younger, the tales about the great Tricksters. I was fascinated while still an elementary school student by the stories of Old Man Coyote of the Plains tribes and Wabosso or the Great White Rabbit of the Midwestern tribes. Also, Tarzan is a classic trickster (in the books, not the films), and I read all of these available while still in grade school. The trickster theme has, as various critics have noted, been an oft recurring one in my fiction.

And Bugs Bunny, I feel, is a direct descendant of Wabosso and Coyote in this industrial-electronic era and also into this Age of Information.

The daily and Sunday comic strips of my childhood and youth also influenced me and shaped somewhat my literary mind. Among the many, perhaps the strongest, was George Herriman's Krazy Kat. This was started in the Hearst newspapers in 1916, but I didn't become aware of it until about 1925.

Two demons sit on my shoulders while I write—and during other times, too. One is Bugs Bunny, the anarchist trickster, who crouches like Socrates' demon on my shoulder. He doesn't dictate what I should say or do, but he does make suggestions, and he counsels me. It was Bugs, not the wise men of the orient or the ancient Greek, Heraclitus, who revealed to me that anarchy and irrationality pulse and writhe and rage just beneath the surface of order and rationality, the skin of what we see as Reality.

Bugs sits on my left shoulder and asks me, "What's Up, Doc? Or down, as the case may be?"

The demon who sits on my right shoulder is Krazy Kat, who loves law and order but is also obsessed with love in the abstract and the particular. And Krazy Kat makes suggestions to me and counsels me. But, even when his voice (or her voice, since the strip never makes Kat's gender clear) happens to be stronger than Bugs' I keep envisioning the brick which the tricky Ignatz Mouse forever hurls at the back of Kat's head. I wince, and I feel as protective of Krazy Kat as Offissa Pupp was. And I think, Is that brick sometimes aimed at me?

It could be said that the tension created by the contradictory suggestions and counsels of these two demons makes me write.

Maybe, one day, their cries and their whispers will mix to make one voice, a unique voice. The sentence just spoken ended my essay in *Liberation*. However, I feel compelled to add to that. I must add: But my voice, like that of any writer's voice, is unique.

Thus, what I should say is that the two voices may mix to make not only a single voice, an Other's voice, but also a better voice.

This text was written in 1984 and published in French in 1985. I'm still waiting for the two voices to meld and make a single and thus better voice. I may be harsher in judgment on myself than others. I don't know. But, essentially I have to satisfy myself.

So, I've decided that the current fantasy novel I'm working on will be my last in that genre. I will keep on writing short stories in the science-fiction and fantasy field. My novels, however, will be mainstream or mystery. After all, when I began writing in the 1940's, my ambition was to be a mainstream writer despite my lifelong love of science-fiction. But things went awry; I became a science-fiction/fantasy writer. So, at the age of seventy-four, I'll start a new career. If that doesn't work out, I'll be eighty-four by the time that I find out.

Maybe I'll throw those two rascals from my shoulders and go shopping for brand new demons.

THE BRUECKEL/HARWOOD LETTER
PHILIP JOSÉ FARMER

The following letter to Frank J. Brueckel and John Harwood, dated March 16, 1973, provides a rare glimpse into the process of Phil's meticulous world building. Note that the Khokarsan spellings are not yet in their final form, and that Dennis Power's theory about the derivation of the name Sahhindar is proven herein.

Dear Frank and John:
(Frankie and Johnnie?) (Lovers of ERB, anyway.)

In between novels and catching up on correspondence. This makes the 56th letter in three days, and in the meantime a number of others arrived demanding answers. This one doesn't demand; I'm doing it because I want to.

At odd moments, and some have really been odd, I've been working on the notes for The Ancient Opar Series. Here, without my consulting them, depending upon memory that is rapidly deteriorating with age (along with my typing ability), are some of my thoughts.

First, the overall term for the ancient civilization around the two inland seas of Africa is Karkhosan. I derived this from Beirce's Carcosa, and indeed the Carcosa seen by Bierce's narrator may have been Karkhosa. (I'm not responsible for Bierce's eccentric spelling.) Kar-kho-sa. Literally, tree-Kho(the Great Goddess)-hill. The hill of the tree of Kho. The original Karkhosa was a hill overlooking a harbor on the north side of the island near the northern

187

shore of the upper sea, Kemu (the great water). Kem, meaning water –u, meaning great or large or splendid, depending upon the context.

The tree on this hill, according to the religion, was where Kho first created birds and later changed some of them into human beings. One of these human beings was Sahintar (the grey-eyed god), who became Kho's first consort. He was the one who gave mankind the knowledge to domesticate plants and animals, to weave, to make bricks, cut stones, erect large buildings, make bronze, write, make ships with sails, and so on. The religion has it that he angered Kho because she had planned on doing all this but in her own good time. Thus, she drove him away. But he still comes back now and then. He was also the one who brought in the plants which are the basis of Karkhosan agriculture. As I've remarked to John, central Africa circa 10,000 B.C. had no, or almost no plants, which could provide enough food for a civilization. But, Sahintar, according to myth, brought in millet, sorghum, barley, emmer, the olive tree, and showed them how to grow a berry which does exist in the rain forests of central Africa. Also, some nut-bearing trees.

Sahintar means: grey-eyed god. Literally, god-eye-grey. Sah=god; hin=eye; tar=grey. Actually, this "god" was Gribardsun of *Time's Last Gift*. When asked by the aborigines (a miserable bunch then) what his name was, he replied, "Zantar." As we know, this was Tarzan's real name, ERB rearranged the position of the syllables for euphony. The aborigines had no z in their speech, and the name sounded so much like Sah-hin-tarh to them that that was how they pronounced it. It fitted, anyway. By the time the first novel opens, the aspiration had been dropped from the terminal r, and the two h's were regarded as one.

Sahintar is a minor character in the series, however, appearing in some as a deus ex machina and not appearing in others at all.

The two basics in creating the civilization were agriculture and language. I had to find some way or bringing in the plants that were needed; Sahintar is a convenient means, since at that time the few very small tribes that would have been in this area would have had no means for transporting the plants from Egypt to the near East.

I wanted to construct a non-Indo-European language, one which has no relationship to any other now known. And I wanted to set up a language which would be consistent and within which I would operate without discrepancy. So I've created the phonology, the syntax, the limitations, etc. When I get this all written, I'll send you a copy.

Similarly, the religion, architecture, social setup, artifacts, history, chronology, superstitions, etc. must be outlined to avoid discrepancies and to give the feel of a real culture. (When I get the history and chronology completed, I'll send you that, too).

Of course, the descriptions of Opar and its colonies (Xuja, Cathne, Athne, etc.) by ERB and your speculations in The Flaming God article determine the Karkhosan civilization. In addition, Haggard's Kôr and Zu-Vendis are shaping factors, since these will come in near the end of the series. Keep in mind that all these cultures have changed considerably since 10,000 B.C. and that they do not necessarily represent the original civilization. The architecture of Opar and Kôr represent the original, but the language, religion, and society will have changed.

Opar, by the way, is a non-Karkhosan word. It is meaningless; it is what the aborigines replied when first questioned by the Karkhosan explorer who encountered them. He asked them, "What do you call this place?" and they replied, "Opar." But they did not understand the alien speech, of course, and it is probable that Opar meant something like, "I don't dig your gibberish," or "Get to hell out of here."

My reconstruction of the original religion goes something like this. The Flaming God was a male, yet his chief vicar is female. How come? La is the head priestess, and the priests are subordinate to her. Nowhere else do we find a chief patriarchal god and a chief priest who is female. When the dominant deities are male, the dominant vicars are males. When they are female, the vicars are female. The cultures preceding the invading patriarchal Indo-Europeans and Semites were based on the worship of a Mother

Goddess, and the priestesses were the chief vicars. When, after a long struggle, the patriarchs succeeded in seating their male gods in the highest stations, female deities still had their temples and places, but they had a lower station (many were masculinized).

According to my reconstruction, the original Karkhosans worshipped a prime deity, Kho, the Earth goddesses. There were, of course, various aspects of her, goddess of the sea, the trees, of various plants, birth, fertility, death, etc. In an early stage of their civilization, when they were confined to the island of Karkhosa, a great earthquake shattered them. During this time, a patriarchal tribe, dwelling in the mountains above the northern shore (the present Tibesti mountains?) moved in, seized the main seat of power, and established a dynasty. The kings, however, retained power only by marrying a queen of the ancient blood, of the family which claimed direct descent from Kho and Sahintar. (This parallels ancient Egypt; no man could hold the throne unless he married a woman of divine blood. Hence, the custom of marrying sisters and even daughters; it was a device to ensure the right to the throne.)

The conquering tribe, by the way, had had contact with Sahintar. He had shown them how to make bronze. They called him Res-u, and in their mythology he was a son of the sun, which they visualized as a great bird with flaming wings. At the time of the first novel, *Hadon of Ancient Opar*, there is a power struggle going on between the priests and the priestesses. There is a widespread prophecy, originated by the priestesses, that if Kho is supplanted, She will destroy the land with a great earthquake.

Our hero, Hadon, asks Sahintar if this is true, and he is shocked when Sahintar says that the land will be destroyed and the people of Karkhosa will be scattered. Only Opar will be spared, and its people will become beasts.

After the cataclysm, the religion of Opar evolves into a compromise; the Flaming God is male but his chief representative is a female. She, always called La, is Opar's insurance against another cataclysm. La, by the way, is the changed form of the original: Laleela. The last two syllables were dropped.

After the original earthquake and conquest, the Karkhosans spread out from the island, first to the northern shore and then along the west and east sides of Kemu. They establish cities and towns and absorb the aborigines, some of whom speak related tongues and some of whom speak entirely unrelated languages.

I'm going to modify your map. It seems to me that it would be more realistic if there were not such a wide opening between the Kemu and the Kemunarpeth (the Chad and Congo seas). There would be a low mountainous barrier with access through a narrow chasm created by the original earthquake. Or perhaps the travellers between the two seas have to go through a valley. I haven't made up my mind yet.

Theoretically, the king of Karkhosa has suzerainty over all the peoples along both seas. Hence, his boast that his rule extends over the waters from where the sun rises to where it sets. And hence La's statement, based on a misunderstanding of an ancient and necessarily distorted legend.

The Karkhosans do not have bows and arrows. Originally, they did, but both religious and civil authority tabu them now. The myth goes that during the early years of conquest by the Sons of the Eagle (their name for themselves), their king shot the high priestess with an arrow. He dropped dead immediately thereafter (probably from a heart attack if the story is true), and a plague followed in a few days. Kho is supposed to have forbidden the use of the arrow thereafter. This may or may not be true, but the situation is that archery is forbidden. However, in the religion, Sahintar is always depicted as carrying or using a bow.

As I said, the king of Kharkhosa claims to be the chief ruler. Actually, the history of the land is full of revolts by various cities against the king, and during the course of the series other revolutions will occur. And while all cities do pay tribute, in practice are independent. There are also wild hill tribes that raid the country or are hard to keep in hand.

Narpethsa, the city founded by the original explorer of the southern seas, is in a very strategic place. It commands the gateway to the southern sea and hence the flow of commerce between

Opar and the cities of the northern sea. It had revolted twice and been put down with great slaughter of the citizens. When the first story opens, it's been quiet for a long time, but the king has ambitions.

Another major character is Khonan, Hadon's giant somewhat mad cousin. Khonan comes from Kho and nan, slave. Slave of Kho. Originally, I was thinking of making him a takeoff of Conan, but now he'll be based on Hercules and Gilgamesh. Hadon has a lot of trouble with him; in fact, everybody does.

That's all now. More later. Feel free to comment. All the above is subject to change, of course. I've made a dozen since I first started to think about it.

Kaor,

Philip José Farmer

WHITE WHALES, RAINTREES, FLYING SAUCERS
PHILIP JOSÉ FARMER

Several of the previously unpublished stories that have appeared in the pages of *Farmerphile* are representative of a period when Phil had not yet begun to write the works of science fiction and fantasy for which he is now so well known, respected, lauded, and loved. Perhaps more than any other examples of his writing, the following two selections—one an essay, and the other a reply to that essay—illustrate Phil's complex, often seemingly paradoxical feelings about writing science fiction and fantasy versus mainstream literature. Here Phil tackles a debate that, over fifty years after he so craftily dissected it, still rages today across the blogosphere: Can science fiction and fantasy be considered good literature, or must it by definition be relegated to a literary ghetto? But so many of the opinions regarding this hot button issue expressed by today's blog pundits seem childish and facile compared Phil's handling of the topic. What is so rare, so cuttingly insightful about Phil's monologue, no, *dialogue* on the question—for between the essay and the reply, Phil carries on a conversation with himself—doubtless lies in his own exceptional ability to balance and fuse the best qualities of both genre and mainstream throughout so much of his fiction.

Collectors of Phil's work may find the history behind this essay and accompanying reply as interesting as their contents. While *Farmerphile*'s main raison d'être is to make available previously unpublished works by Philip José Farmer, upon occasion we have seen fit to print a work that is so rare as to make it virtually unobtainable for even the most diligent prowlers of eBay. "White Whales, Raintrees, Flying Saucers" might not at first seem rare, as an essay under a similar title, "White Whales, Raintrees, Flying Saucers . . ." (collectors, note the ellipsis), appeared on the inside cover of the July 1952 issue of *Fantastic Universe*. The latter essay, though containing some of the same content, clocked in at just shy of 450 words as compared to the former's over 2600 words. This longer version, along with the curious reply, appeared in the Winter 1954–1955 issue of the now obscure fanzine *Skyhook*.

It may also be of no small interest to Farmer aficionados that a third, unpublished version of the essay exists, one only slightly longer than the *Fantastic Universe* version. In fact, the third version of the essay was already prepared for publication in the present issue of *Farmerphile* when the longer version was fortuitously located and obtained. The unpublished medium length essay exists only in manuscript form in the collection of Robert R. Barrett, who also provided *Farmerphile* with the previously unknown manuscripts for "The First Robot" and "Duo Miaule," which appear in this issue for the first time anywhere [page 525].

As for the rebuttal which follows the essay under the title "Parables are Pablum: A Reply to Mr. Farmer, A Letter to Mr. Campbell," it would take over fifty years for the item to appear in Farmer bibliographies. No doubt this is because it was attributed to Tim Howller, whose literary debut in *Skyhook* would precede by nineteen years his appearance as a fictional character in Phil's short story "After King Kong Fell," and by fifty years his published appearance in "The Face that Launched a Thousand Eggs" in the premiere issue of *Farmerphile*. Leave it to Phil to create his own fictional author to critique himself!

P arables travel in parabolas.

And thus present us with our theme, which is that science fiction and fantasy not only may be as valuable as the so-called mainstream of literature but may even do things that are forbidden to it.

Why forbidden? Because parables soar in parabolas. And science fantasy (by which term we will mean both science fiction and fantasy in this essay), being in essence *parabolic* forms, may shoot over barriers which often stop the flight of earthbound *straight* fiction. They adopt certain modes of presentation forbidden to the main-stream and thus strike us harder with their insight.

A definition of a good story should be one that includes both mainstream and science fantasy. The elements that make one excellent also make the other. Any good story creates order out of the chaos of this universe and invests it with a meaning we readers had not noticed before. Entertainment, always the red blood of any good story, comes from the slight and pleasant shock of having our awareness-threshold raised by the author's skill in shaping new patterns of values for us. Or in presenting at a different angle old values so they catch the light in a new splendor.

What do we mean by values? For the limited purpose of this essay, we'll define them as the grasping for good and evil, the tossing away of evil with one hand while we hang on to the good with the other. God and the philosophers know that the problem of value is the most complicated and meandering of all for the reason that it takes in the whole universe, including God and the philosophers. So far, the PhD's who specialize in axiology have not ever succeeded in agreeing on a definition of value. We'll use a makeshift and admittedly arguable definition.

What is good and evil? Good is herein defined as that which breaks down without physical violence the walls that keep out the growth of human life and love. Thus we include all the physical, mental, and spiritual aspects. Fertile fields enough so no one goes hungry; soap and medicine enough so no one need go dirty or ill; science that searches for youth and immortality; love that makes us worthy of living forever so we do not sicken of the sight and rumor of each other and of ourselves.

Good is a growing and protean thing, an evolution of values. It searches and questions, and what once was thought to be good is found evil and goes on the scrapheap of the past. Yet the things that it throws away are the secretions and barnacles that have never really mattered, though we at one time thought they mattered the most. What remains is what all men, with the exception of a few diseased societies, have at least given lip service to. The old cliché, the old thumping from the pulpit, remains. Love thy neighbor as thyself. The rest is background noise, where it should be silence.

One is strongly tempted here to wander off into an analysis of the direction society should take in an effort to make the Rule a living thing. But such a discussion would be too long and would also digress from our theme. It should, however, be clear to any thinking person that man has always tried to throw up walls to hide this Rule. Most of his social inventions have been to make his love a private garden, an exclusive thing, a curbed and bitten thing. Claims to have *the* divine revelation, to be *the* chosen people, to have *the* skin color, to have *the* property rights over land and woman and child, and all the rites and laws and violence that armor and propel these claims: these must be shed like last year's skin. As if there weren't more than one divine revelation, as if all men weren't chosen by God or weren't a peculiar people, as if sun and fog didn't regulate the correct amount of pigment, as if the earth weren't mother to us all, and as if man, woman, and child should not be free to swim in the ocean of love, up or down, to whatever level they breathe easiest in, to whatever school they feel most at home in, not fearing hate or violence . . .

We've digressed enough. Yet the above was necessary so that one may see that when we speak of values, we are not speaking of garments or baggage but of the naked and vibrating flesh, the Golden Rule. If this sounds stuffy and pompous, one can only plead that the subject is a grave one and doesn't demand a laughing face but a steady and unprejudiced eye.

We maintain that the universe is a chaos out of which our senses abstract a world of value. Our thirst for moral values makes us abstract a moral world as well as a physical and mental one. We ignore facts and factors that might interfere with our vision. Thus we see and feel a solid table, though with a keener sense we might see the atomic particles that whirl about each other and get dizzy hanging over the infinite abysses between them. Most of us also allow our children to be smutted and frozen with the beliefs that sex is somehow a sin, that black skin tarnishes status, that war could not be wiped out in one day, yes, one day, and that we could not defeat famine in twenty-five years. All this we allow while ignoring the fact that there have been and are societies which have solved at least temporarily most of our major problems. We refuse their values. Inertia is our original sin.

Most of our fiction, good and bad, is devoted to a reaffirmation of that to which we pay lip service. Even straight adventure fiction displays the conventional values; we follow Hairbreadth Harry, and, if the taleteller's skill is adequate, we are, for the time being, Harry. Courage, strength, skill, keen wits—these primitive but desirable traits we want and admire in our hero. But the pleasure we get from the average story is soon lost. We forget it. The story to which we return is that which gave us a shock because it shaped a new pattern of values.

"Why didn't I think of that? I've always known it, deep down!" we exclaim. Or we say, "What a great truth I've been blind to till now!"

Of course insight without drama is lost; there must be a story-telling skill on the writer's part. But drama without insight is also lost. We know that life is many conflicts, and we hope there's a solution for each. Or at least that the struggle was worthwhile because it meant something. The good writer has a sense of joy even when giving you a dismal play. In the midst of grime and blood and bucking the Juggernaut he says that you are more than just a spark blown upward into the night. Or even if he says this, he says that there is a delight in burning; that the night is brighter for your tiny glow and will not be the same again, though you turn to cinder.

Our major problem here is, can science fantasy fit the definition of good fiction? Can science fantasy wave its magic wand and conjure from chaos a meaningful value-laden picture? Answer: yes. Any bad fiction, no matter the genre, is a wild exercise of the imagination which explodes in the night of our minds, makes garish pyrotechnics, then dies, leaving the night blacker than before. But good fiction is a steady light, even if sometimes a small one. By it we walk without stumbling, and we may return at any time to see under its flare other topographical features we did not understand the first time. (If you say that most of science fantasy is just that, garish pyrotechnics, we can only reply that so is most of mainstream literature. But there are many science fantasy stories that do raise our awareness threshold.)

Thus, a story that deals with unicorns and virgins, demons and talking animals, faster-than-light spaceships, self-conscious robots, or other mythical creatures and creations is not necessarily bad fiction because it uses devices we know do not or cannot exist. If the story clenches the hard core of truth or flashes a facet of life not realized before, it is good. And its magical paraphernalia, far from obscuring its goodness and truth, are the very things that bring them out. Parable in form and essence, sprung from the fairy tale, fable, and myth, it travels in parabolas. Its very mode makes it more than just a jag of fancy. It demonstrates beyond disproof and far more vividly than the so-called realistic down-to-earth story that we are mad if we pursue the White Whale to our destruction; that even if we do find the lost raintree we'll lose it at once unless we keep our innocence; that flying saucers may equate the remoteness of the stars with the abyss of loneliness between each human; that if you do not put a perfect trust in the one you love you will make her less than human; that even if you can't possess the moon yourself you can have no greater love than to break your heart getting it for others.

And always, a good story—science fantasy or no—shows you a hero with whom you can identify. Win or lose, he wrestles with a giant whose mask, no matter how fantastic, conceals our arch-friend or arch-fiend, the recognizable universe.

We need further clarification. Why should science fantasy's peculiar modes of presentation let it soar like flying missiles over reality's limitations and strike from the skies deep into the heart of things with a speed and precision it would not otherwise have?

Our answer is that it is for the very reason that it ignores that which the realistic tale says is impossible. It uses unreal devices to strip reality to its real core, showing us that what we thought was fantastic is not really so. Thus, there was a time when a story that used rays to photograph the living skeleton and organs in action and a voltage detector to graph the waves released by the brain would have been classed as fantasy. Just as a story today in which members of a group use ESP and TK as a means to become a symbiosis, a many-in-one and more than human, is classed as fantasy. Yet what mainstream story has so well struck us with beauty and terror and the possibilities in loving cooperation, or in the power for evil if a symbiotic group has no conscience (another word for love), as Sturgeon's *More Than Human*?

Sturgeon can surpass mainstream limitations because he uses unreal powers to show us the real web of flesh that hangs invisible in the air and pumps blood to all of us from the same great heart. He shows us so well that the result is almost unendurable in its impact. We not only feel the beauty and the evil; we quiver as if he had rubbed a file across our nerves. This is no ordinary tale of people striving to cooperate; these are one flesh and blood in the literal sense, and if one member revolts, he becomes a cancer. And by reading we realize that a man without love is truly a cancer in humankind's body.

Examples are becoming increasingly numerous in the science fiction and fantasy fields; time and space prevent a listing of the better ones and what they have accomplished. The reader who is familiar with the fields, modern and classical, may easily recall many. And I believe that he can take any theme presented in the mainstream and find that, where fantasy treated it, it has more impact *because* of the fantasy. This statement should be taken with the caution that the fantasy must have been written by a good writer. Not necessarily a professional science fantasy writer. Almost all great and near-great writers have experimented in fantasy and almost always have produced an opus that ranks with the best of their mainstream opera. Thomas Mann, Feodor Dostoyevsky, Herman Melville, Charles Dickens, Franz Werfel, Honoré de Balzac, William Shakespeare, Christopher Marlowe, Henrik Ibsen, Nathaniel Hawthorne, Leo Tolstoy, Aldous Huxley, Robert Graves, A. Conan Doyle, Oscar Wilde, Robert Louis Stevenson, Mark Twain, even Somerset Maugham, that cynical and down-to-earth writer. The list is long.

Though the reader may say that some of those named are not great but only prominent, they are at least that and have made a mark on literature. Moreover, some of the fantasies of these greats are still read and anthologized—often in preference to their weightier and more solidly terrestrial works. It is as if the mask they fashioned to put on the face of common things is more ugly or more beautiful than that which it covers because it shows more starkly and startlingly the lines and lineaments we were not able to see before. The classical masks of Tragedy and Comedy are not real faces; they are gargoyles; they leap out and strike us with their essence.

Under science fantasy's unorthodox wrappings, even orthodoxy takes on a new look. Witness Werfel's *Star of the Unborn* and C. S. Lewis' *Out of the Silent Planet*. They take us to far times and places so that we may get a perspective on what is around us now and perhaps even convince us unbelievers that we are missing something in not embracing orthodoxy. Such is the impact of sf when dealing with a world too much for us.

Fantasy we have had from the beginning of man's language. Science fiction, I believe, is only an extension of fantasy, based on science because nowadays we accept the miracles of science but not the existence of mermaids, unicorns, demons. The old myths have lost their force; they are trying to forge new ones. The same psychic powers that created the old are still operating, but they must work through fresh forms.

The writer of science fiction is a pioneer, he has to create "out of chaos a dancing star." I believe that he may do so, but his burden is a difficult one. He has been discredited as a prophet—a role that should never have been his—and it is up to him, not to prophesy, but to invent. Not technological inventions, for he lacks the detailed knowledge of science and access to laboratories, even if he has the inspiration. He must use his knowledge of the workings of the human heart, plus the findings of psychology and social anthropology, and from these pick and choose the social forces that will mold plastic man into a free creature who loves and is free of sin because he loves.

There are many writers in the science fantasy field who will never be anything but hacks, who have the ability to make money in it because they have a brighter imagination than the average writer in other fields. But there are a few who have the insight and energy to create new social institutions—or rather, models of them—and who will display in their fiction how these may be arrived at.

And when these maps for new institutions are drawn, then

the many readers of science fantasy—the engineers, technicians, anthropologists, psychologists, educators, intelligent laymen—will begin to exert their not-inconsiderable influence on society. Slowly but inevitably as the force of mind itself, western civilization will be guided along the new roads. And if this happens, the people of the dawning era will owe much of the understanding and abundance to the once-despised and neglected field of science fantasy. The White Whale will have been harnessed; the raintree found again.

Parables are Pablum
A Reply to Mr. Farmer a Letter to Mr. Campbell
Tim Howller

Torn between bluenosed moralism and rednosed unmoralism, between the faraway thin call of the trumpets of science fantasy and the loud meaty blast of mainstream, Mr. Farmer shows us that he is of no firm conviction. He has left himself so wide open to criticism, and has been so vague, that one is quite sure he is consciously or unconsciously hoping he will be argued out of adherence to sf's claims.

Mr. Farmer's thesis that parables travel in parabolas and thus hop over obstacles that wall in mainstream literature is not at all well founded. From conversations I've had with him I know he can present many more detailed arguments for his thesis. I know that he thinks also that science fantasy will eventually influence the thinking of our intellectuals and technologists and that sf is the best persuader for bringing about the type of society he desires. Mr. Farmer is no fanatic, though there may be statements in his article which might fool one into thinking so. He desires changes, but without violence, and, knows that they may never come about or will do so centuries, perhaps, after we are dead.

He knows that the efforts to divert society into desirable channels will have to be titanic. He realizes that he is no titan, not even a small one. He knows his life on earth may be a relatively happy one if he confines his moralizing and reforming to literary fields. It is hard enough for a man to get food, drink, books, and love. To dedicate one's life to bucking the sociological Juggernaut is to get crushed or be forced to become a Hitler or Calvin. None of these fates is desirable; it is best to accept the limitations of one's self and of humanity at large.

Nevertheless, the angry man has to express himself. Otherwise he burns himself out inside like a smoldering log, or suddenly bursts into destructive flame. Mr. Farmer is at times an angry man, because he is an idealist and a romanticist. Fortunately he has at times a sense of humor, a saving grace which enables him to realize that few things are serious enough to get ulcers over, including literature; and to realize that anger doesn't necessarily make you a good writer, especially if you make the mistake of forever writing about things that madden you. Every writer should—and will, if he's capable of doing so—write for the sheer joy of it, with no moral in mind. Such stories will make one laugh and result in nothing more than a good digestion and firm nerves. And these are quite enough for most of humanity.

For the purposes of this reply to Mr. Farmer, the above considerations are digressive. We are to consider the main thesis. My counter is that mainstream may not only do anything science fantasy can but can do it better and reach a larger audience. Not only that, but those who devote the bulk of their reading to science fantasy are filling their bellies with pablum and refusing the lifegiving meat that is theirs for the taking.

First, I'll agree with Mr. Farmer's definition of a good story: that it creates order out of chaos and invests it with a meaning we had not noticed before. Addendum: that he means by a good story one that has become a classic—or has a good chance of becoming one. Further addendum: that any good story is one that is "blindly seeking with a six inch blade to reach the fathom-deep life of the whale." Mainstream literature is a sharper blade and has more muscles behind it, that's all.

I must protest against Mr. Farmer's choice of *Moby Dick* and *Raintree County* as examples of moralizing fantasy. Moralizing, yes; fantasy, no. Though both novels use fantasy, they work with it merely as a device to put across certain scenes or ideas. The dream sequences in *Raintree County*, the lower case mr shawnessy, the epic fragments from the Cosmic Enquirer, the raintree itself, border upon fantasy, but upon analysis are seen not to be really so. They are exaggerations of what do occur in life.

Just so *Moby Dick*. Here the characters are not realistic in that they are not merely lifesize: they are giants who walk and talk as men never did. Even the mechanically-souled and mediocre, the Starbucks and Flasks, are titans. The men are large as whales, and Moby Dick is great as a mountain. The soliloquies, the stowing away of the Parsees, Queequeg in his coffin, and many other events seem fantastic. But the work is not a fantasy in the sense that we use the term. There is little we can point to and say is impossible. So vast is the work, so overwhelmingly detailed and passionate, that we are convinced where a thinner opus would leave us shrugging with disbelief.

And that brings another point. I am surprised that Mr. Farmer didn't elaborate Dostoyevsky as a fantasist whose works support his thesis. Dostoyevsky uses fantasy to great effect. Such things as the Legend of the Grand Inquisitor, the devil from space who taunts Ivan Karamazov, the saint who had to walk across the galaxy before he could reach heaven—these are characteristic. Moreover, his characters, though not as large as *Moby Dick*'s, are bigger than life; whirlwind events that would take years in real life are compressed into a day; everybody pours out Niagaras of confessions as if they'd been injected with some science fiction truth drug; their dreams are obviously too feverish and contrived to be natural; and many of their motivations can be explained only by saying that Dostoyevsky is writing psychological allegories.

But here, as in *Moby Dick*, it can be shown that there is an explanation which requires only a moderate straining to swallow. And if it is true that both Dostoyevsky and Melville wrote other stories that were pure fantasy, that is beside the point. Their great works are not in that class. *Mardi* and *Pierre*, *The Dream of a Ridiculous Man* and *Crocodile* are not the best work of these two.

What they have done, as have many other authors, is to

incorporate fantasy as a minor device to facilitate certain aspects of their fiction. This, in a way, falls in with Farmer's thesis that fantasy is more striking because it uses modes of presentation forbidden in the mainstream. Agreed. But the fantasy is never used without a possibility of a realistic explanation. Ivan's dialog with the devil could be a projection of his tortured conscience working through his fever; the Grand Inquisitor is a philosophical prose-poem; whales have in fact destroyed whaling ships; Ahabs do try to punch their fists through the visible walls of this universe.

Let's take the other examples mentioned by Mr. Farmer in his article. I read them as "Saucer of Loneliness" by Theodore Sturgeon, "The Lovers" by Philip José Farmer, "The Man Who Sold the Moon" by Robert A. Heinlein. The first is a very moving and poignant story, albeit syruped over with too much sentimentality, as many of Sturgeon's stories are. However, he succeeded in doing what he set out to do, and did it beautifully. The result was—as William Atheling, Jr. pointed out—an original and inspired treatment of flying saucers in which Sturgeon conjured up loneliness with all the artistry of which he is capable, and that is quite a lot.

As for the second, we might wonder why Mr. Farmer could not resist the auctorial egotism of including one of his own tales. We won't, for writers are notoriously publicity-seeking and proud of their own stuff. If they weren't, they wouldn't be authors. I doubt if anybody but Mr. Farmer saw the moral he obligingly points out in "The Lovers." I doubt if he knew it when he wrote the story, or even thought of it until he wrote the article. That it's there may be seen, but it is so buried under a multitude of other things that only a philosopher could deduce it. Nor does the story rank with the other two sf works for smoothness and craftsmanship, though it does, I think, in characterization. It's to be hoped that Mr. Farmer will smooth out the novella for its book publication and develop the wogglebug society as a picture of a desirable society. It is easy enough to portray a puritanical charitableless state; it is most difficult labor to show a convincing utopia.

"The Man Who Sold the Moon" illustrates quite well the point I wish to make. It is not, I believe, a science fiction story.

Though it takes place in the future, it could be *any* time. It is really the story of a man who had an ideal and who moved heaven and earth to make it come true, even though he had at times to subscribe to the ethics that the end justifies the means. The story could just as well have been about a man who wanted to buy a forest land for the use of the people as a public park, or a section of tenements to be remade into a wonderful housing project. That the moon is here a fusing of the symbolic and the literal, as it is in the best of fiction, is a proof of Heinlein's artistry. But the work is not science fiction, for it could be taking place today, and has little of the scientific in it.

Though Heinlein's appreciation of the worthwhile artistic things of life seems to be rather poverty-stricken and philistinish—at least as stated in a recent autobiography in *Imagination*—those who have read him know he is a consummate craftsman with a genuine sense of life. Also, they know he is able to touch the emotions with a few simple words, whereas the consciously artistic and poetic Ray Bradbury fails in this. Bradbury evokes our admiration because of his lyric lines and economy, but he misses the springs from which well tears. Heinlein touches them in a deceptively simple manner. Sturgeon also succeeds, though less often and with more striving for effect. The striving is smooth, but it is worked up to through a complex symphonic method. Heinlein is uncomplicated and uses straightforward, unimpassioned, unepigrammic prose. There is no exploring such as Sturgeon's; no unpeeling of layer after layer of personality, motive, and action until the core lies glistening-wet and naked before us. Heinlein drives straight to the heart and brings the tears—a gift much to be envied; even more so when one considers that he has done his best emotional work in the so-called juveniles.

The fact that Heinlein used the moon in the above-mentioned story did not make it science fiction. Sturgeon, Farmer, and the other writers who put across their various themes could have done even better if they had tried the same thing in mainstream literature. I, for one, would like to see Theodore Sturgeon abandon sf for a while and bring his artistry to mainstream. If he wishes to communicate loneliness and absence of communication, could he not use ordinary people in an ordinary situation, instead of in an unreal situation? Could he not reach a larger audience and reap greater financial returns, thus stimulating him to even higher reaches of artistry, if he tried to work with people as they are and threw away the paraphernalia of magic and pseudoscience?

Could he not use the vehicle of a missent letter instead of a flying saucer? True, it is an old old vehicle, not nearly so original as a disk from space. But missent letters can and have happened; the event is grounded in old Mother Earth.

And what about his favorite theme of symbiosis? Couldn't he show us much more of the evils and good in symbiosis, and teach us how to attain such a state, if he were to apply his literary magic to the Smith family who lives on Elm street? Sturgeon has come to us with a Sermon on the Mount, dressed in a strange disguise and hidden behind a monstrous mask. Couldn't it be just as strange and unconventional if presented to us as a solution to the Smith's dilemma? Undoubtedly that inside-out, Alice-in-Wonderland insight, and passionate prose could be applied to a run-of-the-mill problem to solve it in a way only Sturgeon could. And we might learn and take to heart a rule for our own guidance.

Sturgeon wants to overthrow old idols and hard walls that corrupted and channelled true love. Why, then, shouldn't he move into a larger world, now that he has long ago served his apprenticeship in science fantasy? He has something to say that is worth hearing; let him say it to as many ears as possible and not keep his dreaming jewels in the hands of a few. It is time for him to develop into the first-rate and important novelist he could become.

There are any number of professional sf writers who have served their apprenticeship, who have gamboled long in the joyous waters of science fantasy and who should be ready to take a plunge into other seas. One thinks of Isaac Asimov (who shows an increasing skill in characterization), Damon Knight, Algis Budrys, Cyril M. Kornbluth, Poul Anderson, Arthur C. Clarke,

Fritz Leiber. Why couldn't these men, who have talent both in exploring ideas and portraying character, who have empathy and compassion, transfer to that larger world? There their works will have more chance of bringing wider rewards in readers, money, and endurance.

I mention endurance because science fantasy is rather ephemeral stuff. Little of it deserves to be called great, except in the relative sense of comparison to others of its genre. And those few tales that do tower above the rest were written by non-specialists in science fantasy: *After Many A Summer Dies the Swan*, *Watch the Northwind Rise*, *Earth Abides*, *The Sword in the Stone*, "Peer Gynt," "The Tempest." A curious and debatable mixture, I'll admit. And there are exceptions among the authors: Swift, Rabelais, Cabell, and Dunsany. These specialize. But the first two had to use fantasy because of censorship; Cabell has said nothing he hasn't said in the first of the Manuel cycle, though he has said it extremely wittily and in perfectly polished prose; Dunsany has a wider range—some of his stuff is likely to be read a hundred years from now. Still, he is an exception, and his impact will never be forcible.

Before I hear cries of "Prejudice!" let me say that I love both science fiction and fantasy, that I shall probably read them as long as I've eyes to see, that I do think they have their place in literature. But I wish that those sf writers who love the genre so well they refuse or are afraid to venture into mainstream would take the plunge. Use your golden imaginations and unpeeling insight and ability to shape ideas to take the earth-rooted man and show him as he is and ought to be and *how* to be so—but in terms that everybody will understand and believe. And if you must write science fantasy, let it be a spark blown off the central wheel—bright and joyful, yes, but only a by-blow.

Those who insist that science fiction is the best medium for introducing sociological innovations may find their playground in *Astounding Science Fiction*. For years Mr. Campbell has claimed to be looking for just such authors. But these authors will have to convince him to overthrow some of his taboos, such as those involving sexual situations, and to quit using stories in which parapsychological powers play such an important part in reconstructing society. Or stories in which extra-terrestrial beings overthrow Earth by one little idea.

Such fiction is quite harmless and safe for Mr. Campbell to offer because its basic concepts and situations are so far removed from reality.

Would *Astounding* dare to print a story which depicted a future Union of Colored People, an organization with principles like a labor union which struck against racial discrimination? Such a story would be science fiction because it would be concerned with a sociological invention, one which was an extrapolation from a present day institution. To me such a story would be far more fascinating than one about a star-begotten prisoner of Earth who subtly infects and overthrows his captors' barbaric government with a few well-chosen words.

Would Mr. Campbell dare print such a work, one that might strike a spark in the mind of a Negro sf reader and launch such a movement? And would the many PhD's and technicians among his readers accept such a story? They applaud the narrative of the persuasive philosophical alien, and say yea to liberal and humanitarian views. But what if there is a real and very close danger that the dark-skinned alien who makes enough money to afford the high rents in Dr. Jones' neighborhood will move next door to him and there will be little Dr. Jones can do about it?

What about it, Mr. Campbell? You've long had a vision of changing our culture, of directing it toward the right goals through the medium of your magazine. You estimate that you reach at least 100,000 readers whose influence on our culture is tremendous in many ways: engineers, technicians, psychologists, sociologists, anthropologists, newspapermen, students, intelligent laymen. If they become infected with your ideas, they will pass them on in turn to those who haven't ever heard of your magazine, to educated and uneducated kaffirs alike. Eventually the fictive shadows depicted in ASF's stories will take on legal substance.

There is little difficulty in your present day offerings because most of them lack the fire and heart to convince and stimulate your readership. The characters are too often cardboard figures, and the situations are set in a time and place that doesn't concern us. Such stories are intellectual exercises, and with a few notable exceptions not even good exercises. What about asking for stories set in the near future, based on slight extrapolations of present day living facts, and served with a sense of drama and of flesh and blood?

You have said that you are not too much interested in the literary value of your offerings. What about *becoming* interested? Without literary value your stories will fail in even getting close to your goal of influencing your influential readers.

What about thawing out the icy taboos that have slowly frozen ASF's lifeblood? Compare the quality of the stories Isaac Asimov has been writing for you with that of the stories he's writing for H. L. Gold. Why are those for *Galaxy* so much better? Can it be that Asimov feels your restrictions cramp his style, even if unconsciously so? *Fantasy and Science Fiction* and *Galaxy* have improved or at least maintained a high level. F&SF has presented us with solider and meatier sf stories, tending Campbellwards (the old style Campbell, that is). *Galaxy*, unfortunately, has been running too many light and cute stories, but Mr. Gold's touch is not lost. The hand of Midas glitters yet; there are strange and wonderful things to be read; one blows off the foam and gets to the dark stuff.

ASF has, as a whole, been getting drier and staler and even amateurish, declining steadily for two years. If there are exceptions, such as Tom Godwin's very moving and human "Cold Equations," they form a tremendous contrast to the other presentations and make us ask why we don't get more like them. Yet, ASF is the only magazine that would have published the magnificent "Mission of Gravity," by Hal Clement. Other editors would have cried, Too slow, too dragging, too technically overburdened! And the very fact that you will give the space to develop such a story and do not at all mind a full, microscopically detailed development is encouraging. Perhaps you will allow a writer as much space and time to exhibit character, and the full growth of a psychosociological idea, as you allow for a physical idea.

The point is, "Mission of Gravity" is innocuous, from our viewpoint. It shakes nobody, has little relation to man on Earth. What about a sociological "Mission of Gravity," one as minutely concerned with psychological forces as with physical, as inventive and revolutionary? What about a voyage through another dark and heavy world—*this* world—explaining its perils, suggesting how to slay its dragons? Clement's crawling protagonist revealed his universe; let's get a worm's eye viewpoint of this Earth as we know it.

With the mainstream techniques that writers have learned in your rival magazines, plus the freedom allowed in ASF for symphonic development of an idea, you could do with your magazine what you have always wanted to do. Should western culture—eventually world culture—arrive at peace and under-standing and abundance, it may do so because of the influence of your magazine. And, to go back a step, because you used the despised and neglected science fantasy as your medium, and borrowed the best of mainstream to make the best of possible worlds.

That, Mr. Farmer and Mr. Campbell, is the only way you will harness the White Whale and find again the lost raintree. Realize that flesh and blood man on heavy and dirty earth is himself a parable and his own moral.

Sherlock Holmes & Sufism—
& Related Subjects
A Speech to the Baker Street Irregulars
Philip José Farmer

It is fitting that the following speech about The Great Detective and his possible connections with Sufism was uncovered just as preparations were being made for the first printing in over thirty years of Phil's classic Holmes-meets-the-Jungle-Lord pastiche *The Adventure of the Peerless Peer* (included in *Venus on the Half-Shell and Others*, Subterranean Press, 2008). Throughout the years Phil has worked extensively with The Canon, both as a professional writer and as a fan, so it is not surprising to discover that he gave a hitherto unknown speech on Sherlock Holmes. The subject of the speech, however, if not surprising, is at least extremely intriguing, for here Phil combines his enthusiasm for Sherlockiana with his longstanding fascination with Sufism.

What little is known about the history of the speech must be gleaned with a bit of Sherlockian detection from the speech itself. Phil apparently presented the talk before a local scion of the Baker Street Irregulars in El Paso, Texas—which, with help from both George Scheetz and the BSI Trust, we have identified as The Mexborough Lodgers—during the first half of 1975, the timeframe being indicated by Phil's mention of the upcoming Doc Savage film release in the summer. Phil also mentions he had been in Burbank, California, just prior to flying down to El Paso. This likely places the speech in January 1975, as a citation in *Locus Magazine* indicates Phil, who was residing in Peoria at the time, was to be at an autograph party in Los Angeles on January 11, 1975. January is also the month when the Baker Street Irregulars hold their annual dinner to celebrate the birthday of The Great Detective.

Members of the Baker Street Irregulars, fellow guests, I am indeed honored to be here. And rather happy about it, too. This is for me a unique occasion—so far. This is the first time I've ever spoken at a BSI occasion and is, in fact, my first attendance at one.

I hope that this is the first step, or prelude, to a closer association. I am not a member of any scion, but I hope that some day I will be invited to join one. Unfortunately, my residence is in Peoria, Ill., located about halfway between Chicago and St. Louis (or St. Lewis, if you prefer). It would tax my time and money to travel to monthly meetings. But the main problem is that, so far, no one has invited me to become a member—a consummation devoutly to be wished for.

Perhaps it's just as well. I didn't pass an on-the-spot examination re Holmesiana. Though I've read and reread the Sacred Writings since 1929—the first two stories in that year were "A Scandal in Bohemia" and "The Red-Headed League." I have a bad memory. I'd have to swot for some time before I'd be able to pass a verbal examination. I do better on written tests anyway.

As some of you know, my lifelong interest in Holmes and Watson has resulted in certain unsacred writings. There is much about the immortal twain and related persons—in my biography of Lord Greystoke, also known as Tarzan. Another biography, my *Doc Savage: His Apocalyptic Life*, also contains certain material about Holmes, and his great enemy, Professor Moriarty.

In addition, my science-fictional novel, *The Other Log of Phileas Fogg*, has as its chief antagonist, or villain, that spinner of dark webs, Moriarty, not to mention lesser villains from the works of Jules Verne and R. L. Stevenson.

All three books, by the way, owe much to Professor William Starr, a distinguished member of the Sons of the Copper Beeches, Philadelphia, Penn.

In addition, I have contributed an article to the *Baker Street Journal*—"The Two Lord Ruftons"—in which I pointed out a connection between Brigadier Gerard and Lady Frances Carfax. Gerard, it scarcely needs mentioning, was one of Napoleon's most famous soldiers. Possibly he was also the dumbest.

And then there is my recent, *The Adventure of the Peerless Peer*, in which I achieved my long-desired ambition to bring together Holmes, Watson, and Lord Greystoke. Not to mention G-8, the Shadow, a zeppelin, and certain descendants of certain friends of Allan Quatermain.

I plan a sequel in which Holmes and Watson are deeply involved in a mystery in Ireland—during which they fall in with Leopold Bloom, whose biography was written by the famous J. Joyce. One of the persons the three encounter is, of course, an Irishman named Finnegan.

I have also written into a movie treatment a Holmes-Watson vignette. I returned from Hollywood—or Burbank, to be precise, only two days before setting out for the equally exotic land of El Paso, Texas. With George Pal, a producer at Warner Studios, I worked out—and wrote—a treatment for the second Doc Savage movie. A treatment is a story, in essence, a prose outline on which the script is based. Doc Savage is the hero of 181 pulp magazine novels published during the 1930's and 1940's. He was equal in popularity to the other pulp magazine hero—the Shadow.

Bantam Books began reprinting the Savage supersagas in 1965, and these were so popular that George Pal purchased the options to all 181 novels. Pal, for those of you not familiar with movie producers and directors, made such films as *The Time Machine, War of the Worlds, Destination Moon, The Naked Jungle*, and *The Wonderful World of the Brothers Grimm*.

The first Savage movie, *Doc Savage: The Man of Bronze*, is ready to be shown in the summer. I had nothing to do with that; Mr. Pal and I couldn't come to financial terms.

The second movie, however, *Doc Savage: Archenemy of Evil*, will, I hope, be all a Savagephile could desire. I mention it only because I wrote into it a Holmes-Watson vignette.

While Doc and his fabulous five aides are crossing the Atlantic in their fabulous dirigible, Doc sends a radio message to England. This is to one of the men who taught him the art of criminal detection. The Great Detective, in fact.

Doc wants to find out all about the fabled long-lost city of

Tasunan, located somewhere deep in the Sahara. The Great Detective, now retired, has written a not-so-trifling monograph on the language of the now-extinct Tasunanians.

And so the camera zooms across the seaside Sussex Downs. It closes on a small villa, outside of which are rows on rows of bee hives.

The camera then enters the villa, where Watson is visiting Holmes. Holmes is playing his violin when someone knocks at the door. It's a messenger, delivering Doc's wirelessed inquiry.

Holmes, talking to Watson, reveals that he tutored some promising pupils after he retired. Doc Savage was his best student. He tells them how and why Doc Savage was dedicated by his father to the battle against crime. Doc's father is James Wilder, the illegitimate son of the Duke of Holdernesse.

The scene ends with Holmes opening a book he's removed from a shelf, his monograph on the Tasunan tablet.

I must warn you, however, that it is possible that the scene will be cut before the film is issued. Exigencies of money, movie-length, etc. and the external and infernal interferences from the financial backers—not to mention their wives and mothers-in-law—not to mention the major actors, who are very jealous of any time taken from them—might result in deletion of the vignette.

Let us hope not.

And now to the main subject, *Sherlock Holmes and Sufism*. First I must beg your indulgence. Between the time I was told I'd be addressing you, and the time I boarded the plane for El Paso, I had no time to write this discourse. I was too busy. In fact, I wasn't sure what the subject would be until last Tuesday. It was on that day that I wrote this. The next day I left for Texas.

Thus, I had no opportunity to do extensive research. But I plan to rewrite this part of my trifling effort when I return to Peoria. I will then submit it to Dr. Wolff for possible publication in the *Baker Street Journal*.

As you know, there has been—is—much controversy about Holmes' activities during the Great Hiatus—between May 1891 to April 1894—according to William S. Baring-Gould.

There's no need to go into detail re this before this body of Sherlockians.

Holmes wandered far and wide, mostly in Asia and Middle Asia and northeast Africa, while hiding from Col. Sebastian Moran and his gang of black-handed, red-handed villains. According to what he told Watson on his return ("The Adventure of the Empty House"), he travelled for two years in Tibet, amusing himself by visiting Lhassa and spending some days with the Head Llama. (Incidentally, Watson amused his readers by spelling Lama with a double-l. Though Watson did have a sense of humor, this is undoubtedly one of the many examples of Watson's difficulty with spelling. This orthographic disease is not unknown among many present-day medical doctors, present company excepted, of course.)

Presumably he visited Tibet because of well-established interest in Buddhism.

He then passed through Persia, looked in at Mecca, and paid a short but interesting visit to the Khalifa at Khartoum. Various scholars have objected to the whole account. The late great Edgar W. Smith maintains that *no* European came anywhere near the forbidden city of Lhassa until 1903. And then the penetration of the holy city was made by force of British arms. I say—true, if you count "historically recorded" visits. But Sherlock Holmes was a master of disguise. Just what disguise he could have used is a subject for an article itself, so I won't go into that here. And, possibly, the Head Lama or Regent had read Watson's adventures, though not in Tibetan translations.

He knew of Holmes, after all, "I hear of you everywhere—" and would also know of Holmes' interest in Buddhism.

However, my interest here is on Holmes' visits to Persia, Arabia, and the Sudan. That is, among *Moslems*, not Buddhists. Again, objectioners maintain that Holmes would not have travelled through these countries. Persia was in the midst of troubles: all English and Russians were suspect, since both Great Britain and Russia were struggling to gain ascendancy here. A civil war was raging in Mecca. And the Caliph of Khartoum, Abdullah, would have been more likely to execute any Englishman than to have a friendly chat with him.

But Mr. Benson Murray, an authority on Persian history, poohpoohs Mr. Smith's statements. He presents documented proof as intense or widespread as Mr. Smith claims.

As for Mecca, Mr. Murray maintains again via histories of that period, that there was no civil war in Mecca, merely a struggle between the Ottoman (or Turkish) administration and the Sheriff of Mecca.

Nor were visits to Mecca by Europeans unknown. Twenty-eight (and Holmes' visit) were made between 1503 and 1931. The most famous was probably Sir Richard Francis Burton's Hadj (or Pilgrimage), in 1853. Burton went half-disguised as a half-Persian, half-Afghani hakim (or physician). I suggest that Holmes adopted a similar disguise. Indeed, he may even have prepared himself for this trip by conversing with Burton himself. But this would have been before 1890—the year of Burton's death in Trieste. This speculation, again, will be the subject of a separate article.

We know—or can safely assume—that Holmes' visit to Tibet was inspired by his interest in Buddhism.

But why would he go to Persia and Arabia and Egypt? What was his interest there?

I suggest that it was because Sherlock Holmes was as intrigued by Sufism as Buddhism. Perhaps even more so.

First, what is Sufism?

Webster's New Collegiate Dictionary–1963–defines *Sufi* thus: n. [Ar. sufiy, lit. man of wool] : a Muslim mystic.

The *Encyclopedia Britannica*–1964–contains a page and a quote on *Sufism*. Summarized, it states that Sufism (tasawwuf) is formed from Sufi, applied in the second century of Islam to men or women who adopted an ascetic or quietistic way of life.

It was originally a practical religion, not a speculative system. It is pantheistic. It was heavily influenced by Christianity and Buddhism.

Both *Webster's* and the *Encyclopedia Britannica*, I regret to say, are generally wrong. Sufism, if I am to believe the writings of those who should know, the genuine Sufis of medieval and modern times, is not ascetic, quietistic, nor pantheistic.

Nor is it confined to Muslims. Nor has it been so heavily influenced by Christianity and Buddhism. On the contrary, the influence, the countercurrent, has been much more in the other direction.

And it is true that, though Sufism originated in Arabia, it existed before the birth of Mohammed. It was given an impetus and somewhat revised shape in Arabia during the first two centuries after Islamism was born. But its chief shaping, and propagation, was done by the Moslemized Persians.

It is not ascetic. Though genuine Sufis practice moderation, they do not disdain tasty food. They may marry and often have and do. They can even have four wives. But they are wise, and I've not come across any record that a Sufi ever had more than one wife at a time.

They do not retire from the world to contemplate their navels or live in celibate monasteries. They may withdraw for periods. But they are usually out among them—to use an old Yankee phrase—working in and with people, dealing with life as it is, where it all hangs out. It is, in a sense, an autocratic discipline. This doesn't mean that its candidates are drawn only from the upper crust of society. Man or woman, peasant, fisherman, wealthy merchant or king, black, white, yellow, or brown, Christian, Jew, or Moslem, you can be a Sufi.

But its autocracy consists in this. No one can become a Sufi unless that person is accepted by a Master, one who has himself been the disciple of a Master. The way is long and hard—though not always. Many come to the Master—few are chosen. The Master separates the sheep from the goats, the potential Sufi from the nonpotential.

A Sufi may be a mystic—one who seeks for the ecstasy of direct apprehension of God—or of the True Reality. But this is neither the ultimate—nor even a necessary—goal.

I'm afraid that at this point I must eliminate much about

Sufism which will be in the article. There just isn't time, and I may have stretched your patience already.

So—what is there to indicate that Sherlock Holmes went to Persia, Arabia, and Sudan because he was interested—perhaps intent on—learning about Sufism?

One clue. Holmes' final words in "A Case of Identity," which took place in 1887.

Holmes says, to Watson: "You may remember the old Persian saying, *'There is danger from him who taketh the tiger cub and danger also for whoso snatches a delusion from a woman.'* There is as much sense in Hafiz as in Horace, and as much knowledge of the world."

Hafiz (or Shamsuddin Mohammed to give him his natal native) was not translated in its entirety into English prose until 1890.

Miss Madeline B. Stern (in her *Sherlock Holmes: Rare Book Collector*) suggests that "we must assume that Holmes' copy was either the 1800 Hindley edition of the *Persian Lyrics* printed in Persian and English with verse and prose paraphrases and a catalog of the Gazels, or of the fine 1875 edition containing a verse rendering of the principle poems by Bucknell."

This is fine and dandy, but what about the French and German translations? [I haven't tracked these down yet.] What about Holmes having read Hafiz, a great Sufi poet, in the original? Holmes was an accomplished linguist in French, German, and Italian and probably was competent in Russian. And a man who can write a monograph on Chaldean roots in Cornish must know more than somewhat about Celtic and Semitic languages. Persian is not Semitic (though it uses Arabic writing) but is Indo-European, from the parent tongue of English, German, Sanskrit, Russian, etc. But Holmes may have been as well acquainted with Persian in the original as he was Latin. And as I'll demonstrate in the proposed article, he may have learned much from Sir Richard Francis Burton both about Persian and about Sufism. Burton claimed to be a Sufi, and he wrote a long Sufi poem, the *Kasidah of Haji Abdu el-Yezdi*, nine years before the publication of Fitzgerald's translation of *The Rubaiyat of Omar Khayyam*. Omar, by the way, was a Sufi. Khayyam, meaning Tentmaker, did not indicate that this distinguished mathematician and astronomer made tents. Khayyam had a hidden, or esoteric, Sufi meaning. And Fitzgerald's translation is inaccurate and almost totally misleading.

Holmes certainly did not go to the Mideast or Africa to learn about Moslemism per se. He would have visited Persia, and Mecca, and the Khalifa to learn about Sufism. He would have sought out, and talked with, Sufi masters in Persia and Arabia.

As for the Khalifa, I doubt he was a Sufi. He was a religious fanatic, bloody, violent, narrow-minded, a Wahhabi fundamentalist. But he would at least have had knowledge of local Sufis, and Holmes may have been directed to these by the Khalifa.

Also, this particular visit may have been partly inspired by Mycroft. Holmes' brother would have wanted to find out about the situation in the Sudan. Holmes, always an economist, could have combined a personal mission—a religious one—and a political mission.

Holmes was plainly a somewhat changed man after the Great Hiatus. We hear no more of his cocaine, or of excessive smoking, or of his drinking. And despite what Watson said, he is better tempered, has become more compassionate and tolerant. He even professes a faith in a personal God.

Some have attributed this to the influence of Buddhism during his Tibetan stay. I doubt it. I think that Holmes would have been repelled by the practice of Buddhism in Tibet. Just why I will detail in the proposed article.

I attribute the change in his temperament and attitude to his brief—but powerful—contact with the Sufi masters. Aided and abetted by his readings of Sufistic literature—however. He was not with the Masters long enough to have become a Sufi himself. Not nearly long enough.

But I do suggest here—and will maintain more specifically in the article—that he did suffer a partial strange sea change. And that it was because of Sufism.

JONGOR IN THE WOLD NEWTON FAMILY
PHILIP JOSÉ FARMER

Farmerphile readers are familiar by now with the incredible treasure trove of filing cabinets in Phil's basement. The following discovery was made on a short trip to honor Phil on his 90th birthday in January 2008.

Devoted Wold Newton fans, rejoice! For what follows is an excerpt from *Doc Savage: His Apocalyptic Life*, Addendum 1, "The Fabulous Family Tree of Doc Savage (Another Excursion into Creative Mythography)," which for unknown reasons did not make it into the final published manuscript. A scan of Phil's handwritten family tree accompanies the text.

The character Phil adds to the Wold Newton Family with this unpublished excerpt is Jongor (John Gordon) from the series of pulp novels by Robert Moore Williams: *Jongor of Lost Land* (*Fantastic Adventures*, October 1940), *The Return of Jongor* (*Fantastic Adventures*, April 1944), and *Jongor Fights Back* (*Fantastic Adventures*, December 1951). All three were reprinted by Popular Library in 1970. Jongor is a Tarzan pastiche, a jungle hero who inhabits Lost Land, a hidden world in the interior of Australia, complete with dinosaurs and evil denizens of the ancient and lost civilization of Mu.

If Wold Newton investigator Mark Brown had known about Phil's research, he doubtless would have synched up with Phil's lineage for Jongor in his own essay "The Magnificent Gordons" (*Myths for the Modern Age: Philip José Farmer's Wold Newton*

Universe, MonkeyBrain Books, 2005). As it is, Brown's studies led him to conclude that Jongor's father Robert Gordon was the grandson of Artemus Gordon (from the television series *The Wild Wild West*); Artemus Gordon was in turn the great-grandson of Sir Hugh Drummond and Georgia Dewhurst, who were exposed to radiation at the Wold Newton meteor strike in 1795.

Phil's research indicated that Jongor was a Wold Newton Family member through both maternal and paternal lines. While Brown identified Jongor's mother as an Australian, Margaret Dundee (no doubt a relative of Mick "Crocodile" Dundee), Phil discovered his mother was Elizabeth Rivers, a great-granddaughter of Sir Hugh Drummond and Georgia Dewhurst. Jongor's father Robert Gordon, as seen in Phil's handwritten family tree, was a direct descendant of Fitzwilliam Darcy and Elizabeth Bennet (from Jane Austen's *Pride and Prejudice*), both of whom were at Wold Newton in 1795.

Phil's graphic, which is really an extension of the family tree in *Tarzan Alive*, does not make it explicit, but Delhi Darcy, shown as a descendent of Fitzwilliam and Elizabeth, would have to be a granddaughter, not a daughter. Elizabeth Bennet was born in 1772 (she was not yet 21 during most of the events of *Pride and Prejudice*, which takes place September 1792–Late Autumn 1793 in the Wold Newton timeline). Delhi Darcy was born in 1825 and it is very unlikely that a 53-year-old woman could bear children in the early 19th century. Delhi must be the daughter of Fitzwilliam and Elizabeth Darcy's son, Fitzwilliam Bennet Darcy, as laid out in *Tarzan Alive*; Delhi would be a sister to Athena Darcy. Connecting Phil's text and handwritten family tree, Delhi must have married—de Gordoune, the fifth Lord of Lochinvar; the marriage produced William de Gordoune, the sixth Lord of Lochinvar. The rest of the handwritten paternal family tree leading to Jongor is self-explanatory.

Maybe one day a Creative Mythographer, perhaps Brown himself, will reconcile the two lineages.

Two more short notes about the unpublished text . . . Phil begins with, "A third member of the family might have volunteered for the expedition if Doc could have located him." Conceivably Phil is referring to a possible expedition back to the Earth's center to face the denizens of Hell, as described at the conclusion of the final chapter of *Doc Savage: His Apocalyptic Life*. It also bears mention that the bit in the unpublished fragment about Sir Hector Brandon being a thorough rotter did make it into the final published manuscript, slightly altered. It can be found on page 186 of the Doubleday hardback edition, and on page 210 of the Bantam Books and Playboy Books paperback editions.

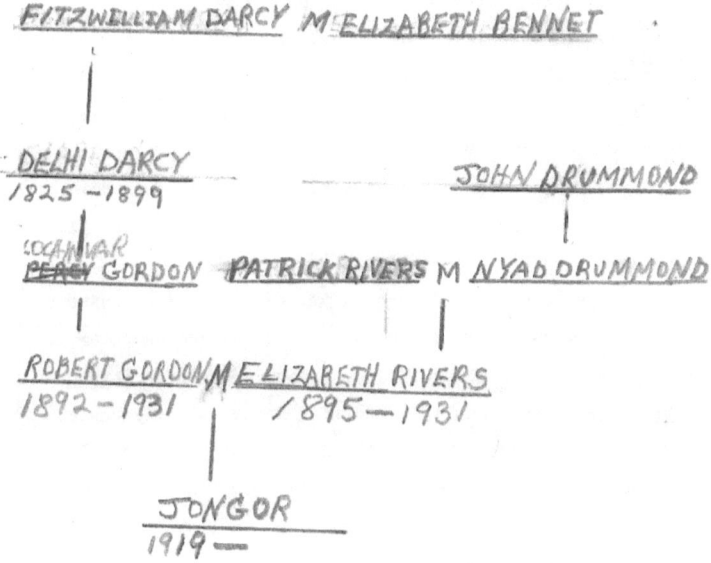

Philip José Farmer

INSERT 258B

A third member of the family might have volunteered
for the expedition if Doc could have located him. This was
Jongor (John Gordon). His father was Captain Robert Gordon,
an ex-naval aviator for the United States.
Robert Gordon was descended on his mother's side from the
ancient Welsh families of Moore and Gronow and on his father's
side from the Scots Gordons. One of his
ancestors was a Macgregor, the infamous Highlands outlaw,
Rob Roy. (Sir Richard Francis Burton was also descended from
him.) Robert Gordon was a member of a branch of the house of
Earlston, sprung from Alexander, the second son of William
de Gordoune, the sixth Lord of Lochinvar. Through
this line Robert Gordon was a descendant also of the youth
immortalized by Sir Walter Scott. He was related to George Gordon,
Lord Byron, through Byron's mother, a daughter of George Gordon
of Gight, county Aberdeen. and also through
the Reverend Richard Byron, the poet's great-uncle,
who married a Mary Farmer.

Jongor's mother, Elizabeth Rivers, was the daughter of
Patrick Rivers and Nyad Drummond. Nyad was the daughter of
John Drummond and Oread Butler. (See adendum 2 of Tarzan
Alive for their genealogy.) Patrick Rivers was the uncle
of Patricia Rivers, who married a Sir Hector Brandon of
Brandon Abbas, Devonshire. Grey eyes seemed to have run in
this family, if P.C. Wren's Beau Geste is to be trusted.
Sir Hector was a rotter but of the landed gentry and was
a scion of a family whose head was Sir Charles Brandon

224

WILD WEIRD CLIME
BALTICON 11 GUEST OF HONOR SPEECH
PHILIP JOSÉ FARMER

Philip José Farmer has been the Guest of Honor at sixteen (mostly science fiction) conventions and has given speeches at countless others. Well, sixteen we know of; since Phil didn't keep track and every so often someone writes into Phil's website telling of yet another con Phil spoke at, often as Guest of Honor.

Even more tragic, Phil did not keep copies of most of the speeches he gave. What we wouldn't give to be able to reprint "SF and the Kinsey Report," the speech he gave at Worldcon 11 in 1953! Or "Now it Can Be Told, the Truth about Kilgore Trout," from the first RiverCon in 1975.

Luckily, however, a handful of Phil's speeches have been preserved. The speech at hand was given in April 1977, during the height of Phil's popularity. He had recently gotten over the writer's block that had stalled the Riverworld and the World of Tiers series for several years, by the trick of writing stories by various "fictional authors," and was still basking in the glow of science fiction's greatest hoax, *Venus on the Half-Shell*. Though still at work on his "fictional-author" series, his gaze turned inward toward the science fiction community at large in the project he speaks of here. It's not surprising, knowing Phil the trickster, that there was some crossover between them.

The title of my speech is: *Wild Weird Clime*, a phrase from Edgar Allan Poe's *Dreamland*. Let me quote the first stanza.

By a route obscure and lonely,
Haunted by ill angels only,
Where an Eidolon, named NIGHT,
On a black throne reigns upright,
I have reached these lands but newly
From an ultimate dim Thule—
From a wild weird clime that lieth, sublime,
   Out of SPACE—out of TIME.

Wild Weird Clime is also the title I've picked for a projected novel. Despite the title, it's not s-f. It'll be a mainstream novel about the wild weird wonderful exasperating troubling many-colored multivaried world of science-fiction and fantasy. I'll be outlining the novel to you.

Some novels about the s-f world have been written. *Herovit's World* by Barry Malzberg is probably the most outstanding. It's very amusing but its range is limited. Its protagonist, like Kilgore Trout, is a sadsack s-f author. Unlike Trout, Herovit is talentless, a genuine hack. Like Trout, he's a miserable cynical person, without any graces whatsoever, social or otherwise.

I have met a few writers like Herovit in the s-f field. But he or she is a *rara avis*, untypical.

Though I've enjoyed the novels about the s-f world, I've been dissatisfied with their narrow range. None make any attempt to cover the entire spectrum of this literary-human phenomenon. None explore thoroughly the wild weird clime, the islands of the sun and darkest Africa, the heights of Mount Everest and the deeps of the Pacific. The Leif Ericsson, the Columbus, the Magellan and the Sir Richard Francis Burton of s-f have yet to make their voyages by sea or foot.

It'll be dangerous for the explorer. One, his voyages may be criticized as lacking in verisimilitude. Two, they may be denounced for having too much verisimilitude. Three, he may be ostracized. Four, he may be sued. Five, he might not find a publisher.

Ignoring the consequences, I'll write this epic cum travelogue cum gossip column. My qualifications are these. One, I've been reading s-f since 1926. Two, I've been involved in the s-f world of writers, fans, editors, publishers, artists, and critics since 1952. Three, I've met hundreds of the denizens of the s-f clime and have known, more or less intimately, both the great and the small.

I won't use my own name as the byline because this is a mainstream novel. My name as author would mean the book probably would go automatically into the s-f section of bookstores. I'd like to reach those readers who haven't had a chance to see the s-f world in all its darkness and glory, its grisliness and beauty, its strangeness and mundaneness. In short, its rich uniqueness.

So, what byline to use? I can't use Kilgore Trout, since Mr. Vonnegut would be afraid that people would think he'd written the book. Trout wouldn't know anything about the s-f world, anyway. Jonathan Herovit isn't capable of writing anything but low-grade space opera. There is the byline of Jonathan Swift Somers III, but that's too long and elegant.

I've thought of a byline. Tom Wode Bellman. Let me give you the derivations. Tom implies, to me, anyway, Tom O'Bedlam, Tom of the Madhouse. I'm especially thinking of the disguise of Edgar, the Duke of Gloucester's son in King Lear, who pretended to be a madman, poor old Tom. "Wode," W-O-D-E, comes from an Old English word meaning "insane" or "mad." From the same Germanic root as Woden or Odin, the chief god of the Old English and the Old Norse.

"Bellman," of course, recalls the bellman in Lewis Carroll's *The Hunting of the Snark*, subtitled *An Agony in Eight Fits*. Bellman is another word for a town crier. He is also the captain of the ship and the organizer of the hunt for the snark. Tom Wode Bellman would also have some of the characteristics of the nameless amnesiac who joined the bellman's crew.

He, if you'll recall, walked with bears and joked with hyenas. In a sense, Tom Wode Bellman will be doing just that.

Let me refresh your memory by quoting some stanzas from Fit the Second, The Bellman's Speech. These are appropriate to the project.

The Bellman himself they all praised to the skies—
Such a carriage, such ease and such grace!
Such solemnity, too! One could see he was wise,
The moment one looked in his face!

He had bought a large map representing the sea,
Without the least vestige of land:
And the crew were much pleased when they found it to be
A map they could all understand.

"What's the good of Mercator's North Poles and Equators,
Tropics, Zones, and Meridian Lines?"
So the Bellman would cry: and the crew would reply
"They are merely conventional signs!"

That last line, by the way, represents to me an essence of s-f. As a literary genre, it ignores conventional signs. Or at least attempts to do so.

"Other maps are such shapes, with their islands and capes!
But we've got our brave Captain to thank"
(So the crew would protest) "that he's bought us the best—
A perfect and absolute blank!"

Well, I don't think that a novel about the s-f world is a ship whose captain has a map which is blank. Some explorations have been made. But I hope to fill in the blank, chart the whole s-f world, go boldly where no man has gone before.

By the way, the protagonist's name will also be Tom Wode Bellman, since this is to be a künstlerroman, a novel about the artist's life. It's a biographical novel, but I assure you that I am not the hero. I'm too inhibited to be the vigorous, bustling, brawling, aggressive, hustling lead character. I suppose some of you are thinking now: Who is it? Harlan Ellison? Harry Harrison? Sam Moskowitz? Ed Earl Repp?

Tom Wode Bellman is a combination of many people. And,

of course, he's not just an amalgam, a figure put together of elements from here and there, that and this. Imagination will be applied to make him a truly fictional character. That is, a real person.

But, if a *Wild Weird Clime* is a künstlerroman, it's also a historical novel. And it's also a bildungsroman, a novel of educational information. In addition it contains some elements of the picaresque novel.

The structure. Should it be episodic instead of straight-line? With such a varied world, populated so heavily by so many colorful people, how can you avoid an episodic novel if you are to show the s-f world in all its variety? But, though *Wild Weird Clime* is an attempt to portray reality, it is fiction. Fiction, at its best, is the compression, the restructuring, the opening of reality to reveal the inner side, the hidden face, the underpinnings, of reality. Writing fiction is somewhat like trying to turn an inflated rubber balloon inside out without untying the neck or allowing the contents to escape. Or it's trying to punch through what Captain Ahab called "the unreasoning mask."

In essence, an impossible task. But some get further than others.

In order to convert almost all facets of the s-f world, and yet keep the novel from becoming a mere travelogue, it's necessary to involve the protagonist in each facet. In the beginning was light. In the beginning was also the fan, the very young goggle-eyed reader of s-f. This will be Tom Bellman, who reads his first s-f magazine story in 1926 with the first issue of *Amazing*. He's only eight, but even though he's a precocious reader, he doesn't understand many of the words in the stories. Nevertheless, he is ecstasized by the illustrations—and what he does understand of the stories also carries him out of himself.

In 1929 he encounters the first issues of the fabulous *Science Wonder* and *Air Wonder* magazines with the exotic Paul illustrations. (You see, this novel is going to emphasize s-f art almost as much as the s-f prose, since the visual impact of s-f approaches the verbal. Especially to the young reader. I haven't forgotten the transports of wonder, the imitations of alien beauty, which the Paul covers gave to me.)

However—there's a structural problem here. Should the story begin at the beginning, as Lewis Carroll's King of Hearts advised the White Rabbit? "Begin at the beginning and go on till you come to the end: then stop."

That's good advice. A straight-line sequence story gives intensity. Just as seeing all the action through the eyes of only one person gives intensity and drive to a story. But in this case I'll probably ignore the King's wise words. I think that in this novel it's better to plunge into the waters, deep though they may be, in the middle of his story.

Our hero is a mess, emotionally, financially, maritally, professionally, ethically. And then as the story progresses, from that point we get flashbacks. These range from his first meeting with magazine s-f at the age of eight to recent events. But these incidents won't be called flashbacks. They'll be in separate chapters titled: *Time Travel, 1926. Time Travel, 1948. Time Travel, 1965.* Etc. This is a legitimate device, since memory is the only possible form of time travel.

The aesthetic problem is: How to get Bellman involved in the entire s-f world, both geographically and chronologically, without the novel becoming a mere tour through a land of essentially static marvels. Such as too often, it must be confessed, happen in the stories of the Gernsback era.

So, Bellman is a man who wants only to be a writer and who naturally gravitates into the writing of s-f. He's a footloose person who would still like to put down roots. Some day. He has a certain stability of character yet is subject to a certain amount of uncertainty, anxiety, egoism, and loneliness. He gets over his initial Don Quixote naiveté but is always too impulsive, rushing in where angels, and E. E. Smith's evil Eich, fear to tread. He's loquacious, often too much so.

He's a liberal, a humanitarian, but he isn't above using current causes or movements to advance his own career. He hates hypocrisy but has to admit that he sometimes is a hypocrite, though he hates himself when he is. He loathes the politics inherent in the writing field and in the s-f writers' organization but his impulsiveness and his hatred of injustice and double-dealing hurl him headlong into situations a cooler head would avoid.

He's born and raised in a small Midwestern city, but when he's thirteen his father moves to the East Coast. And there he joins his first fan club. Later he goes into fanzine publication. One of the fans he meets is Reynard Sheets, nicknamed "Short." Sheets becomes a card carrying Communist, a real firebrand. But he gets expelled from the Cosmoteers Club by Samson "Bullhorn" Tantor, a stentor-voiced young man whose chief ambition is to be the foremost historian of American s-f. And this at a time when American s-f has no history. In later life Sheets becomes an editor, then a publisher, and a devout proponent of capitalism. He has no qualms of conscience about underpaying his writers or taking advantage of them in trickily worded contracts.

Bellman also meets R. Dubious Warfield, who's destined to be an engineer and a prominent s-f writer. He'll be noted chiefly for his humorous fiction, which is strange, since he himself has no sense of humor. But he mechanically takes notes on what makes people laugh and somehow manages to transpose its essence onto paper. Though he can quote whole chapters from Greek and Latin classics, he can't remember the names of people he's met many times. Bellman and Warfield tangle because Bellman can't stand Warfield's air of superiority and his cold aloofness. It's not until many years later that Bellman comes to understand that Warfield is concealing a deep sense of inferiority under this arrogant attitude.

You see, this novel not only will show how s-f itself changes from its beginnings but will also show how Bellman himself changes. Generally, though not always, for the better.

Bellman makes enemies when he publishes his scornful invective-laden editorials and reviews in his fanzine, *The Cosmic Snort.* One of these insulted fan-writers assaults Bellman and damages Bellman's right eye. It's this defect that later gets Bellman a 4-F classification in World War II.

Just before the war, Bellman moves to Burlington, Iowa, where a group of fans are working for a munitions factory. They all live in a rundown house which is something out of Charles Addams by Gahan Wilson. It's owned by a perverted old lady who looks like the bride of Frankenstein's monster. The residents call it The Spam Shack. *Spam!* was the title of the great Preston de Tove's blockbuster serial which had just ended in the magazine *Superior Science Tales*, edited by the great Kenneth Tory MacTarb. Its hero was a spam, a telepath mutant persecuted by the inferior normals, the beastly bourgeoisie. Naturally, all s-f readers identified with spams, since they felt, with considerable justification, that they were regarded as bordering on the abnormal and the persecutable because of their love for the despised subliterary genre, s-f.

The Spam Shack was ahead of its time in being a pre-beatnick, pre-hippie commune. Bellman quickly becomes one of The Spam Shack's accepted inmates—I mean residents. During his stay The Spam Shack is visited by the controversial Hoosier fan Klass Kingman. Kingman is a wild character who preaches the new faith, which he's originated himself. That is, s-f fans are actually a type of mutant, a superior mutant of course. Through s-f, the fan superbeings are destined to rule the world—to be benevolent despots.

Kingman was not only arrogant, he was downright obnoxious, though many fans rather liked his idea they are some sort of spams.

Kingman has neither home, kith or kin. He survives by traveling from fan group or individual to fan group or individual, getting free rent and food and occasionally into the fans' girl friends or wives.

Because of Hitler's distorted preachings of Nietzsche's philosophy, Kingman has chosen a bad time to spread his own faith about the superman potentialities of fandom. I won't go into detail here, but in the novel Bellman and spammates get rid of Kingman. They get him drunk one night and chloroform him, and when he wakes he is bound and blindfolded and being driven around in a car. His abductors are disguised and speak in altered voices.

Having confused him sufficiently, they drive back to the Shack and take him to a room which has been fixed up to look like Dr. Frankenstein's laboratory, including a club-footed hunchbacked assistant. Bellman plays the part of Dr. Cyclops; another the role of Dr. Moreau. And so on.

They tell him he's been judged to be a criminal, and they are members of a secret society, consisting of medical doctors and chemical professors who have spent some time in a mental institution. They've long had their collective eye on him and are now going to operate on him. Their own criminal predilections were cured by brain-operations, so they're going to remove the gland responsible for his insane behavior. (They got the idea for this from the Doc Savage novels, of course.)

After they've opened his skull and excised the gland, they'll send him to a rehabilitation institution where he'll become a respectable citizen. After a suitable display of artificial thunder and lightning and more menacing talk, they anesthetize him. During the process the pseudo-Dr. Moreau is accidentally anesthetized. They carry the unconscious Kingman out and deposit him inside an abandoned house on an island in the Mississippi River.

That's the last anyone ever hears of Klass Kingman.

The knowledgeable among my audience recognize that there was a character like Kingman and there was, not the Spam, but the Slan, Shack. However, both the location of the shack and the identity of its residents have been changed. I'm not using anybody who actually lived in the Shack. They're my friends. Anyway, by making up the Spam Shack characters, I get more leeway in their use.

The Dr. Cyclops-Dr. Moreau incident actually occurred, though not in the s-f milieu and not to the person called Kingman.

Bellman marries one of the Shack's habitués, the first of his five wives. He sells two stories to *Fabulous Scientific Stories* and one to *Thrilling Marvelous*. The Spam Shackers decide to move to Los Angeles en masse, where the weather is paradisical and the landlady won't insist on blowing all of them, male or female. Bellman, however, goes to NYC where the action, that is, the s-f magazine publisher, is.

His wife divorces him because he won't get a steady-paying job and because when he should be talking to her, he's either reading or working out a story idea. Besides, she caught him laying a young fan.

Because of time limitations, I'll skip all but the barest outline of Bellman's career. And by no means can I go into the galaxy of "characters" whom he encounters. I've counted the number of people I know more or less intimately in this field, and so far the number has mounted to two hundred ninety eight. Obviously, the problem here is one of selection and combination. Also, one of disguise. I don't want the reader screaming indignantly, ungrammatically and ambiguously, "That's me! That's me, the son of a bitch!" On the other hand, there will be many who'll be hurt because they don't recognize themselves.

Well, that's my problem.

There is also the problem of balance. As we all know, villains are more interesting than the good guys. Eccentrics are more stimulating than the normal. Absurd and dangerous situations get more attention than the mundane. However, in the richly-colored, many-faceted tumultuous world of s-f, even the normal will seem to the mainstream reader to be abnormal, alien. So a presentation of the s-f mundane to the mainstream reader will strike him or her as quite out-of-the-ordinary.

It shouldn't be necessary to include any but a small number of the bizarre, the near-mad, and the profoundly eccentric characters. And yet . . . and yet . . . should these characters be elided? I mean, what about the editor of a very successful and innovative s-f magazine who locks himself in his bedroom and conducts all his business there because he's suffering from agoraphobia? He's also convinced that there are beings from outer space, aliens disguised as humans, who are out to get his ass. He does come out to play poker with carefully screened friends, but he always wears a mask then, papier-mâché faces which resemble the features of his favorite s-f characters.

What about Lionella Jones, the beautiful young fan whose ambition it is to lay every s-f author and editor in the field—male or female?

What about Portia Oxford, the female s-f writer who's contracted a case of human bondage from a man whose lack of education and alcoholism makes her despise him at the same time she worships him? He's not even a high-school graduate, he doesn't understand s-f, he's unfaithful to her, he beats her. He drinks a gallon of muscatel a day, except on weekends, when he drinks two.

Should I excise the scene where she, her brutal lover, Billy Gowan, and Bellman are on a drinking spree? It's Easter, and so she gets Billy to buy her a giant chocolate rabbit, almost three feet tall. As they are going up the steps from the subway, Billy gets mad at Portia and knocks her down the steps with the chocolate rabbit. Bellman wrests the rabbit from Billy, and knocks him down. Billy gets a broken leg. Portia, instead of being grateful, chews Bellman out, and it's years before they become friends again. She nurses Billy back to health, whereupon he tries to throw her out of a third-story window.

Then there's Hobart "Hobie" Derrick. A man of many though imitative talents. Convinced he can outwrite any s-f author and not backward about saying so. A parasite, a sponger, a charmer whose charm soon wears off with close contact, a lonely and essentially pathetic but often unendurable man. An incredible stud who uses women for his own ends (no pun intended). A comic legend in his own time. How can I not use this character, yet avoid giving the reader the impression that he's typical of the s-f genre?

It's Hobie Derrick, by the way, who supports himself when he's down on his luck by writing *True Love Stories*. But he does this with a gimmick which I happen to know was actually used. He lifts a story from *True Love* or *Ranch Romances*, changes the dialog to action and the action to dialog, changes the name of the characters, and sells the story back to the magazine that originally published it.

Yet he'd rather starve than do this with an s-f story. It is true that it would be much more difficult to do this in s-f, but if he could do it, he wouldn't. Despite all his flaws and character, he does love s-f.

Then there's Caesar Barden, the man who writes poetry-prose, who preaches throughout his works love, compassion, empathy, the need for one lover to meld his/her personality with the other, the propagandist for the group mind. The writer of excruciating tenderness, of the need for hundred percent openness and complete down-to-the-last atom communication. The advocate of peace, pacifism and melting love.

Yet he has six wives and ten children, and he abandons his latest family whenever a new, young, and beautiful worshiper of Caesar Barden hoves on the horizon. He also carries a big switchblade knife and a pair of brass knuckles. He's a strange mixture of the Great God Pan and Jesus Christ, completely oblivious to the contradictions in his character.

Then there's Kenneth Tory MacTarb . . . No, I'll skip him.

But I can't forbear some words on Preston de Tove.

He's the subject of one of Bellman's fables. You see, throughout the novel, samples of prose from s-f texts are given. These start with sections from the Gernsback era and then illustrate, chronologically, the advances made in writing skill and attitudes as s-f itself advances through the years. In addition, we see some of Bellman's parallel-universe fables, little stories or sketches which he makes up in his mind but never puts down on paper.

This example of Bellman's fables is from a story to be printed in the new magazine *Popular Culture*, first appearing in May. The title is "The Impotency of Bad Karma" and its byline is Corwainer Bird.

Nick Adams, Jr. is the antihero, the s-f writer whose virility depends upon the type of fan mail, reviews, and critical articles directed at him. He's at a convention and has been invited to several parties by some of the big-name writers.

"Then, wonder of wonders, the grand old man, Preston de Tove himself, asked Nick to a very select party. De Tove was probably Nick's greatest hero, the man who'd rocked the s-f world in the 40's with his smashing *Spam!* and *The World of Zilch A.*

"De Tove, however, hadn't done much writing for thirty years. He'd been too busy practicing the science of mental health originated by another classic s-f author, old B. M. Kachall himself. This was M.P. (Mnemonic Peristalsis) Therapy, a psychic discipline which claimed to enable a person to attain through its techniques an I.Q. of 500, total recall, Superman's or Wonder Woman's body, and physical immortality.

"Fundamentally, these techniques aimed to keep your bowels one hundred percent open. To do this, though, you had to work back along your memory track until you encountered in all details, visual, tactile, auditory, olfactory, especially olfactory, your first bowel movement. This was called the Primal Urge, or P.U.

"Kachall had promised his disciples, in 1949, that all of M.P. Therapy's goals could be reached within a year. However, de Tove, like all of Kachall's followers, was, three decades later, still taking laxatives as a physical aid to the mental techniques. He had not lost faith, even if he did spend most of his time during the party in the bathroom.

"But de Tove had refused to go along with Kachall's S.P.L. Religion, a metaphysical extension of M.P. Therapy. Perhaps this was because de Tove had to wear a diaper at all times, and attendees at the S.P.L. services were forbidden to wear anything. In any event, the new religion required that the worshipper send his C.E. (Colonic Ego) back to the first movement of the universe, the Big Bang. If the worshipper survived that, he was certified to be an E.E. (End End), one who'd attained S.P.L., the Supreme Purgative Level. This meant that the E.E. radiated such a powerful aura that nobody would dare to mess around with him. Or even get near him for that matter. Aside from having to sit by an open window throughout the party, Nick had a wonderful time." End of quote.

Well, there's the Pumpkin Eaters Poker-Playing and Wife-Swapping Society, composed of New York-based writers, in the 1950's. But I won't go into that here.

And then there's Hendrik Dahl Juve, a real person, a Gernsbackian writer. One of his heroes identified a skeleton as female by counting the ribs. Knowing that God had removed one of Adam's ribs to make Eve from it, he deduced that a male skeleton would have one rib missing . . . Need I go on? That item actually appeared in one of Hugo's magazines, and he prided himself on the scientific accuracy of his publications.

To sum up Bellman's career, he's first a fan, then a fan publisher, then a member of a fan club. He is a member of the committee of a world convention in the 40's. He sells to the early s-f pulps. He becomes an editor and for a while works in an agency. (That section will be an eye opener.) He goes to Los Angeles, is forced to write porn for a while, becomes involved in movie and TV writing and also writes continuity for comics. He's an officer of SWOT, the Science Fiction Writers of Terra. (Another eye-opener, especially when he discovers that two big authors have, in essence, purchased the Quasar Award annually given for the best novel, novella, etc.)

In short, Bellman's career covers almost every aspect of s-f life.

At the end a world convention takes place, naturally. I say naturally because a world con is the focus, the epitome, the quintessence of s-fdom. It's the only appropriate setting in which to end the novel.

Bellman is pro guest of honor of the worldcon in Las Vegas. Finally made it after fifty-two years of citizenship in s-f and thirty-eight stormy years of writing s-f. A novel and a short story of his are up for a Hugo. But there's a crisis. He's been writing an autobiographical novel, *Marooned on the Third Planet*, and word has gotten out that it's unusually, perhaps actionably, frank and candid. The two big-name authors corner him. They want to know if he's going to describe just how they got their Quasars many years ago. I won't tell you his decision.

We find Bellman, shortly before the big banquet and awards ceremonies, looking out of his hotel window. He and s-f have come a long way, baby. He likes some of the changes, regrets others, though they were inevitable. Once s-f was a despised sub-genre—if an s-f story was good, then it couldn't be s-f, according to its snobbish critics, but there was a closeness, a camaraderie, a feeling of belonging to a select group—in itself a reverse snobbery.

But the small groups have expanded enormously, the small

cons where everybody knew everybody else, these exist only in small local cons and maybe not then. At one time it was not only possible to read the monthly output of s-f in a few days, you could reread your favorites again and again. Now the presses pour out a Niagara monthly, and you're lucky if you can read a tiny fraction of it.

It's embarrassing to run into an old friend who's written an award-winning story and have to admit that you haven't read it. Implication being that you probably won't.

S-f has ceased to be the homogenous closely-knit group he knew. It's become fragmented, splintered, specialized, divided into hardcore s-f readers, soft-core readers, Tolkienists, sword-and-sorcerists, comic-book addicts, avant gardists, Lovecraftians, cultists of various kinds, you name it. But then he has always known that s-f was a Protean phenomenon, ever-changing, growing, evolving. Though something has been lost, something has been gained.

Now the once-despised genre has become respectable. Over five hundred universities, colleges and high schools are teaching courses in it. Not that this is altogether good, since there are many teachers who really know little about s-f and some who even dislike it. But he isn't worried about these teachers perverting the tastes of their students or driving them from it. The true s-f fan won't be affected by such monsters.

He reviews the more infamous fan feuds, the Richard Shaver mystery which costs him one wife and some friends, dianetics and scientology, which he tried for a while, the old wave/new wave controversy, the political schisms, the feuds among authors, the SWOT shenanigans. His mind, time traveling, flashes past vistas of despair and ecstasy, humiliation and triumph, sordidness and bravery, hate and love, aspiration for the stars and mud on his feet, not to mention pie in the face.

He thinks of the old days of s-f, when science was a god or the magical tool which would bring about the ideal. Perfect health of mind and body, ease of living, immortality. Power! Power to get to heaven. But the way to heaven is through hell. It's not an either/or choice.

Now the emphasis is on ultrareality, the attempt to understand man's relationship to the universe. To go beyond language, understand the metalanguage even if we couldn't speak it. Perhaps, as with Tennyson and his flower, we could hold the all-in-all in our hands. This wouldn't enable us to control the universe, which includes ourselves. But it would enable us all to live with love, to become as angels are supposed to be.

Was this desire as wrong and as impossible as the earlier desire to gain power, omnipotency?

While thinking these and other thoughts, gazing out at the moon which he, as a boy in 1930, thought he'd be standing on in 1940, he has a mystical experience. He sees the whole universe and knows that *Homo sapiens* is, no matter what happens, one with the world. That everything has been, is, and will be right—though he doesn't understand the how or the why.

Then, wrapped in this glorious feeling, experiencing the ecstasy of the saints who've seen God, he leaves the hotel suite. And he stumbles over a tray of dishes on the floor and falls flat on his face.

But he picks himself up, wipes off the coffee and booze and mayonnaise, and he walks down the hall, if not cockily, at least jauntily.

I thank you.

Doc Wildman's Coat of Arms
Philip José Farmer

From Phil's essay "The Arms of Tarzan" and *Tarzan Alive*, we know of Phil's deep and abiding interest in heraldry, and the symbolism contained therein. While he published a lot on Greystoke's arms, less saw print regarding the arms of Doc Savage, aka Dr. James Clarke Wildman, Jr. In *Doc Savage: His Apocalyptic Life* (DS: HAL), Phil described the coat of arms of the Clarke Wildman family thusly:

> ARMS—Argent, a fesse chequy gules and azure, in chief an alchemical pelican between two fleams, in base a demisavage holding on his sinister shoulder a club. *Crest*—A demihuntsman proper winding a horn gules. *Mottoes*—Free for a Blast; Inicissimus Maleficorum.
>
> The latter motto means: The Greatest Enemy of Evil-doers, a very appropriate motto for Doc Savage.

This description formed the basis for Keith Howell's illustration on page 243, coupled with information in four pages of hand-written notes and drawings by Phil, showing his progressive research on the Clarke Wildman arms (including a lot of non-Clarke Wildman arms scribblings, such as notes for Mayfair and Rassendyll.) On the last page Phil writes essentially the lines from DS:HAL quoted above, demonstrating that these notes do indeed culminate in the final version. With additional research and educated guesses based on Phil's notes, there are a few "charges" (iconic images) added to Keith's final version, which are not reflected in Phil's quote from DS:HAL.

Not coming into this as heraldry experts, by any stretch, required a lot of study. What does this all mean? In heraldry, coats of arms have formal descriptions that are expressed as a blazon. Tinctures are the colors which blazon a coat of arms. Argent is the tincture of silver.

The escutcheon (also called scutcheon) is the shield in a coat of arms. A fesse is a wide horizontal band across the middle section of the escutcheon. Gules (pronounced with a hard "g") is the tincture of red. Chequy is a small alternating pattern of squares of two tinctures. A fleam is a handheld instrument used for bloodletting.

The fleams and the alchemical pelican evoke the cycle of life, blood, and rebirth. In this way, the alchemical pelican is similar to the Ouroboros. "The female pelican was believed to wound her breast with her long, curved bill, drawing blood to feed her young. For this noble act, the bird became a symbol of piety, self-sacrifice, and virtue. It also symbolizes the duties of a parent or parental love." *Somewhere in Tyme, Coat of Arms Charges* (www.familynamesonline.com/charges7.html).

A demisavage and demihuntsman are depictions of the upper half of the body of a savage and a huntsman; the symbolism in the context of the Wildman family is clear. The motto "Free for a Blast" is common among the arms of Clarke and Clerk families. With Phil's description from DS: HAL covered, two charges were added based on Phil's handwritten notes:

- A boar's head couped (a straight line at neck as if cut by a guillotine) sable (black), above the fesse chequy gules and azure; this is called "charging" the shield with the boar's head couped sable;

- Above the fesse chequy gules and azure, two clubs saltirized (crossed, as in an X) proper ("proper" means in their proper or natural color, in this case brown).

Some thirty-five years after Phil first did his painstaking research, *Farmerphile* (with a lot of work by Win and Lisa Eckert, and artist extraordinaire Keith Howell) is proud to present the illustrated Wildman arms.

Buddha Contemplates His Novel
Or, God and Humankind Redefined
A Lecture & Notes
Philip José Farmer

Based on the reference to the then forthcoming September release of *The Unreasoning Mask* and Phil's quoting from September 1981 issue of *Heavy Metal* magazine, the following fascinating and previously unpublished lecture found among Phil's papers likely dates to a currently unidentified event that occurred sometime in the late summer of 1981. As the manuscript ends abruptly, we have substituted Phil's notes after the break in lieu of the lecture's conclusion.

When I was asked to title this lecture, I facetiously replied, "Buddha Contemplates His Novel."

But I am never more serious than when I'm facetious or fecetious.

What I had intended to do was to tell you how science-fiction takes in all fields of human thought and activity. I was going to demonstrate this by postulating a slightly different, or parallel-world, universe in which Gotama or Siddhartha or the Buddha was born in a time somewhat more technologically advanced than that we call "this universe."

In that other universe, Buddha lived and suffered and acted much as he did here. Except that he traveled by train or automobile, and he had a portable typewriter. And he was writing a novel.

The novel was pedagogic, basically educational, though Buddha was too good a writer to ignore a rather fast-moving plot, three-dimensional characterization, suspense, and all the elements that make for a readable if not perhaps a great novel. Of course, he would publish his philosophy in it, but more by implication, more through the actions and concise talk of his characters than through direct propagandistic lecturing.

"That," as they say in India, "is another story."

I won't tell you about it in detail, but I hope to write it some day.

Science-fiction is not just what you might think it is if you know it only through the movies. Nor is science-fiction prophetic. It doesn't, generally, try to tell you what the world will be in the future. No. Science-fiction is about the limitless world of imagination, and, like mainstream, mysteries, westerns, gothics, you name it, it contains stories ranging from very bad to very good and, sometimes, great.

Let me quote a small part of a review of my Riverworld series by Robert Anton Wilson. This review is in the current issue of "Heavy Metal" magazine, a periodical which deals much with science-fiction. Wilson was co-author of a series of books I highly recommend for those who like to be entertained at the same time they're educated and mentally and emotionally stimulated. I recommend the Illuminatus trilogy, *The Cosmic Trigger* (nonfiction, well, almost), *Masks of the Illuminati*, and the trilogy, *Schrodinger's Cat.*

Quote: The Riverworld novels of Philip José Farmer—*To Your Scattered Bodies Go*, *The Fabulous Riverboat*, *The Dark Design*, and *The Magic Labyrinth*—have a multitude of virtues. They boast as much smashing-and-bashing melodrama as ten years' worth of old *Doc Savage* magazines, they are full of odd and interesting bits of historical and anthropological knowledge, and they raise all the important questions of philosophy within the context of a hero's quest that is both exciting and metaphysical. Best of all, taken together, they weigh just enough to make an ideal bludgeon to batter the head of the next person who tells you that science-fiction is not serious literature. Unquote.

I've read this to demonstrate that science-fiction covers more than just space opera or monster movies or scenarios of the dismal future. The Riverworld series could be called theological-eschatological science-fiction.

Permit me to quote another section.

Quote: . . . but Farmer's greatest achievement, accomplished with brilliant understatement, is to make us gradually realize that our own situation here on Earth is just as mysterious as anything on Riverworld, or that the answer to the enigmas of the Riverworld might also be the explanation of the paradoxes of our own particular existence here and now. Once again . . . Farmer demonstrates my pet theory that sf is the only serious literature around these days, because it is the only literature that grapples with the ultimate questions of who or what we are and how we got here. Unquote.

While I don't agree in every detail with what Wilson says, I do agree with the essence.

In September, a new novel of mine, titled *The Unreasoning Mask*, comes out. I mention it because it is a philosophical-theological-eschatological science-fiction work. And because, during its writing, I found or discovered or flashed on or created what I believe to be an original concept in theology. To the best of my knowledge, it has never been voiced or printed. Even if it has, I've independently invented it.

What is this brand-new concept?

It's this. If God exists, He may be omniscient, but He is not omnipotent.

Why isn't He omnipotent, that is, all powerful?

Because he cannot *be* you. Or me.

No matter how powerful He is, He cannot be you, cannot become you. That is a deed beyond Him.

God could make a body exactly like yours in every detail, physically and mentally. He could then, I suppose, inhabit it. But He still would not *be* you. The gulf between you and your simulacrum is infinitely wide, and I do not use the word "infinitely" lightly.

Think about this concept. If you have arguments against, you may voice them during the question-and-answer period. Please stick to the statement I made, though, don't stray far afield; don't appeal to Scripture as an authority. Remain within the logic embodied in the statement: If God exists, then He may be omniscient, but He is not omnipotent.

Which means, of course, that the definition of God needs restatement. You can't say that God is near-omnipotent. Either God is omnipotent or He is not. Just as a woman is either pregnant or not, not just a little pregnant.

During the preparation of this lecture, I conjured up all the arguments I could think of to refute my concept. But I'm not going to state them now, as I did in the original draft of the lecture. That would take far too much time.

However, though I may be an amateur theologian, I am a professional writer of fiction. And it was almost inevitable that the concept I stated in *The Unreasoning Mask* should be percolating or circulating through my minds, my conscious, unconscious, and daemonic. And so I'll write a story which uses the concept as a springboard. Tentative title: *The Bronze Serpent*. It'll be a theological private-eye story.

One of the basic assumptions: That God decides for various reasons I won't go into here to become, for a while, the exact duplicate of an existing human being. To do this, He has to suppress completely His own knowledge that He's God inhabiting the body. So He compresses Himself, as it were, into the narrow compass of an individual's mind and body, and He also makes Himself unaware He is doing this. But, of course, when He is finally released from the body and becomes the expanded God again, He'll remember everything that took place when He was in the body and mind.

He also implants in the body's unconscious a command to free Himself of the duplicate body at a certain time, either in twenty years or at the death of the body, whichever comes first. While in fleshly bonds, He is as subject to the course of events as any other being, to accident and coincidence, or synchronicity, if you prefer that term. And He can't foresee what will happen. For story and philosophical purposes, I assume that God is not omniscient, that he can't see into the future, though He probably knows more about statistical probabilities than anyone else.

This is not a story about Jesus. Jesus has no relevancy to the story except through historical influence, and, indeed, the story will take place in near-future time.

An accident—or is it an accident?—destroys the preset command in His unconscious. And He has already been injected with the recently invented elixir which stops aging, as have all citizens of the United States. Barring accident, homicide, or suicide, He'll live forever. The story ends when the private eye turns the God-inhabited person over to the police, who then read Him His rights.

God will be sent to a prison for the criminally insane, and He won't be released until He's cured. But He won't be cured, though it's possible that science will some day discover how to cure such as He.

The Bronze Serpent is actually only in the stage where I'm making notes and abortive outlines for it. By the time the story is written, it may be, in form, plot, and character, somewhat different. But the basic assumption and logic will remain the same.

I don't want to get deeply into the argument advanced by C. S. Lewis, an amateur theologian/philosopher, and some professionals. That is, that God with one sweep of His eye can see past, present, and future because all events have already taken place, as far as God is concerned. But we humans are still caught up in the flow of time. Still going through our paces, as it were, still totally ignorant of what's ahead of us and not too knowledgeable, really, about what's behind us and more or less bewildered by the present.

As I said, this isn't the time or place to detail that theory. I'll just say that it won't wash, that it can be refuted logically. So, for the purposes of the story, *The Bronze Serpent*, I'll assume that God can't see the future though He probably knows more about statistical probabilities than anyone else.

Some of you are probably thinking, or should be thinking, "But what about Jesus? Wasn't He God in a human body?"

Let's assume, for the purpose of the story, that God was indeed Jesus in a human body. Let's dodge all the arguments and theories that come along with that, the unitarian, duotarian, trinitarian theories, the difference between the human and godly nature or their union, etc. That Jesus might or might not be such is of no interest to me or the reader. The point is that, if God did parthogenetically fertilize Mary's egg so that it produced a male baby, and if God somehow wholly or partially inhabited Jesus' body, God still was not attempting to be anybody dead, then living, or now living or potentially living.

Thus, the example of Jesus has no relevancy to the story.

What does is that, in the story, God decided to reincarnate once more. When He became reincarnate or inhabited Jesus' body, He went through the foetus and baby and childhood and adolescent stages of the body. And He was in an extraordinary situation, a prophet, a founder of a Jewish cult, and one who claimed, if we believe his chroniclers, to be destined to sit on the right hand of God.

But in the story God duplicates the body of a man who's just died, does away with the body, pretends to be resuscitated after being legally dead, and takes the place of the man, continues with his life, as it were. He does this because He wishes to empathize as fully as possible with the problems, wretchedness, meannesses, and also the victories, compassions, and glories, such as they are of a human being.

And, as I said, to be as nearly as possible like the man He's replaced, He buries deep in His unconscious mind the knowledge that He is God. Also buried is the preset command for the knowledge to come to the conscious mind after twenty years. Or at the death of the body, whichever comes first.

I won't go into detail about this story except to say that an accident—or is it an accident?—destroys the unconscious command. Also, scientists have found an elixir which stops aging and which, theoretically, will allow a person to live forever barring accident, suicide or homicide. The story ends when the private detective turns the God-inhabited character over to the police, who then read him his rights.

The intimation here is that God will be sent to a prison for the criminally insane and not released until He is cured. But He won't ever be cured and thus will be imprisoned forever or at least until the sun novas and destroys Earth . . .

The Bronze Serpent will be an example of theological s-f.

Let's go now to another example that is, the Riverworld series, though that is also more than just theological s-f.

This has many themes, basic conceptual threads running thru it. But the one I'd like to talk to most, though briefly, is this. One that's been explicit or implied in some other books or series of novels of mine. That is, that if God has not arranged matters so that all sapients, which includes Earthpeople, have immortality or salvation, then perhaps the sapients will do the job. These stories suggest that humankind has the potentiality for bestowing upon itself immortality and the means for making immortality worthwhile.

Perhaps that is evolution's goal as designed by God, if there is God and there is evolution. There's an overwhelming amount of evidence for the existence of both God and evolution, but the existence of neither has yet been proved in a truly scientific sense.

Re evolution, you should keep your mind open. Perhaps, some day, some genius will take a look at the Mt. Everest of evidence for evolution and say, "Hey! You've all been wrong! You've not looked at the evidence right. Both the creationists and the evolutionists are wrong!"

Keep an open mind. As Ouspensky said, "Think in other categories."

As for the existence of God, that can neither be proved nor disproved. Not thru scientific means, anyway. But there is more than one mode of knowledge, science is only one of them.

For those who may not have read the Riverworld series, it consists at the moment, of four novels and one novella. *To Your Scattered Bodies Go, The Fabulous Riverboat, The Dark Design, The Magic Labyrinth*, and the novella, "Riverworld."

The basic concept in these, along with other basic concepts, is that I spoke about a moment ago. That humankind, may be able to provide physical or spiritual immortality if it gets tired of waiting for God to provide it.

Every human being on Earth who's lived, between 150,000 B.C. and A.D. 1983 and who died after the age of five is resurrected at approximately the same time. If they died after the age of twenty-five, they're resurrected in rejuvenated bodies. Those they had or should have had at the age of twenty-five. Children above five are resurrected at the age they died and then grow normally until they reach maturity and then don't get older.

Apparently, the resurrection takes place on a planet which is Earthlike but not Earth. It's been remade by someone unknown into a ten million mile long river valley, and the resurrectees are scattered along it. People from different times and places find themselves mixed together in the various areas along The River.

The planet is mineral-poor, esp. iron and copper poor. They're forced to live in a stone age.

There's not room enough for thirty-five or so billion resurrectees and land to grow crops. But they don't need the great acreage of soil to plant . . . Every kilometer, on both sides of The River, is a metal-rock toadstool shaped structure which discharges vast quantities of electricity three times a day. The resurrectees have indestructible containers which, when placed upon the structures, called grails, holy buckets, etc. convert the energy into matter. That is, food, liquor, and other various goodies.

Most of these grails can only be opened by their original owners.

If a person is killed or dies, he or she is then resurrected at a distant place along with a new grail. Apparently, the place of the new resurrection is picked by some mysterious random method.

The human beings have no idea who has resurrected them or why. Much of the action and plot consists of several curious characters trying to find out.

In the end, explanations come, but they're too complicated for me to talk about them here. I suggest those who haven't read the series do so, reading them in chronological sequence, starting with *To Your Scattered Bodies Go* and ending with *The Magic Labyrinth*. "Riverworld," the novella, may be read at any time after reading the first of the series.

I've been told that many of the audience had read the series, and that some have questions. I'm ready to answer them as well as I can.

Essex House, Tarzan, and Time's Last Gift
An Appreciation of Philip José Farmer
Bob Zeuschner

I have had the honor and privilege of writing a book for which Philip José Farmer wrote a brief preface. This would never have happened if it were not for Essex House books, and I would like to share the tale of how this came about. It began in the 1950s, took a sharp turn in the late 1960s when Phil Farmer began writing erotic fiction for Essex House, and concluded in 1996. Allow me to explain these interconnected threads.

I had discovered Tarzan and John Carter in 1952, more than fifteen years before Philip José Farmer's first Tarzan book appeared. In my attempt to acquire and read every one of Edgar Rice Burroughs' tales, I sought first editions and the actual pulp issues with ERB's original stories. I did not restrict my reading just to Burroughs, but also read the mysteries of Edgar Wallace, the risque fiction of Thorne Smith (creator of "Topper"), and others such as Talbot Mundy and Sax Rohmer. In the 1950s most of my books were the result of frequent trips to Goodwill stores, the Salvation Army, and the many used book shops which filled Pasadena, California. I read Asimov and Heinlein and was in high school when inexpensive paperbacks appeared, and now I was reading Mickey Spillane, Alan Watts, D. T. Suzuki, plus J. R. R. Tolkien, Theodore Sturgeon, Robert Scheckley, and every other major s-f author. I still have hundreds of those old paperbacks, many with the great Richard Powers covers. I certainly read a few books by Philip José Farmer.

Virtually all the pulp authors of the 1920s, 1930s, and 1940s read the pulp fiction of Edgar Rice Burroughs, tried to imitate Burroughs, or were inspired by Burroughs to begin their own writing careers. The list of influenced authors would be lengthy, but it would most certainly include Robert Heinlein, Isaac Asimov, Robert E. Howard, Ray Bradbury and especially, Philip José Farmer who was born in 1918. More than anyone else, Philip José Farmer extended the various fantasy realms of Edgar Rice Burroughs.

Philip José Farmer Writes for Essex House. The 1940s and 1950s were still Puritan times in this country. In the name of "protecting readers," prudish American and British censors routinely emasculated literature which ventured into sexual waters. In the 1950s and 1960s books like James Joyce's *Ulysses*, Henry Miller's *Tropic of Cancer* and *Tropic of Capricorn*, and D. H. Lawrence's *Lady Chatterley's Lover* had only recently become available to American readers, as a result of the famous Supreme Court decision of 1933.

Science fiction was no exception to this pattern of repressing all matters sensual. In the pulp magazines of the period, although sexuality was implied on the cover of each issue, or implied by John Carter of Barsoom rescuing the scantily-clad yet incomparable Dejah Thoris from a "fate worse than death," within the text actual sexual experience never went beyond a passionate kiss. Sexual attitudes might be utilized as background to a plot, social attitudes and prejudices might be lampooned but as far as the reader could tell, no hero or heroine ever actually engaged in a physical sexual act. Apparently neither John Carter nor Tarzan ever had a sexual fantasy, which as any young American male knows, is impossible.

Due to British and American editorial prudery, many classic novels with sexual content were printed in the English language in Paris by Maurice Girodias' Olympia House, titles which included Terry Southern's *Candy*, Nabakov's *Lolita*, Lawrence's *Lady Chatterley's Lover*, works by Alexander Trocchi and Samuel Beckett, and J.P. Donleavy's *The Ginger Man*.

In the 1960s the literary landscape in America was beginning to become more relaxed and open. One of my very best friends, Brian Kirby, was hired to be the editor for an audacious erotic literary press called Essex House and another press called the Brandon House Library. Not only is Mr. Kirby a great editor, but he is also a jazz musician, a film historian and collector of screenplays, a scholar of contemporary literature, and a collector of the great novelists of the second half of the 20th century. He is also a connoisseur, reader and collector of science fiction. It was the late 1960s and as a pioneer in the effort to expand literary limitations, Brian Kirby sought out many of his favorite authors, and inquired whether they would like to do a book which was not only free of editorial limitations, but in which the author was encouraged to liberate himself or herself from the common Puritanical restraints of the genre and the time period.

Mr. Kirby knew Phil Farmer, and contacted Phil and asked him to write several books that went well beyond anything Farmer had ever done, experimental books written without restraints. Would Phil write a book that could be read seriously but which could also be read as a sarcastic poke at the prevailing limitations of science fiction, or fantasy, for which sexuality was anathema? Farmer did not need to use circumlocution and euphemism. In fact, he was encouraged to explore all the full range of human experience without fear of prudery or editorial limitations. Brian encouraged Phil to be outrageous!

Mr. Kirby also hired knowledgeable scholars to write fascinating and learned introductions to the Essex House books, designed to demonstrate that the popular equation of "erotic literature" = "unimportant dirty books" was simply false. Erotic literature is literature, and science fiction which is sexually stimulating with erotic content is no less science fiction. I recall when my friend Brian told me that Phil had accepted the commission to write a Tarzan tale, and I looked forward to reading each of Phil's books as Essex House published them.

The result was several Philip José Farmer Essex House science fiction books exploring startling and outrageous erotic terrain, including *The Image of the Beast*, *A Feast Unknown*, and *Blown*. This literary freedom seems to have sparked Phil Farmer's creative juices, for in quick succession several non-Essex House titles appeared including *The Lord of the Trees*, *Lord Tyger*, the *Mad Goblin*, *Tarzan Alive*, and *Time's Last Gift*.

Philip José Farmer Writes the Preface for my Burroughs Bibliography. The primary tool for a Burroughs collector was the wonderful 1964 bibliography by Henry Hardy Heins. However, as the decades passed, new Burroughs works continued to appear every year, and unpublished tales had surfaced and were in line to be published. I kept accumulating the new bibliographical information while I waited for someone to put out an addendum to the Heins book, but no one did. Finally, in the late 1980s I began compiling my information and over a period of seven years, I finally had it all in publishable form. I wanted a preface for the book, and Brian Kirby, the Essex House editor, suggested that I contact Philip José Farmer. I wrote to Phil, explaining that I had written a new Burroughs bibliography and that I was hoping he might find the time to write a short introductory piece. Although I had no money from the publisher or my own pocket to pay Phil, he very kindly produced the brief introduction that I had requested. He had done it for the love of Burroughs, and I was deeply indebted to him for his kindness. Philip José Farmer is not only a science fiction author with an extraordinary imagination and a gift for startlingly new concepts, he is also a true fan of Edgar Rice Burroughs, and a kind gentleman.

Time's Last Gift. When I first read *Time's Last Gift* in the 1972 Ballantine edition, I had no idea that the book had any relationship to Edgar Rice Burroughs. The theme was time travel (one of my favorites), and that combined with the amazing imagination of Philip José Farmer made it certain that I would enjoy the book. The opening page described the time traveling vehicle, the *H. G.*

Wells I, which traveled back 14,000 years into the ancient past. In the opening pages of the book the characters are slowly revealed, including John Gribardsun, who seemed strangely familiar to me. Farmer reveals that Gribardsun spoke with a British accent, but he had an underlying accent which even the world's foremost linguist, von Billmann, could not quite identify (an oblique reference to Gribardsun's original language, that of the mangani group who raised him in his earliest years). Gribardsun appeared to be about thirty years old, with very black hair and grey eyes. He had the body of an Apollo. The door of the *H. G. Wells I* was opened, and Gribardsun sniffed the air as if he were a great cat. The tingle of recognition stirred my imagination. Then Phil Farmer tells us that Gribardsun was much older than he looked, and had memories of Africa and Asia when there were still pre-literate groups inhabiting certain areas. He couldn't fool me; this had to be my Tarzan! Phil Farmer had extended Tarzan's universe, not forward into the future, but back into the past.

This was not the outrageous Tarzan of the Essex House books, who shattered the prudish boundaries of science fiction. No, this was more like the fiercely intelligent Tarzan that Burroughs wrote about in the early decades of the 20th century. However, *Time's Last Gift* was not quite Burroughs. In Philip José Farmer's world, Tarzan can smell the odor of human excrement, and body odors are clear to Gribardsun. This sort of descriptive detail was omitted by Burroughs, although Burroughs himself was very much aware of it and even referred to such things in interviews. In the second chapter, Gribardsun observes a lion with a golden mane, which reminds him of a pet lion he once had. Every ERB fan knows the name of that golden lion! Philip José Farmer's vast knowledge of Lord Greystoke's adventures through twenty-three books written by Ed Burroughs serves him in good stead in this novel. This was the Tarzan who had the elixir of immortality, but this immortal Tarzan has no place in the future world where all lost civilizations have been found, where the wild animals are all in cages or extinct, where the skills that allow a man to survive were related to computers and keyboards. So, Tarzan is taken where he belongs, into the past, into the world where the skills of a lone jungle lord could be tested against nature.

I do want to thank Philip José Farmer for providing Tarzan the proper playground for the jungle lord. Tarzan continues on in my imagination, and in the imagination of Philip José Farmer too. Thanks also for writing that foreword. Thank you, Phil.

THE TRICKSTER AWAKENS:
PHILIP JOSÉ FARMER AND
VENUS ON THE HALF-SHELL
TRACY KNIGHT

More than eighty years ago, a sleeping two-year-old named Philip Farmer had a dream, one that evermore has remained pristine in his memory. In the dream, Phil lay in his bedroom when he heard the downstairs doorbell ring, then a violent pounding on the front door. He arose, walked to the door and opened it. "It was night outside, but a single streetlamp outlined a tall thin man with a high hat of curious shape. He held in one hand a bulky shapeless case. He said, 'I can come in or you can come out.'" Even at that tender age, something within Farmer was insisting that he accept secrets from this mysterious stranger. Throughout his stellar writing career, Philip José Farmer has traveled with this mysterious stranger always nearby, utilizing the stranger's secrets to embolden and enrich his writing and his life. On at least one occasion, however, Phil Farmer stepped outside himself and joined the stranger in his own world, in the shadows, becoming one with him.

May, 2004.[1] Nearly thirty years has passed since the release of *Venus on the Half-Shell*, a science fiction novel ostensibly written by Kilgore Trout, a character appearing in several of Kurt Vonnegut's novels. *Venus'* true author, Philip José Farmer, eighty-six years of age, smiles with a muted expression of ageless mischief playing across his face and a startlingly luminous twinkle in his eye. As a warm spring breeze plays through the screened-in porch of his Peoria home, he steeples the fingers of his large hands, tips back his head, closes his eyes and chuckles softly. Then he sighs. Some details of his *Venus on the Half-Shell* adventure have taken flight with the years, but its essential legacy abides: "What I remember most is how much fun I had writing it," he says. But when invited to share the most surprising lesson he learned from writing the novel, he falls momentarily silent before saying with a hint of resigned sadness, "It's amazing how so many people can create so many grounds for becoming angry."

What began as a joyous brainstorm—writing a novel under the pseudonym of fictional author Kilgore Trout—ended as an absurdist account of the human condition on two distinct levels of reality: the reality given life within the mind of the reader by a work of fiction, and the external reality we all share. In writing the novel, Farmer actively explored his decades-old fascination with the mythological Trickster figure. Most amazing, however, was the aftermath of the novel's release, which culminated unexpectedly in Farmer fully incarnating—as *himself*—the very figure he so revered.

In 1972, Farmer was reading Kurt Vonnegut's novel *God Bless You, Mr. Rosewater* for the fifth time. In the novel, Fred Rosewater comes across one of Kilgore Trout's books in the adult section of a bookstore (since Trout's novels were published by World Classics Library, a pornography publisher). The novel, *Venus on the Half-Shell,* sported a photo of Trout on the back cover—"an old, bearded man looking 'like a frightened, aging Jesus'"—as well as a brief description of a hot sexual scene from the book. Nothing else about the fictional novel was revealed. According to Farmer, "rereading this part, a pitchfork rose from my subconscious and goosed my neural ganglia. In short, I was inspired. Lights went on; bells clanged." That instant, Farmer imagined a Vonnegut fan whirling a paperback rack and being stunned and delighted upon encountering an actual, physical novel entitled *Venus on the*

Half-Shell by Kilgore Trout. Asked whether he foresaw anything beyond that astonished reader happening upon the book, Farmer states, "No, I never even thought about it. I just sat down and wrote it. It's a book I would love to have found on a book rack myself." Farmer also wrote the novel to demonstrate his admiration and respect for Vonnegut's earlier works.

Farmer identified quite strongly with Trout: "I'd been ripped off by publishers, had to work at menial jobs to support myself and family while writing, had suffered from misunderstanding of my works, and had to endure the scorn of those who considered science fiction to be a trashy genre without any literary merit."

Phil sought Vonnegut's permission to write *Venus on the Half-Shell*. After some gentle verbal wrangling, Vonnegut acceded, asking only that his name not be associated with the novel in any way, and that he not receive any royalties from its sale. Farmer did not reveal to Vonnegut any details of the plot he was even then constructing for the novel: "At least I had enough brains not to tell him," he says.

Previously shackled by an episode of writer's block, Phil was creatively freed by the pseudonym's cloak; he opened his imagination and ideas flooded out as spectacularly as the deluge that drowns humanity in *Venus'* opening scene. Phil's wife Bette frequently heard raucous laughter ascending in great waves from Phil's basement office as he wrote. Within six weeks, he completed *Venus on the Half-Shell*, the story of Simon Wagstaff— Space Wanderer, bad banjo player—who, the last human survivor on Earth, departs in a Chinese rocket ship (the *Hwang Ho*) and travels the universe, encountering all manner of unusual worlds and unique aliens, his sole goal being to find a definitive answer to his question, "Why are we created only to suffer and die?"

Philip José Farmer was the perfect person to write *Venus on the Half-Shell*, not only because he so deeply identified with Kilgore Trout. At the time of the writing, Farmer already had blurred the distinction between reality and fantasy by writing books, articles and short stories appropriating fictional characters other authors had created, for example by writing biographies (e.g., *Tarzan Alive, Doc Savage: His Apocalyptic Life*) or including them in new adventures of his own creation (*The Other Log of Phileas Fogg, The Adventure of the Peerless Peer*).

To create *Venus on the Half-Shell*, Farmer submerged himself in the persona of Kilgore Trout, a fictional character, to produce a work that would be released under that character's name, Farmer remaining coltishly in the shadows. He even maintained his Trout identification far beyond the book's release, often to hilarious effect (see the "Trout Letters" article in *Farmerphile No. 5* for an intriguing chapter of that story). Considering his lifelong fascination with and love for the mythological Trickster figure, it is unsurprising that such a project appealed to him.

The Trickster Motif. In his book *The Trickster: A Study in American Indian Mythology*, Paul Radin wrote, "The Trickster myth is found in clearly recognizable form among the simplest aboriginal tribes and among the complex." Descendents of the Trickster include both Bugs Bunny and Mork. Carl Jung noted that chief among the Trickster figure's enduring traits are "his fondness for sly jokes and malicious pranks, his powers as a shape-shifter, his dual nature, half animal, half divine." Despite the fact that the Trickster often frustrates and confuses those with whom he interacts, his effect on the cultures where he appears is essentially positive: "[H]is seemingly asocial actions continue to keep our world lively and give it the flexibility to endure," wrote Hyde in *Trickster Makes This World*.

For Farmer, fascination with the Trickster began when he was young:

> "When I was about 10 years old I found a bunch of books in the children's section of the Peoria Library, which devoted four or five books to the North American Trickster: the Old Man Coyote of the Plains Indians; Raven of the Northwest; and the Great White Hare of the Midwest Indians, among others. I got very interested in that. I also, at a very young age, began reading *The*

Odyssey. Odysseus is the supreme Trickster of classical literature. When I began writing science fiction I sometimes used the Trickster figure, especially in the character of Kickaha in the *World of Tiers* series; he's based on the North American Trickster. I conceived of that figure in 1936, when I was a senior in high school. Instead of studying in study hall, I was writing notes about his universe and what kind of a person he was, but I didn't use it until about 1965."

In a 1988 television interview, Farmer said,

"[The Trickster] seems to represent verbally the unconscious of humanity. He's always playing tricks, much to their detriment, but occasionally his tricks backfire on him."

By embracing the persona of Kilgore Trout, he invited himself to give expression to those cast-off parts of himself—the more primitive, the less intellectual, the Trickster-like—and to instill a sense of gleeful absurdity into *Venus.* The novel was written in a less intellectual style than his other works, was filled with a cascade of created worlds and aliens, and tilted at the windmills of God, existence and the human being's quest to understand the meaning of suffering. All with a wry smile.

Even the character of Simon Wagstaff is fundamentally a Trickster, according to Farmer. Wandering from planet to planet and typically without much forethought or intent, Wagstaff frequently wreaks havoc on the alien societies with which he interacts, just as the Trickster, who accomplishes his goals by acting in absurd, provocative ways. Farmer did this in his writing of *Venus on the Half-Shell,* and Simon Wagstaff embodies these characteristics within the novel's pages.

It didn't stop there. Through a Fortean turn of events, Philip José Farmer *became* the Trickster. And, as in the myths, the trick backfired on the Trickster.

The Fallout. A 1975 issue of *Science Fiction Review* featured Richard Geis' scathing review of *Venus on the Half-Shell*, in which he excoriated the author for having the nerve to create this "hatchet job" that so cruelly satirized the science fiction community. Only one problem: Geis assumed Kurt Vonnegut was the author. In a review of the book in *National Review*, a writer "proved" that Vonnegut had written the novel. The UCLA *Daily Bruin* published an article in which the writer established Vonnegut as the author "with 100% certainty."

While Vonnegut was an early suspect for understandable reasons, others soon joined the list: Philip K. Dick, Harry Harrison, Isaac Asimov, Ted White, Harlan Ellison. Philip José Farmer was never mentioned as a possible culprit. "The funniest thing to me," Farmer says, "was that there were all these people guessing who had written it, and none came near the truth. Not even close."

Vonnegut's eventual indignant reaction to the novel likely was born when Vonnegut watched a televised interview conducted by William F. Buckley with literary critic Leslie Fiedler, who said that Farmer had told him that he had been committed to writing the novel, with or without Vonnegut's permission. Perhaps this misunderstanding of a comment Farmer had made to Fiedler during a visit led Vonnegut to believe that Philip José Farmer lacked good intentions and proper respect for Vonnegut and his creation. There is no way to know with certainty, since Vonnegut has never spoken to this point. Regardless, Vonnegut's soured attitude lingered long after *Venus* made its appearance. In a 1987 interview, Vonnegut was asked about the book, and responded:

> "This Farmer wanted to forge on and write a whole series of books 'by' Trout—and I understand he's capable of knocking out a pretty decent Vonnegut book every six weeks. I hardly know Mr. Farmer. I've never met him and most of our contacts have been indirect, so I asked him, please, not to do it . . . I understand he was really burned up about my decision. I heard he had made more money in that one 'Kilgore Trout year' than he had ever made before."

It was not true that Farmer had planned an entire series of Kilgore Trout novels. He had planned only to write one other, *Son of Jimmy Valentine*. However, upon learning of Vonnegut's negative feelings, he immediately abandoned the project. It also is untrue that he made more money from *Venus on the Half-Shell* than he had ever made before. A single novel in his *Riverworld* series, among many others, had provided Farmer with considerably more income than *Venus*.

Farmer received much less money from the novel than Dell had indicated he would, and the most recent edition of *Venus on the Half-Shell* was released by a publisher who did not provide the promised number of copies to the author, printed more copies than contracted for, and never has given Farmer the twice-yearly royalty statements they had promised. In fact, Farmer's agent can no longer even locate the publisher. Like the ancient Trickster, Farmer's trick backfired: "I'm destined to suffer the fate of the fictional Trout. In some respects, anyway."

During my 2004 interview with him, Phil said, "What surprised me was here was a project that I did in honor of Vonnegut and all I did was make him mad. I had no way of knowing it would offend him, and there was no reason it should have." This is perhaps the most unfortunate aspect of *Venus on the Half-Shell*, that it inadvertently created a chasm in the nascent relationship between Farmer and Vonnegut that has never been repaired.

What, then, is the residue of this saga, after all the angry responses, the praises, the pans, the sales? For Philip José Farmer, it is the pure, indestructible remembrance of unbounded joy that accompanied the novel's creation. For readers, it is the novel itself, which is a satiric masterpiece.

"Good science fiction writers try to show how we could become human beings," Farmer wrote in 1984. *Venus* accomplished that, revealing the humanness (for better *and* worse) of Vonnegut, the readers, the science fiction community, and even Philip José Farmer himself.

In writing *Venus on the Half-Shell*, Philip José Farmer answered that door he dreamed of as a toddler and greeted the mysterious man who invited him to share in hidden mysteries from his shape-less case. The young Philip Farmer was challenged: "I can come in or you can come out" (which, you'll notice, leaves no option but to accept the stranger's gifts). *Venus on the Half-Shell* allowed Farmer to step fully outside himself and become one with the mysterious stranger, the Trickster. Like the Trickster, Farmer shifted shapes and visited a wry prank upon the reading public, a prank both animalistic and divine and, in doing so, made for a livelier world.

Judging from Its middling creation talents and the fact that It wandered off, forgetting that It constructed our universe (thus falling prey to Its own trap), the God ultimately revealed in *Venus on the Half-Shell* is perhaps the greatest Trickster of all. Perhaps that God is still at work. On August 10, 2002, the Peoria Public Library hosted a 50th anniversary celebration of the publication of Phil's groundbreaking novella *The Lovers*. I was given the respon-sibility of inviting Phil's peers to write letters of congratulation, which I read to the audience and then presented to Phil and Bette at ceremony's end.

One uninvited letter arrived without a postmark. It read, in part:

> "I don't understand what the big deal is. Years before Farmer sold a sex story to a science fiction magazine, I was selling science fiction stories to sex magazines . . .
> Kilgore Trout
> P.S. I'm not dead. I just smell funny."

So it goes.

---

[1] This article is an abridged version of a paper Tracy delivered in 2004 at a Science Fiction Research Association conference held in Skokie, Illinois.

ON A RIVERBOAT WITH THE FARMERS
GARY K. WOLFE

W ell, it wasn't *exactly* a riverboat; it was actually a water taxi in Fort Lauderdale, and it wasn't only with the Farmers, although memory fails me as to who exactly was in the boat with us. I know the fantasy writer Stephen R. Donaldson was there, and I'm pretty sure David Hartwell and Kathryn Cramer, and possibly Joe and Gay Haldeman as well, and certainly one science fiction scholar from Kuwait (probably the *only* science fiction scholar in Kuwait, come to think of it), and a few others. But by the end of the evening, it had turned into a genuine Farmerian adventure, with perhaps a few elements of Joseph Conrad as well.

For years, my wife Dede and I had been trying to persuade Phil and Bette to join us at the annual meeting of the International Conference on the Fantastic in the Arts in Fort Lauderdale. This was (and remains) a remarkable gathering of writers, editors, critics and scholars which had begun in 1979, under the sponsorship of Florida Atlantic University, as a memorial conference with funds donated by the mother of the late fantasy writer Thomas Burnett Swann. By the early 1980s, the conference had given rise to its own association, and over the years its list of guests of honor had become a who's who of writers, both genre and non-genre: Stephen King, John Barth, Isaac Bashevis Singer, Harlan Ellison, Brian Aldiss, Gene Wolfe, even Tom Stoppard and Doris Lessing. I'd been attending it since nearly the beginning, and I wanted to get Phil on that list.

Eventually, Phil and Bette attended two of these conferences, in 1990 and 1992, the latter as Guest of Honor. The water taxi escapade occurred during the first of these, but it requires some context. On at least two prior occasions, the conference had attempted riverboat excursions, and each had turned out to be such a disaster that, in conference lore, riverboats were coming to be thought of as something of a curse. The first riverboat ride, organized when the conference was briefly displaced to Beaumont, Texas, ran out of food before the boat had even left the dock, and grew increasingly grim as it became apparent that the main sights to be seen consisted of flaming refinery burn-off towers, industrial waste, and the rear ends of rusty barges. The second was organized in 1989, after guest of honor Doris Lessing expressed interest in seeing what a Florida cruise ship was like. What she had in mind, I'm sure, was a day cruise on a *Carnival*-style ship, but what she got was something called the *Jungle Queen*, an ersatz Mississippi-style tourist-trap riverboat which chugged up and down the inland waterway, often being mooned by contemptuous residents of the fancy houses along the way. It took us to a rat-infested island (I still have a photo of Doris Lessing with a rat) where we got off to eat bad barbeque and listen to an appalling succession of accordionists and polka bands.

We told Phil and Bette about the latter adventure, and Bette immediately decided that we should book some sort of more sedate and civilized river cruise for ourselves. And we all enthusiastically agreed. We learned that the water taxis were a cheap and enjoyable way to barhop along the inland waterway, and soon assembled another band of adventurers to explore the taxi system after dinner at a fine restaurant on the 17th Street causeway. The taxi zipped us right across for drinks at another restaurant, and then another, and soon we tired of hopping on and off for drinks and simply wanted to enjoy the ride. The next time we climbed back on, Bette told the pilot (captain? skipper? watercabbie?) to take us "to the end of the line."

What none of us realized at the time, and what the pilot never bothered to explain, was that the end of the line for these taxis is apparently somewhere in Manitoba. As we chugged further north, away from the cruise ships, away from the restaurants of the Strip, away from the fancy houses and into the darkness, a few of our number began to get nervous. Fifteen minutes passed, then a half-hour. Finally, one of the passengers stood up: "I must get back to the hotel!" But by now all the conference programming for the night was over, and we asked why. "*You don't understand!*" he shouted. "*We must turn back!*" He didn't exactly say we're all going to die, but there was more than a bit of B-movie dialogue flavor in his increasingly assertive pleas. Maybe he just needed a bathroom, but the taxi showed no signs of slowing or turning around, and by now the pilot had pretty much stopped answering our queries altogether. We reassured each other that none of us was really worth hijacking, but there was nevertheless a growing sensation of being trapped in some Florida tourist version of *Apocalypse Now* or *Heart of Darkness*, with an hysterical shipmate and a mysteriously silent pilot taking us into a region that by now wasn't even recognizably Fort Lauderdale.

Finally, an exceptionally considerate passenger—Steve Donaldson—persuaded the pilot to stop at the next waterside tavern, where he disembarked with the disturbed passenger and took him in a taxi back to the hotel. Not long after, we started the long voyage back. We never learned the source of our companion's agitation, and he never mentioned the incident for the rest of the conference. The water taxi ride, however, had entered the lore of the conference by the following afternoon, with all sorts of gothic embellishments and with any number of people claiming to have been along.

Phil, though, became a big hit at the conference. Taking the academic aspect of the conference more seriously than most writers, he even delivered a scholarly paper on ibn Tufayl, an "Arabic Mowgli," and two years later was invited back as guest of honor. A high point of that 1992 convention was an energetic discussion (which I moderated) between Phil and the conference's recurring special guest Brian Aldiss. Before climbing to the stage, Phil paused in front of the sizeable audience, took a deep breath, and let out a thunderous Tarzan yell that sounded nothing like Johnny Weissmuller, but probably what Tarzan himself must have sounded like. Aldiss, rarely nonplussed, responded with his own lumbering imitation of the Frankenstein monster (the film of his novel *Frankenstein Unbound* had been released only a year or so earlier). The discussion which followed was among the most freewheeling I've ever heard among writers at any conference, and I've wondered ever since if a tape of it survives somewhere in the ICFA archives.

A brief footnote: The following year, Dede and I were visiting Phil and Bette in Peoria, reminiscing about the water taxi, and talking about getting them down to the conference at least one more time. In the car on the way to dinner, Phil complained that he was getting too old for traveling to conferences, and Bette said, "For heaven's sake, Phil, everyone gets old."

"Tarzan doesn't," said Phil.

HERITAGE OF THE FLAMING GOD
A CLASSIC ESSAY, LONG FORGOTTEN, INSPIRED FARMER
Alan Hanson

In his article in *Farmerphile No. 3,* Christopher Paul Carey stated that Philip José Farmer's *Hadon of Ancient Opar* miniseries is a "unique and original work based on and extrapolated from numerous sources." At the risk of compromising Christopher's promised future article on the nature of those sources, I thought Farmer fans might enjoy the story of how a long forgotten essay, which Farmer identified as the most important source of his Hadon novels, was rediscovered and published in recent years.

O n the back of the title page of *Hadon of Ancient Opar,* published by Daw Books in 1974, appears the following acknowledgement by the author.

> I am grateful to Frank Brueckel and John Harwood for writing the article, which sparked the inspiration to create Hadon of Opar and the Khokarsan civilization. I thank Hulbert Burroughs for his kindness in permitting me to launch this series of novels. The basic debt, of course, is owed to Edgar Rice Burroughs, without whose tales of Opar and other lost cities this book would never have been written.

Any curious Farmer fan who might have tried to find the "article" that inspired Farmer to create Hadon would have been disappointed in 1974, as well as throughout the quarter century that followed. Brueckel and Harwood's article, which Farmer read in manuscript form, went unpublished for twenty-eight years after the two men completed it in 1971. During those years, the existence of the essay was known only to a handful of elite Edgar Rice Burroughs fans. By 1998 I had been an active Burroughs fan for twenty-five years and had never heard of it. Once a copy of it came into my hands, however, it drew me for the first time into the world of Philip José Farmer and ultimately to my publishing of the essay for the first time in 1999.

It's been my experience that Burroughs fans, like Farmer fans, are a generous lot. Most are more than willing to pass on information or offer assistance when they can. In the spring of 1998, Ken Webber, a fellow Burroughs fan in Colorado, contacted me. Knowing my admiration for the work of late ERB fan-writer John Harwood, Ken wrote to tell me that he had a copy of an unpublished essay on Opar that Harwood had co-authored. The sample pages that accompanied Ken's letter so fascinated me that I quickly wrote back asking Ken to send me a copy of the entire essay.

Entitled *Heritage of the Flaming God: An Essay on the History of Opar and Its Relationship to Other Ancient Cultures,* the treatise ran eighty-six typewritten pages and included three maps. It only took a few pages for me to become completely absorbed in the manuscript. Harwood's co-writer was Frank J. Brueckel. Both men were very familiar to me as prolific and scholarly writers for Vern Coriell's *Burroughs Bulletin* of the fifties, sixties and seventies. I knew, therefore, that their Opar essay had been written at least twenty years previously, but I was at a loss to understand why such a quality piece of Burroughs scholarship had remained unpublished for so long.

A month or two after I first read the essay, chance answered some of my questions about its history. One day, while reorganizing some fanzines in my office filing cabinet, the name "Frank J.

Brueckel" caught my eye in a headline in *Gridley Wave #68,* a Vern Coriell publication. Having recently read Brueckel's Opar essay, I stopped to look at the article. It turned out to be an obituary for Frank, who died in 1976. When I saw that the article's author was John Harwood, I sat down to read it, hoping it would shed some light on the mysterious Opar essay the two men had written. Sure enough, Harwood's remembrance included the following passage.

> We worked on the article from 1966 to 1971 with Frank doing most of the writing. I'd send in a five or six page version of a chapter and he'd rewrite it in his own words containing the essence of my ideas plus material added by himself. Frank sent the manuscript to Vernell Coriell in July of 1971 to be published in the *Burroughs Bulletin.*

While the article explained how and when *Heritage of the Flaming God* had been written, it added confusion to the essay's publishing history. Following the obituary, Vern Coriell included a bibliography of Brueckel's fan writings. According to that listing, *Heritage of the Flaming God* had been published in *Burroughs Bulletin #24.* Coriell was well known, however, for skipping numbers in the sequence of the *Bulletin,* and a quick check revealed that #24 was one of the issues that, for some unknown reason, had never been published.

Once I had established that Brueckel and Harwood's classic essay was unpublished, I decided to attempt issuing it myself. Previously I had self-published a couple of Burroughs related volumes under the amateur publishing banner of Waziri Publications. Before explaining the road traveled to publish it, however, let me comment briefly about the forgotten Opar essay itself.

Heritage of the Flaming God is divided into four parts, the first and last of which had the most impact on Farmer's Hadon novels. The first part, entitled "Dawn of Empire," fleshes out something that Burroughs only hinted at in his Tarzan novels—the history of the empire that founded Opar thousands of years ago. Using their knowledge of science and legend, and injecting a good dose of imagination, Brueckel and Harwood tackled many questions that Burroughs had left unanswered about Oparian history. Who built Opar? When, why and how was it built? How came it to fall into decay? What was the nature of the "great calamity" that overcame the empire and left Opar an isolated colony in central Africa?

Using what scanty information Burroughs provided, Brueckel and Harwood created a timeline for Opar's founding civilization. Borrowing an idea from Willy Ley (*Engineers' Dreams,* Viking Press, 1954), they speculated that Opar's maritime founders sailed not the Atlantic Ocean, as Burroughs reported, but instead two great central African seas that existed thousands of years ago. The accompanying maps showed these two great seas and Opar's location at the southern end of them. One need only compare these maps with the one included in *Hadon of Ancient Opar* to see how Farmer made use of the African geography that Brueckel and Harwood conjured up in *Heritage.* Part 1 ends with the authors speculating on the nature of the "great calamity" that destroyed Opar's parent civilization to the north. Since Farmer intended to bring his Khokarsan society to a catastrophic end in a future, never written volume in the series, he only foreshadowed that final calamity in the two Hadon books.

In parts 2 and 3 of *Heritage of the Flaming God,* Brueckel and Harwood dealt with the differing physical appearances of Oparian males and females, and tried to tie other lost cities in the Tarzan novels with Oparian history. While little of these subjects can be found in the Hadon books, the subject of the essay's fourth and final part, titled "Mysteries of Opar," clearly influenced Farmer. In it John Harwood addressed some enigmas about Opar found in the Tarzan novels. For instance, Harwood asked, "Why didn't the Oparians use bow and arrows?" And, "How did Queen La retain her youthful appearance through the years?" In the Hadon novels, Farmer gave his answers to these and other questions posed in the final segment of *Heritage of the Flaming God.*

When I first started preparing the essay for publication in the summer of 1998, I wasn't focused on its connection with Philip

José Farmer. In the letter that first informed me of the existence of *Heritage*, Ken Webber had included copies of the essay's two maps. At the top of one map, Ken wrote, "Enclosing the two maps that illustrate the article. I don't know how they jive with the inland sea that P.J. Farmer wrote about in his ancient Opar books." I knew of Farmer's Hadon of Opar books, and even had copies on my bookshelf, but I had never read them. So, originally, I didn't pay much attention to Ken's note, especially since I was focused on the Brueckel and Harwood essay, which I hadn't even read at that point.

Several months later, however, after I had read the *Heritage* essay, Ken's comment was recalled when I came across that previously mentioned Frank Brueckel obituary. The listing of Brueckel's fanzine articles contained the following note by Vern Coriell about *Heritage of the Flaming God*:

> Philip José Farmer read this article in manuscript form and changed his plans for a book he was writing. He was working on his *Time's Last Gift* and the historical section of the Opar article gave him the idea of rewriting a few pages. This, in turn, led to him starting a series of books based on the article. So far, two of the volumes in the series have been written. *Hadon of Ancient Opar* was published in April of 1974 and *Flight From* (sic) *Opar* will be published sometime in 1976. A third Hadon is in the works.

Now I was interested in the Farmer connection, and decided to write an Afterword to the *Heritage* essay comparing it with Farmer's Hadon novels. So that winter of 1998-1999, I read Farmer's Opar novels twice each, taking notes. It was obvious early on that Farmer's stories were clearly based on the vision of ancient Africa detailed in *Heritage of the Flaming God*. There were the two great central seas and many of the other geographic features that Brueckel and Harwood had envisioned in Africa of twelve millennia ago.

The further I read in *Hadon of Ancient Opar,* however, the more
I noticed how Farmer went far beyond Brueckel and Harwood's
ideas and gave greater depth and life to the ancient empire that
founded Opar. One weakness of *Heritage of the Flaming God* is
that it lacks a human vision. It explains ancient Opar but ignores
the ancient Oparian. In his novels, Farmer added that missing
human element. We get to see and experience Opar when it was
at the height of its glory and to sail the great inland seas with its
sailors as they traveled back and forth between Opar and the
empire's capital. In addition to taking its setting from Brueckel
and Harwood, Farmer's vision of ancient Opar borrows heavily,
and imaginatively, from Burroughs as well. Through the course
of the two novels, there are several surprises thrown in for Tarzan

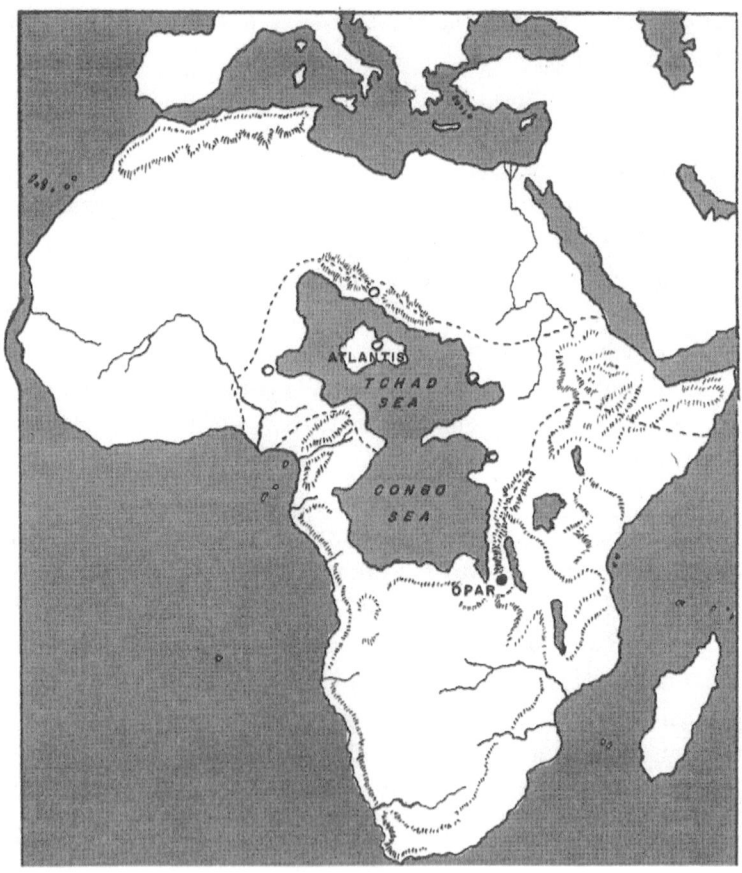

fans, which for me helped make Farmer's Hadon of Opar books interesting reading. I doubt, however, that I would have enjoyed Farmer's Opar novels as much had I not read *Heritage of the Flaming God* first. The essay and the novels are virtually companion pieces, each complimenting the other.

My "Afterword" comparing Brueckel and Harwood's essay with Farmer's Opar novels ran over twenty pages. When I finished with my analysis, however, I still had some questions, so I wrote Philip José Farmer hoping he could satisfy my curiosity on a few issues. On the eve of his eighty-first birthday, he kindly responded with a long letter. In addition to answering my questions about incidents in his novels, he commented on several other related issues, including why he ended the Hadon series after only two

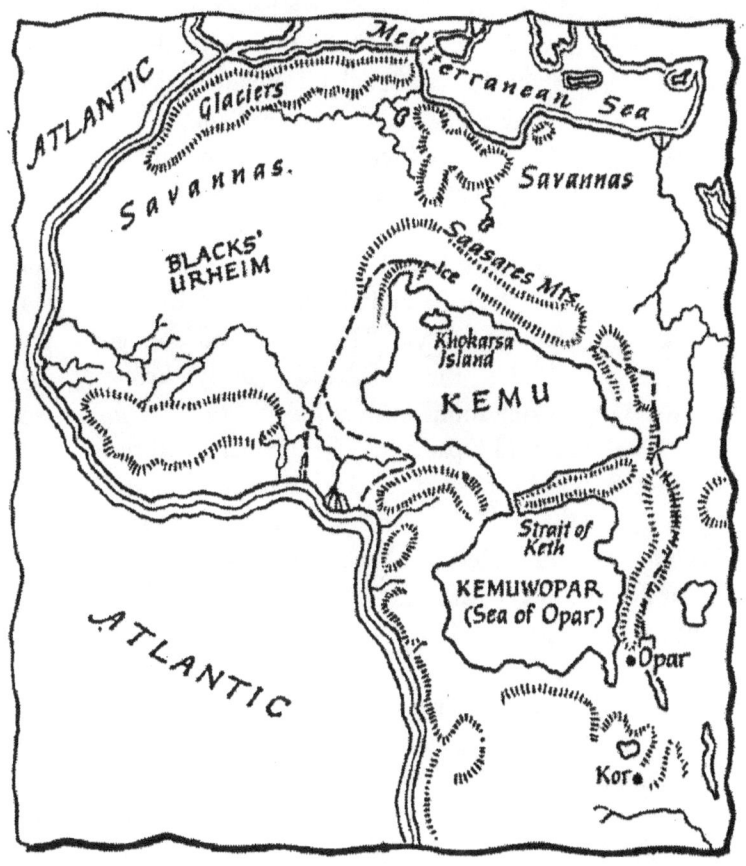

books when he originally intended to write a series of ten books. Without going into the details here, suffice it to say that Farmer blamed Burroughs fans for the premature end to his series. The entire Farmer letter can be found as an addendum to my Afterword in the *Heritage of the Flaming God* volume.

Months earlier, when my publishing plans for *Heritage* were still sketchy, I received a phone call from Ken Webber. Having learned I was planning to publish the essay, he thought I should talk with someone else who had the same idea. Ken put me on the phone with Mick Winger, another ERB fan living in the Denver area, and before we were done talking, we had decided to collaborate on the publishing project.

The following months were filled with dozens of letters, notes, packages and phone calls back and forth between us. There were lots of decisions to make. Waziri Publications would still be the publisher, and I would handle all the financial details. Mick, whose desktop publishing skills far exceeded mine, would be in charge of graphics and producing master copies of the book's pages for printing. Both of us would write supplementary material for the book. I would still write the Afterword about Farmer's Opar books, while Mick would contribute two other articles on the destruction of Atlantis and the history of Central Africa. Another ERB fan, James Van Hise, was kind enough to put me in contact with his printer in Florida. Finally, there was a call to artist Tom Yeates about a cover illustration. We wound up using Tom's beautiful Opar scene, the original of which is owned by Bob Zueschner, who contributed an article to *Farmerphile No. 3*.

In June 1999 the first ever publication of *Heritage of the Flaming God* was made available at the Burroughs Bibliophiles annual meeting in Los Angeles. Of course, as soon as I received the book from the printer, I sent a copy to Philip José Farmer. A couple of months later, I received a short letter from Phil, in which he addressed some comments I made in my Afterword concerning what I personally felt was an over emphasis on violence and sex in his Hadon novels. In my defense, I was writing from the sheltered viewpoint of an Edgar Rice Burroughs fan. In that world Tarzan's actions are marked by a mixture of savagery and reason, but always guided by an inherent sense of right and wrong. That ran counter to the sometimes unemotional, sometimes religious-based fervor with which Farmer's Hadon killed. Additionally, the uninhibited sexual behavior in Farmer's ancient empire contrasted with Burroughs' style, in which sexual activity, if mentioned at all, took place discreetly off stage. It was in reference to these subjects in my Afterword that Phil addressed the following comments to me in his letter of Sept. 8, 1999.

> . . . I did note your objections to Hadon's character and to the temple prostitutes. I have only, just now, a word about these two points. Don't identify a man of an ancient culture, really ancient, with a man in the U.S.A. or, in fact, with any man of any modern Earth. They're different. And the women of Khokarsan culture would view temple prostitution as a holy duty, just as the women of ancient Canaan and other mid-east cultures of that time did. In other words, think in other categories.

I understood the point. After all, I've learned that much of the allure of Farmer's work is that it always challenges the reader to "think in other categories."

In the end, all of the time, money and effort that Mick and I put into publishing *Heritage of the Flaming God* was well worth it. In closing his letter to me, Phil wrote, ". . . your book is magnificent, very well thought-out, a tour-de-force." This essay had waited twenty-eight years for its first publication. Mick and I wanted to be sure we did justice to it, and to its authors, both of whom had passed on years ago. I like to think that Frank and John would approve of how we handled their labor of love.

CALIBAN
WILL MURRAY

I t's one of those interesting coincidences of life that I first discovered Philip José Farmer in the same Boston variety store where I purchased my first Doc Savage novel. Only a year or so had passed, when spinning the wire rack, my eyes fell upon the *Mad Goblin* side of an old Ace Double.

"What is this?" I wondered.

That title sounds like a Doc Savage title. That guy on the cover looks like a cartoony Doc Savage. Years later, I realized that artist Gray Morrow had painted it from an old production still of Steve Holland as Flash Gordon. Holland was the model James Bama used for his Doc Savage covers. He had played Flash in a short-lived 1950s TV series prior to becoming the Man of Bronze.

The other side was *Lord of the Trees* by the same author— unusual for Ace doubles. But this was a very unusual book.

I was slightly put off by the odd, unfamiliar name, but my curiosity was piqued. I bought it, and started reading with *The Mad Goblin* side.

My memory has faded of my exact impressions in my first encounter with Phil Farmer. I recall being bewildered by the interlocking stories, and never suspected both sequeled *A Feast Unknown*, of which I had never heard. No wonder I felt a little lost along the way.

I do remember being puzzled by his choice of name for his Doc Savage simulacrum, Doc Caliban. The reference escaped me,

283

then a teenager. When I subsequently discovered the derivation (Shakespeare's deformed monster from *The Tempest*), I was just as baffled. It seemed, well, unDent. It was my first inkling that Phil Farmer and I saw Doc Savage—if not the world—through very different eyes.

On the other hand, I like Lord Grandrith better than Lord Greystoke for the Ape Man.

Farmer next came to my attention when he released the fascinating *Tarzan Alive*. I was a big Burroughs fan, although I preferred John Carter to the Ape Man. I admit that Phil's conceit that Tarzan was not only an actual person, but still living enthralled me with its sheer audacity. I enjoyed *Tarzan Alive* better than I liked some of Burroughs' Tarzan novels.

Then came *Doc Savage: His Apocalyptic Life* in 1973.

I was delighted to read a book on the Man of Bronze. But once again bewildered by some of it. Farmer's mix of history and personal fantasy with its impossibly ever-shifting lines prompted me to write him a letter. He was kind enough to respond to my foolish fan letter which elected to pick some bones that probably can't be picked. I had recently discovered a number of the Docs had been ghosted by unsuspected writers, which accounted for a lot of the puzzling factual discrepancies Phil had wrestled with. Phil sent me an autographed copy of the Corgi edition of the book, and I offered to help him straighten out the authorship issues in any future edition of *Apocalyptic Life*.

After several years I finally tracked down *A Feast Unknown*. Its reputation had preceded it. I wish it hadn't. It spoiled the story for me. I can see how one writer might give Tarzan the edge over Doc Savage. But I'm not that writer.

We fell out of touch until Bantam Books asked me to write new Doc Savage novels in 1990. I had submitted one in 1980, based on a Lester Dent outline. Ten years later, Bantam ran out of original novels and wanted *Python Isle*, and more. But first, they told me, Phil Farmer was doing *Escape from Loki* to kick off the new series.

I'll admit to a mixture of intrigue and apprehension when I

learned of his plans. A prequel story set in World War I. Once again, I was struck by how differently we approached Doc Savage. Phil was drawn to the backstory. I wanted to tell classic-style Doc Savage adventures set in the '30s.

I will confess that had I been Phil's editor at that time I would have pleaded with him to please write a science fictional Doc adventure set in say, 1936. Make it as wild as imagination can conceive. But no, Phil wanted to tell the wartime tale of how Doc and his men first met. He had planted the seed in *Apoclyptic Life* and it was time to harvest the fruits. Few Doc fans understood that the entire Camp Loki meeting was a Philip José Farmer myth. But a persistent one.

Although Phil had originally planned to write only one Doc, he caught the bug. He expressed to me an interest in working with Dent material. For a while we were talking about him rewriting an old Lester Dent manuscript, to turn it into a Doc. I selected a novelette set in the North Pole called "The Polar Corsair," as the most appropriate to his gifts. With its Polar submarine and naturalistc setting, it was not only Dentian, but Burroughsian. A perfect fit.

But it was not to be. The series proved to be short-lived, a victim of the great Midlist Implosion of 1992-93.

I finally met Phil at the 1993 Pulpcon, where he graciously consented to an extended two-part interview that ran in *Starlog*. It may be one of the longest interviews with Philip José Farmer ever done. Probably only half of it saw print.

We fell out of touch after the Doc Savage series ended. While I continued to write, I drifted into the frontiers of human knowledge, learning Remote Viewing from one of the Stargate pioneers and going on to teach RV as well as doing related *ahem* non-local operations.

At one point, the spectre of writing a Tarzan novel reared its head. Dark Horse had acquired the rights to the legendary unfinished Burrough's Tarzan novel. I lobbied for the opportunity to finish it, knowing in my heart of hearts that Phil Farmer was the only man on earth truly worthy to squeeze in ERB's boots.

To my horror, it went to a writer who seemed the anithesis of Burroughs' heroic pulp tradition. My curiosity overcame my skepticism. I gave the finished book a shot. When in chapter 1, I came upon the UnBurroughsian word "Sasquatch," I quietly closed the book forever . . .

Later, I read a letter in the *Burroughs Bulletin*, where Phil paid me the ultimate compliment of suggesting that only he or I could have done justice to Burroughs. Let me repeat for the record: Philip José Farmer is the only living writer worthy of ERB's boots.

I was delighted when he got to write a Tarzan novel to call his own.

Recently, I was hurled back into time, back to 1970 and that magical spinner rack where I first saw the name of Philip José Farmer. I was going through the carbon to Lester Dent's early Doc Savage novel, *The Squeaking Goblin*. My purpose was to discover any deletions Dent's editors might have made.

I found one in Chapter IX, THREE SKYMEN. It was a modest cut, as those things went. Four words. In the passage below, it follows the word "launch." Four words. But they struck me like a thunderbolt. I will italicize them for you:

Jug took advantage of the respite. He jumped up and down in the launch, *an animated elephantine Caliban.*

Philip José Farmer, how could I ever have doubted you?

Phil & Bette Farmer, Jack London, a Wife and a Baby, a Clean Well Lighted Hotel Room
Joe R. Lansdale

Once upon a time, in a world far, far away, when I was still developing my career, struggling along, trying to write full time, being a house dad while my wife dispatched at the fire department, in that world far, far away, and in that time that now seems prehistoric, I met my hero.

I have a number of writers I admire, and for different reasons, but Philip José Farmer, man, I've said it before and I'll say it again: He throws sparks. He sets the world on fire.

There's something about the way he thinks that's addictive. The thing I like best about it is that his work does mental gymnastics with the brain. His ideas are so wild, and yet, somehow so logical and appealing, that once you read the man, his works hook to your skull and feed you bursts of light and shadow from that point on; it's like an endless morphine drip. Not many writers do that.

I don't know when I first read Farmer's work, but probably in the late sixties or early seventies. I think "The Lovers" was the first thing I read by him, and for a kid raised on a steady diet of Ace Doubles, I was astounded. I then discovered there were Ace Doubles of his work. These were a little different, adventure stuff, more in line with the norm, but even in these there was some kind of iconoclastic worm digging beneath the pages, and you could sense it, and baby, that thing, though harnessed, seemed at any moment ready to snap its bonds and break free, and bite.

I got hooked on Farmer. And the more I read, the more I discovered how varied he was. Some of the novels seemed designed to make a living. Which is not to say they were bad, they were not. But for all practical purposes, they were in line with the rest of the Ace Doubles, at least on the surface. But the more I probed, looking for his work, the more amazed I was. There was a pornographic tribute to Doc Savage, as well as a non-pornographic version of the same character. Same for Tarzan. There were brilliant idea stories like "The Alley Man," and stories like "The Jungle Rot Kid on the Nod," and "The Henry Miller Dawn Patrol." These stories smacked of something more than ray guns and bug-eyed monsters and women who couldn't keep their breasts in their shirts; these were the works of a man who was well read and shared many of my interests, which, of course, made him all the more appealing. Fact is, the short stories were and are, my favorites of his work. Farmer can pack more ideas into a short story than an insecure rocker can pack socks in his underwear.

The man explodes with ideas. It's like someone set off the entire contents of a fireworks stand, then put gas on what was left and set it on fire with a flame thrower.

And this guy, this genius of the written word, one of my main inspirations, I got to meet him.

More than once. But the time that matters was in Dallas, and I guess this was the early eighties, because my son, Keith, was young, a baby, and my wife and I were, as new parents often are, tired.

I had just started to make a bit of a name for myself, and my short stories were beginning to get a smidgen of attention, so for this reason I was invited to be a guest at a Dallas Science Fiction convention. I don't believe they paid the hotel room or gas or food. I think we decided to do it as a kind of vacation. And even more important to me was this: Philip José Farmer was there.

We stayed in a different hotel than the one where the convention took place. Too poor then to pay anything above Motel Six rates. We had to drive to the convention hotel, and lug our baby around in his carrier. We traded off with the baby so I could go to panels, or meet writers and editors (I think there were editors there), to try and make contacts, find out who was buying what and when, maybe learn something from the sage advice on the panels. Or at least I hoped it would be sage. When my wife had had enough, I took over, gave her a chance to cruise the dealers room, go to the bathroom, and stretch her legs.

Phil Farmer had a book that was being released there. It was an old porno novel done in gold and silver, two different editions, one more expensive than the other, if I remember right, and I may not. I don't remember anything else about it, except I wanted one. I had only so much money, however, and I remember my wife and I counting it carefully, trying to figure if we could afford to buy that book. In my memory I think the price was something like thirty-five dollars, early nineteen eighties money. So it would probably be double that price now. A lot of money for new parents, one of them a struggling writer with a hand to mouth career going, the other a small town dispatcher. I wanted that book, bad. It was Farmer and I hadn't read it. Anyway, I went by the table where it was displayed many times. I believe the gold edition was more expensive, and keep in mind, my memory on the colors and price of this book could be off. It's been some years ago, but this part is accurate: It was a rare Farmer book. It was expensive—at least for me at that time—and I wanted it.

Finally, after the panel I was on was over, and we had wandered around, and my wonderful wife had watched our son while I attended panels and met people, we crashed in the large foyer of the hotel, trying to decide what to do next, figuring if we could afford lunch somewhere cheap. So we're thinking and discussing this matter, and a shadow fell over us.

I looked up.

Jesus. It was Philip José Farmer and his lovely wife, Betty.

"You two look tired," Phil said. "Would you like to come up to our room and cool off?"

We thanked him and hustled up the elevator with him, sat in his hotel room, which was much nicer than our little dog run, which seemed the sort of thing that was hosed out more than cleaned out, and we sat there in cool comfort and drank sodas and talked about Jack London. Karen visited with Phil's wife. I have no idea what they talked about, but Phil Farmer and I were Jack London fans and readers, and we talked about that, and I'm sure I gushed about his work, but in time we were cooled and we thanked our hosts and left. Keith, who was often a rowdy baby, was sweet as sugar this time. It was as if he knew that this was an important moment for me.

I walked on air for the rest of that convention.

And then what happened? Another interesting moment.

A book and magazine signing. I was given a spot near Farmer where I mostly twiddled my thumbs, and there he was, signing that new book, the stack of it disappearing, and my mouth is watering, and I wanted that book, and I asked him something about it, and this is the odd moment. I think it's because he knew my situation at a glance.

He told me not to buy it. That it wasn't that much of a book, or words to that effect.

I don't remember much else, but that's what he told me. And I didn't buy it. But I did buy a couple of paperbacks of his work I could afford, and he signed them for me, along with the others I had brought, and though I'm not an emotional goop, I damn near had tears in my eyes.

Phil Farmer had turned out to be just the sort of man I had imagined him to be.

Betty had turned out to be wonderful too.

Okay. I met him another time. Briefer story.

Years later, at a convention, I think Chicago, but I could be wrong. After a while these conventions, cities, etc., run together. Anyway, I came across Phil in an elevator. I said, "You don't know me, but—"

He said, "I know you. You're Joe Lansdale."

I forgot I was wearing my name badge.

Anyway, I told him about the event in Dallas. He just smiled. Kindness for him was all in a day's work. I liked him even more. We got off the elevator.

❧ ❧ ❧ ❧ ❧

I have a postscript to all of this. A kind of thank you, a love letter if you will, to Farmer's work. I did this because his writing has been a big influence on me, and I did it because I wanted to say just that, and talk about how wonderful his work is, and I also wanted in a way to thank him for his and his wife's kindness to me and my wife and son so long ago by doing a small service. It's not tit-for-tat. What his work has done for me I can't equal with a simple introduction, but I wanted to do my bit, and I did just that when *The Best of Philip José Farmer* came out.[1] I had to do it. I begged Bill Schafer at Subterranean Press that this book be done way back, begged Bill to do it on bended knee. I didn't have to beg too hard. Mike Croteau and I came at him from different directions with the same plea. Mike and I wanted this maybe more than Phil. And Bill Schafer, well, it was a ball Mike and I were tossing that he wanted to catch anyway. No real work in that department.

What a marvelous collection of Phil's work this book is. I'm so proud to have made my one small contribution, and I'm sure Mike feels the same.

[1] See "Philip José Farmer: The Man with the Electric Brain" by Joe R. Lansdale in *The Best of Philip José Farmer*, Subterranean Press, 2006.

SKETCHES FROM THE RUINS OF MY MIND
ROBERT R. BARRETT

It was the summer of 1952. I was fifteen years old and had read my first story by Philip José Farmer, "The Lovers," in the August issue of *Startling Stories*. I was also in the early stages of what would turn out to be a lifelong passion for the works of Edgar Rice Burroughs. And I was discovering science fiction and buying many of the science fiction pulps and digests at the corner drugstore. Although I'm sure that I read other stories by Phil in the years that followed, "The Lovers" was the only one, at that time, that stuck with me.

In 1955 Ray Palmer, owner and editor of *Other Worlds Science Stories*, published an article entitled "Tarzan Never Dies," which dealt with his desire to publish a new Tarzan novel, "Tarzan on Mars" by John Bloodstone, a pseudonym for Stuart J. Byrne. Palmer asked each of his readers to send him a dime to help defray the cost of publishing the novel, and to write to Edgar Rice Burroughs, Inc., to ask them to allow the novel to be published.

By 1956 it appeared almost certain that the novel would not be allowed to be published, but in the April 1956 issue of *Other Worlds* a letter was published by Phil Farmer which brought him fully to my attention after many years. In his letter Phil mentioned that he was enclosing his dime for the Tarzan novel, but further stating that "if this is another hoax Ray, if this novel has been written by you, I'm coming up all the way to Amherst, clad in my leopardskin, and tearing you apart. It had better be what you say it is. In grade school my nickname was Tarzan because I spent so much time in the trees playing at being him. I'm thirty-eight now and haven't climbed a tree for a long time, but my hands are still strong, and I can utter the victory cry over a dead profaner of the blesser of my childhood."

I thought, "Gosh, if Farmer is a Burroughs fan, I'd better pay more attention to his writings!" The next year, 1957, I picked up *The Green Odyssey*. I liked it a great deal, and believed that it was quite Burroughs-like in execution. I didn't find another Farmer novel until 1961. By that time I was serving in Germany as part of the Army Corps of Engineers. I was browsing through the English publications in a German store that catered to GIs with such offerings as *Playboy*, etc., when I noticed a Galaxy-Beacon paperback entitled *Flesh* by Phil. Of course I purchased it immediately and went back to the barracks to begin reading. Certainly a wild story but, once again, I found the essence of Burroughs.

I returned to my hometown of Wichita, Kansas, in the spring of 1962 and shortly thereafter made the acquaintance of Vern Coriell, father of Burroughs fandom and the publisher of *The Burroughs Bulletin*. During a trip to Vern's Kansas City home in early 1963, while we were visiting in his living room talking about all things Burroughs, the mailman brought a small package addressed to Vern from Phil Farmer. On opening the package Vern discovered that it contained a signed copy of Phil's latest book *Cache from Outer Space/The Celestial Blueprint* plus a short letter. In the letter Phil explained that *Cache from Outer Space* was actually a sequel (sort of) to Part III of Burroughs' novel, *The Moon Maid*, entitled "The Red Hawk." Phil even named Benoni Rider's horse "Red Hawk." (Note that Hadon also translates to "Red Hawk.") It was this short novel that turned me into a full-fledged fan and collector of Phil's stories.

It wasn't until 1972 that I first met Phil at the Mid-America Con in Kansas City, Missouri. During the course of our short conversation there I discovered how upset Phil was with Doubleday because of their totally inappropriate dust jacket for *Tarzan*

Alive. After I returned to Wichita I began to toy with the idea of creating my own dust jacket for the book, one that I felt would be more appropriate to this stunning *tour de force.*

I enlisted the help of my best friend, Lynn Sutton, who was an amateur photographer, to photograph the portrait of Lord Greystoke by Jean-Paul Goude and the Greystoke coat-of-arms by Bjo Trimble. (I once posited to Phil that Jean-Paul Goude was a friend or relative of Paul D'Arnot. He replied: "That's a good idea about Jean-Paul Goude being a friend, and probably a relative of D'Arnot. If you don't mind I'll mention it in an article for one of the Burroughs fanzines, giving you credit for the idea, of course.") I decided to use a pen and ink drawing of Tarzan, that Frazetta had done for me, on the spine. After finishing the dust jacket, I made five copies of it: one for myself, one for Lynn, one for Phil, one for Vern Coriell, and once for Camille Cazedessus, Jr.

After sending the dust jacket to Phil, the reaction in his August 24, 1972, letter was: "I was completely flabbergasted, overwhelmed, and joyous when I unwrapped your package and saw the dust jacket." To say the least, I was enormously pleased by his reaction.

I also sent photographs of the dust jacket to Doubleday and received a reply from Diane Cleaver dated April 25, 1973: "I like your dust jacket of *Tarzan Alive* much better than ours, I really do. It's distinguished and terribly appealing."

From that time I enjoyed a long period of correspondence with Phil. Some of that correspondence dealt with the creation of his Ancient Opar series—although it would sadly shrink from a series to only the initial book and its sequel.

Phil's letter of February 5, 1973, brought up the fact that Donald Wolheim had asked him if he was in the mood to "go ahead" with the Doc Caliban story (this would have been *Some Unspeakable Dweller*). However, Phil had come under the spell of a long essay by John Harwood and Frank Brueckel entitled "The Heritage of the Flaming God" and dealt with the possible history of the lost city of Opar, as well as several other lost cities found in the works of Edgar Rice Burroughs. "I thought, well, hell, here's the sequel to *Time's Last Gift*," wrote Phil. He went on to explain that he had contacted Hulbert Burroughs to obtain permission to write this Ancient Opar series and stated that Hulbert had replied "if he wanted to do it, fine!" In this letter Phil had tentatively titled his novel, *The Quest of the Grey-Eyed God*. And he was calling the Khokarsans—"Khrakhosans." This was a long, interesting letter presenting in two pages a simple outline of what he planned.

For the next several months Phil continued, in his letters, to lay out aspects of his proposed series, revealing many of the fictional characters by other writers that were the inspirations for his own characters in the series. For example, the mad tyrant king, Minruth, may well be the original for Nimrod. Kwasin, the immensely strong, insane cousin of Hadon was a mingling of Hercules, Gilgamesh, Conan, and Kwasind, Hiawatha's strong friend. Kebiwabes, Hadon's bard friend is based on Hiawatha's singer-friend, Chibiabos, with a bit of Homer thrown in. And, of course, the great meteorite axe fashioned by Wi for Pag in H.R. Haggard's *Allan and the Ice-Gods* would be the same axe given by Pag to Kwasin in the Opar novel.

By March 24, 1973, Phil had settled on *Hadon of Ancient Opar* and the title, and had asked Don Wollheim if he could cross out the Doc Caliban title on his contract and substitute the Opar title, which was okay with Wollheim.

In one of my letters to Phil I brought up the fact that I found it strange that the bow and arrow were not among the arsenal of weapons used by the Khokarsans. I mentioned that I thought Gribardson may have placed a religious taboo on the bow and arrow and would punish any who defied the taboo by invention of such implements, but Phil replied that, while Gribardson may well have imposed the taboo, he just wasn't around that often to mete out any punishments.

Hadon of Ancient Opar ended with a real cliff-hanger. It wouldn't have been so bad if the next book, *Flight to Opar,* had come out sometime during that following year, but readers had to wait two years to get Hadon off his sword! Phil had agreed to too many commitments to write other novels and just couldn't squeeze *Flight to Opar* in. Sadly that would be the end of what

Phil had planned to be a long series. I certainly wasn't the only Phil Farmer or Burroughs fan who was disappointed that the saga was doomed to end without the full history of Opar presented.

I once broached the subject of why he didn't continue the Opar series,[1] and Phil replied, in a letter dated March 31, 1987, that he still intended to write sequels to the Opar series as well as the Lord Grandrith/Doc Caliban series but his contractual obligations had been so heavy for such a long time that it was just impossible for him to get to these. He did remark that: "Actually, I had a contract with DAW to do the 3rd Opar book but I finally got out of that, mainly because I wasn't happy with Don Wollheim."

It has often been speculated as to why Harwood and Brueckel's essay was never published in *The Burroughs Bulletin*, even though it had been advertised. Vern published *The Burroughs Bulletin* on a shoestring and his publishing dreams were always exceeded by his lack of finances. Many times his printer held onto the current issue until Vern was able to pay for the printing costs. Thus his subscribers were forever griping because the wait between issues was just too long. Harwood and Brueckel's essay was over eighty pages long, including notes and bibliography. *The Burroughs Bulletin* was rarely over twenty-five or thirty pages.

Vern had commissioned a professional Kansas City architect, Larry Hanks, also a Burroughs fan, to make a drawing of the Oparian Temple of the Sun to accompany the essay. The result was beautiful—but it was drawn on three separate panels, 21" x 23", 28" x 23", and 21" x 23". Vern just couldn't figure out how to publish a drawing that large! Luckily I own the originals for "The Temple of the Sun," so they are not lost. The essay languished until Michael Winger and Alan Hanson published it in 1999. The architectural drawing has never been published!

In his January 1999 letter to Alan Hanson, published in *Heritage of the Flaming God*, Phil wrote that he could "never get any encouraging words from prominent ERB experts on finishing the Opar series even after I'd decided to write a third book ending the series." I think Phil may have believed it at the time he wrote it, but it just isn't very realistic. For one thing any group of fans, especially Burroughs fans, cannot make or break any book and for an author to feel that he can't write a book because he's not received any encouragement from some fans just doesn't fit with reality. If Phil had actually believed this I doubt that he would have been moved to write *The Dark Heart of Time*. Burroughs fans certainly hadn't been breaking down his door to write a Tarzan novel, even though he had made it known for years that it was his desire. And one mustn't forget that *Hadon of Ancient Opar* and *Flight to Opar* have each been reprinted four times in English editions, and probably many more times in foreign editions. Not a bad publishing history! My biggest regret is that age and age-related illnesses have slowed Phil down to the extent that he has stopped writing. But, God in Heaven, am I ever thankful that he's given us as much as he has!

[1] The third Opar novel, *The Song of Kwasin*, was completed by Christopher Paul Carey from Farmer's partial manuscript, outline, and notes, and published in 2012. Since then Carey has written three novellas set in Ancient Opar: *Exiles of Kho*, *Hadon, King of Opar* and *Blood of Ancient Opar*.

Smoke Gets In Your Nose

Spider Robinson sometimes places characters from other authors' work in his books—something Phil Farmer has certainly been known to do! Spider's story "Dog Day Evening" has the first, of many, appearances of Ralph von Wau Wau, the talking German shepherd with the 200 IQ. Ralph was of course first seen in *Venus on the Half-Shell*, by Kilgore Trout and later in two short stories by Jonathan Swift Somers III. Here Spider tells an unusual tale of meeting one of his heroes.

It was in the last days of the Sixties, in 197(mumble), shortly after the rediscovery of unsliced bread—so long ago, Tom Doherty was probably still working for Ace Books, instead of the other way around.

But not in Toronto, he wasn't. The Ace rep for that territory back in that geologic epoch was . . . how can I put this charitably? A Hipster Wannabe? No, I think I'm gonna have to go with Dork. Assigned (God knows why) to shepherd Judith Merril, Philip José Farmer and myself around Toronto to and from assorted promotional assignments that have mercifully passed from memory, this large sweaty comb-overed chap decided to impress us with his big-city sophistication by hauling out and passing over his shoulder, less than thirty seconds after we had all piled into his big cream-puff gunboat of a car, an elegant cigar box. And when I opened it, it was filled to the brim with joints the size of Italian cigars.

At once I was filled with sharp antinomy. ("conflict between two equally urgent and necessary propositions." Rock above testicles, hard place beneath. If it involves sex it's known as a Dilemma Of The Horns.)

Judith and I were friends—and both heads. But I had never met Phil Farmer . . . the first time I'd ever laid eyes on him was thirty seconds earlier, getting into the back seat while he got into the front . . . and I was intimidated almost to incoherent paralysis by the prospect of meeting the man who had first put functioning genitalia on science fiction characters and adventure heroes, and thus on us writers, and had furthermore perpetrated some of the most monstrous puns of our time. Judith was a great writer, but Phil was one of my personal gods. He seemed unimaginably old (younger than I am now: you should see the portrait in his attic!), and serious, and vastly dignified—more than anything I wanted to avoid striking him as a dolt, for if I were, of what value was my praise?

On the other hand, those were some of the fattest joints I'd ever seen, with an intriguing bouquet. Our sweaty writer-wrangler wouldn't stop talking: there was no conversation to maintain. If we just rolled the windows down Phil might not even notice the funny smell.

I think Judith grokked my problem. And God bless her, she was—as Spider John Koerner once sang of Lady Day—a fast-life woman who didn't let nobody get into her way. And lived half of every year in Jamaica. She took the cigar box from my hands, pulled out a crooked cylinder like an albino Parodi, a bone as thick as my . . . thumb, put fire to it, shortened it an inch and a half with her first inspired inspiration, and offered it to me. I glanced at the back of Phil's white-haired head, then at Judith's sharklike grin . . . took the joint from her and sucked in smoke—

In front, Phil tilted his head slightly, then slowly turned it all the way round to regard me over the seatback. He blinked owlishly.

Aw shit, I thought, and kept inhaling. In for a penny, in for an ounce . . .

"That's reefer, isn't it?" he asked gravely.

"Yes Phil," I croaked in that odd whispered seal-bark that results from trying to talk without exhaling.

Judith's was more like a hoarse walrus. "*Good* reefer."

He got a distant look. "It's been more than thirty years . . ." He sighed and held out his hand. "May I have a toke?"

Between the smokespraying and the laughing and the huge coughing and the *really* laughing, Judith and I scared the *poo* out of that poor Ace salesman. He screamed and nearly hit a parked car, while his car belched vast incriminating clouds of smoke from all four windows like something in a Cheech and Chong movie, and he thereafter declined any of his own weed, and spoke to us only when necessary. I never heard from or of him again. (And since then, any time I've been in Toronto promoting an Ace book, I take cabs and get receipts.)

His loss. Phil and Judith and I got righteously *silly* together, one of the most memorable stones in a lifetime unusually blessed with them—a privilege I will never forget as long as I live. Even Judith was impressed by Phil's laugh, and her own had been measured at Force Ten. The only other science fiction Grandmasters I've ever gotten high with (on first meeting, anyway), let alone *that* high with, were the late great Bob Sheckley, and it was Sheck's weed, and Ted Sturgeon, who'd got his from his next-door neighbor, David Crosby.

I wouldn't be at all surprised if that was the last time Phil ever smoked pot. I was a Celebrity Judge at the 2001 Cannabis Cup. I'd love to get mildly drunk with him, one day—"somewhat over-served," Peter O'Toole would say—and though I haven't done it in decades, he's one of a bare handful of people I'd be willing to trip with—but honestly, I'd be happier just to hang out with him for a couple of days without taking any drug at all. The only thing I *can't* quite imagine is us ever being *sober* together. (Or separately.) We were both born giddy.

And some sort of telepathic connection has apparently been established between us, because a beautiful young time-traveler calling herself Josie Bauer, who claims to be an unrecorded daughter of Phil's, has been spotted in a few of my own Callahan's Place stories. I'm not even going *near* that one . . .

I suspect Philip José Farmer is actually many centuries old, and if so I'll bet he once served in the Sherwood Forest Irregulars, with Robin of Locksley. He is unquestionably a Merry Man.

(He may even be the original model for the character with the big staff, known as Tryer F___ . . . who, according to Made Marryin', was definitely *not* a little john.)

(Just don't let him get started tying knots in it. He's known as the show-off, a knotting ham . . .)

Happy birthday, Phil! I hope you're the first Grandmaster to attend his own Centennial. And not the last. See you upriver . . .

—Spider Robinson,
at an undisclosed location in British Columbia

On Not Going There
Howard Waldrop

"Like most things from the Seventies, this is Philip José Farmer's fault . . . If you don't like it, don't write me. Write to Philip José Farmer." Thus begins . . . and ends, Howard Waldrop's introduction to his story "The Adventure of the Grinder's Whistle," reprinted in his collection *Night of the Cooters* (Ursus Imprints, 1991). After finding a statement like that in print, we just *had* to hunt Howard down and beg an article for *Farmerphile*.

The above quote refers to Howard writing a story to be included in a "fictional author" anthology he heard Philip José Farmer was putting together. Sadly the anthology never happened, but you can read all about that in *Venus on the Half-Shell and Others* (Subterranean Press, February 2008).

> Producer (to director Sullivan): It won't play in Peoria.
> Sullivan: What do they know in Peoria?
> Producer: In Peoria, they know what they like.
> Sullivan: If they knew what they *liked*, they wouldn't be in Peoria.
> —Preston Sturges, Sullivan's Travels (1940)

A nd what was it like, I hear you ask, breaking into writing in the SF and fantasy fields in the late 1960s and early 1970s? It was *tough*.

Though there were more markets then, what with a plethora of original anthologies (the series ones: *Orbit* edited by Damon Knight; *New Dimensions* ed. by Robert Silverberg; *Universe* ed. by

Terry Carr; *Chrysalis* by Togerson; *Shadows* by Charlie Grant, and other less viable ones), part of the problem was that at least a quarter of all the original anthology market was in the hands of the late Roger Elwood, who, though he did convince otherwise stolid publishers to at least dabble in the SF and fantasy fields, when they'd never tried them before, he was (in the current parlance) a right wing Christian who had many many taboos in the guidelines for writing for his anthologies. The thing about Elwood's projects, was that among the safe dreck, there were at least one or two incredible stories in each of them. (Lupoff, Lisa Tuttle, George R.R. Martin, *even*, yes, even Phil Farmer.) You had to search and search, but you'd eventually find them.

And there were diegetic considerations when you tried to do *anything* in the field.

If you were trying to do something stylistically; or with the narrative, or trying to tell stories like they'd *never been told before*, you would find, on opening a new magazine or anthology, that Robert Silverberg had *just* gone there, and done what *you* wanted to do, only *first and better*.

(Silverberg's famous dictum of the time: "I believe a story should have a beginning, a middle and an end. Not necessarily in *that* order." He had just written "Sundance" which was about guilt, racism and parallels between the SF of planetary settlement, Vietnam, and Manifest Destiny; "Passengers" in which half the narrative was *not there*, and had to be filled in by the reader, and was a better story for it. "And so on, and so forth," as Professor Marvell would say.)

You couldn't do *anything* stylistically or narratively without having Silverberg cut you off at the knees. And he was doing it without even breaking a sweat. He just *did* it.

There was another place you couldn't go; your childhood and your cultural roots.

That's because of a guy of the opening epigram: He *knew* what he liked AND he was *still* in Peoria. And he made you like it, too.

It wasn't really his fault he'd written *I Owe for the Flesh* in the early Fifties and he had had a (in the words of *2½ Men*) drive-by colonostomy in a prize-novel contest (it went on to appear) run by hyenas and civets, with some well-intentioned innocent dupes as fall-guys.

Somehow, he'd fought his way back from *that* for fifteen years or so, speed-bump (more like a berm) as it was to his career, and by the late '60s had turned that Urbook into what became the Riverworld series of novellas and prize-winning novels.

That of course was not even a quarter of what he was doing. He was writing the definitive story about King Kong. He was mining territory Melville (no slouch) had left untouched. He (somehow) brought the world of Henry Miller into a nursing home. He took on the worlds of Burroughs (*both of them*) and told of a Tarzan as by William Burroughs in "The Jungle-Rot Kind on the Nod."

Farmer was mining his childhood and cultural roots.

That was a *good* thing.

He was also mining *mine*, and *everybody else's*.

That was *bad*.

I had a novella I wanted to do about Cyrano de Bergerac, a real person, and a proto-SF writer (and unlike in Rostand's play—a tremendous piece of work, the mythic weight of which has overshadowed the truth of Cyrano's life—he died, unlike in the play, at the age of 35. His nose looked more like a turnip than like the late James Durante's. Etc.)

Then all of a sudden—BLOOIE! Cyrano shows up in the Riverworld. (The brilliance of the Riverworld is that it can contain *all* people, *all* times and *all* situations. Did *anyone* ever invent such an elastic place?)

Steven Utley (who started at the same time as me, and who was so full of beans and vigor that we collaborated *all the time* when we'd finish our *own* work) would commiserate with me. "Damn that Farmer," he would say. "How does he do it? He's tapped into the *Zeitgeist*. Mine, anyway."

"Mine, too," I'd say. "How can we go anywhere, when he gets there first?"

Well, we did "Custer's Last Jump!" which was written in 1972 but not published until 1976 (in Silverberg's shorthand phrase "due to complex but uninteresting reasons.") and then was up for a Nebula (against, of course, Asimov's first Robot story in twenty years . . . no reason to attend *that* awards ceremony, was there?).

And we managed to write, somehow without him gumming up the works, a "Farmer-like" novella with references to Mary Shelly, Burroughs, Rafael Sabatini and H.P. Lovecraft in a sort of stylistic nightmare form (à la Silverberg; in fact Silverberg published it in his *New Dimensions 7*, called "Black as the Pit, From Pole to Pole"—which in a later state of high cognitive dissonance I would wake at 4 A.M. in a cabin in Washington state, to hear on NPR a lawyer reading from W.E. Henley's poem we'd used as a title when they croaked Timothy McVeigh for the Oklahoma City Bombing. It took the media about ten minutes to identify the poem McVeigh had left as his last testament, not me. Or Utley. Or for that matter, Silverberg or Farmer, who'd probably both had to memorize and recite "Invictus" in some long-ago sixth-grade class . . .).

"Wow!" we'd said when the story had been published in 1977. "Stole a march on Phil Farmer!" We felt All Grown Up as writers. We thought there should be someplace handing out Certificates of Achievement, or something.

(Joanna Russ' famous review of the story in F&SF referred to us as "The Malaprop Kids, Adrift in the Classics." Touché!)

The shadow of Farmer stretches like that of Goya's giant all over the field. ("He blots out the sun for miles 'round." as *They Might Be Giants*, the 1970 play has it.)

Of course with the Wold Newton link, he's come up with *another*, infinitely stretchable, all-encompassing background for *any number* of stories. How many people have come up with just *one* great concept in their careers, *much less two*?

I pity young writers starting out *now*. Farmer's concepts now stretch so far back they're part of the SF furniture. We had to react to every new Farmer pillage of the culture *right then and there*. It was in our faces, every time we sat down at the typewriter.

Now, he's what people grow up reading. To new writers, he's as established as Burroughs or Conan Doyle or Tolkien was to us. They'll be fighting tradition if they enter Farmer Territory (and it's hard to imagine anywhere Farmer is "traditional").

Happy Birthday, Mr. Farmer. You'll go on frustrating young writers for at least another thousand years or so.

There's *nothing* you can do about it.

Get used to it.

We Were Introduced by Sherlock Holmes
George H. Scheetz

I first met Philip José Farmer—at least in person—in 1977. We actually were introduced by Sherlock Holmes the previous year.

However, this story really begins five years earlier, with the publication of *Tarzan Alive: A Definitive Biography of Lord Greystoke,* which included two items of particular interest to this story:

> Addendum 1, "A Case of Identity, or The Adventure of the Seven Claytons," by H. W. Starr; and
> Addendum 2, "A Case of a Case of Identity Recased, or The Grey Eyes Have It," by Philip José Farmer.

Starr theorized that John Clayton, who drove a hansom cab in *The Hound of the Baskervilles,* was actually the grandfather of Tarzan. Farmer took this theory and expanded it somewhat.

The confluence of two of Phil's great interests—Sherlock Holmes and Tarzan—in "The Grey Eyes Have It" apparently gave him the notion of starting a scion society,[1] as well as its name: The Hansoms of John Clayton. It was several years before the first known announcement of Farmer's quest appeared in print.

In the meantime, another scion society, the Double-Barrelled Tiger Cubs,[2] was founded on 22 July 1975 at the University of Illinois at Urbana-Champaign by Doug Highsmith, Chuck Huber, and me; we sent a letter of intent to Dr. Julian Wolff, Commissionaire of the Baker Street Irregulars, which we thought was necessary to achieve official status. Doug Highsmith suggested the name and persons now unknown suggested the officer titles: Murray (as President) and Stamford (as Secretary-Treasurer).

Unfortunately, Dr. Wolff never responded to the letter, or a second letter (28 August 1975), which led *practically* everyone involved to believe that the Double-Barrelled Tiger Cubs had been rejected by New York. Undaunted, a few loyal souls drove to Chicago for a presentation of *Sherlock Holmes* at the Shubert Theatre, starring Leonard Nimoy and Alan Sues.

To everyone's joy, the March 1976 issue of *The Baker Street Journal* carried an announcement of the new scion society at Champaign-Urbana. Shortly thereafter, letters were arriving asking for information. Thus inspired, Doug Highsmith, Mike Clark, and I met on 20 September 1976 to discuss plans for the organization of the Double-Barrelled Tiger Cubs. After three organizational meetings, bylaws were adopted on 11 October 1976, and elections were held. I became the first Murray and Mike Clark the first Stamford.

A logo was approved on 12 October 1976, and the first regular meeting was held on 18 October 1976, at which time the society viewed *Sherlock Holmes in New York* on NBC-TV. I was the first editor—uncredited—of *Afghanistanzas,* the official bulletin of the Double-Barrelled Tiger Cubs, the Premier Issue of which appeared on 31 October 1976.

Earlier in 1976, in his introduction to *The Adventures of Herlock Sholmes* (Mysterious Press 1976), Farmer reported:

> Recently, I decided to found a scion chapter of the Baker Street Irregulars in my home town, Peoria, Illinois . . . A local newspaper published an interview of me, incidentally noting that I was forming the scion. The response was startling. Apparently, Holmes plays well in Peoria.

Robert C. "Bob" Burr, a neighbor of the Farmers who was interested in things Sherlockian, read the aforementioned interview (Peoria *Observer*, 7 January 1976), introduced himself to Phil, and expressed an interest in the scion society.

Yet another notice, targeted to sf fans, appeared in *Moebius Trip Library's S. F. Echo*, #25 (April–August 1976. p. 4), a fanzine published in Peoria by Edward C. Connor:

> PHIL FARMER is organizing a SCION SOCIETY of the BAKER STREET IRREGULARS (to cover Peoria and surrounding area) to be called: "The Hansoms of John Clayton." Interested parties may telephone Mr. Farmer at 688-5701.

Sorry, folks! Phil no longer has that telephone number—Editor.

A cosmic juxtaposition of the Double-Barrelled Tiger Cubs and Hansoms of John Clayton occurred in March 1976, when *The Baker Street Journal* published Philip José Farmer's address and intent to form a scion society in Peoria. Thus inspired, I sent him the Premier Issue of *Afghanistanzas.* To everyone's surprise and delight, the creator of Riverworld and the World of Tiers actually joined the Double-Barrelled Tiger Cubs on December 6, and sent an LOC—"letter of comment" to those not familiar with fanspeak—in reply:

> Philip José Farmer: Thanks for the premier issue of *Afghanistganzas* . . . (signed) Sherlogically. P.S. I was disappointed that you did not include in your list of new books *The Adventure of the Peerless Peer*, John H. Watson, M.D., Farmer, editor, Dell. [Editor: Oops! Consider the oversight seen.]

Just one month later (on 1 February 1977), I arrived in Peoria, Illinois, to begin my career as a professional librarian. By summer, I had worked up the courage to call Phil, who invited me to visit. I recall Bette baking cookies—lots and lots of cookies. Among other topics, Phil and I discussed the organization of the Hansoms of John Clayton. The details of that first encounter are a bit fuzzy; Phil mixed a phenomenal screwdriver—it had very little orange juice in it.

In August 1977, the late John Bennett Shaw, BSI,[3] his wife,

Dorothy Rowe Shaw, and Theodore G. Schultz, BSI, of San Rafael, California, stopped overnight in Peoria. I had the good fortune to join the party, which included Phil and Bette, for dinner.

On 27 October 1977, Bob Burr, "tired of waiting for Farmer and Scheetz," called both and arranged the first meeting of the Hansoms of John Clayton, which took place on 17 November 1977, at Burr's home. In attendance were Philip José Farmer, Bette V. Farmer, Robert C. Burr, George H. Scheetz, Alex Ciegler, and Emily Sutton. These six, plus Tom Simpson, who was invited but unable to attend, are considered the charter members.

Farmer's interest in Sherlock Holmes, as well as Tarzan and the other great pulp heroes, dates to his youth in Peoria. However, his first published Sherlockian article ("Oft Have I Travelled," in 1969, the year he returned to Peoria), actually related to the world of Sherlock Holmes' successor, Solar Pons, and the faithful Doctor Parker, created by August Derleth.

By the time of the first meeting of the Hansoms of John Clayton in Peoria, Farmer's Sherlockian oeuvre had grown substantially. In addition to books, stories, articles, and other miscellaneous publications, Phil even had made a presentation to The Mexborough Lodgers, the now-defunct Sherlock Holmes Society of El Paso, Texas, in 1975. And, of course, he had devised the Wold Newton genealogy, a source of endless fascination.

Over the years, Phil and Bette hosted numerous meetings of the Hansoms of John Clayton at their home. On 7 July 1979, the 2nd Annual Picnic was held at the Farmers' home, which began a long tradition of the Farmers hosting the annual event nearly every summer. (Another great picnic tradition was the annual egg toss, but that is a story for another day.) Even after moving from Peoria, I enjoyed the periodic opportunity to return for the annual picnic.

In December 1977, Phil was invited by John Bennett Shaw to attend the annual dinner of the Baker Street Irregulars in New York. Phil, to his great regret, had to decline. He was invited a second time, in December 1978, but was unable to attend for personal reasons. I regret to report that Phil, despite his many contributions to the world of Sherlock Holmes, has not been awarded an Investiture as a member of the Baker Street Irregulars[4]—a tragic oversight.

In December 1982, I was invited to attend the annual dinner as a guest of Ronald A. DeWaal, BSI, but I too was unable to attend for personal reasons.

In 1977, I seriously began to collect the works of Philip José Farmer when I found a copy of the original 1968 Essex House edition of *Image of the Beast* in a little shop near the campus of Bradley University. As I recall, I paid the magnificent sum of $4.00 for it. The proprietor of the shop was J. D. Drake, a Farmer aficionado in his own right.

It was during this time period that I began work on *Philip José Farmer: The Authorized Bibliography*. Phil opened his personal library and files to me and provided moral support as I worked on this project over the course of several years. Bette and Phil asked me to house-sit and care for their pets—Geordie, the Shetland sheepdog, and Samantha, the Siamese cat—on several occasions as they traveled, and Phil allowed me to use his IBM Selectric typewriter to work on the bibliography and fanzines. I remember producing most of the third issue of *Farmerage* during one such stay—not to mention Sam's expressive displeasure at my using Phil's typewriter!

By the mid-1980s, I had commissioned a critical introduction for the bibliography from Edgar L. Chapman, indexed the book, and submitted it to Greenwood Press. The book was accepted, but never published.

This project earned me the bittersweet title of Official Bibliographer and enabled me, over the years, to answer sundry questions regarding Phil's work—many from Phil and Bette. One such outcome occurred in early 1998, when the Farmers invited me to help organize an exhibit of Phil's life and work at the Peoria Public Library. I was pleased to loan several hard-to-find items for the exhibit, and I compiled a detailed, twelve-page checklist, "The Works of Philip José Farmer," to accompany the exhibition. My favorite factoid from the checklist: As of April 1998, Phil's work had appeared in twenty-four languages (including English) in forty-one countries.

In early 1978, I organized the Philip José Farmer Society and began to publish a fanzine, *Farmerage,* in June. Over the course of two years, I produced three issues. At the same time, I was editor of *Wheelwrightings,*[5] the triannual journal of the Hansoms of John Clayton; the first issue appeared in May 1978. Both were produced on IBM Selectric typewriters—at least until May 1981, when Bob Burr decided to hire a compositor to typeset *Wheelwrightings.*

For the first cover of *Wheelwrightings*—with the permission of Jack Tracy, the copyright holder—we used a fantastic illustration of a hansom cab by Philip C. Thompson and Ned Shaw, which appeared in the *Sherlock Holmes Calendar 1978* (New York: Doubleday & Company, Inc.).

I began the first issue with "a special letter from our Founder . . ."

11 May 1978

Not so long ago there was a president of the United States who used to ask his cronies, "Will it play in Peoria?" He was referring to political and economic issues, of course. But Peoria, Illinois, was considered to be the epitome of Averagesville, a dull, middle-class Midwestern city to be used as a laboratory for reaction to national issues and policies. What Peoria felt was what the majority of Americans would feel. Or so went the theory.

Peoria had many things, the vast industrial complex of Caterpillar Tractor, Hiram Walker (the largest distillery in the U.S.), a Pabst brewery, a scenic drive which Theodore Roosevelt called the most beautiful in the world, a pigeon-dirt-spotted bronze statue to Robert Ingersoll, and the honor of being the oldest white settlement west of the Appalachians.

What it did not have to make it truly cosmopolitan was a Baker Street Irregulars Scion Society. Happily, that grave lack has been rectified as of late last year. The Hansoms of John Clayton is (are?) wheeling along fine, thank you, and stopping now and then to pick up more fares. May it (they?)

never wear out, and may the passengers always enjoy the ride.

If this issue should happen to fall in the hands of a very old bee-keeper in Sussex, we extend an invitation to you to visit us any time—expenses paid. And [an] honorarium of no small size. Or, my dear Holmes, if you can't make it, we'd be happy to come to your place. Just send the address.

—*Philip José Farmer.*

I compiled a tribute to the Founder, "The Sherlockiana of Philip José Farmer," which appeared in the second issue of *Wheelwrightings* (September 1978).

The Hansoms of John Clayton met every other month; the July meeting was always a potluck picnic and the September meeting was always the annual banquet. The First Annual 2704 Banquet took place at Shady Oaks Restaurant in Peoria. The evening of 23 September 1978 saw 17 members and guests—including Phil and Bette Farmer and me—gathered to celebrate John Clayton's famous ride. Following the meal, the meeting was opened with the reading of The Clayton Ritual, devised by Robert C. Burr:

What was his name? *John Clayton.*
Where did he live? *No. 3, Turpey Street, the Borough.*
What did he do? *He drove a hansom cab.*
And what was its number? *2704.*
Whence came the cab? *Out of Shipley's yard, near Waterloo Station.*
When was his famous ride? *September 26, 1888.*
And who was his infamous fare? *Rodger Baskerville, alias Stapleton, alias Vandeleur.*

"Feature of the evening," reported Burr, "was Phil Farmer's . . . thought-provoking talk in which he proposed a parallel world theory in which Holmes and Watson might be criminals."

In March 1979, I was nonplussed—and very honored—when

Phil added a dedication to the new edition of *Inside Outside* (New York: Berkley Books): "For George Scheetz."

Two incidents occurred later in 1979, which led to the publication of *Riverworld War: The Suppressed Fiction of Philip José Farmer*. The first involved the novel, *Jesus on Mars,* which was scheduled to be published in abridged form in *Isaac Asimov's Science Fiction Magazine* for December 1979, prior to its book publication. However, the book was released early, and the abridged version was killed.

The second incident involved *The Magic Labyrinth,* when the editor deleted a major battle from the manuscript—thus "Riverworld War." I proposed the idea of publishing both pieces in a book, and Phil agreed. We worked out the contractual details and I commissioned Joan Hanke Woods to produce a cover illustration based on the Riverworld story. David Pichaske, then an English professor at Bradley University who had published several small press books, agreed to publish *Riverworld War* under his imprint, Ellis Press. I served as the book's editor (uncredited).

The book was issued simultaneously in two states: Trade, 1,500 copies ($4.95); and Limited, 500 copies, which were signed and numbered by Farmer on p. 109 ($11.95). Due to a printer's error, three versions of the trade state exist: (a) all copies were printed in error with the limitation statement on p. 109; (b) the printing error was compounded in an unknown number of the above, in which "MEMO FROM DONNA JEANNE" was also printed below the limitation statement; (c) p. 109 was removed from an unknown number of the above by the publisher.

In early December 1980, Bob Burr and I were interviewed by Terry Bibo for the Peoria *Journal Star.* Terry wanted to illustrate her article with a special photograph, so, on December 17, six loyal Sherlockians gathered at Bob Burr's home to pose for the *Journal Star.* The article and its delightful photograph appeared on December 28.

I sparked a controversy at the March 1981 meeting, when I served as quizmaster at the request of Norman V. Kelly, who had won the previous quiz. I included non-Canonical questions in my quiz on "The Copper Beeches," which (as later reported by Bob Burr) resulted in "a veritable brouhaha and near donnybrook" between members of the society. At this same meeting, as I recall, my father, who was visiting Peoria, fell asleep and interrupted a dramatic presentation of "The Speckled Band" by snoring—on cue!

The following April, several members of the Hansoms of John Clayton—Bob Burr, Brad Keefauver, Tom Simpson (by proxy), and I—met to discuss methods to improve the bimonthly meetings and involve additional members in the society's operation. (Frankly, we did not want the Executive Secretary—Bob Burr—to burn out.) Little did we know the firestorm we unwittingly would unleash!

At the May 1981 meeting, the proposed changes in meeting format and first-ever election of a president—to be known as The Big Wheel—to run the meetings were presented for discussion. The purpose of the changes, according to the proponents, was to ensure the longevity of the organization, but not everyone

"Outfitted with deerstalker, pipe and magnifying glass is Kathy Scheetz. She and other members of The Hansoms of John Clayton look over a Sherlock Holmes bibliography. The others pictured are (from left) Lucy Sommerfield, Bob Burr, George Scheetz, Bette Farmer and Philip José Farmer.
Photo by Alan Harkrader."—*Peoria Journal Star*, December 28, 1980

understood it that way. In fact, Bette Farmer considered it a coup attempt, for two reasons: the Founder—Phil Farmer—was not invited to the meeting, and (in her opinion) Bob Burr was being pushed aside—notwithstanding that Bob was one of the "gang of four" that proposed the changes in the first place.

Bette called me at work (at the Lakeview Branch Library) the following week and engaged me in a long and highly charged conversation, in which I did my best to assure her that Phil's absence from the meeting was an honest oversight, which everyone regretted, and no one, least of all me, wanted to displace—or replace—Bob Burr. By the end of the telephone conversation, we had cleared the air.

In keeping with the original plan, Bob Burr announced the election of The Big Wheel in the August 1981 issue of *Plugs & Dottles,* the society's monthly newsletter. No candidates came forward and Bob continued as the sole officer of the Hansoms of John Clayton.

A major element of each bimonthly meeting of the Hansoms of John Clayton was the quiz, which was based on the story selected for that meeting's discussion. By tradition, the winner was the next quizmaster. Phil won his first quiz at the fourth meeting on 4 May 1978. Bette won the quiz at the 14th meeting on 18 January 1980. I finally won a quiz at the 25th meeting on 20 November 1981.

As it happened, the following meeting (15 January 1982) was my last as a resident member. I was moving to Ames, Iowa—ostensibly a career move, but, in reality, I intended to found another scion society: The Lying Corn-Chandlers. Up to that point, only two members had attended every meeting: Robert C. Burr and me.

I presented a talk, "The Sherlockismus," at my last regular meeting, which was accepted some five and a half years later for publication in *The Baker Street Journal.*

Many of my greatest friends were introduced to me by Sherlock Holmes while I played in Peoria, including two who are always in my heart: Philip José and Bette V. Farmer.

We Were Introduced by Sherlock Holmes

[1] The word *scion* is defined as "a descendant or heir." In this case, scion societies are local organizations affiliated in spirit and custom with—and descended from—The Baker Street Irregulars, a not-for-profit organization founded in 1934 by Christopher Morley (1890–1957), an American journalist, novelist, essayist, and poet. Most scion societies take their name from a Holmes story, character, or event.

[2] "I endeavoured to cheer and amuse her by reminiscences of my adventures in Afghanistan; but, to tell the truth, I was myself so excited at our situation and so curious as to our destination that my stories were slightly involved. To this day she declares that I told her one moving anecdote as to how a musket looked into my tent at the dead of night, and how I fired a *double-barrelled tiger cub* at it [emphasis added]."—John Watson, in *The Sign of Four*.

[3] The Baker Street Irregulars (BSI) is an organization of Sherlock Holmes enthusiasts. Members convene every January in New York City for an annual dinner, which forms part of a weekend of celebration and study. The BSI has published *The Baker Street Journal*, an "irregular quarterly of Sherlockiana," since 1946. Members are entitled to use the initials "BSI" after their name.

[4] An investiture is the "act or formal ceremony of conferring the authority and symbols of a high office" (*The American Heritage® Dictionary of the English Language, Fourth Edition,* 2000). The Baker Street Irregulars does not accept applications for membership. Instead, membership and an "Irregular Shilling" are awarded as an honor to those who have made a name for themselves in the world of Sherlock Holmes. When membership is conferred, in addition to the Irregular Shilling, the recipient is awarded a Canonical title—that is, an Investiture. As of April 2008, 601 Irregular Shillings have been awarded, and there are 307 living Irregulars, including two members of the Hansoms of John Clayton: Robert C. Burr, 1987, as "The Rascally Lascar"; and Brad A. Keefauver, 1989, as "Winwood Reade." Note to the Baker Street Irregulars: "John Clayton" is available and Philip José Farmer is deserving of Investiture!

[5] I provided the titles for both *Afghanistanzas* and *Wheelwrightings*. Apparently I have a penchant for plays on words. The title for *Farmerage* is a real word, albeit a nonce word, meaning "the body of farmers collectively," which can be found only in the *Oxford English Dictionary, Second Edition.* A nonce word is a word occurring, invented, or used just for a particular occasion. Of course, now it has been used on *two* occasions.

Escape from Loki Again, and Again, and Again...

Steve Mattsson

This is the second of three articles Steve Mattsson wrote for *Farmerphile* examining the overlooked topic of Philip José Farmer and comic books.

There are many renditions of Doc Savage and his Fabulous Five's escape from the German POW camp Loki during the Great War.

The first recorded version of the escape was published in 1973 as part of the chapter titled "Son of Storm and Child of Destiny" in Philip José Farmer's *Doc Savage: His Apocalyptic Life*. Briefly—Doc, a teenage combat pilot, was shot down during a mission. He was captured by the Germans and sent to Camp Loki. There he meets the Fabulous Five and together they are able to pool their skills to escape the "escape-proof" camp.

In 1976, Lin Carter's third Prince Zarkon book was published under the title of *The Volcano Ogre*. During the story, Prince Zarkon demonstrates knowledge of the first meeting of Doc and his aides and their escape from Camp Loki. How did Zarkon come by this knowledge? The answer is obvious if we interpret Prince Zarkon and his Omega Team not as unique characters, but as Carter's symbols for Doc Savage and the Fabulous Five. They know because the events happened to them.

In 1989 DC Comics published the *Doc Savage Annual* #1.

This forty-six page story was written by Mike W. Barr, penciled by Gabriel Morrissette, inked by Rick Magyar, and colored by Tony Tollin.

The story features a one-page prologue which recaps Clark Savage, Jr.'s birth aboard the schooner *Orion* and his grueling training from childhood to become a crime-fighting superman. The prologue also introduces Dr. Gunter Asch, a German scientist who supervises Doc's initial development for Doc's father. Dr. Asch eventually steals all of Savage, Sr.'s notes on his son's training. Savage, Sr., speculates that Asch must intend to train his own Übermensch.

The story flashes forward to New York City in 1936. Nazi agents attempt to assassinate Doc and his aides. The agents commit suicide when they fail. The only clue Doc has as to why is the name "Siegfried." This causes Ham to exclaim, "But he's Dead, Doc—He and Dr. Asch!"

Flashback to Camp Loki in the year 1918. Mike W. Barr tells a version of Doc and his aides' first meeting and the escape from the prison camp. He uses much of Farmer's version from *Doc Savage: His Apocalyptic Life* until towards the end when he chooses to have Doc's, rather than Monk's, pending execution by firing squad act as the trigger for the escape.

Barr also adds a sequence where the sixteen-year-old Doc is reunited with Dr. Asch in the prison camp. With Dr. Asch is his new student, "Siegfried." Asch has refined Savage, Sr.'s techniques and created what he feels is a superior version of Doc.

Doc and Siegfried fight during the escape. Siegfried retreats in an attempt to save his surrogate father, Dr. Asch. Both appear to die in an explosion.

Flash forward to 1936. Doc and his aides have followed the Nazis' trail to the Berlin Olympics. Doc battles the very much alive Siegfried in the deserted Olympic stadium. Doc breaks Siegfried's will before he beats him physically. Dr. Asch shoots his "son" for this weakness. Siegfried falls through the Olympic torch and embraces Dr. Asch. They both burn to death in the symbolic flame of Prometheus. Barr chooses to end his version of the story with the horrible visual pun of Dr. Asch becoming ash. Perhaps this pun is Barr's not-so-subtle signal that "Dr. Asch" is not this character's true name.

In 1991 the definitive version of the escape saga was published as Philip José Farmer's novel *Escape from Loki*. If the story was fiction then there would be no contradictions between Farmer's initial outline and his novel, but this is not the case. Farmer switches Doc's enlistment in Army Air Service to a "French aerial combat unit." He changes the layout of Camp Loki from "a series of caves . . . with a fortress built over the entrance" to more traditional architecture (as did Barr and Morrissette). He altered a scene of Monk being poked in the crotch with a rifle by a guard to Monk being whipped in the face with a riding crop by the Camp Adjutant. Are these contradictions because Farmer was able to obtain more accurate information between 1973 and 1991? Or was Farmer too close to the truth in 1973 and was required to obfuscate the facts during the intervening years?

Escape from Loki has been thoroughly analyzed elsewhere. Please see Christopher Paul Carey's articles; "Farmer's *Escape from Loki: A Closer Look*," "Loki in the Sunlight," and "The Green Eyes Have It—Or Are They Blue? or *Another Case of Identity Recased*" archived at www.pjfarmer.com. I won't rehash that material here, but I do want to highlight a few of Carey's less controversial theories:

- Doc thinks analogically and symbolically.
- The mysterious and sinister Colonel Baron von Hessel uses symbols and code to communicate with Doc.
- The coded message that von Hessel is sending Doc is, "I am your Grandfather!"[1]

If this is true then von Hessel is an even stronger father figure to Doc than Dr. Asch was to Doc and Siegfried. Also, if von Hessel is using symbols to communicate with Doc, then perhaps Farmer, Barr, and Carter are using symbols to communicate with the reader. We'll explore this more later on.

So, on initial analysis it appears that Mike W. Barr simply did his homework after being granted the assignment of writing Doc's adventures for DC Comics. All Philip José Farmer fans and many Doc Savage fans would have been disappointed if someone in Barr's position had not read *Doc Savage: His Apocalyptic Life*. Even so, it appears almost plagiaristic that that DC Comics did not give Farmer any credit for his contribution to the *Doc Savage Annual*.

But does the escape from Loki saga actually originate with Farmer? In *Doc Savage: His Apocalyptic Life*, Farmer writes, "It's too bad that Dent never got around to writing of this highly ingenious and exciting breakout. Perhaps someday Condé Nast will give its permission for an author (myself, I hope) to write this very first of the supersagas." It seems clear that Lester Dent had access to the Loki material and chose not (or was directed not) to use it. Farmer appears to have discovered the Loki notes while researching *Doc Savage: His Apocalyptic Life*, but how did Mike W. Barr gain access to such esoteric information?

One of Barr's collaborators on the *Doc Savage Annual* was colorist Tony Tollin. This is the same Anthony Tollin who, along with Will Murray, is currently reprinting the Shadow and Doc Savage pulp classics through Sanctum Productions/Nostalgia Ventures. Tollin is one of the privileged few who have been granted unfettered access to the archives of both Walter B. Gibson and Lester Dent.

It is obvious that Farmer's sinister German scientist Colonel Baron von Hessel and Barr's sinister German scientist Dr. Asch are symbols for the same man. They both have secret laboratories hidden in Camp Loki. They both wear a monocle and both have blue eyes!

Now let's take this a step further. Farmer goes out of his way to compare Doc to Richard Wagner's Siegfried in his expanded version of the escape from Loki. So, it is not much of a stretch to view Barr's Teutonic Siegfried as another symbol for Doc, like Carter's Zarkon. At this stage of his development the adolescent Doc is dangerously close to becoming Nietzsche's Übermensch rather than the Bronze Knight of the Running Board whose adventures were recorded by Lester Dent. Barr's story isn't really about Doc's physical struggle with his German counterpart. It is about Doc's internal struggle to become what his father, not what von Hessel/Asch, wants him to become.

Farmer's seminal version of the Loki escape predates Barr's by sixteen years, making the DC Comics treatment apocryphal at best. Thematically, however, there are no contradictions between Farmer's and Barr's expanded versions of the escape saga. Both deal with symbolic father figures of Doc attempting to create a Nietzschean Siegfried. Both tell the tale of Doc's maturation from prodigy to superhero through trial by combat.

Perhaps Philip José Farmer, Mike W. Barr, and even Lin Carter all used the same source material to tell their versions of this coming-of-age story. Coincidentally, they all chose (or were required) to use symbols to record the truth about the mysterious escape. If so we all may need to be content with knowing the truth about the escape from Loki without ever knowing the facts.

[1]And Wotan (or Odin), XauXaz, Capt. Nemo, Prof. Moriarty, Wolf Larsen, Baron Karl, and Dr. Karl Linningen.

Editor's note:

Steve Mattsson plays "The Game" very well throughout his essay, maintaining the Wold-Newtonian façade that it all really happened. Some excellent examples of this are Steve's discussions about the possibility of Doc Savage pulp scribe Lester Dent having notes on the Loki incident, and writers Philip José Farmer, Mike W. Barr, and Lin Carter using symbols to communicate with the reader about the truth of an historical event about which they are all writing.

Here at *Farmerphile* we are all for playing The Game to the hilt, treating Doc as a real person, the Loki events as real, tracking down "sources," and so forth. However, in fairness to Phil, we must briefly step outside The Game to acknowledge that the ideas about Doc Savage's first adventure at the German prison Camp Loki are all Phil's. In fact, the Loki story in the DC Comics annual generated several letters from Phil's agent to DC, notifying DC that they had used Phil's source material without permission. In the same vein, it should be recognized that Carter's reference in the Prince Zarkon book was a tip-of-the-hat to Phil's Loki idea, rather than Phil, Carter, and Barr all using the same source material.

"But does the escape from Loki saga actually originate with Farmer?" Outside of The Game, the answer is an unqualified yes!

Bibliophile—A Discussion on Tongues of the Moon

Heidi Ruby Miller

Because I have a degree in anthropology, I probably approached Philip José Farmer's *Tongues of the Moon* from a different perspective than some readers. The pages of this 1965 Pyramid novel, which originally appeared as a novella in the September 1961 issue of *Amazing Stories*, provide numerous examples of cross-cultural comparisons, not only within the alternate history of *Tongues*, but also within our present world.

Farmer gives us a likeable ethnographer in Broward, the book's protagonist, who is a Soviet American medical officer, physical anthropologist, and proclaimed atheist. With Broward as participant-observer, we examine many aspects of culture, including political systems, nationalism, religion, and procreative roles.

The majority of this fast-paced book focuses upon Broward's search for an ultimate weapon that will bring the Soviet Russian-American allies victory over the South Atlantic Axis, run by the Argentineans.

The story opens on a lunar base with the Soviets battling the Axis after a nuclear weapon of some sort has destroyed life on Earth, leaving humanity to fight amongst itself for total domination on the Moon and Mars.

As a reviewer mentioned of the book in the July/August 1971 issue of *Luna Monthly*, "Farmer seems to be saying that humans will fight, even if there are only two left in the world."

But, within this vie for power, I found Farmer's hint about the roles of women impacting me most and left me thinking about the story long after I finished its one hundred forty-three pages.

In an ironic attempt to perpetuate the species during this time of war, the few women left on the Moon may be forced into a sort of polygamy.

There are two basic forms of polygamy still practiced in areas of our own world today, *polygyny* and *polyandry*; when one man is married to multiple women at the same time, he is practicing *polygyny*; *polyandry* is the opposite, the marriage of one woman to two or more men simultaneously. Farmer uses a twist on this latter form.

What the surviving Soviets, both men and women, propose is not that the women take on multiple husbands, but multiple breeding partners, whether they are willing or not. Even if the fertilization of the womb takes place through artificial fertilization, some women and men stand firmly opposed to the idea of forced breeding.

If the characters were part of a society in which this was "morally" acceptable, in other words multiple partners being part of their *mores*, or societal laws, the concern for their plight would be minimal. In normal "*Tongues*" society, however, Farmer represents marriage as monogamous pairings and shows that not everyone finds multiple sexual partners a desirable type of intimacy.

For example, Broward feels disgust and shame upon discovering that a woman he was having an affair with was also having sexual relations with many of the other men on the lunar base. He shares these views with his present love interest Ingrid Nashdoi, understanding that she will be asked to take other partners in order to ensure the rejuvenation of the gene pool.

Concerned not just with the perpetuation of the species, but of countering inbreeding, the group's argument is a strong and logical one, but does not take into account the discord of human emotions strongly associated with multiple partner relationships, such as jealousy, dominance, and interpersonal rivalry. The humans have obviously shown they can't overcome these obstacles even in the face of total species annihilation considering they are still fighting a war among the scant survivors.

The Earth's destruction left the Soviets with few females on the Moon as they made up a disproportionately small amount of the engineers, scientists, and military personnel originally stationed there. Broward even comments on this situation after a female officer dies of wounds sustained during the lunar battle. Looking around the dome and noting the females within the vicinity, he says, "Only three women left. If the ratio is the same on the rest of the Moon, we've a real problem."

With the immediate lunar Argentinean threat and a larger threat from Mars looming, little attention falls upon the potential procreation crisis until the group realizes humanity may destroy itself before the next generation has a chance to be conceived; thus the vote for polyandry, minus the marriage factor.

In the cultures of our own world, often the need for polyandry arises for exactly the same reason as in *Tongues*: a constant or sudden shortage of women.

Ethnographer Gerald Berreman posited in the 1960s and 1970s that this was the reason for widespread polyandry among the Pahari of Jaunsar Bawar in northern India. India is one of several places in South Asia where polyandry has been more commonly observed. Other areas include Tibet and Nepal.

This low ratio of females in the population may arise from a number of factors, including but not limited to geographical remoteness, famine or rampant sickness, or warfare, as is the case in *Tongues*.

In the end, Broward manages to save himself, Nashdoi, and what's left of the human race by helping to overthrow the problem factions within the Axis government and his own by using the ultimate weapon as a *cold threat*, thus allowing the populations from the Moon and Mars to come together and solving the problem of the women to men ratio.

Broward's heroics, however, leave the rest of us in the wake of Farmer's incredible adventure to ponder that subtle and uncomfortable question: *If the only way to perpetuate the human race is through forced polygamy, can we rationalize virtually enslaving the unwilling part of the population to do so?*

To Be, or Not to Be
Tom Wode Bellman

I t is as hard not to exist as it is to exist. That much I can tell you from experience.

When I was asked to write the foreword to Phil Farmer's latest collection, *Venus on the Half-Shell and Others*, I hooted with glee at the chance to honor a cherished friend and peer. I had no idea the kind of worm-can I was opening. How could I have? Outside of a single fan blog devoted to my writings, I was all but forgotten to the science fiction community. How was I to know of the complications that would arise from the hoax Phil and I had perpetrated thirty-some years prior at Balticon 11? That *Farmerphile* would three decades later publish an excerpt of Phil's long forgotten novel about me under the title of "The Light Hog Incident"—an excerpt which indicated by all measures that I didn't exist . . . ?

But thanks to Minowski and Einstein, Time has shifted along with Space, and I am again transported back to that spring day in 1977 as Phil took the podium in Baltimore and with only the magic of his words transmogrified my very real physical form into the thin, ghostlike wisp of a fictional character.

In truth, my metamorphosis into non-Reality had already begun long before that day at Balticon 11. As I mentioned in my foreword to the new collection, though I had been a prolific writer for many years, I never achieved the level of success that Phil did. In fact, I never had much success at all with my writing, with the possible exception of my novelette "Through Love, Darkly" (later expanded into a novel brought out by a fly-by-night publisher of such quality that they misspelled the book's title on the title page). In fact, some at the time even compared my story with Phil's own "The Lovers," although more often as a hackwork copy of Phil's story rather than the deferential tribute it was. But soon the only magazine which regularly published my stories, *Striking Science-Fiction Stories*, folded under and I joined the obscure ranks of so many other writers who were never to be known again. True, I continued to submit and have published my stories of inter- and intra-dimensional rifts, space-krakens, and the metaphysics of macrocosmic stellar-wombs, but by the time of Balticon 11 my work was relegated to Xeroxed and stapled one-shot fanzines which paid only in contributor copies. Indeed, to many I was already a non-entity. In fact, I was on the phone with Phil the week before Balticon discussing how *The Magazine of Fantasy and Science Fiction* had rejected my story "The Wee Weepers of Mu" as by Gabriel Weltstein (the narrator of Ignatius Donnelly's early sf dystopia *Caesar's Column*) which Phil had wanted me to write for his planned fictional-author anthology. Instead I had been forced to give the story to a sub-pro fanzine with the inauspicious name of *Kukuanafan*. While Phil and I were discussing this, I remarked with little thought that I felt as insubstantial as a fictional author myself. There was a long pause on the line, and then I heard Phil's hearty haw-haw.

Phil's laugh might have been the Bellman's toll warning of the approaching of a particularly dangerous Boojum—for from that moment, like the Baker in Carroll's poem, my corporeal self was destined to vanish and never be seen again. Then and there the plan was hatched and my fate sealed. Phil would go behind the podium at Balticon and announce that he was writing a book about a fictional author named Tom Wode Bellman. I would, of course, be seated in the audience, trying to restrain from laughter at the ingenuity of Phil's Swiftian satire on the wonderful world of science fiction and how it "takes care" of its own.

So that's the short of the short of how I came . . . not to be. Nonexistence has caused me a lot of trouble, but alas, the way to heaven is through hell.

A WHALE OF A TIME
LEO QUEEQUEG TINCROWDOR

It always takes longer to get to Peoria from Busiris than I think it will, so naturally I arrived late that Saturday in July for Farmercon 90. Unfortunately, I missed the Wold Newton panel, which apparently took up most of the morning. I arrived in time for the Mystery Panel, however. I slipped into a seat in the back row as unobtrusively as can be done while tripping over a power cord that was running to the video camera stationed very obtrusively in the middle of the aisle. Power cords!

Imagine my feelings when it was made plain that the Mystery Panel revealed news of three new novels and one short story begun by my friend Philip José Farmer, which are now being completed by some of his friends.

I wished I had known about this earlier. As one of the very few people to have ever collaborated with Phil, I may well be the world's expert on the subject. It was during our ill-fated attempt at a second collaboration in the early 1980s that I commented I was the only author lucky enough to have this honor. Phil then set me straight.

He explained that his first collaboration was with Randall Garrett, written back in 1953, while Randall was actually living with the Farmers. They wrote a novel together, entitled *The Ballad of Hilary Boone*. This came from a poem about a space pirate by the Gernsbackian writer Charlie Tanner. The novel was sold to

Startling Stories, the magazine that published Phil's first sci-fi story, "The Lovers." This was *Startling*'s first serial. They had already paid for the novel but after sixteen years, the magazine suddenly folded. The manuscript was then sent to Phil's new agent, but she passed away and the manuscript was lost.

I was thus his second collaborator when we wrote the short story "Osiris on Crutches" in 1976. Since then, unknown to me, he had collaborated with someone else. "The Remarkable Adventure" was an article written with Dr. Beverly Friend, a college professor and book reviewer, published in *Science Fiction: Contemporary Mythology, The SFWA-SFRA Anthology*. This article examined the use of the journey in science fiction as a story-telling device.

Next came our aforementioned attempt at another collaboration, "The Kofa Coyote Girl." Phil wrote about a girl who was abandoned at the age of four in the 665,400-acre Kofa Wildlife Refuge in Arizona. As I recall, she had a knife scar on her throat and was afraid of people. She had been suckled by a coyote and most of her vocabulary consisted of words she made up. She would have been about fourteen at the time of the story.

My part of the story was about an engineer in his fifties whose daughter was married to a bore, a dentist. Dentists!

The dentist had a big ego, drank too much, and among his many sins, liked to poach in the wildlife refuge. Although my engineer didn't like to hunt, his son-in-law dentist talked him into going hunting on the refuge. My guy agreed only because he planned on pushing the jerk off a cliff; this was after he discovered his grand-daughter's mistreatment. I don't recall how we planned on bringing these two storylines together. We may never have gotten that far.

While most of the people reading this will be familiar with Phil's collaborative novel with Piers Anthony, *The Caterpillar's Question*, few know many details about its genesis. Sure, if you read the author's notes at the back of the book, you know that it was originally going to be a round-robin novel called *Light Years*, with a dozen big-name science fiction authors. You also know that it didn't work out, so Piers bought everyone out and asked

Phil to finish the book with him. But why didn't it work out? I'm here to tell you. Remember, as I said, I am the expert on this subject. Experts!

Piers wrote the first chapter and Phil the second, more or less as they appear in *The Caterpillar's Question*.

First Piers introduces the characters, Jack and Tappy. Jack is hired to drive Tappy, a thirteen-year-old blind, mute and maimed girl—missing ear, leg brace—cross-country to a clinic in New Hampshire. As he gets to know her, he has second thoughts about the job, and they stay longer than they should at a nearly deserted motel in the mountains of Vermont. Despite Tappy's young age, they have sex. (Piers knows Phil's work.) She says strange things in her sleep, and the next morning urges Jack to go up into the mountains. Just as the sun strikes a particular boulder, she walks through it, pulling him along with her. End of chapter.

A terrific setup for the next author, don't you think? Phil picked up the story on the other side of the boulder.

Jack and Tappy are no longer on Earth. Phil establishes a world with strange flora and fauna, and large cliff walls covered with gigantic figures and symbols—that sometimes move. Though blind, Tappy leads Jack through this strange place. She is able to communicate and barter with the sentient beings through a series of honking sounds. One morning they awake to find a "honker" pressing something into Tappy's chest. It pokes Jack with a thorn-like projection from its tongue. An enormous space ship arrives and Jack discovers Tappy's leg brace is actually a weapon; he shoots a tree and it vanishes, leaving only a ghostly wavering image behind. They hear human voices coming towards them . . . Again, a great place for the next author to start off.

I won't name any names but the next three chapters shot off in different directions. In a plainly different narrative voice, chapter three begins with Tappy grabbing the leg brace/weapon from Jack and shooting *him* with it! Jack feels himself being pulled back to the boulder, back to Earth and to the motel, where he sees Tappy's "aunt" chastising the motel caretaker for letting them go through the "gate."

A nearly incomprehensible section followed, with aliens in the space ship. We then return to Tappy, who wakes up a now ghost-like Jack. They eventually escape the vicinity of the ship. To be clear, there are now two Jacks: one on Earth, who can pass through objects and can't be seen, and one on the alien planet, faintly visible, who can float around. We also find out that mating with Jack and the thing pressed into her chest are two of three things Tappy needs from donors to morph into her next state. Morphing!

The fourth chapter takes place back on Earth. Jack is in the back seat of Tappy's "aunt and uncle's" car. The uncle, who we abruptly learn is an android, has the feeling he's being followed (actually caused by Jack breathing down his neck). They drive to the "clinic" where Jack was supposed to deliver Tappy, but their superiors order them back to the motel. The uncle is to kill the caretaker and the aunt must then kill whichever one survives.

Adding a new twist, their instructions come through the use of odors, but are they the odors they had been instructed to expect? Odors!

On the way back, still a stowaway in the back seat, Jack learns that the world on the other side of the gate is a refueling station for ships that travel at light speed. Back at the motel, two of the three are killed, but Jack doesn't know which ones since he is pulled back to the boulder.

Things really fall apart in the fifth and final chapter. Jack, once again fully corporeal, wakes up in a hospital bed, in a futuristic and hi-tech room. The nurse and an androgynous porter, both of whom Jack is oddly attracted to, can walk through the dissolving door, but Jack can't. When he wakes a second time, a military man is in the room, in a black metallic-looking Confederate uniform. The Colonel, a "Paratime Marine," explains that the Confederacy has been using "Dimensional Wormholes" for over a hundred years. All hell is about to break out because a Vampire Breeding Vessel is on its way to Earth Paratime Line-Three, which is where they happen to be. Vampires!

Some potential good news is that Earth Paratime Line-Four

has clone warriors, but they may not believe the Vampires are a real threat and so may not help. Then, believe it or not, things get *even weirder.*

Jack is told that the sting the honker gave him (back in chapter 2) was a hallucinogenic. Not only has everything he'd seen since that moment been a hallucination, but the condition is permanent. Now that would be bad news, at least after the first few days. Jack suddenly wakes up back on the alien world next to Tappy, who looks at him and starts screaming, as she is also having a hallucination. Reminds me of my first wife.

That's all we know, and it's more than enough. No doubt *The Caterpillar's Question* was a better book than that mess.

Of course, more recently Phil collaborated with his grand-nephew Danny Adams, when Danny completed *The City Beyond Play* (PS Publishing, 2007). In the unlikely event you haven't read that book, I can't recommend it highly enough. I only wish Phil had let me see that partial manuscript when we were working on the Kofa girl story.

All of this leads me back to the Mystery Panel at Farmercon 90. I could hardly believe my ears: four new collaborations! Three new Phil Farmer novels to look forward to! A book about Hadon's much more interesting cousin Kwasin. A Gothic mystery novel about Doc Savage's daughter, called Wildman here. Right at the end of the panel, the author Win Eckert said, "Oh yeah, I forgot to mention, Phil started this novel in the late sixties or early seventies and while it's not on the level of *A Feast Unknown* . . . it is erotic!"

And—can you imagine it?—an author named Tracy Knight is completing a *Western* that Phil began. Phil has taken nearly every other form of literature and turned it on its head. I can't even imagine what he could do with a Western, although Mr. Knight did give us some tantalizing hints.

We learned from questions asked of the four fortunate authors facing the audience that the short story, "Getting Ready to Write," by Phil and Paul Spiteri, and an excerpt from the novel *The Song of Kwasin,* were in the current issue of *Farmerphile.* I was first in line the moment the panel ended. I bought a copy and went to my favorite place to read, the bathroom, where I devoured the short story found at the back of the issue. I howled with laughter all the way through it. Tears of joy actually ran down my face.

I then turned to the front of the issue to read the fourth chapter of *The Song of Kwasin*. I was so impressed, I swear my feet started to tingle. Then I read the interview with Christopher Paul Carey, about the painstaking attention to detail he took writing the novel, and my admiration for him only grew. I knew I'd be setting aside some serious time to read the rest of the issue. Charles R. Saunders and Tom Wode Bellman! I haven't thought about either of those guys in decades.

Back at the con, I caught the end of a long line of Phil's friends and readers talking about how he and his books had come into their lives. Hardly anyone came to him from the same direction. At the end of the formal speeches, they asked if anyone from the audience would like to get up and talk. I was sorely tempted but couldn't wait to read Saunders and Bellman, so I headed back to the bathroom on numb legs, then went back to see about buying other back issues and what else was on the agenda for Farmercon, and, well, everyone was gone! I had spent too much time in the bathroom. Bathrooms!

I tracked down the publisher of *Farmerphile* and offered to write a "con report." I nearly balked when he told me what the payment for my efforts would be. I'm used to nothing, and he was only offering half that. But he promised to give me an advance look at the excerpt from *The Evil in Pemberley House* found in this issue and, well, a writer's got to write. Writers!

THIS PLAYED IN PEORIA?
ART SIPPO

I remember the first time I bought a Phil Farmer novel. That day is still fresh in my mind as one of the memorable days of my youth. It was thirty-nine years ago and I was sixteen. On a summer Saturday in 1969, I had gone to Manhattan to hit the bookstores and look for the next Bantam Doc Savage reprint. I went into the old Bookmasters store on Times Square (which has been closed now for twenty years). In the Sci-Fi section I found three odd looking books from an outré publisher. Two of them had very strange pictures on their covers and titles to match. They did not look like anything in which I would be interested. The third one, though, gripped my imagination. On the cover were two naked men wrestling, one of whom looked suspiciously like Jim Bama's version of Doc Savage. The title of this book was *A Feast Unknown* and the author of all three of these odd volumes was Philip José Farmer.

I was familiar with the author's name, but not his work. I had read science fiction for several years, but usually the classic authors: Asimov, Heinlein, Clarke, Anderson, and the like. This Farmer guy had written some strange books and I found their storylines kind of . . . scary.

But this new book was different. I had been obsessed with Doc Savage for four years, devouring every word of every novel. This had been my gateway into a lifetime love of books, which my family still doesn't understand. The Doc revival was so successful many other pulp works were being reprinted and I was devouring two or three books a week. At the end of that school year, I had read *Tarzan of the Apes* for the first time. It had been my "relaxation" book during exam week. All that summer, I was reading the Tarzan sequels along with The Shadow, G-8, The Spider, Captain Future, and of course Doc Savage. The blurb on the back cover of this new book made me realize upon whom the characters Lord Grandrith and Doc Caliban were modeled. I couldn't resist.

I must have read *A Feast Unknown* three times in the next week and several more times that summer. I was alternately fascinated, repulsed, impressed, disgusted, and intrigued. It was obvious that Mr. Farmer was well-read, and a master storyteller. It was also obvious that he was as obsessed with Tarzan and Doc Savage as I was. Furthermore, it was also obvious he was an iconoclast who wanted to explore dimensions in these characters that the mores of earlier times did not permit.

I was a young man coming of age in a culture poised on the brink of a sea-change in self-awareness and self-identity. I was—and still am—a very conventional person and I was more comfortable in Lester Dent's imaginary world than the one in which I lived. Well, *A Feast Unknown* helped to shatter that illusion. Though I did not understand the concept at that time, Phil had deconstructed the two great heroic myths of our time: the Noble Savage and the Technocrat "Man of Tomorrow." Compared to Burroughs' Tarzan, Lord Grandrith was far more savage than noble. And Doc Caliban was more Machiavellian and Nietzschean than Lincolnesque or Christlike as Dent had tried to make Doc Savage. In that sense, Grandrith and Caliban were more realistic than their fictional namesakes and it was far more frightening to contemplate Phil's Ape Man and Übermensch walking among us than it would be for the earlier heroic characters created by Burroughs and Dent.

Phil also subverted the whole notion of moral authority and cultural heritage in the antagonists of the piece, the Nine. (It would be several years later before it finally clicked with me who the Hebrew member of the Nine, born in 3 B.C. and named Yeshua, was supposed to be.) The Nine were the scions of the established order that had surreptitiously ruled mankind from its inception. Grandrith and Caliban were each given the opportunity to replace the Germanic Father god XauXaz at the head of the pantheon of the real gods of mankind. But only one could do so. The price would be for the victor to destroy his rival and thus suppress forever the weltanschauung the loser had represented. Such was the fate the gods had decreed for the future of humankind.

In the battle that ensued, Grandrith came out on top (which as a Doc Savage fan annoyed me to no end); he was the more primal of the two and the one closest to the natural man. He was least likely to be seduced by the promises of progress. Caliban was too far gone in the bloodlust and hubris from the Immortality Elixir to think clearly and he was, after all, the torch-bearer for the vaunted schemes of the man-made world. Ironically, Grandrith's infrahumanity was much closer to true human nature and it gave him the perspective necessary to see the truth. The feral man knew that the "either/or" choice they had been given was a false dichotomy. In the wild, one survives by adaptation, not by conformity. The machinations of the Nine be damned. Either/or was not the only option. It could also be a "both/and." But to do that, the two standard-bearers of humanity's potential would need to be allies and the Nine would need to be destroyed so that their strangle-hold on human history would be abolished forever. As a true Farmerian hero, Grandrith made his own choice and did not sell out to the Establishment and its plans for him. Instead, the hero made his own way in the world, resigned and willing to live with the consequences. Grandrith and Caliban would never be the puppets of the Nine again.

I got that message loud and clear. It gave a sixteen-year-old a lot to think about. I have wrestled with the implications of it over the years. One result was that Phil Farmer became an instant favorite and a guru. In the years that followed he wrote an amazing succession of books: *Lord Tyger, To Your Scattered Bodies Go, The*

Mad Goblin, The Lord of the Trees, and *Hadon of Ancient Opar.* His two non-fiction classics *Tarzan Alive!* and *Doc Savage: His Apocalyptic Life* began the Wold Newton movement, which is now a worldwide phenomenon. I also finally had the courage to read some of his earlier works like *Night of Light, The Lovers, The Alley God,* and "Mother."

That sixteen-year-old boy back in 1969 would be envious of me being here at this celebration of Phil Farmer's life and work in his home town of Peoria. So would the twenty-, thirty-, forty-, and fifty-year-old men whom he became and who all appreciated Phil's work in their own ways. All of them are standing here today to honor Phil Farmer for the fun, the ideas, and passions he has shared with us. He has helped to make our beloved pulp characters immortal and he has given us the Wold Newton Universe, which has changed the landscape of adventure fiction forever. For this and so much more, Phil has become an immortal himself in the Literary Pantheon. Phil, thanks for the ride! You will be remembered.

THE VOICE OF FARMER IN MY
VERMIFORM APPENDIX
RHYS HUGHES

I can't remember exactly how I first discovered Philip José Farmer, but I suspect I read *about* his work in an encyclopedia of science fiction before actually reading his fiction. I liked the idea of a river one million miles long on whose banks all of humanity had been resurrected; also a series of worlds balanced on tiers above each other.

Those concepts seemed impossibly grand. But the first Farmer piece I definitely recall reading was on a much more modest scale—"The Sumerian Oath" in the anthology *Nova #2* (1972) edited by Harry Harrison. That short story stood out from the others in that book. Not only was it more pithy and concise and funny and disturbing, but I'm still more than half convinced that its outrageous central hypothesis is true.

"The Sumerian Oath" is one of Farmer's "polytropical paramyths," very brief, neat and startling tales that have the power to change, or at least unsettle, minds forever. Everyone with too much respect for medical "experts" should read "The Sumerian Oath" as a kind of safeguard. That's my opinion anyway. Farmer's other polytropical paramyths are no less impressive and have the feel of a unique subgenre, though apparently the Czech writer Karel Čapek evolved a similar style in his collection, *Kniha apokryfů* (1955).

I can't make any judgments about that, as I've read very little Čapek (what I have read is very good) but Farmer's paramyths rely on a single extreme and rapidly expanding idea that controls the growth of the story in the same way that a gene controls the development of a living organism. By itself that's not enough to make his paramyth a distinct form. But the sparkling language Farmer employs lifts them into a distinguished realm that is wholly *his*, a frantically paced prose full of allusions, wordgames, surreal banter, winks and nods and wiseguy cracks.

Not everything I encountered by Farmer grabbed me instantly. In an anthology with a title and theme that have escaped my memory, I chanced on "The Jungle Rot Kid on the Nod," a reinterpretation of the Tarzan myth in the style of William (as opposed to Edgar Rice) Burroughs. Having read neither Edgar nor William I thought the story was berserk and meaningless. Years later I returned to it and finally understood the jokes, appreciated the twisted and improbable cleverness of the double pastiche. But it was only when I went out and bought the "World of Tiers" omnibus that Farmer became one of my favorite writers, so influential that I find myself constantly judging the worth of my own concepts by comparing them to his. I even felt compelled to include Farmer as a character in several of my stories.

My short story "God in a Basement Flat" was directly inspired by Farmer and I adopted many of his techniques while composing that piece: the sardonic but broad eschatological nature of the backdrop, the mix and match personages from any period of Earth's history (I used Yukio Mishima, Meredith Monk and D.H. Lawrence as my central celestial protagonists), the inherent ironies and paradoxes of pocket universe science.

And the language. I am a lover of wordplay and frequently am castigated by critics for my excessive attachment to puns. I believe (perhaps not modestly) that I have created some spectacular puns in my time, and yet my favorite pun in any work of fiction can be found in Farmer's "J.C. on the Dude Ranch." The three words that form that pun are "assault of pillars" but you'll have to read the story to get the joke. It's obscene as well as clever: my preferred combination!

Many other stories I have written will surely show some trace of Farmer's influence if they are analysed properly. Such pieces include "The Taste of the Moon" and "Chuckleberry Grin" among a more or less unruly horde. Farmer was also an inspiration to me when it came to choosing titles for my tales. His "Riders of the Purple Wage" made me realise that *existing* titles might be manipulated into something new and humorous or collided with other existing titles to produce a weird fusion that was both familiar and unique.

Using this method I have written stories with titles such as "Where Angels Fear to Bake Bread," "As I Walked Out One Mid-summer Night's Dream," "The Unbearable Lightness of Being a Dirigible," "The Taming of the Old Woman who Lived in a Shrew," "Orpheus on the Underground," "An Awfully Bubonic Adventure," "The Non-Existent Viscount in the Trees," "Venus and Stupid," "Von Ryan's Daughter's Express," "Oh, Whistle While You Work, and I'll Come to You, My Dwarf" and many others.

But the first time I actually included Farmer as a character in a story was when I started writing a short cycle of Tarzan stories. This cycle consists of three linked tales, each of which belongs to a different cycle. The way I work is often rather complicated! Thus the first of my Tarzan stories, "Tarzan at the Apple's Core," is also the fourth part of a novella entitled "The Court of Fictional but Very Serious Crimes," and my second Tarzan story, "Tarzan of the Chardonnay," is also chapter eleven of my forthcoming novel *The Pilgrim's Regress*. Philip José Farmer appears in several other chapters of that novel. My third Tarzan story, "Tarzan on Helium," will also be one of the "Tales of the Counter Earth" that will form a new story collection entitled *Ditto and Likewise*. I can't be entirely sure at this stage which other stories of that collection will feature Farmer, but I believe that "Gin and Chthonic" and "Nat King Cole Abhors a Vacuum" probably will.

Another story cycle I'm working on also features Farmer in each of its parts. Early in 2008 I was asked to write a Hellboy story for *Oddest Jobs*, a Dark Horse Books anthology. I produced a tale called "The Feet of Sciron" in which Farmer had a cameo role.

I knew nothing about Hellboy before I was given the commission but I knew at once that I wanted to write a story with overt Farmerian influences.

Farmer was really an intellectual writer who had no hesitation in taking inspiration from pulp forms, from comics, films and other expressions of popular culture. He accepted the protagonists and ideas of such genres on their own terms but he also played postmodernist jokes with them. So when I wrote my Hellboy story I used Farmer as my general guide. I therefore included Farmer as one of my characters, the sort of thing *he* liked to do with real people. There's a circle there, or part of a circle, or a shape approximating a circle: maybe an ellipse . . .

My story was accepted for publication but I had to edit out the stronger sexual scenes. After the story was published I decided I wanted to re-insert the cut scenes, rewrite the whole thing and create my own mythos. It has to be sufficiently distant from Hellboy to stand as an original creation. Hellboy is a demon, so my own "hero" will be a golem, a golem who accidentally falls into a vat of nitro-glycerine before his clay has set, turning him into a giant stick of living dynamite.

I know that this golem's name is Twisthorn Bellow, also that his sidekicks will be Hapi Daze and Miss Abortia Stake, but I don't know much else apart from the titles of the other stories in the cycle ("The Wings of Phoebus" and "The Skin of Marsyas") and that Philip José Farmer will feature in all of them, and may even turn out to be the real hero, or villain, or both!

WRITING "GRACELAND"
ALLEN STEELE

"Graceland," my contribution to *Tales of Riverworld*, is a story with one foot in two worlds.

In June, 1991, I had just finished moving into a house in suburban St. Louis that my wife and I bought only a few weeks earlier, right after I'd sent off my fourth novel, *Labyrinth of Night*, to my publisher. To celebrate becoming a first-time homeowner and also completing another novel, I'd bought tickets to a two-day Grateful Dead concert in Bonner Springs, Kansas. Our moving expenses had been a little higher than I'd anticipated, though, and it would be a while before my publisher coughed up the acceptance check, so I was beginning to regret springing for a road trip that would crimp the household budget even more.

As luck would have it, the morning my wife and I were to leave for Kansas, what would appear in the mail but a letter from Martin Greenberg's office in Wisconsin. Signed by Philip José Farmer, it began: "I'd like to invite you to do a story set in my Riverworld universe. This would be for a two-book deal I have with Warner Books, who promise to make this a major publishing event. I'll be doing an original story for each volume, and I'll be editing the books as well." The offer was for a ten-cents-per-word advance against royalties, and the deadline was early the following November.

I hadn't yet met Phil Farmer, so I don't know how my name came to be plucked from the hatful of writers who could've contributed to this anthology. Not only that, but I'd publicly sworn that I'd never again write a story set in another author's universe; I'd done something like this only a couple of years earlier, and the result was so dismal that I've never reprinted that particular story in any of my collections. I needed the money, though . . . and besides, there was something else as well.

I'd found *To Your Scattered Bodies Go* when I was a teenager, and considered it to be one of the most profound novels I'd ever read. The book haunted me for years, with the concept affecting me at some deep emotional level. So if I was going to break my promise to never again write for a shared-universe anthology, it would have to be for a good reason . . . and doing a story for *Tales of Riverworld* seemed to be it.

So I quickly wrote a reply to Phil and Marty, accepting their invitation, then I helped my wife pack the car for our trip. As an afterthought, I grabbed a spiral notebook, a bunch of pens, and my copy of *To Your Scattered Bodies Go* and threw them in the back seat. Before we got on the highway, I stopped by a local comics shop that sold role-playing games and bought a copy of the Riverworld gaming manual published by Steve Jackson Games. The letter had said that this would be the writers' bible for the anthology, and I decided not to wait until I received the copy that had been promised to me.

During the long drive across Missouri, I sat in the passenger seat, skimming both *To Your Scattered Bodies Go* and the game manual, and otherwise brainstorming what I'd write for the anthology. As usual when we're making a long drive, my wife brought along a cassette box stuffed with tapes of classic rock albums—the Who, the Beatles, Jefferson Airplane, the Band, and so forth—and somewhere along the way, an idea began to coalesce from these two influences: what happened to all the rock stars who'd been resurrected on the Riverworld?

Linda is not only my wife and muse, but she's also a radio disc jockey with a encyclopedic knowledge of the history of rock 'n' roll. I began bouncing my story idea off her, and together we came up with a list of rock musicians who'd passed away; in my notebook I jotted down their names and their likely outcomes following their after-life revival. By the time we pulled off the highway, the story had gelled.

We had a reservation at a Holiday Inn on the outskirts of Kansas City, Missouri; after dropping by to drop our bags in our room, we proceeded to Bonner Springs, just across the Kansas state line, where we joined the tens of thousands of Deadheads waiting for the gates to open. As it turned out, the concerts were being held at an outdoor amphitheater located in a closed-down fairground; mobs of longhairs, most of them stoned on one thing or another, wandered between boarded-up concession stands and livestock barns. It was very hot and dry, with very little to do before the show started; I didn't want to get high, nor did I want to succumb to heat exhaustion before the show began, so I parked myself in the shade of a wooden shack and pulled out the notebook and pens I'd brought with me. And there, over the course of the next two days, I wrote most of my Riverworld story.

According to my handwritten first draft, it was originally called "Long Live Rock, Be It Dead Or Alive," a quote from a Who song that I later decided was too cumbersome to serve as a story title; in its subsequent final draft, I re-titled it "Graceland"... also a song title, this time from Paul Simon's repertoire. While I worked, Linda fetched lemonade, and after a while I attracted the attention of Deadheads who'd come over to share my shady spot. One guy was interested enough to keep dropping by to see how I was doing, and on the afternoon of the second day I gave an impromptu reading to him and a couple of his friends. They enjoyed the story, even though none of them were familiar with Phil's novel; I like to think that I might have sold a couple of copies of *To Your Scattered Bodies Go*.

Nonetheless, I wasn't satisfied with "Graceland," even after it was published. It wasn't my best work, and it only caused me to renew my vow to never again write for a shared-universe anthology. A few years ago, though, I revisited the story, and found that it wasn't as bad as I thought. So I rewrote it a bit, tweaking a few things here and there, and included it in my collection, *American Beauty*. If anyone decides to read this story, I hope they'll track down the revised version.

All in all, my brief excursion to the Riverworld was a lot of fun. It's a minor contribution to Phil's signature world, and I hope he doesn't mind the people I brought there.

Editor's note:
   Once while discussing Phil's influence on Jimi Hendrix and the song "Purple Haze," Phil stated that while he didn't like rock music very much, he did think Jim Morrison was a very good poet.

THE FACE THAT LAUNCHED A THOUSAND EGGS
PHILIP JOSÉ FARMER

There is perhaps no better way to unveil the premiere issue of *Farmerphile* than with the first-time publication of "The Face That Launched a Thousand Eggs," a story which makes use of all the wit, derring-do, and reference to mythology that readers have come to expect from the Wizard of Peoria. At a very young age, Phil Farmer devoured Homer's *The Iliad* and *The Odyssey*, and even before discovering Tarzan or John Carter of Mars, Phil would let loose his unbounded childhood imagination by pretending to be Odysseus. After setting off to college, Phil transferred from Bradley Polytechnical Institute to the University of Missouri so he could take classes that would enable him to read Homer in the original Greek. While Homerian currents run throughout many of Phil's stories—from his first novel *The Green Odyssey* to "Heel" to *Time's Last Gift*—there is perhaps no more clever tribute to the ancient Greek bard than "The Face That Launched a Thousand Eggs." Here Homer's Greeks are metaphorically woven throughout and meshed with the fraternal "Greeks" of college campus life. Of course, the title of the story is a play on Helen of Troy's sobriquet.

And what of the protagonist's name, Tim Howller? Could this be the very same Tim Howller who appeared in Phil's story "After King Kong Fell"? There can be little doubt. We know that Tim Howller was thirteen when he witnessed the real live King Kong plummet to his death from the Empire State Building, and that the Tim in this story is nineteen in 1937. This would indicate that both characters were born around 1918 (incidentally the same year as someone else we know).

Both Tims are from the Midwest: in "After Kong Kong Fell," young Tim Howller can't wait to get back home to Busiris, Illinois (or Peoria, Illinois in the revised publication of the story) to tell his friends about the giant ape, while in "The Face that Launched a Thousand Eggs" Tim attends the University of Shomi (i.e. Missouri, the "show me state"). Further evidence that the two characters are the same person lies in the fact that the Tim who witnessed Kong's death is described with the same shyness and sensitivity that Charlie razzes Tim about in the story at hand.

Written in 1953, the year following the debut of Phil's classic science fiction story "The Lovers," it is a newly discovered gem based upon the real life story of a young Phil Farmer after he transferred to the University of Missouri. Phil has elsewhere described the incident behind this story as one of the big highlights of his life. Seeing the real King Kong must have been one of the others.

N o Charlie," said Tim Howller, "I haven't a date for the political rally tonight. I'm going with Mark and some Phi Delts and Thetas who're going to try to steal the Black's banner."

Over the half-shield of an arm raised to permit smearing of deodorant on his right armpit, he looked at his mirror-self. It stared back, a Judas-pink on its forehead and cheeks.

Charlie Bluepress' eyes squinted sidewise from their trenches of fat while he forced lather and blue whiskers off his blade with running hot water.

He rumbled, "Is it true you'll be carrying the biggest torch at the rally?"

"Torch?" Tim said.

He lowered his arm and looked at Charlie.

"What biggest torch?"

Charlie slapped his enormous thigh.

"Haw!" he shouted. "I mean Francis Uquart's big torch!"

The bathroom rang with laughter.

Charlie's bellow subdued the rest.

"Look at him blush! Like a virgin—if there is such a thing. My gawd, kid, don't show all of your emotions. Toughen up. It's

May 1937, you're nineteen, big enough, old enough to be a man. Be like me. Triple-bound in brass Charlie, they call me."

Tim quickly raised his left arm, ostensibly to rub on deodorant. His crooked elbow hid his nose and quivering mouth.

He said in a flat voice, "Triple-bound in brass Charlie? You mean hippo Charlie don't you? Two-ton Tony with the triple-tiered 'testines."

Laughter gurgled up from the cavern of Charlie's stomach and shook his breasts like thunder in a jelly bag.

He rumbled, "Got under your hide, haven't I? So you try to dig under mine by calling me Fatty. Won't go, Howller. I can look my belly in the face. But if you had my paunch, could you look it in the face? No. You can't look anything in the face. Why, you don't dare consider the fact that, though you've fallen for Uquart, you haven't the guts to ask her for a date."

"Sure," Keith Huston chimed in, "if I liked that luscious peach, I wouldn't stand back in the shadows, sucking my thumb."

"Looking like a dying calf," said Art Fey.

"Knees shaking," said Mark Hazar.

"Heart thumping," boomed Jack Phillips.

"Afraid to step up," sang Art Fey.

"Hot and cold . . . like running water . . . oh, my fevered brow! . . . writing poetry about her but afraid to show it to her . . . Byron himself . . . Dante and Beatrice . . . Petrarch and Laura . . . Ulysses and Helen . . ."

Charlie whacked his thigh.

"Red Helen!" he shouted.

"Yeah!" Keith barked. "That's right. Hey, Art, didn't you tell me that's Howller's most secret, most poetic name for Francis? Red Helen?"

Tim glared; Art paled.

"Wow!" chortled Keith. "I'm hot for Red Helen!"

"Listen, fellows," Charlie shouted, waving his hands and blowing his whiskey-breath in Tim's face. "Who is Francis Uquart, or, as this frightened poet who nests in our midst calls her, Red Helen?

"I'll tell you. A Junior in the University of Shomi, majoring in dramatics, social chairman of Kappa Kappa Gamma, fashion editor on the school paper, Queen of St. Patrick's Ball, Sweetheart of Beta Phi Theta, Homecoming Princess, and a string of etceteras as long as my arm.

"Moreover, this Titian-haired beauty, whom all of you have no doubt seen many times strutting her stuff—what stuff!—in the Workshop plays, has got a potful of dough. That is,"—Charlie leered—"she will have as soon as she finds some well-heeled sucker to marry her.

"And she almost did, for as *tout le monde* knows, not so long ago she wore the governor's son's frat pin. Think of it. Don Blairston, son of the governor of this glorious state.

"But, fortunately, Francie and Donnie quarreled, and she had to hand back the pin. And the potful of dough she might have had.

"But don't worry, gentlemen. She'll get another. A woman with her superb character is bound to win some great and rich man. Yes, she has a superb character, which I will now describe. It consists of a build that holds a candle to nobody's. Can a figure hold a candle? And it also consists of tresses, oh, so auburn they burn, or so burning they auburn.

"So, gentlemen, ta-ra, ta-ra, ta-ra, I give you the one and only—Red Helen!"

"Hooray!" shouted one of the boys.

"Wait, fellows," bellowed Charlie though no one had moved to leave. "We know Miss Uquart. But who is Tim Howller, this latter-day Ulysses, this would-be Paris? I'll tell you, though"—Charlie's voice quavered—"it's like tearing out my heart-strings. He's a freshman, a measly Lambda Lambda pledge who has no friends that amount to anything, no talents except for getting into trouble, no money, no nothing.

"So-o-o-o, brother Greeks, fellow Lambda, why blame the poor suffering guy? If you were this insignificant mote in the beam of Shomi campus life, would you ask Miss Uquart for a date? No. You wouldn't. So, why blame him?

"Bu-u-u-ut, he is in love. Capitals I-N-L-O-V-E. He's standing in the midst of a great blaze of passion as intense as any the martyrs burned in.

"And she"—Charlie raised a finger for emphasis—"she doesn't even know he exists!"

The bathroom stormed with laughter.

"Aw, that's a lot of hooey!" shouted Tim. "She does too know me!"

At Tim's first words, loud and hoarse, Charlie had stepped back and raised his hands in a half-warding gesture. But when Tim's voice trailed off weakly, Charlie stepped up. His hand slapped down on the youth's shoulder. A crimson five-petalled flower bloomed briefly on the white skin.

"Then," Charlie said in a tone half-paternal, half-condescending, "you've no excuse for worshipping her through binoculars. Ask her for a date."

"Yeah . . . yeah," chanted the others. "Date . . . date . . . boom-boomety-boom. Datity-date. Rate a date! Date a rate! Boom-boopity-date!"

Tim snarled, "You guys know where you can shove it."

He picked up his razor, deodorant, towel, brilliantine, tooth-brush, paste, and comb and walked out. Voices followed him down the hall.

"Red Helen . . . wow! . . . unrequited passion stalks the ivied halls of Shomi . . . Howller carries a mean torch . . . torch!"

As quickly as his fumbling fingers allowed he dressed. He flashed glances in the mirror. Was it true? Had their banter been merely a means to put across what they really believed? Was it true? No talents, no brains, no looks, no money, no guts. Especially no guts.

In a moment Art Fey came in. The light behind the smile and mockery he'd had in the bathroom was cut off: the upcurve of lips and squinting of eyes were caricatures of themselves.

Tim looked contempt at Art, scowled, and refused to look again. Inside, he was hurt. He had once, in a burst of over-whelming need to discharge some of the turmoil burning inside him, confided in Art. He had told how much he loved Francis

Uquart and how, whenever he thought of her, he called her his "Red Helen," because that was so intimate, exclusive, and poetical. That even she didn't know of it made it all the more valuable.

Having eased somewhat the tension, he had not thought it necessary to swear Art to silence. Like himself, Art was sensitive. Why should he think that Art would ever do such an unspeakably gutterish trick?

Art arranged his toilet-set on the bureau-top, all the while looking at his roommate out of the corner of his eyes and shifting weight from one leg to the other. After a silence unusual for Art, he broke out, "Look here, Tim, I don't want you to think I showed everybody that poem you wrote about Uquart. You know I wouldn't do a thing like that. I appreciated the fact that it was something intimate that you wanted only your best friends to see. I didn't betray your confidence. It's true I did show it to Mark Hazar, but he's one of your best friends, close-mouthed and sympathetic. If he mentioned it to anyone, I can't help that."

Tim grunted and finished buckling his belt.

Art bit his lip and said, "Well, I might have mentioned it to Traje Courke because he's one of your best friends, and I thought I could trust him. But outside of those two, and maybe Jack Littley, I—"

Lower lip sucked-in, two deep creases parenthesizing the inner ends of his brows, Tim walked out.

II

Tim slammed the screen-door and walked out to the railing of the frat house's front porch. Mark Hazar followed him. Looking up at Tim he said, "What kept you from taking a poke at blubber?"

"He'd been drinking and wasn't too responsible. Anyway, nobody seemed to think he was out of order. I noticed you were in the chorus yourself."

"Sure," Mark said, "I feel Charlie is right when he said you shouldn't be afraid to ask her for a date. Still, I think he went too far."

"You know me, Mark. I have to be pushed hard before I'll fight."

"Charlie knows that," said Mark. "But for a moment he thought he'd pushed too hard. Did you see him get ready to take off? He ought to pick on somebody who can't beat the tar out of him."

"Why did he pick on me in the first place? I've done nothing to him."

"Cripes!" Mark exploded. "That's easy to see. After Francis Uquart split with Blairston, Charlie asked her for a date. She turned him down. He never said so, but I know he thinks it is because he is so fat and ugly. He's jealous of you because he knows you could get a date with her if you had the guts to ask her."

Tim turned quickly and put his hand on Mark's shoulder.

"Do you really think so?"

He was smiling.

"Cripes! I know it!"

Tim removed his hand and wrinkled his forehead.

"I don't think so. Charlie was right. She's got everything. I've got nothing."

"Nuts!" barked Mark. "You're a man, aren't you? Tim, you're too self-analyzing, too self-conscious . . ."

Mark cocked his head and said, "But then I'll have to admit this Uquart gal can get a guy muddled up. Look at the present political situation. It's partly her fault. You know the Betas were once in the Gold coalition, didn't you? That was when Zinter, the Sig prexy and Blairston were both rushing Uquart. When Blairston pinned her, Zinter got so nasty that Blairston lined up the Betas with the agricultural frats and talked Uquart's Kappa sisters into joining them. Now, even if Francis and Donnie are parted, the Black coalition still stands.

"Zinter and Charlie hate Blairston, and they're out to win the school government election, hook or crook. They've been whipping up such high feelings there's no telling what might happen. Both Blairston and Zinter have been popping off about having a show-down and beating hell out of each other.

"And if you and I, Tim, and those other guys that are going with us tonight, succeed in stealing the Black's banner, there'll be hell to pay. The last two years the Black's have run us off, but in my freshman year I was with a gang that stole the banner. The Blacks found out where we were hiding, and they came after us. Cripes, what a brawl! Paddle-fights, fist-fights, rotten tomatoes thrown, a fire-hose dousing the crowd, and, finally, the police called. I got a bloody nose and my shirt was torn off, and I was soaked with tomatoes from head to foot. Cripes, what a brawl!"

Laughing, Mark walked out to his Model T, the Tin Centaur, parked by the curb.

He said, "I'm going to pick up our gang from frats here and there. Want to ride along?"

"No, thanks," Tim said, "I'll meet you in front of the Pi Phi's."

Tim Howller walked in the dusk towards the Pi Phi house, from which the Gold parade was scheduled to start. His scowling silence contrasted with the smiles and chatter and shouting and laughs of the crowds on the sidewalks and in the narrow streets. Boys and their girls walked along swinging their locked hands. Gangs of yelling boys charged through the crowd, stumbling and falling and knocking each other down. Clusters of girls giggled and screamed and yelled at the boys.

Many carried blazing torches which lit up white banners and signs on which broad black letters were painted.

VOTE FOR WALKER. VOTE GOLD. WALKAWAY WITH WALKER. YEA GOLDS!

When Tim was walking past the Acacia house, he was stopped by a big man wearing a black sweater with a big gold S on its chest. Speaking loudly and officiously, the athlete tried to force a flaming torch on Tim.

Tim muttered, "No, thanks."

"Here, take it, bud. Get into the swing of things. You're not one of those damn Blacks are you?"

Tim swallowed and awkwardly took the torch. But when the athlete had gone, Tim threw it in the bushes. He didn't care whether or not the bush caught on fire. He walked on.

When Tim came opposite the Kappa House, which lay across

the street, he stopped, facing it, and his eyes raked the brick façade. Two lights glittered, one on the first floor in the front room and one upstairs. On the latter he fixed his eyes. While the crowd broke to flow around him, and while girls yelled at him to quit standing there gawking, and while boys accused him of window-peeping, he stood statue-like, seemingly unhearing.

Suddenly his rigidity disappeared in a spasm. Clutching at his back and giving a cry that was half-grunt, half-yell, he jumped a foot forward.

Behind him rose raucous, parrot-like laughter. That, plus the undignified and vulgar method of introduction, was enough to tell Tim that it was Trajan Courke.

Tall, lean Traje with the narrow skull, the sharp nose with a shallow pit on each side of its bridge as if thumbs had squeezed there while the bone was yet soft, and the yellowish-brown hair combed Mephistophelean into two horn-like waves.

The ever present cigarette jerked in the corner of thin lips. He chuckled. He said, "By God, Tim. Caught you again. I'll bet you were dreaming of your lovely Uquart doll, weren't you? I won't ask just which lovely portion you were mooning over."

"Darn it," said Tim. "Do you *have* to sneak up on a guy and do that?"

He made an upward stabbing with clenched fist and extended thumb.

"Best method in the world for recalling a guy to his present surroundings. Listen, Tim. What's the matter with you? Standing here in the midst of all this activity, teeming with possibilities for an enterprising young man, and conjuring up all sorts of scenes in which you are Antony and this Uquart doll is Cleopatra.

"Not history but herstory; the tale of a woman's attempt to become again a rib, warm and snug and well-fed and without worries. Yes, Tim, that's true. And I've nothing but a big sneer and profound contempt for these pantywaists who stand in awe of a skirt, who don't know that it's the slugger who gets in there and fights for her that she admires. It's action she adores, my boy . . ."

Tim said, "Yeah, I know."

He glanced with seeming desperation from side to side as if looking for an excuse to leave. When he saw the Tin Centaur rattling towards him, he grinned and heaved a sigh. The passengers, jammed into the topless car until they had to lean over the sides to make room, yelled, "Hey Howller, plenty of room. On the hood."

Tim blurted, "So long, Traje," and ran off.

Traje called out, "Don't forget, old buddy. It's action that gets the woman. Action. Action."

III

While the election rally was breaking up in a tumult of cheering, whistling, and wild waving of torches, Mark Hazar yelled at Tim, "Come on. We're gonna go after the banner!"

But Tim shook his head and said, "I—I can't. I've got a—a date."

Mark shouted, "Huh? Since when?"

Tim reddened, hesitated, then said loudly, "I didn't quite tell you the whole truth, Mark. I do have a date, but it's not with a woman. It's—it's with action! Yeah, that's it! With action.

"You see, all the ribbing I took from Charlie and the boys, and the advice I got from Traje, have convinced me that maybe I am a dweller in shadows, a guy who lets others make off with the prizes and the girls. So—I got an idea. Instead of letting others make history, I'm going to make it. And I'm going to do it right now!"

He began to walk away before Mark could object.

Mark yelled after him, "I don't get it! Hey, Tim! You're missing out on a lot of fun!"

"Not on this date," said Tim.

Ten minutes later he walked into Campustown with his hands in his pockets and whistling with a merriness he didn't feel. A crowd was gathered on the sidewalk and street before the drugstore, grocery store, beer-joint, hamburger-joints, and jelly-joints huddled into one short block called Campustown. As the black rally was over, most of the boys and girls milled around aimlessly. Many boys carried pine or oak or walnut paddles of the kind used in fraternities to thwack bent-over pledges. The paddle-swingers were mostly Agricultural students, for the Black coalition consisted of all the Ag frats, in addition to the Betas and three sororities.

Tim eyed the blue-jeaned men, half-apprehensive they would challenge him, even though common sense said they would have no way of telling a Black from a Gold. He stood around, hands in his pockets, listening, watching. Then he began drifting towards the banner strung high across the street between two iron power poles. In big black letters was: Barker For President.

That banner was the challenge, and Tim, raking it from end to end with his eyes, felt like a spy in enemy country. He was conscious that he had a heart, for it beat furiously. He felt sweat trickling from under his armpits, despite the deodorant, and his belly was closing in on itself like a fist.

Calm down, he told himself. Nothing's happened. And from the looks of things nothing is going to happen. How in the world could I, alone, drag that banner down from those poles and make off with it through this crowd?

Obviously, he couldn't. But he could hang around until the Aggies took it down for him. And then, if he combined the serpent's cunning with the dove's speed, he might be able to catch them off guard and, who knows, run off with the banner as Jack did with the singing harp. The only difference between him and Jack was that he had no axe to cut down the route of pursuit. It was a big difference.

He decided to talk with one of the guards and find out when they planned to lower the banner and where they would carry it. But the guards suddenly shouted, "Look out!" and ran off in different directions.

Tim half-turned. He cried out in alarm. He flung up an arm, a useless, late gesture, for the blazing torch missed him by a foot. It slammed into the street-pavement and rolled over and over, bumping to a stop against the curbing, where it burned fiercely.

Three other torches described burning trajectories close to the path of the first.

Behind Tim, girls screamed.

One of the Ags, a big blonde with a paddle in each hand, shouted, "Let's get those damn Golds!"

He ran off toward the dark, cupolaed James Hall, the university administration building. Three paddlers ran after him. Their destination was a group of boys standing under the bushes by the hall's big porch. Evidently, the torches had been flung by that bunch.

Tim, straining his eyes into the dark, thought he could make out Mark Hazar's short, broad figure.

Another Aggie called out, "Hold it, Jim. It's just a ruse to get us to leave the banner unguarded."

Jim stopped and came back. He said, "You're right, Bob. But those damn fools might've burned somebody bad."

Bob said, "Anything's likely to happen tonight."

He glanced at his wristwatch and then called to two other paddle-swingers. "Almost ten. We've given the Golds enough of a chance. Let's take the banner down."

"Yeah," said Jim. "They've got no guts."

Jim dropped his paddles, pushed aside a guard, and began climbing up the steps of one of the iron poles. Another boy ran across the street to the west pole.

Tim turned to see the women who had screamed. His heart had waxed and waned fast before; now it began the furious squeezing of blood, accompanied by a tightness in chest, that it always experienced at each fresh sight of Francis Uquart.

She was standing in a group of Kappas who had just come out of the Yellow Sable. Her large blue eyes locked with his; Tim opened his mouth to say hello, remembered that she might wonder what he, a Gold, was doing there, closed it, and half-turned to go as if he hadn't seen her.

But she said, "Hello, Tim Howller."

Her voice was curiously deep for a woman's, throaty, husky, vibrating, and hinting at the substratum of energy and emotion that would be well worth the effort a man would have to take to tap it.

Her voice reached out with strong, but delicate, fingers, and plucked at him. He felt the squeezing of blood and the tightness of chest, and he felt also something go *strum*! within him as her strong, delicate voice-fingers plucked a string.

"Hello, Francis," he said.

His voice sounded all right to him, just loud enough to sound confident and deep enough so she wouldn't guess how she shook him and friendly enough but not too friendly. He had never yet allowed it to betray him, but he could never be sure of himself until he had spoken.

He said, "Did one of those torches almost hit you?"

She laughed with a slight note of anger. She said, "Oh, yes. One of them just whizzed by my head. What's the matter with those nitwits? Don't they know they might seriously hurt somebody?"

"They're nitwits, all right," said Tim, despising himself for not thinking of something clever, something that would convulse her and the rest of the girls with laughter.

He stepped back to let big Jim off the pole. Jim had untied the east end of the banner, and it had fallen into upstretched hands below.

"O.K.," said Bob. "Fold it in two and roll it up tight. We'll put it in my car around the corner. Those yellowbelly Golds aren't going to try to steal it."

The banner consisted of a thin lath about ten feet long from which hung a rectangle of thin white cloth. The lath was broken in two and folded. The cloth was rolled around the lath into a tight stick about five feet long. Then the banner was picked up by two men who held opposite ends, even though one could carry it easily. Around it gathered six paddle carriers.

"Now," said Bob. "Honor-guard, forward! To the armored chariot. Ta-ra-ta-ra-ta-ra! Boom-boom-boom! If the Golds try any last minute raids, beat hell out of 'em!"

Tim had a vision of himself sinking in a sea of arms, each of which held a paddle thudding dust and pain from the seat of his pants.

His saliva dried, but sweat pebbled his forehead, soaked his armpits and the area between his shoulders.

Nevertheless, he began walking by the side of the guards, and he said, "Didn't the Golds make any real attempts to get the banner?"

"Yeah," one answered. "A bunch of guys in an old Model T drove down the street close to the banner, but we stood in front of it and scared them away by throwing our paddles at them."

He laughed. "I hit one right on the head. You should have seen him bleed."

Tim gulped. So Mark Hazar and those other guys had tried. And failed. The men of action had failed, and now it was up to Tim Howller, man of inertia, man who stood in the shadows and sucked his thumb, to carry out the rape of the banner.

He gulped again and ran his tongue over the dry stalactites of tension that seemed to hang from the roof of his mouth. Now or never. The banner had been carried around the corner to Bob's sedan. The backdoor was open, and the banner was about to be shoved in. Once that door was closed on it, he would have lost all chance to take it. And to ask the guards where they were driving it to on the off chance that he might be able to sneak it out of their hiding place, would be to expose himself to their suspicions.

He glanced over his shoulder to see if any paddlers were directly behind him. Lord! Francis was standing on the corner, and she was watching him! If he failed now! If he didn't have the guts! He'd lose forever his chance to distinguish himself enough to be able to ask her for a date.

Now or never.

The man holding the banner's front end was ready to shove it in the back seat. But his back was turned to Tim. And the man holding the rear end was laughing and looking away from Tim.

Now or never. Too many times now had slipped through bashful-fingers and never come home to roost.

He sucked in a deep breath, sucked in the now with the oxygen. Then, the now penetrating his blood, threaded with it so that it would not come out, he released his breath in a wild warwhoop. And at the same time that he gave that scream which he hoped would unnerve the guards, he leaped upon the banner.

His outstretched hands clutched it, felt the cloth and doubled lath, and tore it with the force of a hundred and eighty pounds of track-tempered physique and an immeasurable amount of determination and desperation from the slack grip of the carriers.

Around him the guards stood like men in a broken-down film, shock-suspended, bewilderment-frozen.

Then they were behind him, there was no one in front, and he was running down the middle of the street, the banner clenched in his right hand, whipping and swaying and vibrating like a white lance launched straight for the Lambda Lambda house.

Shouts and curses rose behind him. A hard-flung paddle spun by, narrowly missing his head. Another slammed into a tree-trunk on his left.

"Get him! Get him!"

Feet slapped the pavement behind him.

IV

Between 10:20 and 10:45 that night, telephones rang in the frats in the Gold coalition. Those answering were surprised to hear Charlie Bluepress' loud authoritative voice. He demanded that they round up all their available men, arm them with paddles and eggs, and get them down in front of Sigma Chi house as quickly as possible.

"What's the matter?" they asked.

The receivers bellowed: "What's the matter? Man, I was in a bull session with a bunch of politicos at the Sig Chi's, when Jack Littley phoned. He said there's three hundred Aggies and Betas in front of the Lambda house. They're bombarding it with eggs.

"Yeah . . . that's what I said . . . eggs . . . eggs . . . old rotten eggs they must've gotten down at the warehouse, or maybe from the Agricultural Labs . . . yeah . . . my gawd, Littley says the house-front is plastered . . . broken-in screens . . . cracked windows . . . smeared the hallway's walls and rugs . . . our housemother's in hysterics . . .

"Why? . . . haw! haw! . . . one of our pledges stole their banner! . . . yeah, isn't that delicious? . . . I'll bet they're really frosted . . . snatched it right from their hands . . . ducked down alleys, ran like a stripe-tailed ape . . . outran them all the way to our house . . . then collapsed inside . . .

"Some of them trailed him, and now Litttley says there's a mob outside howling for their banner and the guy who stole it . . . they're threatening to come in and get him and shave his head and maybe tar and feather him and ride him around town on a rail . . .

"Naw . . . they won't do it . . . Littley and Weiss were in the house when the pledge got there . . . you know how big and tough they are . . . they'll clip the first guy that steps inside . . . but those Blacks are making a mess with the eggs . . ."

Charlie's voice switched off the bellowing joviality and became crisp and commanding.

"Enough of this blabber . . . hop in your cars and get over *tout de suite* . . . the touter the sweeter . . . and come with paddles and eggs . . ."

The receiver banged down.

V

At 11:10 P.M. a loose phalanx of excited and determined students, numbering between four hundred and five hundred, left from in front of the Sig Chi's and marched down School Avenue towards the Lambda Lambda's, three long blocks eastwards.

These Greeks, however, unlike Agamemnon's or Achilles' warriors, were armed with pine paddles and paper sacks and wooden crates of eggs, referred to as pullets' pellets. Fortunately, the Aggies had not had the foresight, or the money, to buy out the entire stock, and the Golds had therefore caught the amazed operator of the downtown warehouse before he had closed up again. Putting off his questions about the sudden run on hen fruit with a multitude of witty and totally irrelevant answers, the Golds had seized his remaining stock, paid off, and taken off.

Now, heroically armed, they went into battle as so many heroes of the past had gone—with a song on their lips. It was a song that is, in one form or another, traditional on the campuses of the larger colleges. There at the University of Shomi it was entitled "Uncle Tom, What Makes the Grass Grow So High on the Beta Lawn?", and it was a song derived from the tradition that the Betas were one and all inclined to look down their noses at other frats. It is a song that is usually sung when non-Betas are tipsy or just feeling good, or, as on that night, looking for a fight. It is sung with the hope of enraging the Betas into retaliatory songs and imprecatory poems, or, even, into violence. It is usually a forlorn hope, for the Betas are too Olympian to reply by word or fist to mere mortals.

Though most versions of the song are earthier, it runs something like this:
"Oh, we'll all go over and do what the dogs do,
　　Do what the dogs do,
　　Do what the dogs do,
　　On the Beta lawn.
"Oh, we'll all go over and do what the dogs do, etc.
"We'll growl, growl, growl,
　　howl, howl, howl,
　　growl, growl, growl,
　　On the, on the, on the Beta lawn.

On this occasion, however, reflecting the high tension and bad feelings that had distinguished the election, and the fact that, inasmuch as Barker, the Black candidate for president of the student government, was a Beta, and that, therefore, the rape of the banner was a blow in their face, the Betas had come out of their ivory tower. They stood with the Aggies, facing the Golds.

Tim Howller, from the vantage point on the roof of the Lambda's porch, could see the whole situation. He was lying flat with his head raised and peering through the bars of the white-painted little railing that kept the boys from falling off when they sun-bathed or slept outside at night. Beside him was a sack of eggs that he had taken out of the kitchen refrigerator and which he was ready to drop on any Blacks who tried to invade the front door, three stories below.

Around him were the white broken shells and yellow yokes of

unsuccessful attempts to pierce the third story windows beyond the porch-roof. None had hit Tim, for he had not come out of his retreat in the attic until Littley had reported seeing the Golds marching down the street. Now he watched. He saw Blairston, the governor's son, tip a bottle to his lips and then smash it against the pavement. He saw Barker going through the crowd trying to find out how many eggs were left. Unfortunately for the Aggies, they had launched most of them at the house and were now left with nothing but fists and paddles for defense. Evidently they felt naked, for an uneasy mutter ran through their ranks, and some loud voices counseled immediate flight.

Then the army of Golds marched to within ten yards of the Blacks. At a ringing command from Charlie Bluepress, they halted, after which they shifted uneasily, gripping eggs and watching the Blacks for sudden moves.

The Gold big shots stepped forward to confer with the enemy leaders. Zinter and Blairston put on a sideshow by arguing.

Tim watched them anxiously. He disliked both, for they had once dated Francis Uquart. Blairston had beat Zinter out by putting his fraternity pin on Francis. That was the beginning of the well-known feud between the two and the boasts of both that when it came to a showdown, each would kick hell out of the other.

Tonight, stimulated by the banner's rape, the damage done by the eggs, and the consequent excitement, not to mention a dozen beers and half a pint of whiskey, Zinter had decided to have it out.

Blairston stood with clenched fists and red face listening to the names Zinter was calling him. When he was accused of being a Judas because he had pulled the Betas out of the Gold coalition the preceding semester and lined them up with the Aggies, Blairston barked back angrily. Then everybody could see that the governor's son had also been hitting the bottle, for he mumbled and slurred and swayed.

Tim mentally hugged himself and hoped Zinter would swing. He'd like nothing better than to see the old stuff knocked out of Blairston. The guy deserved that and far more, for he had spread stories about Francis since their split-up that nobody but a liar and a degenerate and the tail-end of creation would permit to pass his lips. Especially when they were about Tim's Red Helen!

But shortly it became apparent that neither of the arguers had guts. Both were contenting themselves with calling each other names that should have aroused them to an instantaneous and blinding urge to kill. But they swayed and repeated each other's insults.

Nor was Charlie doing anything to urge his men on. He stood immobile, a huge fat Buddha, blinking and looking from side to side and talking in a very restrained way for him with Barker. Tim couldn't hear them above the drunkard's bickerings or the catcalls and insults passing back and forth between the main bodies. But he guessed by their gestures and the seriousness of their faces, revealed by the light of the arc-lamp above them, that they were discussing peace.

Disgusted, Tim rose to his feet.

"Ah, those lousy men-of-action!" he muttered. "They'll stand there talking forever and then slink home."

He picked an egg out of the sack, a nice extra-large one, balanced it in his hooked fingers, made a rapid estimate of the distance involved and force required, and sailed it out in the night.

The white oval rose, became black against the sky, suddenly dropped, and was white again.

Tim's eyes were focused on Blairston. He confidently expected the trajectory of the pullet's pellet to end in an explosion of yellow yolk against yellow hair.

Then he gasped. His aim was way off!

Charlie Bluepress let out a bellow of surprise and anger that drowned the shrill bickerers and dull mutter and hoarse jeering of the crowd. He wiped at his cheek and cursed. Then he plucked something from a paper sack in his left hand and cast it viciously.

Splop!

Even from his third-story height, Tim could hear it. And he could see a suddenly silent Blairston pawing at his dripping face.

Then Charlie shouted out an order and pulled out another egg and splop! And Barker was pawing at his face and cursing.

There was a roar from the Golds. A cloud of white pellets sailed from them, broke and rained over the Blacks. There was another cloud—and another—and then a thunder of feet and a tumult and a shouting as the Golds rushed the Blacks.

Tim didn't see much after that, for he was struck with a laughter that seized him and pulled him to the roof and made him roll back and forth, shouting and holding his aching ribs. Then, when the convulsions lessened, and he could sit up and wipe his eyes and wheeze for breath, he noticed that he had rolled through the sack of eggs and that he was soaked with yolk. And that brought on other gusts of laughter that shook him until he was too weak to laugh anymore.

"Old Charlie got it! Big fat Charlie! Right in the kisser! Ha! Ha! Maybe that'll teach the overgrown hippo not to prate of action. Action! He wanted action, and he got an egg!"

He wiped his eyes.

He shouted, "Ha! Ha! I'm not sure now that my missing Blairston was unintentional. Ha! Ha! I'll bet that if Charlie could have seen what razzing me was going to lead to, he wouldn't have opened his big mouth."

And he laughed until he could laugh no more at the thought it was he, and he alone, supposedly inert, actionless, thumbsucking, shadowdwelling Tim Howller who had started the battle that was making clamorous and bitter and eggy the street in front of the white façade of Lambda Lambda.

And, of course, the shadowy card-player in the back of his mind had flipped out the inevitable Daliesque ace on which Tim-Paris sat on a topless tower of Ilium, leaning on his trusty lance, resting on his laurels, laughing at the thought that his desire for the most beautiful woman in the world, Red Helen, had started all this, and watching with Olympic aloofness the poor mortals of Greek and Trojan mix it.

VI

The next afternoon, Tim Howller, shaved, shampooed, showered, shined, and shining, dressed in new green-brown herringbone tweed pants cuffed at the ankles according to the vogue, a sport coat of gray-green herringbone tweed, a white shirt, and a green and red dotted bow tie, stood outside the jelly-joint. Grinning broadly, he looked like a very fresh and confident, almost brash, young man. Part of that effect came from the pseudo-spiritual feeling a clean body and clean clothes give; part, from an inner light.

The light was the glowing of a nimbus—a nimbus which soaked him through and through with a joy and an aggressiveness that had been largely lacking in that shy, moody youth. Much of the glow came from his previous night's exploit. That alone was enough to fill him with satisfaction and confidence. But much also fountained from the keen interest and joy displayed by his frat brothers—their urgings to tell and retell the story of the rape of the banner, how he snatched it from under the suspicious noses of the Blacks, how he outraced them, how he started the battle outside the Lambda's by accidentally striking Charlie. That brought roars of laughter from all, from Charlie most of all. He slapped Tim hard on the shoulder and bellowed that he'd make a politician and a big-man-on-the-campus out of Howller yet.

The only grey thread in the gold of the nimbus had been Tim's worry over the damage to the house, which he could not keep from blaming on himself. But that was dissolved, for Charlie said that the Ag leaders had agreed to pay for the damage. Their offer, said Charlie, wasn't as noble as it seemed, since Charlie had sworn to them that if they didn't cough up, the Golds would make similar raids on the Ag frats.

So it was that young Tim Howller rode in on a wave of glory much as young Lochinvar rode on his steed, rode into the Yellow Sable, jelly-joint par excellence.

The booths lining the walls were filled with couples or four-somes, or even sextets, who had dropped in for a jelly-date, local parlance for a cheap date during which one sipped on cokes, listened to the band, if there was one, and danced on the raised floor at the back of the joint, shouted at each other or whispered in soft, amorous tones, saw and were seen, and, in the dark corners, went through a series of facial contortions and nuzzlings known as smooching.

Though he was smiling buoyantly, Tim's heart was beating as fast at the idea of asking the hitherto unapproachable Francis for a date as it had when he was on the verge of stealing the banner. He had no such ideas as smooching. Not yet. It would take enough nerve to talk to her.

But he was determined to do it. After all, his name must be on everybody's lip, and she would be standing in reflected glory by being seen with him. The worst that could happen would be her refusal to date him.

He looked through the thick clouds of cigarette smoke. From long surveillance of her, he knew it was her habit to drop in there after her noon classes. He looked around and couldn't find her. For once, she had failed to come. He didn't know whether to feel disappointed or relieved. Then, as he walked around a counter, he saw her bright-red hair at a booth in one of the darker corners.

She was alone. He was lucky. It wasn't often that this girl was unattended. The chances were, she was waiting for her date, whoever he might be, to enter now.

Quickly, before he would lose his determination, and before some boy would come up and beat him to the draw, he walked up to her.

"Hello, Francis," he said, smiling at her.

"Hello, Tim," she said, smiling back.

"Mind if I sit down," said Tim, "I just happened to drop in and saw that this is one of the few spots unoccupied by a fanny. I'll buy you a coke."

"Of course, I don't mind," she said. "I always like company."

He didn't care for that. He didn't want to be considered just company.

"Is that a new dress?" he said. "It really is beautiful. That bright green with the yellow collar really goes good with your red—uh—auburn hair."

"Yes it's new. I'm glad you like it."

She smiled and patted her hair and said, "And you may call it red. It is. Auburn sounds so affected, don't you think?"

Tim said, "Yes. I think so."

The waiter came. Tim ordered a lime coke for Francis and a plain coke for himself. While they waited, he talked slowly and hesitantly, trying to keep the door shut on the bursting sea inside him. He wanted to ask her immediately if she would go this coming Saturday night with him to see Robert Taylor and Greta Garbo in "Camille."

But first, he had to know he was swimming in safe waters. He had to hear her words of praise and of wonder at his exploit and her breathless inquiry about what happened after he ran off with the banner. And he expected to send her into laugh after laugh with his comic account of the egging of Charlie Bluepress.

He waited, but she did not speak. Some of the nimbus chilled. Was it possible . . . ? Oh, no!

"Wasn't that an idiotic thing for those boys to do last night?" he burst out. "I mean, throwing the torches like that. They might have hurt somebody. They almost made me ashamed to be a Gold."

"Oh yes," she said. "One almost did strike me. But you know how boys are. Besides, they were anxious to get the banner."

He waited with beating heart. But she spoke of her part in the forthcoming Workshop play. At another time he would have blotted up every word, but now was no time to talk of the stage. Not unless he was on it.

"Listen," he said sharply in the middle of one of her sentences, "haven't you heard about the Black's banner being stolen last night?"

She raised eyebrows.

"You don't say? Well as I—"

"But, but," he said desperately, "it happened right after those torches were thrown. Surely you must have seen who ran off with the banner. You were standing right there watching!"

She looked around, saw someone she knew, waved. She spoke, her eyes roving, everywhere but on Tim. She spoke, and the nimbus chilled and turned to grey, and Tim knew that the now was flown and the never had come home to roost.

"Oh, no. Right after those torches were flung I decided it was too dangerous with those silly boys showing off, so I walked back to the Kappa House."

THE UNNATURALS
PHILIP JOSÉ FARMER

One of Philip José Farmer's childhood ambitions, to write and have published his own Oz novel, was fulfilled in 1982 with the publication of *A Barnstormer in Oz*, a rollicking, funny, sometimes irreverent extrapolation of the idea "What if L. Frank Baum's *The Wonderful Wizard of Oz* was based on real events?" In the mid-1970s Phil used the name "Leo Queequeg Tincrowdor"—a sly reference to the Lion, the Tin Woodman, the Scarecrow, and Dorothy—as both a character and pseudonym. But even before this, Phil wrote a touching tribute to Baum's Oz in his 1954 essay "The Tin Woodman Slams the Door." In that essay he discusses how his childhood love for the Oz series was tempered against his growing maturity as a writer. But that is not the end of the essay. Phil goes on to express that his creative muse eventually reopened the dialogue with the innocent wonder of his childhood. The Oz-verse had endured throughout the years and survived into the present, albeit cloaked in a new and modernized language.

"The Unnaturals," published here for the first time, but written in 1973, nearly two decades after Phil's essay on Oz, is an example of how an artist successfully retranslates myth so that it is meaningful to current generations. Myth is not a static thing—it must live and breathe if it is to survive—and this is something that Phil knows and addresses throughout all of his work with an intuitiveness that is, frankly, stunning. The story you are about to read illustrates this talent and provides the reader with an allegory which resonates as well today as it would have had "The Unnaturals" been published in 1973.

Although it had no brains, it thought all night.

Always, there were problems. Before it was made, it had no problems. It had neither existence nor essence. Then existence came along, or it came along to existence, and it was. And with its being were problems.

When its eyes were painted on, it saw the light. It saw the sun and the little man in blue who had buttoned him into being and painted in the doors to its senses. At one time, it had imagined that, just as the farmer had buttoned and painted him into life, so the sun must have brought the farmer into life. And who had buttoned and painted the sun?

The biggest problem, though not the most pressing, was: Who am I?

After a while, the more practical problems had concerned it.

How do I get down off this pole?

The pole was stuck in its back at one end and into the ground at the other. It was unable to twist around and release itself, so it hung there. The days and the nights had gone by with sun, clouds, rains, moons, clouds, rain, and wind. As it swayed at the end of the pole, it thought that the wind was the force that pushed the light and darkness along.

Then it thought that the pressure of the light from the sun pushed the wind. At times, it seemed that the crows pulled in the dawn or pushed it ahead with the flutter of their wings. When they left, the night flowed down from the sky in the same way that water had to fill a hole in the ground.

Then along came Miss Twinkletoes, and she got it down off the pole. Ever since, it had determined to do everything for itself. It would not have to depend on anybody; a Twinkletoes might not always come along. The best way to be independent was to get a brain. Then it would be able to think out the answers to its questions.

But here they were, only halfway to The City, if there were a City. Some people said the City did not exist any more than the gray country of Kansas that Twinkletoes was always talking about.

However, here they were, in an abandoned hut on the edge of

a little farming community. Three of the party had to sleep, and that was that, even if they could not afford to waste time. Behind them, baying on their trail, were two groups of men. These were at war with each other, but both wanted Twinkletoes. Ahead, beyond this tiny village, was a dark woods filled with huge carnivores and monsters. Somewhere at the end of this narrow winding rundown brick road was the person who could give four of the five what he, she, or it wanted.

All night it had stood in the corner, thinking these thoughts. Once, it had moved briefly to kick the little black dog sniffing around its leg. Its boot struck the ribs of the dog, which shied away, unhurt. Although the boot was leather, the foot inside was cloth and straw and the cloth and straw leg was not powerful.

"Why doesn't he try to piddle on you?" it said to the figure standing in the opposite corner. Its voice was muffled, as if strained through a cloth sack.

The figure replied in a metallic voice, "Because he thinks I'd chop him in two with my axe. He knows I'm heartless."

The dog trotted out into the cloudy night. After a while, having found a tree that did not try to beat him away with its branches, he returned. He burrowed between two large figures by the wall. One, partly hidden under a blanket, was a girl of nine. The other was a giant bushy-maned lion.

It stood unmoving, listening to the breathing of the three. In and out. Up and down. Life depended upon movement of itself and the movement of other life. Even when a thing of flesh and blood and bones was absolutely still, the inside of its body was moving. Organs expanded and contracted, blood rushed around as if it were on its way to put out a fire. Actually, it was on its way to start fires. Oxidation.

It backed up a step then, as if it saw a flame before it. Fire was the only thing it feared.

Why? What did it care if it went up in brightness and blackness? Why did it want to stay alive?

Life was the desire to keep living. To keep moving.

Even the night had to move. It slid away, and the dawn, equally helpless to stop, moved in, tied to the night's tail. The shiny white-gray figure in the other corner said, "Will they ever wake up?"

"You were once flesh and blood, Stan," it replied.

"The name is Jack."

"Stan for stannous. Stand-all-night Stan."

Twinkletoes cried, "Good morning!" and got up from under the blanket. The dog crept out a moment later. The lion abruptly stopped snoring, opened his eyes, and yawned. The girl and the dog yawned, too.

The lion left to hunt for some poor deer or horse or cow. A farmer would be enraged and come tracking Shivernshake, and there would be more problems.

Twinkletoes and the dog ate some scraps left over from supper. Then the two went off in the woods to do what flesh and blood had to do.

It thought about this. All life needed input of energy and output of waste, itself a form of energy. All except Stan and itself. Why were they the exceptions? Magic was the answer. Either magic side-stepped the basic requirements of life, or magic supplied them with energy of some kind. This was nice for them, unless the magic was suddenly withdrawn or collapsed. Everything was uncertain.

The girl and the dog came back in. Shivernshake padded in about ten minutes later, looking a little less ribby and licked his whiskers.

"Come on, Innocent," Stan said to his companion of the night. "We have to load up and roll 'em out!"

It did not object to the nickname Stan had given it. Tit for tat, was the rule of life, one of the first he had determined through observation.

Stan and it loaded the lion with the folding platform, the folding chairs, the drums, the guitars, the xylophone, and the blankets. The lion grumbled, saying, "Here I am, King of the Beasts, burdened down like an asterisking ass."

"You're not King, remember?" Stan said. "You're The Yellow Streak Kid. Champ scaredy cat of the year. The gutless wonder."

A tear crawled down the lion's big nose. Stan said that he was sorry. He had not meant to hurt his feelings and please don't cry.

Stan managed to feel compassion despite his lack of heart. Perhaps he was operating on the memories of his lost tenderness.

Twinkletoes made a joke then and teased Shivernshake and got all in a better mood.

She was a wonder, it thought. A beauty, a joy. If only she knew how it loved her. But it did not dare to tell her. Humans had too many mysterious reactions for it to take a chance and tell her again that it loved her. She had been scared when it had first tried to kiss her. That was the first day they knew each other. It had been overly grateful or overly eager to display its gratitude, and it had come blundering and bending and bobbing at her so that she thought that it would be better if she initiated the kissing.

They left the hut and followed the yellow road. They passed a farm house and, a half a mile more, another. Then the farms were side by side, and, presently, they were in the village square. While they set up their platform, chairs, and instruments, the people drifted in from the stores, the blacksmith shop, the livery stables, the granary, the town hall, and the houses. Others were driving in from the farms, having seen the group pass by.

Few of the men were taller than the little girl. All were inclined to be roly-poly, and most wore clothing of one color; blue. Some of the more daring youths wore shirts and hats of other colors, but they were the recipients of sarcastic comments from their elders.

Twinkletoes wore her only dress, a gingham with blue and white checks and a pink sunbonnet. These were clean and the holes and tears had been sewn up. Her silver shoes were beautiful and were the main attractions of the group for the crowd. Even out here, they had heard how she had gotten those shoes.

Innocent took the megaphone and climbed up on the platform. It looked around at the crowd, which numbered perhaps fifty. More were coming however.

It yelled through the megaphone, "Come on, folks! Now's the time! This is it! Where it's happening! Where it's at!"

It put the megaphone down and placed the strap of the guitar around its neck. It felt the weight of the instrument unbalancing it. Actually, it did not feel the weight but knew through the up and down movements of its body, visually detected that the weight was difficult for it.

"If I had any brains, I'd learn to play the xylophone," it said to itself.

It pulled out of its pockets the gloves with the plectrums sewed into the tips of the fingers. Without these, its boneless fingers would have been useless in playing the guitar.

Shivernshake was at the drums, using his paws instead of sticks and the tip of his tail for a brush. Twinkletoes was at the xylophone. Stan adjusted the base guitar. The dog, of course, would do nothing. Strictly nonutilitarian, it thought. Why did Twinkletoes keep it around? Love? How could anyone love anything so useless?

Then it remembered what its farmer father/maker had said about it and its failure in scaring off the crows. It felt ashamed.

Twinkletoes tinkled out a few bars by way of getting the crowd's silence and then spoke to it.

"O.K., folks. We're the Unnaturals, and we're here because we dig all you tillers of the soil, you brave sons of the dirt, in your simple dignity, great courage, and closeness to Nature, Mother of Us All, even us Unnaturals. Also, we really dig this simple rural community, this village of . . . of . . . uh . . . what'd you say it was, Your Honor? Pasadena? Peoria? Punchy?"

"Punchkin!" His Honor cried.

"What's in a name?" Twinkletoes said. "It smells as sweet."

Aside to Innocent, she muttered, "Swinekin'd be a better name. Whew! Couldn't we have gotten upwind from the pig pens?"

Smiling, she shouted, "Punchkin's a great little wide spot in the yellow brick road, folks! We dig it! We're out of our minds with joy to be here!"

There was more of the spiel with Twinkletoes doing better as she went along. The kid was still stoned from eating that purple flower with lavender berries she'd found on the roadside, but she was coming out of it.

Innocent took over from her as she went back to the xylophone. It strummed a couple of fast chords and then said, "We call ourselves the Unnaturals, folks. You can see why. We're straight from a long engagement at the palace of the Wicked Witch. In fact, this little lady, Twinkletoes, I call her, was out of sight, folks. Too much. She really killed them, especially the Wicked Witch, our late ruler. You might say her performance brought down the house, hah, hah!"

Shivernshake beat a tattoo on the drums and clanged a cymbal. Innocent went a-one, a-two, a-three, a-four, and they broke loose. It played its tenor guitar and sang with its curious muffled voice.

"Who am I?

A wandering minstrel
A being of straw
An unnatural

Tripping
On the yellow hard butter
Of the slippery brick highway
Headed towards
The Great Green Glass Cutter

Where the Grand and Glorious
Optimumflummorious
Frightful and Awesome
Metaphysician operates.

Hidden in a bubble
In the Big Green Glass Glitter

Where brains for me
Courage for Shivernshake

Heart for Stan
And a ticket home
For Twinkletoes
Await

Oh, who am I?
And what the price
For finding out?

Call me Frankenstein
Call me Dracula
Call me

I won't be home

I'm tripping on the yellow hard butter
Of the winding gold-brick highway

Wandering
Wondering
Who am I?

A Wandering minstrel
A thing of straw
An Unnatural."

The concert was not a sell-out. It was more like a cop-out. Twinkletoes passed the empty picnic basket around, but only a few coins were tossed in. The group received a loaf of old bread, half a dozen eggs, a piece of cake, a chunk of cheese that had been set aside for use in the rat traps, and several pieces of horse meat that the house cats had disdained.

"Thank you all, kind sirs and ladies," Innocent said. "Punchkin once again lives up to its reputation for generosity."

A tall youth at the back of the crowd shouted, "We dug your chords, scarecrow, but our folks won't let us have no money!"

The mayor's face had turned red. He shouted, "That's enough

of that smart talk. You refugee from a cornfield! We're poor folk around here! What the wild beasts and birds don't get of our crops, the bandits take! And what the bandits don't get, the tax collectors of the Wicked Witch snatch."

"The Witch is out of it now," Innocent said. "Or haven't you heard?"

"We ain't that isolated, sackhead! We heard! She was a bad and vile ruler and taxed us unmercifully! But better a bad ruler than none at all! Now anarchy strides rampant throughout this once fair and peaceful land, and revolution runs riot! This nation is torn with division, brother against brother . . ."

Innocent beat out some loud chords of a music that was favorite among the youths but forbidden by law of the land. "Who Blew My Blue Hugh?"

"Hey, politician!
Will you talk forever,
Promise destruction on one hand
And peace and prosperity with the other?
Straddle the fence,
Keep your ear on the groundswell,
Your eye on the main chance,
While your mouth runs
Like a kid who's eaten green corn?

Hey, politician!
Ride your ass out of town
Or vice versa
But don't make no speeches.
Tell me,
What's really behind
The big wind,
The fastest mouth in the East?"

The mayor jumped up and down and screamed. Innocent began to regret having told the truth. Or was it The Truth? What was The Truth? Oh, if only it had intellect, gray matter!

A number of little men with spears, pitchforks, and a few blunderbusses surrounded them.

"Off to jail!" the mayor screamed. "Lock them up! Throw away the key! They're monsters! Spies! Criminals! Revolutionaries! Foreigners! Nonhumans! Corrupters of our youth and our morals! Besides, did anybody sell them a license to give a public concert?"

Twinkletoes was crying and holding her dog tightly in her arms. She shouted at Innocent above the roar of the crowd. "The mayor's doing this just to use me for his own gain! He'll try to get my silver shoes away! Or sell me to those men that're after us!"

"Don't worry, baby," it said. "Nobody can hurt you as long as you're wearing those shoes."

"Yes," she sobbed, "but they can hurt those I love. Or make me do what they want by threatening you and Stan and the lion and my dog."

"Gee, why didn't I think of that?" it muttered as the group was forced towards the jail. It looked around over the heads of the little men and women. The young men and women and the teenagers were standing to one side and scowling and gesticulating.

Then the group was inside a brick building and going down a gray urine-stinking hallway and then was in a big bare room with rickety wooden bunks and dirty blankets and one window with heavy iron bars and one steel door with bars. The door slammed behind them, and the keys clicked in the lock.

Innocent looked out the window. A few minutes later, soldiers charged into the square on their big horses. They were led by a skinny man with slick black hair, a skimpy black moustache, and eyes even bluer that the painted eyes of Innocent. He wore a tricorn hat and bandoliers and two flintlock pistols and a stiletto and a sword and a knife in a sheath in back of his neck and a knife in a sheath in his boot. Twelve men guarded him every minute.

The jailer said, "That's Joe Hunchmerker. Only he calls himself Anonymous Legion now. He's the head of G.O.D., the Good Old Days party."

General Legion waited until the villagers were assembled before him, and then he made a speech. He promised to fight until peace and law and order and prosperity were restored. He would use a firm, even harsh, hand on the bandits and the unruly youths and provocateurs from foreign lands. There were cheers from everybody except the young and one old man who shouted, "Will the taxes be cut?" The old man had run away then with a dozen of Legion's men lashing at him with their cat-o'-nine-tails.

Legion marched into jail with a small brass band playing behind him. His speech this time was short. Twinkletoes must give her silver shoes to him because he alone would use them with the benefit of all in mind. She and her friends could then go unharmed, although they should all be hung, if justice were to be truly done.

"Go ahead and hang me and Stan," Innocent said. "If it'll make you happy. Then let us go. We're on our way to see the Whiz-Wiz and get our heart's desire from him."

Twinkletoes wanted to hand over the shoes, but Innocent refused to let her.

"I haven't been alive long, and I'm not very smart. But I know that very few humans keep their word. Certainly not Anonymous Legion, who is a soldier and a politician both, which makes him doubly untrustworthy."

"Give them to me," Legion said. "Or I'll burn this sickening unnatural immoral product of hellish sorcery, this stack of blue-eyed straw, first thing in the morning. And if it burns, and you still won't give me the shoes, then we'll see about getting a big enough can opener for your sardine can of a friend. And if you're still stubborn, then that quaking shaking pussycat there will undergo some unpleasant experiences, fatal, too. And then your dog . . ."

Twinkletoes cried and said she'd give up the shoes. Innocent, Stan and Shivernshake said no. She'd be crazy to do it.

Legion stormed out, shouting that the scarecrow would go up in flames right after breakfast.

The jailer said, "You may not have to worry about him, honey. I hear that The Underground Revolutionary Null Over Nil party is hot on the trail of Legion. Not that it'll make much difference eventually to you. They'll want the same thing Legion does. And either way, the villagers lose."

Night came. The moon, a cool substitute for the sun, sauntered across the sky. The square was bright with torches and noisy with people talking and shouting. The soldiers ringed the jail and regarded the milling townspeople with hostile eyes and sharp spearheads. The little girl cried a while, then lay down and sang songs to her dog, who seemed to understand the unintelligible references to things Kansan. Then she fell asleep. Innocent kissed her softly and patted the dog. The lion paced back and forth and swore he'd knock down the walls and carry them all to safety. Stan tried to pull the bars of the door apart.

Innocent looked out the window. The youths stood at one end of the square and talked among themselves. Innocent remembered what the youths of every town the group had passed through had said. They were tired of the wicked old witch and their elders and the men who wanted to take over after the witch was killed.

Innocent watched the square for a long time. The torches made it shiver inside, as if mice were crawling around its straw. This is living, it thought. You live the most when you see the end of living.

It took the guitar and sang through the window.

"Hey, firebugs!
The scarecrow'll burn in the dawn!
There'll be two flames in the morning.
The big one, the sun.
The little one, me.
Nobody notices the sun.
It's so big you forget it.
It comes up and goes down
Every day
Like a monkey on a stick.
But the little flame
Me, the scarecrow
Will burn for a few minutes
In the dawn

And a hundred years
In the middle of men.
It's nice to be a symbol
But I'd rather just
Be."

The youths drifted closer to hear, and then Legion charged out and ordered them to disperse. Sullenly, the young people back away, and soon they disappeared into the shadows. Innocent felt despair. He had hoped they would storm the jail.

"We're on our own," Stan said. He clanked back and forth, his head bending creakingly in thought. "We got to find a way out."

Innocent hit the chords.

"If there's no way out,
How about a way in?"

"What's that mean?" Shivernshake growled.

"Old Legion has guards all around the building and a dozen in the room in front," it said. "But no one's watching us at this moment. So stuff me through the bars."

Stan looked astonished, even if his face was stiff tin.

"Why didn't I think of that?"

"You're pretty weak, Innocent," the Lion said. "You won't be able to put up much of a fight."

"I'm weak, true, but on the other hand, I never get tired," it said. "Let's get on with the disassembly."

It felt peculiar, and frightening, to be unbuttoned and taken apart and spread out. Its head, straw enclosed in a cloth sack with painted blue eyes, red nose, blue ears, and a red mouth, lifted at the end of Stan's metal arms. It could see its body, the jacket and trousers and boots, and gloves, in a pile and the straw in another pile. Then things became blurred as its head was rolled up and passed through the bars.

Stan's arms were the only ones thin enough to go between the bars. Even if Twinkletoes had been awakened, she could not have gotten her chubby arms through.

The process of stuffing it and buttoning and setting it up and patting it into shape again took about five minutes. While this was being done, a roar came through the window. The lion said, "Here come the kids with torches and placards. They'll get massacred."

It wanted to hear more, but now was the time to act. Legion and his soldiers would be occupied with the youth. It walked softly down the hall, though not as softly as it wished. Its lack of sense of touch and pressure forced it to proceed by use of its eyes. Though it had considerable skill in walking thus, it could never do it automatically, as humans did.

Just as it got to the jailer's office, it saw Legion and some soldiers go out the front door. It peeked around the corner and saw the keys. They hung on a peg on the wall to the right and were flanked by two burly spearmen. Stan's big axe lay on the jailer's desk, which was on the left. The jailer was at the desk, furiously writing on papers and muttering, "Red tape! Red tape! Forms! Triplicates! No matter the master, the paperwork piles up like fat on a drunken housewife's skillet."

The front door of the jail could be secured on the inside by a big wooden bolt. Innocent stood a moment, thinking, and then gave a yell and ran towards the door. The jailer jumped up, scattering papers. Innocent lifted the latch and pulled the door open with a great effort and shot through. Behind it, the two guards shouted and their shoes slapped on the stone floor. They ran out through the door, and Innocent, who had stood by it, ran back in as soon as they passed it. It pulled the door shut and slammed the bolt in, though only by an effort that threatened to split apart the seams of the gloves which acted as its hands.

The jailer looked as if he were going to attack Innocent. It said, "Better not get involved, fuzz. The villagers are on the march, and you know what happens to collaborators!"

The jailer's blue eyes became glassy with indecision. Innocent removed the keys from the peg. The jailer started forward, Innocent said, "Don't, fellow!" and ran down the hallway. The jailer shouted and ran after it. Evidently, he had decided that Legion was going to be a winner.

Innocent ran swiftly, gracefully for once, and coolly put the key into the lock of the cell door. This was one time when lack of nerves paid off. Then the jailer had seized it by its shoulder and plucked it backwards and spun it down the hall. It hit the wall and crumpled. But when it got to its feet, it saw that Stan's metal arms were between the bars and gripping the jailer by the neck.

There was nothing weak about Stan's hands; the tin fingers were like vises. Twinkletoes, awakened by the noise, was screaming at Stan not to kill the jailer.

Stan said, "I don't like to hurt people. That's why I'm killing him."

He opened his hands, and the jailer, purple-faced, tongue hanging out, fell to the floor. Innocent turned the key, and they were all out of the cell. Stan picked up his axe from the desk, and he and the great lion, who was shivering and shaking, went outside. The soldiers were getting the best of the youths when the tin man and the lion hit them from behind. Stan, acting at Innocent's orders, made for the general. He bowled the bodyguards over and those who did not fall at the impact of his body collapsed a moment later under a meteor shower of axeblows. The soldiers, seeing their chief captured, broke and ran.

Anonymous Legion was still struggling in the grip of one of Stan's hands when Innocent approached them.

"You! You!" Legion sputtered. "You've lost your chance; nobody's fault but your own! It wasn't the girl I really wanted. It was you! I would have made you my prime minister; you would've lived off the fat of the land!"

"But I don't eat fat or thin," Innocent said.

"I wanted to find out how you magicked into life," Legion said. And then I was going to liquidate all humans and have a nation of scarecrows! They don't eat, and there'd be no problem with food or garbage. They don't breed, so there'd be no population problem. And they . . ."

Innocent looked around quickly. Twinkletoes wasn't in sight, so what was going to happen wouldn't horrify her or ruin her image of it and of Stan.

"Kill him!" it said. "Quickly!"

"In cold blood?" Stan said. "Have a heart!"

"That man would kill Twinkletoes and every human in the world to get a perfect world," Innocent said.

"He's sick in the head," Stan said. "Anybody with brains can get sick in the head. Including you. So you'd better consider again your desires when you face the Fabulous Whiz-Wiz."

"Any advantage has its shadow," Innocent said. "No risk means no gain. And I could go on with enough platitudes to pave this road twice over. What puzzles me, though, is why Legion didn't tell me his idea for scarecrowifying the world until now."

"I wasn't going to burn you!" Legion gasped. "Not unless you turned me down. I thought I'd try to get the shoes from the little girl first, because, if I had them, I could rule the world and do with it what I wanted. If she refused, *then* I was going to propose my plan to you."

"Miserable as I am, stupid as I am, I still like being me. And I don't want a million duplicates around, drowning me in non-individuality. Kill him, Stan!"

"You do it," Stan said.

It felt the straw inside it move around, as if some mice with very active feet were building nests.

"Let him go," Innocent said. "I can't do it."

"He'll kill more people before somebody does your job for you," Stan said. "Maybe Twinkletoes. Many little girls and boys, you can bet on that."

"He at least ought to have a trial," Innocent said. "Let's jail him, and when we come back from The City, we'll hold the trial. By then I'll know what to do with him. I'll have brains."

"It takes more than just brains to know whether or not a man should be killed," Stan said. "All right, Legion. March! Back to jail!"

Innocent watched the metal man guide the general by the neck to the red brick building. There went another problem which had to be faced someday. But not now. Maybe somebody would solve it for Legion and for itself. The townspeople had suffered much during the hour or so of Legion's invasion. Perhaps they would get tired of waiting for the group to return and would settle matters themselves.

"There's nothing like refusing to face an ethical issue," Innocent said. "I must be getting more human by the minute."

The next morning, the group set out on the yellow road. The forest seemed to engulf them; it was deep and dark and cool and quiet except for strange and frightening cries now and then. Twinkletoes kept up a merry chatter for a long while, but, by they third day, she was wondering if they would ever get to their goal. Innocent hit the chords and sang,

"Hey, Anxious Voyager!
The end comes fast enough!
Too asterisking fast!
Ask your grandma!
She'll tell you!
The end comes fast enough!"

You'll be grown up, little girl, it thought, and looking for a real man, not a scarecrow or a tin man. And I, who ache with love for you, and ache because there is an ache I can't experience, will have to let you go. Oh, if only Stan knew how lucky he is not to have a heart.

Twinkletoes cried, "It's so gloomy and spooky here, in this great dark silent forest, Innocent! Sing me a song! Make me as happy as you look with your big happy painted blue eyes and your big painted red smile!"

"Sure thing, little lover," it said.

"Somewhere, this blue leaks out
At the end of the winding
Yellow brick road
And then it'll be green.
Come on, blue sky.
Green sky,

Philip José Farmer

Give me a different color
A color I've never seen before
I'm tired of
Blue moods,
Green moods,
Yellow moods,
Purple moods,
Black moods,
White moods,
Brown moods,
Scarlet moods,
Come on, blue sky
Green sky
Give me a different color
One I've never seen before.
I'll be grateful
For a little while."

THAT GREAT SPANISH AUTHOR, ERNESTO
PHILIP JOSÉ FARMER

First written in the early 1940s and completed many years later, this story is a pastiche of sorts, though not about Tarzan or Doc Savage or Sherlock Holmes, or any of the characters Phil is famous for writing about; neither does its style echo that of any of the creators of those characters. While most of Phil's readers are doubtless aware that wit, subtlety, and literary allusion are common throughout his work, we are sure you will agree that "That Great Spanish Author, Ernesto" is one of the finest examples illustrating just how artful and diverse Phil's writing can be.

The captain told me that the loading of the bananas would be finished in thirty minutes. I had time for several drinks and some more conversation with Sancho. Why waste it here? I left the ship and walked up *La Avenida del Conquistador Blanco*, a street which does not deserve its magnificent name at its waterfront end. Along both sides are mean adobe ranchos and bleached wooden huts on stilts and many black *zopilotes* with silver-tipped wings. As the big birds swing upwind from you, they radiate the stink of sun-rotten garbage.

Sancho's is a cleaner *posada* than you would expect from the neighborhood. There you can get cold drinks and entertainment by rubbing elbows and buttocks with tourists and representatives of every social stratum in Ticimarra, capital city of Huitzil.

Since it was mid-morning, there were only three in the place. Sancho, behind the bar, and two women at a corner table. Sancho smiled at me with a touching sincerity and joy. When he bobbed his head, his family of four chins, the two parents, the adolescent and the embryo, bobbed in unison.

"*Buenos días*, Sancho,"

"Don Felipe!" said Sancho in Huitzilian Spanish, the only tongue he could speak well. "How goes it with the bananas and with you?"

That was our private joke. I replied, as always, "The bananas ripen. I ripen. Soon, we rot. Then, we stink. All goes well; all goes as it should."

For some reason, he always laughed.

One of the women left her table and walked towards me. I said to Sancho, "Still out of Scotch?"

He shook his chins. "Just out. I am always just out of Scotch. But if you can't make up your mind what else to drink, the simple thing to do is to take the next best thing, Mexican beer."

He talked much of the simple thing. Sancho himself is a simple. Simple does not have the meaning in the Central American nation of Huitzil that it has in the United States. In Huitzil, a simple is not an imbecile. He is one who looks at life with such simplicity that the complexities drop off like a leper's flesh, and the simple bones are seen. The simile, Sancho's, is gruesome, but it fits. Life walks on bones. Flesh is needed but not rotten flesh. Get rid of the rotten. Better yet, see the bones first, and then you will understand the flesh.

The philosophy of the simple takes some time to understand and more to practice. Most people find it too painful to pare away the rotten flesh.

The Mexican beer was too sweet and heavy, but it was cold, and that was what I wanted.

The woman, María, sat down on a stool by me.

"*Buenos días*, Don Felipe."

The title of don was mercenary flattery, but it pleased. It deserved a drink. Sancho set out her rum. And the other woman, a peroxide blonde also named María, walked over.

The dark María turned swiftly.

"Take thy greediness elsewhere."

The blonde María said, "Thy greediness! It was my turn!"

It seemed there was a violation of ethics.

"It was not thy turn. It was mine."

"*Puta!*"

"*Ramera!*"

"*Aborticidia!*"

"*Onanista!*"

They seemed ready to pull out the knives from their stockings. Sancho did not like that. Blood so early in the morning would upset his customers. He considered the simple thing to do. Either buy them a drink or throw them out. I thought it cheaper to throw them out. Sancho agreed. They knew better than to talk back; they got out.

I said, "For a moment, I thought I was going to see a scene à la Hemingway."

Sancho's heavy lids fluttered up like a window-shade.

"Hemingway? Ernesto Hemingway? The great Spanish author?"

I coughed up beer.

Sancho said, "Ah, Don Felipe, it is true that I read only the newspaper. But once a Yankee traveling book-salesman to whom I had given too much credit, may God forgive me for that, and who had run up a great liquor bill, parted with his private collection of Hemingway as payment for half of his bill. When he surrendered the books to me, he wept. It was true that he was given to weeping, especially late at night. But I thought that if this author could wring such tears, he must be worth reading. And, truly, he was."

"You mean the Ernesto who was born in Oak Park and who wrote stories based on his boyhood days in Michigan?"

"Michigan? I believe the foreword in that highly technical and philosophical book on bull-fighting—you have read it?—mentioned some such place. I thought it was a Basque town because his name sounds Basque or, perhaps, it was another spelling for the Mexican state of Michoacan. Which is it?"

"His name is not Basque. He was born in North America. Give me another beer."

"So, he is Mexican, even if he did love the country from which his ancestors came more than his native land. Ah, the next time I visit Mexico, I would like to make a pilgrimage to his native town. Is it remote?"

"It is remote."

"Too bad. Perhaps, some day, I will have the time and the means to go there. But this Ernesto is magnificent. You have read him in Spanish? No? In English, then. You should read him in the pure Castilian, a language not corrupted by Americanisms. I imagine he loses potency in translation. Spanish is the language for power and grace and beauty.

"Ah, Don Felipe, I loved all his books. The one of the technicalities and philosophy of bull-fighting. The novel of the drunken castrado. The tragedy of the Yankee who kissed war goodbye forever. The novel of the rum-runner. That great romance of the lovers and the bridge in the Spanish Civil War. And the one about the old fisherman and his big fish. All I loved and wept over.

"To me, they are almost faultless. Indeed, I have but one criticism. Too many of his characters are not Spanish, or of that descent, but are Yankees."

"That is the fault of many young writers," I ventured. "They love to idealize their heroes. And, since they know their countrymen too well to idealize them, they make their heroes foreigners."

"That is well said. I can see that now. And when Ernesto matured and rid himself of his youthful romanticism and became a realistic writer, he dropped the impossible foreign heroes. He wrote in his old age only of his great and glorious ancestors and of his ancestral country.

"I refer, of course, to that mighty work: *Don Quixote*."

I choked the grandfather of all chokes. Sancho shook his chins.

"The beer is not of the quality it used to be. Ah, yes, Don Felipe, when I read that of the old fisherman and the sea, I knew that Ernesto was destined to write what he should have been writing. But I did not think that he would ever surpass himself, that he had started too late. It seemed to me he must have poured out all the mighty juice of his life into those books. I thought the last would be a repetition of the others. And the others were so great it would be a—a—"

"Anti-climax?"

"*Gracias.* But I was wrong. The last was the best. *Don Quixote* was so magnificent, so truly Spanish, that the others seemed the work of an apprentice author."

"Pardon me. You said one of the books had a foreword about Ernesto. Did *Don Quixote* also have a foreword saying anything about the author?"

"There was none. The Yankee salesman had cheated me with a damaged copy. The cover, the back, the title page and the foreword were torn out. It is nothing. I am content."

A customer came in. Sancho served him and returned.

"Quixote's servant had my Christian name. A trifle flattering, no?"

I nodded.

He said, "Sancho Panza, like me, was a simple."

I said, "I thought Don Quixote was the simple."

Sancho's eyes twinkled.

"In the Yankee sense that he was somewhat of a fool, though like all Spaniards, fearless, yes. In the Huitzilian sense, no. Some day the word simple and the philosophy simple as we mean it, kindly and uncomplex and unselfish, will spread to the north. And then Huitzil will have the credit for civilizing North America, yes?"

I choked. Sympathetically, Sancho's chins shook. I recovered and looked at my wristwatch.

"The bananas will almost be loaded."

"*Vaya con Dios,*" said Sancho. "I will see you on your next trip."

"If God wills."

I laid down four quarter-huitzils, three for drinks, one for Sancho's conversation, and walked off. Sancho followed me to the door.

He said, "I cannot recommend too much that you read *Don Quixote* again. This time, in Spanish, the tongue it was written in, the only tongue strong enough to bear up under Ernesto's power. And remember, when you read, that that great author has, I am sure, portrayed himself in the character of Sancho Panza. Panza is a simple. Ernesto, too, is a simple. You agree?"

"I understand that he has striven all his life for simplicity," I replied cautiously. "But I think that Ernesto was also Don Quixote. He had a bravery that Panza lacked. But the good Don was also one of the brave ones."

"Perhaps you are right," said Sancho. "Yes, I know you are! What insight you have, Don Felipe! Ah, the great old knight!"

And tears flowed down his bulging cheeks.

I studied Sancho, wondering. Then, knowing he would hear, sooner or later, I said, "Ernesto is very ill. He had left Cuba and gone to Idaho."

"*Aydajo*? Where is that?"

"In the United States," I said. "He has a home there because it reminds him of Spain."

"That makes me sad," said Sancho. "But I am sure that he will face *la muerte* as fearlessly as all his heroes, especially Don Quixote, did."

"He will not shrink," I said. "He will do the simple thing."

For one second, I thought of presenting Sancho with his own moment of truth. Then, cowardly but perhaps wisely, I closed my lips. If he was happy, and he was, why should he not stay happy? Let the drunken joke of a drunken salesman live. I wanted to remain Sancho's friend. Not from me would come any shattering revelation.

I walked away, but before I had gone far, I turned for one more look back up the street. Sancho, standing in the doorway, waved. His family of chins waved. I waved and turned away and wondered if the twinkling in his eyes was his general good nature or something deeper. Also, I wondered which one of us was the simple.

In the Yankee sense, of course.

THE ESSENCE OF THE POISON
PHILIP JOSÉ FARMER

Philip José Farmer's reputation is built, in part, on tackling issues few writers would dare to touch. From Hal Yarrow's intimate encounter with an alien female in the groundbreaking sf tale "The Lovers" to the sexually and violently explicit adventures of Lord Grandrith and Doc Caliban in *A Feast Unknown*, Phil's stories often challenge us to look in uncomfortable directions.

"The Essence of the Poison" is one such story, though of a different theme. Written in 1941, as the United States was about to be drawn into World War II, this early example of Phil's mainstream fiction confronts the infectious nature of prejudice head-on with no apologies. Writing in the October 31, 1941 issue of his college newspaper, *The Bradley Tech*, Phil strays from the topic of his trip to New York City (to thank radio host Fred Warring for writing his school's fight song) and addresses the plight of the Jewish people in the face of the war: "Hitler is raping all that they and civilization are doing to lift mankind up." Then he adds, rather coyly, "Please excuse this digression, but one's thoughts cannot be helped." Certainly, they could not, and as Phil wrote the story at hand surely his thoughts lay heavy before one of the darkest chapters in human history.

Those who have read "The Face that Launched a Thousand Eggs" in Issue No. 1 of *Farmerphile* may perk up at the mention of the Shomi-Upper Ozark Railroad in this current feature. For those who may have forgotten, Tim Howller, the protagonist of the former story, attended The University of Shomi. Since Howller also appears in Phil's "After King Kong Fell," we may also safely place "The Essence of the Poison" within the continuity of the Wold Newton Universe. Further, we may marvel that Phil was already well on his way to creating his own inter-connected universe by the youthful age of twenty-three.

Be forewarned: this story of a man tortured and obsessed by his own narrow-minded intolerance raises uncomfortable issues that, unfortunately, must still be addressed today. While Phil's writings indicate that he is a realist—that he knows well human nature has long carried with it a predilection for prejudice it still has yet to abandon—his stories also cry forth a great shout of hope, an undying optimism that humankind can exercise its little used free will and change for the better. The challenge lies in awareness, and Philip José Farmer dares to make us aware.

Outside his great-uncle's house, under the light of the street-lamp by the high, wrought-iron gate, Richard Bodkin ran into Pete Fabel. Pete, cocky in a straw hat, a black red-dotted bow tie, red-and-white striped shirt, and white duck trousers, grinned widely. He said, "How's the boy, Bodkin?"

Richard said he was all right. He started to pass Pete, not caring to talk because he had always disliked, and at times hated, Pete. Pete had been, and was, a loafer, a wisecracker, a bully.

Pete put out a detaining hand on the bulging brief-case under Richard's arm. His whiskey-clotted eyes twinkled; his lips, pale and rubbery as chewing-gum, stretched in a half-smile, half-sneer.

"Goin' in ta see that . . . uncle of yours?" he asked.

Richard understood that the pause was to be filled in by himself. Crazy, nutty, off-the-beam . . . any one of those would block the gap.

Richard gave him a hard look. "Yeah?"

He looked from Pete to the house. Inside it, filling it as if it were a vessel, was the essence of the poison that was infecting the world.

The essence of the poison . . . a dense, heavy fluid through which his uncle swam, blind, groping, choking, doomed to drown. The essence of the poison of hate and fear, the essence of a self-loathing, self-torturing, too venomous and burning to be contained, spilled out and projected into the form of a people conveniently different and weak, unable to fight back.

Inside that house was the concentration, the condensation, the distillation, of an insanity of the world, the essence of the poison.

He looked back at Pete Fabel, the loafer, the bully.

Pete was saying, "They oughta be run out of the country . . ."

Outside, here, was the poison.

"What's it look like I'm doing?" Richard said.

"Yeah? Don't get on your high horse. People might get mad. People might say, O.K., it's time your uncle went to the bughouse."

Richard, six foot three of gaunt, stoop-shouldered, hollow-cheeked, bespectacled college student, blinked. Behind the stolidity of his narrow, hawk-nosed face was a hatred for Pete.

Richard said, "And some people, including my uncle, might say it's time some people went to jail for spreading malicious slander."

Pete snarled, "Yeah? Yeah?" and backed up a step.

Richard wondered why he had let Pete push him around when they were kids. Probably because Pete always had a gang behind him.

He mocked, "Yeah? Yeah? Whatever you might say, my uncle still swings a lot of weight in this town. President of the bank. Chairman of the town council. Rotary Club. Elk. Chamber of Commerce. Boardman of Y.M.C.A. Temperance Union. And so on. What he says in Bodeau, goes."

Pete contorted his face into a friendly smile. He said, "I didn't mean nothin'. Forget it. Listen. How're you comin' with your college work?"

Richard wondered how this low-lifer had heard of his reason for visiting his uncle. If Pete knew, the whole town knew. And he had thought he had been tight-lipped. Beyond the understanding of man were the wondrous workings of the small-town grapevine.

Richard said, "I'm doing O.K."

He was not, but he did not want to give Pete any cause for malicious joy over his failure.

Pete said, in a disappointed tone, "That's fine. I guess you're the only one that ever got any place with your uncle, huh? Wasn't there another student from the University that came to see your uncle about his book? Yeah. Haw! I remember. Little Jewish fellow. Got scared and jumped over the porch railing. Sprained his ankle. Haw! Didn't know what he was running into, did he? Haw! Served the kike right, don'tcha think so?"

Richard grunted noncommittally. He remembered. He had been walking across the campus when he had seen Mose Goldstein limping along, a cane in his right hand. Mose had stopped him and had said, "Listen, Richard. Is your uncle crazy?"

Richard had said, "Not exactly. Why? I didn't even know you knew him."

Mose said, "Yes, I do. Look. I was wondering what subject I was going to write on for my doctor's thesis in history. All of a sudden I remember that your uncle was once vice-president of the Shomi-Upper Ozark Railroad.

"I remember that when that line was absorbed into a larger one, your uncle retired to Bodeau, Oklahoma, and set himself up in the banking business. He took with him the records and ledgers of the S. & U. O. R. R. He's the only man with access to them.

"So, I figured it would make a swell thesis if I wrote a paper telling the exact number of spikes used in the building of the line during the years 1879-81."

Mose put his tongue in his cheek. "A real contribution to knowledge, see? It'd make quite a stir in the academical world. The beauty of it would be that I would not have to go all over hell and back to get my information. It'd all be concentrated in the attic of your uncle's house."

Richard had stiffened. He said, "You louse. I was going to use that for my doctor's thesis."

Mose had nodded somewhat shamefacedly. "Yeah. I know you were talking about it. That's what gave me the idea. I had no scruples about lifting it because Jake Silvers told me you stole his subject for a master's thesis. I figured turn about would be fair play."

Richard flushed. "Yes. I used it. I didn't think Silvers had the ability to develop it properly."

Mose said, "That's O.K. There's no honor among scholars. Anyway, I hopped a train to Bodeau. There, I went to the bank, but your uncle was home because the bank was closed for a legal holiday. I went to his house. I knocked on the door. Naturally, I thought it would swing wide open with the traditional Oklahoma hospitality you're always telling me about.

"Not so. A peephole in the door slid open. A big eye, black pupiled with a lot of white around it, stares through the peephole. I said, 'Does Mr. Porphyry Bodkin live here?' The eye said, 'He might.' The voice was deep and sent shivers up and down me. I said, 'I'm Moses Goldstein. Did you get my letter?' The eye said, 'What did you say your name was?' I said, 'Moses Goldstein.'

"With that, the eye disappeared. All of a sudden I heard a howl, high-pitched and quavering like a wolf whose tail was being twisted. It came from behind the door. Presumably, the howling was being done by the owner of the eye. Or else he was torturing a dog. Whoever was howling, he—or it—set my nerves to shaking. You know I'm the nervous, sensitive type.

"Then, I saw something in the peephole. It wasn't the eye. Not the eye of a human being, anyway. It was the muzzle of a gun of some sort. What sort I did not wait to find out, I'm not interested in calibers, .25, .30, .32, .38, .45, .155, six, ten, twelve inchers, I don't care. A gun is a gun.

"I took off. Naturally, being in a hurry, I ignored the steps. Especially since, if I ran down them, I'd be in sight of that gun.

"I darted off to one side and ran kersmack into a rusty old pot-bellied stove sitting on the porch. It knocked me down. Undaunted, I got up and ran around it and made an athletic leap over the railing.

"I did fine until I hit the ground. There, I sprained my ankle. At the time I did not notice it. I kept on running. In no time at all I reached the railroad station, purchased a ticket, and beat it on back here.

"Listen. What the hell is it all about? Can you tell me?"

Richard looked at the humorous, inquiring face. He shook his head. He said, "Sorry, Mose. No can do." And walked away. Behind him he heard Mose yelling, "Hey, Bodkin. You must know something, don't go away sore."

Richard had not been angry, just embarrassed. He could not find it in himself to explain the true cause of Mose's bewildering reception. It would hurt himself, and it would hurt Mose. It was better just to say he did not know what was wrong.

Now, six months later, he was outside his uncle's house on his sixth trip in his efforts to gather enough information to complete his thesis. He hoped that this would be his last. It had better be. If he did not get what he wanted this time, he might as well give up and choose another subject.

When he had selected this one, he had thought he was very clever, for the simple reason that of all the million or more college students in the U.S. he, Richard Bodkin, was the only man who would have access to those ledgers and files stored in the attic.

Any other scholar, he had thought, would not have a chance, no more chance than poor old Mose Goldstein had had. But now it looked as if he, too, were going to fail miserably.

Thinking this, he gritted his teeth and vowed inwardly that this trip he would outbluff, outsmart, or outsomething-or-other his uncle. Anything to transfer that information from the records to his notebooks.

Pete's whining voice, begging Richard not to tell his uncle what Pete had said about him, jerked Richard from his reverie. He said, "See you later, Pete." He hoped he would not.

Pete whined, "So long, Richard. Don't tell your uncle."

Richard did not reply. Let Pete worry. It would be a small payment for all the beatings, bullyings, and sarcasms he had endured from Pete when they were children.

He went up the steps, observed that the rusty old stove was still parked on the porch, knocked on the door, and waited. His heart was beating fast.

The floorboards in the hall creaked. There was a fumbling sound at the door. The peephole shot back. An eye, gleaming white by the light of the streetlamp outside, appeared. A voice rumbled, "Ah, Richard, it's you."

The eye dissolved into a blackness; the peephole shot back into place; the door opened; his great-uncle Porphyry Bodkin embraced him with two long arms and a long beard. Then he released him, pulled him inside, shut the door, bolted it, and led his nephew into the parlor, lit by the feebleness of a kerosene lamp.

Richard saw a man six feet tall, thick-bodied, bull-necked, with the fierce, arrogant, hawk-nosed, thick-lipped, square-bearded face of an ancient Assyrian. Making him look much younger than his almost eighty years was his thick, curling, jet-black hair, streaked here and there with grey.

Porphyry wiped a tear from his fierce black eyes and said, "Ah, my boy, you don't know how glad I am to see you."

Richard said he was glad to see him, too. Under his uncle's urgings, he sat down on the horsehair sofa while his uncle poured a cup of hot tea. In view of the ordeal that was coming, Richard would have preferred a shot of whiskey, but his uncle was a rabid prohibitionist. A request for anything stronger than caffeine would have resulted in Richard's immediate and violent expulsion.

The old man held a saucer in one meaty palm, and with the other he clutched the cup, meanwhile straining tea through his whiskers with a loud slurp. In between he asked Richard how his folks were coming along, how he was doing with his studies, what he thought of the Yankees' chances, what was Russia going to do next, who would make the best candidate for the G.O.P., wasn't this an especially hot summer, and why didn't the nincompoops at Washington ever use their brains?

To each question Richard replied as best he could. So far his uncle was like everybody else, talked rationally, even with gusto and wit. Richard replied. And waited.

The hot tea warmed his blood and stomach and brought out sweat on his forehead that collected on his lean jaw and trickled down under his tight collar. It brought out sweat under his armpits that crept warmly, like little insects, down his ribs. He squirmed, wishing it would dry up and go away. He squirmed, watching his uncle.

He waited.

And it came.

Midway in a discourse on the necessity for converting the black natives of interior Africa to Christianity, his uncle stopped speaking, put down cup and saucer on the black walnut coffee table, slid off the chair and dropped onto his hands and knees on the floor. There, he laid his ear flat against the thick nap of the rug, listening intently.

Silence swooped through the house. There was nothing to be heard; nothing, nothing at all; it was as quiet as the spaces between the stars.

At last, the old man, who must have been repressing his breath, gave a great sigh. Richard jumped, causing the sofa to squeak. The old man glared at him. Richard attempted to control the shakings of his legs.

Suddenly the old man leaped up with a howl.

"They're stirring!" he cried. "They're stirring! The devils. Always at ten o'clock at night they wake up. They wake up and begin their evil work. The devils. Listen, Richard, can't you hear them?"

Richard listened. Of course, there was nothing to hear. There could not be. Not to a sane man. Yet, and this disturbed Richard much more than he cared to admit, there were times, brief seconds, when he did hear something. It was a scuttling, a footfall, a sharp clink as of metal on metal, a grinding, as of a borer twisting into wood. It was one of these; he heard it; but he knew he should not hear it. It was this that frightened him, hearing and knowing he should not.

"Listen to them," howled his uncle. "They're starting to dig. They're thinking, tonight, tonight's the night they'll get their talons on the records. Tonight and tonight and tonight."

Richard said, "Take it easy, uncle."

This was what he had been waiting for. This was what every visitor who was admitted to Porphyry Bodkin's house, and who stayed for more than twenty minutes, was subjected to. At first, everything would be normal. There would be small talk and big talk, perfectly commonplace, perfectly rational. The unsuspecting guest would be at ease, thinking himself in the presence of a gentleman and scholar, perhaps a little old-fashioned, like his house, but an aristocrat, nevertheless.

Then, bit by bit, as the old man talked, there would be little discrepancies sandwiched between normalcies, vague references, mysterious looks, hints. The guest would be puzzled until, all at once, the old man would spring up from his chair, roaring a demand for silence. Next, down on all fours he would go, his ear clamped to the rug.

The guest would look, listen, and wonder. What was coming? He had not long to guess, for Porphyry Bodkin, rising, eyes bulging, thick lips working, would launch into a tirade against the Jews in his basement, of how they had burrowed into it, and how, even then, even then, they were crouching, bearded, hook-nosed, and evil little men, crouching in the cellar, kneeling on the beams, their eyes laid flat against the floor, listening to the sounds above, waiting for an opportunity to burst forth.

They would burst forth, he howled, seize him, seize the Shomi-Upper Ozark Railroad records, and burn the house down.

In order to spy on him, he declared, they had bored holes in the walls and floors. To prove this statement, he pointed out mouse holes along the baseboards. He showed them stains around these holes, discolorations resulting from acid he had poured down them. For hours, he said, the burned and blinded Jews had screamed in the basement. He knew, because he had heard them, his ear against the floor.

He would chuckle at the memory and declare he had surely given them what they deserved. Then, he said, he had boarded up the holes. But he was always on the lookout for more. If he found them, he would drain more acid down them.

"That'll teach them," he would mutter.

He refused to go down in the cellar to shovel coal into the furnace. Until recently his negro servants had done so, but they, one after the other, had quit. His warnings to them to look out for the evil little men, the numerous bolts and shackles he had installed on the door in the kitchen that opened onto the cellar steps, his insistence on searching the negroes, immediately after they had fired the furnace, for Dictaphones and time-bombs planted on them by the Jews, all this had frightened them until they began to share his delusions.

They, too, heard noises behind and under them and listened furtively and with a pounding heart for the tapping and scratching of picks and shovels in the basement and the grinding of wood as borers screwed spy holes in the walls. Unhappy, nervous, they had quit, declaring the house was "haunted." So effectively did they spread the bad word among their friends that, in a short time, Porphyry Bodkin could hire no colored servants.

In the winters, servantless, he shivered in his cold house, stubbornly declaring he would freeze to death before he would venture down in the basement and thus place himself in the "talons"— talons was the word he always used—of those Jewish devils.

The old-fashioned Franklin stove he had ordered to be installed in the front parlor had gotten no further than the porch. Alarmed at the Semitic features of one of the laborers who had brought the stove, he had driven them off. In the exact spot where the startled workmen had dropped it before fleeing, the stove sat, and rusted.

Uncle Bodkin declared it was a pity he had to freeze every winter, but he would endure it, for it was doubtless part of the plotting of those in the basement that he should go stoveless. Moreover, he could not abide anyone who looked like a Jew. This statement, in view of his own thick, black hair, slanting brow, great hook of a nose, and thick lips, should have been comical. But he was mad and not to be laughed at.

Some there were who asked him why Jews should be hiding in his basement, what they were after.

"The records! The records!" he would growl, his eyes blazing. His tone and bearing dissuaded most from further inquiries, but a few foolhardy people, mostly women, professed ignorance of the records. Uncle Porphyry, in the manner of a teacher in a school for the feeble-minded, explained softly and in detail, that those who had the key could decipher from the records the date of the coming of the Beast.

As everybody, thoroughly cowed by this time, did not have the temerity to ask just what beast he meant, they kept quiet and listened, waiting for their chance to leave.

Meanwhile, the old man's voice would lose its softness, and he would howl, "It's hidden there. It's hidden. But, damn them, they won't get the records. They won't. God is on my side."

And he would glare at the visitors as if he would strike them down if they contradicted him. Nobody did.

Yet, despite this clear indication of mental unbalance, Porphyry Bodkin was respected enough, not only to keep out of the asylum, but to retain his position as president of the bank. Perhaps this was due to the fact that outside his house he never referred to his obsession. Any tactless remark about it by somebody who had been in his house only called forth a blank look as if he knew nothing of it.

Probably he did not. Outside his house he seemed normal. It was not until he entered his bachelor household that the terror dropped on him.

The genesis of this "quirk," as the natives of Bodeau were kind enough to call it, was unexplainable to many people. Richard, however, suspected that the depression of '29, which had almost wiped out the old man's fortune, and the consequent death of his wife, who pined away from worry and anxiety over lack of funds and loss of social prestige, was, in the main, responsible.

The old man had always been an anti-Semite, neither less nor more violent in prejudice than the ordinary American citizen. When the Big Crash came, Uncle Porphyry, like many people, had been unable to face the fact that his own wild speculations were responsible. Instead, he had found it much easier to blame the devilish machinations of Wall Street Jews for his misfortunes. His wife's death was another blow, which he attributed to the same cause.

He had sat in his dark, creaking old house, brooding for a long time, thinking what thoughts no one knew or cared. Then, all of a sudden, he had quit glooming and seemingly forgotten his sorrow and hate. Aided with government funds, he had gone back into the banking business, where he once more came into money, power, and prestige. His wounds had seemed to be healed.

Then, one hot summer's day, as he was entertaining some friends, he dropped his tea cup, lunged from his seat, fell to his knees, and pressed his ears against the rug.

There followed the by-now familiar ravings. Evidently his broodings and recriminations had succeeded in taking audible, if not visible, form. He was convinced there were those things down in the cellar, and no amount of contradictions cancelled his beliefs. On the contrary, they confirmed them.

Despite this, Richard had induced his uncle to let him search through the records and ledgers. Old Porphyry was certain none of his flesh and blood would be hand in hand with the Jews, but he steadfastly refused to allow his nephew to remove the records from the attic. There was, he claimed, too much chance they might fall into hostile hands.

When Richard countered that the Jews in the basement would never be able to get to the records if he took them to his room four hundred miles away at the University, old Porphyry was silent. He pursed his thick lips and looked as if he were thinking desperately. At last he burst forth with the statement that undoubtedly the Jews would burrow their way from the basement to that of Richard's fraternity house. Besides, didn't Richard know they had an underground system that extended all under the world?

Richard shut up. Plainly, his uncle wanted to be tortured with the fear. He gloried in it. It tasted good in his mouth. To take away the cause of the fear would be to deprive him of a drug and an ecstasy.

If the old man wanted to be insane, wanted to be terrified, let him be. There was nothing for Richard to do except ignore what he could, swallow the rest, and use all his cunning to dig out the desired information from the records.

He said, "Take it easy, uncle. Let's go up to the attic."

The old man's eyes lost some of their fierceness. "A good idea, my boy." He said. He walked into the hallway, seized a lighted kerosene lamp resting on a table, and led Richard up the stairs to the second-story floor, down the silent, gloomy hallway to its far end, where he unlocked a door which opened to a steep flight of stairs, climbed the steps, pushed open a trapdoor, and entered the attic.

Here, while his nephew searched through the shoulder high mass of ledgers and papers, the uncle stood behind him, lamp in hand. When Richard complained about the weak light, the old man said, "I don't allow any of that devilish electricity in my house. Those Jews have death rays they could project through the wires. I tell you, my boy, I have to be on my guard all the time against their cunning wiles."

Inwardly, Richard cursed. His weak eyes were strained, his back ached from his squatting position on the floor, his buttocks stung. Added to this was the rage engendered by the knowledge he would never find what he needed for his thesis in the short time his uncle allowed him.

He wondered what mad, fantastic reasoning could induce his uncle to part with the records.

A sigh disturbed him, he looked up. The old man was staring with glittering eyes at the records.

"Are you getting anywhere, Richard?"

"No, uncle. It will take months."

"Months? I tell you, you'll have to find the key before then. Why, he—the Beast, I mean—may come tomorrow! Tonight! It'd be too late. And those that are below might break loose before then. Recently, I've been hearing increased activities. I've lain with my ear on the floor and heard them muttering and stirring and creeping about. And chanting.

"And I've heard them sharpening the knives.

"The knives!" he suddenly howled. "The knives!"

He stopped to look furtively about. Hunching his shoulders as if he would hug a secret close to himself, he dropped to his knees and put his mouth against his nephew's ear to whisper, "Know what? That knife sharpening has warned me what they're planning. Who are they going to use those knives on? Not their boy babies, for I've listened and heard nothing but the voices of men. Who, then?"

A chill passed over Richard. He clenched his jaw to keep from chattering. So sincere, so intent, was old Porphyry he almost convinced Richard. Something in his demeanor showed, mad though he was, that there actually were those noises.

The kerosene flare threw a flickering light over the dusty books and furniture piled the length and breadth of the attic; a stuffed owl sitting on one of the low beams reflected a red gleam from its glassy eyes that was similar to that in his uncle's; down at the far end, dimly seen in the jittery shadows, a dressmaker's dummy, used by the old man's wife, still clad in one of her white dresses, leaned against a chair like a headless and drunken ghost; the old man's rapid, hoarse breathing sawed the silence in two; the clutch of his frenzied fingers was like a monster's.

"Listen!" he said. "Who're they sharpening those knives for?"

"I don't know. Who?" Richard's voice shook.

"For me. For me. When those devils burst loose, they'll tie me to the bed and take their knives and perform a certain ancient ceremony on me. You know what I mean."

Even in the grip of his terror the old prude would not let such a word pass his lips.

"You know what I mean. They'll do it. Then, I'll be one of them. My soul . . . lost forever. One of them."

Tears stood out in his eyes, welled over, ran down his wrinkled face and sopped his beard.

"Listen, my boy. You're smart. You can find the key to the code that I know is hidden in the calculations in those ledgers. Those figures add up to something the Jews would like to find out—the day the Beast comes.

"But if you can decipher the code, we'll have them licked! They'll have to retreat, abandon the cellar, and leave me free from fear. I'll be so happy then."

Though Richard doubted very much that his uncle would ever be happy, he was sensible enough not to say so. His uncle took a large, white handkerchief from his pocket and blew his nose with a tremendous, almost comical noise that helped relieve Richard's tension somewhat. He looked at Richard with large, red-streaked eyeballs.

"If they break through the floor or the walls, my boy, I'll be outnumbered. I'll smite them hip and thigh, my boy, my blows will be for God and right. I'll stand them off.

"But what if the cowards sneak up on me while I'm asleep. They'll crush me with their numbers. They'll strap me down. They'll perform their hebrewifying rites. I'll be lost.

"Why, boy, on Judgement Day how do you think the Lord is going to separate the sheep from the goats? Why, we'll all be stripped naked, man and woman, naked in our shame. And how do you think Christian will be told from Jew? How?"

With the tip of one index finger he made a rotary motion around the tip of the other.

"That's how he'll tell. Aha! Now you see. Where'll I be? Because of what those cellar-devils have done to me, I'll be judged to be a goat. Before I can explain how it happened, I'll be cast into the fiery pit. There'll be so much weeping and wailing and gnashing of teeth, my little voice won't be heard among the multitude.

"Think of it. One little snip. My soul lost . . . one little snip."

Richard asked, "Is that all that differentiates you from those below? One little snip?"

"Yes. One little snip . . ."

Richard was frozen with fear and shame. Never had he heard his uncle rave so much. The old man's mind was giving way fast.

Unable to look any longer at the pitiable object, he averted his eyes and pawed over the letters heaped before him. He picked one up and saw that, by the miracle of chance, it contained all he wanted to know. It was a letter from the chief clerk of the S. & U.O. Line to the president, describing the number of spikes, the number of ties, the number of rails, their cost, and, in short, everything Richard needed.

He looked at his uncle to see if he had noticed anything. He was afraid his sudden elation would break through the stolidity he was trying to keep on his face.

Old Porphyry had noticed nothing. But Richard knew that if he attempted to carry the letter out of the attic, those sharp eyes would detect any such motion, and that feverish old brain would attach a tremendous importance to said communication.

"Listen, Richard. Decipher . . . decipher. You have to. If you don't, your poor old uncle will be one of them. Think . . . the pain of body . . . unbearable anguish of soul. I won't be able to stand it, I'll go crazy . . . crazy."

Ignoring the babble, Richard twisted his head around to stare over his uncle's shoulders. His eyes widened. Slowly, he opened his mouth. Wide. Wide. His forehead crimsoned, became almost purple with a terrible effort. He looked like a man who was trying to voice a warning and could not because his sheer terror congealed him.

Suddenly, he broke through the crust of his paralysis and pointed a long finger behind his uncle. Simultaneously, he shrieked, "Uncle! There's one of them!"

The old man understood. He yelled. He jumped up. At the same time he attempted to whirl around. Unable to complete either maneuver, he tripped and sprawled, howling, on the floor.

The lamp slipped from his hand and rolled away. Afterwards, Richard thought that it would have been a fine thing if the kerosene, spilling out, had set the house on fire. The old man had plenty of money; he could afford to build another home. And the destruction of the old, silent, creaking, brooding house might have also sent up in mental flames his uncle's obsession.

Later reflection assured him, however, that it would have made no difference. Wherever Porphyry Bodkin went, there went the fear.

As it happened, the lamp did not shatter. It was extinguished, leaving the two in a darkness that put unreasoning panic into Richard.

In the brief flickering of the flame before the lamp went out, old Porphyry saw, crawling towards him on its hands and knees, one of the horrible creatures he had often heard but had not up to then visualized.

It was hideous, with a maggoty-white face above a black, priest-like beard, its thick, greasy lips writhing in hatred, a long nose flaring with distended nostrils, and eyes bulging with whiteness and madness.

Old Porphyry thought he saw a knife in its hand.

He screamed.

Then, the light went out.

Without bothering to jump up, he scuttled on all fours towards the attic trapdoor. Behind him, also on hands and knees, came his nephew, equally desirous of getting out.

When old Porphyry felt Richard's fingers on his pants leg, he must have thought the devil was laying talons on him. He roared, "Save me. Save me. Avaunt, avaunt!"

Richard panted, "It's me, uncle." but the old man had fallen through the doorway and down the narrow flight of steps. With a scream and a thump, he stopped at the bottom.

Afterwards, Richard was to reflect that, first, the lamp could have burned down the house. It did not. Second, the old man, in falling, could have broken his neck and put an end to his worries. He did not. Nothing was working out the way it could have. However, that was not unusual. It never did.

After his uncle had slammed shut and locked the attic door, and, leaning against it for a while, his ear against the panel, listening, his breath coming in great sobs, echoing up and down the shadowy, dust-grey hall, his breath finally becoming quieter and more controlled, the old man turned from the door.

He said, "I'll board this up. That fiend will be left to starve, and it'll serve him right. The beast! I can hear him groaning now. Did you see him? He was crawling towards me with a knife in his hand. Ready to perform the rite. My soul had a narrow escape . . . narrow . . . too narrow. He almost got me. But I was too slick for him. Too slick. The beast!"

The harsh, hate-filled enunciation of this last epithet seemed to pierce him as suddenly and painfully as the knife which he had been dreading. He stiffened; his face twisted like crumpled linen; he clutched at his heart.

"My god, boy!" he breathed. "The Beast!"

He released his heart to put his hand over his eyes.

"Of course. He wasn't one of Them. He was It. The Beast Himself. It was the Time for Him to appear and lead the Jews out to conquer the world. The Time. The Beast."

"Take it easy, uncle," said Richard, wondering how often he had repeated that warning.

"Of course I will, Richard. Why not? I've got him safely locked up where he can't get out and where they can't get to him. He'll starve. It'll take a long time, but He'll starve. And I'll be free forever of my fear."

He took Richard's hand. "Come, my boy, we'll go outside to the woodshed and get some boards and nails and block up this door. Come."

He led his nephew down the hall. "Ah, Richard, wasn't it a wonderful coincidence that we should have happened to be in the attic at the same time the Beast appeared and thus were able to forestall Him. Such luck!"

Richard said nothing. He could have told his uncle that what Porphyry saw crawling towards him was his own reflection in a dusty, old mirror. He decided not to, because, in the first place, he would not be believed, and, in the second place, maybe his uncle was not so far wrong. Maybe it was the Beast he saw.

It was too bad the attic was no longer open. The basement door had been boarded up. Now, the attic door. Next, something else would occur to cause him to board off the second floor. Then, different rooms on the first. Finally, one room left, and the terror closing in on that, and, in the end, the old man being dragged off, screaming, to the asylum.

Richard patted his coat-pocket, which contained the letter he had deposited therein when the old man had been tricked into looking away.

He said, "Guess I'll be going, uncle. I'd help you to nail up those boards, but I've got to catch a train. You're sure you'll be all right, though?"

Old Porphyry cackled and fingered his beard.

"Yes, my boy, I'm all right. I've got the situation well in hand. Nothing more to worry about. A glorious future. I told you I was too clever for them."

Richard could have told his uncle that there was nothing to keep those who were in the basement from trying to tunnel their way up through the walls to the attic. He refrained because he realized his uncle would in too short a time come to think of that possibility. Also, if he were to point it out now, his uncle, frantic, might insist he stay in the awful house with him, thus causing him to miss his train.

Richard merely said, "See you later, uncle." Knowing he lied, knowing that now he had the long-desired letter there was no use in visiting this old house again.

Outside, he breathed in the quietness and strength of the night air. What he had gone through in the last few hours seemed incredible. He turned around. The old house looked like an old house, not what it really was: a pocketful of poison.

He walked away and pushed open the iron gate.

Pete Fabel was still hanging around, leaning against the street-lamp. He was looking up at the moths and midges whirling around the hot aura of the globe. Hearing the gate creak, he straightened up, adjusting his bow tie.

"Hi, Richard." he said. He smiled ingratiatingly, his lips pale, twisted, and wet as discarded chewing-gum. Evidently he had loitered there to ascertain if Richard had reported his words to old Porphyry.

Pete nodded at the house. "How's he doing?"

"Uncle? He's fine."

"Yeah. That's good. You know, your uncle goes a little too far with that stuff about them bein' in the basement, but he ain't so far wrong. In fact, 'twouldn't really surprise me if they were down there. Why shouldn't they be? Those damned Jews are everywhere else. They're running the country—ruining it, too. They're everywhere—business, politics, movies—running and ruining the country."

Richard gave him a hard look. "Yeah?"

He looked from Pete to the house. Inside it, filling it as if it were a vessel, was the essence of the poison that was infecting the world.

The essence of the poison . . . a dense, heavy fluid through which his uncle swam, blind, groping, choking, doomed to drown. The essence of the poison of hate and fear, the essence of self-loathing, self-torturing, too venomous and burning to be contained, spilled out and projected into the form of a people conveniently different and weak, unable to fight back.

Inside that house was the concentration, and condensation, the distillation, of an insanity of the world, the essence of the poison.

He looked back at Pete Fabel, the loafer, the bully.
Pete was saying, "They oughta be run out of the country . . ."
Outside, here, was the poison.

THE DOLL GAME
PHILIP JOSÉ FARMER

"The Doll Game," along with most of the shorts published thus far in *Farmerphile*, is another example of Phil's attempt to break into the mainstream market early in his career. As Phil relates in his autobiographical essay "Maps and Spasms" (*Pearls from Peoria*, Subterranean Press 2006), *Story* editor Whit Burnett liked it very much but Burnett's wife vetoed the sale, saying it was "too rough," doubtless referring to the subject matter, not the writing.

Later, Phil sent the story off to sf editor and author Judith Merril, who accepted it for inclusion in a mainstream anthology. After Merril's publisher withdrew support, the manuscript of "The Doll Game" was presumed lost until a copy was recently uncovered in Phil's basement.

A nd now, children," said Mrs. Williams, "what have we learned from our lesson this Sunday?"

She looked around the circle of little faces.

"Would one of you want to tell the other the moral of the story I have just told you?"

Some faces were intent and straining; some, vacantly smiling; others, bored. Mrs. Williams suppressed a sigh, smiled, and said, "Kathy, would you tell the others? I'll help you just a little. The story I told you has the same moral as last week's lesson."

Kathy Sievers, tall for her nine years, rose. She spoke emphatically, as one with authority.

"Jesus meant the same Moses did. Moses said we should love everybody that lived in our block or something like that."

"That's close enough," said Mrs. Williams. "And what did Jesus add to that?"

"I thought he said the same thing."

"Yes, but he went even further than Moses. He said we should love everybody, everybody in the whole world."

"Oh, yes, now I remember," said Kathy. "If we love everybody then everybody will have to love us. And we won't have any fights or wars with anybody or bad things like that."

A buzzer rang in the hallway. Mrs. Williams stood up.

"That's very nice, Kathy. I wish everybody could remember your lessons as well as you. Now, children, before you go, let us . . ."

A few minutes later, Mrs. Williams, standing at the Sunday school exit, called to Kathy Sievers and her friend, Jeannie Grant.

"Girls, aren't you going to stay for church with your parents?"

Kathy shook her head and said, "Our Daddies and Mommies didn't come today. They were too tired. We dressed ourselves and got our own breakfasts and came together."

"Oh!" said Mrs. Williams.

"Our Daddies and Mommies gave a big party last night," said Jeannie. "It was at Kathy's house, and there were lots of people, so Kathy stayed at my house all night. We played dolls, and we sat up late in bed, talking and having a good time because our baby-sitter fell asleep watching TV. But we weren't too sleepy to come to Sunday school."

"You're both very nice girls," said Mrs. Williams. "I hope your parents are able to come to church next Sunday."

Afterwards, as they walked the three blocks to their houses, Kathy said, "You shouldn't have told Mrs. Williams about the party. She'll be mad because she lives so close and wasn't invited.

"I heard Mommy tell Daddy she couldn't invite Mrs. Williams because Mrs. Williams was a stick-in-the-mud and a creep. She said she'd be a skeleton at a feast."

Kathy giggled.

"She is kind of bony. And when she laughs, she doesn't laugh from the inside out."

Absently, Jeannie shook her blonde curls, "Uh, huh. Kathy, do you want to play dolls some more?"

"Sure. Only, I'll get some ice cream out of our freezer and bring it over to your house."

"You mean we'll eat it *before* lunch? Mommy never lets me have any before lunch."

"Mine doesn't either. But she also said if she didn't get up on Sunday mornings I could get anything I wanted to eat as long as I let her sleep. So there. See you in a minute."

Kathy ran up the curve of the walk, through the front entrance of the tri-level, and turned in the doorway to shut softly the door. She glanced around the room, wrinkled her nose over the heavy odor of tobacco smoke and stale beer, and began blazing a trail around the empty beer bottles, ash trays, rolled up throw rugs, crumpled towels, and chairs that had been moved from their accustomed places.

Four times she paused. Once she stuffed a handful of cheese crackers in the pocket of her skirt. Three times she lifted a cocktail glass to drain the liquor left in it. Two made her shudder, but the third, a brandy, brought a smile.

Smacking her lips, she proceeded down the hall to the kitchen. Here in the chaos and mess she saw to her liking a bowl of crab-meat paste, ran her finger through the white stuff, licked off the gob, made a face, wiped off the finger with a dish towel, and went on to the freezer. From this she took a pint carton of fudge royale. After putting it in a paper sack, she left the house by the side door, again taking care that the door was shut softly.

Between her house and the white picket fence was a walk, a strip of grass, and rose bushes, all bright in the noon August sun. Kathy ran to the fence, hit the gate hard with the palm of her free hand, and hurtled into the Grants' back yard. The white garage with its Buick Special and MG was at the rear of the lot; along its side was a thick row of bushes. Kathy stopped running and squatted to frown into the denseness of the bushes. She did not hold the pose long but straightened up and walked through the back door of the house.

To get to Jeannie's room, which was on the second story and in the rear, Kathy had to go through the front room. This was much tidier than her parents', but there were two martini glasses on the coffee table, and the ashtrays on the table were full. A spindly heeled shoe lay in the middle of the floor, as if it had been kicked or thrown there.

Kathy picked up the glass that wasn't quite empty and drained it. Nibbling at the olive, she walked on up the steps and along the hall, where, noticing that the adults' bedroom door was half open, she stopped to glance in.

Jeannie's mother, fully dressed except for her shoes, was sleeping face down on the bed. Jeannie's father, also dressed, was slumped in a chair by the wall. He was snoring; one hand, dangling down, almost touched the edge of a martini glass which stood at the base of the chair.

Cautiously, Kathy closed the door and went to the end of the hall, where Jeannie's room was. Eyes narrowed, she stood in the doorway.

"Your Mommy's bedroom door was shut when we went to Sunday school. Did your Mommy or Daddy get up after you came home?"

"No, but the door was open when I came in."

Kathy frowned and said, "It must have been your Mommy who got up to go to the toilet. If your Daddy had gone, he wouldn't have gone back to sleep in the chair. He'd have made your Mommy move over so he could sleep on the bed too."

She shook her head. "Maybe. Maybe your Daddy's still mad at your Mommy. Maybe he was so mad he wanted to sleep in the chair, anyway."

"Sure. You ought to know why. They came home real late last night—this morning. 'Cause I woke up when I heard them come in, and they talked a long time downstairs. Least, I think so. I went back to sleep before they must a come up to bed. But they sounded like they were mad at each other."

Jeannie shrugged her shoulders and said, "Oh, well, they get mad lots a times when they think I'm not around or can't hear them.

"Sure," said Kathy. "My Mommy and Daddy do too."

Jeannie took from her friend the sack, opened the carton in it, and began spooning the ice cream into two bowls she had previously brought up from the kitchen.

"Do you want to play dolls after we eat?" she said.

"Uh, huh," said Kathy. She was standing by the big window, which looked out on the backyard. From her second-story vantage she could see clearly the space between the garage and the rose bushes.

"The ice cream's ready," said Jeannie.

"Oh?" said Kathy. She blinked, turned away from the window, and sat down at the little table with Jeannie.

Jeannie giggled.

"Kathy, how can you stand to drink those awful icky tasting whiskey sours and martinis and then eat fudge royale on top of them?"

Kathy shrugged. "I got a strong stomach. I can eat pickles and ice cream or fish and ice cream, too, and not get sick or have nightmares. Daddy says anybody can do it. He says people can stomach anything if they're taught to when they real little. And they get sick on other things because they're told they ought to get sick.

"Well, I get sick just thinking about some things," said Jeannie, "and I don't remember anybody telling me to get sick."

"You don't remember your Mommy changing your diapers either," said Kathy scornfully. She pushed her empty bowl away. "Do you want to play Daddies and Mommies with our dolls? Or Robin Hood and Maid Marian? Or Matt Dillon, Chester, and Kitty? Or . . .?

"Let's play Daddies and Mommies."

"O.K. Let's play they're having a big party."

"O.K."

Swiftly, the two arranged the doll furniture, the tables, chairs, sofa, TV, stove, refrigerator, sink, and cupboards as they were in the living room and kitchen of the Sievers home. On tiny tables they set up the tiny plates and cutlery, the tiny glasses, cups, and saucers. Into these they poured water colored with Kool-Aid.

Then, in very thin, very high voices that sounded as if they came from the Lilliputian throats of the dolls themselves, they began the drama.

Kathy's Daddy and Mommy were busy running between the living room and the kitchen, setting up things for the party. Jeannie's Daddy and Mommy, supposedly in the bedroom of their own house, were dressing or being dressed on the floor at the other end of Jeannie's bed. Kathy, in her high piping voice which became thin or thick as she spoke for her mother or father, launched into a discussion about Mrs. Williams. Mr. Sievers said that no, she shouldn't be invited, she'd chill everybody, chill and kill 'em. Mrs. Sievers said that Mrs. Williams was nice to the children but that she might become nasty to them if she wasn't invited. Mr. Sievers piped that she'd better not get nasty. If she did, she'd be a hypocrite, preaching love thy neighbor and all that and then hating two sweet kids because of something their parents did.

Mrs. Sievers said that she supposed so and then she made Mr. Sievers cross his heart and hope to die and might lightning strike him right up you know where if he got you know what with too many of what put him under the table too soon. And he also had to swear on a stack of Bibles higher than Mt. Everest that he wouldn't make any passes at you know what and especially at you know who, because God knows it's only next door and for the sake of our . . . well, never mind, just watch it 'cause I'm watching you.

Kathy then turned on Jeannie's 45 RPM player, and while Frankie Sinatra spun out *Autumn Leaves*, Jeannie walked Mr. and Mrs. Grant into the Sievers home. There was some fast high-pitched conversation between the two couples. Jeannie, like the long arm of God, reached down and snatched Mr. and Mrs. Grant through the ceiling and into the outer air. However, a moment later, she floated them back to Earth just in front of the Sievers' door. Now they were Mr. and Mrs. Peaton, who lived across the street.

"Hiya, Joe . . . Hiya, Ginny . . . How's the kid? How's the hardware business . . . Couldn't be better, how's the legal eagle business these days? . . . You know me, Peggie, make mine very dry, wave the bottle over it, haw, haw! . . . I'll have a scotch on the rocks please . . . Oh, Martha, you should have seen this blouse and skirt . . ."

Then up rose Mr. and Mrs. Peaton and soared through the roof and walked in through the front door as Mr. and Mrs. Silvan who lived three houses away. The record played; the cups were filled and refilled; dancing began; Nat Peaton insisted on standing on his head; over he went and over went the coffee table and a dozen drinks; he apologized and apologized; everybody laughed and began dancing, shouting laughing, screaming.

Suddenly Kathy dropped Mrs. Sievers and took Mrs. Grant away from Jeannie.

"What are you doing with her?" asked Jeannie.

"Here you take my Mommy while I use yours," said Kathy. "They're going out the side door."

Stooping, holding the heads of each one, she walked them out of the house and across the Sievers' backyard and through the gate. The Grant's backyard, where they now found themselves, was in the corner, under the monogrammed Now I Lay Me Down To Sleep on the wall, which Jeannie always read by the light of the nightlamp before falling asleep every night.

"Kathy," said Jeannie, "what . . ."

"Sh! They're talking."

She began her piping speech.

"Won't they notice we've left together?"

"No. They're all loaded out of their skulls."

"Darling, isn't the moon lovely?"

"Too lovely. Too damn bright. Let's get out of it."

"Where can we go?" said Mrs. Grant.

"Over there. It's dark behind the bushes," said Mr. Sievers, his stiff plastic arm lifting, his stubby flesh-colored fingers pointing.

Mrs. Grant giggled, but a moment later she said, "Ouch! Honey, the thorns hurt."

"Here, I'll hold them apart for you, I can't feel anything, anyway."

Kathy placed the female doll on its back so that the weighted eyelids slid over the staring blue eyes and it looked as if it were asleep. The she placed the male doll face down on top of the female and began raising and lowering the male doll by the back of the shirt.

"Kathy!" cried Jeannie. "Don't do that!"

Her voice broke. "Quit it! Quit it!"

Kathy looked up at Jeannie and smiled.

"Mrs. Williams said we should love our neighbors, Jeannie. It's all right."

"It's all right honey. All right. Anything's all right if it's done for love. Just love me."

Keep Your Mouth Shut
Philip José Farmer

"Write what you know." How many times has this advice been given to fledgling writers?

Phil Farmer worked for Keystone Steel & Wire Company from 1942 to 1952. During that period he struggled to support a family, finish his B.A. in English at Bradley University, and light the flame that would ignite his writing career, all the while laboring amidst the muck and slag of the steel mill. In "Keep Your Mouth Shut," probably written between 1946 and 1955, Phil certainly writes from the pit of his white-hot, fire and brimstone experience at Keystone. It is no coincidence that the name of the story's protagonist, Danny Alliger (who is also featured in Phil's 1962 novel *Fire and the Night*), sounds remarkably similar to "Dante Alighieri." Be careful not to get scorched as you read on.

Sometimes I think about Jimmy Maharg's murder, and I wonder how bad a time I might have had if Vogler or Rugford had not kept their mouths shut. For a long time afterwards I used to sweat about it, and every once in a while I'd wake up groaning from a nightmare in which Jimmy had been pointing his finger at me.

Only two months ago, over eleven years after Jimmy died, I dreamed I was working in the steel mill again. An open hearth door opened before me, and I saw Al Vogler and Barrett Rugford standing within it on top of the lake of white-hot molten steel, scooping out the stuff in a sieve while Jimmy stood behind them, spitting tobacco juice on them.

You might say I have a conscience, and I'm trying to work off my guilt by writing this story. I don't care. You're probably right, and nobody'll be hurt by what I'm telling. Vogler dropped over dead two years after Jimmy's skull was crushed. Two months ago Rugford fell or jumped off a boat while fishing in the Illinois' backwaters and wasn't found until a week later. Jimmy's wife was taken by cancer. And none of the three had any immediate relatives.

It all started for me the summer after Pearl Harbor. Medically discharged from the Navy, I returned to my native mid-Illinois city and applied for jobs at several industries. Within a week I reported for work at 7 A.M. as a labourer for Helsget Steel and Wire Company.

When the whistle blew, Moose Larkin, a foreman, opened a locker in our shanty and gave four of us shovels, picks, and rakes. We trailed after him across the smoky steelyard to the railroad tracks that ran around the east side of the open hearth building. There Moose put us to raking up the ashes between the rails that dropped from the yard locomotives like red hot puppies from an iron bitch. We shovelled the ashes into a wheelbarrow and dumped them against the foot of the levee about ten yards away.

This is easy, I thought. Where is that backbreaking labor they tell you you'll find in a steel mill?

At that moment, as I bent over my rake, I heard a voice that was loud, harsh, nasal, and hissing at the same time.

"S-s-say, Moose-s-s, I need a couple of boys for the furnaces-s-s."

I looked up.

Jimmy Maharg was a little old man about five feet four, and, as I later found out, close to seventy. Stoop-shouldered as a question mark, he looked as if he'd spent all his days hunkered down deep in the three feet high dust tunnels under the open hearth furnaces.

He wore a dirty high-crowned once-grey hat. Beneath its broad flappy brim his long white hairs bristled to form a shelf over his ears and the back of his frayed shirt collar. The chief thing you remembered about his long lipped Irish face were his eyebrows. Thick and woolly and black, they contrasted strangely with his white hair. Always in motion above his heavily lidded and pale blue eyes, they twitched and wriggled, rose and fell, writhed and squirmed, a pair of epileptic caterpillars. They seemed to be geared to his jaw, which chomped savagely upon a handful of Red Man.

Moose waved a huge and negligent hand and said, "O.K. We ain't got much to do. Take Vogler and that Alligator kid there."

"The name's Alliger," I said.

"Yeah," Moose boomed in a voice like a lion's with a sore throat at the bottom of a well. "Haw, haw! That's what I said! Alligator!"

I didn't mind Moose's laughter, because there was nothing mean in it, but I didn't care for Maharg's dry crackling laughter which sounded so much like radio static and had about as much real mirth in it. I said nothing, however. Putting my rake and shovel over my shoulder, I started after Maharg.

He spun around and shouted, "For cryin' out loud! Put them tools down! You won't need them where you're goin'!"

I was surprised and angered at such irritation, for my mistake was natural for a rookie. But I kept my face stony. Al Vogler, who'd leaned his rake against the side of the building, walked up, grinning.

He spoke in a high-pitched whining voice. "Stung you, didn't he, Alligator? But you did right, kid. Keep your mouth shut and stay out of trouble. Me, I talk all the time. I got to, else I'd blow up from here to Kingdom Come. But you keep your mouth shut and just laugh inside yourself at Jimmy. That's best, 'cause he hates college kids."

He spat and said, "He 'n' I don't get along so well. Long time ago I worked here, and he fired me for nothing at all. If it hadn't been for him, I could a been a boss here by now, too. And had a lotta seniority and retirement pay coming up in ten years. As it is, I got nothing."

Vogler was tall and lean and as nervous as an old alley tom. He had a hooknose and a grin with long yellow-and-brown teeth. The grin seemed painted on because it was almost always there. Even when he ate, he'd be smiling at you, teeth and food and all.

"Why'd you come back here to work?" I asked.

"Oh, this is the third time in twenty-three years I worked at Helsget's maybe it's because I hate Jimmy so much I hope he'll say something that'll make me mad enough to tie into him. Or maybe get something on him."

He paused to give me a peculiar look, his narrow head cocked slyly to one side. "You'll be hating his guts, too, before the day's over. He's easy to hate."

Another hesitation, then, casually, "Some day somebody'll drop a brick on Jimmy."

The next moment, we walked into some of the hardest work I'd ever done, and I forgot his words. For a while, that is.

Helsget's had three open hearth furnaces that ruminated on iron scrap and poured out molten steel, white and hot as Hell's own milk. These took a terrific punishment, and in time the bricks that bound the inferno within them weakened. Cracks formed and widened. Sections of the brick roofs fell in and had to be hastily and temporarily repaired. Parts of the walls collapsed. And after a while the heat was escaping so fast through the fissures and faults that it took too long to melt the scrap.

The furnaces ran six months before getting to the point where they just had to be rebuilt. They were shut down in order, one being torn down while the other two kept on operating. On the biblical principle that the last shall be first, we attacked No. 3 first. It had been cooling since Saturday morning, but by Monday morning the bricks still sizzled if you spat on them.

The furnaces were two stories high, towering stories. Jimmy's gang of six worked on the charging floor with several other gangs, wrecking the upper half. The thick grey insulation plaster on the outside of the furnace's walls was scraped off, put in large cardboard boxes, and carted away. Then a horde of demons, goggled, and masked in bandannas and respirators, charged the walls with bars and sledges and shovels. At the same time, other fiends pried apart the arching roof. Great clusters of bricks, mortared together like souls clinging desperately to each other in their fall into Hell, tumbled down into the big bowl of the furnace floor or into the slag pocket far below.

Heat like little pitchforks rose and stung the delicate linings of our nostrils. Hard driven, sharp edged bars and falling bricks clattering against each other knocked dust and chips into the air. Before long I was blinded by sweat filling my goggles. I was forced to stop every other minute, remove the goggles, and wipe them out. Then sweat mingled with the thick hot dust to form mud on the kerchief I used for cleaning. Soon, like the others, I left the goggles up on my forehead and took the chance of a chipped-off fragment hitting my eyes.

Vogler grinned at me, his face red as a steak just put on the pan.

"Just like tearing down the walls of Hell itself, ain't it? Matter a fact, this is a department of Hell. The whole world's Hell. Ever stop to think we already died some place else and came here to pay for our sins? And that religion's something the devils fixed up to keep us from blowing out our brains, so we'll go on living and suffering? Me, I don't believe in an afterlife, not really, but if there is one, I'll bet it's just as bad as this one. If that's possible."

Rugford, the big Negro, looked up from his sledge and said, "Vogler, you a flap-mouthed atheist. You don't wanna blaspheme that way, or you gonna catch it where it's *really* hot."

Vogler jerked a thumb at Rugford. "He used to be a preacher," he said.

Suddenly, Jimmy Maharg was standing behind us and shouting, "You won't tear down no furnaces with your mouths!"

We went back to our work, but Vogler whined, "This is Hell, and Maharg's one a the demons."

By mid-afternoon the walls of the upper half had been tumbled. Jimmy then took us downstairs to the open hearth pit, in front of the slag pocket. It was here that most of the bricks from the wall had fallen, burying the slag beneath it in a great pile. Jimmy ordered us to jump in and start clearing away the debris. To show us how to do it, the bent old man began picking up the bricks as fast as he could, using both hands. The broken ones he threw into the open end of a large iron pan outside the pocket; the good bricks he tossed onto a pile to one side.

When sweat had stained the armpits of the thick grey jacket he always wore, regardless of the heat, he straightened up and panted, "That's the way to do it, men."

His was a favorite trick of the foremen. Work fiendishly for five minutes and then tell the gang to keep up that pace for the rest of the day. Greenhorn though I was, I didn't fall for it any more than the old timers. I threw bricks until I was hot, then walked around the furnace to the other side, where I could get a salt pill and a drink of water. Moose Larkin hailed me and gave me a slip of yellow paper.

"That's a requisition for two new shovels for Jimmy's gang!" he bellowed against the Niagaraish roar of the gas flaming in the nearby furnaces. "He'll sign it and probably send you after the shovels."

But when I returned, I couldn't find the old man. I walked around, searching, and finally located him in the narrow and murky canyon between No. 2 and No. 3 furnaces. I came up close to him from behind and shouted, "Hey, I got a requisition!"

He jumped and whirled, then struggled visibly to recover his dignity. I couldn't help grinning, for I knew he'd been spying on his gang to make sure they were working while he was gone.

He took the requisition in both hands and peered at it.

"You're holding it upside down," I said.

"Oh yeah? I know. I know."

Quickly, he turned it over and then ran his left hand over the breastpocket of his jacket.

"Must've left my glasses home. Besides, it's too dark here to read."

It wasn't so dark I couldn't read it. And earlier that day he'd bragged that his eyes were as good as when he was a young man.

"Who gave this-s-s to you?" he asked, angrily.

I told him what Moose had said, and he took out a pencil and printed a very neat but heavy J and M. Then he glared at me, his brows rising and falling like angry sea waves.

"What're you grinning at, Alliger? Just 'cause you went to college, you needn't think you're so smart."

I raised my own eyebrows, took the slip, and walked off to the storeroom. Later, I told Vogler of the incident.

He whinnied with laughter and said, "Yeah, he's illiterate, but he won't ever admit it to the men. The other foremen make out his time cards and slips for him, but they don't dare sign them. If they do, he blows his top, just like a ten inch firecracker."

Jimmy couldn't read or write, but there was nothing wrong with his lungs. All day long he raved at the top of his nasal and crackling voice, raging about this and that. One man didn't work fast enough; another took too long to get a drink; another, he swore, was goldbricking in the toilet; another didn't handle a shovel right; another threw too many good bricks into the dump pan.

I endured that rasping voice, but I never did get used to it. The point was, the heat that weakened and the dust that choked and the noise that deafened were enough to grind the skin off your nerves. But they were impersonal. Though heated, they were mechanical; they didn't radiate that different, human heat of passion. You could dislike them, bitch about them, but you didn't rage against them.

Jimmy Maharg had a devil of a whirling, snarling, grinding passion in him. And passion in a human being will strike off sparks in another—whether it's the passion of love or hate. I've found it possible to be indifferent sometimes to love but almost never to hate. I think this is true of most men.

"What's the matter with Jimmy?" I asked Vogler.

"Hell, he's always been that way. At eleven he ran away from his home in the Kentucky hills because his folks beat him and because they wouldn't give him an education. He's never been back, but he never went to school, either. He's a mean old bastard, and the only two times I ever saw him smile was when he got news his father died and the day after he came back to work from his first wife's funeral."

"Life must be hell for his second wife," I suggested.

"That's what you think. Jimmy's dumb, never learns. His first wife watched him like a hawk. Took his paycheck and gave him back enough to buy two sacks of Red Man. So what happens? Less'n nine months after she's died, he's hitched to a woman less'n half his age. And she pulls the same squeeze play on him.

He never goes anyplace except to work, the store, or home, and he gets enough money for chewing tobacco. That's all."

Rugford said, "Maybe he'd drink all his money away if she didn't watch him."

"Ha-a-a, not him! He won't touch a drop. He's agin liquor just like he's agin everything."

When I came to work the next morning, I found the second and third shifts had cleared away the rest of the bricks and exposed the slag. It was a dull black mass about six and a half feet high, ten broad, and fifteen through. Our job was to blast and pry it apart so the new furnace would have a place to deposit its burden of impurities.

Jimmy showed Rugford and me how to drill a hole for a dynamite stick with an air-hammer in the lava-like stuff. While we pressed the yammering heavy tool downwards, we stood upon boards. Only a few inches below its surface, the slag was red hot. Imprisoned for six months, the heat now soaked through and over the boards, making ovens of our shoes. We endured it long enough to drill half a hole, then climbed down from the pocket to get a drink and cool our feet.

Rugford was a heavily built man about forty years old who looked like a black-skinned Jiggs. His blarney completed the resemblance, for he talked even more than Vogler.

Did I believe in the gospels, brother, in the savin' blood of the Lamb? Not in the way he did, huh? Well, he wouldn't argue. Not yet, anyway. But he went to church twice on Sundays, and I was welcome to come with him. We was all one color in the eyes of the Lord. He'd been a preacher himself, five years ago, but his lying deacons had run him out of town. Why? It didn't matter, brother, didn't matter. That was all past and forgiven, and the road to heaven looked straight and near to him.

He was by no means always serious. Usually, he was joking and laughing loudly, and when he was with Vogler it was a contest to see who could outtalk and outlie the other. Vogler had a slight advantage because he was an atheist and loved to dig Rugford's theological ribs. Rugford didn't mind a joke about God too much, but he was easily angered if anybody questioned His existence or Rugford's belief in Him. Then he'd argue loudly without a thought of backing down simply because Vogler was a white man. He was right, and he knew it, and his pride was based upon the unshakable authority of the Scriptures.

Moreover, despite his chatter and his frequent breaking into singing of hymns, he was as good a man as any and a harder worker than most. When the rest of us, weak and burning, stopped, he labored on. More than once he remained at the handles of the air-hammer while I went off for a drink, and when I came back he was outlasting another partner.

By lunch time, aided by Rugford's strong back and Jimmy's crackling unceasing voice, we'd blasted and carried away a quarter of the slag.

"No wonder," complained Vogler. "We're working our tails off. And Jimmy'd let you fall over before he'd tell you to take a break."

At twelve-thirty we returned to prying away at a huge wedge-shaped chunk that towered almost to the top of the pile. It would rock back and forth but stubbornly refused to be barred loose, remaining as tightly locked as if Jimmy's dynamite had driven it into the clifflike face of the pile instead of blasting it free.

There were three or four inches of sand between the brick flooring and the bottom of the slagpile, laid there as a cushion to prevent the hot slag from fusing with the bricks.

"Vogler," said Jimmy, pointing to the chunk, "dig that sand from under it. That'll make it easier to pry loose."

"Hell, no," said Vogler. "I ain't gonna stand right underneath that boulder. If it fell, I'd stand a fat chance of getting away."

Jimmy snarled, "For cryin' out loud, you afraid of that? Go ahead. Dig. That chunk couldn't fall over in a thousand years. Ain't we almost ruptured ourselves barring away at it? Go ahead.

"Damn it, don't then! Give me a shovel, somebody. I been working this slag for thirty years. Nobody knows more'n me about it. Here. Give me that shovel. I ain't afraid of that."

I started to hand him mine, but Vogler, red-faced, his grin gone, began taking the sand out with a long handled shovel. Jimmy at once picked up a bar, stuck it in the gap between the great poised boulder and the pile, and shoved.

Just as Vogler turned away to toss a scoopful of sand behind him, the chunk began to topple over.

I yelled, "Watch it, Vogler!"

He froze for a second, then jumped away. The black slab rushed out at him, fast, fast. He yelled and threw his hands up at the same time he was in the air. When he came down he touched the ground just before the black end of the chunk crashed. His right foot was caught, the metal of the shoe's safety toe pinned. And then he was screaming like a wounded horse, his face twisted, and his lips rolled back over his long yellow teeth in another painted grin, only a grin this time of agony.

"For chrissakes, get if off! My leg's burning up!"

He didn't have to tell me that. I'd smelled the same odor last December 7, and it did the same thing to me now that it had done then. I seemed to go crazy; nothing mattered except getting that man off to a place where he wouldn't have to stand being cooked alive and where he could quit that terrible screaming.

I leaped forward, and when Jimmy got in my way I shoved him aside so hard he fell over on his back. Then, along with three other men, I seized the chunk in my gloved hands and rolled it, somehow, off Vogler's foot. The odor of scorched cloth mingled with that of burning flesh, but it was over with quickly and we snatched off our gloves and threw them down on the floor.

Jimmy got up. "You knocked me down, Alliger."

"Shut your damned mouth," I snarled.

Shortly afterwards, the first aid men carried Vogler off in a stretcher to the company ambulance. We stood around and talked about the accident until Jimmy returned from the yard superintendent's office, where he'd been making his report.

"For cryin' out loud," he shouted, giving me a hard look, "he ain't killed. Get back to work. The rest of you ain't hurt. You think the company's paying you for standing around with your thumbs in your mouths?"

Rugford scowled and said, "It ain't paying you, Jimmy Maharg, to bar a chunk down on a man while he's digging out from under it, either."

The old man turned grey as his workjacket. He thrust his contorted face upwards towards Rugford, a rocket of sputtering incoherent rage, blowing out dark wet shreds of tobacco.

"You—nigger!" he screeched.

Rugford gave a roar and lifted his long handled shovel straight above him to bring the edge of the scoop down on Jimmy's head.

"I don't allow nobody to call me that! 'Specially trash like you that can't read or write!"

His pausing to tell Jimmy off before he killed him gave us time to act. Three of us fell on him at once. I grabbed the shovel and hung on, not because I cared if he split the old brute's skull but because I wanted to protect Rugford from himself.

"Don't do it!" I yelled in his ear. "He isn't worth going to the chair for!"

That did it. He stopped struggling and allowed his shovel to be taken away. Like a dog coming out of water, he shook himself free of his rage.

"You right, Alligator boy," he said huskily. "I ain't no blood-thirsty heathen. I almost spilled my brother's blood. *Vengeance is mine, saith the Lord.*"

For a moment he watched Jimmy walking away fast across the yard, then added, "But the Lord sometimes works through the hands of us human beings."

Maharg was not—as I'd hoped—fired. He did get a severe reprimand, but the company felt it had to back its foremen—especially its old timers. And it satisfied its conscience with a hundred dollars for Vogler.

During his time in the hospital, however, Vogler had no money coming in. Moose Larkin organized a collection to help him. Jimmy's name, in Moose's handwriting, was down on the list for a dollar. And that, I was sure, was all he ever contributed, for Vogler would have been sure to mention it if he had.

Meanwhile, Rugford and I refused to work for Maharg even if it meant being fired. Word had gotten out about our run-in with him after the accident, however, and somebody, Lemore the superintendent or Moose, figured that the old man had it coming to him. So we went to work for the other yard bosses during the rest of furnace repair. When we met Jimmy, which was often, we stared through him, and he paid no more attention to us than we did to him. Finally, the hearths were rebuilt, and we all went back to our regular jobs. Once away from him, my intense dislike for him sank into a mere unpleasant memory.

Six more months. Furnace repair again. Production slowed, and those with low seniority were bumped back to the yard. There I saw Vogler. Except for a slight limp, he was his old self. I asked him why he was now working again on Jimmy's gang.

"Maybe I can get him in the same kind of spot he got me in," he replied through gritted teeth.

I considered that statement for a while, then I said, "I've been thinking what you said about dropping a brick on Jimmy. That is, purely as an academic problem, understand? But an interesting one. And I've been thinking it wouldn't work. If he was down in the pit, and you were on the second floor, you'd be too exposed to view."

His yellow painted grin was wider than ever. "You been getting a dream-revenge, too?"

"Don't get me wrong," I replied seriously. "I think murder is wrong. But I am a rabid detective story reader. I'm interested in the fine art of murder—technically speaking."

"Don't you think the world'd be better off without a stupid selfish sourpuss like him?" Vogler asked, still grinning.

"It might be, but I'm no judge. Let's consider this as a problem. For instance, what's the best place around here to kill a man? I'd say the tunnels beneath the furnaces are because he's always prowling around them, hoping to catch somebody loafing. You could finish him off there and make it look like an accident."

Rugford, who'd been listening, said, "Man, don't you know *thou shalt not kill?* 'Tain't good even to make jokes about such things."

"Jimmy's an old devil, isn't he?" I asked. "What if you killed a devil? That's different than killing a human, isn't it? And you wouldn't call Jimmy a human, would you?"

Rugford looked thoughtful. "I don't know. I confess I ain't never forgiven him for what he called me. And when I think of it, I get mad enough to bash his head in, even if it is a sin. But how would you do it 'thout getting caught?"

"Here's how," I said, getting interested in the technical aspects and caught up in the thrill every man, no matter how law abiding, gets when he thinks of pitting his wits against the police.

"You know that when you clean out the tunnels under the checker-pockets of No. 3 furnace you throw the dust and broken bricks into an enclosure between the two pockets. The enclosure is on the basement floor. The debris is put into two large buckets and hoisted out by the charging-floor crane, three stories up. It drops its hook through two square holes in the second and ground floors. The hole on the charging floor is usually covered by an iron plate. But the hole on the main floor is open, though it has a railing around it to keep a man from falling through to the basement.

"That hole is way back in the shadows; you can't see anybody back there unless you're there yourself or flash a light into it. And the plate that's supposed to be over the hole is usually left propped up against the railing.

"I'd wait until Jimmy went down there to examine the tunnels. Then I'd walk off the job under the pretence of going to get a bit to eat at the tool shanty, where we leave our lunch buckets. I'd get a sandwich, stick it in my pocket so I'd have an alibi, and run back to the hole.

"I'd crouch down behind the big propped-up plate. Jimmy'd only take a couple of minutes to complete his inspection. When he came out of the tunnel, I'd have a little bucket full of broken bricks poised above his head. Down it'd come. End of Jimmy. And even if you missed he couldn't see you because you'd be in the darkness and he'd have to look past that bright light in the enclosure. Either way, hit or miss, I'd hurry back to my job.

"I'd return through that little corridor that runs behind the checkers, and I'd walk out when nobody was around. When I went back to my job, I'd be eating my sandwich, which would explain my absence. If done properly, I could have it all over in five minutes of less."

"Where'd you get the bucket?" asked Vogler. "You can't have everybody see you lugging it around."

"While we were working on No. 2, I'd hide that bucket behind the propped-up plate, using my work gloves all the time, of course. It'd be there waiting for you."

"What about your footprints in the dust around the hole?" asked Rugford.

"As soon as Jimmy's body would be found, there'd be a commotion. If he was found on my shift, I'd go up to the hole and look around. There'd be some of your buddies tagging along, and they'd make so many prints that the police'd have nothing to go on. Anyway, there's always any number of tracks around there during a repair."

Vogler grunted but said nothing, which was unusual. Rugford muttered that the Lord had said an eye for an eye and a tooth for a tooth but that had been in the Old Testament.

Jimmy shuffled up, brows working, his pale blue eyes stabbing through Rugford and me as if we didn't exist. "Come on, Vogler, let's roll. You won't make no money standin' around like this-s-s."

A few days later we finished No. 2 and went on to 3. Most of the time I was unloading bricks from the freight cars for the masons, so I saw little of Maharg. But one morning Moose sent me back to Jimmy's gang because two of his men hadn't showed up for work. I didn't object. I figured I could get along with him for the little while left for furnace repair. I walked down to the electricians' shanty in the south end of the building and found his gang just leaving it, having finished their nine o'clock "sandwich" break. Jimmy, they told me, was inspecting the tunnels. On hearing this I didn't have any flash of premonition, but I did wonder where Vogler was.

"Went upstairs to get a coke," said one man.

I forgot about his absence until a few minutes later when we started down the spiralling iron stairway into the enclosure. It was then that the leading man yelled, "There's Jimmy! He's hurt!"

I wasn't nearly as surprised as I should have been. I'd pictured his hypothetical murder too vividly while describing it to Vogler and Rugford that I'd retained a still-scene in my mind, a prophecy of the real thing.

Jimmy lay between the big five-foot-high buckets, flat on his back, his face upturned to the harsh glare of the naked bulb on the wall, the top if his head crushed in, the blood still wet, though forming a dark red-grey mud, being mixed with the steel dust. Not far from him lay his hat and a large bucket on its side, broken bricks spilled out in a frozen stream from it.

I stood around for a while, getting sicker and more trembly all the time, then went up to the opening from which, presumably, the bucket had dropped for sixteen feet before striking Jimmy's skull. There I found Vogler and Rugford among the crowd around the railing. This, too, followed my outline for murder, for any footprints left by the killer were now mixed up with a dozen other pairs.

The two didn't see me, for they were standing shoulder to shoulder, their heads turned towards each other. On their faces was an intent look, one of tightened lips and of narrowed eyes, out of which they glared at each other.

Their expressions said, Did *you* do it?

Then, as if by command, their heads swivelled, and they looked across the open well of the enclosure, across the body of Jimmy twenty feet below, straight at me. And under the shock and focus of their accusing stare, I cringed for just a second and gripped the iron bar of the railing. Then, I suddenly realized that I had upon my face exactly the same look.

We made a pretty picture for one who could read us—a triangle as eternal as the other kind and one whose ties were even more binding. One of us was guilty. I knew I wasn't, not legally, anyway, though I might be morally. But one of the other two was wondering which of us had done it, and one of them knew but he was pretending to be suspicious. And at the bottom of our hearts we'd all wanted Jimmy to be dead. He was now, and he no longer counted. What did matter was that we must keep our mouths shut.

If we didn't, we'd all be in for a bad time; I, because I'd proposed the plan and dreaded the publicity and scorn I'd get if it were known; the murderer, for obvious reasons; the other, because he wasn't really concerned with justice and because he was glad Jimmy was dead. There was a web in which we were caught, and in that three-cornered look we vibrated the strings so that each understood the unspoken vow of silence.

The police came and began their questioning. They got no place. Thirty men could have committed the murder, and there was scarcely anybody who'd worked for Jimmy who hadn't had one or more violent quarrels with him. Rugford was grilled about his attempt to hit Jimmy with a shovel, but they had nothing definite to pin on him. Everybody had had access to the enclosure; everybody had had a few minutes in which to do the deed.

I sweated for a while, and I suppose I looked guilty when I talked to the sergeant. But so did many other men.

Afterwards, the three of us avoided each other as if we were unclean or lepers. Only when our work demanded it did we speak and then as briefly as possible. And when our glances unavoidably clashed, each had that curious stony cast of features which hid his wonderings or his pretended wonderings.

Time went by, and after a while I managed to lock Jimmy in a compartment of my mind. After I quit Helsget's, I could forget him entirely. That lasted for years until Rugford's drowning seemed to have jarred loose that drawer in which I kept the body of the old man with the crushed skull. As I said in the beginning, I've been seeing him again in my dreams. I'm writing this in the hope that his ghost will be banished once and for all, and so I may get a good look at what happened. I want to decide if I, too, in a way, held that bucket above his head and then dropped it.

THE FRAMES
PHILIP JOSÉ FARMER

Written in early 1970, "The Frames" is the first piece of pure science fiction by Phil thus far published in *Farmerphile*. Parallels between the present story and the Dayworld series are abundant and clear. The ever watchful eyes of Big Brother haunt the citizens of both Farmerian worlds in a future Manhattan where the government uses trendiness as a tool to manipulate and sedate the masses. Even the semi-comic tone of "The Frames"—with its references to Krazy Kat, TV Plutarchs, and the Federal Bureau of Felonious Law Enforcement—is in direct sympathy with the pop-gut humor of Dayworld. But while suspended animation "stoners" have not yet materialized in our civilization, one can hardly argue with the fact that Phil Farmer anticipated reality TV by thirty years, not to mention CGI and the very real dangers of electronic data manipulation.

Phil submitted "The Frames" to Robert Hoskins, senior editor at Lancer Books, for the anthology *Infinity Two*. Hoskins wrote back to express interest and offer comments, and these comments intrigued Phil enough that he rewrote the story's ending (this is the version which appears here). Phil, in his letter to Hoskins, reveals that most of the elements in the story, including its title, have a double meaning, and that the story is "essentially an illustration of where the electronic duplicity of our communications might go, though there is much more to the story than that." In typically Farmerian style, Phil also offers a number of intriguing alternate titles for Hoskins to consider: "Simulation" or "Duplication and Duplicity" or "The Cheshire Katz."

While ultimately the story never saw print in *Infinity Two*, "The Frames" looms today in brilliant clarity before the mirror of the present. We can't say Phil didn't try to warn us.

U niformed policemen blocked ten exits. Plainclothesmen moved through the two thousand people in the Folk Culture and Goods Plaza. Their goal was a shifty figure in a shifting jungle of men, women, and children.

Newsmen, moving their heads from side to side, panned the crowd with the flashlight-sized double-antennaed TV cameras set into the helmets on their heads. While they spoke into chest mikes, they also manipulated hand cameras.

A woman shrieked. A man yelled. The crowd swung towards the south side of the Plaza like a school of fish disturbed by the scent of an intruder. A camera took advantage of a brief opening and held for several seconds a man, presumably a plainclothesman, staggering backwards. It also caught the shover, a bronze-skinned, dark-red haired, eagle faced man about 190.50 centimeters high and built like a panther. Then the crowd collapsed in on itself, and the bronze man was gone.

The Plaza had walls which bent inwards from the floor, twisted and disappeared upwards seemingly into infinity. The whole looked much like the inside of the closed end of a conch shell. The floor, which covered six-tenths of a hectare, was a varicolored mosaic of abstract animal heads. Glittering hexagonal balconies projected from the walls. The bottoms of the balconies were 121.440 centimeters above the average height of the male population. Slender poles projecting from the railings held streamers which quivered in the flow from the air conditioners.

The entrance-exits were wide arches. The two trefoil arches were tube entrances. The two ogee arches were shaft entrances. The other opened into the Folk Theater, the Folk Distribution Center, the Folk Dance Hall, the Folk Tavern, the Democracy Hall, and the Zoo. The light pulsed randomly and varicoloredly from the walls. Electric tricycles were parked in ferris-wheel stacks near the entrances.

Except for the sudden appearance of the police, it was a normal scene at any hour.

Whistles shrilled but were heard only by the police, each of whom wore in one a ear a plug to detect the lower frequency of the whistle. They converged towards the center of the disturbance. One fell bleeding when a women slapped him alongside the head, just below the helmet, with a bag that contained a brand new recorder-projector. He became the first martyr of the Tenth Level, No. 8 Zone, Forty-Second Street, April 1, 2012 A.D. Riot Aiding and Abetting the Escape (Not Again!) of Hilary Katz, Arch Criminal.

The news casters danced around the outside of the crowd.

Shrieks, yells, grunts, cries of, "Stop in the name of the Law!" "Take your dirty paws off of me, you filthy blueface!" and "There he goes! Get him!" came clearly over one hundred million sets. (Bells were ringing in three billion apartments over the Earth, announcing an extraordinary event, everybody come a-running, we aren't crying wolf this time.)

In a momentary opening, a camera sucked in the image of a man with broad shoulders, almost kinky dark red hair, and aquiline features worming towards the nearest arch. Then the man disappeared, but the cameraman lay on his side and pointed head and hand cameras between the brilliantly painted legs of men and women and past the painted faces of some scared children. The bronze man was crawling on all fours, moving swiftly, stopping only once when a woman, overcome by hero worship, dropped to her knees and kissed the back of his neck as he passed her. The voice of Meister "Faster Than Light" Garcia had been narrating from the beginning.

"And now, like Douglas Fairbanks, Sr., Errol Flynn, and Barton Drummond all rolled into one, Hilary Katz explodes like an old-fashioned rocket from the crowd. He leaps out, jumps onto the back of a policeman trying to get to his feet after being trampled on by three women, and soars up from the human diving board. His outstretched hands catch the edge of the balcony on the left of the arch leading to the Folk Theater, one hand frees itself and grips the base of the streamer pole, and he pulls himself up and over in a single fluid movement all grace and beauty, ignoring the proffered help of the men and women who only a moment ago were sipping drinks. Replay that magnificent jump, Donald. Folks, you think Tarzan . . ."

At the bottoms of all screens—now 800 million according to the Instantaneous Ratings Bureau—flashed: SIMULATION.

The voice of Garcia's assistant: "Though this scene is enacted, it is being shot only ten minutes after the actual events. TB brings you the fastest news anywhere. If TB can't shoot it when it happens, TB shows you how it was, before reality has a chance to cool off."

Michael Stark, Ph.D., Chief of Manhattan Federal State Metropolitan Police, did not take his eyes off the screen. He spoke out of the side of his mouth, past the cigar.

"Kowolsky, how accurate is the simulation?"

"Good enough," she said. "Garcia, as usual exaggerates for dramatic effect. And to denigrate the police. Katz's escape was fifteen minutes before the simulation, not ten. Garcia'll get called down for his lie, but he'll blame it on his scapegoat, as usual. The viewers won't even hear about it, and that is what matters."

The floor of the control room covered 18.6 square meters. The walls swirled conchoidally upwards towards the ever-receding tip of infinity. The walls had been painted in the glaring colors by a policeman shortly before he went mad. The murals depicted famous cases in Manhattan's criminal history (rather, history of crime). Crimson and scarlet and sickly orange blood flowed and spouted and dripped. Green-yellow-purple intestines spilled out. Crystalline hearts were pierced with vibroknives. Scrambled-egg brains spilled out of skulls blown open with homemade guns. Men hung in showers, their lower extremities swollen and dark with collected blood.

Around the walls were giant transparent screens dotted with tiny glowing stars and threaded with bright white worms and hydras. The pale grids on the screens marked streets and apartments and tube and shaft entrances and plazas.

Two revolvable platforms, kidney-shaped, occupied the center of the room. The smaller was the chief's. He sat in a high-backed chair before a huge crescent-shaped desk on which were twenty videophones. The larger platform held fifty chairs for visitors and university students when the chief lectured.

Chief Stark heard Kowolsky's report. Garcia had used members of the original crowd, hired on the spot (payment: their names would be listed in the credits), actors rushed in on Emergency Tubes, and he had even tried to used policemen who had been in the riot.

Stark told Kowolsky to send in the usual complaints through the usual channels. The usual response, of course, would be that the matter would be looked into.

A finely detailed map of the tenth level scaled to represent one kilometer per two meters dominated the great screen on the north. Differently colored pulses, moving through the streets and tubes on the map, marked the location and identity of search groups.

Kowolsky stabbed a slender gentian-violet finger at the central screen on the desk before the chief and said, "Old Faster Than Light wants to speak with you."

Garcia, a tall pale-skinned man with sleek dark hair, a golden glittering forehead, crimson moustache, and a double-shafted cigarette in his thin mouth, was looking directly into the camera.

"Folks, I've been trying to get *Doctor* Stark for some time, but apparently *Doctor* Stark's too busy trying to catch Hilary Katz. Folks, it looks as if once again our elusive shadow, the Robin Hood of our tight little isle, Manhattan, has slipped through the clutches of the Sheriff of Nottingham."

Stark bit down on his cigar and grunted, "Very funny fellow."

"I put through a complaint about his editorializing," Kowolsky said.

"Already?"

"Ten minutes ago. I knew he'd be saying something about this, something like this, so I jumped the gun a little."

"Notice how he emphasizes my degree. There he goes again! *Doctor* Stark! Always *Doctor*! He knows that doesn't help my image any! Thos illit . . ."

He stopped, and then he mumbled, "I won't let him get me down."

Kowolsky touched his skin with the end of her finger, which

had accidentally—at least he thought it was accidentally—gone through the star-shaped hole in his right sleeve.

"Chief, the Commissioner."

On a screen to his right, the brown fleshy face of Dillman appeared.

"Stark! Garcia wants to know if you've got anything to tell the people! He also requests permission again to latch in on Katz's call when he calls you the next time. He says that the people have a right to on-the-spot when-it's-happening news. They're getting tired of simulations. And of tapes."

"The people!" Stark said. "You mean Garcia! Tell him no! He'll get a tape of the call, if Katz calls. That's all. If Garcia knew exactly when Katz was talking to me, he'd have his own men trying to trace the call and his own men looking for him. He'd screw us up, just as he did on the Abdullah case. You . . ."

"Chief!" Kowolsky spoke in his ear. "Screen No. 3!"

"Speaking of the devil," Stark said. "Here he is."

"Garcia?" the Commissioner said. "He's still on my line."

"The other devil," Stark said. "Hilary Katz!"

Dillman swore and then said, "Latch him in to me."

Stark looked at Screen No. 3. The big dark-bronze devil was grinning at him. But he was sweating.

"You won't tie in Garcia with your line?" Stark said.

The Commissioner growled, "You're insulting, Stark! If I did so, I'd tell you!"

"Sorry," Stark said. He gestured to Kowolsky to connect Dillman with Katz. Then he leaned forward and said, "What is it this time, Katz?"

The voice that replied was deep and soothing. It was the voice that rocked the gonads of the world, as Garcia put it. And the handsome eaglish face knocked every woman's phosphenes loose from her eye to her pelvis, again as Garcia put it. Shooting stars from the sexual nervous system.

"Hello Doctor Stark! Chiefey-wiefey! I just watched the simulation of my escape from the bloodhounds of the law. Pass my congratulations on to Mr. Garcia, will you? It's very authentic.

There are a few inaccurate points. But I'll have a friend pass them on to Garcia, and he can have a one percent simulation for the 13:30 newscast."

"What do you want?" Stark said harshly. "You didn't call me to review Garcia's show. Or did you?"

Kowolsky, out of range of the screen, shook her head. Her expression said that he was not playing it cool enough.

"It's like this," Katz said. He smiled, aware that his beautiful white teeth and melting dark-brown eyes and almost kinky dark-red hair would be flashing on three billion screens in half an hour. "I'm the hare and you're the hound. And every now and then the hare likes to take a breather. Likes to sit down in some nice well hidden hole, you know, and talk things over with the hound. Get to know the mutt, you might say. After all, you have a job to do, and I don't hold it against you. I even feel sorry for you . . ."

Stark snatched his cigar from his mouth and said, "I don't need any BLEEP to feel sorry for me!"

Kowolsky rolled her violet eye and her chartreuse eye in agony. The police monitor—on Screen No. 7—waggled a finger at him. Katz was wanted for the slaying of one policeman, but he had not been brought to trial and convicted. The word *murderer*, along with a list of others, was tabu. Katz could sue through his lawyer and force the Federal State Bureau of Felonious Law Enforcement—and who thought that title up?—to discharge Chief Stark and offer an official apology.

Hilary Katz smiled again and said, "Careful there, Doctor. I can read lips, you know."

Stark looked at Screen No. 7. The monitor passed a finger horizontally over his lips, indicating that Stark's mouth had been blurred out.

Stark sighed deeply and he said, "Are you ready to turn yourself in, Katz?"

"Not as long as I can't get justice. I'm not psychotic. I killed that policeman because he was trying to kill me. He was the psychotic, not me. I was only defending myself."

Stark had not fully taken in Katz's words. He had been

watching the big north screen. The little white star on it represented Screen No. 3 on his desk. The twisting white thread that ran north from the star indicated the progress in tracing the call along the videophone lines and stations. The thread was out of the original scaled area, and the map had been widened to show the crawling outwards. Katz was calling from more than two kilometers away. He had traveled swiftly indeed after he had escaped through an as-yet undetermined exit of the Folk Theater. He could not have taken a tube. Every station for a half a kilometer around the Plaza had been guarded within two minutes after Katz had been sighted in the crowd.

He could not have slipped through the police there. Not even the Master of Disguises, the Shadow of the Great City, the Bronze Pimpernel, as Garcia called him in his less inspired moments, could do that. Every person entering a tube station or a fall shaft had to pass by a scanning beam. And the police sets had indicated a negative for every one. None of the brain waves detected matched Katz's.

Katz's words finally touched off an alarm bell in Stark's mind. He became aware of what he had said. He straightened up, and he said, "Wait a minute! You admit that you BLEEP Officer Pauls? You admit that you BLEEP him?"

"Don't put words in my mouth, Chief," Katz drawled. "You police are always trying to put words in other people's mouths so you can convict them and get high ratings on your civil service jobs and all the extra goodies that go with the ratings. And so you can puff up your already overinflated green-at-the-edges egos. As so . . ."

"Yes, folks," Garcia was saying on Screen No. 4, "Our Hero, the only hero in this age of No Heroes, has sworn to stay on Manhattan Island. *This is my home. Here I was born. Here I will live and here I die.* Those were the words of Hilary Katz, spoken defiantly to Doctor Stark only two weeks ago."

Beside Garcia appeared the superimposed face of Katz, the lips moving soundlessly.

"And then Hilary Katz said, *Man is not a cipher. It is still possible in this world of overwhelming mass production of things and of human beings for man to be an individual. I am I. Hilary Katz is Hilary Katz. I am not an insect, a faceless two-legged bug. I wasn't duplicated from a tape. I am unique. There is no other Hilary Katz. In the words of the philosopher Descartes,* Cogito ergo sum.

"That's what Hilary Katz said, folks. That *Cogito ergo sum* is French folks . . ."

"Latin, you illiterate swine," Stark murmured, and he saw on Screen No. 5 that the monitor had not blurred his lips.

Katz had heard Garcia. He grinned and said, "Did I really say all that? I must've, since Garcia doesn't make anything up, does he? The news as it happens, before reality cools off."

"*I think, therefore I am a man,*" Garcia said. "That's what the ancient Frenchman said, folks, and that's what Katz . . ."

"*Non cogito ergo sum Garcia,*" Stark murmured. Aloud, he said, "All right, Katz. You admit you BLEEP Officer Pauls? Damn it, monitor, you can censor the tape, but don't censor me! I am discussing a hypothetical case with Mr. Katz, if that'll help the situation any! Now, Katz, you admit you killed Pauls, but you claim self-defense? So why don't you surrender to the proper authorities?"

"Because I wouldn't get a fair trial. I'd be railroaded to the hospital. It'd be years before I'd be released as certifiably sane. If I ever *was* released. How about the shortage of doctors and nurses, heh? And the shortage of good psychiatrists? It'd be years before I could get effective treatment.

"But that is not the point. The point is that I am not insane. I just got fed up with going along with what everybody said was right. So I stole some painting. Stole some from supposedly burglar-proof places. And then Pauls caught me and he was going to kill me. He was the psychotic, and . . ."

"Pauls had taken all the tests," Stark said. "He had been cleared of any suspicion of neuroses that might have interfered with his competency in a highly demanding and sensitive profession. He could not . . ."

"I say, the hell he could not! He did! He did! Either the tests are invalid, or Pauls developed into a psychotic after he became a police officer. In which case the tests are invalid. But I'm glad that he did go psycho, because it shows that you people don't have all the answers! You can't predict one hundred percent how a man's going to turn out! How he's going to act in every situation!

"Look at me! I was cleared by the tests, too, before I took a job teaching history in the junior high school! Yet, I stole works of art. And I killed! And I know why! I struck out at you, at the government, and at you Doctor Stark, who is part of the government, because I felt that I had been one hundred percent classified. And I wanted to show you that I wasn't one hundred percent classifiable! Maybe that's why Officer Pauls was going to kill me! He wanted to prove the same thing!"

Stark sighed and slumped a little. Katz's speech was for the benefit of those who would see the tape during *The Noose of Time* show, Garcia's show, Reality Before it Cools. Stark had heard this lecture before. There was only so much you could say about individuality and freedom or any of the abstractions. Most of what was said had to be clichés. Abstractions were clichés.

He looked up at the big screen. The glowing thread he split into a dozen going up and down and out to the north, south, east, and west.

Kowolsky had walked to the east side of the room to speak to an officer who had just entered the room. She was coming back now. She had long legs and a sway that usually delighted him. But now she was just a woman bringing him bad news.

"He's got ten lines, or more, hooked into that one. That one is in an apartment on the fourth level, East 108th. There's nobody home. The occupants, people named Beal, are being traced down. But . . ."

"But they'll claim they know nothing about it, and we won't be able to prove they do. And maybe they don't."

One of the ten threads lengthened westwards.

He spoke into a screen. "Expand that thread in sector 4."

The big wall screen seemed to jump. The other threads shot out of sight past the lower left-hand corner. A few seconds later, the thread, which had ceased to grow, squirted out again. It stopped only a few blocks from the little star representing the set on his desk. Its terminus was, however, on the fourth level.

Katz stopped talking. Stark said, "You finished with the rhetoric?"

"Never," Katz said, grinning. He locked his fingers and pulled and the snaky muscles writhed under the bronzish skin. "I think I better put on some fat. I can disguise myself better if I look like most everybody else. Hardly anybody has to work, and everybody can eat and drink themselves sick if they want to, so we got a land of fatasses. Me and the police are the only people in shape. How are you coming with the hunt, hound?"

"As if you don't know exactly where we are," Stark said. "Katz, you may be Robin Hood to some people, but to me you're just a BLEEP BLEEP who's BLEEP once and who'll BLEEP again unless he's caught. Monitor, damn it, censor me afterwards! I want him to know exactly what I'm calling him!"

Officer Crighton, the monitor, shook his head.

"And a merry BLEEP to you, too, High Sheriff," Katz said. "Well, folks, a good friend has just handed me a note. The bluefaces are closing in. I have to go now, but I'll be keeping in touch with you, courtesy of the police. BLEEP bless you for your kindness and moral support and all those tender loving messages you send me through that noble and good-hearted man, Meister Garcia. I watch his newscast religiously, and I get your messages. As long as there are people like you, there's hope for mankind. Good night, all!"

The screen went blank. Stark put his head between his hands and leaned forward until his elbows rested on the desk.

Kowolsky's voice was soft but insistent. "Chief, I hate to tell you this. But guess where they finally traced the call?"

"My home?"

"How'd you know?"

He dropped his hands on the desk with a loud noise and looked at her. "I didn't! I was just being sarcastic! My own home! My God! That man is making a laughing stock of me! But, he must not be too far ahead of us?"

"Every corridor and tube shaft is being blocked, Chief. But he knew how much time he had, and the fact that he let us get so close might mean that he's confident he can get past us."

"Might mean?" Stark said, and he groaned.

"The mayor, Chief."

Mella's broad big-nosed face filled the viewplate in the center of the desk. "Stark, we have to do something! Fast! That Garcia gave me a hard time! Did you see the interview?"

"No, I was too busy trying to track down Robin Hood. Haven't they told you yet?"

"Told me what?"

Stark told him.

Mella's face became even darker, and his nose seemed to swell.

"The election's only eight months away! Garcia's making noises about running against me! What do you think this is going to do to me? Your own place!"

Do to you? Stark thought.

He said, "Do you want me to resign?"

"Would you if I asked you to?"

"No. I'm a Federal employee, and I can't be ousted without a lot of red tape. But I can be moved laterally or vertically, as you and I well know. And you could bring enough pressure. But I want to catch Katz. He's made a monkey out of me, but he's going to slip up. He's cutting things too close; he's too sure. I want to be the one that grabs him."

"I'll give you a little more time. But if he ever calls from your place again . . . the next place'll be the control room of the police department."

Mella faded out. Stark remained at his desk for six hours. By then it was apparent that Cheshire Katz (another of Garcia's titles for the outlaw) was holed up some place. Stark went home. This involved dropping down a shaft near the control center to the fourth level and then walking ninety meters down a corridor.

Once he had had a wife and child. Now the child was an adult and married and living in a tenth level apartment in New Guinea. His wife had left him for a man who did not work. She had not objected to the extra goods and the prestige resulting from his job. But she had objected to his spending twelve to sixteen hours a day at his desk, and so they had said farewell. He had loved his work too much before Katz came along, she had said. But since Katz had killed Pauls when he was caught stealing a Picasso from the Manhattan Federal State Museum of Historical Classics, Katz had occupied Stark's mind to the exclusion of almost everyone else.

"Yes, folks," Garcia said on a special Sunday evening cast. "It's true that Hilary Katz had been robbing public and private collections for years. The man had a deep seated need to do so. He stole because the works of art were there. This modern age offered him nothing thrilling, nothing challenging. And who was he hurting? Didn't he always give back the objects of art a year or two after he had stolen them? Didn't he just keep them for a while to enjoy them in the privacy of his own apartments? Wasn't he just a type of Robin Hood, robbing the rich to give to the poor?"

Stark had never figured out how Garcia justified his reasoning. It just could not stand up under logical analysis. Yet Garcia's audience seemed to swallow most of it. Stark supposed that that was because his audience wanted to accept it and so shunted any analysis off to a dark corner of the mind.

He took a tranquilizer. At 01:30 the phone rang, and its light went on. He flicked the ON switch. Then he sat up and swore.

"Hello, Chief!" the big bronze man said. "Did you ever figure out how I got into your apartment?"

Stark rubbed his eyes and yawned. The yawn was to relieve tension, not sleepiness.

"No," Stark said. He suspected that some Katz sympathizer in the police department had looked into the records and then passed on the frequency of Stark's lock to Katz.

"What do you want, Katz?"

"Did you see the late Garcia Gas?"

"I see too much of his shows during working hours."

Katz frowned.

Stark was surprised. He did not remember ever seeing Katz

anything but cheerful, except when he was making a speech for the benefit of Garcia's audience.

"He reviewed my life again," Katz said. "You know, the capsule biography bit. But he did a new thing. He capsuled your life, too."

Stark swung his legs around and sat on the edge of the bed. He leaned towards the screen. "Come again."

"He outlined our lives in parallel, as if he was a sort of TV Plutarch."

Stark was surprised again. He had never guessed that Katz had read anybody who wasn't required in school, and he knew that Plutarch wasn't required, not even for history majors. But the breezy informal style of Katz's talk had probably been adopted to suggest semiliteracy to Garcia's audience.

"He started off with photos and films of both us when we were babies, outlined our family backgrounds, took us through school. Everything. Kept flashing back and forth, sometimes had both of us on at the same time. He showed what a similar background we had, how much alike we were in many ways. Then he speculated on what made us take different paths. Why one went wrong and the other didn't."

"And he never really said which one of us went wrong?"

Katz smiled briefly and said, "How'd you know?"

"Even Garcia wouldn't have guts enough—or be dumb enough—to wave the flag for crime. But I'll bet the audience had no trouble knowing whom he thought was wrong, right?"

"Right! I'm the hero of the people, and Garcia knows it!"

Stark said, "You poor donkey! You're the hero of the people because Garcia *made* you the hero! You got it all backward!"

Katz had grinned again. Evidently he was anticipating the explosion of Stark with great pleasure. Now the grin faded away like a reverse Cheshire Cat, the grin the first thing to go.

"And I'm the villain because Garcia decreed it so. Of course, he knows it's easier, and far more popular, to cast a criminal as the protagonist. Even those few who are screaming for your blood envy you, way down in their unconscious. Every man would be his own Robin Hood. At least, every man would like to be the lone fighter against the great hydra of society, the Hercules, the Siegfried against the dragon, the Tarzan against the lion.

"But if Garcia awoke tomorrow with a new idea—which isn't likely to happen—and started after breakfast to reverse your role and mine, he could do it. In the eye of the public, anyway, and that is what counts. It would take time. He'd have a lot of resistance to overcome, resistance he carefully built up. But he built it up and he could tear it down. Katz! Where are you going?"

The screen was blank.

"I must have really shaken him up," Stark muttered. "But, my God, I thought he knew all that! Maybe he isn't as smart as I thought?"

He smiled. For the first time in many months, he slept long and well.

The next two days he received no calls from Katz. However, he thought much about him. Why was it Katz had never directly phoned Garcia? Garcia was his chief supporter. Yet Garcia had to depend for his information about Katz on Stark, the man he decried. The caster must have thought this peculiar, but he had never commented upon it. And if he had wished to speak to Katz, he had only to say so on his program. Katz would get the message.

It was possible that Katz and Garcia did talk to each other, but they let no one know of it to avoid an accusation by the police department that Garcia was aiding a criminal. If so, neither had ever slipped.

There was one splendid moment, like a mystic seeing heaven unroll before him, when Stark thought he comprehended everything. Garcia and Katz were the same man!

He abandoned that theory as reluctantly as a saint giving up his halo. Both of them had been on videophones on his desk at the same time many times, and they been on live. Yet the idea was so beautiful. What a fabulous positive feedback. Garcia propelled himself to greatness with his support of Katz, who was, in fact, Garcia. And Garcia, as Katz, relieved the tensions of the criminal drives that existed in every man who had the slightest connection or involvement with public relations or mass communications. But if the two were not the same man, they could be partners. They were working one of the greatest con games ever.

That had to be it. And they were so cautious, they never spoke directly to each other in public. They used him as their intermediary. And, of course, they were laughing themselves silly at the role he had been forced to play.

That would explain why Katz always eluded the police nets. Garcia notified Katz exactly where the police were. The few times Katz had been surprised were the results of chance.

Stark sat for five minutes, chewing a dead cigar while Kowolsky delayed incoming calls. Suddenly, he smiled and touched several buttons on the control panel on his desk. He issued crisp orders and then sat back. The campaign to establish a connection between Garcia and Katz had started. No man, no matter how quicksilvery elusive, could escape unceasing surveillance, provided the Federal State Bureau of Felonious Law Enforcement knew where he was. And the Bureau might not know Katz's location, but it knew Garcia's.

Stark was twenty minutes too late. A sergeant reported that Katz wanted to speak to him. Stark had a premonition which drained the satisfaction from him. He told the sergeant to put the call through, and when he saw Katz's huge grin, he knew that his premonition had been correct.

"Chief, you sure had me downed for a couple of days! But I'm up now! I'm going to show you that you're wrong! I don't need Garcia to make a man out of me! I'm all it takes to make me a man!"

"I said he was making a hero out of you," Stark said. "I didn't say a thing about making a man out of you."

Katz was not paying him any attention. He was stepping away from the screen so Stark could see the bedroom.

Sitting on the bed, his arms behind him, obviously bound, and a piece of tape across his lips, was Garcia.

Katz's face filled the screen again, and he said, "You might as well call off the men hanging around Garcia's apartment. He isn't home, as you can see. I guess I beat your men by about fifteen to twenty minutes. If they'd come sooner, they'd have grabbed me. Maybe!"

Stark put his hands below the edge of the desk so Katz would not see them shake. He shredded the end of his cigar and then leaned over sidewise and let the cigar fall from his lips into the funnel opening of the atomizer by his chair. He wanted to light up another cigar, but he would not let Katz see his hand shake.

Katz was still grinning. He said, "You're trying hard, Chief, but you aren't making it. You're really mad, aren't you? I got to you, didn't I? You look like you'd like to dive through the screen at my throat, like a character in a cartoon."

Stark pushed back his desire to shout, and he spoke quietly. "Can you prove that's Garcia?"

Katz quit grinning. "You accusing me of simulating! You think I'm a news caster?"

"Bring him close to the screen so we can photograph his ears, retinas, and fingers. And take that tape off. I want a voice print, too."

"No voice," Katz said. "I won't take the tape off. I'm sick of hearing that voice."

Stark was able to smile and to light up a cigar. After the first puff, he said, "Of course you wouldn't want to hear that voice. It'd remind you that it was the voice that made you into a hero."

"Think what you want, blueface," Katz said.

"You always called me Chief or Doctor before. All right, Robin Hood, what do you want?"

"I don't want a thing except that the news casters know that I'm holding Garcia. I'm keeping him out of circulation for a while. Keeping his big mouth shut in the only way I know, short of killing him. But you might tell Garcia's replacement how I took him right out from under the noses of the police. Who is his replacement, by the way?"

Stark gestured. Kowolsky turned up the audio on Screen No. 5.

"Hello, Chief Stark! It's me, Abel Able. You know me and my nostalgic sports program, Able's Fables. I'm taking over *The Noose of Time* program, Chief. What's the latest on the kidnapping of Garcia? You heard from that BLEEP, Katz?"

Able's long big-jawed face receded, and the broad brown face of Commissioner Dillman appeared beside his.

"Stark, I want to know—immediately—what you plan to do about Katz! That man is a menace to public health, a Typhoid Mary in many respects! He must be caught and quarantined!"

"Katz is on the line now, sir. Would you like to speak to him?"

"Nothing doing." Katz said. "I talk to you and you only. You're the only man in the entire establishment I got any respect for, and that isn't much. See you later. At my leisure."

He faded away.

"I heard that!" Dillman rumbled. "This is very peculiar! Why won't he talk to anyone but you?"

"I don't know," Stark said. "Why didn't you ask me that when Garcia was bugging me?"

"What?"

"Never mind. What can I do now I couldn't do before? An apartment-to-apartment search would require 200,000 men minimum and thirty million search warrants. Our only hope is to turn the people against Katz. Let those who made him a hero make him a villain."

"Are you saying Garcia was responsible for Katz's freedom?"

"I'm not saying a BLEEP thing! You know who the BLEEP was responsible! What I'm saying is that Katz went too far! He made the big mistake of his life when he turned against Katz. Which, by the way, proves . . . pardon me, *indicates* that he could be found BLEEP by a competent board of psychoanalysts."

"Yes," Able said, "he would have to be BLEEP . . . damn it, monitor! The official attitude is that Katz is BLEEP! Just a minute, Stark!"

The screen became a red and black waffle pattern for sixty seconds, and then the two faces appeared again. Able said, "That's straightened out. No bleeps, no circuitous phrasings. Crazy, crazy, crazy! Krazy Katz, how's that? No, Krazy Kat is a sympathetic character. Killer Katz, how's that? But he'd have to be crazy to kidnap the best friend he ever had. My God, Garcia was a news caster! You don't touch us!"

"Not unless you're crazy," Stark said. "All right, Commissioner. Give me six days. If somebody doesn't turn Judas by then, I'll resign. If Katz isn't in my hands by the end of the sixth day, I'll eat crow on Able's program."

"No public apologies, Stark!" Dillman said. "That'd make the Bureau look bad."

Five days passed. The rings under Stark's eyes deepened. Though the networks were referring to Katz as a dangerous psychotic, a potential Jack the Ripper, and a man who despised the public, nobody had phoned in to reveal Katz's hiding place.

Nor had Katz called Stark. And this, he realized was the worst part of the new campaign. Something had been painfully cut out of his life.

And then, the afternoon of the fifth day, he stopped in mid-stride before his desk and swore. Kowolsky, who was taking his calls while he exercised, said, "What's wrong?"

"Divorce hurts," he said, and he resumed his pacing. Kowolsky raised her gold-sequined eyebrows but said nothing. Doubtless, she was wondering why the thought of his ex-wife was so painful after six years. Or why he should be thinking of her at all.

He did not undeceive her. He stopped behind Kowolsky and grunted. She looked up at him after half-turning in the chair. He said, "Listen. A fish lives in the water but never knows it, right?'

"I don't know," she said. "I've never been a fish."

"You're smart," he said. "You know when you can get away with a crack like that and when you can't. You know me. In a way, I'm your water and you are my fish."

"Nobody's ever called me a fish before," she said. "Cold blooded, yes."

"As soon as a fish becomes aware it's living in water, it ceases to be just a fish. It still has limitations, but it's become a superfish. Now it knows something the other fish don't know."

Kowolsky was busy with a call from the 8th Precinct, Fourth Level, and then she said, "I can smell something fishy. You're about to produce something really rotten."

"If you were a true policewoman at heart, you'd say brilliant, not rotten."

"Stinking and shining like rotten mackerel? Or something like that? Whom am I quoting?"

"John Randolph of Roanoke, Virginia. No poet. A statesman only, though I guess you could call him a poet of invective. He'd be a nonentity today, bleeped out of existence. Never mind him. We live in these skyscraping plastic cubes connected to each other by many multileveled bridges. We're in black boxes which are all light inside. All light and sound. That's our water. The light and sound of instantaneous communication. Garcia knew that. All of us should know that, since it was spelled out for us long ago. But a fish who's been told he lives in water still doesn't understand it. He has to feel the water to comprehend it. When he's aware of the water, he can then do what the other fish can't."

Stark resumed pacing.

"Able's practically said that Garcia has been murdered by Katz and that the people who're hiding Katz are in danger themselves. If he'll turn against Garcia, who won't he turn against? And Able suggested that Katz was responsible for that bomb scare on the third level, Zone No. 2, Broadway Plaza. And he hinted that Katz may be responsible for the mutilation murders of those two girls on 58th, seventh level.

"Katz can't tell anybody the real reason why he kidnapped Garcia. Everybody would think he *was* crazy. And maybe he is. But I'm not sure. He may be the only sane man in Manhattan."

"Chief!" Kowolsky said. "Do you realize what you're saying?"

He came up behind her and put his hands on her thin shoulders.

"Reality that hasn't cooled off yet," he said. "I have to grip it for just a minute."

"I don't mind," she said, looking up at him. The ash blonde hair in its psyche knot, the right eye—deep green today—and the retroussé nose and the edge of the bright yellow lips were enticing.

"I'm twenty-five years older than you," he said. He turned, walked a few paces, and then wheeled. "What's the name of that actor that played Katz in Garcia's simulations?"

"You never forget a name," she said. "But it's Guy Bronze Horse."

"Is he really an Indian?"

"He got the courts to declare him one. He could prove he had an Iroquois great-grandmother. The networks have to use a certain percentage of Indians, and since the Indians prefer to live in the federal parks, it's hard for the networks to fill the quota. Since he became a certified Mohawk, Bronze Horse has been working steadily."

"He looks enough like Katz to be his brother, and Katz is no Indian. Get him."

"Katz?"

"You're mad at me," Stark said. "You know who I mean."

At 01:30, the phone rang, and the light shone through his eyelids. He woke swiftly because he had been expecting the ring all night. He had dreamed of it. Still not sure he was not dreaming, he sat up and flicked the ON switch. He also pressed a button on a device he'd had installed two days before. No one would be monitoring this conversation.

"Hello, Katz. Where's the Cheshire grin?"

"You're real smug, aren't you?" Katz said. "You've been playing footsie with reality and really ruined my image. Most of my *friends* have turned against me. But not all of them. And as long as I've got a few left, you'll never catch me."

"Why don't you give Garcia up? That way, you can prove you're innocent. And you'd make me look like a real villain."

"It's too easy. You're up to something. Especially this trick that . . ."

"You watched Able's show last night, of course?" Stark said. "There you were, handcuffed, brought in by the police after being caught in an apartment next to the apartment where those two girls were murdered. And no Garcia, though there were plenty of signs that he had been there. Including a pool of his type of blood on the bathroom floor."

"You stinking blueface! You lying degenerate blueface! You set up the whole fakeroo scene! But how long do you think you can get away with it? You have to produce evidence that your prisoner is me! Then where'll you be?"

"No worse off than I am," Stark said coolly. "Besides, I've given the Prisoners' Rights Safeguard Commission all the prints, and they're satisfied that the prisoner is Hilary Katz, ex-hero of the people, Robin Hood in the red."

"They didn't check that you actually took the prints off of the man in jail, of course! The dumbos! Well, Stark, I'll let Garcia loose, and he'll tell everybody what a liar you are. You'll not only be disgraced, you'll be a criminal yourself!"

"Why don't you do that?"

The silence was long.

Finally, Stark said, "You don't have Garcia. He escaped."

Katz shook his head as if he were trying to dislodge something. "You knew that all along. So you must have him. But why haven't you told the news casters? And why is he willing to stay hidden? I know that bigmouth. He'd want to get back in front of the camera. He'd want to kick Able out before he gets too established."

"We found Garcia," Stark said. "And we moved him to another apartment. Only four of us know about him, and they're not going to say anything. You're not the only one has friends, Katz. He thinks he's still your prisoner. He saw Bronze Horse, and he thought Bronze Horse was you."

As if he were hoisting a rusty drawbridge, Katz closed his jaws. He glared at Stark and then he said, "You're the criminal, not me! What's Garcia going to do to you when he learns the truth?"

"Nothing. Garcia isn't going to say a word. He has an image to preserve. He'll know he'll be a laughing stock if the truth got out."

Stark took a cigar from the box on his table and pulled the plastic tip off. The end glowed red, and he sucked in smoke. It tasted good, though not as good as the carcinogenic cigars he smoked when he could get them on the black market.

"As soon as you tell me where you are, I'll send somebody to pick you up. Bronze Horse will go out the back way as you come in the front, disguised as a police officer, of course. And Garcia will then be rescued with much attendant publicity.

Katz said. "I'd say you were crazy, except . . . You sure learned from Garcia, didn't you?"

Katz lit up a cigar, too. Stark was pleased to see that his hand trembled. Then Katz blew out so much smoke that Stark could barely see him. Was he going to dance away behind the clouds? No, there he was.

Katz said, "We've never once met face to face. Never once in the flesh. And if I did meet you in the flesh I still wouldn't believe it was you. I'd say to myself, 'Hilary Katz, that's not the real Michael Stark, Ph.D., Manhattan Federal State Chief of Police. That's a simulation. Better looking than the original and guaranteed to project charisma!'"

"Are you surrendering?"

"Why should I? All I have to do is phone old Abel Able and tell him the truth. And then you're not only out of the job, you're in jail and headed towards the federal state hospital, the old skull garage."

"I'll guarantee that your call would be only one of two dozen from men claiming to be the real Hilary Katz. You'd be just another crank, another repair job for the skull garage. Give up. If you do, I'll see that your image is protected. You'll have to spend only a few years in the hospital. It's very comfortable there. There's nothing you can't get there, so you're just as well off there as in the so-called outside world. And you'll still be the living legend, the Robin Hood of Manhattan. There'll be shows about you, maybe a series that could run for years. You'll be able to watch them in the hospital."

"No!" Katz shouted. "No! No! No! I won't! You can't force me! To hell with you and your images! To hell with my image! I won't give myself up, hero or no hero, villain or no villain! And the truth will out! Eventually, it will out!"

"Then they'll find the mutilated body of Garcia. It'll have his retina and ear and finger prints. These things can be arranged if you know certain biologists. They have a supply of corpses. The public will be outraged, and I doubt very much that you'll have any friends left. Not enough, anyway."

"And you'll keep Garcia a prisoner all that time? That makes you as much a criminal as I am."

"The psychic exchange between criminal and policeman is somewhat osmotic," Stark said. "Or you might say that when we come into contact, our magnetic fields overlap and cause mutual induction. But that analogy may be wrong. In electricity, like repels like, and opposites attract, whereas in our . . ."

"I won't go along with you!" Katz said. "I'm my own man! Set up your simulations as you will, you won't get me to imitate them or agree they're valid! I'm living out my own life as I wish."

He breathed deeply and said, "I'm leaving now. I know your tracers are about to locate me, but I'll be gone when your dogs get here. And I'll be calling Able and spilling the whole incredible story."

"Incredible is right," Stark said. "Who'd believe you?"

"You have to release Garcia sooner or later, unless you're going to kill him. Garcia will tell it the way I tell it, whether or not he believes me. And Garcia's audience will believe him because they'll want to believe him."

"We'll see," Stark said. He looked at Katz as if he were trying to see him in the flesh, without the intervention of metal and carbon and flying electrons.

"I'll hear from you again?" he said.

Katz said, "I'll call you at the hospital now and then, though I don't expect them to let me through to you. They might consider me an upsetting factor. I might interfere with your therapy. Isn't that a laugh? You've been trying to catch me to ship me off to the hospital, and I'll be free, and you'll be there instead."

"Call me anytime, no matter where I am," Stark said.

Katz grinned and said, "Do you know, I actually think I'll miss you?"

He faded away. This time, Stark would have sworn that his rictus hung in the center of the screen for a half second after the other features were gone.

Then he smiled.

He rolled out of bed, put on a single-piece suit, and strode through his apartment door and into the street. An electric tricycle was waiting for him. He sped down it, leaped off it at the end the street, and took the police tube to the Central Manhattan Detention Ward, still often referred to as *jail*. All details had been arranged, so it took only a few minutes to get Bronze Horse out and then to announce the escape of Katz. Chief Stark, of course, assumed all blame and all responsibility. But he pointed out that his men had found Garcia only a few minutes after Katz's escape.

That morning, Kowolsky tried to sympathize with her boss. But he only puffed gently at his cigar, smiled, and nodded his head in time with the old tunes he was humming.

"I don't understand it, Chief," she said, being over close to him so that the monitors could not hear. "Everything's blown up in your face. Katz told Garcia the truth, and Garcia's screaming that you're a criminal. And he's right, according to the law. What they don't understand . . ."

"So my simulation didn't work!" he said. "But you'll have to admit it was brilliant. Even Garcia admits, in private, that it was brilliant."

"But you act as if you're happy, Chief! Don't you realize that you'll be going to the hospital? My God, maybe they're right! Maybe you are . . . unbalanced. This has been an awful strain on you. Yet you seem so happy. Why are you so happy?"

Stark sat back and sighted along his cigar as if he were aiming at a target somewhere in infinity.

"I know a man who means it when he says No. I wonder if he'd like me to join him."

The Light-Hog Incident
Philip José Farmer

The following is an excerpt from *The Man Who Loved The Great Wizard*, an uncompleted semi-autobiographical novel about life in the science fiction community (not to be confused with the also uncompleted *Wild Weird Clime*, which is also set in the world of science fiction fandom, but is more fictional). What follows is the musing of the novel's protagonist, science fiction writer Tom Wode Bellman. It represents just one in a seemingly infinite array of staggeringly creative, neuron-charged ideas that Phil abandoned in his half a century of writing groundbreaking science fiction.

He hadn't been able to sleep. He lay there thinking while Barbara snored gently, and soon he had an idea for a story. It would be novelette length, say about 15,000 words, and he could sell it to Stanley S. McDonald, the great editor of *Striking Science-Fiction Stories Magazine*. McDonald paid three cents a word, and at 15,000 words—hell, make it 20,000—that would be six hundred dollars. McDonald should like the story very much, provided he never caught onto the basic premise.

The story would be called "The Light-Hog Incident." Our hero, Hilary Boone, is captain of a space liner which is attacked in interstellar space by a horde of strange creatures, gigantic, barrel-shaped, mouthless, noseless, earless, and eyeless. These beasts, called light-hogs, actually inhabit outer space. They are adapted to live, thrive, and move in the near-vacuum and near absolute zero of the space between the stars. They don't breathe air or eat, of course.

They get all their energy by browsing on light as they move over the three-dimensional meadows of space. They absorb light—or any radiant energy—and the chemistry of their internal organs converts the absorbed photons into hydrogen atoms. (He'd have to work the chemistry out in scientific, though not too specific, detail. That would be a pleasing intellectual challenge. And it would please McDonald, too, who always liked his stories to be based on scientific fact.)

The herd of beasts would excrete the hydrogen atoms to get rid of them, both as refuse and as energy to propel themselves through space.

The herd of beasts would have been attracted by the spaceship's emission of energy from its atomic-powered jets, and the hogs would suck all the electrical and atomic power right out of the ship. Next, they'll suck the energy out of the crew and passengers, if they can get to them. But Hilary Boone saves the day, of course, and this gives the optimistic ending that McDonald insists on.

But the kicker was that Boone discovers that the light-hogs are in fact, responsible for the existence of galaxies or, indeed, for all matter in the universe. They take in light and excrete hydrogen atoms. And, as everybody knows—well, practically everybody— the continuous creation theory maintains that hydrogen atoms are, somehow, produced continuously in space from some un-known mechanism. These individual hydrogen atoms eventually fall together, form molecules, attract even more atoms, and after eons form cosmic clouds of dust or clouds of cosmic dust.

Out of these truly mind-staggering nebulae, suns and their planets and other phenomena form. The pressure of matter in objects of a large enough size cause fission and then fusion. Suns, stars, are born, and planets also form out of the accumulation of gases. The hydrogen atoms, the basic building blocks of the uni-verse, begin to form complex elements, helium, iron, and so forth.

Half-asleep, he had chuckled so loudly that Barbara had jerked in her sleep and muttered something crossly.

The unstated premise of the story was that the universe was created from hog shit.

A Spy in the U.S. of Gonococcia
Philip José Farmer

Issue No. 2 of *Farmerphile* featured Phil's previously unpublished story, "The Unnaturals," a surreal Wizard of Oz pastiche about the creative individual caught up in the madness of the system. A similar motif is found in "A Spy in the U.S. of Gonococcia," another rescued pearl written between 1978 and the early 1980s. This ironic tale of ultimate societal paranoia echoes all the dystopic absurdity of Phil's Hugo Award-winning novella "Riders of the Purple Wage" and Dayworld series, only in this case the dystopian society described belongs not to the science fiction future but rather to the Cold War past. Though best known for writing fantastic fiction, Phil shows here that he is at heart a realist when it comes to human nature.

M y own outfit, the KGB, was after me," the black man said. "So were the CIA, the FBI, the Black Muslims, a Salvation Army soldier, and the Reverend Uriah Bucket. Except for the FBI, and its agents were hoping for a shootout, all meant to kill me on sight."

The wedding guest did not know if Si Tomkin was talking to himself or to him. It made no difference. Though his two friends were urging him to catch up with them, he could not tear himself away. His reporter's antennae quivered; his newshound's nose twitched; his Adam's rod, which was, like most journalists', sexually confused, swelled slightly.

The big black man, Tomkin, sat in a folding chair at the edge of the huge lawn. He wore a white shirt, red tie, black leather jacket, and blue jeans. His withered right leg was encased in steel braces. His head was shaved, his long bushy beard was gray, and his eyes glittered as if glass fragments had been shot into them.

The wedding guest had been told that Tomkin was woo-woo, but he *knew* he had a story in front of him. His boss would never allow it to be printed. No matter. The guest meant to write *That Novel* some day. Here might be the springboard from which he could dive in the waters of literary luster and loot.

What the guest knew about Si Tomkin was not much but was intriguing. Mr. Kohlback, the bride's father, a wealthy importer and politician, had accidentally shot Tomkin while on a hunting trip in the state of Washington. How he could have mistaken Tomkin for a duck was never explained. Kohlback, not wanting any bad publicity then because he was under Congressional investigation, had hushed the matter up. After paying off a doctor to treat the wounds and keep his mouth shut, he had brought Tomkin to his estate north of San Francisco and given him a job. Tomkin did more drinking than gardening, but his boss did not seem to mind. The job was a salve for Kohlback's conscience and a bribe for silence.

"As I lay face down, bleeding in the marsh mud," Tomkin said, "I wondered if I was dying. And I thought of my family and friends in Kiev."

"Kiev? In Russia?"

For the first time, Tomkin's eyes seemed to focus. He looked at or perhaps through the guest. He picked up a bottle of Wild Turkey from the lawn and drank deeply. After putting it down, he said, "There are twelve million Negroes in the U.S.S.R., descendants of slaves owned by wealthy Russians. When the Tsar ruled. You didn't know that?"

"I'd heard something about it," the guest said. He was not going to admit that this was a revelation.

"My birth name is Rodion Ivanovitch Kazna," Tomkin said. I was black, and so my future looked bleak and limited. I could be a factory worker, a janitor, or soldier. Being a soldier meant my permanent post would be Siberia. Russian blacks were never stationed in the west. It also meant that I couldn't rise higher than a captain, and my command would be all-black.

"But I was very ambitious and intelligent and a natural linguist. By the time I was thirty, I became a member of the Communist party, one of twelve out of twelve million of my race to be so honored. I spent three years in a language training school in east Russia. When I graduated, my superiors had no doubt that I was one hundred percent sincere in my belief in Marxism. They were right, but what they didn't know was that I was so sincere I was a counterrevolutionary. A fundamentalist. I subscribed to the pure primal Communism as inscribed by our great German-Jewish Moses, Karl Marx. Not the class-ridden, corrupt, hypocritical state ruled by power-hungries who talked much about the withering away of the state but would never permit that because they'd lose their power. I was determined that some day conditions would be changed. I was eager to go to America to help overthrow the capitalists.

Tomkin grinned and took another drink. One of the guest's companions walked up to him and said, "What's keeping you? Larry's asking for you."

"Be along pretty soon," the guest said, as his friend walked away.

"Not if you hear me through," Tomkin said. "It's a hell of a long story."

"If you're really a Russian spy, why're you admitting it? Aren't you afraid of the FBI and all those people you mentioned?"

"Have a snort," Tomkin said. "No, I'm not. I'm like a fox that camouflages himself as a fox. He looks like one but no one believes he is because it's obvious he's crazy. A crazy something pretending to be a fox."

"I can speak Russian fairly well," the guest said. "Want to tell me your story in Russian?"

Tomkin laughed and said, "You'd know then that this old beat-up American nigger was a real Russian then, wouldn't you?"

"I ought to go," the guest said.

"Go then. Anyway, three weeks after graduation, under the name of Bill Williams, I slipped off a Polish freighter docked at

Manhattan and plunged in the wilds of Harlem. My mission was F & A . . ."

"F & A?"

"Foment and Agitate. But I wasn't to contact the American Communists. If I did that, I'd have the FBI down on me like Simon Legree on Uncle Tom. Besides, the KGB despises the white American Communists as ineffectual toadies and lickasses. The black Communists were too unruly and independent. My colonel, the school head, told me the American blacks didn't fully trust the Russians because they were white. He said they were racists and none were quite sane."

Tomkin smiled and downed more Wild Turkey. "This stuff beats vodka all hollow."

At first Rodion-Williams-Tomkin lived rather quietly. He had to get the feel of Harlem, learn the power structures there, and immerse himself in the behavior, customs, and language, which were not always exactly what he had learned in the training center. He hung around the street corners, taverns, and churches, and attended many meetings of various organizations. He said little and listened much. Three weeks after his arrival, a KGB contact told him via phone to meet him in the Empire State Building lobby.

"I told him I didn't have enough money for busfare for the bus or subway. The reds were sending me just enough of the green to pay rent in Vermin Villa and to eat hamburgers and French fries and have a beer or two. Which I don't like anyway. The KGB was a real tightass, the Russian equivalent of Scrooge. I was getting real horny, but I couldn't afford to speak to a whore, let alone pay for one. The free ass wouldn't even look at me because I didn't have any money to show them a good time. I didn't jack off, no real man ever did that, I thought then. I hadn't been Americanized enough.

"And I was lonely. That was maybe worse of all. Worse than not getting any pussy. Well, maybe not. Anyway, I was homesick for my family and friends in the Kiev ghetto. Harlem was full of people of my color, but they were of another tribe. Black—but American. I was black—but Russian.

"My contact, a fat white man with garlic breath, didn't want to listen to my financial problems. His excuse was that the police and the FBI might wonder where my money came from if I lived affluently or even well. I wasn't being paid to loaf, he said. I should get my ass in gear and join the Black Muslims. I felt like hitting him in the face. Did this Charley asshole really think I was dawdling in the lap of luxury?

"I got hold of myself and told him I needed some seed money. What I really meant was that I need to spill my seed, as the Bible says, but I didn't tell him that. A week later, the tightasses did come through with fifty extra bucks—real big deal—and instead of buying some decent clothes I bought me a whore for an hour. The fifty was blown, among other things. And ten days later I had the clap."

He had by then joined the Black Muslims. If, however, the Muslims, who were rigid moralists, found out that he had gonorrhea, they would kick him out. He kept quiet about his disease and went to a free clinic for massive penicillin shots.

"How was I to know that the doctor there was an FBI informer, and he reported every young black male patient infected with VD? I don't know why. Maybe the FBI confused VD with subversiveness? Maybe they were running some sort of statistical survey. Whatever, the KGB found out about me from their man in the FBI, and I got called in, this time to the Chrysler Building lobby. The KGB had a thing about skyscrapers, some sort of phallic symbol, I suppose. The contact reamed me out for consorting with capitalistic whores. I asked him if he knew any communist whores I could go to, but he didn't think that was funny. He told me to go the next time, to a clinic where the staff wasn't working for the FBI. I didn't tell him it was already the next time. I'd caught a second dose from a woman in my apartment building. Her husband worked nights and though I was broke, she didn't care. She didn't dare be seen with men on the streets, but inside the building, in my room, oh my!

"The penicillin wasn't very effective. I was in bad shape. Believe me, clap's worse than a bad cold. You can blow your nose, but do you blow your cock? Five or six times a day you have to go through the painful rites of pissage. One day, while I was softly moaning in front of a urinal in the Muslim headquarters, a man entered. I didn't hear him, but he heard me. He asked me what was causing me such distress.

"One thing led to another, mostly my inability to explain my dripping penis—they didn't accept my story that it was from straining myself while lifting a heavy weight—and I was out on my ass. I couldn't lie to my contact about why I'd been kicked out because the other agent in the Muslims would have told him the truth. So the contact chewed me out again. What he didn't know was that I now also had the syphilis, from the same bitch gave me the clap. Man, she was something."

His contact told him that, so far, he had been a great disappointment, completely ineffectual. He had better start spreading propaganda around instead of VD or else.

"Or else meant I'd be called back to Russia and probably end up in Siberia freezing my ass off guarding the Chinese border. Or maybe picking coal in a mine. He did let me R & R, some R & R!—in my apartment until I'd been cured of the gonorrhea. Not to mention, which I didn't to him, the syph. I almost went crazy shut up in there. I read a lot but that got tiresome, and the TV set had more bands than a May Day celebration. I got very horny, but I didn't dare to let that sex-crazed, diseased woman in. In fact, I had to not only lock the door but pile furniture in front of it to keep her from breaking in. She was something else. I wanted her, but the only thing she hadn't given me was the crabs, and I could do without that. I'd never heard of herpes. Blacks aren't supposed to catch that very easily, but if only one in the U.S. had gotten it, it would've been me."

When Tomkin reported that he was cured and ready for action, he was told that he had to go to Los Angeles. The FBI was investigating him, and the CIA had him in its files as a suspect. Also, the Black Muslims were wondering if he might be a Federal agent. All this the contact knew because of the KGB agents in all three organizations.

"My new mission was to infiltrate the Black Muslims in L.A. I protested. I told him the Muslims had high ideals, but being a Communist wasn't one of them. I'd just be trying to butter the butter if I agitated to make them hate whites and the U.S. government. They were also religious fanatics who despised the godless Soviets. One word of pro-Marxist propaganda from me and they'd be suspicious. I could get killed."

The fat man told him he was a coward, and he gave him a ticket for cross-country busfare and enough money for two weeks' food and one week's lodging in L.A. An agent there would get in touch with him at some now unspecified place and time.

"'A bus, for God's sake!' I said. 'Why not a plane?'

"'It would attract too much attention,' my contact said. 'You're on welfare. How would it look if you suddenly had money to buy expensive airfare?'

"'They'd think I stole it,' I said, 'but they wouldn't be able to prove anything. Come on man, have a heart. This is America.'

"Nothing doing. At least, I didn't have to travel in the back seat of the bus, though I did anyway. I met a good-looking black girl who was going to Hollywood to get into the movies. The second night out, we screwed in the back seat. A week after I got there, I had the clap again."

He laughed uproariously.

"I was thinking what I'd tell the folks back home some day when enough time had elapsed that it wouldn't hurt to let them know I'd been abroad. 'How is America?' they'd ask me, and I'd say, 'Everything's free including the gonorrhea.'"

"The penicillin and other drugs didn't seem to be doing any good. My contact finally came up to me when I was sitting at a table in a taco stand. He said he'd expected me to try to join the Muslims before then. I told him why I couldn't. 'If they found out I was clapped, kaput for me,' I said. 'They're worse than holy rollers.'

"'They won't like that,' he said. I knew who *they* were.

"'Tell them to kiss my ass if they don't like it,' I said.

He said, 'I'll do you a favor and won't report exactly what you said.'

"He slipped me an envelope. I opened it and counted the money. Just enough for a week's rent in my cockroach-ridden skid row room, and a week's supply of hamburgers and French fries. No cigarettes, no booze."

He decided that, somehow he was going to smoke and drink up a storm before he joined the Muslims. What the contact had said about the FBI thinking he might have stolen the money to buy the airfare gave Tomkin an idea. That night, when the contact came home, drunk, Tomkin mugged him.

"The neighborhood he lived in, he should have expected it. He had a roll of bills big enough to choke a hippo. He sure didn't get it from the KGB. I found out later he was peddling drugs so he could live in a style he wanted to be accustomed to. But he hadn't really had the nerve to move into a better neighborhood because he was afraid his superiors would ask questions."

His gonorrhea would fade away, and he would think that he was cured, and then it would return.

"The doctor hinted that I was a curious case. He wanted me to come in for a battery of tests. Free. I think he was on to something, a medical phenomenon he could write about in a journal. But publicity was the last thing I wanted. And then, as if the clap wasn't bad enough, I developed a gastric ulcer."

"From tension?"

"I think so. Anyway, I pretended to convert to Black Islam, and I got a job as a grocery store clerk so I'd have a visible means of support. My contact stopped giving me money then. He said I didn't need it. Days, I worked. Evenings, I spent listening to lectures, working out in the gym, and taking judo and karate lessons. I was an expert, but I had to pretend I was an ignoramus. After a while, I became an instructor.

"I should've been in great physical shape, but I started drinking and smoking secretly. I could hardly wait until I got home. I grossed out until I passed out. Mornings, I'd wake up with the alarm clock beating my brains out and my belly wanting to crawl into a hole and die."

In the meantime, he got a new contact. The old one had been shot dead in a dark alley. Tomkin did not know if his superiors had expressed their dissatisfaction with the man in this fashion or a criminal had killed him for his drugs and his money.

"There was one danger I hadn't anticipated. Suddenly, my rock-fast atheism was sinking in the sands. I found myself wondering if perhaps the *Koran*, the Muslim holy book, was *not* just a paper bouquet of crazy visions and perverted history. Could it be that Allah *had* sent the angel Gabriel to Mohammed to launch him on a mission of salvation? No, I told myself. It's the emotional atmosphere here. It's getting to you, overcoming your rational mind."

While fighting this, Tomkin uncovered a black FBI infiltrator. He kept the discovery to himself until he could tell his contact. Before that man showed up, Tomkin became convinced that the infiltrator had penetrated his disguise. He wanted to tell his contact about this, but he had to wait until the man got in touch with him.

Before he could do this, he collapsed while giving a karate instruction. An intense pain struck him in his upper stomach, and he passed out. When he awoke, he was in the hospital. The surgeons had already operated on his gastric ulcer.

"Bad enough became the worst. Harun Zee, one of my students, a really nice guy, visited me, but he didn't bring chocolates and cheer. First, he told me that I'd been denounced as an FBI infiltrator. Guess who'd done it? The real FBI man. He'd beaten me to the punch. That, you might say, was the good news.

"Harum told me that Omar Ya, a big shot in the ruling inner circle, had sworn a mighty oath by Allah to kill me. First, though, he was going to cut my dick off and stuff it in my ass. An Arabic custom, I guess. Harun told me that Omar had caught the clap from his wife. He'd beat hell out of her, and she finally named the dude who'd given it to her. *Me!* I was innocent, but she was protecting her lover. Since I was in the hospital and in the doghouse with the Muslims, she'd picked me as the fall guy.

"I told Harun I was innocent. He said it didn't matter. Omar Ya was convinced I was guilty, and he was going to get me."

Tomkin was discharged (owing huge medical expenses he could not pay), and then he was kicked out of his apartment because he could not pay the rent. The KGB contact had not appeared yet, probably because he was afraid that the FBI was closely tailing Tomkin.

By then, Tomkin had shaved his head and grown a beard, more to hide from Omar Ya than from the Federals. Broke, he slept in doorways and alleys and ate at the Salvation Army mission. Desperate, he pretended to convert to Christianity. He made such an impression that he was given odd jobs around the station. After a while he joined the Salvation Army and played the flute in the band.

"I looked great in my uniform, if I do say so myself. And I was actually enjoying myself. The soldiers of God were good people. Kind-hearted, dedicated, and highly moral but not obnoxiously so. I felt they genuinely liked me and didn't look down on me because I was black."

Six weeks passed, and the KGB contact had not shown.

"Then, what do you know? I couldn't believe it. My gonorrhea came back!"

He went to a free clinic, where the doctor asked for the name and address of the person who had given him the disease. The doctor laughed scornfully when Tomkin told him that he had not had sexual intercourse with anyone for three months and that he must have gotten the germs from a toilet seat.

Tomkin tried to explain his was a special case. The germs have been lying dormant in him, waiting to break out when his defenses were down.

"He really chewed me out, but I stuck to my story. Finally, he gave me a tremendous jolt of penicillin and told me to come back for regular scheduled shots. And I was *not* to screw anybody until he was sure I was completely cured. I wasn't even to pound my pud."

The resurgence of the disease was the first surprise. The second was that he suddenly became genuinely converted to Christianity. Just as the gonococci had been quietly expanding in his flesh, so the conversion had been quietly gathering strength in his psyche. And, like the gonorrhea, it burst forth one day.

"I don't know," Tomkin said, shaking his head. "I don't know. I almost converted to Black Islam. I would've if I'd stayed with the Muslims. And now—bang!—while I was eating breakfast and not even thinking about religion—I was worrying about my VD—I was blinded by a great light, couldn't see the end of my nose through it, and I began weeping with joy, and I leaped up, spilling my soup, and began shouting, I'm born again! I'm born again! Oh, great and good Jesus, this time I'm really in your bosom! Sweet Jesus, take me now!"

But, though he had become a Christian, he was still a Russian. He had no intention of spilling his guts to the FBI. However, if he ran out on the KGB, they'd be hunting for him. And the FBI would also be looking for him, not to mention the CIA and Omar Ya.

He did not think about that at the time. He was too happy with his unexpected state of grace. He did have some difficulty explaining to the S.A. soldiers what had happened. They had assumed that he had been born again at the time that he joined the Army. But he babbled something about a deeper grace, and they accepted that.

"Then, wouldn't you know it, the trumpeter, Corporal Rachel Ogg fell in love with me. She was no Major Barbara, but she wasn't bad looking. I could tell there was a lot of sweaty passion under that white scrubbed-clean face. It was ready to burst out like, well, like my clap and conversion. All I had to do was say no, tell her I wasn't in love with her, but I didn't have the heart. Or maybe I was selfish. I needed an intimate and warm relationship. I would've married her, but how could I when I couldn't get rid of my gonorrhea? I sure wasn't going to take a chance on infecting a lovely woman like her. I'd have deserved to be stood in front of a firing squad."

He continued taking penicillin, and the disease suddenly vanished. The symptoms anyway. He was convinced that it had gone into hiding again and would rage forth some day like the Assyrians on the Hebrews. He got engaged to the corporal, and he was pleasantly surprised when he found out that she thought sexual intercourse was not unbearably wicked if it was with the man you were going to marry.

Two days after the engagement party at the S.A. station, the KGB contact showed up. He got on the same bus with Tomkin and sat down beside him. After looking around, he put his hand on Tomkin's wrist.

"At first, I thought he was a queer making a pass, but he started tapping with his finger on my wrist in Morse code. In Russian. He told me his superiors were very disappointed in me. My incompetence and my penchant for getting into apolitical messes made me security-dangerous. But they were going to give me another chance. In San Francisco. There I had better display a level of competence high enough to at least earn my pay—I almost laughed then—and keep away from the filthy imperialist whores.

"He told me I'd find money in my locker at the mission. It would pay for two weeks' lodging while I found a job. There was no bus ticket in the package. It had been decided that it would be safer if I hitchhiked because the FBI might be watching the bus stations. That was ridiculous, and I told him so. He ignored that remark and transmitted that my San Francisco contact would get in touch as soon as I got a job. He gave me the password and left. But when I went to my locker, I found that somebody had broken in and taken my money.

"I was flat broke and no way of getting more money from the KGB. So, I sort of replaced it. When I accidentally saw my contact leaving a restaurant, a fancy one, I followed him. First chance I got, I knocked him out with a brick. He had a big roll, enough for a plane ticket and two months' food and lodging, tobacco and booze, and some goodies. I figured it was owed me."

But he was suffering from guilt at deserting Corporal Rachel Ogg. He tried to bleach out its intensity with six glasses of champagne and two small bottles of Johnny Walker Black on the flight. His guilt rode him as hard as before. But, the moment he stepped out of the plane, he quit believing in his recently found religion and his guilt evaporated.

"I recommend the champagne flight if you have religious and emotional problems. It clears your head, heart, and nerves."

He found a cockroach-and-bedbug-swarming room, coated his intestines with Maalox, and went out on the town. Sometime during the night, he got into an argument with a man in some dingy bar and was invited out into the alley to fight. He accepted, and then the man and five of his friends jumped him.

"I'm a hell of an alley fighter, if I do say so myself. But I was loaded out of my skull and outnumbered. I woke up in a hospital ward with three broken ribs, a fractured skull, a concussion, two broken fingers, a broken hand, five teeth knocked out, aching balls, and, worst of all, anal gonorrhea, though it didn't show up right away of course. They'd raped me, given me the clap fore and aft, not to mention shredded piles. As if that wasn't bad enough, the KGB or maybe Omar Ya or Rachel sent me a box of poisoned chocolates. I didn't eat any, but the nurse I gave a chocolate to almost died. That brought the police around, and then some men I was sure were FBI and CIA questioned me. I got a lawyer, sort of, he was a drunk, to stand by my bedside while I was being interrogated. He couldn't remember if my name was Smith or Williams—I'd gone back to Williams—and eventually he was dragged off to face a charge of three hundred unpaid traffic tickets."

Corporal Rachel Ogg showed up. She had gotten leave from the Salvation Army and had hitchhiked to San Francisco.

"Thumbed rides, for God's sake! It's a wonder she wasn't raped half a dozen times on her way up. Maybe her uniform kept her safe, though there were plenty of perverts would've been turned on by it. She claimed that God had protected her. What God should've been doing, He should have been protecting me. That sweet woman, that gentle Christian, wanted to kill me. Not because I'd run out on her without a word of explanation. That had broken her heart, she said, but that wasn't why she was going to shoot my prick off as soon as I got well enough to be killed. I'd given her the clap! That was the unforgivable sin, she said, and she felt indescribably soiled.

"I was surprised. Until then I hadn't known my disease had broken out again. I hadn't had any symptoms. Maybe, I told myself, the sneaky little bastard had just come out for the occasion and then retreated again."

He sank deeper and deeper into self-loathing as she raved loudly on. The other patients in the big ward were all grinning except for two dockworkers who were upset at the spectacle of a white woman degrading herself over a black man.

"I think that if my lawyer hadn't showed up then, the fascist dockworkers would've started the riot instead of him."

"Your lawyer?" the guest said. "But you said . . . ?"

"This was another, a black named Hubert Renal. He said he was a public defender. I found out later he was lying. He'd been sent by the KGB to case the joint and determine if I should be liquidated in the hospital then and there or at a later time and place. The KGB screwed up though. He was a black American Communist, but he was also a virulent anti-Semite. He began raving and ranting about what the Jews had done to the blacks in America. Rachel stood open-mouthed, and the two dockworkers clapped and yelled encouragement. I couldn't believe my ears. According to Renal, it was the Jews and Jews alone who were responsible for the plight of Negroes. Not only that, they were secretly and insidiously pushing the two superpowers into a nuclear war so that they could seize power and rule the world thereafter.

"Man, I've met some crazies in my time, but that dude . . ."

Tomkin shook his head and took another drink.

It took the pseudo-public defender three minutes to antagonize everybody in the ward except for the two white dockworkers. Even the orderly who entered in the midst of the triage, Howland, a harmless and totally pacifistic homosexual, was grinding his teeth and clenching his fists.

During his loud remarks, the pseudo-public defender called Rachel a Jewish slut and rebuked Tomkin for consorting with her.

"She was pure Scotch-Irish, if there is any such thing, but she fitted the stereotype with her black hair, black eyes, big nose, and just then, her big loud mouth. The moron should have wondered what a Jew was doing in a Salvation Army uniform, but he wasn't thinking straight, of course."

Rachel, wild-eyed, red-faced, and screaming, slammed her hand-bag on the side of Renal's face. He staggered back, then cursing, came around the bed to get at Rachel. Just as he did so, an old man slammed him in the back of the head with a bedpan. Its contents spilled on Renal and the floor.

"He was a survivor of Dachau: he'd had a double hernia operation two days before."

Stunned, Renal went down on his knees. The old man fell on the floor screaming because he had torn open his stitches. An old wino with liver cirrhosis crawled out of bed and grabbed Renal's tongue with long dirty fingernails and yanked, loosening its roots somewhat.

Two black orderlies, attracted by the commotion, burst in. They assumed from what they saw, wrongly of course, that one of their brothers was being attacked. They might have done some damage to Rachel and the wino if the two dockworkers had not gotten out of bed and hobbled swiftly to intercept them.

"If I hadn't been so afraid of being injured again, I would've been laughing. One of the rednecks had a concussion and a broken nose, among other things. The other had an arm in a cast and something wrong with his intestines. Probably rotten with beer. He swung his cast against the side of the big black's head and staggered him and swung it down and up against the crotch of the small black, who'd just rebroken the other redneck's nose. Then he was dancing around screaming because he'd hurt his arm again."

The larger orderly pulled a switchblade knife out. The dock-worker, whirling, accidentally struck him again on his head with the cast. The orderly reeled back and fell backwards over the body of the man with the broken nose. When he fell, his head struck a bed-railing, and that put him out for a few minutes.

Renal had gotten to his feet again, his eyes still crossed. He reached inside his coat and pulled out a .38 automatic. An old man whose face was covered with tendril-like tumors dashed an ashtray full of butts and ashes in Renal's eyes. Renal fired the gun into the ceiling, dropped the weapon, and clutched his eyes.

Down came Rachel's bag on his head, once, twice, thrice. The tumorous old man slipped on a turd on the floor, and began gnawing Renal's ankle. Renal kicked him away, grabbed Rachel's handbag and tore it from her grasp. Howland, the white orderly, hurled himself screaming at Renal. They fell against the bed next to Tomkin's and Renal struck his head on the railing. Half-stunned, Renal got to his knees, pushed Howland away, and began groping for the gun. Rachel picked it up and fired a shot close enough to Renal's ear to burn it. She later claimed that she had only wanted to fire a warning shot.

The bullet ricocheted off the floor through the mattress of a bed and stuck, half-exposed, in the ceiling plaster.

Unfortunately, Rachel did not release her trigger finger at once. Three more bullets were fired before she dropped the gun and started weeping. One bounced off a bedpost and zinged by the dockworker still standing. He threw himself on the floor, causing further injury to himself.

A hospital security man burst in, a revolver in hand. The last ricochet took his cap off. He whirled and ran out yelling for the police.

Almost everybody who had strength enough to drag himself out of bed was hammering away feebly at whomever was within reach. There were more casualties, most of them caused by catheters violently pulled out, as patients hurled themselves into the brawl.

"Man, it was right out of Dante's *Inferno*. Such screaming and screeching and cursing you never heard. There was blood all over the floor, urine from bedpans used as weapons, ashes, cigarette butts, vomit, and crap voided because of the excitement. The wino had smuggled in a pint of muscatel but somebody had broken it over somebody's head, and the barefooted patients were stepping on the pieces of glass. You should have seen them hoping around, swearing and yelling."

Renal must have been sure that Rachel was going to shoot him. For that matter, so did everybody else, except Tomkin, who thought she would be taking a shot at him next.

"When Rachel started shooting, I got so scared I lost control of top and bottom, which caused me great pain. Urination and defecation were both very painful for me."

Tomkin winced as if the memory hurt him.

Then, the nurses, orderlies, and doctors moved in. Bedlam continued for quite a while. The patients had to be gotten back into bed and the catheters and IV tubes reinserted. Amidst more screaming, and the more badly injured were taken to the emergency room.

"The police arrested everybody except me. Obviously, I couldn't have participated. They even arrested a doctor who'd slipped in a pool of urine and was carrying on like a madman. But, even though I wasn't formally charged, I was questioned at the hospital and after I'd been discharged. But I kept mum, and a real public defender steered me to safety. Meanwhile, the KGB sent another assassin after me. He was a white with a heavy Slavic cast of features, looked like Khrushchev's twin, only younger, and that was enough to put me on guard. I would've been suspicious of him anyway. Why would an insurance salesman come to me, a down-and-out jobless black with a history of 'accidents' and trouble with the police and gonorrhea-proneness? I might've just thought he was FBI. But that face and his ill-fitting suit and the garlic on his breath identified him.

"I think he was going to shoot me with his silencer-equipped .45 automatic as soon as my apartment door was closed behind him. But I hit him over the head with a full quart of dago red just as he reached inside his coat for the gun. I kicked him in the balls and then knocked him out completely with a massive volume of Marx's *Das Kapital*. Poetic justice."

Tomkin took the man's gun and his wallet, which held three hundred dollars. After taping the man's mouth, he taped his feet together and his hands behind him. He filled the bathtub with cold water, then hoisted the big heavy man into the tub.

"Just as I did, I felt a burning pain in my groin. It was the first indication of my right-side hernia, which had to be operated on two months later. 'What next?' I told myself."

He then taped the man's penis and connected it tightly with a rope around his neck.

"When he came to, I told him not to get a hard on or he'd strangle himself."

He then wrote KGB AGENT on a piece of paper and taped it to the bathroom mirror. An hour later, he was on a bus to Seattle. There his gonorrhea was cleared out after a long treatment. But, for some years, every time he had a ready woman, his penis shriveled up like burned bacon.

"*It* was afraid of catching the clap. So was *I*."

The wedding guest glanced at his wristwatch and looked at the dancers and the rock band at the other end of the lawn. The loud guitars called him.

"I really must be going."

"Yea, sure. But wait a minute. I'll cut it short. I took another name, never mind what, got a job, and settled down in a middle-class mixed-race suburban area. I married a fat but good-looking jolly woman, a real church-goer though. I got a job, stayed out of trouble, tended to my garden, let the world flow by my front yard. No children, the clap had made me sterile. But I didn't have to worry about that—I thought. How was I to know that my obese, cheery, God-fearing, choir-singing wife was a nymphomaniac? Or that she'd get my most unfavorite social disease from a lover, pass it on to me, and then on to our minister, Reverend Uriah Bucket? How was I to know that the reverend would blame it on me and come after me with a shotgun? Also, I couldn't foresee that Rachel Ogg would attend a S.A. meeting in Seattle and just happen to see me walking down the street. Or that her old hatred and fury would rouse, and she'd forget the Christian dictum about turning the other cheek and would track me down and come after me with a .32 revolver? How was I to know that she'd also turn me in to the FBI, and the CIA and KGB agents in the FBI would notify their superiors? Or that she'd also tell the Black Muslims and Omar Ya would come after me to fulfill his vow of vengeance?

"Hell hath no fury like a woman you've clapped up. I was sitting in my front room when the picture window was blown apart by a blast from a shotgun. I got a glimpse of Reverend

Bucket with a smoking shotgun in the front yard, of Rachel, in her uniform and holding a revolver. At the same time, two cars speeding in opposing directions slammed head-on into each other by the curb in front of my house. A black man, must have been Omar Ya, pulled up on a motorcycle at the same time.

"I dived just as Bucket emptied a second barrel, and I crawled across the floor while pistol shots banged and bullets struck the wall above my head. I got to the back door and ran like all the demons of hell were after me, which they were. I got the car out of the garage and away, though not before the rear window was shattered by Bucket's pellets. And then the chase was on.

"You've seen all these car chases in the movies and on TV? Burt Reynolds couldn't hold a candle to me. Four cars and a motorcycle were after me. Once, looking back, I could see Rachel's bonnet. She'd jumped into a car, but I don't know whom she was with, the CIA, FBI, KGB, or Bucket."

"I really must go," the wedding guest said, though he could not leave until he heard the end.

"Hold on a few seconds. I got way out into the country and then I ran out of gas. So I took off into the misty woods and just as I was congratulating myself on having eluded all those assholes, I saw a flash of red. My heart stopped. I thought the red was the sun glancing off the lining of Rachel's bonnet. But it must have been a cardinal I saw. Next I knew I was lying face down in the mud in the marsh, in shock but with enough sense to wonder who had gotten me. Not that it mattered. And then Mr. Kohlback turned me over. He was yelling that it was an accident, his shotgun had gone off when he stumbled over a log. He was half-drunk, I could smell the Scotch on his breath, he'd forgotten to put the safety on. The rest you know. Or can surmise."

Tomkin lifted the bottle to his lips again. The wedding guest said, "I'm stunned. Only, what does all that, your story, mean?"

"Haa! Good stuff, Wild Turkey! Smoo-oo-ooth! What does it mean? Are you one of those moralists always has to have a meaning, a message, in a story? If anything, it means what you already know. Life is savage, comical, and absurd, all at the same time.

"What it means to me is that I'm unfortunate but unique. I'm the only spy in the world who defected, not because of ideology, but because of the clap."

The guest said so-long to Tomkin but as he walked away, he muttered that he thought he had just been had. The old black was half-looney or having fun with him or both. If he had made up the tale, he had a hell of an imagination.

The guest talked to the bride and groom and his friend, the best man. Then he got into a conversation with Kohlback, the host.

"That man," the guest said, indicating Tomkin with his thumb.

Kohlback smiled and said, "Which story did he tell you? The one about his being a Russian spy is my favorite."

"Yes, that one. Mr. Kohlback, just suppose it's true?"

"Then I'd be harboring a fugitive from justice, wouldn't I? However, he suffered enough, he's paid for his crimes, paid for them before he committed them you might say."

The guest closed one eye and skewered Kohlback with the other. "I'm a reporter, you know, and I can sniff out things other people can't. I got an instinct. Tell me, Mr. Kolhback, just as a hypothetical case. If Tomkin's story is true, then some of the people who were after him surely must know he's here. But he's harmless now, and there's no sense doing anything about him. Still, they'd want an eye kept on him. Tell me, just in a hypothetical sense of course. Which outfit is using you as his keeper?"

"Hypothetically? Well, maybe the FBI or the CIA or the KGB."

"Come on. Off the record. Which?"

Kohlback smiled. "You take your pick."

The Rebels Unthawed
Philip José Farmer

A faster-than-light starship expanding and bursting outside of the universe. An alien idol which affects one's memory in a very intriguing way. A one-hundred-page manual for Gene Roddenberry's forthcoming Star Trek series, detailing what is and is not scientifically possible. A drab metal filing cabinet in the basement of an unassuming home in Peoria, Illinois. A window into the magnificent imagination of Philip José Farmer.

"The Rebels Unthawed" is a treatment that Phil wrote in early 1966 for Gene Roddenberry's *Star Trek*. For the uninitiated, a treatment is a prose synopsis used to pitch an idea for a television or film screenplay. "Rebels" has been reworked for publication here, but provides an interesting footnote to both Star Trek and Farmerian history. Until now, it was widely thought that Phil wrote only two treatments, and the aforementioned and unused manual, for Star Trek.

Phil explains in his introductions to "The Shadow of Space" and "Sketches Among the Ruins of My Mind" (*The Grand Adventure*, Berkley Books, 1984) that those stories also originated as treatments for *Star Trek*, but were rejected by Roddenberry as unworkable, too far out. Regular television viewers would not understand them, and the special effects budget would be astronomical. At this point, Phil tells us, he said to hell with television treatments and stuck to prose, where he could exercise his imagination to his heart's content and do justice to his own ideas.

Which is essentially true, but not quite. Phil proposed at least one more idea for Roddenberry's show, the treatment at hand.

One of the main characters in Phil's "Rebels" is Dr. Paula Eden. A black doctor who is the chief doctor's assistant is also mentioned. Phil could have been anticipating. Two female ship's medical doctors appeared during *Star Trek*'s run: Dr. Elizabeth Dehner ("Where No Man

Has Gone Before") and Dr. Helen Noel ("Dagger of the Mind"). In *Star Trek*'s second and third seasons, a black doctor, Dr. M'Benga, served as McCoy's chief assistant and was featured in two episodes ("A Private Little War" and "That Which Survives").

It is not inconceivable that the creators of these episodes came up with these characters independently—and certainly fleshed them out in a way that goes beyond Phil's brief mention of a "Negro doctor who assists the chief doctor." However, it is equally conceivable that some of the ideas in the ostensibly unused manual and treatments actually did filter into the collective consciousness of *Star Trek*'s writers and producers. Another possible explanation is that many *Star Trek* writers could have been given source material and instructed to construct their own versions of the same stories and subject matter.

In any event, "The Rebels Unthawed" stands as a treatment that actually could have been filmed for *Star Trek*. The story is a character-driven melodrama demonstrating the folly of unchecked ego and misplaced patriotism, right up 1960s *Trek*'s alley. Although we'll never know why it was not accepted—or did Phil withdraw it from consideration after the previous two rejections?—it is interesting to note that the plot bears no little resemblance to a first season episode of *Star Trek: The Next Generation*, "The Neutral Zone," in which the *Enterprise* crew finds floating in space the cryogenically frozen bodies of several humans from 1990s Earth. Upon thawing and revivification, one of the characters is revealed to be arrogant and ego-driven, causing a minor amount of chaos aboard the ship.

In this regard, then, Phil's plot for "Rebels" serves as another excellent example of his talent for anticipation.

TEASER:

The *Enkidu* detects an object in space. It is going at half-speed of light but is under no apparent drive. Catching up with it, the *Enkidu* finds it to be a spaceship of alien make, wrecked by collision with some large body, perhaps a meteor. Boarding it, the *Enkidu*ans discover the space-frozen bodies of sapients. They also come across a chamber which is partly wrecked and occupied with other dead. But these are the bodies of animals and people of Earth: buffalo, lions, elephants, bears, Europeans, Indians, Chinese, Africans, Arabs, etc.

The bodies are dressed in the garments worn during the mid–19th century. This is amazing enough, but the crew finds twelve bodies unharmed by the explosion or collision. Apparently, all the Terrestrials had been kept frozen in a jelly, in suspended animation. The accident had ruined all but twelve humans, who are still preserved in the jelly, which has been maintained by the cold of space.

Several of the men are clothed in Confederate and Union uniforms.

Taken aboard the ship, the twelve bodies are scientifically unthawed, administered adrenalin, hearts stimulated, and brought back to full life.

The resurrectees' first reaction is shock, wide-eyed and silent amazement. But one of the women, seeing First Officer Jubal's alien features, begins to scream.

ACT I:

The resurrectees' story: They were all picked up at night by the aliens and placed in deep-freeze. This happened in April, 1862, around the time of the Battle of Shiloh. The aliens were apparently picking up terrestrial specimens at random over the entire planet. Their ultimate destination must have been the home planet of the sapients. Three men and three women are southerners; three men and three women, northerners.

The Confederates are:

    (1) Rawson, an Alabama cavalry major

    (2) Mrs. Theodora Dutton, a Virginian housewife, close to giving birth to a child

    (3) Sergeant Jeannot, Florida

    (4) Beulah Radine, a poor white Georgian

    (5) Lt. Wilson, Texas artillery, a rancher

    (6) Michele Burton, a Mississippi planter's daughter

The Union members are:

    (1) Kegan, a New York cavalry captain

    (2) Crawford, a Rocky Mountain fur trapper

    (3) Elizabeth Van Groot, a Michigan grocer's wife

    (4) Sergeant Dooley, an Indiana infantryman

    (5) Mrs. Mueller, Iowa, a riverboat captain's wife

    (6) Willetta Mueller, 17, daughter of the above

The thawees are still in sick bay but recovering fast. The Negro doctor who assists the chief doctor tells them what has happened since they were abducted. Most of them seem relieved that the issue of the Civil War has been settled, since their hearts were not really in it. It is evident, however, that Kegan and Rawson are firebrands unquenched. These two are enemies from the moment of recovery from the shock. It is seen later that the patriotic issues are really pegs for the personal drives of these two, rationalizations for their behavior.

The thawees react with embarrassment and sniggering comments to the dress of the crew, especially that of the female crew. Catapulted headlong from the mid–19th century into the mid–21st century, the thawees are continually shocked by the (to them) near-nudity and outrageous speech and attitude of the crew. The only exception is Mrs. Dutton, the pregnant Virginian. She is remarkably adaptable and broad-minded, cheery despite her situation.

Another doctor, the beautiful Paula Eden, attracts both Kegan and Rawson. While feuding with each other, they make a play for her. Each has been quite a Don Juan, so there is the additional rivalry of sexual competition. Neither, though, is capable of admitting that a woman is their equal. Yet Dr. Eden is obviously their intellectual superior. She is friendly with them but quietly puts them down when they get too familiar or condescending.

Kegan shows his alcoholic tendencies almost at once. He asks for a drink, is given one, and demands more. Rawson makes a remark about Yanks needing Dutch courage to go into battle. Dooley, the Indiana sergeant, comments pointedly on this. He saw Rawson running for his life during Shiloh, remembers him because he shot Rawson's horse from out under him. Rawson has a scar on his cheek and long golden flowing locks, thus enabling Dooley to remember him.

Rawson is indignant and shouts the sergeant down. Dooley quietly says that it was no disgrace for raw troops to panic in their first battle. Thousands on both sides have done it; he himself did in his first battle. But it takes a man to face up to it and to return to battle.

This theme is developed during the story. Rawson cannot forgive himself for his running away and hence overcompensates with aggressiveness now. He has to prove he's not a coward.

Kegan keeps the feud going with a remark about illiterate southerners. This further enrages Rawson, who went to the University of Heidelberg.

Dr. Eden tries to settle them by saying that the War has long been over and is only a history-book event now. But Kegan can't keep quiet. He chortles, yes, we won it. Rawson starts to get out of bed to attack Kegan but is restrained by two corpsmen. Rawson says that it's like a blue belly to hide behind a woman's skirts, which causes Kegan to point out that Eden is wearing pants.

Captain James Kinnison enters sick bay during the latter part of the quarrel. He strikes up a conversation with Mrs. Dutton to take everybody's mind off the tension between the two men. He suddenly excuses himself and goes to his cabin and looks at his collection of microfilmed books. Magnified on his viewing screen is the cover of the Kinnison Family Genealogy. Pages flash by, showing text and photos of the family, jumping from the present (2066 A.D.) and going back until Kinnison stops the machine. There is Mrs. Dutton with a two-year old baby boy. Date: Jan. 26, 1861. Kinnison has an enlargement made and takes it to Mrs. Dutton. He tells her they're related; she is his great-great-great-great-great-great great grandmother. She loses her cheerfulness and bursts into tears. He apologizes for having caused her sorrow, but she dries her tears and smiles, saying she couldn't help it. The photo was just too much for her. After all, her son was only two then, and now she learned he died at the age of seventy in 1929. And here is his brother or sister about to be born two hundred years later.

Kinnison jokes with her. He'll have a great-great-etc. grand uncle 30 years younger than himself. Mrs. Dutton asks him if he doesn't think she's remarkably young-looking.

The thawees get out of bed. Kegan and Rawson put on their uniforms. Kegan steals a bottle, gets loaded, and corners Dr. Eden in a room. She fights him off. He gets angry and tells her that he hasn't any money to pay her. Obviously, any woman who dresses as she does and talks so freely must be a prostitute. He tries again, and she throws him over her shoulder and onto the floor. At the same time, Rawson, who has been trailing them, bursts in to rescue her. Kegan gets up and knocks him to the floor with his fist. The slight Dr. Eden thereupon half-kills Kegan with a display of judo and karate. Rawson is amazed, also ashamed, and a little frightened of this modern woman.

ACT II:

Mrs. Dutton, with Eden's help, is putting on lipstick and some eye makeup. The others, men and women both, get upset and make some insulting remarks. Willetta Mueller, the seventeen-year-old, then tries the makeup despite her mother's objections.

Kinnison enters. He tells them they can't be returned to Earth by his ship. They can be dropped off at a naval base and from there can take a ship back. Nobody wants to return to Earth. It's changed too much; they'd be completely lost there. Moreover, they're aware by now that the crew, though considerate of them, essentially regards them as museum pieces or living fossils. Modern terrestrials would have the same attitude.

Kinnison suggests two possible homes. One, an agricultural type planet with a small Earth colony. Or, two, Americus, an M-type world uninhabited by sapients and hence open to colonization.

Kegan and Rawson make sure that the colonists will be allowed to set up any type of democratically agreed-upon government and society they wish. Kinnison says yes, as long as the rights of the citizens are observed. Also, the Federation conservation laws must be kept. There must be no wasteful slaughter of animals or stripping of soil and forests. A Federation official will check on them from time to time.

Rawson and Kegan are elated. Rawson intends to set up a new Confederate States; Kegan, a New U.S. Kinnison says this is ridiculous. They're going to have a rough enough time if they band together. If they split, they may go under.

Mrs. Dutton is also against setting up two states. She wants her baby boy (lab tests show it's a boy) to have a fighting chance.

And she doesn't want him to grow up in a world where there's a chance for another civil war. She lost her husband in a war that was totally unnecessary. If it hadn't been for a few hotheads on both sides, it need not have happened.

Rawson reproaches her for disloyalty to the C.S.A. She answers that she can't be loyal to something that died two hundred years ago.

During the hot discussion, Kegan shows up and apologizes to Eden. He goes into an old-fashioned, sentimental, purple prose discourse on the evils of Demon Rum, his fight against it, etc. Eden says he can be cured of alcoholism if he wants to be. A metabolic exam will disclose the physical deficiency if the alcoholism originates from a physical cause. If the cause is psychological, the psychiatrist can help him, at least until they get to Americus.

Kegan is affronted by the suggestion that he might be insane (his misinterpretation of her remarks). He stalks off. Rawson is delighted at this and tries to be charming to Eden. She's cool towards him.

Except for Rawson and Kegan, the thawees agree that it'll be best to forget past divisions.

Rawson goes to Kegan, brooding alone. He tells Kegan that they may hate each other, but if their ideals are to be realized, they'll have to work together for the time being. Kegan agrees, and they plan out the future. Both have grandiose ideas, see themselves as combinations of Napoleon and messiahs. Kegan even half-jestingly says that they could be the founders of new dynasties. How does King Paul Kegan I and King Vickers Rawson I sound?

They ought to drink a toast to this. Rawson produces a small bottle he has brought along to get Kegan into an agreeable mood. They drink, and then Rawson brings up an unsolved problem. Both want the lovely Dr. Eden. They also need her in the group because she's a doctor. God knows what strange and awful diseases exist on the new world. But who's to get her for his mate?

Rawson says that gentlemen in his day solved some disagreements by duel. To the death? Kegan asks. To the death, Rawson replies. Kegan laughs and says he's no swordsman and knows

Rawson is an excellent one because he's heard him bragging about his saber skill. But Kinnison will undoubtedly give them beamers for hunting and for protection against the large ferals of Americus. They can settle this after they land. Winner take all, Eden and the whole group into the new state, C.S.A. or U.S.A.

They agree. Neither considers Dr. Eden's feelings in the matter. Despite what's happened in their relationship with her, they are confident that they can make her love them. Also, it is evident that the mid–Victorian attitude of regarding a woman as an object or an inferior is strong in them. They haven't learned better. Rawson and Kegan leave each other. Rawson sees Kinnison and Eden enter Kinnison's cabin. They're going to discuss the group, but Rawson is sure they're up to no good. A man and a woman can't be alone without evil intentions. In this attitude, he projects his own desires. He paces back and forth outside the cabin for a while, then beats upon the door. Kinnison opens the door and becomes justifiably angry. Rawson makes an ass of himself. He slaps Kinnison in the face and challenges him to a duel. Kinnison tells him this is not the mid–19th century. Moreover, as captain, he can have Rawson jailed and taken to a base for trial.

But if Rawson thinks he's so great with the saber, why don't the two have a match in the gym, with masks, etc.? Kinnison intends to show Rawson what would have happened in a real duel. Eden asks him if he will tell Rawson that he was an Olympic and Naval champion before or after the match. Kinnison replies that he won't tell him either time.

The observers in the gym include the thawees, some ship's officers, Eden, and Jubal. Jubal is the referee. Kinnison and Rawson exchange salutes, there's a brief encounter, and Rawson, a huge powerful man, knocks Kinnison's saber out of his hand. Kinnison bends down to pick up his saber. Rawson, instead of stepping back, lifts his saber above Kinnison's head. His expression is demoniac.

ACT III:

Jubal interposes himself between the two. Rawson laughs and says he only intended to frighten Kinnison, to show him how dead he would have been in a real duel. Rawson taunts Kinnison, but Kinnison wins the match. Rawson takes this very badly. Not only has he been defeated for the first time in his life, it's before Eden. Kegan jeers at him. Rawson says he will make Kegan pay for the remarks when they get to Americus. Rawson thereupon goes into a sulk.

The other thawees are getting fed up with their self-appointed leaders. Lt. Wilson, the Texan, and Sergeant Dooley, the Indianan, talk to Kinnison about it. Kinnison says that if the group sticks to their intention of colonizing Americus, it'll have to settle Rawson and Kegan down at the start. Dooley, a farm boy, and Wilson, a rancher, are far more interested in the agricultural and husbandry potentialities of Americus than in perpetuating the quarrels of the past. There are terrestrial wild cattle, deer, buffalo, and horses (also wolves and mountain lions) on Americus. Twenty years before, Earth zoologists placed these animals on Americus as an experiment in adaptation. Dooley and Wilson are delighted by this.

The *Enkidu* takes up a stationary orbit above Americus over an area like Southern California. The thawees are reluctant to be beamed down and need reassurance. They look to Rawson and Kegan to demonstrate their leadership and courage by going first. Kinnison deliberately stays out of the discussion, knowing that if the two fail in courage now, they've lost their chance to be leaders.

Kegan and Rawson summon up their nerve. Pale and trembling, they get under the dematerializer. Kinnison and Eden then take their places alongside them; and the others follow. They're materialized near a mountain (or wherever necessary for the least costs and most convenience in filming this). They have food, medicine, seeds, tools, beamers, inflatable tents, and even a g-car, loaned by Kinnison.

Kinnison has decided to stay a couple of days with the group to make sure they get off to a good start. Also, he hopes that Mrs. Dutton's baby will arrive as predicted within the next two days. Dr. Eden can assist in the delivery and give the baby a smooth launching into its future. Crawford, the fur trapper, Rawson, and Kegan, armed with beamers, go hunting. Beulah Radine, the Georgian woman, comes into camp and describes how Rawson and Kegan are slaughtering the buffalo and cattle and how Kegan shot a mountain lion. Kinnison goes after them. He sees dead buffalo at a distance.

Crawford slips up on Kinnison and tells him that if he had been an Indian, he would be dead and scalped. Crawford is just as furious as Kinnison at the slaughter, since he has respect for animal life. Together, they go after the two.

A beam fired from a rock almost hits Kinnison, who is pulled down just in time by Crawford. A search fails to uncover Rawson and Kegan. But it is evident that the two were having their duel. There are boulders cracked apart or destroyed by the full beamer power. Where are the duelers?

On returning to camp, Kinnison finds the two there. They were so frightened by the awesome effects of the beamers, they both sneaked back to camp. Now Kegan is drinking and Rawson is in a fury (both reactions caused by shame). It was possible that the near-hit was an accidental shot. Kinnison reads the riot act to both. He has deep misgivings about allowing them to remain on Americus. Legally, he can take both to a naval base and turn them over to Federation conservation authorities.

Rawson challenges Kinnison to a duel with sabers. He is out of his mind with self-reproach and humiliation for his cowardice. Eden's attitude of silent but obvious disdain further enrages him. Kinnison tells him to grow up. Does he think he can solve every problem by killing? Besides, the new society will have to abide by Federation laws, which forbid dueling. Rawson smirks at this and stalks off.

Kinnison tells Eden they'll stay one more day and then take off. He's still undecided about arresting Rawson and Kegan. The group needs all the members it can get to survive. But it may be better off without the two troublemakers. Kegan overhears this and goes off to inform Rawson.

All go to bed on a dark moonless night, each in his own tent. Wolves howl, a mountain lion screams, and there are weird cries from the Americun beasts. Rawson and Kegan leave their tents to confer under a tree. They agree again to follow their plan. While they're talking, shadowy figures sneak into the camp, prowl around the tents, examine the tools and the g-car.

Rawson and Kegan start towards Kinnison's tent. They're silently walking, beamers in hand, when they startle a prowler. It bolts away. The two men fire, and by the light of beam energy they glimpse a humanoid figure, furry from the waist down, short-tailed, rabbit-eared. The intruder gets away unharmed, however.

ACT IV:

Other prowlers run away into the darkness. Kegan and Rawson keep on firing. The camp comes awake. Kinnison runs out of his tent, his beamer ready. Rawson and Kegan are shaken, but they go ahead with their plan. They get the drop on Kinnison. Then it is seen that neither trusts the other enough to put down his beamer and tie up Kinnison. Impatient, Kegan knocks out Kinnison with the butt of his beamer. Rawson points out that he could have adjusted the beamer to stun-power to make Kinnison unconscious. Kegan says that it is far more satisfactory to hit him. Kegan then orders Dooley to tie Kinnison up. Dooley hesitates, and Kegan urges him on with a bolt near his feet.

Dr. Eden is disarmed by Rawson. Sergeant Jeannot, apologizing, ties her hands behind her. Kinnison comes to and asks the two what they intend doing. Rawson tells him and the others at the same time. Some object, notably Mrs. Dutton. Rawson says they have no choice now. Neither of the two say anything about the half-human prowlers, thinking that knowledge of this will scare the others into wanting to go back to the ship. And Rawson says that Eden will be taken along because she's a doctor. This doesn't fool the others, who know the real reason, but they're shouted down.

Eden asks if she'll be released later. Rawson and Kegan grin, and Kegan says sure. Kegan then insists that Eden put on a long coat to cover her scarlet-woman nakedness.

The two decide the group had better start off at once for the forest on the mountain. They can hide out there until the *Enkidu* crew gets tired of looking for them.

The supplies and Mrs. Dutton are put into the g-car; the

others walk. Mrs. Dutton feels the first labor pangs. Rawson tells the others to quit hanging back. The die is cast. It's like the firing upon Fort Sumter. To which Mrs. Dutton replies that they haven't learned a thing.

A dimly seen figure watches the group depart. It then leaves the tree behind which it has been hiding and approaches Kinnison. He is out in the open, his hands and feet tied, and his beamer and radio taken by Kegan. He struggles. He hears the grass rustle and sees several silhouettes creeping up on him. He shouts, and the things run away. Several times during the night, he has to shout to scare them away.

At dawn he frees himself of his bonds. He can't communicate with the ship. He can either follow the colonists or wait until somebody is beamed down to investigate the radio silence. He writes a note and puts it on the end of a stick held upright by rocks. Then he goes after the group. As he leaves, a hand, furry and thickly nailed, pulls the note off the stick.

The colonists are on a hilltop in the forest. Mrs. Dutton is giving birth behind a boulder, Dr. Eden attending. Kegan is drinking whiskey, filling himself with Dutch courage for the second showdown with Rawson. Rawson himself isn't too eager, since he's trying to convince Kegan they should use sabers. Kegan refuses.

Crawford enters the camp, driving a strange being before him. Crawford says, "I got me an Injun."

It's no Indian, although its face is painted and it has several feathers stuck in its long hair. It's humanoid, short, and is covered with brownish fur from the waist down. From the waist up, it's hairier than a man but less hirsute than a chimpanzee. The nails on fingers and feet are very thick, almost claw-like. It has a stub tail, white on the end. A lion-like mane of yellow-brown fur covers its neck. The head hair is long, and it has a frizzly beard. The nose is round and black, covered with fine hairs, like a Siamese pussycat's nose. The eyes are slanted. The ears are rabbitish but not nearly as big in proportion to the body as a rabbit's. The teeth are rodent's. In fact, the whole head gives a rodent appearance, as if on this planet a branch of rodentia or lagomorphs had developed into sapients instead of a simian branch as on Earth.

Crawford says he scared off a group but managed to capture this one. They were all carrying stone axes, clubs, spears, and knives. He heard them speaking a language of some kind. Dr. Eden tells the group that now they'll never be permitted to stay on Americus. It's against Federation law to colonize a planet already inhabited by sapient life, no matter how few the numbers or how primitive the technology. Rawson says that Kinnison informed him that Americus had no sapient life. Previous explorers and the zoologists didn't see any. Eden replies that they didn't see any, yes, but now they've shown up, and there's no arguing about the point.

Rawson says that, by god, the colonists are going to stay here. And these sapients, if intelligent enough to speak and to make weapons, can be used for slaves. Lt. Wilson objects to this. Rawson asks him if he's a true Confederate or not. Wilson says that he *was*, but that he, like so many Southerners, was basically opposed to slavery. Besides, Rawson and Kegan are crazy if they think they can buck the Federation. They can't hide forever.

Kinnison locates the group just as Rawson and Kegan go into the forest to try to settle who is going to lead the group. He works up close to them. Eden, climbing a rock, sees all three. She shouts to warn Kinnison that Kegan is sighting in on him. Kegan whirls and shoots at her, and tears her arm off with the beam. She falls down behind the boulder. Rawson kills Kegan. Kinnison tries to work his way through the thick underbrush to get to Kegan's beamer.

Rawson, searching through the brush for him, flushes out an aborigine. The sapient hurls a stone axe, which stuns Rawson. He drops the beamer and staggers off. Kinnison gets to Kegan's body in time to see three aborigines, two dragging the body away and the third holding the beamer. The native obviously doesn't know what the beamer is; he's holding it like a club. Kinnison charges them, shouting, and all three take to the brush. They drop Kegan but keep the beamer.

Kinnison removes Kegan's saber from the scabbard. He encounters Rawson, who is now recovered from the blow by the axe. They go at it with sabers. Kinnison slashes Rawson's face and arm with the saber, but, again, Rawson knocks Kinnison's saber from his hand.

Kinnison doesn't dodge around, ducking the strokes of the saber, as so many unrealistic TV fights between an unarmed man and a swordsman portray. A swordsman within range of a weaponless man is not going to miss.

Kinnison runs like hell towards the hill, hoping that the group will come to their senses and help him.

Jubal and other crew personnel appear in the distance in a g-car. They've come down to see why Kinnison didn't make his scheduled call.

Kinnison picks up a rock and hits Rawson with it. Rawson comes on anyway. There's a shout from above. Wilson and Dooley are threatening Rawson with their beamers. Rawson, realizing that this is the end, shouts a Confederate warcry and charges Kinnison. This leaves Dooley and Wilson with no alternative. Rawson is too far away to use stun-power, so they both cut him down (apart, rather).

There is a silence, broken by the cry of a baby.

TAG:

The *Enkidu* is orbiting above the agricultural planet. Eden is up, having been gotten to by the ship's doctor in time. Her new arm is already starting to bud. The colonists are getting ready to be dematerialized. Mrs. Dutton says goodbye to Kinnison and kisses him. He promises that whenever he gets a chance, he'll visit her and little Kinnison Dutton, his great, etc. grandmother and his great, etc. granduncle.

A Peoria Night
Philip José Farmer

This story was written in early 1983 for submission to the Nelson Algren Award contest, an annual competition run by the *Chicago Tribune* in honor of the author whose 1951 novel *Chicago, City on the Make* painted a vivid picture of the Windy City's backstreet inhabitants and corrupt politicians. Ironically that novel raised the ire of the newspaper that would many years later go on to sponsor the award. As you read on, picture, if you will, if Phil had won the contest and his story had appeared in the pages of the *Tribune*. Anyone familiar with Phil's past attempts at challenging antiquated mores in literature would hardly be out of bounds to wonder if, in depicting with such colorful realism Peoria's red light alleys, he may have deliberately forfeited a chance at winning this prominent contest to make a point.

George Harrier had never heard of the wheelchair whore when he started looking for a woman for his legless brother.

While driving over the Franklin Street Bridge to downtown Peoria, he was not thinking of the quest. The hot still air and the Illinois River below reminded him of the Philippines jungle in 1944 when he was fighting the Japs. Then, faster than Tarzan's arrow, his mind was in 1926. The quarter moon, its lower half in a cloud, was a treasure ship looted by Doug Fairbanks in *The Black Pirate* and upending just before it sank. Then the crescent was Fairbanks' scimitar rising above the dust of battle in *The Thief of Baghdad* 1924.

As the van left the upslope and crossed Adams, George glanced at the corner street sign in the lamplight.

"Franklin Street is William Kumpf Boulevard now, Joe! Things have changed since we were here . . . 1972?"

His brother muttered, "You'd think there'd be a thousand whores in East Peoria."

"There were, and not one would take you on. I was downright embarrassed, yelling above that damn rock and roll at all those whores. It's even more embarrassing when I drag them out of the taverns, and they take one look at the tub of lard that's my brother, and they get a whiff of him and walk away. Why'n't you take a bath once in a while?"

"In a while? Why not in a tub?"

"Ho, ho, ho!" George said. He looked like Santa Claus on a binge. His gray hair fell to his shoulders, and his white beard and moustache framed a big raw steak nose, shaggy gray eyebrows, hazel irises, and sunrise eyeballs. He was short and heavy-boned and had big muscles slopped over with fat. His beer belly pushed out a white T-shirt bearing a loin-clothed man swinging on a vine and the legend: "Tarzan Loves."

Joe was another but much fatter Santa Claus. He wore a black T-shirt, immense black chinos, and dirty white shoes.

George, waiting for a green light, looked up and down Jefferson. "Jeeze! They've torn down almost everything, looks like Berlin after the bombing. What's that big building? The new Civic Center I read about?"

"The El Dorado tavern's still there," Joe said, pointing to the left. "Why'n't they tear that dump down, too?"

He swallowed half a can of beer, belched, and said, "I ain't been here for years."

"Don't worry," George said. "They're not still looking for you. They closed up the State Hospital years ago."

"I never was crazy, you know," Joe said. "Just because I took the TV set out into the street on account of its stupid programs and smashed it with a sledgehammer . . ."

"Ho, ho, ho. So you jump out of the hospital's third-story window and bust your feet and *then* try to walk home. Ten miles! No, you weren't nuts! You stagger into that tavern, get drunk on the money you stole from the nurse, get thrown out, take a shortcut through the woods, start crawling, and then you decide to commit suicide, so you lie down by the railroad tracks. Dummy! You don't stick your legs on the tracks if you want the train to kill you. You stick your head on them."

"Knock it off," Joe growled. "You think you're Tarzan because you smell like ape shit. You know I wasn't trying to kill myself. I passed out, but it wasn't the booze did it. It was the pain in my feet."

George stopped the van by the curb, got out, and looked around.

Joe stuck his head out of the window. "What're you doing now? For God's sake, I got a hard on big as the rock of Gibraltar."

"You're in good hands," George said. "You'll get your piece of the rock. Take it easy."

The broad empty spaces where the buildings had been, the new ones thrusting up, and the quarter moon reminded him of the desolate and grotesque landscape in the Krazy Kat comic strips. Bare flat stretches and towering rock monoliths. The street lamps here were the cacti. He could almost see Offisa Pupp strolling along, swinging his billy, and Krazy Kat being powed by a brick thrown by Ignatz Mouse.

No pedestrians or cars were in view. Far off, a police siren wailed, and a tugboat blew its deep whistle.

"Coma reigns," George said.

"Rain? What you talking about? Come on, George. I ain't as young as I used to be."

"Who is?" George said. He got back into the van and drove up the boulevard with Third and Fourth Avenues to his left. When he had been a kid, he had lived on Third. The only change he could see was that there were houses missing here and there and those remaining looked even more like live-in roach traps. He was tempted to swing into the neighborhood to see if the Harrier house was still there. But he had business to attend to, and he did not want to drive through that area at night. When he was young, a little kid could walk through it late at night and be safe, but not now. There was no place like that now, not even in the small village of Imwintu where his mother and brother lived.

Another reason he could not waste time tonight was that his mother did not like them to stay out after eleven. She complained that they woke her up when they stumbled in and she could not get back to sleep. Mom never asked them what they had done, though George suspected that she knew. When George came from Florida on his infrequent visits, he took Joe to Pekin or East Peoria to get his rocks off. This time, they had had to keep cruising until they came to Peoria. Peoria, which he avoided because of painful memories.

It was here, when he was nine, that his father had told him that Mom had deserted her husband and five children, that she had left a note saying that she could not take the gypsy circus life any more. She wanted a permanent home and stability, not just a place to live in during the winter or when times were bad. What she had not said in the note was that she could also no longer put up with her husband's infidelities. George knew that. Too often, he had tried to sleep while his parents shouted in the next room.

Mom had gone to her native Imwintu, thirty miles from Peoria, to live with her parents. After they had died, she had married a hardware store owner, a nice old guy though not the real man George's father had been. After Mr. Quigley died, Joe lived with her when he was not in the VA hospital. George drove to the right onto a short street that had not existed the last time he was here, turned at Main and Monroe, and, after crossing Madison, passed by a rubble heap that had been the Palace Theater.

"Is nothing sacred?" George said, and he groaned. The ghosts of a thousand singers, comedians, jugglers, tumblers, and tightrope walkers, among the last, himself, were still doing their act in the empty lot. Something rang in his ears. Phantom music or his high blood pressure?

"Why'n't you drive up to the bluff?" Joe said.

"You crazy? The whores there are too high class for you, and the amateur talent would take one look at you and puke. Besides, if they knew you were psycho . . ."

"Damn it, don't insult me just because you're doing me a favor. I ain't crazy! Anyway, if I was, it wouldn't be my fault. It runs in the family. It's generic."

"Genetic!" George bellowed. "Not generic! Genetic!"

"Ah, who cares? I know you never got past the third grade. Just because you read a lot and use big words, you think you only fart Chanel Number Five."

George laughed and affectionately punched Joe's shoulder. He turned the van onto a sidestreet. A firefly was zigzagging across a trash-littered lot at the corner of the short block. Next to the lot was a one-story brick building with a big sign in front of it. *Acme Plumbing Service.* The firefly was looking for a mate, like Joe, and was flashing his code, all dashes, no dots, for any female which could take care of his plumbing. Mayday! Mayday!

"Dumb insect!"

"What'd I do now?" Joe said.

"Nothing. That lightning-bug. It's heading for downtown. There's nothing there but concrete, badlands for him."

He turned the corner and started to go by a paved alley bounded by the backs of the *Acme* building and of a three-story brick building and the side of a two-story white frame house. There was a big wooden sign in front of it: *Holy Church of the Burning Bush.*

Joe said, "Hey, slow down. What's that at the end of the alley?"

George, looking at the flashing red light, said, "It's too low and too small to be a cop's flasher. O.K. We'll see what gives."

He backed the van, turned the wheel, and drove into the alley. The headlights showed a woman sitting in a large motorized wheelchair at the end of the alley. Metal tubes projecting above its back supported a flashing bulb on a horizontal tube. The light was not much larger than a Christmas tree light.

The woman put her hands over her face, pale in the headlights, and yelled, "Turn it off, assholes! You trying to blind me?"

"Not exactly sweet-voiced," George said. He stopped the van a few feet from her, switched off the lights, and got out. Approaching her, he said, "Pardon me, lady. Does the red light mean what I think it does?"

He sniffed. Only a whore would use perfume like that. It must be, ho, ho, ho, ho, Chanelcat Number Five.

"How do I know what you're thinking?" she said.

She reached into a box attached to the side of the chair and pulled out a flashlight. Its beam blinded him for a moment, then went to the van. George turned and saw Joe, blinking, speared in the light. Then the light was cut off.

"I have to make sure," she said in a softer, now attractive, voice. "I'm not worried about being run in, but there is one cop who likes to hassle me. Sometimes, he puts others up to it."

The sky was bright with reflected city lights, and the flasher added some illumination. Her dark hair, which had been henna-red in the headlights, was too long for a woman her age. She had good bones, delicate and aristocratic, and she must have been a hell of a good looker when she was young. She could have been an aging Elissa Landi—*The Sign of the Cross* 1932—if poor Elissa had lived that long. She wore long chandelier-like earrings and a thin red blouse with nothing under it. Sweat made it cling to large but sagging breasts and huge nipples. A thin red blanket with a green intricately embroidered design covered her legs.

She had looked a hard fifty in the headlights, but in this dimness she could pass for thirty-eight or so. Whores aged fast; time was for them the bottom of a deep sea squeezing the juices from them, juices which hardened into ugly protective shells.

Though she had not answered his question, it was not necessary. George said, "What's your name, baby?"

"Sally. Sally in the alley. You've heard of her."

"Ho, ho, ho, have I ever! Listen, Sally, I'm not your man. I'm here for my brother. He's the one wants his ashes hauled."

"The other Smith Brother?" she said.

George laughed and said, "You're dating yourself, Sally. The young punks nowadays never heard of Smith Brothers Cough Drops."

"What's the matter with him? He's shy or just too fat to get out of the van."

George started to explain, but she said, "What's painted on the van, sweetie?"

George grinned with delight. "Just the old things I love. Tarzan giving the victory cry over a dead gorilla. Doc Savage, Man of Bronze. The Shadow. The Spider. Doug Fairbanks. Hairbreadth Harry and Belinda. Tom Mix, and . . ."

The chair motor whined again. She circled the van, her flashlight beam playing over the crowded mobile metal canvases. "Well, well, Sherlock Holmes and Conan the Barbarian."

George was astonished and delighted. Very few whores he had known had read much, and none knew about the pulp characters or Holmes except for the movies about him.

She returned to her original location. "My father had a roomful of the old magazines, *Argosy*, *Bluebook*, *The Shadow*, *Weird Tales*, all that stuff. I never read them, but he talked a lot about them. He was like you, out of it, a dreamer."

"You must've seen I painted Humphrey Bogart as Sam Spade and Warren Williams as The Lone Wolf," George said. "And Claude Rains as the Invisible Man. Of course, you can't see him, ho, ho, ho."

"A real joker, aren't you, honey? Well, I've seen your etchings. Now let's talk business. My rates are very reasonable, considering inflation. Thirty dollars for a piece of ass. Forty-five for a blow job. Nothing else doing. I don't go for kinky tricks."

"My God, I remember when you could get blown in a Peoria alley for fifty cents during the war."

"This isn't the good old days, honey, or haven't you noticed? You better make up your mind fast." She gestured toward the street. "Otherwise, my man gets uptight if you waste my valuable time."

George looked down the alley and across the street. He thought that he could make out a dim figure inside the shadows of a gutted brick building.

He turned and said, "No kidding, *you* got a pimp, too? I still don't see any reason for rush. Business isn't exactly booming, you know."

"Don't be fooled, Tarzan. There are johns out there aching to screw a woman in a wheelchair. Plenty of them are from the country club set, too."

George laughed and said, "Sure there are. Now. I'll explain about my brother. His legs are cut off just below the knees, but he's got artificial legs, wood and metal ones that fit onto his stumps and are strapped to his upper legs. He used to be an acrobat, so he's got a hell of a good sense of balance. He can walk on the fake legs like you wouldn't believe once he gets on his feet. When he's screwing, which isn't often, ho, ho, ho, he usually lets the woman get on top. But he can do it on top if he has to. You . . . if your legs are paralyzed and you can't move your ass, he'll have to do the work. No way he can do it with you in the wheelchair. I'll have to put you in the back of the van . . . unless you got an inflatable mattress."

"It had a blowout," she said. "It's in the bike shop getting repaired. That doesn't stop me, though. My legs are dead, Tarzan, and so's my ass. But I moan and scream a lot; I'm a real pro. What do you want for thirty bucks?"

George went to the van and explained the situation. Joe said, "Why'n't you tell her I don't like being blown?"

"How do you know unless you try it?"

"I get disgusted just thinking about it. Forget it, George."

George laughed, and he went back to Sally. She was smoking a cigarette and gazing up at the sky as if she expected something to drop from it. Manna? UFOs? The Second Coming? Prince Charming on a white horse?

Sally lowered her eyes and jerked the cigarette from her mouth. "Well, well, here comes that big prick, Simon Pure!"

George turned again—he was beginning to feel like a spinning top—and he saw a black-and-white blocking the alley. A uniformed cop with a flashlight turned on was going around the car. The driver was still at the wheel.

"Don't panic," she said. "Stay the course. As long as we're just talking, he can't get us for anything. Anyway, no matter what we were doing, he couldn't do much about it."

She laughed. Her cackle sounded like Margaret Hamilton, the Wicked Witch of the West, planning to put a monkey on Dorothy's back.

"Why not?"

"Because I got two brothers protecting me. They hate my guts, but they don't want any scandal. They make sure the fuzz don't bother me except for a little harassment. One brother's a big shot businessman. He's got a lot of political pull, and he'd keep his ads out of the newspaper if it printed a word about me. The other brother, hold on to your whiskers, Tarzan, he's a priest."

George resisted the impulse to turn around and look. To hell with the cop. He wasn't going to give him any satisfaction.

"You called him Simon Pure?" George said. "That his name?"

"Simon Parr, a young cop of African persuasion. We call him Simon Pure because he isn't on the take. He's really pissed off because I'm protected."

Shoes rang hard on the pavement. George determinedly kept his back turned. The shoe steps stopped, and the cop, who had gone a step past George, shone the beam into George's eyes. George said, "Do you want to blind me?"

When the beam swung to center on Sally, George could see the man's silhouette. He was about six feet and three inches tall and broad-shouldered. He would have made a great Waziri warrior, a faithful follower of Tarzan, George thought.

"You want us go in kill them motherfuckers, Bwana?"

"No, Mzula, there's not more than a dozen shitpants Arab slave dealers there. I'll take care of them myself."

"Anything you say, Lord of the Jungle."

A deep rich voice—Paul Robeson's *The Emperor Jones* 1933, *Sanders of the River* 1935—said, "Well, Mrs. Elizabeth Barrett Browning, on the loose again?"

"There's nothing worse than an uppity educated black," Sally said. "Why don't you get going, Simon Pure Legree, and leave us poor white trash alone?"

"May I see your driver's license, please?" Parr said to George.

Having been through this many times, George did not have to be told to remove the license from his wallet and give it to the cop. Parr looked at it in the beam and handed it back.

"Come all the way from Florida to enjoy the cool climate?"

He had not gone back to the squad car to run a check on the license plates. No one in his right mind would steal a van that stood out like a pickpocket in a nudist camp. Besides, he was so accustomed to Sally and her customers that he had probably gotten lax about proper procedure.

"You better turn off your light, Mrs. Browning," Parr said. "It'll run the battery down."

"Hell, I forgot!" Sally said, but she did not follow his suggestion. Too stubborn, George thought. She had to defy him even if what he said made good sense.

Parr said, "O.K., Mr. Harrier. You and that leviathan in the van move on. Don't come back here. I'll be around, watching for you."

"We were just leaving, officer," George said.

"He hasn't got any right to shove you around," Sally said. "You stay here. We can talk anywhere we want to."

Joe stuck his head out of the window. "Come on, George. I gotta piss something awful."

As George walked to the van, Parr said, "Don't let me catch you pissing in public. Do it in a public convenience or in the privacy of your stately mansion."

Jeeze, he reads *Batman*, George thought. No, probably saw it on TV.

George got into the van and started the motor and turned on the headlights, but he waited for the squad car to move away from the entrance. Joe said, "I'm gonna piss in my pants."

"Nobody could smell the difference."

The cops were parked by the corner, waiting to make sure that the Harriers were leaving. George waved at them as he passed them. He drove straight down to the river—thank God, the cops were not following them—and parked in a lot where trees gave good cover. Cursing, Joe got down from the van and, hanging on to the door handle, relieved himself. George got rid of his load, too. When Joe had heaved himself back in and got his tun-shaped body settled, he said, "I don't know, George. Life just ain't worthwhile since I committed suicide."

"Aha, you son of a bitch!" George said. "So you *did* try to kill yourself!"

"Just a manner of speaking," Joe muttered. "I been in and out of the VA hospital since then, everybody acts like they're scared of me, they think I'm psycho, when I'm home with Mom she nags and whines me to death, my stumps hurt unless I can get soused and I got to wait until you come home before I can get a drop of booze, I have nightmares so bad I wet the bed. Maybe I ought to kill myself."

"Don't forget which end is which if you do. Remember, your brains are in your head. At least, I think they are."

George started laughing and kept on until he choked. Joe said, "You think it's funny? I can't get sympathy from my own brother. You're hard-hearted, George, you got a lump of ice for a heart."

"No," George said, wiping his eyes with the back of his hand. "I was just thinking how you could try to kill yourself. That boomerang you used to use in your act and carry it in your belt under your shirt for protection. You still carrying it?"

Joe nodded. "So what?"

"Well, I was thinking you could commit suicide with that. That'd be absolutely unique. You'd go down in history as the only man ever killed himself with a boomerang. And you'd have plenty of time to change your mind while it was curving back at you. You could always duck. You can't duck with a pistol held to your head."

"*That's* what's so funny? You're made out of stone, George, stone."

"No, it's just that I got to keep laughing. Laugh, clown, laugh. If I was pissing and moaning all the time like you do, you'd get even more depressed. I got to keep your spirits up."

They were silent for a while. Then Joe said, "When're we going back to Sally?"

"Not right now. The cops'll be coming back to check on her."

"You believe that story about her brothers?"

"Well, ordinarily I wouldn't. I don't know about the young

whores, but you remember how they used to be. They always came from wealthy families with stately mansions, and they went to schools like Vassar, Wellesley, Stephens, so on. If you believed their stories, those schools graduated more whores *Magna, come louder* than the U. of I. does Ph.D.s. They always fell among evil companions or were abducted by white slavers, and then they were forced to become prostitutes. I'd think Sally was lying except she talks like she was educated and that black cop was afraid to run her in. What's the difference? They all got stories to keep them warm and well lit."

George was driving up Main then. Going past the Madison Theater again reminded him of how shattered he had been when his father had told him that his mother had run away. He had left the house so that his father would not see him crying, and, after wandering around downtown for a while, had bought a ticket for the movie showing at the Madison. The dimly lighted high-ceilinged cathedral of the flicks had made him feel vaguely as if he were in church. (How would he know? He had never been in one except when he got married the first time.) But there he had seen *Tarzan and the Golden Lion* with James Pierce and Dorothy Dunbar. His mother's leaving had been one light going; the movie, his first Tarzan movie, had been another light moving into the darkness and emptiness.

Tarzan, he liked to tell his friends now, had become in that magic house and in that golden hour his mother substitute, ho, ho, ho. Tarzan was strong and clean and always victorious, and he never deserted those he loved. And Tarzan had also lost his mothers, the natural and the adopted, when he was young.

George turned left onto the street leading to the Acme Plumbing Service. Joe popped open the last can of beer, drank, belched, and said, "You catch that?"

"What?"

"Sally and Simon Pure was snarling at each other. But I think underneath it all they kind of like each other."

"Yeah, I caught that. You aren't such a dummy after all, Joe. I don't care what everybody says about you, I think you're alright."

"Jesus! Even when you compliment me, you gotta spoil it with insults."

"I calls 'em as I sees 'em."

"The great referee of life," Joe said. "Only nobody's paying you off under the table."

"Life's the payment, Joe. That's all I need."

He passed the lightning-bug just before he came to the alley entrance. It was describing big circles over the street. Maybe its insect mind thought that curved lines were straight. Maybe they were.

Just before entering the alley, George swung the van to the left so that its headlights would sweep over the building in which the pimp had been. He was back, standing in the front of the open ruin with a walkie-talkie to his ear.

Laughing delightedly, George turned the van into the alley. "You see that? I can't believe it. He's got the big black floppy-brimmed hat and a big schnozzola just like The Shadow's. He must think he's the Lamont Cranston of the pimps."

"It's made your day, hasn't it?" Joe said.

"Yeah, only I wonder why he didn't use the walkie-talkie when the cops came. Maybe he didn't see them because he was taking a piss or shooting horse."

George stopped the van a few feet in front of Sally and turned off the headlights. Her light was still flashing. He got out of the van and said, "O.K. I'll get her in the back, and then I'll go to the street and help the pimp watch so cops don't catch you *in flagrant delicious*."

"I sure hope they don't show. I got a hard on like King Kong's."

George laughed and said, "Sally isn't any Fay Wray. If she was, I'd take her on myself."

He opened the back doors of the van and went around it to Sally. She was putting her walkie-talkie into a large box attached to the right side of the chair. She closed its lid and said, "Here's Tweedledee and Tweedledum again. I thought Simon Pure scared you off for good."

"No, it isn't those two little fat boys," George said. "It's the March Hare and the Mad Hatter come to visit the Queen of Tarts."

"Thanks. You didn't say The Ugly Duchess. First, some coin of the realm."

George got his wallet out, and, standing close to the flashing light, counted three tens. She took them and turned the flashlight on them to check. She folded the bills and dropped them in the slot of a small box attached to the left side of the chair.

George looked behind him. Joe, a Moby Dick silhouette, was trying to force his way between the two swinging chairs in the front of the van. George turned back to Sally just as she opened the lid of the big box again. He went to it and saw that it held a plastic half-gallon bottle of water, a bar of soap on a dish, a roll of paper towels, a jar of Vaseline, a spray perfume bottle, a douche bulb, a case for glasses, and several Silhouette romances.

"There isn't enough water," George said. "He needs to be hosed off first."

"If he's that ripe, you can have your money back. I'm a real pro, but I don't have to take just anything that comes along."

"You can wash the part that matters," George said. "Only . . . don't back out now. He's really horny, and if you back out, he'll go ape. I'm not kidding. I know my brother."

"My man'll take care of him if he makes trouble. He's mean as the devil himself. You tell your brother that."

Sally took the walkie-talkie from the box and spoke softly into it. George went to the van and looked through the open door at the struggling and cursing mass within.

"What's the matter now?"

Panting, Joe said, "I'm stuck!"

"Why don't you just back out? The chairs'll swing free then."

"Damn it, I'm in too deep. They won't go forward, and they won't go backward!"

George laughed and said, "I'm paying for this and getting nothing out of it, and I got to do all the work, too? You want me to screw her for you?"

Joe screamed, "Get up here, and help me, or so help me God, I'll kill you!"

George hesitated, and Joe began bellowing and striking the tops of the chairs. That told George what was coming for sure. He went back to Sally.

"Listen, there's no telling what he's going to do now. You better get going while the going's good."

"How'd I ever get involved with you two clowns?" Sally said. She had picked up the walkie-talkie, but she did not need it. Pulled by Joe's cries, the pimp came running down the alley. Huffing and puffing, he leaned on the van and said, "What's going on, honey?" His voice was thin and high, not at all what you'd expect from The Shadow. He glared at George. "They giving you any trouble?"

Sally started the motor, and, as the chair moved past George, said, "Let's get out of here before someone calls the cops. I'll explain on the way."

"Hey, you got my money!" George said. "I want it back!"

While the chair was still moving, Sally reached into a pocket on her skirt and pulled out a key. By the time that she had unlocked the small box, she was ten feet past the van. George ran after her, past the bellowing Joe, and he shouted, "The money! The money!"

Perhaps the pimp misunderstood and thought that George wanted all the money, or perhaps he suddenly decided not to give any back. Whatever his reason, he pulled a knife, silvery-black in the flashing red light, which Sally had forgotten to turn off. George should have stopped and explained—he told himself later—but something took over, and he kept running. He did a forward flip, his spine crackling, and his feet struck the pimp in the chest. The man fell heavily to the concrete, the knife flying from his hand. Joe hit the concrete on his back, and his breath was knocked out of him.

By the time George had recovered enough to get up, the pimp had also gotten his wind back and was on his feet. The knife lay equidistant between them, but more than his breath had been kicked out of the man. He fled after Sally, who was just turning to the left onto the street. A siren started whooping somewhere far off in the direction Sally was taking. The pimp took off to the right and disappeared.

George could see people at the windows and on the front porches of the houses down the street to his right. Someone had called the police, that was for sure.

George ran to the van and got into it. With much panting and pushing, he wedged himself between Joe and the dashboard. That was a dumb move. He had no room to pull Joe backwards, and he had to struggle to get loose. Finally, he squeezed himself out, climbed over the back of the chair, and got in front of Joe. His brother was still yelling and pounding the chair tops. When George put his hands against his brother's chest to shove him, he was knocked reeling back by Joe's fists. George said, "Don't hit me again, or I'll leave you here, you hear?"

Joe did not seem to hear him. George breathed in deeply, roared like Tarzan charging a kill-crazy gorilla, and, bending forward, ran at Joe with his arms held stiffly out from him. His hands struck Joe on the chest, and Joe fell backwards, hit the dashboard with his shoulders, and fell sidewise on the chair to the right. Grunting, he pulled himself up onto the chair, twisted, and started to get out of the van. George went out through the rear and came around the side. Joe, hanging onto the open door, looked wild in the half-light.

"It's only thirty dollars," George said. "We'll lose more than that if the cops come. We got to haul ass."

"Thirty dollars!" Joe said. "You mean . . . she's still got the money?"

"It doesn't matter. Let's get out of here!"

"I'll kill her," Joe said, but he turned around to get back into the van. George trotted around it and started to climb in but stopped. Joe was not in sight. And a scream that would have made Tarzan himself look for cover came down the alley.

"Oh, no!" George said, and he ran to the back of the van. By then, Joe was moving his wooden legs at a rate of speed he could never have managed if he had been in his right mind. George groaned and ran after his brother, but his left ankle bent as he stepped on something, and he fell to the concrete. He started to get up but, moaning, sat down. His ankle felt as if fire ants were attacking it. The culprit, the knife, was beside him. Its broad hilt guard had caused his foot to turn and twisted his ankle.

He rose and, wincing, hopped on one leg. When he got to the van, he grabbed the wheel and pulled himself inside. After starting the motor, he turned on the headlights and backed the vehicle out of the alley quickly. His ankle hurt even worse when he pressed down on the brake.

He saw in the headlight beams three bills on the concrete. Sally had thrown them down on her way to safety.

When George straightened the van out and started it forward, he could see Joe trotting—his stumps must be hurting with every step—and he could see, half a block ahead of Joe, the chair, the back of Sally's head, and the flashing red light. She was headed down the gently sloping street for the next intersection. Joe would stumble or run out of breath soon. In any event, George intended to overtake him and tell him that Sally had not kept the money. If that did not work, he would brush Joe lightly with the van and knock him over or stick his arm out of the window and shove him.

No, he would not have to do that. Joe had stopped. But what was he doing? Teetering, Joe was reaching behind him and under the tail of his shirt. George groaned again and stepped on the accelerator. Joe had braced himself, had thrown the object, and now was falling on the street. George stopped the van beside him and looked through the windshield. Twinkle, twinkle in the bright streetlights, the boomerang was a tiny star in orbit, a silver-colored bat, a deformed tea tray, a whirling UFO.

"Oh, no!" George said. "Oh, no!"

He knew that the weapon would end its curving path with the wheelchair.

Enter, a siren whooping, a black-and-white from the left. It was going fast and headed for Sally.

George could not hear the glass breaking, but he saw the red light disappear.

Even without the siren, the screeching tires as the car maneuvered to avoid hitting the chair would have drowned out any other noises. As the car skidded to a stop, its swinging rear end blocked George's view of the wheelchair, but he saw Sally flying out from behind it, her skirt flapping like the cloak of the Phantom of the Opera as he leaped into the sewer to escape the vengeful mob.

While George was watching the cops get out of the car and put Sally back into the apparently undamaged chair, he heard Joe yelling at him to get out and get him back on his feet. George explained why he could not do so. Joe crawled to the van and pulled himself up on the hood. Breathing as if there were not enough air left in the world for him, he walked around the van. He got in and, panting, said, "Did you see that? I couldn't do it again if I tried a hundred times."

"Yeah, I saw it," George said. "You O.K. now, Joe?"

"Yeah, sure. I'm over it. The money, though . . ."

While George drove down to the intersection to park by the curb, he told Joe that the money was in the alley and that they would go after it later. Just now, he wanted to make sure that Sally was all right.

The white cop was in the street directing cars with curious passengers through the intersection. Sally seemed to be unhurt except for some scratches and smudges on one side of her face. The black cop was writing on a form while he talked to Sally. George, knowing he might get into trouble if either of the two noticed him but helpless to fight his curiosity, drove across the street and parked near them.

"Simon says! Simon says!" Sally jeered.

"Yeah, that's right. Simon says. Simon says that at last, by God, you're going into court. I told you I'd get you some day. You were not in the crosswalk, and you ran a red light."

"The ticket'll be fixed."

"No it won't. I'll raise a stink God Himself couldn't put a lid on. If I have to go to your brothers myself, I'll see to it you get off the streets. Sally, you're *retired*!"

The boomerang was under the car, a tip sticking out. George decided to leave before the cops found it and started asking questions. A few minutes later, he drove the van into the alley. The knife and the money were gone; someone had been there first.

George laughed and said, "Well, that's one on me."

"Ain't you going to look for another woman?" Joe said.

"You kidding? We've used up all of tonight's luck, such as it is. Besides, Mom wants us home by eleven."

He laughed, then said, "Only one thing's bothering me. How in hell does Sally do it in a wheelchair?"

Joe said, loudly, "Gotcha, you little son of a bitch!"

George was startled by Joe's sudden violent movement and his cry. He looked at Joe and said, "What the hell's the matter now?"

Joe held up his hand to show George the firefly gripped gently between his thumb and forefinger.

"He came at me through the window like I wasn't here. I'll teach him."

Joe was looking at the firefly, not as if he was appraising a diamond but as if it was something he had picked from his nose. The insect did not seem to know that it was in danger; it kept flashing its dashes, Mayday, Mayday.

"Look at you," Joe said. "Happy, happy, happy. You just think so, bug. You just think you're going to get some glow-worm ass. Well, you ain't. I don't, you don't. This is it, Mr. Bug."

George grabbed Joe's wrist.

"No!"

Joe reared back and stared at George.

"No? Why should he get it if I don't?"

"Listen, Joe. Don't ever put anybody's light out."

THE FIRST ROBOT
JEANNETTE RASTIGNAC
(PHILIP JOSÉ FARMER)

In this short but poignant tale, Phil engages in what he is perhaps best known for: expanding the often all-too-narrow horizons of genre writing, in this instance in the field of prehistoric fantasy. Like Jack London's *Before Adam* and H. Rider Haggard's *Allan and the Ice-Gods*, "The First Robot" uses the backdrop of a primitive past to narrate social commentary; but instead of London's stark portrayal of Darwinian ethics, or Haggard's parable of the dangers facing great reformers, Phil's story imagines the origin of one of humankind's most prevalent and yet darkly hidden societal maladies.

It is certainly a high literary crime that "The First Robot" did not see print after it was first written, presumably in the first half of the 1950s. If it had been published then, the story very probably would have been highly anthologized, and might have reached the same critical acclaim as Phil's "Sail On! Sail On!", which contributed to the winning of his first Hugo Award. As it is, "The First Robot" does have a direct connection to one of Phil's quintessential classics, namely "The Lovers." Curiously, the penname on the original manuscript of "The First Robot" is "Jeannette Rastignac," the same name as that of the alien woman from the planet Ozagen in Phil's groundbreaking debut science fiction novella. We think those familiar with "The Lovers" will quickly see why Phil chose to write the story under Jeannette's name.

Trarg was beating the woman again, and her screams rolled the tribe from its sleeping-bags. Ansha, crouching by a fire, said, "It is bad for Trarg to strike her. What if he cripples their unborn child?"

Ganag said, "Trarg would never hurt her so much she couldn't work for him."

Ansha replied, "Why beat her? She works hard; she bears healthy children. What more does he want?"

Ganag stammered, "She . . . she lives in the cave with Trarg. Nobody else can live there unless he says so. He allows her to live there and gives her protection and food. She is . . . is . . ."

His hands waved, his fingers clutching as if he were kneading the air into new but known shapes. Almost, the word for property was born.

"She does all a good mate should do," Ansha answered. "Does she beat him?"

Ganag laughed. "Her? She is too small."

"Lusha is small, but she beats her mate."

"That is because he's a lazy hunter, and they often go hungry."

"He could beat Lusha in return."

"He knows he deserves her blows."

"But Trarg's woman deserves a caress, not a club." Ganag shrugged. "I don't understand."

"Neither do I, but I don't like it. What if all the men, well . . ."

They quit talking. Trarg had appeared in the narrow opening of his cave. He was a man who commanded silence, for he was tall and lean and had a thin nose curved like a sabertooth's claw and green eyes in which calculation burned coldly.

Without pausing for greetings, he walked into the forest, his flint-tipped spear in hand. He had a long day ahead; a man had to use all his strength and wit to bring in enough to fill today's mouths and store a little for tomorrow's. When winter came, the smoked strips of meat hanging from the cave-roof would be very much appreciated.

Trarg roamed until noon, empty-handed. Then he heard a low rumble which erected the hairs on the back of his neck—lightning rods spurting the lightning of fear. Nevertheless, he walked softly toward the noise. Meat wasn't caught by running away from it.

The scene he came upon thrilled his hunter's heart. A bear had stuck his head into a hole in a hollow tree and could not get it out. Trarg wondered why the shaggy eccentric hadn't scooped out the honey with his paw, but he didn't stop to do his thinking. Swiftly, he severed its spine with a spearthrust, then skinned it and hacked off a leg and cut out the heart, liver, and kidneys. While doing this, he paused. Why not watch this tree and catch other honey-stealers unawares? But a moment's reflection convinced him that nobody could be spared just to stand around and watch. And even if a child were posted, he'd need a man to guard him from the big cats and bears.

He resumed cutting. A minute later, he stopped again. Out of the clouds roiling in his brain had appeared a bright and solid picture. He'd once seen a pony run into a liana thicket and strangle itself to death. Now, if you were to fashion a noose . . . thus . . . and set it on a game path so an animal's head entered the hidden ring, as the bear's had the hole in the tree, and if that noose could be set so that no matter how the creature struggled, the liana didn't come loose but tightened more and more . . .

On the way home, his green eyes swam, hot and moist as the drippings from the fat meat he envisioned. Not just one trap could be built. Many. Many. And they'd all be working for him like the woman in his cave while he was out hunting.

Head thrown back, chest swelling, he walked back to the cliff-side, dumped the load of meat wrapped in the bearskin on the floor, and told his woman to get to work. Busy washing her baby, she did not do at once what he ordered. He struck her. She snarled at him, and he hit her again.

Silently, she covered the baby with a fur and began working. He helped her. His hands did their required duties, but his mind was only partly connected with them.

A big rock or a heavy log could crush a bear or a lion. What if you balanced a boulder so delicately that just touching a small stick connected to its base would cause it to fall. The beast would bite down on meat tied to the stick; the rock would fall . . .

"Trarg!" said the woman.

"Shut up! I'm thinking!"

"But—"

He slapped her across the mouth, and she froze with terror, her lips bleeding.

"You must learn not to interrupt me," he said. "You're a woman; you're weaker; your place is obedience. I am the man, the planner, the strong. I will feed and protect you and our children, and you must do everything I say. Understand?"

"I'll go back to my parents," she muttered.

"They can not help you!" he blazed. "They are old and feeble!" And he struck her on the jaw but not hard enough to injure the child in her womb. She held her face and moaned, her eyes dull. Then, slowly, her shoulders sagging as if they'd never lift again, she picked up one end of the bearhide. Thereafter, she never spoke to him except to reply to direct questions. And when they lay down to sleep that night, she was a tongueless statue, her back turned, allowing him to talk without interruption.

He felt vaguely dissatisfied, but he didn't long think about it. He planned just how he'd build this thing that would work for him while he was not there to watch it. His heart beat faster at the vision; it did to him what his woman could not.

Next morning, he told her he'd be gone most of the day, and he gave her detailed instructions about the work she was to do. Though it was enough to keep two women running all day, she did not argue.

A little later, Trarg talked to Lusha's mate, the lazy one. That man then told Lusha he'd have no more of her backtalk and beatings. Afterwards, though he had to work himself into a screaming fury before he could do so, he struck her with his fists until she could not stand up.

Trarg grinned at her outcries and at the uneasy look in the women's eyes. They, like him, could see the beginnings of a new age. Then he strode into the forest and picked a spot on a game-path for his noose-trap. When dusk came, he was finished. Proud with what his male hand and brain had done, he picked up axe and knife and left the world's second robot behind him.

At home, inside the cave, moving efficiently but mechanically, operating upon preset instructions, devoid of the spark of love and hope, was the first.

Duo Miaule
Philip José Farmer

From January through October 1954, the magazine *Fantastic Universe Science Fiction* published four Philip José Farmer stories, "They Twinkled Like Jewels," "Rastignac the Devil," "The Celestial Blueprint," and "The Wounded," as well as the essay "White Whales, Raintrees, Flying Saucers . . ." A letter to Phil from *Fantastic Universe* publisher Leo Margulies, dated March 3, 1954, does not mention a backlog of Farmer tales as a reason for his rejection of "Duo Miaule," although certainly such a surfeit may have been a factor, especially considering the enjoyable tale that follows.

In the course of his distinguished career, Phil has written science fiction, fantasy, supernatural thrillers, and private eye mysteries. "Duo Miaule" combines all of these genres in an entertaining, humorous, and tantalizing mix. Like Phil's fictional-author mystery "The Volcano," the present story blurs the line between science fiction and fantasy. Are the transmutations witnessed and experienced by the story's characters the result of a science so advanced it appears like magic? Or instead, are such claims of magic a sham? The protagonist plainly states that he believes in magic, but as the reader will soon discover, Dirk Cannon, much like Philip José Farmer, makes a living—in part—based on his abilities as a trickster.

D irk Cannon was a private eye and a good one, too. He had savoir-faire, gallantry, quick reflexes, and a keen wit. He was straightforward and highly moral, though not inflexibly so. What was more to the point, he was broke.

So, upon this bright and early February morning that paved with sun and frost a large west coast city, he entered his office. His thoughts were not upon wine, women, and song, as any respectable private eye's should have been, nor was he meditating upon his preprandial devotions, as all men should. No, he pondered upon unpaid bills and creditors, and the queer state of affairs in which his fame was noised abroad but he yet had no rich clients.

Thus pensive, he stopped in his outer office to speak to Telva, his secretary.

"Any calls?"

Telva's voice was smooth as cheese but monotoned. She showed no signs of having stayed up all night.

"At seven-thirty this morning I received a call from an anonymous cat."

He considered this while he lit a cigarette.

"Yeah? What did it say?"

"It said for you to lay off the Cathcart case."

"Hmm. That's surprising. I'm not even remotely connected with the case. I'd like to be, though."

His mental fingers itched for the reward, forty thousand dollars stacked high and green and crisp, prettier than lettuce and good enough to eat.

He ordered Telva to run off the recording of the call, then went into the inner office to watch it. The screen on his desk showed a mangy grey tom cat squatting upon the table before the viser of a public booth. Beyond the glass window of the door was the interior of a drugstore. None of the customers were paying any attention to the cat. This was understandable, for they were Californians.

The tom talked intelligibly enough, though he had difficulty with some of the consonants. Being a cat, he could handle the vowels easily enough. A good thing it wasn't a dog, thought Dirk. As he understood it, the psychologists who had trained canines to talk had reported that they slurred their vowels.

Dirk winced while he listened to the recording. Such language! The tom snarled in the roughest backalley phraseology, threatening immediate disembowelment of Dirk and other picturesque methods of execution if he did not stay away from the Cathcarts.

When the screen had flickered off, Dirk sat behind his desk and blew smoke rings. Whoever was in the cat's body must have had advance information on what was going to take place. He might have consulted a seer about Dirk's future moves, but Dirk doubted that. Undoubtedly, the fellow knew somebody close to the Cathcarts and knew that they planned on calling Dirk into the case.

And for reasons of his own, the cat didn't want Dirk Cannon to stick his short Irish nose into the affair.

The phone's buzz cut into his thoughts. Telva said, "Another call. An anonymous lady."

Dirk switched on his desk-screen. It showed the head and shoulders of a beautiful redhead with a triangular face and slanting rusty-brown eyes. Her distraught expression meant that she was in trouble and needed his help. Dirk's heart leaped with joy. He favored beautiful and smartly groomed female clients, but he loved those with money.

"Mr. Cannon," she said in a low voice that would have been sultry if there had not been a slight quaver in it, "I've checked on you, and I know I can trust you. So I'll tell you everything."

"That won't be necessary," he replied. "For instance, you won't have to tell me who you are, Mrs. Cathcart."

The slanting eyes widened.

"How did you know who I was?" she gasped.

"It wasn't a little bird that told me," he replied in the manner of the traditional wisecracking private eye.

Somewhat recovered, she waved disdainfully at him. "Oh, you detectives are all alike, all playing Sherlock Holmes. You're not so mysterious. You saw my picture in the papers."

He was content for her to think that. "The Cathcart diamond-a-day case has been rather publicized."

Mrs. Cathcart didn't seem displeased. "Oh, yes, everybody knows about us. However, it's not true that we've been missing my jewelry at the rate of one article a day. We've only had four robberies in the past three weeks. So far we've caught nobody in the act, despite a constant guard over the house. Anyway, you know all that, if you've been reading the papers.

"I may as well tell you, Mr. Cannon, that I'm not speaking from my home. I'm in a public booth downtown, and I had to sneak away from my bodyguard in order to make this call."

"Why?"

"Because Georgieboy—that's my husband—is a jealous old man who keeps a constant watch on me. Everywhere I go, and at home, too, his thugs shadow me and inform Georgieboy about what I do. I think I got away from them today, and I came downtown so I could ask you if you'll please help me. The police have failed, you know."

"Mrs. Cathcart, if they can't crack it, there's little chance I could. Their resources are very much greater than mine. However, why should you feel compelled to be so secret about the matter?"

Though his face was expressionless, his heart was hammering. He was tired of the dullness of routine cases, and this sounded exciting. Moreover, breathed there a man with soul so dead he didn't think he had more brains than the entire police force?

"Well," said Mrs. Cathcart, pursing up her lips in a manner meant to look thoughtful but failing to be anything but very sensual, "it's this way. Georgieboy spends a lot of money on me. But he won't allow me to carry any around, and he won't give me a checking account. He keeps a very tight fist on the purse strings. When I suggested calling you in, he blew up and said it'd be a waste of money. Of course, Dirk—may I call you Dirk?—I reminded him of what a wonderful reputation you had. Everybody has heard of your Case of the Unlocked Room. They say your methods are unorthodox and work like magic."

He chuckled. "You *could* say that. And thanks for the compliments. Now, if I understand you correctly, you wish me to take the case without Georgieboy's—I mean your husband's—consent?"

She glanced through the window behind her, presumably to look for her shadows, then faced him again. "Yes, that's right."

"Mrs. Cathcart, I'm a practical man. How would you pay me?"

Dirk Cannon, gallant soul that he was, felt the bite of shame that he should have to ask such a beautiful dame, obviously in distress, such an unchivalrous question. But there was rent and the grocery bill, and there was Telva, too. Unless he got some money soon, he'd have to let her go.

Mrs. Cathcart said, "My husband has offered forty thousand dollars for the return of the jewels. I think that is worth taking a gamble for."

She looked at him appealingly with her slanting rusty-brown eyes and her full, slightly pouting red lips. Inwardly, he groaned. Did she think the days of knighthood were yet in full flower, or did she take him for a sucker, or was there any difference between the two concepts?

"Look, Mrs. Cathcart . . ." he began.

"You may call me Fleena," she interrupted. "All my friends do, and I'd like very much to have you as my friend."

"Sorry, Mrs. Cathcart, but this must be strictly business." To his surprise, her eyes filled with tears, and she choked back a sob. "But I need your help desperately!" she wailed. "And what's wrong with calling me Fleena?"

"Nothing, nothing," he replied hastily. "There, there, don't cry—uh—Fleena. Damn it, I can't stand a woman's tears. And you must know it," he accused, "else you'd not be using them so quickly."

She stared innocently. "That's not true. I *really* feel bad!"

"O.K., O.K. Now, I'm going to tell you just why *I* think you've come to me despite your husband's wishes."

His green eyes narrowed, and his lips pursed as he searched through his memory for what he had heard of her.

"You're an ex-stripteaser, a nationally famous one. You used to do a dance wearing nothing but some trained cats. You met old man Cathcart at a party, and he fell in love with you. You married him about a year ago and gave up your profession. And why not? Your husband is seventy-five years old and worth millions—even after income taxes are taken out. He's a reputation for being tighter than a banjo string and suspicious as the devil himself. The information you gave me rounds out the picture a little. He'll spend money directly on you, but he won't allow you to go out and blow it yourself.

"Now, didn't the police question you on that? Weren't they suspicious that you might have sold the jewels yourself to get some pocket money? *Some* pocket money, too! About one million dollars' worth, wasn't it?"

"Yes, they were nasty about that," she replied with dignity. "But why should I do such a thing when he'll authorize anything I want to buy, even if I never see the money myself? Besides, his two thugs vouched for the fact that I'd done no such a thing. I couldn't," she added bitterly, "not when they were watching me so closely."

"I'll be frank with you," Dirk said. "I know Nick Sukavitch used to be your boy friend. He couldn't be blackmailing you, could he? And you've paid him off with your jewels?"

She paled, but he didn't know whether it was because he'd hit the truth or because she resented the accusation.

"Mr. Cannon, Nick was my lover, long ago. But I've not seen his face since the day I married Georgieboy. And I haven't smuggled out any jewels to him. I swear it."

"Then you're on the level?"

"Yes, very much so. And I'm desperate, because my husband thinks the same as you do about Nick, and I have to convince him I haven't paid Nick any blackmail."

He thought, If you don't, you lose all those millions.

Out loud, he said, "Well, Fleena, I'll think about it. It's a long gamble. I'll call your home later on."

"But a home call will be tapped."

He shrugged. "So? What objection can your husband have if he's not paying me? To him, I'll be just another reward-seeker."

Her expression became even more desperate. "You don't understand. The thief shouldn't know you're working on the case. He must be someone living in the house or someone intimately connected with us inmates—I mean, tenants. If he doesn't know you're on the case, he might give himself away."

He hesitated a moment, then said, suddenly and firmly, "O.K., forget that, Fleena. I'll get in touch with you, somehow, and I'll find a way to look over your house. So long."

Before she could object, he flicked off the screen, then punched for Telva.

"Dial the Bureau for information on the Cathcart Jewel Case."

"Yes, sir. But your credit is low there."

He sighed. "I know it, but try it anyway."

A minute later, his phone rang. He knew Telva was still talking to the Bureau, but she was a wonderful secretary. She could handle several calls at a time.

"Mr. Cathcart wishes to speak to you."

Dirk's eyebrows rose. So, the old boy had not only shadowed his everloving wife to the public booth, he had tapped the call. Though difficult to do, enough money could do it, and Mr. Cathcart had more than enough.

A bald head shaped like a radish appeared upon the screen.

It had two tufted eyebrows, deepsunken eyes with purple bags beneath their hollows, a nose like a question mark, and a chin that looked sharp enough to cut hard wood. His voice exploded in the office, jumped with energy, and spoke as one with authority.

"Mr. Cannon, I am not sure what my wife is up to, but it does not matter. I would like very much to hire you. Two hundred a day plus expenses. What about it?"

Dirk blinked and replied slowly, "I like your terms. But what do you want me to do?"

"I want you not only to investigate the robbery. I want you to report if my wife is unfaithful to me."

Dirk looked the old man in the eye. Usually, when a husband requested this type of work, he was unable to meet Dirk's gaze, almost as if he shared his wife's suspected guilt or as if he felt ashamed to come to another man to do his dirty work for him. There was none of this in Cathcart's craggy face. He glared fiercely at Cannon.

Reluctantly, seeing the two hundred plus slipping off into the horizon of things-too-good-to-be-true, Cannon said, "Sorry, no can do. I never touch that adultery stuff. Some of the grime always comes off on the shamus."

He thought again of the two hundred plus. Tears almost came into his eyes.

Cathcart sneered, "Perhaps your heart is pure, Mr. Cannon. I won't argue with you about that. But what if you come across evidence of her infidelity while you're investigating the jewels? Would you turn over that knowledge to another detective working for me?"

"No," Cannon replied, wincing at the vision of the greenbacks winging away into the wild blue yonder, "I keep my hands strictly clean. I'll have nothing to do with divorce proceedings."

The old man's voice was grim. "Who said anything about a divorce?"

Dirk was taken aback. Was the old guy figuring on dealing with her as the sultans of Baghdad did with their unfaithful harem women? Or was he just planning on cutting off all her money and keeping her locked up in his mansion while she endured her imprisonment in the hope he'd fall over dead and she'd inherit his fortune? Whatever Cathcart intended, Cannon was intrigued. He scented violence, dark and evil plottings, mystery, romance, and, of course, cash.

"O.K.," he said, "if we go on the understanding that I handle only the jewels, I'll take the case."

"Very well," snapped the millionaire. "You're hired. I'll expect a day by day progress report, an itemized account of expenses, and no fooling around with my wife."

Cannon stared coldly at him. "You overheard our conversation; you know I told her it was strictly business with me. Aside from that, if I solve this, I still get the forty thousand reward, don't I?"

"Naturally," barked Cathcart, and he punched the button that ended their conversation. Cannon was angered, for he had wanted to ask the old man if he knew a grey tom cat. However, there was no doubt that Cathcart was an eccentric and that getting along with him was going to be difficult. Cannon shrugged and decided he'd do just as he wanted to and tackle the problems as they came up.

He punched for his secretary. "Telva, do you have all the info?"

"Sure, boss. I'll just give you the stuff you don't already know. Fleena Cathcart loves jewels and cats. She keeps twenty pedigreed felines in her luxurious suite in Cathcart Mansion. The house is guarded so well a mouse couldn't slip through, let alone a jewel thief. The old man is very occupied with his business; he doesn't see much of her. Occasionally he takes her out to the opera or to a cat-show, but never to a night club. Her ex-lover, Sukavitch, was down on his luck for a long time, but in the last month he's suddenly prosperous again and dickering to buy a gambling-house."

"Well, well," breathed Dirk. "Let me see. Sukavitch might have been waiting for the old man to die so he could marry Fleena. But he became impatient and wanted money right away. Fleena slipped him her jewels to fence. She did so willingly or because he knows something that would cause the old guy to get rid of her."

Dirk rose and put on his hat. On his way through the outer office, he patted Telva's behind. Telva did not squeal with delight or swing on him. She regarded him dispassionately. She was not tall and curved and blonde, nor did she lust after her boss' flesh. She was short and squat and square and brown, and her only desire was to be an efficient secretary. Not altogether the typical private eye's amanuensis, perhaps, but at least nobody would be trying to abduct her, and there was no chance of an office affair with her. IBM would have objected.

Just before dusk, Dirk Cannon was walking by a row of rundown houses on whose peeling and dirty-windowed exteriors were signs that told of those who plied their dubious trades within: astrologers, palmists, phrenologists, levitationists, yogis, prophets of doom, aura-photographers, mind-readers, metaphysicians, dowsers, cultists, anything you wanted. Dirk paused before a door which had no sign and looked around for the dozenth time to make sure he had no shadowers. Then he knocked. A minute later the door squeaked open, and from the dark hallway appeared a bald head with very bushy and grey sideburns.

"Hello, Dirk," said the Wizard of Booze. His breath struck

Cannon with all the force of the windward side of a brewery. His protruding and red-veined eyes blinked.

Dirk followed him into a large and moldy-smelling room.

He pulled a quart of Old Blowtop from his overcoat pocket.

"You get this for nothing if you tell me whether or not Nick Sukavitch or Fleena Cathcart have been your clients," Dirk said.

The Wizard of Booze drew himself up to a ragged facsimile of dignity and outraged pride.

"Puh-lease, Mr. Cannon!"

Dirk drew another quart from his pocket and set it down by the first. "This change your mind?"

The Wizard's mouth fell open and he licked his lips. But he shook his head.

"No? Well, here's a third bottle. You don't even have to tell me what I want to know. Just shake your head yes or no."

The Wizard's fingers curled, and he smacked his lips. Nevertheless, he replied, in a quavering voice, "Mr. Cannon, this is highly unethical. I'm surprised that you think you could tempt me or that you'd even try it. No, when I pledge secrecy, my lips are closed until death do them part. Besides, if I opened my big yap, I'd get knocked off, tootsweet."

"That sounds like Nick," said Cannon. "O.K., Wizard, no hard feelings then? Good. Keep the bottles, anyway. I want you to work on me."

Dirk told him what he wanted him to do.

"When you gonna give me credit for your successes?" grumbled the Wizard.

"If I do, I won't be able to use you," said Dirk. He lay down on a broken backed sofa. The Wizard stooped before a large square machine with many dials and flashing lights.

"Don't bother with that," said Cannon. "I know it's just a pseudo-scientific prop to impress your superstitious customers. Go ahead, give me the straight stuff. I'm Celtic as they come; I believe in magic."

The Wizard rubbed his hands and smiled a toothless smile.

"It's a pleasure, Dirk. You don't know how I hate to use that damned out-of-Frankenstein-by-H.G.-Wells gimmick. But in this machine age a successful practitioner has to pretend he's dealing with biomagnetic forces and cyclotrons and theta and mest and orgones before he can get his client to believe in him."

The Wizard picked up a piece of typewriter paper and handed it to Dirk. "You forgot to sign this."

Cannon had seen a paper like it before, but he never signed anything without reading it first. This repeated the statement that the Wizard's client would release the Wizard from any ill effects that the client might suffer while under the spell.

"You understand, don't you," said the old man, "that if your temporary body suffers any injury, your permanent one is liable to have corresponding stigmata? And that if you're killed, your soul might not be able to find its way back to this room? All I guarantee is that I'll make an effort at the end of twenty-four hours to summon you back."

Dirk nodded. He'd gone through this once before when he'd been a horse.

"Hmm," said the Wizard. "Let's see." He walked to his 33 ⅓ player and picked out a disc from the shelf beneath it. "This is Ravel's *The Child And The Sorcerers*," he explained. "There's a part in it which Ravel marked *duo miaule musicalement*, where a black tom cat is calling from a window to his lady love, who is in the backyard. Extraordinary thing! I'll play it to get your soul in the proper mood for the transition."

The needle came down, lightly, upon the exact spot desired. Meerow! Meerow! went the record. Sppt! Fttui!

"Isn't it wonderful?" said the Wizard. "You can't tell whether it's a violin or a human voice imitating two amorous cats." He tipped one of the quarts of Old Blowtop to his lips, gurgled, put it down, wiped his mouth, picked up a big black leather-bound book, and, peering shortsightedly at it and scattering a black powder around the room, began reciting, "Come forth, O soul, and soar through the night air and end thy fearful arc in the body and fleshly sheath of that which thou seekest for temporary and dangerous lodging. I conjure and invite you by Bast and by . . ."

Dirk slipped off with the Wizard's incantations and the meerow-spuffitt of Ravel's music ringing in his ears. There was a deep and dark abyss which he crossed, and then a light.

Like Jackie Robinson sliding into third base, he slid into a strange body. Instantly, the room around him exploded; there was a thunderous sound; light blazed into his eyes. He cowered and then arched his back and snarled. His soul rattled inside the new body, further confusing him.

Then, abruptly, he became aware that he was not in an enormous room but that he himself was small. And the thunder was merely the blare of a radio paining his unhumanly sensitive ears; and the light hurt him because he had not adjusted his pupils to it.

In short, he was inside one of Fleena Cathcart's cats, inside her suite.

It took another moment to fit into the grooves left by the dispossessed soul—or consciousness—of the body, and then he began casing the joint. In this case, it consisted at first of getting over the embarrassment of seeing Fleena parade around in the nude. He was a gentleman who did not like to take an unfair advantage of a lady, and while there was some doubt about her status as such, he still did not care for his position. Moreover, though he was as much a cat as it was possible for a male human to be, having his body's memories and conditioned reflexes and instincts, he had retained his human desires and lusts. And Fleena was undoubtedly built as one would wish a stripper to be built.

She must have noticed something strange in his behavior, for she walked to him, saying, "Ah, Sum Kid, is 'oo scared of som-fing? Poor 'ittle Siamese, don' be frightened."

"For chrissakes, cut out the baby talk!" he snarled at her, and then gasped as he realized that not only had he answered her in cat language but that she had questioned him in the same tongue. It had been pure reflex; his human responses had been translated into feline.

She pouted and said, "Ooh, naughty-waughty. Such bad talk. And to your Big Mother."

Before he could leap away, he was picked up and cuddled between the mounds of her magnificent breasts. He flushed and tried to squirm away, but she misinterpreted his protests as a display of affection and held him the more tightly. He didn't know what to do next, for he didn't want to spoil his chances of spying by clawing her and thus, perhaps, being imprisoned. Moreover, it would have hurt his aesthetic sense to have marred that perfect bust.

At that moment a huge red tabby slunk into the room and leaped upon her shoulder. "Take off, Buster!" it spat. "Or I'll rake you fore and aft!"

"Sez you," snarled Dirk, but Fleena had released him, and he jumped to the floor, glad of a chance to get away. Then he leaped upon the sofa and watched the woman and the tabby. She had carried the tom to her bed, where she sat down and talked to it in low tones. Anxious to hear them, Dirk bounded back onto the Oriental rug and sauntered carelessly by them. They both stopped their conversation to watch him.

"Beat it, Bub," said the tabby from its white nest. "Big Mother and I are having a tête-à-tête."

"Don't get jealous, Sum Kid," said Fleena, smiling at Dirk. "Mommy 'oves 'oo, but she has business with Machiavelli. By and by Mommy'll gi' 'oo a 'oving."

"Sfft 'oo!" hissed Dirk, which meant in feline just what it sounded like. Fleena's eyes widened, and she said, "Oh, 'oo naughty pussy. 'Oo hurt Mommy's feelings."

Machiavelli snarled, "Say, Fleena, if I didn't know this Siamese was just another cat, I'd be getting suspicious. You sure you ain't doublecrossing me, too, like you're doing to your old man?"

"Why, don't be silly," she cried, kissing Machiavelli on the mouth. "You're getting as jealous as Georgieboy."

She shrieked as the tabby dug its claws into her shoulder, and she threw him away from her so he soared out over the rug. He landed spitting beside Dirk.

"Don't compare me to that feeble old goat," he said. "Or I'll give you a real going over tonight that you'll never forget."

Dirk pricked up his ears. If there was a rendezvous tonight, he'd be there, too. He purred with satisfaction. This case was progressing even faster than he'd expected it to.

Fleena soothed the cat's feelings for a while, then rose and walked into another room. Machiavelli trailed her and Dirk slunk along behind him. Unfortunately, she closed the door on his nose, leaving him glowering and frustrated. A minute later, however, the door opened again, and the red tabby trotted out. Fleena followed him. There were tears in her eyes and another furrow of oozing blood upon her thigh, and she was rubbing her third finger, left hand, now bare of its great wedding ring.

"When Georgie discovers that that is gone," she said softly, "there'll be hell to pay."

"Sorry, Fleena," said the red tabby out of the corner of its mouth, "but I need more cash and I need it now. That damned fence takes half of what I get, and you know it. So kindly shut up!"

The tabby headed for the little door built into the lower part of the big one for the benefit of Fleena's pets. But before he could get there a black and white thunderbolt struck him in the side. It was Dirk Cannon, intent on proving a theory he had about the identity of Machiavelli.

Siamese and tabby went over and over, a tangled and snarling ball of red and white and black fur, until they fetched up with a thump against the door. There Dirk sprang away and raced towards the glittering object which he'd seen fall out of the tabby's mouth when it had tried to bite him. As he had guessed, it was Fleena's ring.

Almost without pausing, he took it within his own mouth and raced away into the next room. Before the red tabby could catch up with him, Dirk had whirled and slammed the door shut and then sped through five other rooms. He closed the door of each and, when he came to a dead end, he dived under a bed. Trembling, yet exultant, he waited for the two to find him. He hoped that by that time they'd be so upset they'd involuntarily give him some information. Excited people weren't noted for being close mouthed.

He was disappointed. He waited for about half an hour, yet neither Fleena nor Machiavelli—whom he suspected of being Nick—came into the room. Nor could he hear their voices. At last, unable to stand the suspense, driven by the tension of his feline nerves, he crept out from under the bed and scratched on the door, mewing loudly the meanwhile.

Presently, the door swung open, and Fleena looked down on him.

"Sum Kid, you naughty tom," she said, "Machiavelli will kill you when he catches you. You shouldn't have taken that ring from him."

Suddenly, she stooped and picked up Dirk and cuddled him to her breasts while tears fell upon him. "But I love you for it," she said softly. "You must love 'our Mommy an awful 'ot, don't 'oo?"

"As long as you lay off the baby talk," he growled. He looked around, but he couldn't see the tabby. "How'd you get rid of Mach?" he asked.

"Oh, he realized he was a naughty boy," she replied, innocently. "He slunk out when I told him I'd have one of my bodyguards throw him out. He hates cops."

Dirk could imagine that, especially if the tabby really housed Nick's soul. He supposed that the truth was that Nick had threatened to get her that evening if she didn't bring the ring along to the mysterious affair they'd hinted at earlier. When he saw Fleena place the ring upon the sofa instead of putting it back on her finger, he was sure. Nick was a coward and would avoid a battle, if possible. A natural born pimp, he'd use a woman to do his dirty work for him.

Dirk speculated about telling Fleena his true identity, then decided against it. He wasn't sure yet just what sort of game she was playing. For instance, if she wanted him to help her, why hadn't she told him about Nick? And why had she lied about not seeing Nick any more? Technically, she hadn't, for you couldn't really say the gambler was a cat. But morally she was guilty, just as she was guilty of infidelity to old man Cathcart, even if her human body was faithful to him.

Dirk stood still for a long time, petrified in thought like a feline Socrates. He was an Irishman and, consequently, a hair-splitter and a natural-born Jesuit. The more remote implications of this case troubled him. If Fleena did spend her nights out in another form, making love in backyards and howling at the moon, was she legally unfaithful? Whom could her husband sue as co-respondent? A cat? Nick? Nick in a tom's body? Would a jury convict her? What kind of jury would you have? If she were tried by her peers, would she insist upon a human jury or twelve cats tried and true?

After a while, his head swirling, he gave up and decided to stick to business. He watched Fleena's every movement, an easy job for she had crawled into bed with a mystery thriller. At eleven she got out and took a bath and put up her hair. Every now and then she talked with one of her pets, mostly about the important event that would take place that night. Dirk listened in, but he could learn little.

"Full moon tonight," said a Persian in a whisper.

At eleven thirty Mr. Cathcart's radish head appeared on the phone's screen. "I won't be home until twelve-thirty," he told her. "Don't wait up for me."

"Business?" she said with a faint wail in her voice.

"Yes, I have a small deal on. Won't net me more than a few hundred thousand, hardly worth staying up for, but I've been wanting for a long time to put one over on this Smith character."

"I'll see you in the morning then," she said, blowing him a kiss. Cathcart's rocky old face collapsed into a smile, and he blew her a kiss back. Then his features fell once again into line, like veterans who hated to be out of step.

Afterwards, Fleena swallowed a sleeping pill and crawled between the sheets with a pocketbook edition of the *Necronomicon*. She read it for a while, then the book dropped from her hand, and her head rolled to one side, her eyes closed.

Dirk sat watching her in an agony of indecision. How could he tell into whose body she'd slip? At the moment there were only tom cats in the room, and she wouldn't be limited to a choice of them. If she took one of those outside the room, he'd not be able to trail her.

Then his eyes alighted upon the ring on the sofa. He smiled. She'd be sure to pick that up before she left. It was obvious that Nick had given her orders to bring it along when she got it back from Dirk.

He wasn't mistaken, for a moment later a Persian, Zeenab, she of the flaming red-orange hair and the bright copper eyes, leaped upon the sofa and put the ring in her mouth. Then she disappeared through the little door with the others close behind her. Dirk padded after them.

The caravan of cats paced silently out of the huge mansion, past the guards at the front door, and out into the streets. They trotted quickly down a sidestreet, where they were joined by another large group. All were deathly silent and seemed intent upon getting as swiftly as possible to their mysterious destination. Dirk loped among them, trying to keep Zeenab—or Fleena—in sight. It was not an easy task, for other cats were constantly joining the throng, flowing from alleys and sidestreets into the mainstream, felines of all kinds, sleek and groomed purebloods, ordinary house cats, and long and mangy alley denizens with ribs sticking out and quick deadly ways. Commoner, pariah, and royalty jostled softly against each other, nor did the pedigreed Angora sniff insultingly at the fishy fur of the wharf lounger. Tonight the great glowing moon painted all in equalitarian silver.

Dirk moved in the midst of the ever swelling current, pacing always behind the orange Fleena and keeping a round and glowing eye out for a red tabby or for any other cat who might suddenly join her and by his actions betray the soul of Nick Sukavitch. He saw nobody who filled the bill, though he was excited several times when great-headed toms slid up beside her, rubbing flanks and meowing indelicate suggestions. But each time Fleena told them to take off and not bother her until they reached their destination.

Dirk was becoming increasingly curious about where they were going, but he was afraid that if he asked, he'd give himself away.

So he bided his time, a practice in which every son of Sherlock is steeped.

Sometimes the procession was broken up when automobiles raced down the street, their headlights suddenly striking hundreds of fire-laden eyes. Brakes screeched as the startled drivers slowed down to investigate, but always the dense mob exploded to both sides, and the two parts, as if shifting silent and velvet gears, spurted forward.

After an hour or so, they had come to a country road over which they did not travel but instead paralleled its course in the grape arbors on both sides. And soon Dirk smelled a strong odor of garbage and knew, through the joy that sprang up in him from his body's suddenly tapped stores of memory, that he was approaching their previously unknown goal, their full moon gambol, the Walpurgisnacht of the slit-eyed tribe, the annual crowning of the city's Pharaoh and his Queen! All praise and glory to Bast and her brood, and let all hell bust loose!

The moon looked down upon the city's sprawling and stinking dump heap, piled with Himalayas of refuse and pyramids of battered and rusty stoves and beds and car chassis and tin cans. Over it swarmed a thousand pygmy Sphinxes dedicated to a frenzied combat for mastery in those sports with which the cat worships the bright goddess of the night: singing, fighting, and lovemaking.

Dirk, in those first few mad moments, tried to preserve his detachment and to cling to his duty. He ignored the yowling, leaping, clawing throng and the heavy pungent odor of lust-crazed cats in a determination to take stock of his surroundings. After leaping to comparative safety on top of a cracked commode, he noticed that there were only two others who stood aside from the raging mêlée. These were an enormous brown Abyssinian tom and a white Persian female. They crouched upon the apex of a pile of old lumber which reared up from the center of the heap and from which they could view the entire ritual-orgy. Dirk guessed that they were last year's Pharaoh and Queen and that they were judging the contestants for this year's positions.

At that moment a grey thunderbolt knocked Dirk off his perch. For a few seconds he was locked with the stinking alley-dweller, then he raked the old veteran fore and aft and sent him off, howling. Immediately after, a sexy tortoise-shell slunk by, glancing invitingly and uttering the mating call, the *a* and *c* notes above the middle *c*. Dirk's nerves quivered in response, but his human inhibitions allowed him to run away and take refuge on a heap of decayed potatoes. A tiger tom sat there, caterwauling, his head lifted to the moon. Dirk thought he could best escape the fighting and the lovemaking if he joined in the singing. Everywhere were *a capella* choirs, sextets, quartets, duos, solos, making the night harmonious for feline ears. Dirk joined in with the tiger, striking a note exactly an octave apart from his comrade.

But just as they made the time-honored switch to another key, he saw an orange Persian that looked like Fleena. Deserting his partner, he leaped after her, only to find himself facing the big red tabby, Machiavelli-Nick.

"You again?" snarled Nick. "Beat it, Bud, or I'll scoop out your guts and make you eat them."

"I'm not taking any more of your stuff," spat Dirk, and he launched himself at the tabby. From then on he had a very hazy notion of what went on. At the first clutch and shock of tangling with the hated body of the other, he lost all his human inhibitions and became a frenzied furred catherine wheel who fell upon tom or female alike, though he vented his fury in different fashions.

He ripped at Nick until the tabby turned tail, and he chased him over a big pile of junk, losing him on the other side. Then the Catpurgisnacht opened up and swallowed Dirk, and he was lost. After what seemed an endless pandemonium of screams, bites, scratches, blows, thrusts, and curses, he saw Fleena. She was standing in the midst of the screech and tumult, looking upon the ground for something and paying no attention to those around her. Dirk disengaged himself from a ten-tom brawl and pounced upon her. She lost her detachment and fought for her virtue, as would any honorable female. Dirk, however, had just about mauled her to the point where she would say yes when he and

Fleena were overwhelmed by a fur-and-claws avalanche and swirled away from each other.

The rest was nightmare. Hours later, seemingly, Dirk, staggering, bloody, ragged, was seized by a dozen toms. Exhausted, he could do nothing but chew feebly upon one of his antagonist's forelegs.

"Quit biting," said a brown tabby. "We're your guard of honor." Dirk didn't know what he was talking about. Dazed, he allowed himself to be hoisted into the air and carried up to the lumber pile on which sat the Pharaoh and the Queen.

"Congratulations," they murmured.

"S-s-oo wa-a s-s-saa! All hail the new Pharaoh, best of fighters, greatest of lovers, and most melodious of caterwaulers!" sang the multitude in a single deafening voice. And the deposed king and queen leaped from the lumber to make room for the mauled but triumphant Siamese, Dirk Cannon.

And presently, borne by a number of females, appeared the other new monarch—Fleena.

After she was seated, the assemblage began a sort of saraband, a dance that looked almost formal and might indeed have been meant to be so. But there were so many staggering around and bumping into each other or else lying down and panting, they took away from the intended effect.

Dirk bowed his head and smiled from time to time, but out of the corner of his mouth, he said, "This is Cannon speaking to you, Fleena."

Fleena's back arched, and her orange hairs bristled. Then, seeing he had made no move towards her, she relaxed. "O.K.," she said, "so you're even smarter than I thought you were. What are you going to do about this mess?"

"First, tell me why you called me in on this case. No, wait a minute! Have you given Nick your ring yet?"

"I lost it!" she wailed. "Nick'll never believe it, though. There's no telling what he'll do to me!"

"Never mind that," said Dirk. "I had thought I could trail Nick after you gave him the ring. But if you'll tell me the truth about hiring me, I'll help you with Nick. But I have to know what I'm doing."

Fleena recovered her poise. She gave him a wicked sharp-toothed grin.

"I'd heard that you'd solved some of your cases because you used magic," she said. "So I figured you'd be the only one who could help me get rid of Nick."

"Wha-a-at?"

"Yes, of course. Just before I got married to Georgie, Nick found out I knew how to talk to the cats in my act, and that I'd also learned how to use one of their bodies. It's an ancient Egyptian secret, and one that the witches of the Middle Ages knew very well. Why do you think they kept cats around? Just to provide atmosphere? No, they left their own bodies at night and rode around in their pets'.

"Well, after I married, I couldn't stand being locked up all the time, and Georgie didn't come home very often. So I began leaving the house through the courtesy of Zeenab. And don't tell me I'm being unfaithful to my husband. Would he want a cat to be loyal to him? Besides, it's practically impossible for a feline to be moral. You've heard of Mehitabel haven't you?

"Anyway, one night, while I was singing to the full noon, I was picked up by a big-headed red tabby. He beat me up and then afterwards told me he was Nick Sukavitch. I couldn't imagine how he managed to get into a cat's body, but he told me he knew a drunken old scientist who did it for him."

"The Wizard of Booze!" cried Dirk. "I thought that skidrow Faust was working for Sukavitch, too! Damn him and his professional ethics. He could get me killed!"

"Yeah," she said. "So Nick said I was still his girl, and he didn't want any back talk about it, and he was broke, and he wanted money right now. I couldn't give it to him, but I could pass my jewels on to him. I hated to do it, but I had to. And I tried to cover up their disappearance, but Georgie takes a monthly inventory of everything in the house, and you can't lose a pin without his knowing it, and him with his millions."

"I guessed all that," said Dirk, "but you still haven't told me why you called me in."

"I needed you because Nick said he wanted to make me a rich widow whom he could marry later on. And I wouldn't go for that. Blackmail, yes, but not murder. I don't love my husband, though I could go for him if he spent more time with me. He is a powerful domineering man, and I love that kind. Especially when they have dough."

"Ah, yes," replied Dirk. "Fundamentally, Fleena, you're a real pussy—sleek and beautiful and selfish and sadistic-masochistic."

"Uh, huh. Whatever that last means. Anyway, Nick wanted me to sneak into Georgie's room some night in Zeenab's body and bite him in the jugular vein. I said I wouldn't, so he said he'd do it himself. And there wasn't anything I could do about it. I couldn't tell the police, of course, because they'd never believe me. Then I heard of you and wondered if you could use magic to fight magic."

Dirk growled, "Nick called me up before you did. How'd he know you were going to get in touch with me?"

"Oh, I got mad and threatened him with you. I thought maybe I could scare him off. It didn't work. However, as I was saying, even if I was mean enough to let Nick kill Georgie, I still wouldn't want Nick around, for I'm sure he'd find some way of killing me after I'd inherited the money. Then he'd have it all."

"How could he get it? He can't force you to marry him."

Fleena opened her mouth to reply, then gaped in astonishment.

Dirk followed her gaze and saw below them, at the base of the pyramid of lumber, the red tabby, Nick himself, staring upwards at them. Behind him crouched a giant black tom with flaming orange eyes. This fellow was remarkable not only for his size but for the fact that he was the only unwounded feline on the place. A latecomer.

"Who's that?" whispered Dirk.

"I don't know, but I'll bet it's Blackie Garsoni, Nick's torpedo," she whispered back.

"Do you mean I have to fight him, too?" said Dirk, cringing in spite of himself. Abruptly it had come to him that forty thousand dollars couldn't be collected if he were nothing but scraps of cat strewed around the garbage dump. Also, he realized that Fleena was hoping he'd knock off Nick so her problems would be solved. And it made him furious that she could so blithely and neatly push him into this no-quarter-given struggle.

"Fleena," crooned Nick, "come on down. Playtime's over; I want that ring now; it's time to go home."

Fleena and Dirk looked around for help. What was the use of being Pharaoh and Queen if you couldn't get protection? But the dump was fast being cleared; the thousand shapes had dwindled to a few dozen at the far end of the area; everybody was trying to get home before dawn.

"We'll have to make a run for it, babe," he said. Before she could protest, he gave a terrific screech and leaped over the heads of the two below him. Behind him he heard another scream from Fleena and an answering yowl of fear and rage from Nick. Then the chase was on.

Junk and garbage raced by; then, grape arbors. From their rear rose the cries of the pursuers; but as time sped by and they needed every atom of breath, there was silence. Presently, the two hunted ones left the country road and crossed a paved highway, narrowly escaping being run over by a truck. Dirk hoped his chasers would be blinded by its lights and be smashed. No such luck. On they came.

Nevertheless, Fleena and he gained some time which enabled them to reach the outlying backyards of the suburbs. After that, it was hide and seek, but the two were sobbing so loudly for air that they could not long keep their locations hidden.

Finally, after they'd traversed a dozen alleys and twice that many fences and driveways, Dirk stopped in a driveway between two houses. He panted, "Damn it, Fleena, my Irish blood is up. I'm not going to run like a coward until I fall over. I'm making a stand here, come what may."

He paused and then, always the gallant, said, "But you go ahead."

"Not me," she answered. "I'm sticking with you. After all, what good will it do me if Nick lives? He'll knock off Georgie and me, too, afterwards, and get all the dough."

"Don't marry the nogoodnick," said Dirk.

"Oh, I won't have to. I'm *already* married to him. How do you think he's been blackmailing me? He's been threatening to tell Georgie that he never gave me a divorce and that I'm a bigamist. And if he kills Georgie, he'll remarry me later on because he knows I can't say a thing without the police suspecting I was his partner in the murder."

At that moment Nick's big red head came around a corner. Dirk, seeing it, thought of all the millions that would go to the crook while he, Dirk Cannon, the honest private eye, died with forty thousand just beyond the grasp of his paws. The thought infuriated him and poured adrenalin into his tired and quivering limbs. Unconsciously, he screamed the ancient feline warcry, which contained the insult sublime.

"En garde, you *son of a bitch!"*

The Siamese and the tabby tangled, whirled, became a blur and a snarl. Dirk fought as if he came from Kilkenny instead of the Orient, confident that even in his exhaustion he could whip Nick, hoping against hope that the black tom had been separated from his boss. For if that had not happened, Dirk would be easy prey for the fresh and unwounded Garsoni.

And then, during a very brief lull in their struggles, as the two panted for air and renewed strength, he saw the enormous jaws of the black gaping above him, ready to close upon his throat. Dirk cried his last and feeble challenge, "May the dogs chase you in hell!" He could do no more; he was too tired.

A glittering object dropped from the big tom's mouth. Dirk blinked as he watched it roll down the concrete driveway, then he jumped with fright as one of the cats screamed. His heart pounded with hope. Had Fleena launched herself against the black?

A glance showed him she had not. But the big male had closed its teeth upon the back of Sukavitch's neck. There was a crunching sound, and the red tabby dropped, lifeless.

"Move over," said somebody in a thin, wispy voice that tickled Dirk's ear, tickled terror in him. Despite his tiredness, he leaped squalling into the air. And on the way down he realized that he had not heard the voice outside his body but *within*.

"What's the matter?" growled the black tom.

"Nick's soul tried to muscle into my body," said Dirk. The tom raced up and down the driveway and peered beneath piles of dead leaves and in the basement windows of the two houses.

"Where'd he go? Where'd he go?"

"What's the matter?" screeched Fleena.

Though dazed by the sudden turn of events, Cannon was able to understand part of what was going on.

"Nick's soul can't go back to its human body until the Wizard summons it," he explained. "Meanwhile, it has to find temporary lodging."

Something small and grey skittered out from beneath a tin can. A mouse. The black pounced on it and squeezed its life out between his jaws. And a thing white and transparent in the moonlight arose, wailing almost inaudibly, and disappeared into the darkness behind the house.

"Nick is lost for good," said the tom. "He'll never find his way home now."

"Who are you?" demanded Fleena.

The tom looked slyly at her and then grinned savagely. "I'm Georgieboy, your old and decrepit husband, darling. Aren't you glad to see me?"

Fleena screamed. A window rose above them, and a shoe sailed by them. They ran off. Once out of range, Fleena whimpered, "Georgie, what're *you* doing here?"

Mockingly, the tom said, "Fleena, what're you doing *here*? I left you home, sleeping in bed, and now I find you out catting around with this disreputable private eye and an even shadier gambler, now deceased. Do you think that that is right?"

Fleena regained some of the spark in her copper eyes. Lifting her head defiantly, she said, "How did you find out?"

"I had Cannon shadowed because I wasn't sure that your

calling him wasn't a ruse on your part to meet some handsome and vigorous young man. When he didn't come out of the Wizard of Booze's house for a long time, I investigated. And when the Wizard was given a whole case of Old Blowtop with the promise of more to follow, he showed me how I, too, could do as you had done. However, he would not allow me to know in which of his rooms you, Cannon, and Sukavitch were. I didn't care. As soon as I was in this magnificent and virile body, I followed the parade to the dump heap. There I saw you drop your ring, Fleena, and I picked it up. And it was an easy matter to find Sukavitch and you two."

"What do you intend doing about it?" she asked saucily, giving her bushy tail a flirt. One thing about her, she was fast on the bounce.

Cathcart bared his sharp teeth in a threatening smile.

"Well, for one thing, dear, I think I've solved the secret of making you happy. We'll go out more often at nights—without spending a cent—and I'll be able to keep up the high level of amorous activity which you have always demanded and which, I'll confess, has kept me away because I couldn't match you. But now I've nothing to fear. However, just in case you get any ideas of running away from me and stepping out with some other tom, I think I'll show you right now what will happen."

Like a lion, he leaped forward and grabbed Fleena. Dirk watched the mauling for a moment, then, shuddering, he limped away. It was none of his business; strictly a husband and wife affair; besides, she deserved a roughing-up. Nevertheless, he felt bad about the forty thousand dollars. With the prospect of no rent for them, IBM would soon be coming along to take back Telva, his secretary.

The following night, Dirk Cannon slipped back into his body in the Wizard's room. Stiffly, he rose and hobbled towards the door. He wasn't surprised to find bandages around his arms and ankles, and band-aids on his face and ears, for he knew that wounds upon the temporary body often appeared as stigmata upon the permanent. Evidently, the Wizard had had quite a first-aid job to do on him.

Two of the whiskey bottles that had been on the table were gone. Beside the empty one that remained there was a large package wrapped in brown paper. On top of it was a note addressed to him. He read it.

Dear Mr. Cannon:

While I may not legally be held accountable for delivering the reward money to you, I feel morally bound to do so. Moreover, I am grateful to you for having inadvertently presented me with the solution to my marital problem. Because of you, I'm sure I'll be very happy with Mrs. Cathcart from now on. Provided, that is, that she behaves, and I believe she is now convinced that it is to her best interests to do so. We two are now, as you would probably phrase it, able to "get our kicks" while out singing to the moon from backyard fences. But, believe me, there will be nights when we remain in human form when I'll reach over and wake up Mrs. Cathcart to make sure she is there. You know what I mean.

Meanwhile, here is your forty thousand. And when you arrive home, you will find Fleena's six male cats awaiting you upon your doorsteps. Knowing you are an ailurophile, I've taken the liberty of sending them to you. As you can see, I couldn't very well allow my wife to keep them around the house.

Sincerely,
George C. Cathcart

GETTING READY TO WRITE
A POLYTROPICAL PARAMYTH
PHILIP JOSÉ FARMER & PAUL SPITERI

The following story is a special treat, the first new Polytropical Paramyth to be published in over thirty-five years! The genesis of this story is very similar to *The City Beyond Play* by Philip José Farmer and Danny Adams. Phil wrote sections of the story, had notes for the rest, but never completed it. When Danny sent his completed novel to Phil's agent, the agent purposely read the novel without knowing which parts were written by Phil and which by Danny. When he couldn't tell where Phil ended and Danny began, he knew the novel would be an easy sell.

We took a similar approach when reading Paul's newly completed version of "Getting Ready to Write." It had been over a year since Chris Carey, Michael Croteau, and Win Eckert had read through the original story fragments and notes, so it was felt we could read the story without remembering which specific parts we had read before. The funny thing is, we read the story—with our vague recollections of the original—and not only could we not tell what was new, at first we weren't really sure *any* of it was new. However, after comparing the original version to the completed, we were amazed at how seamlessly Paul fleshed out certain sections and inserted ideas, not only from Phil's notes, but a few of his own, into the story which is now more than twice its original length!

Paul has written nine persuasive "Bibliophile" articles for *Farmerphile*, but we think you'll agree, after reading "Getting Ready to Write," his real forte may very well be fiction.

William Mungo Canine had hammered out the outline of the novel on the anvil of his typewriter. It was now a beautiful trefoil shape, though there were dents and filemarks here and there. They would polish out as the work took its final shape. One or two small notches would remain (or be introduced); nothing was ever perfect.

He reached over to his array of whiskey bottles and, after checking their levels, poured himself a pinkie of Macallan (a particularly aromatic twelve-year- old malt that smelled of moon-dust and rainforest sunshine) into a Scarecrow emblazoned shot glass. He placed the bottle back in its position. Twelve bottles, all whiskies and bourbons, the liquid level in each diminishing down the line starting with an almost full bottle of Tullamore Dew along to the last dregs in a bottle of Glenfiddich. He picked up his lucky pencil (the one with a flame-headed gonk on its end) and rapped the business end down along the bottles. The sonorous cascade pleased him. The bottles responded by whistling a short refrain of "Auld Lang Syne." Out of tune, he thought, next time I need to take half an ounce from the Maker's Mark.

He downed the shot and held out the glass at arm's length. The Scarecrow gave him a wink. Canine winked back at him and replaced the glass on the desk upside down. He pulled his lips back over his teeth, stretched his hands out in front of him and settled in his chair.

He glanced over at the mirror and saw his shirt, but the reflection was clear through where his head should have been. His Timex hovered over the keys, a dis*arm*ing sight that Canine was now used to. All would be well soon.

So, all was ready. Go! His fingers tripped lightly and out of the paper, pulled by the keys, came the title, *They Laughed When I Sat Down in Babylon*, his byline, and a number 1, for the first chapter. The dance of the digits ceased for a moment. Zero hour. The watches had been synchronized, the artillery barrage had ceased, the bayonets were fixed, a moment's silence and the whistles had been shrilled. Over the top!

At that moment, the papers, the top copy, the carbon, the second sheet, rolled out, sliding past the restraining bar with a clacking sound, and flew to the ceiling.

Canine sighed with relief, though he could have cursed. Now he had an excuse. How could he write when the story was itself fluttering bat-like around the ceiling? And now had gone through the door of his basement study into the big recreation room? It was better than sitting there with his hands dropping, fingers poised, like a vampire about to seize the throat of his prey, but paralyzed by the unexpected advent of daylight. How many days had he sat thus, everything ready, the notes, the outline, everything clear in his mind, the story a hill to be sledded down upon, THE END waiting at its bottom? And sat and sat?

But he had his pride and his conscience. Besides, upstairs in the kitchen was a wooden container on the wall marked BILLS, its throat jammed with envelopes and their loathsome meretricious contents, choking, clutching, crying for oxygen, for payment.

Carefully, he reached under the long desk by his typewriter stand and pulled out a big butterfly net. Slipping his leg out of the leg iron he rose and, whistling softly, strolled into the recreation room. Out of the corner of an eye he saw the sheets hanging upside down from a dark part of the room. Slowly, he walked past the pool table, the net behind him, and stopped near the area where the papers now appeared to be sleeping. He pulled out *The League of Frightened Men* from a shelf containing detective novels and turned away as if to take it to a nearby easy chair. Then he whirled, "Aha!" But the canny thing had taken off as soon he'd turned his back to it, and the net whooshed emptily.

This was going to be tough. When it had been in the larval form of an outline, but still very much aerial, it had evaded him for two days on end. Now, wise from much dodging and hiding, it had taken refuge behind a shelf holding the complete works of Thackeray. It was smart of the thing to do that. Canine hadn't gone near Thackeray for years and didn't want to now. The last time, he'd been overwhelmed by a gush of boredom, a sting of apathy. It'd taken weeks before he recovered enough to write; the weeks-long convalescence had resulted in the reading of many mystery novels and some science-fiction. But the typewriter had collected dust and one spider's web.

Ah, well. Perhaps the thing knew better than he. It was aware that his unconscious wasn't ready yet. Why fight the ancient wisdom of the primal brain?

Yes, but there was his correspondence. He went back into the study, which seemed so desolate now that the thing had flown away. Against a wall was a garbage can into which dropped letters to be answered. Six hundred by his estimate; it was too depressing to count them. Every six months he went through the pile, removed those which had to be answered, and dropped them into a wastepaper basket. The remainder went out onto the curb for pickup, though the deed gave him a pang of conscience. But what was conscience? He that had it Wednesday got rid of it in the toilet Thursday morning.

He picked an envelope out of the paper basket. The red ink caught his eye. "URGENT" it proclaimed to no-one in particular; certainly Canine had ignored it so far. He tore open the envelope, giving himself a small paper cut in the process. Perhaps it would get infected, infested, gangrenous and down-right sore. Could he type with seven fingers and two thumbs? Maybe he should practice in case the situation arose. Suppose he lost two fingers? Or three? What if . . . ? He grabbed his Ideas Book and made a quick scribble. The idea factory was churning them out though he sometimes felt the quality control team might need to buck up their ideas. He dated the entry and, out of habit, opened the jotter randomly. "The ritualistic pencil sharpening that turns into a sexual orgy. The masochism of sharpening one's own pencil. The shavings turning to flesh, a wooden briss ceremony." Canine smiled and closed the well-thumbed notebook.

Canine put his finger in his mouth and relished the ferrous tang. His eyes went back to the invoice contained within the blood smudged envelope. It was from *Hamelin Extermination Service* "We lead, the worst follow." He read:

Clearing of roof space of all fans (Variety: SF. 3 blonde, 5 brunette)
    $55.00
(Plus droppings)
    $25.00
Sealing of roof space to prevent re-infestation
    $30.00
House sprayed with newsprint oil to deter re-infestation
    $23.00
Humane trapping of newborn ideas (returned to client)
    $18.00 (9 ideas at $2 each)
Request to exterminate mother-in-law
    Request denied
5 mousetraps set (3 corpses subsequently removed)
    No Charge

Total $151.00
Tax (3.14159%) $4.74
Total Charge $155.74

Note: Redhead discovered in coat cupboard left at client's request.

All work guaranteed for 90 days.
Payment now due if legal proceedings are to be avoided

He'd have to pay this one under the radar, the wire, the table. His wife might see the funny side of the mother-in-law jibe (though he doubted it) but she would ask questions about the girl in the coat cupboard. The redhead was astonishingly well-read for an SF fan and just went into raptures over his autographical cursive m's (and I go into raptures over her, he thought). He wanted to talk more with her when he had time. Besides, she had a great rack.

He felt a little regret over the blondes and brunettes. It had been fun at first but they'd become a right royal pain. How many autographs can one person want for chrissakes! He'd originally just wanted them removed but the exterminator had said he didn't go in for any "catch and release bullshit" as he put it, so Canine had agreed to have them exterminated, killed, rubbed out and eradicated. Moving them on would just mean they'd come back anyway.

He wrote out a personal check, using his flowery book-signing signature just for the hell of it, and put it in an envelope along with the invoice on which he had scribbled "Up and down yours buster. Any idea how to exterminate an exterminator, you trouble-making SOB?" He sealed the envelope, grimacing at the bad taste of the gum and popped the envelope in his jacket pocket. He'd have to make sure he posted it today. He suspected his wife of going through his pockets while he slept at night and wouldn't put it past her to steam open the envelope to read the contents. He didn't want her getting hold of the redhead before he'd finished his discussions with her.

As he stood looking into the garbage can, trying to wind up his sense of duty as if it were a watch, an old family heirloom, he heard the phone ringing. He went back to the recreation room, having put the phone there instead of by his desk stand so that he could get some exercise. One red eye shone behind and above *Vanity Fair* and ducked back down. Becky Sharp's hand reached up from the cover of the book and poked a finger in the eye. Canine heard the squeak and Becky's laugh as he picked up the phone. Good old Becky, as petulant as ever.

"Hello," a squeaky voice said. "Mickey Mouse here. How're you and yours?"

"Fine," Canine said. "Couldn't be better. How's Minnie?"

"Pissed-off at me. She says I spend too much time at the Watering Hole. Which is where I am now. There's quite a gang here. Socrates was asking after you, d'Artagnan sends his regards too, so I thought maybe you'd like to come down and join us. If you ain't working."

"Gee, I'd like to, but I'm working my ass off on a book that's a month overdue. Maybe later."

"Nietzsche's been buying drinks for the house. It may not happen again, you know how tight he is. Which is why—hee, hee!—he's flashing his Marks like he just won the Irish sweepstakes. Cleopatra's on her fourth martini and muttering about Sigmund's Indian wrestling with her asp while she belly dances on the table."

"Sorry, Mickey!" Canine almost sobbed. "But I have to discipline myself. Work comes first."

"Marciano has finally agreed to take on Samson—at arm

wrestling, he says he doesn't box any more, Abe is going to umpire, and, can you believe it, Mohandas is running a book!

"Old Bill and Kit are having a graffiti match in the men's room, you oughta see the stuff they're knocking out, you'd roll on the floor. Boney's beating hell out of the Duke on the pinball machine, and Scott's tinkling the ivories like you wouldn't believe."

"I can hear him," Canine said. "It's tearing my heart out, Mickey, but duty calls. I got to go."

He had no sooner hung up than the phone rang again.

"No wonder I can't get any work done," he muttered.

"Mr. Canine?"

"No. It's not *Kay*-nine. It's Kuh-*nine*. Just like it's not Min-*nee* but *Min*-Nee. I'm going to change my name one of these days."

"Sure, Mr. Kuh-*nine*," the squeaky voice said. "Listen, have you seen that silly three-fingered son of a bitch? He's not there, is he? I called The Watering Hole three times, but that lying bastard bartender says he's not there. The prevaricating drunken villain!"

"If Francois says Mickey's not there, then he's not, as far as I'm concerned. No, he's not here. This is my working time, not visitor's hour."

After he'd gotten rid of her, Canine went back after his story and tried to sneak up on the thing. He had to get going, he'd wasted enough time already, but the thing plastered itself against the back of the bookcase. After trying three times to reach over *The Luck of Barry Lyndon*, and each time being seized with a powerful impulse to sleep—narcoleptic poison delivered via more paper cuts—Canine retreated. For a moment he almost surrendered to it. He reached out to turn on the TV, but after a brief near-epileptic shaking, he withdrew his hand. He remembered a dialog at The Watering Hole.

Alcibiades: "Master, what is the lowest form of human life?"

Socrates: "Someone who watches daytime TV?"

Then, as he passed a corner he smelled something rotten. Looking behind the chair that hid the corner, he found a dead dream reeking of sperm and coal oil. Born by night, dead with the dawn. This one, however, had died a natural death, unlike the one killed last week by the cat. He picked up the carcass by its tail, held it out at arm's length while turning his face away and deposited it in the wastebasket. Tonight, he'd take it out with the garbage if the stench didn't make him act earlier.

His private phone rang.

"Hallo, Meester Canine?"

"No. Kuh-*nine*, not Cah-*nee*-nay. I'm not Italian."

"What's wrong with being Italian? You WASP *bardassa*."

"Actually, I'm Sicilian," Canine said. "*Capisce?*"

"In that case, I'll have to have the money in advance, Meester Canine, and no checks. So, who do you want terminated?"

"There's a New York critic, Abel Snydewell, who's been pretty nasty about my last two books . . ."

After making the necessary financial arrangements and precise identification of the victim he fell silent. He didn't feel especially good. For one thing he couldn't afford to hire any more killers. For another, what good did it do? As soon as you knocked off one creepy crawly critic, another took its place. There was one born every minute.

His wife's voice bellowed through a bullhorn at the top of the steps. "Who was that, dear?"

"Just hang on a second," Canine said down the phone and hit the secrecy button.

Canine remembered to reach down and shake the chain so that his wife would think he was walking over to the foot of the stairs. Old Marley's ghost.

"It was just the exterminator, dear. I can't imagine how he got my unlisted number. He's chasing payment, I'm telling him he needs to come back and do a better job."

"About time," she blared. "I don't see how you can work in that horrible place with all the horrid things sliding around down there. We can smell the decay from here."

Canine didn't answer. He could hear his mother-in-law, no doubt standing at his wife's elbow, breathing heavily through the bullhorn. She could have made a fortune as a professional obscene phone caller.

"How's the work coming?" his wife thundered. "I haven't heard a sound from you in the last two hours!"

"I'm working in longhand today, my dear. I forgot to get a new typewriter ribbon."

"Stay away from the bar!" his wife yelled, and the door at the top of the stairs closed. Canine jumped, and the thing flew out from behind the books mewing pitifully.

It flew around and around, its senses dazed by the many decibels and utter savagery of the voice from on high. The door at the top of the stairs closed. Though his ears rang, Canine could still hear his mother-in-law's evil cackle.

"Is that it?" asked the hired gun, his voice slicing the settling silence.

Canine had momentarily forgotten the line was still open.

He took a deep breath and reactivated the line. "There's one other thing I want taken care of."

"Oh yes?" said the Gunman.

"It's my wife's mother . . ."

The arrangements made, Canine hung up and immediately switched off the ringer on the phone. He did the same with the house phone in the rec room. He needed to concentrate on his novel before the whole day was a complete washout. He decided to give up on his first attempt. He could hear the story fluttering madly behind the bookcase; maybe the cat had got hold of it. Good!

He prepared a new set of papers and fed them around the roll and under the restraining bar. This time he remembered to put a line of X's along the top of the page. That would keep the buggers in their rightful place till he was finished with the page.

Again he typed the title, the byline and the page number. His hands above the keys, his fingers dripping stalactites, he paused momentarily. He smiled and his digits descended in a crescendo of clacking ferocity. He whipped out the first page before the last letter key had settled back to complete the demilune within the typewriter's casing.

In went the second page. No need for the row of X's this

time. Canine was typing ferociously; he could see the papers tugging to pull free but the unrelenting pounding from the keys trapped the paper. As long as he didn't stop all would be okay. He continued to feed through page after page. The sweat gathering on his brow remained unmopped, the itch on his nose went unscratched, the gathering pain in his lower back was ignored.

He glanced at the mirror and could just see the outline of his arms as they worked over the keys. He looked into his own eyes and although not yet fully realized, at least his head was there in outline. His writing was giving him corporeality.

Within a couple of hours a stack of pages had risen untidily by his right hand. They started to flutter and, quick as a flash, Canine brought up his right leg and planted his foot on the pile before they gathered enough momentum to fly away. Little Richard would be proud of his contortions! Canine's emanations might not be as pleasing on the ear as the ivories fondled by Mister Penniman but the pounding at the typewriter keys was music to his literary soul.

As the tidal wave abated and Canine's tsunami flattened out he slowed down his writing. He kept hold of the pages and felt them try to escape. Not this time! He tidied up the sheaths, pushed them into a folder and stuck the package in his drawer where he could hear it beating softly. He checked himself in the mirror one last time. He was whole!

Eleven whole chapters completed, and good ones too. The back of the book had been broken. That thought brought to Canine's mind the punishment Jamuka had requested from his former friend, the infamous Genghis Khan. This literary ending was not as permanent, death would linger a while longer before this book could be laid to rest.

Time to join Mickey and the gang for a drink. Just a quick one and a rushed sandwich. Today was a good writing day, he was going to get back and do some more. Of course he might not get away with just having one drink, if he bought for his friends he'd wait to have the favour reciprocated. He'd worked hard this morning, perhaps he deserved more than just a sandwich. And on the way back he would pop into that bookshop on Locust and see what new titles were in. Surely the bookseller would offer him a coffee and they would sit and talk a while. By the time he got home it would be too late to restart his writing, maybe it would be the right time to open the coat cupboard.

As he looked again at his reflection he started to see the edges fuzz and fade.

CONTRIBUTORS

Danny Adams is the coauthor, with Philip José Farmer, of the 2008 British Fantasy Award-nominated novella *The City Beyond Play* (PS Publishing, 2007) and the novel *Dayworld: A Hole in Wednesday* (Meteor House, 2016). He has published many poems and short stories, including "Whiteness of the Whale" a sequel to Farmer's novel *The Wind Whales of Ishmael*, which appeared in *The Worlds of Philip José Farmer 4* (Meteor House, 2014). He is also a speculative fiction reviewer for Publishers Weekly. He is an assistant reference librarian at Ferrum College in Virginia and is currently working on a series of historical novels. He lives in the Blue Ridge Mountains with his wife Laurie, numerous cats and dogs, and a Phil Farmer-inspired library. Find Danny online at facebook.com/madwriter.

Robert R. Barrett is retired from the Boeing Airplane Company where he worked as a graphics artist and analyst. He has lived in Wichita, Kansas, his entire life, except for two-and-a-half years with the Army in Ashaffenburg, Germany. He has contributed art and articles to various Edgar Rice Burroughs fan publications since 1963. He has also written numerous Philip José Farmer book reviews for *Erbania*, as well as one essay about Lord Grandrith, "Tarzan by Edgar-Philip-Rice-José-Burroughs-Farmer," for *The Jasoomian*. His first book is *Tarzan of the Funnies*, a history of the Tarzan newspaper strips from its inception in 1929 to 1950, the year that Edgar Rice Burroughs died. He also worked as a consultant for Danton Burroughs, working with Phil on *The*

Dark Heart of Time. The title of his article is from Phil's subtitle to his novel, *Blown*. Robert used it for many of his essays for the *ERBapa* when he was a member.

Tom Wode Bellman is the author of the novelette "Through Love, Darkly," (*Striking Science Fiction*, 1952) later expanded to novel length and published by Rubicon Classics (1961). He and Philip José Farmer became friends from often running into each other at science fiction conventions throughout the '60s and '70s and Phil proposed using Tom as the main character in a novel he was going to write about science fiction community. Tom wrote the foreword to Farmer's fictional-author collection, *Venus on the Half-Shell and Other Stories* (Subterranean Press, 2008).

Christopher Paul Carey is the coauthor with Philip José Farmer of *The Song of Kwasin*, and the author of *Exiles of Kho, Hadon, King of Opar*, and *Blood of Ancient Opar*, all works set against the backdrop of the lost civilization of Khokarsa. His short fiction may be found in numerous anthologies. He is a senior editor at Paizo, working on the award-winning Pathfinder Roleplaying Game, as well as the Pathfinder Tales novel line published by Tor Books, and has edited numerous collections, anthologies, and novels. He holds a master's degree in Writing Popular Fiction from Seton Hill University. Chris lives in Western, Washington. Visit him online at www.cpcarey.com.

Michael Croteau is an avid book collector, the long-time webmaster of pjfarmer.com, author of *Collecting Philip José Farmer, The Illustrated Guide, Vol 1*, (1998) and the former publisher of *Farmerphile: The Magazine of Philip José Farmer*. He is currently the editor of *The Worlds of Philip José Farmer* series (four volumes to date), and one of the owners of Meteor House. He is also a co-literary executor and caretaker of Philip José Farmer's "Magic Filing Cabinet." He and his wife Lisa and children live outside Atlanta, Georgia. When he's not publishing books, he plays drums in two local cover bands.

Win Scott Eckert is the coauthor with Philip José Farmer of the novel *The Evil in Pemberley House*, about Patricia Wildman, the daughter of pulp hero Doc Wildman, the bronze champion of justice (Subterranean Press, 2009; Meteor House, 2014). Pat Wildman's adventures continue in Eckert's sequel, *The Scarlet Jaguar* (Meteor House, 2013). He is the editor of and contributor to *Myths for the Modern Age: Philip José Farmer's Wold Newton Universe* (MonkeyBrain Books, 2005) and author of the critically acclaimed, encyclopedic *Crossovers: A Secret Chronology of the World 1 & 2* (Black Coat Press, 2010). His short fiction has been published by Moonstone Books, Black Coat Press, Meteor House, and Titan Books. Win is hard at work on the unfinished fourth novel in Farmer's Secrets of the Nine series, *The Monster on Hold*, furthering the titanic saga of Doc Caliban's ongoing battle against the dark manipulators who hold the secret to eternal life, the Nine. Find him online at winscotteckert.com and @woldnewton (Twitter).

Bette Farmer and Philip José Farmer were married for sixty-seven years. She was in the Lambda Phi sorority at Bradley University (Red Helen?) when Philip José Farmer threw himself down a flight of stairs, repeatedly, to get her attention. She and Phil married on May 9th, 1941, and she went on to receive a degree in Medical Laboratory Technology. She worked for several years while Phil began his writing career. She raised two children and then renovated and sold the houses they lived in, always moving up in house and neighborhood. When the Peoria Public Library held a 50th Anniversary Celebration for "The Lovers" in 2002 she invited many of the fans who traveled to Peoria to visit their home. After that Bette was the driving force behind the annual FarmerCon that included a picnic in the Farmer's back yard. Bette passed away June 10th, 2009, just a few months after Phil.

Philip José Farmer certainly needs no introduction here. He is the three time Hugo Award-winning science fiction Grand Master, whose writing has inspired every contributor in this book to one degree or another, presumably those reading it as well. His debut science fiction story, "The Lovers," appeared in the August 1952 issue of *Startling Stories*, and is noted for breaking the taboo on sex in science fiction, as well as for earning him a Hugo Award for "Most Promising New Talent." From the mid-'50s until the moon landing he moved around the country with his family working full time as a technical writer, selling science fiction stories and novels in his spare time, and winning a second Hugo Award for the novella "Riders of the Purple Wage." In 1970 Farmer moved back to Peoria with his family, began writing full time and his career took off, soon winning a third Hugo Award, for *To Your Scattered Bodies Go*, the opening novel in his bestselling Riverworld series. The next two decades were his most productive with over forty books published including series and stand-alone novels, pastiches of his favorite literary characters, fictional biographies, short story collections and much more. The unpublished and unfinished work he left behind is an ongoing gift to those of us who can't get enough of his dexterous imagination and daring literary conceits.

Alan Hanson is a retired public school teacher, turned freelance writer, living in Spokane, Washington. Since 1977 he has contributed several dozen articles to Edgar Rice Burroughs fan publications, including *The Burroughs Bulletin*. He is a charter member and former editor of the Edgar Rice Burroughs Amateur Press Association, which formed in 1984, the author of *A Tarzan Chrono-log: A Chronicle of Lord Greystoke*, and along with Michael Winger, the editor of *Heritage of the Flaming God* by Frank J. Brueckel and John Harwood.

Rhys Hughes is a prolific writer of wildly entertaining short stories. In fact his goal is to write 1,000 of them, all somehow interconnected despite crossing multiple genres such as absurdism, fantasy, OuLiPo, and science fiction. He has used Farmer as a character in several short stories and his story, "The Pollinators" is a sequel to Philip José Farmer's "The Lovers" (*The Worlds of Philip José Farmer 1*, 2010). Much of his work is surreal, absurdist, metafictional, and shows a mishmash of far-flung literary influences such as Italo Calvino, Milorad Pavić, Jorge Luis Borges,

Stanislaw Lem, and of course, Philip José Farmer. His two most recent books are *Cloud Farming in Wales*, a novel length tribute to Richard Brautigan, and *Salty Kiss Island*, a collection of the offbeat love stories he has written in the past two decades.

Tracy Knight is a clinical psychologist who currently teaches and directs a free clinic at Western Illinois University in Macomb, Illinois, where he lives with his wife, Sharon. He has authored two novels, the western tale *Beneath a Whiskey Sky* (Leisure, 2001) and *The Astonished Eye* (PS Publishing, 2001), a compelling blend of fantasy, SF, and horror. He has also released a collection of his short stories, *Trace Elements* (Perfect Crime Books 2014). He was a close personal friend to the Farmers and was one of Bette's favorite writers.

Joe R. Lansdale is the Mojo storytelling author of novels and stories in many genres, including Western, horror, science fiction, mystery, and suspense. He has written forty-five novels and published thirty short story collections along with many chapbooks, comic book adaptations and animated television shows scripts. Several of his novels have been adapted to film and the Hap and Leonard series is currently being adapted into a TV series for the SundanceTV channel. His awards include the Bram Stoker, British Fantasy, Edgar, American Mystery, International Horror Guild, Horror Critics, and the 2007 World Horror Grand Master Award.

Steve Mattsson has written and colored for Marvel and DC Comics. He slipped a few Philip José Farmer and Wold Newton references into the Boris the Bear series when he was writing it for Dark Horse Comics during the mid-'80s. He wrote three articles for *Farmerphile*, all regarding Philip José Farmer and his connection to comic books. He is a contributing editor to World Watch One, the Buckaroo Banzai newsletter. Steve made a mid-life career change and became a Paramedic and Certified Alcohol & Drug Counselor. He is the director at the Hooper Detox Center in Portland, Oregon. He is also a SAG-AFTRA eligible actor. He and his wife, Shaune, like to climb mountains and SCUBA dive.

Heidi Ruby Miller uses research for her stories as an excuse to roam the globe. Her books include the popular Ambasadora series and the award-winning writing guide *Many Genres, One Craft*. In between trips, Heidi teaches creative writing at Seton Hill University, where she graduated from their renowned Writing Popular Fiction Graduate Program. She is a member of The Authors Guild, International Thriller Writers, Pennwriters, Littsburgh, PARSEC, and Science Fiction Poetry Association. Follow Heidi's adventures with her husband, Jason Jack Miller, on their youtube travel and lifestyle channel Small Space, Big Life.

Will Murray is the author of over seventy novels, including seven posthumous Doc Savage collaborations with Lester Dent, under the name Kenneth Robeson, for Bantam Books in the 1990s. Since 2011 he has written fourteen additional Doc Savage adventures for Altus Press, two of which co-starred The Shadow, as well as a solo Pat Savage novel. His 2015 Tarzan novel, *Return to Pal-Ul-Don*, was followed by *King Kong vs. Tarzan* in 2016. Over fifty of his articles and essays on Doc Savage have been collected in one volume, *Writings in Bronze*. He is also the co-editor of Sanctum Books' Doc Savage and Shadow reprint series. As the Literary Agent for the estate of Lester Dent, Murray is dedicated to keeping the Missouri author's works in print.

Dennis E. Power is a master at one of Philip José Farmer's favorite literary tricks: taking two or more apparently unconnected stories/novels/mythologies and finding a link between them. His real knack, however, is finding these connections between seemingly unrelated stories and novels by Farmer himself. Long active in Wold Newtonry, three of his articles appeared in *Myths for the Modern Age: Philip José Farmer's Wold Newton Universe* (Monkey-Brain, 2005). Many of his articles can be found at www.pjfarmer.com/secret/content/secret-articles-alphabyauthorb.htm.

Spider Robinson has won many awards for his writing, from the John W. Campbell Best New Writer Award in 1974 to the Robert A. Heinlein Award for Lifetime Excellence in Literature in 2008;

with three Hugos, a Nebula, and many others in between. He has been a regular reviewer for several science fiction magazines but is best known for his beloved Callahan's series. He collaborated with his wife Jeanne Robinson on the Hugo- Nebula- and Locus-winning Stardance Trilogy, concerning zero-gravity dance. In 2006 he became the only writer ever to collaborate on a novel with Robert A. Heinlein, posthumously completing *Variable Star*. Visit him at www.spiderrobinson.com.

George H. Scheetz is a librarian, bibliophile, and the publisher of the first Philip José Farmer fanzine, *Farmerage*, and the collection *Riverworld War: The Suppressed Fiction of Philip José Farmer*. He began his career in Peoria, Illinois, and served in various positions at Bradley University and the Peoria Public Library from 1977 to 1982, at which time he met Philip José Farmer and began work on a bibliography of his works (completed for Greenwood Press, but not published). Since December 2004, he has served as director of the Batavia Public Library in Illinois. He has an abiding interest in local history, Sherlock Holmes, the movies, and the works of Thorne Smith and (of course) Philip José Farmer.

Art Sippo is a longtime Doc Savage fan who loves Philip José Farmer's various takes on the Bronze Man, even those that many Doc "purists" find sacrilegious. He has participated on panels and given lectures regarding Farmer & Doc, and one such speech was published as the afterword to Titan Books' 2012 edition of Farmer's novel *A Feast Unknown*. Art has also written the novel *Sun Koh: Heir of Atlantis, Vol. 1* (available as a Nook ebook and as an Apple iBook). He hosted many episodes of the Book Cave and Art's Reviews podcasts (artsreviews.libsyn.com). For more of Art's imaginative essays on Doc Savage and the Wold Newton Family, visit his site, speculations-in-bronze.blogspot.com.

Paul Spiteri was a close personal friend of Phil & Bette Farmer. He and his family traveled many times from England to visit the Farmers in Peoria, including his infamous "Just One Day" trip when he flew over for Phil's 90th Birthday. Paul edited the mammoth collection of Farmer rarities, *Pearls from Peoria* (Subterranean Press, 2006) and coauthored, with Philip José Farmer, the Polytropical Paramyth "Getting Ready to Write" (*Farmerphile No. 13*, July 2008). Paul also penned two stories: "The Time Distorter" (*Farmerphile No. 15,* January 2009) and "Le Maréchal" (*The Worlds of Philip José Farmer 1*, 2010) featuring Phil Farmer as a time-traveling Eridanean agent.

Allen Steele is primarily known for writing hard science fiction, including the Near-Space series, which looks at the blue collar grunt work involved in building things like space stations and moon bases, and the Coyote series, which shows plausible events leading to mankind's first space colony. He has served on the Board of Advisors for both the Space Frontier Foundation and the Science Fiction and Fantasy Writers of America, and has testified before Congress in hearings regarding space exploration in the 21st century. He is the winner of the Robert A. Heinlein Award, three Hugos, and many other awards and is one of the most popular and acclaimed writers of hard science fiction today.

Leo Queequeg Tincrowdor is the first author to have published a collaboration with Philip José Farmer, the short story, "Osiris on Crutches" (*New Dimensions 6*, 1976). He has a lot of detailed knowledge about Farmer's career. In addition to the article found in this book, he also wrote the article "Desires Denied" (*The Worlds of Philip José Farmer 3*, 2012) which detailed the truth behind Farmer's long lost novel, *As You Desire*. Leo is best known for his novel *Sphinxes without Secrets*, which, like most of his work, he says was too racy to be reviewed in the local town paper. He lives in Busiris, Illinois.

Howard Waldrop has long been considered one of the most unusual writers working in science fiction. Many of his stories are heavily-researched alternate history, while others are considered unclassifiable. They often contain very obscure references. He is "famous" for being unknown, but has been nominated for nearly every genre writing award and has won the Nebula and a World Fantasy Award for his story, "The Ugly Chickens." He has taught at the Clarion Workshop and written movie reviews for Locus Online. He has been called "the most startling, original, and entertaining short story writer in science fiction today." He lives in Austin, Texas, but does not own a computer.

Gary K. Wolfe is one of the preeminent scholars of the science fiction today. He has received numerous awards for his studies of the field and has written over two hundred essays for various periodicals and books. He is currently a contributing editor and senior book reviewer for Locus Magazine and has published three collections of his reviews, as well as several other books about the genre. In 2016, he taught the course "How Great Science Fiction Works" for The Great Courses series of audio and video lectures. In 2017 he retired from Roosevelt University where he had been a Professor of Humanities since 1971.

Bob Zeuschner began reading and collecting Edgar Rice Burroughs in 1952. Based on his own collection and the help of other collectors, he wrote *Edgar Rice Burroughs: The Exhaustive Scholar's and Collector's Descriptive Bibliography*, with a foreword by Philip José Farmer (McFarland, 1996). He worked as the assistant to the editor of the *Burroughs Bulletin*, and contributed numerous articles to it and other fan publications. He wrote the captions for the art book *Grand Master of Adventure: J. Allen St. John* (Vanguard Publications, 2005). Bob is a professor of philosophy at Pasadena City College in southern California, and has written a college textbook on ethics, *Classical Ethics: East and West* (McGraw-Hill, 2000).

Meteor House Titles

PHILIP JOSÉ FARMER ANTHOLOGIES
Edited by Michael Croteau

The Worlds of Philip José Farmer Volume 1: Protean Dimensions
The Worlds of Philip José Farmer Volume 2: Of Dust and Soul
The Worlds of Philip José Farmer Volume 3: Portraits of a Trickster
The Worlds of Philip José Farmer Volume 4: Voyages to Strange Days
The Best of Farmerphile: The Magazine of Philip José Farmer

WOLD NEWTON SERIES

Doc Savage: His Apocalyptic Life by Philip José Farmer

The Khokarsa Series
Exiles of Kho by Christopher Paul Carey
Flight to Opar (Restored Edition) by Philip José Farmer
The Song of Kwasin by Philip José Farmer and Christopher Paul Carey
Hadon, King of Opar by Christopher Paul Carey
Blood of Ancient Opar by Christopher Paul Carey

The Pat Wildman Series
The Evil in Pemberley House by Philip José Farmer and Win Scott Eckert
The Scarlet Jaguar by Win Scott Eckert

The Phileas Fogg Series
Phileas Fogg and the War of Shadows by Josh Reynolds
Phileas Fogg and the Heart of Osra by Josh Reynolds

SCIENCE FICTION ADVENTURE

The Abnormalities of Stringent Strange by Rhys Hughes
Airship Hunters by Jim Beard and Duane Spurlock
Dayworld: A Hole in Wednesday by Philip José Farmer and Danny Adams
Man of War by Heidi Ruby Miller

CHAPBOOKS

Being an Account of the Delay at Green River, Wyoming, of Phileas Fogg, World Traveler, or, The Masked Man Meets an English Gentleman by Win Scott Eckert
The Adventure of the Fallen Stone: Being the First Part of the Account of The Dynamics of a Meteor by Win Scott Eckert
Watch Your Back, Mr. Minamoto by Frank Schildiner

NONFICTION

Crossovers Expanded, Volume 1 by Sean Lee Levin
Crossovers Expanded, Volume 2 by Sean Lee Levin

meteorhousepress.com